The Destroyermen Series

DESTROYERMEN

RIVER OF BONES

TAYLOR ANDERSON

ACE
New York

ACE
Published by Berkley
An imprint of Penguin Random House LLC
1745 Broadway, New York, NY 10019

ISBN: 9780399587528

Ace hardcover edition / July 2018
Ace mass-market edition / May 2019

Printed in the United States of America
3   5   7   9   10   8   6   4   2

Cover art © Studio Lidell

To my family for understanding why, sometimes, they have to sneak through the house like some terrible "booger" might get them if they make a peep. Sadly, sometimes they're right. But at least *this* booger is big enough to say "I'm sorry." I love you all.

ACKNOWLEDGMENTS

Thanks again to my friend and agent, Russell Galen, and my incredibly sweet, patient, and understanding editor, Anne Sowards. They're the real crew that keeps this ship steaming along. I also have to thank all the great, imaginative folks who visit my website (taylorandersonauthor .com) and comment on the wide range of ongoing topics. (I'm sorry I forgot to mention Joe, Leo, "the Steves," and "GSW" last time. . . .) Shoot, I probably forgot some more, and there'll *be* a lot more by the time this hits. Nothing for it. But the point is, whether their ideas and suggestions inspire me or not, their *participation* and *enthusiasm* certainly do—as I'm sure they do the *many* other people who read their posts. (I'm the one with the counter. If they had any idea how many people hang on their every word, they'd probably clam up forever!)

Finally, I have to thank all of you out there who love this yarn as much as I do. Russell and Anne might keep the steam up, but you're the ones who give me the fuel, inspiration, and motivation to keep dashing forward through rough seas or fair.

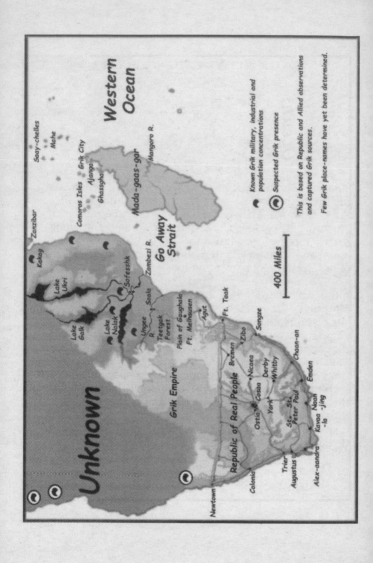

Western Ocean

Unknown

Go Away Strait

Soay-chelles
Mahe
Grik City
Comoros Isles
Ajanga
Ghasshga
Zanzibar
Mangoro R.
Mada-gaas-gar

Kakag
Lake Ukri
Sofesshk
Lake Galk
Lake Naluk
Ungee R.
Zambezi R.
Soala
Taetgak Forest
Plain of Gaughala
Ft. Melhausen
Grik Empire
Agat.
Ft. Traak

Newtown
Republic of Real People
Colonia
Trier
Augustus
Alex-aandra
Ostia
York
Cosaa
Nicaea
Ste. Ste.
Peter Paul
Kawa
Naan
-la
-jing
Derby
Whitby
Bremen
Zibo
Songze
Chaan-on
Emden

400 Miles

● Known Grik military, industrial and
population concentrations

◉ Suspected Grik presence

This is based on Republic and Allied observations
and captured Grik sources.

Few Grik place-names have yet been determined.

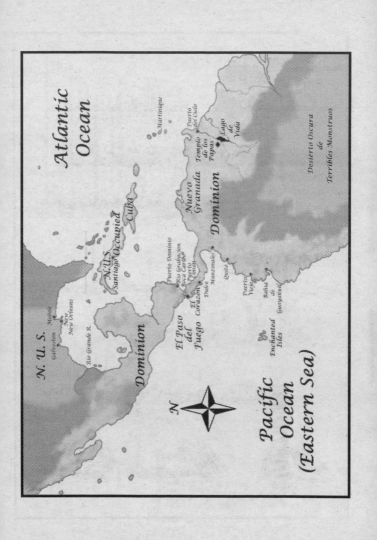

Recognition Silhouettes of Allied Vessels

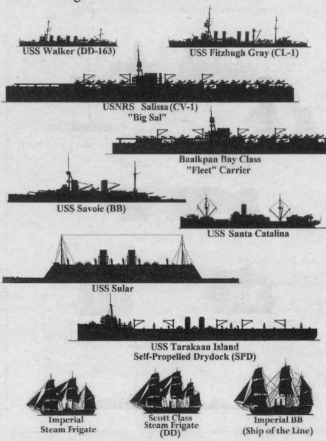

USS Walker (DD-163)

USS Fitzhugh Gray (CL-1)

USNRS Salissa (CV-1)
"Big Sal"

Baalkpan Bay Class
"Fleet" Carrier

USS Savoie (BB)

USS Santa Catalina

USS Sular

USS Tarakaan Island
Self-Propelled Drydock (SPD)

Imperial
Steam Frigate

Scott Class
Steam Frigate
(DD)

Imperial BB
(Ship of the Line)

Recognition Silhouettes of Enemy Vessels

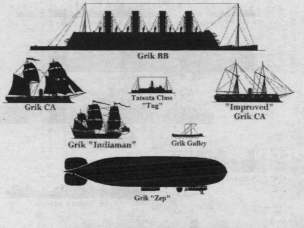

Grik BB

Grik CA

Tatsuta Class "Tug"

"Improved" Grik CA

Grik "Indiaman"

Grik Galley

Grik "Zep"

The "Holy Dominion"

"Dom" BB (Ship of the Line)

"Dom" DD (Frigate)

"League of Tripoli"

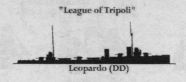

Leopardo (DD)

U.S.S. WALKER
(DD-163)
(Per Oct./Nov. 1944 refit)

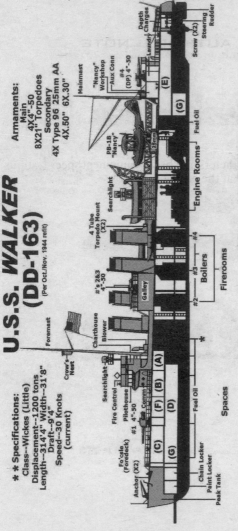

Armaments:
Main
4X4"-50
8X21" Torpedoes
Secondary
4X Type 96 25mm AA
4X.50" 6X.30"

✳✳ Specifications:
Class—Wickes (Little)
Displacement—1200 tons
Length—314'4" Width—31'8"
Draft—9'4"
Speed—30 Knots
(current)

Foremast
Crow's Nest
Charthouse
Blower
Searchlight
Fire Control
Pilothouse
Fo'c'sle (Foredeck)
Chain Locker
Paint Locker
Peak Tank
Anchor (X2)
#1 4"-50
Fuel Oil

4 Tube Torpedo Mount (X2)
Searchlight
#'s 2&3 4"-50
Galley
#2 ---- #3 ---- #4
Boilers
Firerooms

PB-1B "Nancy"
NB-1 "Nancy"
25mm
Mainmast
"Nancy" Workshop
Aux Conn
#4 (DP) 4"-50

Engine Rooms
Fuel Oil
Depth Charges
Laundry
Screw (X2)
Steering
Rudder

Spaces

(A) Captain
(B) Officers
(C) Chiefs, Warrants, P.O.s
(D) Fore Crew
(E) Aft Crew
(F) Wardroom
(G) Storage/Magazine

✳ Temporary fuel bunkers fill the space for #1 boiler

✳✳ New Construction DDs such as USS *James Ellis* have similar specifications but are 5-7 knots faster and 150-200 tons heavier

AUTHOR'S NOTE

A cast of characters and list of equipment specifications can be found at the end of this book.

OUR HISTORY HERE

By March 1, 1942, the war "back home" was a nightmare. Hitler was strangling Europe, and the Japanese were rampant in the Pacific. Most immediate from my perspective as a . . . mature Australian engineer stranded in Surabaya Java, the Japanese had seized Singapore and Malaysia, destroyed the American Pacific Fleet and neutralized their forces in the Philippines, conquered most of the Dutch East Indies, and were landing on Java. The one-sided Battle of the Java Sea had shredded ABDAFLOAT, a jumble of antiquated American, British, Dutch, and Australian warships united by the vicissitudes of war. Its destruction left the few surviving ships scrambling to slip past the tightening Japanese gauntlet. For most, it was too late.

With several other refugees, I managed to board an old American destroyer, USS Walker, *commanded by Lieutenant Commander Matthew Reddy. Whether fate, providence, or mere luck intervened,* Walker *and her sister* Mahan, *their gallant destroyermen cruelly depleted by combat, were not fated for the same destruction that claimed their consorts in escape. Instead, at the height of a desperate action against the mighty Japanese battlecruiser* Amagi, *commanded by the relentless Hisashi Kurokawa, they were . . . engulfed by an anomalous force, manifested as a bizarre greenish squall—and their battered, leaking, war-torn hulks were somehow swept to another world entirely.*

I say "another world" because, though geographically similar, there are few additional resemblances. It's as if whatever cataclysmic event doomed the prehistoric life on "our" earth many millions of years ago never occurred, and those terrifying—fascinating—creatures endured, sometimes evolving down wildly different paths. We quickly discovered "people," however, calling themselves Mi-Anakka, who are highly intelligent, social folk, with large eyes, fur, and expressive tails. In my ignorance and excitement, I promptly dubbed them Lemurians, based on their strong (if more feline) resemblance to the giant lemurs of Madagascar. (Growing evidence may confirm they sprang from a parallel line, with only the most distant ancestor connecting them to lemurs, but "Lemurians" has stuck.) We just as swiftly learned they were engaged in an existential struggle with a somewhat reptilian species commonly called Grik. Also bipedal, Grik display bristly crests and tail plumage, dreadful teeth and claws, and are clearly descended from the dromaeosaurids in our fossil record.

Aiding the first group against the second—Captain Reddy had no choice—we made fast, true friends who needed our technical expertise as badly as we needed their support. Conversely, we now also had an implacable enemy bent on devouring all competing life. Many bloody battles ensued while we struggled to help our friends against their far more numerous foes, and it is for this reason I sometimes think—when disposed to contemplate "destiny"—that we survived all our previous ordeals and somehow came to this place. I don't know everything about anything, but I do know a little about a lot. The same was true of Captain Reddy and his US Asiatic Fleet sailors. We immediately commenced trying to even the odds, but militarizing the generally peaceful Lemurians was no simple task. Still, to paraphrase, the prospect of being eaten does focus one's efforts amazingly, and dire necessity is the mother of industrialization. To this day, I remain amazed by what we accomplished so quickly with so little, especially considering how rapidly and tragically our "brain trust" was consumed by battle.

In the meantime, we discovered other humans—friends and enemies—who joined our cause, required our aid, or posed new threats. Even worse than the Grik (from a moral perspective, in my opinion) was the vile

Dominion in South and Central America. A perverse mix of Incan/Aztecan blood-ritual tyranny with a dash of seventeeth-century Catholicism favoring technology brought by earlier travelers, the Dominion's aims were similar to those of the Grik: conquest, of course, but founded on the principle "Convert or die."

I now believe that if faced with only one of these enemies, we could've prevailed rather quickly despite the odds. Burdened by both, we could never concentrate our forces and the war lingered on. To make matters worse, the Grik were aided by the madman Kurokawa, who, after losing his Amagi at the Battle of Baalkpan, pursued a warped agenda all his own. And just as we came to the monumental conclusion that not all historical human timelines we encountered exactly mirrored ours, we began to feel the malevolent presence of yet another power, centered in the Mediterranean. This League of Tripoli was composed of fascist French, Italian, Spanish, and German factions from a different 1939 than we remembered, and hadn't merely "crossed over" with a pair of battle-damaged destroyers but possessed a powerful task force originally intended to wrest Egypt—and the Suez Canal—from Great Britain.

We had few open conflicts with the League at first, though they seemed inexplicably intent on subversion. Eventually we discovered their ultimate aim was to aid Kurokawa, the Grik, even the Dominion, just enough to ensure our mutual annihilation, and simultaneously remove multiple threats to the hegemony they craved. But their schemes never reckoned on the valor of our allies or the resolve of Captain Matthew Reddy. Therefore, when their Contre-Amiral Laborde, humiliated by a confrontation, not only sank what was, essentially, a hospital ship with his monstrous dreadnaught Savoie, but also took hostages—including Captain Reddy's pregnant wife—and turned them AND Savoie over to Kurokawa, we were caught horribly off guard. Tensions with the League escalated dramatically, though not enough to risk open hostilities that neither we—nor they—were ready for. (We later learned such had already occurred in the Caribbean, between USS Donaghey and a League DD, and that 2nd

Fleet and General Shinya's force had suffered a setback in the Americas at the hands of the Dominion.) But we had *to deal definitively with Kurokawa at last, and do so at once. As powerful as he'd become, and with a battleship added to his fleet, we simply couldn't risk our invasion of Grik Africa with him at our backs.*

Captain Reddy conceived a brilliant plan to rescue our friends and destroy Kurokawa once and for all, and in a rare fit of cosmic justice, the operation actually proceeded better than planned, resulting in the removal of one long-standing threat forever, and the capture of Savoie *herself. The battle was painfully costly, however, and the forces involved too exhausted and ill placed to respond when word came that the Grik were on the move. It became clear that all our hopes for victory depended on a heretofore reluctant ally; how quickly we (and Shinya) could repair, reorganize, and rearm; and the insanely, suicidally daring defiance of some very dear friends aboard the old* Santa Catalina. . . .

Excerpt from the foreword to Courtney Bradford's
The Worlds I've Wondered
University of New Glasgow Press, 1956

PROLOGUE

"*T*o the cookpots with any who fall out!" gasped Jash, heaving his burden along with the rest of his warriors. He was a Senior First of One Hundred, now sometimes referred to by the odd-sounding words Taii or Ka'tan, and commanded three hundred of First General Regent Champion Esshk's New Warriors. The New Warriors were still sometimes derisively called the hatchling host by long-established regents and the elite Hij of Old Sofesshk, which was the First City and old/new capital of the Ghaarrichk'k Empire in Africa. But they had been schooled from birth in the radical new ways of the Hunt and were the best equipped, best trained, most lethal warriors the Grik ever made, all for the purpose of this Final Swarm they were about to embark upon. Their mission was to slaughter a most tiresome "worthy prey" once and for all, a prey that had made the *Grik* prey for the first time since before their racial memory began, and was now threatening the holy city of Sofesshk itself.

Jash knew all this, or most of it, as well as the fact that he owed his rank—probably his very life—to the military reforms of First General Esshk and not, also for the first time in history, to the Celestial Mother, or Giver of Life, who ruled the Empire in name. This was particularly remarkable for a warrior not quite three years old, with precisely zero combat experience and who was only beginning to sprout the bristly crest of adulthood on his head. Like many his age, raised as he was, it was his intellect that so quickly elevated him to the exalted rank of First of One Hundred, then Senior (Ka'tan), and he was *very* clever for a Grik not "of the blood." Under normal circumstances, even if he'd survived the cannibalistic melee of traditional hatchlinghood in the nest, he would've risked being arbitrarily sent to the cookpots by some disinterested chooser. If he avoided that, the best he could've hoped for was a brief, brutal life as an ordinary Uul warrior or laborer. He owed *everything* to Esshk, he believed, and it was for the Regent Champion that Jash felt the urgency of (and responsibility for) completing his current task in the allotted time—whether or not he fully understood why his three hundred warriors must *carry* the inverted weight of a seventy-foot, eighteen-ton wooden galley to the waters of Lake Nalak, west of Sofesshk.

"The warriors tire, Senior," another First of One Hundred, named Seech, wheezed beside him, hacking a gobbet of dust-stained mucus on the ground. He didn't add that they were thirsty as well. He didn't have to. They'd been carrying the galley all night, down twisty trails in the vine-choked brush south of the lake, from the place it had been hidden from view from above ever since the prey, the . . . enemy, discovered the covered slips on the lake. To prevent their destruction, all the galleys—maybe twenty or thirty hundreds; Jash had no idea—were quickly carried ashore or sunk in shallow water. Most were stashed in places it was hoped the enemy flying machines wouldn't look, but some were even buried. The latter didn't fare well, quickly rotting in the living soil, but all this was accomplished none too soon, since the enemy returned a few days later with more flying machines and bombed the slips into a roaring inferno. As far as anyone could tell, however, they hadn't found any galleys, and rarely diverted their efforts from bombing more obvious targets bordering the lake and the Zambezi River.

Jash glanced at Seech, one of only thirty-odd under his command that even had a name. Names were earned by rank or achievement, and only Firsts of Ten, Fifty, or a Hundred had them yet. Looking harder, Jash realized it was dawn at last, because he saw Seech's tongue lolling from his tooth-studded jaws, moisture around his red eyes made muddy with dust, the young plumage on his tail dragging the ground. The gray armor and tunic over his dun-colored feathery fur wasn't stained with sweat, but they'd crossed several streams, and the dark dust had stuck. Somehow he'd kept his weapons clean; that was something whipped into them since infancy. There was dust on the shiny-bright barrel of his musket (called a "garrak" for the loud sound it made, and because the near-lipless Grik couldn't do Ms)—but there wasn't a speck of rust. Jash expected nothing less. He and Seech had been nestmates and, according to the old way, would've torn each other apart if they could have. Prevented from that and raised together, they'd developed a certain . . . fellow-feeling between them that was difficult to define. Jash was smarter, and Seech expected him to display wise leadership. Seech was possibly stronger, and Jash relied on him to swiftly enforce his commands. Being closer to the ranks, Seech was also expected to have a better feel for what the warriors could endure. The relationship worked, and Jash knew Seech wouldn't have spoken at all if their warriors didn't absolutely require a rest.

"Very well," he panted, then called a halt with a loud, guttural bark. "Hold them here," he said, "but do not allow them to lay their burden down." He hesitated. Able to do simple sums, he'd calculated that each of his warriors had been supporting upward of 120 pounds with their arms and heads since dusk the night before. "They may never lift it again," he added resignedly. "I will look at the trail ahead." He nodded at the peak of the rise they'd been working toward.

"As you command," Seech huffed.

Jash stepped out from under the bow of the galley, his arms and legs suddenly rubbery, and staggered several steps before firming his stride. Looking back, he saw the graying, raw wood bottom of the galley and wondered how badly it would leak when it touched the water again. For the first time, from his slightly elevated perch, he observed dozens more upturned hulls snaking back the way they'd come like a line of huge grayback beetles drawn to carrion. He resumed his trek to the top of the rise, where he stopped and stared, breathing hard.

Before him, stretching almost as far as he could see,

the opposite mountain shore a hazy smudge of darkness against the brightening horizon, was Lake Nalak at last. He'd seen the lake many times, of course, and it always had a few of the great iron-covered ships lying at anchor or moving smokily about its surface. Now it was packed, and he'd never seen it so densely covered with anything other than the fat, floating, flying creatures that teemed there twice a year. There were iron-covered ships to be sure, more than he'd imagined existed, and most were chuffing columns of dark smoke high in the calm orangish morning air. But hundreds of galleys were already on the water as well, some rowing east, forty oars on either side flashing in the bright light of the rising sun. It was then that Jash fully grasped the scope of the undertaking of which he was such an insignificant part.

We made it, he thought. Gauging the distance to the near shore below and conscious that other galleys might soon start stacking up behind his, he scrambled back down the trail. "We are almost there," he said loudly, voice carrying easily to his entire command, "just over the rise and hardly five more lengths of our burden. As soon as it is righted, set in the water, and the way cleared for those behind, all may rest!"

Seech looked at him with widened eyes. "Truly?" he asked.

Suppressing irritation that his subordinate might question him, Jash jerked a diagonal nod. "Just so. We will step the mast and emplace the oars, but the galley is liable to sink in the shallows as soon as it is launched. Our warriors can take a short rest then, and refresh themselves in the water by bailing it out. Detail a few to watch for lake monsters while the others frolic." He considered. "And to guard their weapons, of course." Not all New Warriors had garraks yet, and the leaders of those who didn't weren't above raiding other units for them. "Choose those who have endured the best for this task and give them names," Jash decided. "That should inspire others to greater effort in the future."

"How long will we let the boards soak—and our warriors rest?" Seech asked.

"Two hand-spans of the sun, perhaps slightly more.

Less if we must make way for another vessel, of course. The planks should quickly tighten and we will get underway as soon as they do."

As it turned out, it took almost four hand-spans before the galley was upright on the beach, its mast stepped and the great sail-bearing spar raised to its peak. The whole thing was then pushed down across the sand to the water. As Jash predicted, it rapidly filled and settled to the bulwarks in the murky water, the dry seams open a quarter inch in places. But just as quickly, the porous timbers swelled, and before the next galley crested the rise and began its descent, his slightly rested warriors were already tossing buckets and helmets full of water over the side. Quicker than Jash really expected, "his" galley was afloat, though bailing still, and ready to shove off.

None of his warriors had ever operated a galley, but they'd trained intensively on benches arranged for the purpose, practicing with weighted oars. What's more, none displayed the terror of the water that came instinctively to others of their kind. There were monsters in Lake Nalak and the Zambezi, but nothing like what lurked in the salty sea, and they'd trained in water since they could walk, moving in the shallows and even learning to swim, after a fashion. Mere rivers would *not* stop the advance of Esshk's New Army. In any event, the dangers of the water were well-known, even avoidable to an extent, and the warriors quickly adjusted to their new environment as Jash tried to remember the commands regulating their labor. (He'd once crossed the lake in a galley, learning to steer, but never commanded one.) Seech was invaluable in this instance. He may not've been considered as smart as Jash, but he apparently had a better memory. Soon, as the day progressed, the galley was flashing across the water at an astonishing speed as its crew got the hang of working together and Jash relearned the steering commands. He rested the rowers often; they'd already had a long night and day. But they seemed invigorated by their new experience, and he made the most of their enthusiasm.

Other galleys darted around them with sometimes

more, often less, skill. A few occasionally collided, filling the boats and spilling their crews farther from shore than was likely for them to survive. Jash collected forty or so stranded warriors that kept hold of their garraks. He had no use for the rest. If he hadn't retained ship-handling commands very well, he could spew other mantras in his sleep, first and foremost being that firepower dominated this New Way of war, and he wouldn't feed anyone who'd drop his weapon to save himself. Some *were* saved by other Ka'tans who valued quantity over quality, and when one of these almost crashed his galley into Jash's, he gave the order to back oars and pull away. The soggy survivors herded below as ballast belonged to him now, and he'd see what they were made of later.

Finally, with no orders to proceed toward the city yet, Jash decided to take his galley ashore and let his warriors get some much-needed sleep. They were heading toward the beach not far from where they'd launched their ship when First of Fifty Naxa, stationed near the bow, cried out and pointed. Jash rushed forward on the walkway between the rowers and stared at the sky. A distant speck was growing, coming their way. Even as he watched, the first became two, then five. *Six!* Dozens of smoky white streamers lanced into the air, pushing rockets intended to stop the enemy flying machines. They exploded with dull thumps and dirty gray puffs, mostly above and considerably behind the enemy. Jash considered the rockets worse than useless. They occasionally got an enemy machine and probably wounded more, but they did as much damage on the ground as enemy bombs. Still, they couldn't just let them come and go as they pleased, could they? He snorted.

"All ahead full," he shouted, and the drum regulating the stroke of the oars picked up the pace. "A quarter left!" he shouted at Seech, standing by the tiller. A "quarter" corresponded to a mark on the deck, as did "half" and "full." More nuance was required under sail, but under oars, particularly in battle, such increments were considered sufficient. "We will land near those trees," Jash told Naxa, pointing at the beach. "Have line handlers stand by to go over the side and secure the ship."

"As you command," Naxa agreed. Jash trotted back

toward the stern, watching the flying machines roar past. If anything could strike terror into his warriors (and him), it was the enemy planes. These six were of the medium size with a single engine, blue on top and white on bottom, marked with a red dot in a white star, surrounded by a darker blue circle. Red and white stripes festooned their tails like colorful plumage. Shaped like a small boat with wings, they were obviously designed to land on water. Rockets no longer pursued them, though they still rose and flashed over the south side of the distant city, above New Sofesshk, where much of their war industry was. About the time he reached Seech's side, he knew with relief that the warplanes had no interest in his lone galley, but were making for one of the monstrous iron-plated greatships of battle, with four tall smoking pipes rising high in the air. Their target was anchored and seemed helpless—but Jash had seen some of the new things they could do. . . .

Three planes went for the greatship, beginning steep dives, while more peeled off after other targets. Dozens of antiair mortars fired amid a great swirl of smoke, but instead of a short-range cloud of small projectiles, each mortar threw a bomb, or "case," packed with powder and balls. These all exploded nearly simultaneously about half the distance to the diving planes—just as two dark objects dropped from each. To Jash's satisfaction, the cones of projectiles the mortar shells discharged intersected the paths of two of the planes pulling out of their dive and literally swatted them from the sky. Both fell in the wakes of their bombs, trailing shattered fragments and streamers of ragged fabric. All six bombs hit the sloped iron armor of the greatship, exploding and sending jagged plates spinning into the lake. One plane's remains clattered against the armor, while the other dropped into the water. The third plane, which Jash thought was uninjured, began to trail smoke as it turned away to the southeast. Except for one toppled funnel, the ship seemed little hurt.

"Well," Jash said, eyes slitted with pleasure as he searched for the other three planes. A column of smoke towered over an armored cruiser about a mile away, but the planes were nowhere in sight. Either they'd all been destroyed or they'd beat a hasty retreat. Not seeing any more smoky tendrils, he suspected the latter. Still . . . "That worked better than I expected," he finished.

"Yes," Seech agreed, troubled. "But some almost certainly flew away from here"—he waved at the sky over the distant city—"and there. I don't *think* the enemy was supposed to see us assembling like this," he added darkly. "Why else did we do all we did, hiding the galleys and carrying them back and forth, if not to trick the prey? Now they have seen. They will know." He paused. "They will be ready."

Jash shook his head, staring at the vast numbers of ships and galleys spread across the lake. There were at least ten of the greatships here alone, and they'd demonstrated only what they could do to planes. Their new ship-to-ship batteries were even more impressive. More greatships would be nearer the city and there were probably three tens of cruisers and at least four hundreds of galleys in view. He knew many more had been gathered and hidden at Old Sofesshk because the enemy, for whatever reason, didn't bomb there. There was no question he was very young and had little experience with such things, but he didn't think there could've ever been so much power assembled in one place.

Signal flags were breaking out now, punctuated by attention horns repeating the commands of other flags beyond his view. They were probably spaced all the way back to the Palace of Vanished Gods itself. The order had been given, directing the entire Swarm to begin moving eastward, toward the city. "They may soon know," Jash replied, "and they may prepare. But I doubt they will ever be *ready* for this."

"Surprise is lost," the Chooser lamented, crest lying flat. He hadn't had time to have it stiffened or brush the age-defying tints into his facial fur before his attendants warned him of the air raid. Flinging on his macabre vestments, breaking several fringes and scattering tiny bones across the floor in his chamber, he added the belted short sword—not that it would do him any good if the already

restless Hij population of Old Sofesshk chose to riot—
and hurried out to watch. By then the raid was already
past. *They come and go so fast!* he thought. What
prompted his thought wasn't the expected result of the
attack—more dark columns of dirty smoke and hundreds
of wispy tendrils of rocket exhaust, already dissipating
downwind—but how densely choked the river was with
warships and galleys. *The galleys are moving* now, *in
daylight. That was* not *the plan,* he inwardly wailed,
dumbfounded.

They'd determined it was time to launch the Final
Swarm mere days before, but Esshk had said nothing,
nothing about doing so now, under the sun—and the direct observation of the enemy! And what might be in-
calculably worse: a few bombs had actually fallen on the
north shore of the Zambezi, on *Old Sofesshk*, for the
very first time, obviously targeting clusters of galleys being carried from their hiding places in the sacred city to
the water. So far, for some reason, the ancient city, with
its high density of pampered Grik elites, had been spared
the attention of their enemy. And the Chooser had long
dreaded the loss of support they might suffer when that
changed.

Esshk, First General and Regent Champion of all the
Ghaarrichk'k, was already outside the Palace of Vanished
Gods, standing on the smooth stone approach to the
arched entrance and staring at the smoke piling across
the river above New Sofesshk. The handful of wrecked,
burning galleys on the near shore hardly seemed to reg-
ister. The Chooser relaxed slightly when he realized Esshk
was prepared for any reaction by the mob because he
wasn't alone. Second General Ign, Supreme Commander—
after Esshk—of all the Grik armies, stood beside him,
and several hundred of his Guard troops were deploying
around the palace. Esshk looked grim, his jaws clenched
tight, but his crest stood high on his head and his tail
plumage flared beneath his long red cape. His—and
Ign's—were stances of defiance, almost *eagerness* to join
the fray, usually shown only by mid-level Hij commanders.
Grik Generals were supposed to suppress such urges,
keeping themselves apart from the joy of battle, and the

Chooser didn't know whether to be encouraged or panic over that.

Esshk turned to him, eyes flashing, but his voice was unusually mild. "*Complete* surprise may be lost, but not its scope or timing. And I do not think it will matter now," he added cryptically.

"How can that be, Lord?" the Chooser asked.

"There has been a great battle at . . . Zanzi'ar, the Sovereign Nest of Japh Hunters. Our ally, the General of the Sea Hisashi Kurokawa, was utterly defeated and slain." Esshk said the last with what might almost have been satisfaction.

"How? When? Are we *sure*? The enemy has been destroying our airships practically at will, and they were our only means of rapid communication with the Japhs."

"Their General of the Sky escaped with some of his flying machines and landed in the Central Regency, near Kakag." Esshk waved his clawed hand. "It is such a tiny little outpost, I doubt you have heard of it. All it does is make Uul for the shipbuilders on the coast. In any event, the Japhs had a small airfield there, and Regent Consort Agatch'k discovered their presence. He sent the report by airship, flying far inland. It arrived last night."

"What did the General of the Sky say?"

"What I told you. Zanzi'ar has fallen and Kurokawa is dead—but the enemy required virtually all its fleet to accomplish that and suffered sorely in the battle. Little, if any, of its fleet will be available to oppose us."

"That leaves . . ."

"Only the single carrier of flying machines, their *Arracca*, and the one heavy warship, *Santa Catalina*, which have plagued our coast for weeks and launch the swarms of smaller flying machines that come during the day. That also might explain why the larger flying machines that drop their bombs at night have not been here for several such; they were busy elsewhere. Perhaps *they* were all destroyed," Esshk hoped aloud. "But, again, that will hardly matter. By launching the Final Swarm now, much of it will be loose in the strait and scattering far and wide, as planned, by dawn tomorrow. There will be no concentrations for the big planes to harvest. As for the two ships and their inconsequential escorts, they can *try* to oppose the Swarm and be overwhelmed or destroyed, or they can flee. There is no other option for them."

"Brilliant," the Chooser conceded. "But why did you not consult me? It was your decision, of course, but . . ." He didn't continue. It *was* Esshk's decision, but they'd been a team ever since the evacuation of the Celestial City. He felt . . . disappointed.

"You slept," Esshk replied gently. "And might have counseled caution," he continued more firmly. "Of that we have had enough. And air attacks aside, the Swarm will gather itself and proceed more easily in daylight."

"I appreciate the sleep, Lord." The Chooser bowed. "The Giver of Life knows I needed it. And I understand your reason for setting the Swarm in motion with light to see. But I *would* have counseled caution once more, that we wait for darkness regardless. We remain vulnerable."

"In what way, besides a few nuisance attacks and the loss of a few ships and Uul?"

The Chooser pointed at a massive iron-plated battleship chuffing past the palace, red flags streaming proudly from its mastheads. "There are places on the river where the enemy need only sink one or two of those, and the entire Swarm will be caught as if behind a cork in a jug. With daylight, a few 'nuisance attacks' might result in disaster."

Esshk's crest twitched. "They cannot sink such a thing with the puny bombs the smaller planes carry. All will be well. And it will do the coddled Hij of Old Sofesshk good to *see* the unleashing of the Final Swarm. Perhaps now they will cease their mewling. A night sortie would have had less effect."

"But bombs have fallen on Old Sofesshk," the Chooser reminded. "What if that encourages their mewling—and more?"

Esshk glanced at Ign. "Then, as we have discussed, we will begin the long-planned 'final transformation' slightly early. No interference of any sort will be tolerated now. From the Hij of Old Sofesshk . . . or even the Celestial Mother herself." Esshk's eyes narrowed. "Such a strong-willed one, for her age. I never would have imagined it. Given time, she might have been a *great* Mother of the traditional sort." He clacked his jaws. "She still might be great, under our guidance, but she must learn her new place."

The Chooser considered that for a moment, torn inwardly, instinctively, as he always was when they discussed such things. It had been his idea, after all, but it remained difficult to toss aside perhaps thousands of years of tradition and conditioning. And there was no going back now. They were committed. Another thought struck him. "What of the General of the Sky and his planes? I understand some can even be flown by our kind. Can we use him? Them?"

"Possibly," General Ign answered for Esshk, who looked doubtful. "There is fuel for the machines where they landed, but they are few in number and I do not think we could make more like them before the war is decided. All the things to make them fell with Zanzi'ar, and there are none of the bombs or other special ammunition they require, other than what they may carry. Our allies"—he snarled the word—"always made their own and never trusted us with the new types they worked on. We might remedy that with time, but like my lord"—he bowed to Esshk—"I remain . . . unconvinced the General of the Sky will serve us well. He is not as craven or despicable as Kurokawa, and by all accounts gave freely of his knowledge while developing the airships, rockets, and bombs we have. But despite that aid, and other sorts"—he nodded at the passing ships—"all his kind are remarkably refractory at times. I am unsure he will help more than hinder."

"He has little choice now," Esshk pronounced. "And he may be of *some* use establishing ties to the curious League hunters who aided Kurokawa. We know so little of them. If they joined Kurokawa's hunt, might they not join ours? In any event, General of the Sky . . . Hideki 'urina'e has no nest, no support, and few of his own kind remain. He *will* return to our hunt as General of the Sky, for none can match his knowledge, but no other ambitions will be encouraged. He will do that or die."

////// *Baalkpan, Borno*
Capital of the United Homes and Headquarters of the
   Grand Alliance
November 29, 1944

*I*t was a bright, gloriously clear, and pleasantly dry
afternoon when Commander Alan Letts, Chairman of the United Homes and currently the entire
Grand Alliance, came down to the waterfront to watch
their latest achievement, the light cruiser USS *Fitzhugh
Gray* (CL-1), return to port after her high-speed trials.
Accompanying him was Surgeon Commander Karen
Theimer Letts and all their children (one human and two
adopted Lemurian war orphans); Commander Steve
Riggs, who was Minister of Communications and Electrical Contrivances; and Henry Stokes, the director of the
office of strategic intelligence. A Lemurian aide supported a broad, colorful parasol above them, at Karen's
insistence, to protect her husband's sensitive skin. He
"sloughed off skin like a snake," in her words, when he
burned.

   Dozens of Lemurian ministers were there as well, as
was almost every member of the legislative assembly representing the various Homes, or "states," in the Union.
Their furry pelts and wide, bright eyes were as multicol-

ored as the parasol. Most strongly supported Alan as chairman, as did the vast majority of the Union population, but Alan understood and even sympathized with the fact that, with the war increasingly distant, a disconnected weariness was beginning to set in. That couldn't be allowed to take deep root, because the war was in a critical tipping-point phase, and he was fully aware of how quickly it could get dangerously close once more.

Fortunately, many understood this, particularly the ministers and assemblypersons who'd been present during the apocalyptic battle that had consumed this very city. They'd continue to support him as long as his policies were successful. On the other hand, Baalkpan had grown tremendously as labor and troops flooded in from all over the Union, and most of the newcomers had no personal experience with the war besides the hard work they performed to support it. That was the true source of the disconnect. There was a growing desire to get on with the better life promised by the industrial and economic revolution Alan himself had set in motion. Therefore, though he remained highly popular with the people, only the assembly members from Maa-ni-la, Aryaal and B'mbaado, North Borno, Austraal, and Baalkpan itself, of course, were solidly behind him. And of those members, only "King" Tony Scott of the Khonashi in North Borno might be considered a close personal friend, who'd stick through thick and thin. Then again, Tony shared his perspective in a number of ways. Not only had he ridden herd over an even more bizarrely diverse constituency—the Khonashi were a mixed tribe of Grik-like beings and humans, who'd absorbed former enemies into their population—but Tony was also a former shipmate from USS *Walker*.

Members from Saa-leebs in general, and Sular in particular, were generally more antagonistic and stood figuratively and literally somewhat apart on the pier that day. Assemblypersons from Sina-pore and B'taava (which barely had enough people to qualify for independent representation, and then only because Sular had sent so many colonists there), stood close to the delegations from Saa-leebs. Others from Yoko-haama and the seagoing

Homes, many of which were politically united, tended to follow Maa-ni-la's lead. Many more stood squarely in the middle, and Alan longed for the days when there hadn't been so many factions within the cause. *I don't much miss the* reason, *though,* he realized philosophically. *We were losing then.*

Still, it was a mess, and growing more fractious as the war dragged on. But Alan had helped create the monster, and figured in the long run, if the Union survived, the diversity that formed it could only make it stronger. In the meantime, it probably seemed awfully confusing to the representatives of their more . . . monarchical allies, also present. These included Ambassador Bolton Forester of the Empire of the New Britain Isles, and formerly Leftenant, now Ambassador, Doocy Meek from the Republic of Real People. Of the two, he counted Bolton a friend. He'd lingered long after he would've preferred being replaced to help maintain the stability of the Alliance. The Empire was a Pacific power and its Governor-Empress wielded near absolute authority, since the cooperative plots by the New Britain Company and the twisted Dominion in Central and South America resulted in the murder of her family and nearly the entire Courts of Directors and Proprietors. Her nation was chiefly focused on prosecuting the war against the Doms, and there were those in the new Union who considered that theater much too far away to concern themselves with. Fortunately, most knew better. The Doms, though human, were just as bad as the Grik and had been, at least until recently, a more technologically dangerous foe.

Alan didn't know what to think of Doocy Meek. He'd arrived only the day before, after a very long flight from Zanzibar, via Madraas, Andamaan, B'taava, and finally Aryaal, but came highly recommended by Captain Reddy. The Republic, while ostensibly closer to the Union in regard to species diversity and political organization, was really more similar to the Roman Empire, which had undoubtedly, somehow, influenced it at some point. Its aristocratic senators held power over the purse strings of the nation situated on the southern tip of Africa, but its

Lemurian kaiser, Nig-Taak, had the final authority. His senate could choose not to *fund* his policies, but that could be risky, since he and his family were very popular, representing the stability the Republic craved, and there were always other aristocratic families from the various provinces angling for their constituents' approval. Senators were chosen by electors who could be picked by popular vote at any time.

The population was composed almost equally of Lemurians, humans (from very diverse races and even histories, it seemed), and a third species called Gentaa, which legend mistakenly considered human-Lemurian hybrids because they shared physical attributes of each. Courtney Bradford was adamant that this was a myth and the Gentaa were probably imports from yet *another* evolutionary past. In any event, the Republic was in the war at last. After a tentative start, its armies had finally lurched into action against the Grik in southern Africa, giving the Allies a long-needed second front for their enemy to worry about.

Surrounding the already relatively large gathering of officials were thousands of citizens of Baalkpan: sailors, troops, even yard workers who'd momentarily stopped what they were doing to watch from precarious perches atop cranes or other ships at the pier. Everyone was on hand for what had promised to be a triumphant celebration of the completion of the largest, fastest, most powerful modern warship ever built on this world (as far as they knew), but Henry Stokes had discreetly presented Alan with a cryptic report when he arrived that the trials hadn't gone quite as well as hoped. Alan was extremely anxious and had a sinking feeling that the celebration might quickly turn into a morale-pounding flop.

"What's the matter, dear?" Karen asked, noting Alan's furtive glances at the spectators and various assemblypersons.

"Oh, nothing." He managed a smile. "You know me and crowds."

Karen glared at him, sure he was lying, but shrugged.

"How long *now*, Daddy?" piped little Allison Verdia

in her heartwarming toddler voice, tugging on the sleeve of Alan's dress whites.

"Yeah," agreed their older Lemurian daughter, Sandra, fidgeting with her skirt while looking at other Lemurian younglings scampering around. They were all naked, but Karen insisted that *her* children would wear clothes. Sandra, named after Captain Reddy's wife and Karen's friend, was probably about four, but nobody knew for sure. Nor had she known her Lemurian name. Still, Karen figured she'd gained the size and maturity roughly equal to a human child of six or seven, and she spoke perfect English, without the odd pronunciations common among older speakers who learned the language. "I wanna play," Sandra emphasized, watching the younglings shoot up the cranes in marauding packs. They were never allowed in the yard and were taking the rare opportunity to explore it from all angles. "Later, sweetheart," Karen temporized, watching the same younglings with alarm.

Their younger adopted daughter, Seetsi, had a name when they got her but was still just an infant. She was sleeping in a carriage, pushed by their one-armed nanny, Unaa-Saan-Maar. Unaa was a former Lemurian Marine and had left her own younglings in the care of another nanny—with offspring of her own—at the Great Hall.

"I think she's coming in now," Alan said, hearing excited cries from the 'Cats with the highest vantage points. Even before the rest of the crowd caught sight of USS *Fitzhugh Gray*, however, coming through the narrow channel into the bay, the excitement started changing to dismay as word quickly spread, and the air of celebration began to turn.

"What's the matter?" Karen asked, standing on her toes.

"I reckon," began Henry Stokes in a very dry tone, "that no one expected to see the bloody thing *towed* back to port."

Alan glared at him. "Towed? Why? And why didn't you warn me?"

Stokes shrugged. "What difference would it've made?"

"I . . . I might've told them to bring her in after dark," he replied, as the crowd grew more disappointed.

"An' lose half a day fixin' whatever failed?"

Alan had no reply.

"Pick me up, Daddy!" Allison demanded. Without thinking, Alan raised his daughter and plunked her on his shoulders. He could barely see the tops of the tall funnels in the distance now, and the ship's high "fighting top" on her foremast as she was towed past the Baalkpan ATC. He could also see the masts and funnels of the two transports, heavier, beamier versions of Scott-class steam frigates, pulling her in.

"Daddy," Allison said doubtfully, with her better view, "I think that boat is broken."

"What's the dope?" Alan asked Stokes. "What's the matter with her?"

"Why don't we let Commander Miyata tell us himself? He'll be here soon enough an' we'll get the full report." Stokes borrowed a speaking trumpet from a nearby yard foreman and raised it questioningly. Alan reluctantly nodded, and Stokes, a former leading seaman aboard HMAS *Perth* on another world, scampered halfway up the stout timbers supporting the closest crane and raised the trumpet to his lips. "Attention! Your attention, please!" Most 'Cats, in the yard at least, spoke some English. All the ex-pat Impies did. Others had to wait for a translation. He paused while the hubbub died down. "Thanks," he continued. "Now, it appears the *Gray* had a bit o' bother with her engineerin' plant, an' Captain Miyata chose to shut it down before it got worse. That's what sea trials are for; to find problems so we can fix 'em. No worries; it's nothin' serious. On the other hand, reports are that all her weapons're fine, an' work better than expected. Her new fire-control systems're the best we've made." He laughed. "She ain't sinkin', an' we'll have 'er fixed up an' sent out to help Captain Reddy in no time! So give her an' her crew a good onya when she comes alongside. But stand ready to clear the dock so we can get right to work on her, yeah?"

"Karen," Alan said, "Why don't you take the kids home? I might be here awhile."

"Okay. And then I'll head over to the hospital for a while." She frowned. "Let me know what you find out?"

"Sure."

A much smaller crowd did give *Gray* a nice welcome an hour and a half later when she finally touched the dock, but it was more subdued than it would've been if she'd steamed in under her own power. And, as Henry Stokes asked, the onlookers cleared fairly quickly once *Gray*'s lines were doubled up. Even most of the ministers and all but one assemblyperson had gone, leaving a few deputies, some of whom Alan would've wished away. Specifically underscoring this, as soon as the brow was rigged, the deputy assemblyperson from Sular, an annoying pain in Alan's ass named Giaan-Naak, tried to lead the others up the ramp.

"Hold it!" Alan snapped, earning a resentful blink. "That's not how we do it in the Navy Clan, or anywhere else I know of," he reminded forcefully. "You will *not* just stampcde aboard!"

"Thaat's our ship as much as yours!" Giaan objected.

"That's debatable," Stokes murmured. "Far as I know, all Sular's tax revenue has gone to support Sixth Corps in India—where it ain't doin' a bloody thing—an' sendin' colonists to B'taava."

"Enough," Alan said, tired of the ongoing argument. "But it doesn't matter who paid for her; she was built for Captain Reddy's clan. *My* clan," he stressed, "to defend us all. You can go aboard as soon as Commander Miyata's prepared to entertain you. I have official business." He turned. "Mr. Stokes, uh . . . 'King' Scott, and Ambassadors Forester and Meek, will you join me?"

"You take *them*?" Giaan seethed. "All foreigners, and none of them even *people*!" There were gasps, even from some of Giaan's companions, but for the first time Alan realized he was right, in a way. Everyone he'd invited was human. But he was simultaneously stunned and furious because he couldn't remember how long it had been since he even thought like that. "Deputy Assemblyperson Giaan," Alan said icily, "I said you could go aboard soon, but even you must understand that I need the first report." He nodded at Tony. "'King' Scott's not only a

head of state but a full assemblyperson. The only one
still here. If others had stayed, I'd have invited them as
well—but *they* probably get that there's a lot to do, and
I'll give the entire assembly a full and complete report
as soon as *I* have it. As for ambassadors Forester and
Meek, they enjoy the same status as heads of state, as
the senior representatives of their national leaders in
Baalkpan." His expression darkened. "And you'll apologize at once for implying they're not people, or I'll personally and unmercifully pester your boss until you're
replaced and sent home. Is that understood?"

Giaan recoiled amid the shocked chatter around him,
and Alan was perversely satisfied to hear the deputy
from Maa-ni-la tell another: "Indeed. Well said. They
were all people enough for him when Giaan fled to the
Filpin Laands with so many other Sularaans, raather
than fight when the Grik came as far as Baalkpan!"
Giaan must've heard, because he spun and flashed his
hate with fluttering eyelids. Turning back once more,
however, he seemed to have composed himself. "I . . .
aa-pologize if my zealous protection of Sularaan inter-
ests has caused offense."

Alan shook his head. That was no apology at all, but
it was the best he was likely to get and he couldn't afford
to widen the rift with Sular right now. He'd never understand it. Sularaans in general were fine folks, and many
were in the armies and the Navy. *But how the hell did
the same shitbags who ran out on them when the Grik
came get put back in charge when they slithered back?*
Then it dawned on him. *Because most of the ones who
stayed were* here—*or in the armies and the Navy!* Sular
had been a ghost city until the "runaways" returned. He
sighed inwardly. *They'll be in for a shock when the war's
over—if it ever is—and all those veterans go home and
kick their asses out of office.* In the meantime, he'd just
have to put up with their crap. Without another word,
Alan turned and tromped up the bouncing brow. Tony
Scott limped behind him, crutch under one arm and his
ruined leg in a brace. Forester and Meek followed, leaving only Stokes. For a moment he just smiled at Giaan,

who began to blink uncertainty. "C'mere, mate," he said, beckoning him away from the others.

"Anything you haave to say to me, you can say in front of them!"

"Oh, I don't reckon you really want me to do *that*," Stokes suggested. Reluctantly, Giaan stepped forward, and Stokes leaned over to whisper in his long, unusually pointed ear. "Chairman Letts won't say it because he's a good bloke an' just wants ever'body gettin' along to win the war, but Sular, under wankers like you, ain't helpin' nobody but itself. I can't prove it yet, but I reckon you're even doin' things that'll *hurt* ever'body—except the wankers in Sular. Now, here's fair warnin'. Either quit it now an' pitch in, or I *will* get my proof an' take it to the chairman. We'll see how nice he is about it then. Don't let his 'good bloke' act fool you. If he gets good an' mad, if the rest of the *Union* does"—he leaned back and his smile became a grin—"if *Captain bloody Reddy* does, I promise you'll hate what happens next."

Giaan stepped back amid a flurry of frightened blinking but quickly regained his composure. He turned to the others. "I de-maand thaat you bear witness!" he cried stridently. "The director of straa-te-gic intelligence has just *threatened* an aassemblyperson!"

Stokes shook his head as though exasperated, tilted it to the side, and blinked exaggerated pity in the Lemurian way. "You better watch him; he's had too much seep. All I did was make a promise to a *deputy* assemblyperson. No threat at all."

After being piped aboard (with whistles) by a finely turned-out side party that had obviously been expecting them, they adjourned to *Gray*'s wardroom with Commander Miyata and his senior officers. Miyata was stiffly correct but also clearly mortified. Alan doubted if anything that went wrong had been his fault, but Miyata was very sensible to the trust placed in him and took any failure extremely personally. 'Cat stewards brought iced tea and distributed it around the table while Miyata introduced his officers to Forester and Meek. All were Lemurians except the gunnery officer, a rangy, blond-haired former *Mahan* gunner's mate named Robert Wallace. He'd been heading up Bernie Sandison's Department of Experimental Ordnance while his boss was gone, but volunteered to be reactivated—like so many others—to provide a small, experienced core group of officers and NCOs for this very experimental ship. Miyata's XO, Lieutenant Commander Ado-Sin, was a burly, gruff-looking 'Cat with dark, rusty fur, who looked a lot like a younger Keje-Fris-Ar. *Gray*'s engineering officer was Lieutenant Sainaa-Asa, the tallest female Lemurian Alan had ever known. Like Wallace, she'd been too busy in Baalkpan to spare—a project manager at Baalkpan Boiler and Steam Engine Works—until others knew enough to replace her. Alan hated to let any of them go and wished Spanky, Bernie, Campeti, and so many others—and especially Captain Reddy—would come home where they belonged to pass along their irreplaceable knowledge. *Then again,* he supposed, *their* experience *is probably where we need it most right now.* . . . He shook his head.

Several other officers were introduced, including another distant cousin of Chack named Lieutenant Eno-Sab-Raan. He was the torpedo officer and had also worked with Bernie. Gaat-Rin was the final ensign to be named before Chief Bosun's Mate Pepper was introduced. Alan shook his head and smiled at the black-and-white 'Cat. "We're really scraping the bottom of the barrel now," he said.

"Yah," Pepper agreed. "An' me just a cook on *Waakur* before." He'd been a cook ever since, in fact, managing a thriving café and bar called the Castaway Cook in partnership with the absent Earl Lanier. The establishment was very popular with sailors and Marines, and better known by the unofficial name of the Busted Screw.

Stokes chuckled. "You've been runnin' the Screw *like* a bosun, by all accounts. You'll have no worries."

"I ain't worried about bossin' sailors around. Like you said, I do that all the time. I'm just worried how the old Screw will get along—an' my other business enterprises." He blinked suspicion. "Some o' my cousins are *not* the most honest 'Caats."

Everyone laughed at that, even Miyata, but then his expression sobered. "Perhaps, sir, now that the introductions are complete, it is time for me to make my report?"

Alan nodded. "Please."

Miyata sighed. "All was well—much better than expected, in fact—until the full power astern trial."

"If I may, Cap-i-taan?" Lieutenant Sainaa asked.

Miyata frowned. "It was not your fault, but it was *my* responsibility."

Alan cleared his throat. "One thing you still need to get past, Toryu," he said gently. "We don't fling blame around in *this* navy when there isn't anyone to blame. I assume Lieutenant Sainaa observed the casualty first-hand? Let her have her say."

Miyata reluctantly nodded, and Sainaa spread her brown-furred hands on the table. "Thaank you, Mr. Chaar-man. But I *do* have blame. Some of the problem was because my snipes is so inexperienced. I should'a trained 'em bettcr."

"You've had very little time," Miyata interrupted, "and this crew is *very* green . . ."

"Please, just tell us what happened," Alan pressed.

"As he said"—Sainaa glanced at Miyata—"the crew is very green, but they been trainin' haard an' is staartin' to get the haang of things. Still, on top o' all the usual little stuff that craaps out in trials"—she'd participated in quite a few, so she knew what she was talking about—"some things go unchecked." She shrugged. "An' with a whole new kinda ship, there's things maybe we don't *know* to check—or expect. The worst was when the lube-oil pump for the staar-board shaaft croaked an' quit." She blinked anger at herself. "I prob'ly should'a heard that," she confessed, and with her acute Lemurian hearing, Alan didn't doubt her. "But *Gray*'s noisy down below, an' I ain't learned all her sounds yet myself. Caan't blame green younglings—though it should'a been looked over."

"What happened?" Ambassador Doocy Meek inquired, speaking for the first time beyond his greetings. He'd been a ship's engineer himself long ago, in another war on another world, and was keenly interested. Sainaa looked at him. "The bearing croaked too. Seized up the shaaft."

"We believe we secured the engine quickly enough to prevent serious damage," Miyata interjected. "But the bearing, at least, must be replaced. And the pump repaired, of course."

Alan leaned back. "That doesn't sound too bad. What, maybe a week or two in the yard? But why didn't you just bring her in on two engines?"

Gray's officers exchanged looks, and Miyata sighed. "It's not quite that simple, and as I said, it's my responsibility." He hesitated. "Considering the critical shortage of ships at Captain Reddy's disposal and how important it is to take this one to him as quickly as we can, with the shaft secured and the ship in no danger, I . . . chose to proceed with further trials. It's possible *Gray* will lose an engine in combat, and I saw an opportunity to learn how she handles in such a circumstance." He brightened. "The answer is, quite well, actually. On her remaining two shafts she can maintain eighteen knots with ease, and with the center engine directing its thrust at the rudder, she turns almost as sharply as she otherwise would."

"Then what happened?" Alan pressed, and Miyata's face fell. "Perhaps in my exuberance, fueled by this discovery, I ordered emergency full astern." An uncomfortable silence descended on the wardroom, and *Gray*'s officers fidgeted in their seats.

"Oh, for God's sake, spit it out!" Stokes exploded. "We're wastin' time!" Miyata looked at him and nodded miserably. "She answered very well at first, slowing rapidly. Then she began to back." He blinked. "Perhaps it was the uneven thrust, or the rudder geometry itself is problematic, but . . . it slammed hard over, damaging the steering gear and wrenching the rudder shaft out of alignment. That's why we had to request a tow."

"Blimey," Meek murmured.

"What's the breakage?" Alan asked with a sigh.

"Where's Commander Rulk?" Stokes demanded. Rulk was the senior inspector for the Baalkpan Navy Yard and had supervised the trials.

Sainaa waved toward the stern. "Aaft. Him an' his team is still surveyin' the daamage, but he thinks it'll take a month in the dry dock."

"A month!" Alan declared.

"They may haavta rebuild the whole stern, strengthen the shaaft, an' reinforce the framing. He didn't know."

Stokes fulminated, and even Alan simmered. He wasn't mad at Miyata; what he'd done was reasonable. *God knows how many times* Walker *has been down to* one *engine,* he thought. *But still . . .* He'd hoped to get *Gray* squared away and deployed immediately.

"Okay, here's the deal," he said flatly. "Everybody knows Captain Reddy finally kicked Kurokawa's ass, and the Repubs"—he nodded at Doocy Meek—"have won a battle against the Grik in southern Africa and pushed all the way north to the Ungee River, near some Grik burg called Soala. That's only a couple hundred miles southwest of Sofesshk itself. Crossing the river's gonna be a bitch, though, because the Grik have shoved a lot of reinforcements down to stop it—which is what we wanted, I guess: to weaken Esshk's Final Swarm. But the Repubs are in for a bloody slog. All the same, people here are pretty pumped about how things are going, and that's good." He paused and took a sip of tea.

"In the east, in the fight against the Doms"—he glanced at Forester this time—"USS *Donaghey* met up with Fred Reynolds and Kari-Faask. And Greg Garrett's finally getting to know people in the New United States." He shook his head. "That's still so weird. Americans— from 1847!—that've made their own country in south-central North America. Anyway, they're gearing up to jump on the Doms from the east while CINCEAST Harvey Jenks gets ready to hit 'em from the west at that 'Pass of Fire' of theirs." He looked around. "What isn't as widely known is that General Shinya's Second Fleet Expeditionary Force kind of got its ass handed to it, chasing Don Hernan's Army of God. Seems Don Hernan isn't in charge anymore, and the Doms finally have a general who can pour piss out of a boot. Nobody knows where Don Hernan is—he probably got away—but Shinya's pushing hard to catch up with his army and mount a joint operation against the Pass of Fire with High Admiral Jenks. We'll see how that goes."

Alan took a deep breath. "Worse, and what *nobody* knows, is that Greg Garrett confirmed that the Doms and the goddamn *League* have been talking. We don't know what that'll lead to, but it can't be good."

The League of Tripoli was a fascist power composed of a warped alliance between France, Italy, Spain, Germany, and possibly a few others that had arrived in the Mediterranean from a very different 1939 than the one Alan Letts, Tony Scott, and Toru Miyata remembered. And they'd come with a modern *fleet* originally intended to wrest Egypt from the British Empire and take the Suez Canal. There'd been considerable friction, but for reasons of its own the League seemed more intent on subverting its war effort against the Grik and Doms than actually joining the fight. And with the information Matt Reddy had obtained from one of their disaffected German pilots and a few Leaguer prisoners taken when they captured Zanzibar—and the League battleship *Savoie*, which had been given to Kurokawa—a *very* few now knew roughly what the League had in terms of ships, planes, and men. If they combined with the Doms, it could be catastrophic. Alan didn't elaborate on that. Everyone understood the implications.

He took another sip of tea and set the mug on the wardroom table. "Finally," he said, "and worst of all." He glanced again at Meek. "Repubs on the Ungee or not, the Grik are about to launch their whole damn Swarm at Madagascar. We've confirmed that by aerial reconnaissance, and we're talking *hundreds of thousands*, armed with muskets and cannon instead of crappy crossbows, swords, and firebomb throwers. And they're going in *galleys*, thousands of 'em, which they can scatter all over the Go Away Strait if they get out of the Zambezi River."

There was shock in the compartment, and Miyata exclaimed, "But Captain Reddy and what remains of First Fleet are stuck at Zanzibar and Mahe Island, making repairs!"

"Too bloody right," Stokes replied sourly. "Captain

Reddy can't do a bloody damn thing about it. All we have in the way is Task Force Bottle Cap." Everyone knew all it consisted of was the heavy Home-turned-carrier US-NRS *Arracca* and her small battlegroup, which included USS *Santa Catalina*. She was just an old freighter with a few guns and a little armor slapped on. She'd done good work and could handle herself against Grik battlewagons by keeping her distance and relying on longer-range weapons. But she was fat and slow, and no matter how they used her, she wasn't really a warship. Unfortunately, she was the only surface combatant of any consequence on the scene. Against the force they were expecting, she stood no chance.

Alan confirmed their worst fears. "Russ Chappelle is taking *Santy Cat* up the Zambezi to block the Swarm until we can get some help down there. It's suicide," he stated with utter certainty, "but she's all there is." He looked squarely at Miyata. "So I want Commander Rulk in my office as soon as he has hard figures, or inside of two hours even if he doesn't, and you'll get ready to shift this tub over to the dry dock right now. No liberty for anyone until she's out of the water. Then, however long Rulk figures it'll take to fix *Gray* up, you're *personally* going to make sure it takes half that time. Is that understood?"

Toryu Miyata bowed over the table, expression intense. "Yes, Mr. Chairman, it is."

"W hat the *hell* do you think you're doing?"
Lieutenant (jg) Dean Laney practically
roared, shoving his way past the Lemu-
rian stationed at the lee helm on (CAP-1) USS *Santa
Catalina*'s bridge. The 'Cat, his tail arching slightly beneath his kilt and his eyes blinking indignation, almost
shoved back. Almost. Huffing from his climb up the stairs
outside, Laney stopped in front of Commander Russ
Chappelle's captain's chair and glared at the younger man
with light brown hair. Younger he might've been, but
similar to Laney's longtime nemesis, Dennis Silva, Russ
was more than a physical match for the obese engineer
who'd gone considerably to seed. And his moral, not to
mention official, authority towered over Laney's.

Once a mere torpedoman 1st aboard USS *Mahan*
(DD-102), Russ Chappelle had risen to become captain
of the *Santa Catalina*, a former naval auxiliary general
cargo hauler of 8,000 tons that they'd discovered half-
sunk in a Tjilatjap (Chill-Chaap) swamp. Its cargo had
been crated P-40Es, which they'd salvaged and used to
good effect. Sadly, particularly after recent battles,

nearly all of those were gone. But refloated and reconstructed as a protected cruiser and seaplane tender, while
retaining her cargo capacity, *Santy Cat* carried as much
armor as her old bones would support and was armed
with a variety of weapons. Some had been salvaged from
the Japanese battlecruiser *Amagi*, including a breeched
twenty-foot section of one of her main guns. This 10″
rifle was forward, on a robust pivot mount, with spring-
assisted hydro-pneumatic shocks to tame the recoil. It
was a bear to load, having to be returned to a fore-and-
aft orientation and depressed between shots, but with
an imaginative fire-control arrangement, it could throw
an improved 500-pound projectile with surprising accuracy up to ten thousand yards.

Six of *Amagi*'s 5.5″ secondaries had been placed in an
armored casemate, or castle, at the base of *Santy Cat*'s
amidships superstructure. And two 4.7″ DP mounts had
been moved to flank the main gun, somewhat behind and
below on the well deck, when five new DP 4″-50s were
recently installed—four on the upper central superstructure and one on the fantail. In addition, pipe mounts had
been welded to almost half the stanchions and would
accept the twenty new copies of the .30-caliber Browning
M1919 water-cooled machine guns the ship was issued,
in light of the new—hopefully now controlled—air threat
that had been posed by Kurokawa's aircraft on Zanzibar.
Everybody prayed that with the fall of that place, they'd
seen the last of those, but there were plenty of other
threats in the world and lots of things those machine guns
could defend against, in the sky and on the surface. Russ
certainly hadn't clambered to give them back. The only
new thing *Santy Cat* hadn't received that Russ really
wanted was one of the quad-tube torpedo mounts with
the improved MK-6 torpedoes. Her role as a seaplane
tender required her to keep a *little* open deck space, however, and there just hadn't been anywhere to put one. In
any event, bizarre as she was, Chappelle commanded
what was, at least until USS *Fitzhugh Gray* joined the
fleet, the most powerful warship in the Union and Grand
Alliance—and he still had to deal with the likes of Dean
Laney.

"What was that again, Lieutenant?" Russ asked softly, but his tone was full of menace.

Laney, without thinking, blinked something akin to "excuse me" in the Lemurian way. 'Cat faces weren't quite as expressive as human faces, and they conveyed a lot of meaning through blinking, as well as ear and tail positions. Humans couldn't do the ears or tails, but many had incorporated some blinking over time. Even Laney. When he spoke, however, he didn't sound very contrite. "I asked . . . sir, just what the hell you're about to do with *my* engine." He glanced at the compass binnacle and saw their course, 270—due west—and nodded to himself with a grimace. He'd already been ordered to increase speed to 10 knots, practically flank speed for the old ship. "Scuttlebutt is, the flyboys off *Arracca* saw the Grik gatherin' up to come gallopin' out. That's a helluva thing, sure, what with the rest of First Fleet stuck at Zanzibar or limpin' back to Mahe Island. We're on our own." He flapped his arms in genuine frustration. "We kinda been on our own before, an' whupped our way out of the jam. Even the ol' *Santy Cat*'s as fast or faster than those Grik cruisers an' BBs, or whatever they might send out. We got better guns too. We can stay at arm's length an' hammer 'em till they quit, or we get some goddamn help down here. But that's not what *you* got us doin," he accused. "Is it . . . sir?"

"No," Russ agreed. He looked at the bridge talker, a young female Lemurian who reminded him of Minnie aboard USS *Walker*. Even her tiny voice was similar. "Call the XO to the bridge, if you please," he ordered. "Tell him to ask Major Gutfeld for a pair of Marines on the way," he added, glaring significantly at Laney. Laney gulped, possibly realizing he may've gone a step too far this time. *Good*, Russ thought. *Laney rules the roost in his engineering spaces, the one and only place he hasn't been kicked out of. The problem is, he stays there so much that he's begun to think the rest of the ship is just a shell around his engine, not the* warship *his engine pushes around. Well, it's time to straighten him out once and for all—even if it's for the last time,* he considered bleakly, *or finally just relieve his stupid ass.*

"Captain . . ." Laney began.

"Shut up, you. I've had enough. You throw your weight around"—he glanced significantly at Laney's waist—"in your division pretty well. The only thing you've ever excelled at. And you've got all your poor snipes buffaloed because they put up with it. Hell, they must *like* it, God knows why, or they would've tossed you in the wake long ago. But whatever you do, whatever they think of you, you somehow keep the screw turning better than I ever thought you would. That's the only reason I haven't had you up on charges for your shit before. But you *won't* come up here and talk to *me* like that!"

"Cap—"

"No! Shut the hell up. You *will not* say another word. I'm talking to *you* now, see? And you're going to listen." Russ rubbed his face and stood. "You're an asshole, Laney. Probably born that way and can't even help it. I don't know how many postings you got tossed from before you came to me, but like I said, you do your job and I've let you slide. But now we're in a crack and there'll be no more sliding for anybody. It's time for everyone to get together and pull more than their weight." He shrugged and stepped to the aft bulkhead beside the talker, and turned the knob on the intercom to Shipwide.

"Now hear this," he said calmly. "You all know about a week ago, Captain Reddy and First Fleet finally kicked Kurokawa's sorry ass to death." Even on the bridge, they heard a similar roar of approval throughout the ship. Russ waited for it to subside. "You also know First Fleet took a beating in the process and'll take some time to make and mend." He looked straight at Laney. "What some of you have *heard*, that the Grik are gathering around Sofesshk to come charging down the Zambezi in full force—right in our face—is also true," he added. There was silence in the ship now except for the throb of the engine, other machinery noises, and the salty wind gusting around the open, armored hatches on either side of the pilothouse.

"I don't know if they planned it all along," he continued, "or figured out what happened up north and saw an opportunity, with us out here all alone, but the fact remains they're coming. And we *can't* let them out in the strait." He let that hang a moment before continuing. "*Arracca*'s observers reported a bigger fleet of heavies than we've ever run into"—he shook his head, unseen by any except those watching—"which wouldn't worry me by itself. We can sink whatever they send at us, and if anything big got past, what could it do? Their BBs can carry troops, lots of 'em, but none have been reported carrying landing craft. No boats at all. That means they'd have to off-load troops in a deep anchorage at a dock. That won't happen at Grik City because they'd have to get past Fort Laumer. The first one that tried would get sunk in the channel and block it—which they must know, because that's not what they're going to do. That brings us to our problem. Apparently, the Grik've got wise, and it looks like most of their army means to cross in galleys.

"For those who don't know, galleys are small ships with a bunch of oars that can go anywhere they want, with the wind or against it." He paused. "And people, they've got *thousands* of 'em. Those *galleys* are what we have to stop. If they get out in the strait they can scatter, and we can't kill enough to matter. Oh, we'd probably sink a few hundred, between us and *Arracca*'s planes— if we weren't too busy fighting the heavies—but Commodore Tassanna figures even if we got *half*, which I don't think we would, the rest could land wherever they like and our people on Madagascar would wind up facing two or three hundred thousand Grik, probably armed with muskets and the improved artillery Mr. Bradford reported down south. Our friends can't stand up to that," he pronounced simply. "The Maroons and Shee-Ree will fight like hell, but there's only about six thousand of them. General Maraan's Second Corps is still there and that's another thirty-odd thousand, but chances are Madagascar will fall. Then, while First Fleet's still trying to put everything back together, the Grik'd probably keep reinforcing until they can pull the same stunt against Mahe Island." He took a deep breath. "Folks, if that happens, we're *done* out here. All we've fought and suffered for will be for nothing—and we'll probably lose the war."

He didn't need to add that "lose the war" meant

"wind up eaten," sooner or later. He also didn't add that if it just came down to numbers, they were even more screwed than the forces occupying Madagascar. With a little more than half of Gutfeld's 3rd Marines aboard, *Santa Catalina* had 750 people to defend her. All the DDs and AVDs together had about the same, so about 1,500 combined. *Arracca* could send—or, God forbid—*bring* another 3,000, including the rest of the Marines, but that was it. Grand total: less than 4,500. Their only hope was that it *wouldn't* come down to numbers.

He shrugged, again unseen. "So here's what we're going to do: Captain Reddy didn't order it and doesn't like it, but Commodore Tassanna and I *told* him we're going up the Zambezi River ourselves, to put a stopper in it. We'll go upriver, fighting where we have to, until we reach a narrow bend the flyboys spotted at the end of a fat spot, almost a lake. That's where we'll sink whatever comes at us until we choke the river off. Our escorts will watch our flanks and *Arracca* will support us with her planes—and then herself, if she has to. She's still got some guns, you may recall." His voice hardened. "I'm sorry, people. This is a tough one, and I wish I could ask for volunteers. Instead, I volunteered us, and it was a crappy thing to do, but we don't have any choice. We *will* block that river. We have heavy weapons, a strong veteran crew, and the entire Third Marine regiment to help us do the job." Major Simon "Simy" Gutfeld's 3rd Marines were part of General Rolak's I Corps and had come along in case the commodore saw an opportunity for raiding. They hadn't expected anything like this, but Simy was all in. "And make no mistake, Marines," he added for the 3rd's benefit, "you'll be crucial. Galleys can squirm through some pretty tight places, and I guarantee you'll be in the action."

He paused again, for quite a while. Finally, he spoke once more. "I know what most of you are thinking: 'How long will we have to hold?' The answer is, I don't know. Right now, most of First Fleet simply isn't seaworthy. Even if Captain Reddy sent it down—and didn't lose half of it trying—it wouldn't do us any good. He'll move heaven and earth to get here as fast as he can and support us however he can. But we *will* block that damn river as long as we have to—and as long as a single one of us is alive. What's more, if we can do that, we'll be *handing* General Alden a safe place to land his army, close enough to the enemy capital that he can take it with a hop."

He sighed. "Well, that's it. That's the mission. It isn't pretty, but it is for all the marbles. I can only make one promise: however it turns out, nobody will *ever* forget USS *Santa Catalina*." He puffed out his cheeks. "That is all."

Switching off the intercom, he turned back to Laney just as his XO, Mikey Monk, stepped onto the bridge with a pair of Lemurian Marines. Laney was ashen faced, but didn't even look at the 'Cats. He merely shook his head. "I'll, uh, I'll go below now, Skipper, if that's okay. Back to my engine room."

"What? No more bitching?" Monk demanded, goading, almost breathless. His dark hair was disheveled under his hat and he looked like he'd sprinted there. He *hated* Laney and saw his chance to get rid of him slipping through his fingers.

Laney shook his head. "No. I'm done with that." He looked back at Russ, eyes steady. "You're . . . we're *really* gonna do this?"

"Right now."

Laney furrowed his brows. "Yeah." He took a long breath and looked at the overhead, thick with conduits. "You're right, Skipper," he finally said. "I've never been much. Won't ever be. All I've got is my engine. But as long as I'm alive, you'll have it too."

"You realize your engine, boilers, the whole damn ship"—Monk barked a laugh—"an' ever'body aboard, are gonna do have holes shot all in 'em, or get blown up or hacked to death before this is through?"

Russ held up a hand. "That's enough, Mikey. I think he knows."

Laney nodded. "Sure. Sure, I know that," he said distractedly, almost whispering. "But don't say it so loud!" He gestured at the ship around him. "You want *her* to hear?"

"She already knows too, Mr. Laney," Russ told him,

almost gently, watching the sheen appear in the man's eyes. "I think she's known this time would come ever since we found her. So let's treat her sweet while we can, okay?"

"Aye, aye, sir. Am I dismissed?"

Russ nodded.

Almost tripping as he turned the wrong way, Laney corrected himself and stiffly exited the pilothouse.

"He's completely lost it," Monk observed, a little shaken by how . . . let down he felt, and how compliant Laney suddenly was. "You still ought to relieve him."

Russ just waved it away, looking fondly at the Lemurian bridge watch around him, gauging their reactions. Most seemed to approve. The 'Cats got it, and they were in. They knew the stakes. In a way, this was what they'd been fighting for all along. If they couldn't hold the river, they'd probably lose the war. But if they did, and Captain Reddy came in time with First Fleet and all of I, II, and III Corps, they might finally *win*. "Hell, Mikey, we've all lost it," he said. "But Laney'll be all right for now. Long enough, I think. And did you see his face? He'll keep the screw turning as long as anybody on this goofed-up world possibly could, if just to keep the only thing he really loves alive."

He looked out the windows down at the fo'c'sle and watched 'Cats, sailors, and Marines placing narrow sections of iron plate, pierced for riflemen to fire through, between the stanchions. A lot of plate had been captured at Grik City, and Russ scarfed some up and had them prepared. Marksmen would have to crouch down to do it, but they could fight from behind the armor. Netting would be rigged above, to entangle boarders. Higher up, thick, grass-filled mattresses were being strung between the stanchions. They'd stop arrows and musket balls too, for a while. There'd been a number of notable close-quarters fights in this war, and it was almost inevitable that they'd soon face one for the book. He intended to protect his people as best he could. He refocused on the way the purple sea parted before the ship, creaming white down her sides. She was leading the way, the "screen," just four steam/sail (DD) frigates, two of which, having suffered the indignity of having some of their guns removed and becoming small seaplane tenders (AVDs) themselves, were already on the flanks. Frankly, Russ doubted they'd be much help against what lay ahead and was already contemplating how to use them best. Behind them all steamed *Arracca*, the thousand-foot-long wooden aircraft carrier, converted from a seagoing Lemurian Home. She wouldn't proceed upriver yet and would do so only as a last resort. For the time being, she'd linger near the mouth of the Zambezi, with the AVDs to guard her, while she covered *Santy Cat*'s advance from the air. But if she had to, she could probably block the river all by herself for a time. If it came to that, however, it would probably mean they'd already lost. It would certainly mean that *Santa Catalina* had failed—and everyone aboard her and the DDs detailed to accompany her, *Naga* and *Felts*, was dead.

Finally, Russ raised his gaze to the hostile shore of Africa, not so distant anymore. The coastal plain was broad and marshy, with clumps of strange trees surmounting little hills. Tiny in the distance, herds of large animals of some kind roamed the shallow swamps and grassland, unconcerned by their approach or the savage species that made their land its home. Grik didn't like swamps, and even when the Grik used their cooperative hunting tactics, the coastal beasts were fairly safe. Even if the Grik killed one, they still had to get it out. There was easier prey on firmer ground. Farther away, purple mountains loomed, only slightly darker than the sky above.

Everything looked deceptively peaceful; the late-morning sun was dazzlingly bright and the sky was clear, unmarred as yet by any clouds. Colorful lizardbirds flitted among the foremast booms and snatched morsels on the water, disoriented by the ship's passage. There hadn't been any enemy traffic in the strait for some time; even the supply barges carrying food and ammunition to the beleaguered Grik expeditionary force already on Madagascar had stopped after *Arracca*'s planes sank so many. Those Grik troops, under constant attack by the Shee-Ree and their allies (local descendants of all Lemurian ancestors), along with the human Maroons—and, basically, Madagascar itself, in the form of the hostile land and its many predators—were reportedly in very dire circumstances. But to Russ, it was hard to imagine what lay ahead. He'd been in some god-awful actions, but almost always out on the open sea. Somehow, he suspected what was coming within the narrow confines of the Zambezi would be much, much worse.

He debated sounding general quarters but decided to wait. The enemy had maintained a pair of heavy shore batteries at the half-mile-wide mouth of the river, and they were surrounded by the usual clusters of adobelike Grik warrens. Not cities or anything like that—just little villages to support the defenses. *Arracca*'s planes had bombed the gun positions (and warrens) repeatedly and mercilessly when they first came on station, so the batteries shouldn't be an issue. The river quickly narrowed, apparently becoming deeper with a clear channel, based on the estimated drafts of what had been seen coming and going before they arrived. Russ doubted they'd face much resistance at all—for a while. Word had it that the Swarm was coming downriver in a mass, following several Grik BBs, but there wasn't anything between them and the coast. Commodore Tassanna estimated that *Santa Catalina* and her consorts would probably meet the first enemy ships about the time they neared the bend in the river, if they hurried. Ideally, they'd get there first, but that would be tricky without a pilot and they couldn't count on it. No Allied vessel had ever been up the Zambezi before. "We've all lost it, Mikey," Russ repeated quietly, "but without this, we'll lose the whole damn thing."

Russ was wrong about one thing: there *was* something—someone—Dean Laney loved besides his engine. And the problem wasn't that voluptuous, almost stocky Surgeon Commander Kathy McCoy didn't know he existed; she absolutely did. She just could hardly stand him any more than anyone else could. But "hardly" was an important distinction and remained a source of hope for the engineer. Her face was pretty, in a rough-hewn, square-jawed sort of way, though her often tired, knowing eyes unconsciously reflected a lot of the misery the war had shown her. Lately, that was in the form of bleeding, crying 'Cats who somehow managed to set their shattered PB-1B Nancy floatplanes down in the water beside the ship. Though better planes were supposedly in the works, Nancys, a variation of the first aircraft the Alliance ever built, remained the backbone of the fleet air arm. Smaller, faster, pursuit ships, P-1C Mosquito Hawks—more commonly called Fleashooters—could carry machine guns *and* a couple of bombs now, but they couldn't carry a Nancy's load or land in the water.

Kathy's medical division tended the wounded, and the ship's air division salvaged the wrecks or patched repairable planes and sent them back to *Arracca*. Kathy probably should've been on the flagship herself, but most of the badly wounded, like their ravaged planes, wound up on *Santy Cat*, so the grinding pace of the carrier's air operations wouldn't be hampered by dealing with them. That made sense, but it also made sense that she should be where she was most needed. Besides, one reason the word "hardly" was so significant was that she *was* a woman and, by some twist of fate, the only one aboard USS *Santa Catalina*. There were others, mostly Impie gals, in *Arracca*'s engineering spaces and hangar deck, but there wasn't a single solitary human *man* over there. There were few enough on *Santy Cat*: just Captain Chappelle, Lieutenant Monk, Chief Dobson (the bosun), Major Gutfeld, and Dean Laney.

The captain was always courteous and appreciative that she was there, but showed no romantic interest. That was probably as it should be, Kathy supposed, and despite starting out enlisted, Russ Chappelle was very conscious of the behavior required of him as *Santy Cat*'s commanding officer. (This despite how things had turned out between Captain Reddy and Sandra Tucker, but everyone understood those . . . different circumstances, and knew they'd kept things "correct" for a very long time. Kathy could've been resentful, even catty, but was actually happy for her friend and colleague, particularly now that she'd been rescued unharmed.) But that still left her without a man. She supposed she really didn't need one but for a few things, from time to time, but also kind of *wanted* one, and there just wasn't much to choose from. And with things looking so grim . . .

Mikey Monk was the "prettiest" man on the ship, but had an Impie gal waiting in Baalkpan. So did Dobson, though he *did* show interest. *Not happening.* Dobson was enlisted, and even if he didn't care that he had a girl, Kathy did. She didn't know about Gutfeld. He hadn't always been a Marine, but he was now—all the way. He was friendly, even funny, but didn't talk much about himself. And all he seemed to care about was working his Marines, all day, every day, as much as possible. That left Dean, who'd been crazy about her ever since she once showed him a trace of compassion—and cured his hemorrhoids—while chewing him out for being a jerk. And he was *still* a jerk! But he didn't have an Impie gal, he wasn't enlisted, and he'd remained almost droolingly devoted to her for *years* in the face of zero encouragement.

She'd begun to feel her defenses slip. Then came the captain's speech. They were headed for the mouth of a river leading straight to hell, and as she approached the stairs to the bridge, to discuss what she needed to do to prepare for what was coming, she saw Dean Laney's distracted, dejected form shambling down from the pilothouse. "Oh, what the hell?" she murmured, and stepped to intercept him.

"You gonna throw me down the rest of these stairs?" Laney asked miserably, nodding at the companionway leading into the castle below. "I prob'ly have it comin', an' it would just about make my whole damn day complete."

Kathy was taken aback. "No," she said. "What's up?"

"You *heard* what's up. And just now, at the end of my useless life, I finally realized what a heel I've been for most of it. Worse, I gotta trundle my baby's carriage right up to the furnace an' throw her in." Kathy knew he always called the engine his baby.

"It can't be that bad, can it?"

Dean finally raised his gaze and looked at her balefully. "Oh yeah. You're goin' up to see the skipper. You'll see." He waved around at the 'Cats securing mattresses and mounting machine guns on the rails. "We're goin' right in among them hungry lizards, every last one, to feed ourselves to 'em."

Kathy's eyes narrowed. "I don't accept that. I *won't*. Sure, I heard, and I know it's a dicey situation—"

"Dicey?" Laney snorted.

"Don't interrupt! Yeah, maybe it's even worse than that. But I won't just give up." She put her hands on her hips and tilted her head at the Lemurian Marines working nearby. "You see *them* quitting? I don't. And unless you're even less a man than I thought you were, you won't either."

"So you think I'm a man—of some sort, anyway?" Laney ventured, his gloomy expression lightening a bit, with a flicker of an awkward, almost . . . charm she'd never seen before.

"Damn it, Dean . . ." She sighed. "Yeah. I never doubted that. I just never saw any sign you were a *good* man. Prove me wrong. Keep it together, keep your baby going until we get out of this jam, and maybe we'll talk about it. How's that?"

A tentative smile appeared on Laney's face. "Sure, doll, but why wait?"

Kathy pulled at her short hair in frustration. "See? You're such a *jerk*! Don't you *dare* 'doll' me! And we *will* wait—to *talk*, see? Or you can just forget it and go crawl down in the bilge and drown yourself, for all I care." She bulled past him, up the stairs to the pilothouse, leaving Dean Laney staring at her, mouth hanging open.

Arracca and her remaining screen, USS *Kas-Ra-Ar* and USS *Ramic-Sa-Ar*, had begun to shake out into their offshore station. With 'Cats casting lead lines aboard the escorting DDs *Naga* and *Felts*, and others preparing to do the same on USS *Santa Catalina*'s fo'c'sle, the old ship and her two consorts passed the ruins of the shore batteries and steamed upriver, toward the Grik capital at Sofesshk.

CHAPTER

3

"*T*hey're going in," Captain Matthew Reddy, High Chief of the Amer-i-caan Clan and Commander in Chief of all Allied Forces (CINCAF), said simply. Absently, he ran his fingers through sweaty dark brown hair, which was starting to gray at the temples. The face looking up from the message form Commander Perry Brister's XO, Lieutenant Rolando "Ronson" Rodriguez, had brought them would've still looked boyish, however, if not for the deep worry lines around the eyes. There were quite a few people, humans and Lemurians, packed in the small pilothouse of USS *James Ellis* (DD-21), and the aroma was . . . hard to handle. It was raining outside, of course, and the smell of the Lemurian-made "cotton" uniforms was a lot like wet, mildewed wool. Add stale human sweat and the musty, somewhat ironic wet-dog odor of damp, sweaty Lemurians, and it was amazing the funk wasn't visible.

Ellie was another four-stacker destroyer, almost exactly like USS *Walker*. That was understandable, since she'd been copied directly from her in the Baalkpan Navy Yard. The workers there had plenty of experience rebuilding *Walker*, after all, and with all the advancements made in the past few years it had been time to make the jump from wooden warships to modern steel-hulled designs. Using the term "modern" in association with *Walker* was ironic in itself, however, since she was a very hard quarter-century old, but copying her had been at the very cutting edge of what the 'Cats were capable of at the time.

Ellie had been the first of her kind, with many of the attendant prototype issues beginning to surface. Her slightly younger sister, *Geran-Eras*, had already been better—but was also already at the bottom of the Western (Indian) Ocean. Still, two more just like them—with further improvements—were finishing up at Baalkpan, and more had been started there as well as in the Filpin Lands. At the moment, *Ellie* was tied to a shattered dock on the east side of Island Number One in Lizard Ass Bay on the southwest coast of Zanzibar. All her most critical hull damage had been patched in the repair bay of USS *Tarakaan Island*, a massive SPD (self-propelled dry dock) not much smaller than a Lemurian Home. *Ellie* still needed further repairs, but they could be accomplished alongside the dock, and she'd been moved that morning to make room for the Allies' greatest prize: the French superdreadnaught *Savoie*, captured at the climax of Operation Outhouse Rat. One of *Walker*'s torpedoes had started a serious leak in her port engine room, but it had been another that damaged a shaft support, flooded the steering engine, and jammed her rudder, which drove the ship aground at the height of the battle. As soon as her hull and steering were patched, she'd be towed to Mahe Island for more repairs. Only then could *Walker* enter the dry dock for repairs of her own.

Matt glanced almost guiltily at his gallant old destroyer, moored dejectedly alongside *Tarakaan Island*. She'd only recently undergone a fairly thorough refit, and most of the latest repairs held good, but he'd immediately taken her back into the fire and she'd been hammered. Again. Her most serious wounds were a slap-patched pair of massive holes caused by one of *Savoie*'s 13.5″ projectiles, which had skipped across the sea and hit her sideways, causing a lot of structural damage to already age- and battle-weakened frames. It was bad enough that Matt's

XO, Commander Brad "Spanky" McFarlane, feared the patches alone wouldn't prevent the ship's bow from breaking off if she encountered heavy seas. They'd asked far too much of *Walker* in this war, her people too. But she'd become more than just a ship to so many now—a kind of "talisman of the Alliance," a living symbol of victory in the face of impossible odds. They still needed her as a warship, of course, but her mere presence in action was a force multiplier of confidence for those engaged far beyond her actual capabilities. She'd also become an object of dread for her enemies. Particularly the Grik.

Matt straightened and looked out to starboard. Most of the wreckage of Hisashi Kurokawa's dreams of empire were invisible from *Ellie*, the slashing squall ruining the view across the bay, where the bulk of his sovereign nest had been. Hundreds of Allied soldiers, sailors, Marines, and aviators had died taking the place, including Adar, who'd been the former Chairman of the Grand Alliance. *Thousands* of Kurokawa's Grik allies died as his army collapsed and his fleet was destroyed. Some surrendered, including more than a hundred of Kurokawa's surviving Japanese crew, accepting transport to the Shogunate of Yokohama in this world's Japan. A few even volunteered to serve, their old war with Matt's original destroyermen as dead as Kurokawa. And the Shogunate—mostly peopled by Lemurians—was an ally, after all. The wounds remained too fresh to use the experienced Japanese sailors as he'd like just yet, but Matt hoped that would change. Amazingly, persuaded by the Grik-like Sa'aaran Lawrence and a strange little Grik named Pokey who'd been fighting with the First North Borno Regiment, the *Grik crews* of Kurokawa's last four ironclad wooden cruisers even surrendered—something almost unknown in this war.

The rest of the defenders, along with perhaps a hundred more Japanese, fled into the wilds of Zanzibar. Matt doubted they'd survive, cut off from supplies from the mainland, and the Grik wouldn't have to go very hungry before they started eating each other. He suspected the Japanese, their former masters, would be the first in the cookpots.

"Stupid," Sandra snorted bitterly, refocusing Matt's attention. Her sun-bleached sandy-brown ponytail swayed as she shook her head. "Taking *Santy Cat* up that river now, with so little, will only get them all killed." Matt's wife was very small, very opinionated, and very pregnant. Shortly before, she'd been Kurokawa's hostage, and hadn't fully recovered from her long ordeal. Her face and limbs were still tight and skinny, her skin darkened by exposure, her features sharper, with a more ruthless edge. To Matt, she was still the most beautiful thing in the world, and having her back, safe by his side, made him feel whole again. He knew it might be a long time before *she* felt that way. Then again . . . She looked at her husband, and the harsh expression faded and she continued in a softer tone. "Of course, all of you coming here against Kurokawa, with everything *he* had, was pretty stupid too—and I'll always be grateful."

"Had to be done," Matt returned, avoiding her gaze. "Whether you were here or not." Sandra stepped closer to him and put her hand on his elbow.

"*I* think Russ's stunt is brilliant," Perry Brister croaked, disagreeing with Sandra. Despite his youth, *Ellie*'s skipper sounded like an octogenarian chain-smoker. He'd wrecked his voice commanding Fort Atkinson during the frantic maelstrom of the Battle of Baalkpan almost three years before, and a few of the old hands affectionately called him Froggy behind his back. The reference was only partially lost on their Lemurian friends, since there *were* frogs on this world. "If it works," Perry qualified. "I never thought he had it in him," he continued grudgingly, remembering when he'd been engineering officer on *Mahan* and Russ Chappelle was, apparently, just a somewhat lazy torpedoman.

"*If* it works and if we can take aad-vantage of it," agreed "Ahd-mi-raal" Keje-Fris-Ar, Matt's oldest Lemurian friend and commander of the great Home-turned-carrier USNRS *Salissa* (CV-1). In spite of his support, white-furred eyelids blinked worry against his dark rust-colored face. He and Tassanna, high chief of *Arracca*, had joined their Homes politically and were practically betrothed besides. But even though Matt had ordered

Tassanna not to follow *Santy Cat* up the river, everyone knew she'd do it anyway if she saw no other choice.

The hard rain abruptly stopped as the squall swept onward, over the main island to the east, leaving a steaming fog rising from the ship as the blurry sun appeared. Matt stepped out on the bridgewing, under the final drops, with his wife, taking a deep breath of wet, clean air. Keje, Perry, Rolando, and Colonel Chack-Sab-At of the 1st Raider Brigade followed, looking around for a moment. The rain-stilled waters of the bay lapped gently at the charred, skeletal wreckage of Kurokawa's last carrier, just ahead, and beyond was *Tarakaan Island*, with her massive burden, high and, if not exactly dry under the circumstances, already lifted from the sea and resting in the repair bay. *Savoie* was an awesome sight, apparently massing as much below the waterline as above. Tiny rain-soaked figures stood in ankle-deep water, dragging hoses and torching away curled and jagged steel amid bright yellow arcs of molten metal from the underwater hurts Matt's old destroyer had inflicted. Real steam rose around the hot slag hitting the water.

Lucky, Matt thought. *Even improved as they are, just two of our new fish never would've taken that damn thing down if her armor or torpedo blisters stood in the way. Just one lucky hit made the difference between defeat here, the loss of everything I love, and probably the whole war—and victory. Not to mention capturing that ship—which happens to outgun everything else the Alliance has, combined—relatively intact. Considering her age* [laid down in 1914, she was five years older than *Walker*], *she's in top shape. She's clearly had some upgrades over the years and her engines're fine, including the one that got a little wet. Isak and Tabby are happy with her boilers. She has been a bit neglected over the past few months, but only superficially.* He frowned. *The only things that'll affect her combat power, once she's patched up, are that her League crew apparently gutted her central fire-control suite before they gave her to Kurokawa, and the portside gun in her number one turret is missing about nine feet. Campeti thinks we can still use the gun if we cut it off a bit more, but it'll change its velocity and tra-*

jectory. That still leaves us with a heavily armored BB of our very own, with seven and a half 13.5″ guns, eight 5.5″s, eight DP three-inchers, twenty-four 8-mm Hotchkiss MGs, and five quad-mount 13.2 mms. The only problem will be feeding them—though she's got enough ammo for a couple of stiff fights. Almost a full load of a hundred rounds for each main gun, and near-full magazines for her secondaries as well. The small-bore stuff is a little more depleted.... We can handle the 5.5″s, and probably 3″s with help from the Republic, but it might be easier to just replace her machine guns with our own .30s and .50s. And the 13.5″s ... He rubbed his forehead. *They're going to miss a lot if we can't build a replacement for her fire-control computer. We can install a new level-crosslevel as soon as it gets here from Baalkpan. And the Japs were already working on a new computer from manuals. We'll just have to see.*

Looking at her now, particularly her upper silhouette, Matt was reminded of the old New York–class BBs, including USS *Texas*, named after his home state. *I wonder if we should change her name,* he mused distractedly. *That's never been common, even for captured ships. But we've always renamed Grik prizes, and after what* Savoie *did* ... He shook his head. *I'll worry about that later. She should probably keep her name. It's not her fault she did what she did, and it might rub their noses in it if she ever steams against the goddamn League.*

The League of Tripoli, centered in the Mediterranean, was founded by a large force of fascist French, Italian, Spanish, and German assets. There may have been others, but those were the big four. Actually, big three. The League was ruled by a triumvirate, and the German contingent seemed a little less equal than the rest. Matt still didn't understand it all. But the force that became the League arrived after experiencing a similar ... transportation to that which brought various other peoples over time, some friends, others ... not. Up until recently, however, the League had seemed content to merely meddle in the Allies' war against the Grik, Kurokawa, and the Holy Dominion while consolidating its hegemony over the Med—the main goal of its interference, apparently, being to weaken every party involved.

There'd been some costly scraps, but *Savoie*'s activities had been the most overtly hostile. Even then, it was clear from the few League prisoners they took with her that her leadership, including the (dead) Contre-Amiral Laborde and her (wounded, but in custody) Capitaine Dupont, had surpassed their orders when they sank SMS *Amerika*. *Amerika* was an old passenger liner converted to a lightly armed commerce raider in the Great War, and had represented the Republic of Real People in the Grand Alliance. The Republic was a very strange mix of humans, Lemurians, and . . . others, from the disagreeably (to the Grik) cooler climes of southern Africa, and was only starting to build a real navy. *Amerika* had been the only thing it could send east, past the perpetual ship-killing storm that lingered off the cape. Old and fragile, but still relatively swift and comfortable, she'd been serving as a hospital ship when she ran into *Savoie*.

It was from *Amerika* that *Savoie* took Sandra, Adar, and other hostages, before turning them—and herself—over to Kurokawa. That act, and otherwise materially aiding Kurokawa, put the entire League on Matt's "I *will not* forget what you did" list, but the Alliance simply couldn't do anything about it now. They had plenty of war to go around, and according to information Matt received from a disgruntled German pilot named Walbert Fiedler, who—hopefully—remained a friendly source within the League, as well as other leaguers they'd captured here, even *Savoie* would be woefully outclassed if it ever came to open warfare with the League. Matt had a rough list of League assets that he'd shared with very few people, and it wholly justified his desire to "finish the wars we've got, then prepare like mad," before going toe-to-toe with the League. Unfortunately, the campaigns against the Grik and Doms were presently proving to be more than they could handle.

On the plus side, Republic land forces *had* finally opened a long-awaited second front against the Grik, though it remained to be seen how effective they'd be.

The Australian engineer, Courtney Bradford, was with them as an advisor and representative of the rest of the Alliance. He'd reported that they'd (barely) won a battle, and were beginning to draw a lot of attention to their advance. That would make things harder for them, of course, but their allies desperately needed a distraction to thin the Grik Swarm at Sofesshk. Especially now.

"*Savoie* should be out of *Tarakaan Island* in a week," Matt said, looking at Brister. "She won't be ready to steam or fight by then—we don't even have a crew for her! But *Big Sal* can tow her to Mahe. She'll be better protected there, and closer to where we'll need her when she *is* ready. And besides the dry dock, Mahe has better repair facilities. Ideally, we'd send her back to Madras, where they could really fix her up, but we just can't spare *Big Sal*. My question to you is, can *Ellie* be fit for sea by then? We have a grand total of *two* seaworthy Scott-class sail/steam DDs left, and they can't defend such a helpless pair by themselves."

Keje bristled. "*Salissa* is not helpless! Her air wing was badly mauled," he conceded, "but I can keep a strong com-baat air paa-trol overhead!"

"You can't maneuver, dragging *Savoie*, and I'm not as worried about threats from the air as the sea," Matt countered. "There *was* a Kraut U-boat creeping around out here—we know it for a fact. God knows if it's still in the area. Where would it replenish? But we have to assume it is. *Salissa* and *Savoie*, poking along, would make a tempting target. I want *Ellie* and her sound gear prowling ahead of you."

Perry Brister pursed his lips. "*Ellie* could go to sea now," he said cautiously, then shrugged. "Today, anyway. We've got things taken apart that I'd like to secure first. She wouldn't be doing much sprinting, though, and I'm not sure how much good she'd be in a fight. The main battery's all right, but the fire-control wiring got shredded by *that* hit"—he nodded at the gutted charthouse behind the bridge—"and all we've got is local control. The EMs have been twisting wires like crazy, but there's still a lot to do. Otherwise, as you know, we lost one of the twin twenty-five-millimeter mounts. No fixing that anytime soon." All the 25-mm guns in the Alliance had been salvaged from *Amagi*, then *Hidoiame*. Most were going into new construction and there were no spares. New barrels were being made—since they were already making ammunition, it seemed sensible not to change the caliber—but the Baalkpan Arsenal was torn between copying the existing actions or trying to come up with something simpler. Both projects were underway, and trials would determine the outcome. "And the port torpedo mount is a total loss," Perry continued. "I was hoping to get another one installed. *Tara* still has a couple."

"Sure, if there's time," Matt agreed. "What else is left?"

"The forward fireroom is still trashed, and the number two boiler is finished . . ." He hesitated. *Tara* also carried a few entire boiler assemblies, but he didn't even mention it. Replacing a complete boiler would take too long. "We're trying to get the number one boiler up, and probably will," he said instead. "But the forward stack is a sieve. Right now all we have is the aft fireroom, and maybe eighteen knots, maximum. Other than that, the only major issue is the Nancy catapult. It's wrecked." He gestured aft. "In fact, it's gone. *Tara* took it and the shredded torpedo mount off."

Watching Perry, Matt was reading between the lines. "Okay, but what about the 'little things'?"

Perry glanced away, but when he looked back at Matt, his expression was pained. "No skipper likes to gripe about his ship. . . ."

"Stuff is starting to wear out, sir," Rolando finished for him. "Important things. Stuff that isn't *supposed* to wear out."

"Like . . ."

"Like the reduction gears," Perry rasped reluctantly. "There appears to be excessive, uneven wear." He held up his hand. "It's not incapacitating yet, just troubling. I know *Ellie*'s were the first, and still kind of experimental, but we can't tell if it's a surface-hardening or alignment issue without taking the whole thing apart."

"Which there isn't time for," Rolando said.

"Right."

"How bad?" Matt asked.

Perry managed a wry smile. "I've heard the sound they make compared to *Walker*'s reduction gears—it's about the same. And I can say from personal experience that *Mahan*'s weren't as bad."

"So, a few thousand miles have caused as much wear as . . . God knows how many thousands should." Matt managed a smile of his own. "Any chance it's just been a really rough break-in, and they've settled in?"

"That's possible, sir." Perry nodded. "But there're other things. Even the turbines are starting to look rough. Don't get me wrong," he quickly added, "the hull's sound and the patches are solid. *Ellie*'s combat power *should* be almost fully restored by the time *Big Sal* pulls *Savoie* out of here. It's just, as the first in her class, she has . . . issues you need to be aware of that may affect her reliability."

"I see," Matt said, thinking. "Well, relax. Like I said, you'll have at least a week. You're not going anywhere today."

"Whaat about *Waa-kur*?" Chack asked anxiously. Despite commanding a brigade of elite ground forces, probably permanently including the 1st North Borno, he still considered *Walker* his Home.

"Oh, she's in swell shape—except Spanky believes she'll break up and sink if she slaps a wave wrong," Matt answered bitterly. "He thinks a week or so of welding— he *hates* welding—will reinforce her enough, and provide sufficient framing for complete repairs. Then she'll escort *Tara* down to Mahe."

"So . . . two or three weeks, maybe *more*, before we can send help to Russ?" Sandra asked incredulously.

"*Probably* more," Matt agreed with frustration. Looking at the confused expressions and blinking around him, he sighed. "First, we don't know if Russ's stunt will even work. We'll prepare as if it will, and continue getting ready for our own invasion up the Zambezi with everything we've got. But if the Grik roll right over *Santa Catalina*, we damn sure can't get caught with our defenses out of place, or some half-ass reinforcement on the way. The good news is, we should know pretty quick if he was at least partially successful." By "partially successful," they knew he meant that *Santa Catalina* and everyone on her was dead, but her carcass was still blocking the river and slowing the enemy exodus. "If that's the case, we'll plan accordingly."

"Why would the reinforcements be half-assed?" Sandra persisted.

Matt had to remind himself that she'd been out of the strategic loop for a while and was still catching up on their dispositions. "Alan—I mean, Chairman Letts—is running around like a chicken with its head cut off, trying to get every transport and fighting ship we have left on this side of the world sent down from Madraas, Andamaan, even Aryaal, La-Laanti, and Baalkpan itself. And there's some good stuff coming. No more carriers, but more planes, supply ships, even the new cruiser, he hopes. Maybe one of the new DDs, if they can finish it in time. To prove how seriously he takes it, he's even mobilizing almost a Corps' worth of militia to send, people badly needed in the factories of Baalkpan. Another half-trained Corps, probably armed with rifle-muskets, is coming from Austraal. And we'll have more of the big PB-5D 'Clippers' sooner than expected, bringing Jumbo Fisher's Pat-Squad Twenty-Two up to twenty-five planes to bomb the enemy pretty soon. Ben Mallory, Lieutenant Niaa-Sa, and Cecil Dixon are going to the Comoros Islands to help turn the squadron into a wing." He shook his head.

"But most of the ships'll probably take closer to a *month* to get here, and our biggest problem, frankly, is transport. Second Corps, and about a division of Shee-Ree and Maroons, are at Grik City. They have no transport at all." He hesitated. "I've actually been thinking hard about sending *Sular* down to get them." USS *Sular* was a former Grik BB converted to an armored transport. "Evacuate Grik City completely," he continued. "Trying to hold it, so far out on a limb, has been a thorn in our side from the start. Sure, we've got friends on Madagascar," he said quickly, forestalling argument, "but even if the Grik take the city, they won't go after them. They can't for a while, and they'll be more focused on Mahe, anyway. That might even be a plan: let the Grik have the city, then invade Africa behind them."

"Then we would both haave each other's supply lines by the tails," Chack said, blinking distaste, swishing his own brindled tail behind him.

"Yeah, not ideal," Matt agreed, "but we might make it work. We'll *have* to if the Grik get past *Santa Catalina* and the strait, because I won't leave Second Corps to die." He looked back at Sandra. "First and Third Corps are on Mahe Island now. We could probably move both with the transport available, including *Sular*; the new carrier USS *Madraas*; and *Big Sal* when she gets there. But we *can't* send our damn carriers up that river carrying troops!" He nodded over at *Tarakaan Island*, with the French battleship in her bay. "She and *Sular* are really the only things we have suited for landing large forces with all their gear."

"Then . . . throw *Savoie* out and send *Tara* now," Sandra pressed. "Start the invasion *now*, right behind *Santa Catalina*!"

"I would if this war was all we had to worry about," Matt replied with feeling. "Hell, I'd even abandon *Walker* if it came to that."

"You would never do thaat!" Keje blurted, stunned.

"Yes, I would," Matt countered. "If I had to . . . and it would matter. As it is, we're still going to need every ship we can scrape up even if we finally beat the Grik. We can't *afford* to just abandon *Savoie*—or *Walker*." He looked back at Sandra. "Which brings us to the final point again. Without sufficient transport, we could only dribble reinforcements in a Corps at a time—and the Grik would chew them up. When we go, we need to be as fully prepared and equipped as possible, and hit the Grik with at least three Corps, maybe five. Just as important, we'll need a plan and logistics train to land on them like an iron *avalanche*, not a drizzle." He looked around. "That's the deal."

"So . . . even if *Santa Catalina* holds—for a while—we won't send *anything* to help her? To help our *friends*?" Sandra sounded just as incredulous as Keje had.

"I didn't say that," Matt denied.

"Hell, send me," came a bantering voice from behind them.

A colorful blur streaked past Matt's face, and a small, furry reptile with gliding membranes between its fore and hind legs slammed into Chack and stuck to his dingy rhino-pig armor like a grasshopper. Looking up with huge liquid eyes, it must've realized it had misjudged its target and instantly hopped onto Sandra and flowed up onto her shoulder. "Hello, Petey," Sandra said, fondly scratching the creature between eyes that narrowed with pleasure.

"Hell, send me!" Petey shrieked. The laughter that followed was simultaneously amused and annoyed, but everyone turned to watch Chief Gunner's Mate Dennis Silva take the last stair and join them on the bridgewing.

Silva was a big man, much abused by the war, with a black patch over his left eye. Other scars too numerous to count were hidden behind a short blond beard. He was wearing whites, apparently of his own accord, instead of the habitual dungarees and T-shirt, and was unusually presentable. "Not you, you little traitor," he growled at Petey. "I just got him back from that screwball Isak," he complained to the rest. "Had to promise him a cat." He glanced at Chack and Keje. "A *real* cat." Keje grinned, but Chack began to bristle. Silva quickly held his hands about a foot apart, blinking innocence with his good eye. "You know, the little four-leg kind, runnin' around on Impie ships . . ."

Mi-Anakka didn't mind being called Lemurians. Many even called *themselves* that now. And they knew 'Cat was an affectionate diminutive. They didn't necessarily appreciate comparisons to common felines, though, of the sort that crossed to this world in ships that founded the Empire of the New Britain Isles, centered where Hawaii ought to be. And referring to those as "real" cats was clearly intended to rile Chack. "God knows when I'll get one," Silva continued, seemingly oblivious. There were Imperials serving in 1st Fleet, but all their ships were fighting the Dominion in the east, on the west coast of Central and South America. "But Isak—the little twerp—took a IOU. Dumb-ass's been pinin' for a pet since we got here." He pointed at Petey. "Then, after all my finaglin', *that* little shit—pardon m'language—jumps ship first chance he gets, leavin' me holdin' the empty cat bag."

"He'll soon grow bored with me, I'm sure," Sandra said, still scratching Petey's head. "By all accounts, I never spoiled him like you do."

"Chief Silva?" Matt prompted, ignoring the distraction. "What did you mean?"

Dennis blinked and looked at his captain. "Just what I said: send me down to give Cap'n Chappelle a hand." He waved around. "Fightin's all done here an' I ain't got to kill nothin' in *days*. Killin's mighty hard to quit when you been at it awhile," he added matter-of-factly.

Sandra frowned, understanding perhaps better than anyone that Silva wasn't really joking. And everyone listening knew, despite how ridiculous the suggestion seemed, that the big man wasn't suicidal and wouldn't have made the offer if he didn't have something up his sleeve.

Matt was intrigued. "All by yourself?" he prodded.

Dennis displayed a patently disconcerting gap-toothed grin. "Well, maybe not *all* alone. Look, Skipper, I overheard what you said, an' it makes sense. Won't do a'tall, to go tricklin' our big landin' in. We gotta *pound* 'em when the time comes. But we do hafta send *somethin'* to hold the cork in the bottle for them three or four weeks you talked about. . . . If Cap'n Chappelle can stuff one in."

"What do you suggest?" Keje asked.

Silva grinned wider. "I'll take Larry an' Gunny Horn"—his eye shifted lazily toward Chack—"an' tag along with the First Raider Brigade."

"Now, wait just a minute!" Sandra flared. "Lawrence and Horn are both wounded, and Chack's Brigade took almost twenty percent casualties in the battle here. Thirty percent in the First North Borno!"

Silva waved it away. "Larry an' Horn ain't really *hurt*. Just little pokes."

"They were *shot*!"

"So? They ain't shot *bad*. You think they'd rather loll around in a rack or go have fun?"

Chack was leaning forward now. "The First Raider

Brigade is ready," he said. "Cap-i-taan Abel Cook has replaced Major I'joorka commanding the First North Borno, until I'joorka is . . . fit to resume his duties." I'joorka had been badly burned in the fighting here, and they all knew it was extremely unlikely he'd return to combat. He was lucky to be alive. Chack continued, shaking his head. "I know Cook is very young, but the troops trust and aad-mire him. More important, he has proven himself steady, imaginative, and aggressive. I recommend him for the brevet rank of major."

"Done," Matt said. "But no matter how ready you are, your Raiders are still under strength."

Silva winked at Chack. "Actually, they might be a tad *over strength*—after we swoop down by Grik City an' pick up a couple hundred of Will's Shee-Ree an' Maroons."

"You can't be serious," Rolando blurted. "All they've trained for is static defense, and that would further weaken the force we intended to leave there."

"Skipper just said there's no sense defendin' the place if the Grik get out," Dennis replied reasonably. "An' as for 'static,' tell that to the Shee-Ree who helped me an' Chackie hammer *dug-in* Grik on the Mangoro River. Tell it to the Maroons who broke trail for Chack's Brigade through the jungles o' northern Madagascar." He scratched his chin. "They're fightin' fiends, an' none of 'em like sittin' behind the Wall o' Trees at Grik City. Sure, we'll hafta mix 'em in quick, but if Cap'n Chappelle makes 'em somethin' to defend, they'll fight their way to it an' hold it to the end. They got more reason than anybody to keep the Grik the hell off Madagascar for good."

Chack was nodding. His sister, Risa, had fought with Maroons. So had Major Galay. Both told him they were "wasted" in defense. And Silva's point about the Shee-Ree was also valid.

"Okay, say that's so," croaked Perry Brister. "How will you get the whole brigade there?"

"Easy," Silva said. "We take what's left of Des-Rons Six and Ten: *Saak-Fas* and *Clark*. Skipper already said they ain't good for much, escortin' *Big Sal* an' *Savoie*.

There's half a dozen AVDs an' fast transports too, run-nin' supplies up from Mahe." He grinned. "But what I'd *really* like to take is them four Grik cruisers."

"But . . . how can you crew them?" Keje asked, sur-prised.

"With survivors from our other DDs."

Matt grimaced. "I want to put most of them in *Savoie*, as a core of officers and NCOs to build her crew around."

"Still can, Skipper. We don't need many. The new Grik CAs don't need many hands to sail. They hardly *got* any sails. All they need're officers an' gunners. Chack's Bri-gade can handle the guns."

"What about engineers?" Perry asked.

"Hell, use the Grik snipes." Silva waited while their expressions of disbelief spread. "Don't you get it? They ain't warrior lizards a'tall. They just run the machines. They surrendered, an' far as they're concerned, they b'long to us. Those Grik snipes in the tug that pulled Chackie out of Madagascar might'a been the first to do it, but ask Larry or Pokey. They talked the cruisers into givin' up. Hell, ask Gunny Horn how the Griks in *Savoie*'s gunhouse *joined* him in the fight. They'll do their jobs just fine unless more lizards swarm aboard an' take 'em back." He looked thoughtful. "An' after what Horn said, I ain't sure they'd change sides again so fast. Weird."

"You have given this a lot of thought, Chief Sil-vaa. Also 'weird,' considering you usu-ally tend to make things up as you go," Keje observed.

"Doin' a little o' that now, Ad'mral," Dennis con-fessed.

"It could work," Chack urged.

Matt was nodding. "Yeah. *If Santy Cat* survives the night—and however many days it takes you to get there." He looked at Chack, Silva, Keje, then Sandra. "Start putting it together. I want the First Raider Brigade em-barked and underway by dawn." He glared at Chack's surprised blinking. "You *wanted* to do this. There's no point if you get there too late, so you'll have to hustle. I'll send a preparatory order down to Grik City, to get the Maroons and Shee-Ree ready." He paused. "And remember, if it *is* too late, you'll stop wherever you are and whatever you're doing and head straight for Mahe, clear?"

"Aye, aye, Skipper," Silva and Chack chorused. Silva turned and started back down the stairs aft. "Where are you going?" Chack demanded. "We have to plaan!"

"Sure, Chackie. Just a couple things I have to do. First, I gotta go tell Larry an' Horn what they volunteered for. . . ." He was already gone. He hadn't added that he had to tell Pam Cross as well.

"That's something," Matt said, allowing a little relief to enter his voice. He really hadn't known how he was going to support Chappelle, other than from the air. He'd still do that, of course, and it would help, but probably not enough. "Spread the word: the new priority for everyone not actively working on repairs to our ships is to do whatever they can to get Chack's Brigade underway." He rubbed his forehead. "That's about all we can do at the moment. I sure hope we get better news from Second Fleet and General Shinya in the east."

4

////// *USS* **Maaka-Kakja**
2nd Fleet
Eastern Pacific

CINCEAST High Admiral Harvey Jenks and Admiral Lelaa-Tal-Cleraan stood on the high starboard bridgewing of the massive carrier USS *Maaka-Kakja* (CV-4), steaming northeast from the Enchanted (Galápagos) Isles. Two new, slightly smaller fleet carriers, built in the Filpin Lands—USS *New Dublin* (CV-6) and USS *Raan-Goon* (CV-7)—had joined her at last, already sporting the new "dazzle" camouflage scheme the Alliance had adopted and *Maaka-Kakja* had received during her extensive repairs at Albermarl. The sky was bright and almost cloudless, the equatorial temperature moderated by a stiff southwest wind that had turned the Pacific a brilliant marbled blue, its wave tops hazed by blowing spray of perfect white.

Lelaa had to admit that, particularly with the sea so scattered, the ugly new paint scheme was very effective at altering silhouettes. The idea wasn't so much to hide the ships; that was practically impossible, considering their size and vast wakes, which, snowy white by day and phosphorescent at night, would give them away from the air. Mainly, the jagged shades of gray and blue were intended to spoil the aim of enemy gunners by making it difficult for them to estimate ranges. *Faat chaance that I'll take carriers into a surfaace aaction again!* Lelaa thought. She'd done it at Malpelo and probably tipped the scales toward victory, but it nearly cost them her ship. And the months she'd spent laid up had deprived their land forces of vital air cover while fighting the Doms on the South American coast. In retrospect, it might've almost been better to *lose* at Malpelo and preserve *Maaka-Kakja.* The enemy would've still been too badly battered to capitalize on their victory. *But retrospect is too distaant to consider in the heat of baattle when your fleet is dying,* Lelaa honestly assessed, and realized the new paint scheme was a good idea after all. Given the same situation, she'd probably do the very same thing.

"It is a fine sight," High Admiral Jenks proclaimed with satisfaction, nodding at the carriers, steaming in line abreast, and the vast battlegroup surrounding them.

"Indeed," Lelaa agreed. "It's the most powerful fleet ever aass-embled against the Doms. With three carriers together, along with their improved planes, it might be the most powerful fleet aass-embled by the Graand Alliaance."

"With the situation so desperate in the west, it makes me feel a bit guilty . . . almost." Jenks absently twisted the long braided mustaches dangling several inches below his mouth. "I suspect I may manage to subdue my regret, however," he added dryly. The fact was, Jenks *did* feel guilty on behalf of the Empire. It had required far too much in terms of "modern" ships, arms, and even blood from their mostly Lemurian Allies just to hold its own against the evil Dominion. This while the Lemurian Union could ill afford the generosity, facing an existential threat from the Grik on the other side of the world. It shamed him that so few Imperials were helping their friends in that distant, desperate struggle. If this front had been comparatively neglected, Jenks more than understood.

Things were finally changing, though, and the Empire was getting its industrial feet under it in the wake of a brutal Dom attack, civil war, and various domestic upheavals. The three carriers and about half their auxiliaries belonged to the Union and, more specifically, the American Navy Clan, but the rest of the fleet, with a few exceptions, was Imperial. Granted, all the ships of the line were older-style sidewheel sailing steamers, but some of the newer escorts were armored copies of Union Scott-class screw frigates, or DDs. And the factories of the Empire, supplied with their allies' plans, were making their own weapons now. The DDs here and on their way were a stopgap. Armed with technical advisors from the Union, drawings sent by Spanky McFarlane, and the Empire's own inventiveness and impressive steel-making capacity, the shipyards on New Scotland were already working on steel-hulled warships of their own. The lightest would hopefully improve on the *Walker* class, and it was hoped the heavier ships might someday serve as a deterrent even to the mighty League. None of those could possibly be ready in time to impact the current campaign, however. They'd have to fight with what they had for the foreseeable future, and the war might very well be won or lost before the new designs could join them.

Jenks wouldn't complain. In addition to the carriers and their nearly two hundred combined aircraft, 2nd Fleet had twelve ships of the line under Admiral E. B. Hibbs. Eight sailed in front of the carriers, oilers, troop transports, and all the various support ships. Four brought up the rear. Ten of them, including the veterans *Mars*, *Mithra*, *Hermes*, and *Centurion*, represented the Empire of the New Britain Isles, and two were Dom prizes, manned by mixed human and Lemurian, Union and Imperial, crews. In partial recompense for all the gallant escorting DDs the American Navy Clan lost at Malpelo, they'd become USS *Sword*, formerly *Espada de Dios*, and USS *Destroyer*, formerly *Deoses Destructor*. *Destroyer* was commanded by Captain Ruik-Sor-Raa and seconded by Imperial Lieutenant Parr. They and their crew were as inseparable as their previous ships: USS *Simms* and HIMS *Icarus*, still bound by a desperate towline on the bottom of the sea.

Surrounding all was a screen of twenty DDs and AVDs (basically DDs with the capacity to launch scout planes), including the repaired *Ulysses*, *Euripides*, *Tacitus*, and *Achilles*. Jenks and Lelaa couldn't get enough of the awesome sight; the great carriers pounding through the swells, undisturbed by the boisterous sea, the liners a bit more jostled, and the DDs capering with what almost seemed an energetic impatience. All the sailing steamers were under staysails and reefed topsails, taking best advantage the gale, while smoke streamed from the tops of their funnels. Paddle wheels churned the sea at the sides of the older ships.

"If we'd had this much power before Malpelo, including your carriers, of course"—Jenks bowed—"there'd be no Dom fleet left to oppose us at the Pass of Fire."

"Perhaaps," Lelaa agreed, "but if so much had been spared to us then, at the expense of First Fleet, the war in the west would be lost. I too feel guilty and *almost* wish the caarriers had gone to Cap-i-taan Reddy instead."

She suddenly lowered her voice and glanced around to ensure no one was in earshot. "Speaking of feeling guilty, I suppose you read the, uh, con-taact report submitted by *Raan-Goon*'s cap-i-taan?"

Jenks nodded gravely. As soon as *Raan-Goon* and *New Dublin* joined at Albermarl, in the Enchanted Isles, *Raan-Goon*'s captain, Rin-Faak-At, passed on a detailed description of some disturbing radio traffic they'd intercepted three days out of the Filpin Lands, apparently originating from a mysterious flight of Japanese attack planes of some sort. This was confirmed by *Raan-Goon*'s signals officer, who'd come to this world aboard the Japanese destroyer *Hidoiame*. After a brief stay in the Shogunate of Yokohama after his capture, he'd joined the American Navy Clan. No former *Hidoiame* sailors were sent west—the Khonashi had wanted to hang them all, with good reason—but only their officers were "bad" men. The rest were just following orders in a frightening, inexplicable situation. In any event, he'd heard the increasingly desperate calls of his countrymen, somehow swept to this world as well, as they searched for their own carrier. Obviously, it hadn't crossed over with them.

Interestingly, this exact possibility had been foreseen and standing orders stated that no such contacts could be answered. There was too great a chance the Allies' unfamiliar ships—particularly the carriers—would be attacked by the modern Japanese aircraft. Even replying in Japanese might only make matters worse, because the talker wouldn't know any current codes or call signs. It was a terrible calculation, especially since the distressed flight would almost certainly go down at sea when its fuel ran out, but there was really no choice.

Lelaa imagined *Raan-Goon*'s signals officer had faced his worst nightmare and must've been tortured by his inability to assist his countrymen, but the fact he'd followed prescribed procedures eliminated any doubts about his commitment to the Allied cause. She honored and sympathized with him for it, and wished she could reward him. *But that might make him feel even worse. . . . And even though I wasn't even there, I still feel responsible.* "I wish we were with Cap-i-taan Reddy, fighting a clean—*right*—war against the Grik," she suddenly blurted. "Or that Cap-i-taan Reddy was here."

Jenks nodded. "Honestly, I feel much the same. I miss his quick judgment and his instincts. And his confidence," he added, "real or affected." Lelaa looked at Jenks. Obviously, the High Admiral knew Matt Reddy very well. Ironically, Matt's cousin Orrin, who came to this world at a different time aboard a prison ship escorted by *Hidoiame*, chose that moment to step out on the bridgewing with *Maaka-Kakja*'s captain, "Tex" Sheider. Orrin had been a pursuit pilot in the Philippines before they fell and became Lelaa's commander of flight operations (COFO). Oddly, the ship's chief engineer, Gilbert Yeager, was tagging along with Orrin and Tex. All seemed surprised to see Jenks and Lelaa. Orrin and Tex saluted, while Gilbert hung back.

"Sorry to disturb you," Tex said. "We didn't know you were out here."

"No disturb-aance," Lelaa replied, her eyes narrowing. "Unless you brought your aar-gu-ment with you?"

Both men looked sheepish. Tex was a former submariner off S-19 and had been with Lelaa a long time. He was also relatively short compared to Orrin, who looked like a younger version of his cousin. Tex's great ambition before the war was to become a naval aviator—little chance of that, since he hadn't been an officer then—but he remained loyal to naval aviation and had a running dispute with Orrin over which was best: the P-40 or the Wildcat. Sometimes it got fairly heated, to the amusement, and eventual annoyance, of those around them.

"Well, we *were* still discussing the merits of certain aspects of various planes," Orrin conceded, his drawl apparent through his careful enunciation. He, Matt, and Tex, of course, were all from Texas. Surprisingly, though Orrin had moved to California with his family some years before the war, his accent remained the most noticeable of the three. "Mainly whether air- or water-cooled is better. The Air Corps liked water because it allows for better streamlining—our Nancys notwithstanding. Nothing has more drag than they do."

PB-1B Nancys were an increasingly sore subject with their pilots. They were great, reliable little planes, perfect for relatively long-range reconnaissance and capable of landing on the water. They even made pretty good light bombers and ground-attack aircraft. The problem was, nothing else could do what they did, and they'd remained virtually unchanged since their inception. Part of that had to do with a general reluctance to mess with a good thing, but they weren't good enough anymore. Against the Doms, they were vulnerable to attack by lizardbirds, or what the Impies called "dragons," and they were slow enough that the enemy could sometimes bring them down with concentrated musket fire. Other, even more effective countermeasures had to be expected.

And the Grik already had close-in defenses, swatting Nancys down like flies from their capital ships. Worse, the battle for Zanzibar had shown that if they ever tangled with the League, Nancys would become useless, unsurvivable wastes of pilots. The little P-1 Mosquito Hawks, or Fleashooters, had been upgraded several times, and a C model with stacked, air-cooled radials now predominated. Yet another model, bigger and with a more powerful engine, was already in the works now that they'd faced a few League fighters (in Kurokawa's possession) for the first time and their limited hoard of P-40Es had been almost wiped out. But Nancys were still the only small planes they had that could float. There were finally rumors of a new model with a faired-in stacked radial of its own, along with other improvements, but none had been seen and none were expected for some time.

"And the Navy liked air-cooled for simplicity and reliability," Tex supplied. "Not to mention that air-cooled engines—like those in Wildcats—can take more punishment."

"Yeah," Gilbert interjected, his reedy voice so much like that of his half brother, Isak Reuben. Lelaa blinked at him, wondering why he was even there, and why her two most senior officers were putting up with him.

Orrin rolled his eyes. "I don't know how anything could take more abuse than the couple of P-Forties the Japs shot up around me. Stick to your boats, Tex—things you know something about!" Tex's face reddened and he started to respond.

"Gentlemen!" Jenks growled. "That's enough."

"Indeed," Lelaa agreed, "but haaving laid this aside, I thought, I'm curious why you resumed your debate."

Tex shuffled his feet and Gilbert ignored them all, looking at the fleet around them. "Nancys and Flea-shooters, indirectly," Orrin confessed. "I got the dope on the load-outs for *New Dublin* and *Raan-Goon* from their COFOs when they reported. Dern, those kids are green!" he digressed. "About half the new fliers are 'Cats from the Filpin Lands, a few from Austraal too, but the rest are Impies they picked up as the new carriers sailed east. Flight training in the Empire, on New Ireland, is even skimpier than what the 'Cats got, since there's fewer planes to practice in. We have to do some refresher training and joint exercises before we hit the Doms, or it'll be a slaughter."

"Of course," Lelaa agreed. "You can commence tomorrow. The sky priests in the weather division aass-ure me the wind and sea will moderate signifi-caantly. And we will be at Maan-i-zaales for a few weeks, at least, before we move against the enemy. You may continue your training uninterrupted by me until baattle is joined." Manizales was another coastal town that cast its lot with the Allies. Like most communities on the west coast of the Dominion, it included various equally oppressed but somewhat mutually tolerant cultural minorities. They'd been separated—and, until recently, protected—from more frequent persecution by New Granada and the denser populations to the east by vast distance and formidable ranges of volcanically active mountains. Like Guayak, Puerto Viejo, and Quito to the south, Manizales had been lured into rebellion against its Dominion masters by the possibility of Allied liberation. Strategically, Manizales was particularly important because it was closer to the Pass of Fire and had a much better harbor than Puerto Viejo.

Orrin looked relieved. "Good," he said. "My biggest chore will be un-teaching 'em half of what their instructors pounded into them at the Manila ANATC. I know those guys were all veterans when we sent 'em home to teach, but things've changed." He brightened. "The Impies might actually be easier, since they may not've picked up as many bad habits yet." He gestured at Tex. "What got us going, though, like I said, is how the Sixth and Seventh Air Wings are equipped. They've only got a few new C model P-Ones. Most of their ships are like ours—all the early models. It's like we got the rejects left over when the Cs went to First Fleet."

"I know," Lelaa said, "but they're not rejects. They're new air-craaft right off the aass-embly line in Maa-ni-la. They are the *laast* of the early models," she conceded, "but shouldn't go to waste if they're still of use. They are, and I'm glaad to have them."

"You are?" Orrin and Tex chorused.

"Of course. They're aac-tually better suited for fighting Grikbirds. The C models are too faast." Orrin's eyes went wide. Lelaa was right, and he should've thought of that. He was the experienced combat pilot, after all. But even if she wasn't a pilot herself, Lelaa was learning carrier and air combat tactics fast. Grikbirds couldn't even catch a Nancy in level flight. They could almost outdive one because they were so clean, but what made them really dangerous was their incredible agility. Speed was a wonderful thing, and even the earliest P-1s had that advantage over Grikbirds. But they could also—almost—

turn with them. The faster, heavier C models simply couldn't go slow enough to stay with them without stalling. "Besides," Lelaa continued, "as far as we know, the Doms still haave no air-craaft to contend with. Certainly not such as First Fleet recently encountered. Jaap planes, League planes—our best should go to them. They haave few enough ad-vaantages left, while we enjoy many."

"*May* enjoy many," Jenks cautioned. "We must never take that for granted. It has been some time since we fought their ships, and I can't believe they haven't improved them in some way by now." He looked at Lelaa. "But I agree with you. What we have should be sufficient for what lies ahead."

"About that," Orrin prodded. "What's the dope? Where are we going after Manizales? Straight to the pass?"

"Essentially," Jenks cautiously agreed, "but this is not yet to be generally known. There are doubtless Dom spies among our new friends ashore, and we will linger among them long enough for them to report what loose lips reveal. General Shinya and his Army of the Sisters have already reached Manizales and are marching from there to Dulce." Jenks looked thoughtful. "Frankly, we considered embarking General Shinya's army and carrying it by sea to the north side of the Pass of Fire. There's a fortress there, at a city called Ahumada, and there would've been less opposition. But General Shinya convinced me that he must continue to advance up the enemy's only line of retreat and supply by land. We will have to count on New United States forces to prevent supply or escape by sea in the Caribbean," he added doubtfully. "Meanwhile, the new Dom general, a man we now know is named Mayta, is making for the fortress city of El Corazon on the south side of the pass. We have good maps now, some captured and some the result of improved—if costly—air reconnaissance. Do not doubt there are still large numbers of dragons in the vicinity of the Pass of Fire," he warned.

"We haave our own spies now as well, of course," Lelaa put in.

"Right, all those Christian and Jaguar Doms flocking to join Shinya."

"They are not Doms, Mr. Reddy," Lelaa stated definitively. "At least most are not. Some are likely spies as well. But the vaast maa-jority want nothing more thaan our help to throw off the oppression of Don Hernaan's evil church."

"Any word on *his* sick ass?" Orrin asked, then caught himself. "S'cuse me, Admirals. Tex's uncouth ways are starting to rub off on me."

Lelaa chuckled but then blinked frustration. "Nothing. He escaped, as you know, and we must aass-ume he makes his way to the Temple at New Graa-nada, if he has not aal-ready reached it. Saadly, Gener-aal Mayta does not seem to suffer from his predecessor's mili-taary incompetence. He haandled part of Gener-aal Shinyaa's army raather roughly when he caught it strung out on the march to Popaay-an. Worse, the closer Shinyaa gets to El Coraa-zon, the stiffer the opposition may be. And not only from the Army of God." Lelaa shuddered to mention that most inappropriate name. To her, "God" and the "Maker of All Things" were the same, and it sickened her that all Dom depravity was practiced in His name. "By all accounts, the population on the finger of laand leading to the Paass is fiercely loyal to the Dom Pope, and we caan expect the locals to defend it and the fortress protecting El Coraa-zon just as fanaa-ticly as Mayta's army."

"So we'll be waiting while Shinya fights his way *to* the fortress guarding the pass," Orrin guessed.

"Initially, though we'll support him from the air as best we can," Jenks said. "Actually taking the fort and the city will require a rather more complicated joint operation."

Orrin sighed and waved out at the troop transports. "I get it. That's why we didn't just feed more troops to Shinya. Part of the joint operation will involve an amphibious assault."

"Yes," Lelaa confirmed. "But we must deal with whaat remains of the Dom fleet first."

Orrin looked quizzically at Tex. "Looks like we have our work cut out for us. C'mon, let's start working on a training schedule." In addition to directly commanding

Maaka-Kakja now, Tex was also Lelaa's "flag" captain and still, essentially, her XO. Orrin, as "flag" COFO, was likewise senior to all other COFOs in the fleet. They'd have to work very closely to implement Jenks and Lelaa's strategies. Orrin paused, blinking curiosity at Tex in the Lemurian way. "Say," he said, "what's your first name, anyway? I know it isn't Tex. Every Texan in the Navy was called that. I bet they called Cousin Matt that before he got the rank to make 'em quit—if they ever did." He shrugged. "Hell, it was the same in the Air Corps. I was 'Tex' in flight school, even though I was from California by then. Lucky there were already two Texes in my squadron in the Philippines when I got there. So what's your real name? Spill it."

For an instant, Tex panicked, then his face turned red. Looking at Jenks and Lelaa, he knew neither understood. Very few left alive on this world would. He started to go ahead and reveal what he considered one of his darkest secrets, but saw the look of predatory anticipation on Orrin's face. "My name's Tex," he said flatly. "Let's get to work."

"Suit yourself."

When Orrin and Tex were gone, Lelaa was surprised that Gilbert had remained, studiously ignoring them. "So, Lieu-ten-aant Gilbert," she asked, "what brings you here?"

"I ain't no lieutenant," he insisted. "Just an actin' chief."

"I promoted you."

Gilbert shrugged. "So? I don't wanna be promoted. You kept me from quittin' by swearin' you'd transfer me back to First Fleet." He frowned. "Back to *Walker*, where I belong. I kept up my end, helpin' get *Makky-Kat*'s engineerin' division sorted out. Even helped with her refit. But you didn't keep your word," he accused, then shrugged. "I figger my oath's to Captain Reddy an' *Walker*, an' since you won't cough me up, I'm retired. I'm a civilian, just strollin' around, takin' my ease. I can do what I want, like Mr. Bradford."

Admiral Jenks's face reddened, and he started to form a sharp reprimand, but Lelaa raised a hand with a tiny, secret smile. "Very well, Mr. Gilbert. You're right," she said. "And since I did promote you to lieuten-aant, you're free to resign your commission—though your oath to the Amer-i-caan Navy Claan remains in force." Her tone hardened. "As its senior represent-aative in this hemisphere, I *could* keep you as a sea-maan's aapp-rentice if I wanted, but I won't." She waved a hand. "I caan't send you baack to First Fleet. The traans-port simply is not available. But in light of your long and distinguished service, I will graant your wish to become a civiliaan. As soon as we reach Maan-i-zaales, you may go ashore and seek opportunities to occupy your new status as a gen-tlemaan of leisure."

Gilbert almost choked. "You'd *maroon* me here?" he demanded. "'Mongst heathen folks who don't under-stand a word I'd say?"

"If thaat is your desire."

Gilbert took off his hat and rubbed the short, greasy hair on his head. "Well . . . if that's my only choice, why can't I just stay aboard here for now?"

Lelaa smiled. "You mean as a civili-aan volunteer?"

"Well, yeah. Somethin' like that."

Lelaa sadly shook her head. "I'm afraid thaat's impos-sible. *Maaka-Kakja* is not a paass-enger vessel. She's an air-craaft carrier, a waar-ship, the *flagship* of Second Fleet. There's no space for idle haands." She blinked sud-denly, as if something just occurred to her. "Of course, you haave not yet resigned your commission! If you chose to reconsider your retirement and remain aboard *as an officer*, I'm sure something could be aarranged."

Gilbert opened his mouth and shut it several times, then slowly closed his eyes and shook his head.

CHAPTER

5

////// 2nd Fleet AEF (Allied Expeditionary Force)
Army of the Sisters

Rebecca Anne McDonald, Governor-Empress of the Empire of the New Britain Isles, and her Lemurian "sister," Saan-Kakja, High Chief of All the Filpin Lands, exuberantly galloped their horses alongside the seemingly endless column of troops. Both loved to ride and were very good at it, though Saan-Kakja hadn't known horses even existed for long. She'd learned her skill on the backs of vicious me-naaks, the long-legged, vaguely crocodilian beasts her people used for cavalry mounts. Though me-naaks, or meanies, saw extensive use in the West, horses were unmanageable around them and none had been sent east. Horses didn't like paalkas—oversize moose-shaped draft animals used for pulling wagons and artillery—either, but at least paalkas didn't instinctively want to eat them. In contrast, there were many creatures in the Americas that indigenous horses were well accustomed to yet might send me-naaks fleeing in terror. It was all a matter of familiarity.

Rebecca and Saan-Kakja had briefly outstripped their entourage of aides and guards sheerly for the fun of it. Both were young and adventurous—too adventurous for their own good, most believed—witness their presence, as heads of states, on a desperate military campaign. But they'd endured many dangers already and neither could bring herself to send their people to fight where they wouldn't go themselves. Their sentiments were simultaneously considered noble and irresponsible, even by the troops they led, but those same troops adored them all the more for sharing their hardships.

"Your Majesties, please!" came the breathless call of Lieutenant Ezekial Krish, Rebecca's aide-de-camp and leader of the protective detail. Rebecca rolled bright eyes in a grinning elfin face at her companion, whose mesmerizing eyes of black and gold blinked reluctant agreement. Together, they slowed their mounts while Imperial dragoons, the only forces still wearing traditional red coats with yellow facings and tall black shakos, quickly encircled them.

"Really, Lieutenant," Rebecca scolded the young and handsome—if sometimes excruciatingly rigid—Krish. "If we are not safe here"—she gestured around at the hilly coastal plain upon which all of X Corps marched along the winding Camino Militar—"with the might of half our army to protect us, we would not be secure within our own capitals."

"*Safer* here," Saan-Kakja murmured dryly. "You from any lingering plots to murder you for the soci-aal reforms you begaan, and myself from being coddled to death by my dear Lord Meksnaak." She sighed and blinked dramatically. "He caan be most tiresomely protective!"

"With respect, Your Majesties," Krish stated primly, disapprovingly, "even with good visibility all around and better air reconnaissance, General Mayta has already proven our army is not invulnerable to his surprising strokes. You mustn't simply gambol about without a care. War is *not* a lark."

That was the wrong thing to say. Pleasure of any kind had been a rare thing for Rebecca to experience over the past few years, and when she did, it was fragile. She spun in her saddle to face Krish, her sweet expression overwhelmed by fury. "You cannot possibly imagine that I am not aware of that! Or that my sister Saan-Kakja is not! We've seen more of this war than *you*, sir, and watched *thousands* of our people die. Many for my mistakes," she added bitterly. "So do not presume to imply that you alone can prevent us from harm, or that we do not view our situation with the gravity it deserves!"

"I . . . of course not, Your Majesty!" Krish floundered.

"You might just give her a little space from time to time, Lieu-ten-aant," Saan-Kakja counseled mildly. "As she said, we're as safe as the thirty thousand troops around us." She nodded ahead. "And look, there are Sister Audry's troops—just who we came to see! Rest your horses, Lieu-ten-aant. The Vengaa-dores will pro-tect us!"

Krish frowned. "Colonel" Sister Audry's Vengadores de Dios were almost all former Doms, and the core of their force had been captured in the fighting on New Ireland. Sister Audry, a Dutch Benedictine nun brought to this world with the children of diplomats aboard the old S-19, had gone among them and converted them—imperfectly, in Krish's view—to a Catholic version of the same Chris-tianity practiced in the Empire. Their ranks had swollen here, as hundreds of "heretical" true Christians, brutally persecuted by the obscenely twisted version espoused by the Dominion, flocked to join them. Another faith, even older here and equally oppressed, was represented by the Ocelomeh, or Jaguar Warriors, marching beside the Vengadores with Major Blas-Ma-Ar's badly depleted 2nd Lemurian Marines. Krish was torn between which faction he considered more unwholesome, but all had proven themselves in battle, and his Governor-Empress had warned him before that she'd tolerate no offense offered them.

"Very well, Your Majesties," he conceded sourly, holding up a gauntleted hand to stop his dragoons.

"I think he desires you," Saan-Kakja told Rebecca lowly, blinking mischievously as they trotted toward Ma-jor Blas and Sister Audry, who were striding among sev-eral others in the dust beside their troops.

"Nonsense," Rebecca replied, though she imagined it might be true. "And even if he did, do you think for an instant I could ever submit to his boorish attempts to direct me? It does not all have to do with protection, I'm sure." Her fury faded as she recalled Krish's actions at a critical time. "But he *is* loyal."

Saan-Kakja chuckled. "Yes, but you're right. Even if he won you, he'd die of frustration trying to guide you. Or worse, bend utterly to your will and become something you no longer respect." She grinned. "Besides, everyone knows your heart belongs to Abel Cook—a brevet major now, if I'm not mistaken!"

Rebecca's face colored. She didn't think she'd encouraged Cook, though she'd consented to let him write her, and his letters still came in periodic heaps from the far side of the world. In the wake of all the tragedy she'd endured, Rebecca hadn't allowed herself to examine her feelings for Abel Cook, but she knew they were there, and she worried about him.

"Here come your younger sisters," she heard Major Blas-Ma-Ar dryly inform Sister Audry as they approached. The brindled female Lemurian was slightly built, but many considered her the finest soldier in the entire 2nd Fleet AEF. It was also common knowledge that she and not Colonel Sister Audry actually commanded the heavy brigade, including her Marines, the Vengadores, and Ocelomeh. She also, to a lesser degree than Krish, considered Rebecca and Saan-Kakja irresponsible younglings, even though she was little older. But the war—and other things—had aged Blas beyond her years. In Rebecca's view, she'd earned her cynicism and a disquieting, simmering hostility toward General Shinya through her experience and performance. Rebecca would tolerate more from Blas than anyone except Captain Reddy. Her prime factor, Sean Bates; High Admiral Jenks; and General Shinya himself probably made that list as well.

Sister Audry stopped and greeted them with a smile. She was dressed like her troops, in a tie-dyed combat smock held tight to her waist by a belt supporting copies of a 1911 Colt and 1917 Navy cutlass. By all accounts, she'd never drawn either. High canvas leggings protected her shins and calves over brown, rough-out boondockers, and a steel doughboy helmet sat on her head atop light blond hair shorn even with the bottom of her jaw. A large cross rested on her bosom, suspended by a light chain around her neck. Like all the Vengadores, she had another white cross painted on her helmet. Otherwise, the only difference in dress within the heavy brigade—or all the armies of the Alliance aside from the Republic, for that matter—was that humans usually wore trousers beneath their smocks and Lemurians didn't. 'Cats also wore sandals beneath the leggings, of course, to accommodate their differently shaped feet.

"Good afternoon, Your Majesties!" Sister Audry said, saluting.

"And to you and your brave troops," Rebecca replied, bowing in her saddle. The humans cheered her, and the Ocelomeh cheered Saan-Kakja. Even though the Ocelomeh were humans as well, most wore little jaguar icons that looked strikingly like Lemurians. Their faith differed from the others' in that they believed that the same son of God the Christians worshipped had appeared to their ancestors in the shape of a great cat that they hadn't thought—until recently—even existed on this world. The consequent, much discouraged reverence they showered on Lemurians in general and Saan-Kakja in particular could be hard to take.

The men and 'Cats walking with Sister Audry and Blas were all known to the two leaders. Marine Sergeant Koratin had once been an Aryaalan lord but became a grizzled veteran devoted to protecting Sister Audry. He'd been one of the first Lemurians to convert to Christianity and credited it with saving him from despair and corruption. Commanding the Vengadores, and Sister Audry's nominal XO, was the dashing Colonel Arano Garcia. It was he who'd convinced Rebecca of his troops' true penitence and had led them in bloody battles against his former countrymen. Captain Jasso was his new "co-XO," along with Captain Bustos, who'd replaced the dead Ximen as headman to the Christian rebels swelling the ranks of the Vengadores. Captain Ixtli was another dynamic figure who'd been in charge of the Jaguar Warriors. He and his people still had a lot to learn, and they'd been incorporated into the 2nd Marines. The snowy-furred 1st Sergeant Spon-Ar-Aak, better known as

"Spook," was helping Blas groom him into a true combat commander. Blas intended to make him her XO of the 2nd Battalion, 2nd Marines, if he could be induced to take the oath to the Amer-i-caan Navy Clan. All saluted Rebecca and Saan-Kakja as well.

"I know you'd have all preferred a longer rest after your ordeal in the mountains," Rebecca said, pitching her voice to carry, "but at least this march must be fairly easy in comparison." Her deliberate understatement solicited light laughter and she continued. "Let Eleventh Corps enjoy the highland march for a while, though I know the highlands here are not nearly as extreme as those which you traversed." The laughter was mixed with good-natured jeering now, but many troops remained silent, reflective. XI Corps was another mixed force of Imperials and Lemurian Filpin Scouts strung out across the isthmus bisected by El Paso del Fuego, where Costa Rica should've been. Its objective was also to prevent landward escape or resupply of Corazon, and to investigate the east coast city of Puerto Limon. Whether XI Corps' commander, General Ansik-Talaa, would be allowed to attack Puerto Limon depended on what he found there, but it was hoped he'd at least finally make physical contact with covertly approaching ships of the NUS. Either way, it would be a milestone. His would be the first Imperial/Lemurian force to view the mythical Atlantic Ocean from the coast of this continent.

Rebecca considered what she'd said and what some must be thinking: that they'd been through hell, and now XI Corps had replaced them for the easy, exciting part, almost as if they were being punished. She had to squash that notion. "Some of you may even imagine that since Don Hernan escaped once more and we were all deceived by the size of the force you pursued, you suffered in vain during your recent campaign. Not so. You still destroyed a much larger force than your own, composed almost entirely of Blood Drinkers, the rancid cream of Dominion power. Your dogged, aggressive pursuit also convinced the new Dom general, Mayta, that all our army remained behind him, so he was almost as unprepared as we when he came upon us. I shudder to contemplate the scope of the disaster we may have suffered if he'd had more time to plan his breakthrough. All of Tenth Corps could've been destroyed. So never think you wasted your time and blood in the mountains, or that your sacrifice is unappreciated!" A general cheer swept among the troops under Blas and Sister Audry's command, and an unconscious smile even appeared on Blas's war-weary face.

Rebecca considered her next words. There probably were spies among these troops, as General Shinya warned, but the army's objective could be no secret now. She pointed north. "We march for Dulce, approximately two hundred miles distant. If the enemy stands there, we will destroy him, but I expect he'll flee to Corazon, another two hundred and fifty miles more. *You* will follow," she said simply, pointing at the troops, then waved at Saan-Kakja and Sister Audry. "And so will we." The brigade before her had practically stalled, creating a small but growing gap in the column. *No doubt General Shinya will chastise me for disrupting his orderly march,* she thought, *but here on the plain, for the moment, there is no danger. And these troops deserve these words after what they've endured—and what is yet to come.* She looked out at the expectant faces.

"That sounds far; four hundred and fifty, perhaps five hundred miles. But think how far we have come! Some of you were born here and had to find your true path far away before you could return. Others live here still, but have come far in other ways. My people come from the New Britain Isles, far across the sea. Saan-Kakja's from Maa-ni-la, even farther still. Some of you are from distant Baalkpan on the other side of the globe!" She paused for effect. "A few still among us were born on other *worlds*! THINK HOW FAR WE HAVE COME!" she roared, and held up her hands to stall the cheers. "Corazon and the Pass of Fire are a mere stroll in comparison," she said softly. "The battles there, when they come, may not end the war, but they will turn the page to the final chapter on the road to victory. And Tenth Corps . . ." She paused. "And the Sister's Own Division—for that is how

Saan-Kakja and I think of you—*will* be first to break into the city and take the enemy by the throat!"

The cheers were thunderous now, and waving, Rebecca and Saan-Kakja rejoined their dragoons and galloped forward along the column.

"Well?" Koratin roared. "Don't just staand there! The enemy is ahead, as the Governor-Empress said. At the quickstep, maarch!"

"A stirring speech," Blas remarked as the column resumed, hurrying at first to fill the gap. "Aass-uming, of course, the new Sister's Own Division haasn't already had its fill of fighting."

"Have you?" Koratin challenged gruffly, knowing the answer. To the contrary, most were concerned that Blas had come to love it, and his words were intended to assure her that the division had plenty of fight left in it as well.

Blas blinked irony and countered, "Have *you*?"

Koratin sighed. "My fill of fighting *this* enemy will come when they are defeated or I am dead," he said simply.

"As will mine," Sister Audry agreed, surprising them all. She looked at their blinking and the odd expressions of the humans. "You think my enthusiasm for the cause is less than yours?"

"Of course not, Santa Madre!" Arano Garcia fervently denied.

"Stop calling me that," Sister Audrey said in a tone of long-suffering patience.

"Yes, Santa Madre."

Sister Audry rolled her eyes heavenward, but then looked directly at Blas. "Then perhaps some think I do not fight because I do not kill?"

"Yes," Blas said, earning her shocked, reproachful looks from everyone except Sister Audry, who merely regarded her with a sad smile.

"Then, respectfully, Major Blas, I would try to persuade you that is a great mistake. I can't bring myself to kill, but I do most emphatically *oppose* as directly as any of you. With my life." She pursed her lips. "Do you think me a hypocrite because I urge you all to fight and kill when I will not?"

Blas blinked thoughtfully, evaluating her understanding of the word "hypocrite." "Yes," she finally said again, and there were murmurs of anger from the Vengadore officers this time. Blas continued. "As a few here know"—probably only Koratin, First Sergeant Spook, and Audry herself—"there was a time when I was as innocent of killing as you." Her thoughts drifted back to a terrible night in Aryaal that still tormented her dreams. She'd been a young naval recruit aboard USS *Mahan*—and the coarse, dark, gut-wrenching memory of a stubble-faced, bulging-eyed, reeking-breath human . . . "I was once . . . unable to fight," she said simply, quietly. "I tried, but didn't know how. All I could do was oppose, and it didn't do any good." She looked at Audry, her large eyes flashing. "And to this day, though I love and honor them for it, my greatest shame in life remains thaat it fell to others to aa-venge me." She took a long breath in the sudden silence. "Never think I don't respect you, Col-nol"—she tilted her head at the troops they led, talking loudly among themselves and oblivious to this—"or even love you as much as any of them, but I *don't* under-staand you—or how you don't often feel like I do."

"She follows her faith," Arano Garcia hissed, "and sets the example all of us would follow if we could!"

"But what if you did?" Blas countered, shaking her head. "Could we still win?"

"No," Koratin replied firmly, but he was blinking discontentedly, as if searching for an argument.

Sister Audry was still smiling, but tears of compassion filled her eyes. She wiped them away. "My *dear* Major Blas. I *do* feel as you do, in many ways. I daresay I even dimly comprehend a helpless sense of violation related to that which tortures you, because of the despicable way the Dominion desecrates my very faith, clothing their abominable teachings with some of the same trappings of my own. Don't you think I *want* to destroy them for that? Can you imagine how hard it is for me to resist the temptation?" She shook her head. "But I resist. I *must* resist, to prove my church and theirs are not the same, that God is love—not the bloodthirsty sucker of souls *they* revere!

"I never asked for this," she continued, then snorted. "This *command*," she stressed, "because of the inherent hypocrisy you perceive. And contrary to the belief of some, I'm not here on a mission to convert our enemies to my specific faith, though I praise God when they come to His understanding. I no longer even begrudge the pagans among us, because compared to those of the enemy— at least in the sense they have suffered, and would end the suffering of others—their beliefs are as close to mine as are the shoes upon my feet alike." She paused. "Which brings us to the insurmountable difference between all of us and our enemy, Major Blas," she said. "The Doms *revel* in suffering, even to the extent of exalting their own, but their chief pleasure comes from inflicting it on others. This is hateful to *my* God, the same Maker that you, the Christians here, even the Ocelomeh, worship. So, to my mind, we are engaged in a holy crusade made even stronger by its interdenominational nature." She gently touched Arano's shoulder. "Mr. Bradford would be amazed by how flexible I have become toward other faiths since this command was thrust upon me, but I cannot be flexible enough with my own faith to directly cause the suffering I abhor and still remain who I am."

Blinking rapidly and deeply moved, Blas considered that. Then she looked at Spook, Garcia, Koratin. Everyone in their little group had been entirely different people when the war began. In spite of herself, she couldn't keep all the irony out of her voice when she said, "Then I pray to the Maker that you—of all of us—might get through this as something like the person you staarted as."

"Major Blas!" Colonel Garcia said harshly.

"She is right, Col-nol," Koratin countered, "we must all pray for that. And so she *caan* remain the example we need, thaat our enemy—your people—needs, protecting and keeping the Saanta Maadre just the same is as much a part of *our* jobs as fighting the Doms."

CHAPTER
6

/////// Santiago Bay, NUS-occupied Cuba

"*I*t's pretty here," Lieutenant (jg) Kari-Faask observed as she and Lieutenant Fred Reynolds hurried along the bustling Santiago waterfront. In spite of what she said, all her attention seemed focused on the new bar sewn on the hem of her smock, and Fred pulled her back before she was run over by a freight wagon.

"Watch out, wilya!" Fred scolded. It would've been ridiculous to have his friend smushed now, after all they'd been through, particularly by a creeping wagon drawn by something like a small armabuey. Armabueys were basically giant armadillos that the Doms used for heavy draft animals. The ones here, called dillos, had the same purpose but were only half as big, with a thinner shell and more bristly fur delineating the armored segments of their case. In size and general shape (even their long, pointed heads), Fred compared them to a 1940 Ford coupe he'd been saving money for before the war back home. Oddly, likening them to his dream car made him feel vaguely unfaithful to his old world and life.

"Sorry," Kari said, blinking wryly. "I just never been a lieu-ten-aant before."

"How about trying to stay one awhile longer?" Fred quipped.

Coming to the end of the long pier where some of the

mighty NUS steam frigates of its newly organized Caribbean Fleet were docked (Fred wondered if they *had*
another fleet), they veered up Chandlery Street toward
Navy House a couple of blocks away.

The Santiago Bay on the Cuba of this world was situated more to the west, closer to where Manzanilla Bay
should've been, and there were even the same low mountains to the east, jutting surprisingly from an otherwise
low coastal plain. Santiago City was a mixture of NUS
wood-and-brick construction, in a vaguely Victorian
terraced-housing style, alongside earlier, more ornate Dom
buildings fashioned from cut coral blocks. The streets were
also crushed coral, glaring as brightly as the white sand
beaches under the midafternoon sun. The people reminded Fred of those in the Empire of the New Britain
Isles: mostly brown with dark hair, but there was a slightly
higher percentage of light-skinned folk with brown, blond,
even red hair. He understood that was because the "Nussies" had mixed a little with some European descendants
from diverse, insular, and often belligerent tribes scattered
along the East Coast of North America. Fred wanted to
learn more about them, but Captain Willis, of NUS *Con-
gress*, said they were even more disagreeable than the
various Indian tribes with which the Nussies had generally
peaceful relations, even alliances. They didn't seem anxious to invite the easterners to join the alliance, however,
and Fred guessed they had their reasons. That the NUS
wasn't currently at war with any of them was enough to
satisfy him for now. No doubt Courtney Bradford, even
Captain Reddy, would be fascinated and want to meet
them.

"It *is* kind of pretty," Fred finally agreed. "And not
too hot either. Kind of like San Diego . . . ought to be."
Fred had been born in Southern California, but even
Saint Francis—where San Francisco should've been—
was cooler on this world, and wetter. *More like Seattle,*
he thought. Passing a well-dressed man in a fashionable
wide-brimmed straw hat, who escorted a plump woman
wearing a lacy shawl and a lightweight bonnet, Fred
bowed and smiled. The man managed an uncomfortable
smile in return and touched a walking stick to his hat,

but the woman drew away as if frightened. "There you go, scaring the locals again," he murmured to Kari.

She blinked annoyance and turned, still walking, to watch the couple go. "Dumb-aasses," she muttered lowly. "They got no reason ta be scared o' me."

"Sure, but how're they supposed to know?" They'd finally discovered the answer to a mystery that had bothered them for some time. They'd been the very first to meet a representative of the NUS, the enigmatic Captain Anson, who helped them escape from Dom captivity. He'd been intrigued by Kari but not overwhelmed by her strangeness, even though it was clear she'd been the first Lemurian the Doms had ever seen. After flying halfway across South America and landing in the Caribbean, their poor, shot-up Nancy on its last legs and out of gas, they'd met more Nussies who, though also surprised to see her, weren't amazed. Finally, after Captain Greg Garrett arrived in USS *Donaghey* with her Dom prize, *Matarife*—and a whole ship full of Lemurians from the Union and the Republic—it was finally explained that the NUS had known about "felinoids" almost since the very first days they'd arrived on this world, though they'd never been sure where they came from. And regarding those they'd met before, that uncertainty still existed.

It was possible, even probable, that some had been 'Cats from the Republic—long-range traders or explorers who either never made it home or chose to keep their secrets. It was also possible *another* population of Lemurians existed somewhere, the ancient exodus from Madagascar spreading farther than anyone had ever dreamed. In any case, the 'Cats had always sailed small, swift schooners, and though the infrequent encounters had almost always been friendly, there'd been anecdotal accounts of piratical acts against unarmed merchantmen. Even most Nussies suspected these were tall tales, or even insurance scams, but Lemurians had remained sufficiently mysterious to be frightening to some, now that they walked among them.

"Bunch-aa dopes," Kari sniffed, pulling out a cigar and lighting it with the Zippo Fred had given her. Fred rolled his eyes. *They'd kill for real tobacco back home,*

*instead of that nasty crap Isak came up with, and it's to-
tally wasted on me. But Kari took to cigars like she'd
craved 'em all her life, and runs around smoking like a
Chinese coastal freighter.* Ahead was Navy House, second
in size in the city only to the governor's residence and the
warehouses lining the wharves. Four tall, pinkish columns framed a high, dark wooden door that was opened
for them by a guard all in white cotton and leather cross-
belts. The only things on him that weren't white were the
dark blue wheel hat on his head and his black shoes and
cartridge box. "Good afternoon, ah, sirs," the man said
lowly, recognizing them at once. "They're all waiting for
you," he urged.

Fred pulled the watch Captain Willis had given him
out of the pocket on the breast of his faded combat
smock. "Crap!" he murmured. "We're late! I told you to
quit goofin' around with those kids on the beach!"

"*They* weren't scared o' me!"

"They didn't know any better."

Another guard—steward . . . probably guard, since he
was armed with a rifle-musket—marched them to the
same conference room they'd visited a dozen times. Inside, seated on one side of the long table, was Captain
Greg Garrett, his tall, rangy frame folded on a tall-backed
chair, and Lieutenants Mak-Araa, Greg's XO, and Wen-
del "Smitty" Smith, *Donaghey*'s gunnery officer. Next to
them, representing the Republic of Real People, were
Tribune Pol-Heena and his assistant, Leutnant Koor-
Susk. Fred found it amusing that Captain Garrett, Smitty,
and he were the only humans here on behalf of the Grand
Alliance. "I'm sorry we're late, sir," Fred told Greg, then
began to direct his excuse at the Nussies on the other side
of the table. He recognized Admiral Sessions, who'd only
just arrived a few days before, as well as Commodore
Semmes and Captain Willis. He'd met a few of the other
NUS naval officers present, but couldn't remember their
names. Another man sat at the far end of the table, leaning back, and Fred couldn't make out his features.

"It's my fault," Kari began. "We was down paast the
dock, down on thaat saand spit—"

"And got involved in a conversation with some local

fishermen, unaccustomed to Lieutenant Faask's appearance," Fred interrupted before Kari could finish. He doubted their hosts would appreciate that they'd all been kept waiting because he and his friend had gotten caught up in helping some fascinated giggling children catch fish with a cast net. "In the interest of better understanding between our people, particularly when it comes to folks getting used to 'Cats, why, we thought it was a good idea to mingle." He hesitated. "Like we've been doing . . . mingling with folks," he finished lamely. The only ones who seemed vaguely annoyed were Admiral Sessions and Captain Garrett. The latter because their behavior reflected on him and the Alliance, no doubt, but the gaunt Semmes and pudgy Willis only smiled and nodded. They were both used to Fred and Kari's youthful exuberance by now.

"Yes, yes, all for the best I'm sure," Sessions said impatiently, and started to stand.

"I wouldn't count on it being for the *best*," said the man at the end of the table in an amused tone, "but I doubt it did any harm. Those two have the most astounding knack for avoiding unpleasant situations, in spite of themselves."

Fred could only stare. *That voice . . .* Finally, the man leaned forward and turned to face them. He still wore the thick, bushy mustache they remembered, but it had been joined by equally bushy muttonchops.

"Caap-i-taan Aan-son!" Kari exclaimed.

The man smiled. "Not my real name, of course. Not even Admiral Sessions knows that." He looked thoughtful. "But Anson will do." He rose and walked around the table until he stood before them, and extended his hand. "It's good to see you both again," he said as they shook. "The last time was at the Pass of Fire, and you were rowing a small stolen boat out into a sea infested by leviathans!"

"And you just . . . vanished back into the darkness around Corazon, which was lousy with Doms chasing us!"

"Yes, well, perhaps we can reminisce another time," Sessions suggested.

"Sure," Fred and Kari chorused.

Greg waved a hand. "Am I to understand this is the man you met when you escaped the Doms—who told you the NUS would join our war against them right after we kicked the hornet's nest?" He looked at Anson. "We kicked it two or three times and got stung pretty bad for our trouble too, but nobody here had ever heard of us before we showed up!"

"That's not exactly—" Fred began, but Anson interrupted. "I apologize for that," he said. "You know about the adventures your young aviators experienced, but my escape overland was somewhat eventful as well. I suspect it also took considerably longer." He glanced at Sessions. "Then, even after I managed to effect it, I had a great deal of difficulty convincing some in our War Department that not only had the Empire thrown off the unwholesome influence of the 'Honorable' New Britain Company, but it was now fully engaged in an all-out war against the Doms. Even more difficult for some to accept was my report that the Empire desired an alliance with us, and other significant powers were arrayed beside it." He leaned slightly forward and clasped his hands behind his back. None could fail to notice that he not only wore a long, straight sword, but had a pair of large pistols enclosed in flap holsters suspended from his belt. He noticed their attention. "Even here I'm not entirely safe, I fear." He frowned. "Nor are any of you. I understand, Captain Garrett, that you had a demonstration of how depraved our common enemy can be?"

Greg shuddered, remembering the young Dom officer—little more than a child—who'd murdered a Marine on his ship and tried to kill him. "I think we've all seen that," he conceded.

"In any event," Anson continued, "I regret that your people were 'stung,' but I did my best, in good faith, and hope we can move forward in our common interest."

"Me too," Greg said. "Fred, Kari, have a seat." He glared at the cigar still smoldering in Kari's hand as the two found chairs and scooted up to the table, but he couldn't really complain. Semmes was smoking a cigar of his own, and Captain Willis was puffing a pipe. Smitty had accepted an offered cigar, but immediately crammed it in his mouth and chewed it up into a soggy blob. Greg supposed he was swallowing the juice. Then again, he hadn't actually spoken for a while . . .

Admiral Sessions cleared his throat. "Tell me more about your General Shinya and his plans. Is it true you used to be enemies?"

Greg nodded. "He's a Jap," he agreed, as if that explained everything, but then frowned thoughtfully. "But he's a *good* Jap. He's been on our side almost from the start. Even some of the Japs that weren't—Kurokawa's men—have come around. What choice did they have?" He shrugged. "I'll never understand the way some of 'em think; it's almost as weird to me as the Grik or Doms, but honor is incredibly important to them. It looks like helping us is the best, most 'honorable' choice they have left. Some of 'em, though, like Shinya, Miyata, a few others, are on our side because they want to be, and we're damn lucky to have 'em. Shinya, for example, started out on a Jap tin can we sank, but he's more American—like me, in the time we came from—than you are. And he's turned into one tenacious bastard in a fight. Probably as good as any army commander in the Alliance."

"Tin can?" Sessions asked dubiously, and Commodore Semmes leaned over and whispered in his ear. "Ah. Indeed. It seems the two Americas that spawned us are even different enough to produce separate languages! I shall endeavor to interpret yours in context."

Kari chuckled, emitting a stream of smoke, and Greg grinned. "I wish you luck. Allied English has so many 'Cat, Impie, Repub, hell, even Chinese and Filipino words mixed in by now, my own mother would probably have trouble understanding some of what I usually say. I'm trying extra hard."

"I thank you for that. And General Shinya's plan?" Sessions prompted.

Greg turned serious, rubbing the dark stubble already forming on his chin. "As far as we can tell, nothing's changed. He'll keep pushing toward the Pass of Fire on land while High Admiral Jenks prepares an assault by sea. Ideally, their attacks on Corazon will be coordinated with each other—and your attack from this side of the pass. Now that we know the League has ships in the area, we can't transmit anymore, to ask for clarifications."

"No," Sessions agreed uncomfortably, "particularly since the League has aligned itself with the Dominion." There was no escaping that fearful fact now. First, Fred and Kari had aided in the capture of a Dom emissary to the League, named Don Emmanuel. He hadn't revealed any information, but his mission had been clear. Since then, not only had Dom prisoners taken with *Matarife* confirmed that the ship had met two League vessels at Ascension Island, but *Donaghey* and *Matarife*, with only their guns manned while at anchor at Martinique Island, essentially ambushed and destroyed an Alsedo-class destroyer belonging to the League. Her senior surviving officer, a young ensign named Tomas Perez Mole, had been reluctant to talk as well, but even he was discontented with the excesses of the League. Through gentle persuasion and conversation, quite a bit was learned obliquely, not only about the formidable resources at the League's disposal but about their ultimate aims in the hemisphere.

Apparently, with the sea between Antarctica and the horn of South America utterly choked with ice, El Paso del Fuego was even more strategically important than the Panama Canal on another world. The only possible conclusion was that the League was determined to control it either directly or through the Dominion. Though largely confined to the Mediterranean for now, consolidating their control and opposing other powers Mole could not be induced to reveal, leaders of the League believed that possession of the pass would ultimately bring them mastery of the entire Atlantic—and all the shores around it.

"So," Admiral Sessions continued, "whether or not the League is yet prepared to materially assist the Doms, we must assume they will pass intelligence to them in much the same way they did your enemy, Kurokawa. No doubt they suspect your presence here, but we mustn't give them reason to warn the Doms that we are now better able to coordinate our efforts with Second Fleet." He paused. "Therefore, at a time when we desperately need *better* contact between all our peoples"—he bowed his head in acknowledgment of Tribune Pol-Heena of the Republic—"and just as desperately need to conduct reconnaissance of our side of the Pass of Fire, we dare not use the two wondrous assets best able to provide those things: your wireless transmitter"—he looked at Fred and Kari—"and your amazing flying machines."

"Our plane is pooped, anyway," Fred said. "*Donaghey*'s ground crew could probably get it flying, but it'd take most of the spare parts they've got for their plane."

"Which leaves that perfectly good plane you're saying we can't use," Greg said, frowning.

"Not necessarily," Anson countered cryptically. He also looked at Pol-Heena. "You came here with them"—he nodded at Greg—"as a token by your kaiser that the Republic was committed to the war against the Dominion."

"Yes?" Pol-Heena confirmed quizzically. "We are currently fully engaged fighting the Grik, but Kaiser Nig-Taak believed it was important that our allies understand they have our full support."

"Did the description of your assignment detail what you were empowered to do in regard to us, should we meet? In other words, do you have powers plenipotentiary?"

Pol-Heena shifted uncomfortably on the chair, and not just because it cramped his tail. "Yes," he finally confessed.

"Then, since we're fighting the same enemy, are you prepared to enter into a provisional military alliance with the New United States on behalf of the Republic of Real People"—he nodded at Fred—"as Lieutenant Reynolds was empowered to do, on behalf of the United Homes and the Grand Alliance?"

Pol-Heena straightened. "A *provisional* military alliance, for the good of the war effort, yes," he said.

"Very good. In that case, we will immediately dispatch an ambassador to your country for the purpose of better coordinating our efforts"—he smiled at Kari—"and getting to know one another." He glanced at Admiral Sessions, then looked at Greg. "At the same time, I propose that as soon as her repairs are complete, *you* sail *Matarife* into the eastern approaches of the Pass of Fire to discover what forces and defenses the Doms have there."

Greg looked thoughtful. "Makes sense. I'd kind of hoped to use her for something, oh, I don't know, a little more dramatic, I guess. But that seems the best option."

Smitty suddenly raised his hand, looked around, and finally rose and stepped quickly to a window. Launching a huge, thick brown stream on the shrubs outside, he turned sheepishly to face them. "You said *Matarife*'s well-known in these parts. Won't the Doms get wise when she shows up so late, pokes around, and then scrams?"

"I think we might work that out," Greg said, warming to the prospect. "But what about our plane? What do you want it to do?"

"You said your army is advancing up the isthmus toward the Pass of Fire? The land there is easily narrow enough for your flying machine to cross. Therefore I propose that before you approach the pass, you go inshore behind your army's reported line of advance and set your, ah, plane in the water. With no one the wiser, it can then—finally—carry a fully accredited representative of the New US to consult and counsel directly with your own theater commanders."

"Okay. About time too. I hope it's somebody with a clue."

"I myself will go," Anson said. "I know more about the Dominion than anyone who enjoys our president's trust, and am well-acquainted with many of the native resistance forces joining your ranks."

Fred cleared his throat. "Even flying across a narrower stretch than Kari and I did will take a good pilot, Captain Garrett. There's weird winds in the mountains. Weird thermals all the time, for that matter, with all the volcanoes. And then there's the damn Grikbirds. You gotta watch out for them!"

Greg swiveled his head to look at Fred and his eyes twinkled. "*Donaghey*'s pilot is fresh out of flight training and hasn't flown since we left Alex-aandra."

Fred's face fell. "Grab your wallet, Kari, I think we're getting rolled."

Greg shook his head. "Not Kari, just you. Nancys only have two seats."

"Now wait just a daamn minute!" Kari snapped, gushing smoke. "Fred don't fly *nowhere* without me!"

"Right," Fred said stubbornly. "I'd've been dead a hundred times without her. I'm no good by myself, I tell ya! I'm not really that good a pilot. I get so busy just flying, I lose track of what's around me. Grikbirds'd get me—and Captain Anson—for sure!"

"He's right," Kari confirmed sadly. "He's *not* a very good pilot. Not without me."

"Hey! I . . . ah, yeah," Fred murmured.

"So there's only one thing for it," Kari continued. "I'll sit up front with Cap-i-taan Aan-son. It'll be tight, but we caan squeeze in. Fred can fly from the baack-seat."

Anson, Greg, and Smitty all laughed, and Fred rolled his eyes. "Oh, swell."

"Whaat's the maatter, Fred? Ain't you tired o' lollin' on the beach haaf days? I'm ready to get back to the waar!"

"There'll be plenty of war around here, soon enough," Fred grumped. "Won't have to worry about who sees us fly, once the fighting starts."

"Sure, an' we'll prob'ly be baack by then. But I miss our navy, our friends, an' COFO Orrin Reddy too."

Fred had a sudden thought. "Say, Captain Garrett. You said when you met up with Kari that you'd been authorized to give her a hug—or arrest her. We did kind of run off, after all. What do you think COFO Reddy and Admiral Lelaa'll do? They're the ones we ran off *from*!"

Garrett laughed again. "Good question. But since you actually managed to do what you set out to, and they already promoted you, I doubt you have anything to worry about. Other than getting there, that is."

Fred nodded glumly and looked at Captain Anson, who was gazing back with a smile. "Come, Mr. Reynolds. Just think of it as one more adventure together! I'm sure we'll have a wonderful time."

"Yeah. Just like last time," Fred moped.

Leopardo
Northeast coast of South America
Nuevo Granada Province

*I*t was raining when the big Italian Leone-class destroyer *Leopardo* turned into the broad mouth of the River of Heaven southeast of the peninsula called Trinidad on another world. On both sides of the river stood the Dominion city of Puerto del Cielo, and dozens of boats ranging in size from dugout canoes to large, heavily laden barges poled along by a hundred men or more, scattered at their approach. Eventually, *Leopardo* left them and the sea behind and steamed slowly south, followed by a small plodding Spanish oiler.

Capitaine de Fregate Victor Gravois, resplendent in a new dark blue double-breasted coat; sky-blue trousers tucked into brown, knee-high boots; a tall, round-topped hat with a patent leather brim; and a sharply creased tie stared malevolently at the oiler from under the dripping canvas awning on *Leopardo*'s signal bridge. *Those* fools *in the ridiculous Triumvirate,* he brooded, *simply can't grasp the bigger picture! And that they actually chastised me for the loss of the battleship* Savoie *only proves that beyond doubt. Giving her to Kurokawa not only quickly completed my mission to weaken* everyone *contending for control of the Indian Ocean; it ensured the League a relatively free hand in the Atlantic.*

Unfortunately, the Americans and their ordinarily loquacious Lemurian . . . "ape-folk" (as far as Gravois was concerned) allies had finally improved their comm security. And the submarine Gravois left behind to observe hadn't reported anything after it confirmed that a devastating battle was underway at Zanzibar. The outcome of the battle was unknown, and they hadn't heard anything from Maggiore Rizzo and the League aircraft they'd also lent Kurokawa, but Gravois was confident all the forces involved had surely slaughtered one another quite satisfactorily.

The problem was, the mission he'd been given to "redeem" himself had been to divert *Leopardo* from her homeward voyage and proceed directly to the Dominion to finalize the alliance that that Italian imbecile Contrammiraglio Oriani had initiated from his base on Ascension Island. And instead of allowing Gravois to bring the armed tender *Ramb V* to see to *Leopardo*'s needs, Oriani decreed that the old oiler—which *Leopardo* had been forced to take *under tow* when she'd suffered engineering casualties—would suffice. The result had been a lengthy layover at Ascension while the oiler was repaired, then a very slow voyage here. And it was Gravois and, to a lesser extent, *Leopardo*'s commanding officer, Capitano di Fregata Ciano, who'd be blamed for the delay. They were the same official rank in their respective navies, but Gravois was in charge of the overseas branch of French military intelligence and had overall command of the mission.

Contrammiraglio Oriani was well placed in the OVRA—the Organizations for Vigilance and Repression of Antifascism—however, which had increasingly usurped all intelligence-gathering efforts for the League. Gravois would find sympathetic ears among the French contingent, but factionalism was the OVRA's primary target now. Complaints might actually lead to his assassination. Even Ciano wasn't safe, despite being Italian himself. Their best bet was to successfully conclude the treaty—and make a good impression on the Doms.

Leopardo should help. From what they'd seen, the Doms' most advanced warships were basically eighteenth-century sailing ships of the line equipped with crude steam engines and paddle wheels. Gravois knew Captain Reddy's *Walker* had fought the Doms in the Pacific, but doubted anyone in the capital of Nuevo Granada had ever seen her. So much the better if they had, because *Leopardo* was actually designed as a "scout cruiser," or "Exploratori," and was much more impressive than the battered old American four-stacker. Besides looking relatively fresh and clean in her new light gray paint, she was more than seventy feet longer than *Walker* and almost twice as heavy. She also carried twice as many, heavier guns, along with two 40-mm pom-poms, four 20-mm machine guns, and four torpedo tubes. And unlike *Walker*, she could still easily achieve thirty-four knots. Gravois grimaced and glanced back at the rust-streaked oiler. *Now, if only that . . . thing does not too greatly undermine the overall effect . . .*

Capitano Ciano joined him, passing a cup of hot tea. Gravois accepted it, knowing its heat would only add to his misery. This close to the equator, the air wasn't as hot as it would be back home, but the humidity was profound, and Gravois caught himself coveting Ciano's lightweight tropical whites. *Perhaps I can borrow some from him?* he thought. *We are much the same size.* "Were you able to make yourself understood?" he asked instead, gesturing at the pilothouse with his cup.

Ciano scowled. A Dominion officer had been waiting for them at an impressive stone fort at Puerto del Cielo, and came aboard to pilot them the almost 320 kilometers through the snags and shifting channel of the broad, forest-bordered river leading to the Holy City of Nuevo Granada. That's where the Dom Pope, His Supreme Holiness, Messiah of Mexico, and, by the Grace of God, Emperor of the World resided in the holiest shrine of all, El Templo de los Papas. Gravois was appalled by the pomposity of the title claimed by the absolute ruler of the Dominion but also attracted by the unambiguousness of it, compared to the League's Triumvirate. He understood the real power in the Dominion was wielded by a senior Blood Cardinal named Don Hernan de Divina Dicha, recently returned from the fighting in the west, but even he wouldn't hesitate to obey a direct decree by His Supreme Holiness. The arrangement struck Gravois with its simplicity and . . . tidiness.

Ciano rolled his eyes. "My Spanish is not good," he confessed, though Gravois never had occasion to correct Ciano's French, "but, apparently, according to a member of our Spanish landing force I detailed to interpret, neither is that of our pilot." He shrugged. "He makes himself understood, though I think he was disappointed when I refused to let him directly conn the ship."

Gravois barked a laugh. "Indeed?" he asked, amused by the thought of an unsophisticated Dom conning the old but relatively advanced *Leopardo*. He likened it to letting an ape drive a car. Then he grew more serious. "We have to proceed carefully. Like it or not, you and I are quite literally in the same boat and must be of one mind at all times. Our last assignment"—his tone turned sarcastic—"at which we 'failed so dismally,' according to that bloated toad Oriani, was . . . difficult. It was made even more so by Kurokawa's madness. But he was only one man, and his madness couldn't run entirely unchecked by the officers he relied upon." His expression twisted in distaste. "Here we deal with a different kind of madness: an entire culture that celebrates—*reveres*— what we would deem mad." He hesitated. "I doubt you will forget what we saw, on the beach at the base of the fort."

Ciano's scowl returned and his eyes narrowed in disgust. "No," he replied simply, remembering the dozens of corpses, men and women, hanging on charred wooden crosses on the bright, sandy beach. Their withered, disfigured, blackened bodies shrouded in a dark, flapping nightmare of lizardbirds and other flying carrion eaters. People had obviously been crucified, then burned alive. Their pilot had offhandedly referred to them as rebels, lured from God by rumors of the war in the west.

"I asked the pilot how their guilt was determined," Gravois continued—his Spanish also better than the Dom's—and he looked meaningfully at Ciano. "He replied that the townspeople merely told the commandante of the Blood Drinkers in the fort. No further proof was required." He shuddered. "Blood Drinkers are the elite troops of their pope, by the way. In any event, I tell you this so you will know a mere accusation is tantamount to conviction." He rubbed his chin. "We have based our justice on even less during our conquest of the Mediterranean, though I doubt we have been quite so cruel. At the same time, our own people have never been subject to such arbitrary treatment. Caution your crew to do nothing to rouse the locals against us. In fact, it would probably be best if you grant no liberty."

Ciano looked doubtful. "It has been so long. . . . I may face a mutiny if I do not allow them ashore at some point!"

"Then let us get a better feel for things first. We're here to conclude an alliance with these people, not fight them for the release of misbehaving sailors accustomed to the . . . perquisites allowed them as conquerors at home." Gravois considered. "Your men have already witnessed what may befall them if they ignore local customs. If you do allow them ashore, you might promote good behavior if you tell them they go at their own risk and we can do nothing to save them if they cause offense."

Ciano nodded unhappily, watching yet another fort surrounded by a large village passing abeam. "I don't like it, but that might be best. The chart the pilot brought shows more forts, every thirty kilometers or so, each armed with heavy guns. Mere muzzle-loaders, of course, but we couldn't survive them all if we rescued our people and tried to escape."

"I don't like it either, but we didn't come here to escape, in any event. We will *not* fail this mission! We ourselves have too much at stake." Gravois slapped a mosquito on his upper lip beneath the thin mustache he wore. "How long must we endure this stinking river and its pests?" he complained.

"At a paltry five knots?" Ciano snorted. "Several days, I'm afraid. In theory, drawing only a little over three meters, we should be able to go faster where the river is straight. Our pilot is accustomed to the deeper draft of the largest Dom warships, however."

Gravois frowned. "Could he be persuaded by that?"

Ciano made a wry face. "No. Just as we're concerned about offending our hosts, he is most determined not to run us aground. If he did, I suspect he'd face a similar fate to that of the rebels. He won't risk it, and would probably go slower if he could."

Three days later, Gravois was on the bridge with Capitano Ciano as *Leopardo* and its oiler, having gathered a pair of Dom steam frigate escorts, steamed into the north end of a very large lake their pilot called Lago de Vida. Hundreds of small boats were in view, as well as several large warships. More barges were headed toward the river. They'd have to be towed back or wait until later in the season to return. Only a steamer or one of the swift biremes of the Blood Cardinals could move against the current that prevailed for now.

It soon became obvious that here was a major city indeed, probably the largest in all the Dominion. The lake was almost entirely surrounded by buildings of all sorts, mostly of stone. Many were clustered together, forming vast ghettos, while others stood alone—great villas with scenic views on impressive estates, perched on the flanks of mountains rising to the west. Most surprising, perhaps, even the ghettos looked clean and well kept. At least from a distance.

Finally, as they steamed closer to the center of the lake, the pilot raised his hand and swept it to the side in a gesture encompassing the western shore. "Behold!" he said in his odd Spanish. "And give thanks to God as you lay eyes on the glory of Nuevo Granada! You now gaze upon the very gateway to Heaven, which no heretic has ever seen before! Certainly none have ever been *summoned* to view it! Are you not amazed?"

"Indeed. It's quite impressive," Gravois exclaimed aloud. *Almost as impressive as Alex-aandra, in the Republic of Real People,* he silently conceded, *if in a more primitive, less artistic way.* "We're most sensible to the honor." He stepped out onto the starboard bridgewing and raised his binoculars. As he'd been told to expect, a great pyramidal temple rose perhaps fifty meters high, completely dominating the center of the city. It was built of countless massive stone blocks, each approximately seven meters square, judging by the height of the people thronging around it, and the blocks were stacked to create distinctive levels. Studying it, and the rest of the city, Gravois was surprised to see numerous smaller pyramids geometrically arranged around the first. He easily counted twelve, since they were probably twenty-five or thirty meters high and there were no taller buildings in the city. He wondered what significance their size, number, and placement might hold. Scanning closer, he was impressed by the stone wall encompassing the central city—and the many large gun embrasures piercing it. He doubted the wall could stand for long in the face of a determined, concentrated bombardment, even by the heavy muzzle-loading smoothbores the Allies had on their ships. And there was evidence the NUS had large-bore *rifled* guns. But only a very determined bombardment by wooden-hulled vessels could succeed, given the sheer number of well-situated Dom cannon. Gravois smiled to himself. *Of course, even these defenses would be utterly at the mercy of any armored League warship. Perhaps we will find occasion to demonstrate that one day?* He shook his head. *No. We're here to make* friends. *I must stop automatically thinking of everyone I meet as an adversary!*

He leaned toward Ciano and spoke in French so the pilot wouldn't understand. "You know the League, on my advice, never approached Captain Reddy or his Grand Alliance with anything like an overture of friendship. Perhaps the fact that the British and Americans were our enemies on the world we came from influenced that decision to some degree, but in retrospect, it might have been a mistake."

Ciano looked at him, surprised. Gravois nodded. "Though the Grand Alliance tends to keep territory it wrests from its aggressive enemies, none of its members is inherently expansionist." He waved a hand dismissively. "The Empire of the New Britain Isles has a few far-flung colonies, but they are limited and have remained static for a very long time."

"You think we could have . . . cooperated?" Ciano asked.

Gravois snorted. "I doubt that. And we could never have become *friends* with the Union or its allies; we're far too different. With the possible exception of the Empire and Republic, they govern themselves with too much— how can I say? I think the best way to describe it is exuberant, tolerant chaos. And even the Empire and Republic accept more independent thought than we ever could. I believe they all would find the League too . . ." He smiled. "Ideologically demanding. That said, we all have priorities, and it is a vast world. I believe we could have coexisted with the Allies in relative peace for years—before it became necessary to destroy them. We could never have brought them willingly into the fascist fold, particularly with so many . . . animals they'd never abandon among them." He shrugged. "So a confrontation was and is inevitable."

Ciano nodded agreement but spoke cautiously. He disliked discussing politics, particularly with such as Gravois. It was so easy to say something that might cost him his career—or his life. "The Grik, Doms, and Kurokawa as well are expansionist by nature. Conquest seems seared into their very bones. Each believes it their destiny to annihilate all opposition to their ultimate supremacy on this world."

"As does the League," Gravois agreed philosophically. "And like the League, they cannot suffer the existence of examples of another way."

"Indeed. But unlike the Grik, who seem incapable of innovation, or the Doms, who are, but resist it with great tenacity, the Grand Alliance—even the Lemurian ape-folk who make up its greater part—are amazingly innovative and industrious. Given the time a peaceful coexistence could have afforded them, they might soon have equaled even our technology!"

"Exactly why I proposed the path we took—and was probably right to do so." Gravois sighed. "Hopefully, Kurokawa has crushed their First Fleet by now, and what remains will be ripe for the Grik to pick. The Alliance and Grik will continue to slaughter one another until even the victor can be managed. The question remains, however: what of the Dominion? They're religious zealots, crazed by their twisted faith. But are they not also fascists of a sort already? Except for those who resist them from within, they're slavishly devoted to their leaders and gladly sacrifice their very lives on command! If they could be brought to accept a few of the truths we bring them, along with our aid, we might even learn a thing or two from them."

Ciano pursed his lips, unable to imagine anything they might learn from the Doms. He chose to say nothing more as *Leopardo* neared the city and they continued to gaze at the spectacle of it all.

"This is close enough," the pilot said as they drew within a quarter mile of the dock paralleling the waterfront defenses.

"I beg your pardon?" Gravois asked, confused. "Why should we stop here? The dock is there." He pointed.

"It is," the pilot agreed, sounding surprised. "I thought it had been made clear. You *cannot* dock; you must anchor. No heretic can touch the sacred soil of the Holy Dominion and live! That is the Law of God, older than time itself."

"But . . ." It was Gravois's turn to be surprised. "I thought I was supposed to meet His Supreme Holiness."

The pilot actually laughed. "That is impossible! Only Blood Cardinals may gaze upon his holy form, and even then they may not truly *see* him." That confused Gravois even more, but he nodded at Ciano, who cried, "All stop! Call the anchor detail!" Bosun's pipes twittered and feet pounded on the fo'c'sle. Moments later, a great splash accompanied the clattering rumble of the anchor chain. It ran out quite a distance, and Gravois was impressed by how deep the lake was. He turned back to the pilot. "I don't understand, señor," he said. "We were invited."

"Yes," the pilot agreed. "An honor without precedent. Particularly since His Holiness Don Hernan de Divina Dicha himself will condescend to meet with you aboard your fine ship."

"So much for liberty," Ciano told Gravois wryly in French, his tone almost relieved. "I doubt there will be

many complaints once the men understand it means their
life to go ashore!"

"How soon might we be . . . blessed by Don Hernan's
presence?" Gravois asked the pilot, trying to conceal his
annoyance.

"Quite soon. The proprieties must be observed and
a propitious day chosen." He hesitated, actually counting
on his fingers, then he beamed. "No more than three or
four days." Victor Gravois's face turned beet red and his
eyes flashed.

"We should leave at once!" Ciano ground out, teeth
clenched.

"No," Gravois replied. "Whether the insult they offer
is deliberate or not, I'm sure they'd view our departure
as such—and there *are* all those forts along the river to
the sea. We'll stay a few days more and hear what Don
Hernan has to say. That's why we came, after all."

////// *Army of the Republic*
South Soala
Ungee River

*M*ajor "Legate" Bekiaa-Sab-At, commanding the newly amalgamated 23rd Legion of the Army of the Republic, removed her helmet and slowly raised her head to peer over the reinforced breastworks on the south side of the Ungee River. Her careful movements were meant to draw as little attention as possible, since the Grik had moved a *lot* of cannon down to their own forward positions protecting the other side of the river and their half of the Grik city of Soala, about a quarter mile away. Republic troops had found the other half of Soala, on the south bank of the river, utterly abandoned. Though it was obvious the enemy intended to contest their crossing, they'd sensibly chosen not to fight with the river at their back. That implied the Grik leadership knew what it was about, for a change, which bothered Bekiaa a lot. She couldn't help peeking over the breastworks from time to time to see what else they were up to. Grik couldn't see as well as Lemurians, even in daylight, but tended to expend a lot of ordnance on any movement they spotted, and Bekiaa didn't want to bring that down on the people around her. Still, she had to look, and wasn't encouraged by the growing defenses she saw. "Daamn," she muttered, slowly lowering her head. Plopping her helmet back on, she slid into the trench below.

Her aide, Optio (basically lieutenant, as she reckoned things) Jack Meek, regarded her like a wayward youngling. "Still determined ta' get yer 'ead knocked off, I see," he scolded, his expression mirrored by the blinking and disapproving looks of the men and 'Cats nearby. These were mostly members of the 2nd Battalion of the 23rd Legion, who'd originally belonged to the 10th before it was decimated on the Plain of Gaughala. Those who'd been in the 23rd from the start now made up 1st Battalion. Lots of things had changed since the narrow victory at Gaughala, and the reorganization of the various armies of the Republic into one cohesive force had been the most beneficial. But the momentum they'd gained after the battle, and during their increasingly professional and effective push through the terrible Teetgak Forest, had stalled at Soala, and Bekiaa was afraid the initiative was slipping away as well. "General Kim wouldn't approve o' his fair-haired lass pokin' her fool 'ead up like a bloody skuggik, right in front of a hundred an' fifty thousand Grik."

"I'm not fair-haired," Bekiaa corrected pedantically. Like that of her cousins Chack and Risa, her fur was brindled.

"Figure o' speech," Meek stated unapologetically. "An' a fittin' one. General Kim relies more on you than his army"—he corrected himself—"his *corps* commanders, for advice."

Bekiaa grunted. "If thaat were so, we'd've been across this daamn river as soon as we got here."

"An' prob'ly lost half the army doin' it," Meek retorted. "We're just now back up ta the seventy-five thousand we started with."

Bekiaa glanced around. Most of the replacements had endured hard marching and seen some kind of action in the Teetgak. More important, they'd joined the 23rd after the reforms were already in place. She had no concerns about them, and only their slightly less faded and weather-worn fatigues set them apart from the veterans now. "Each soldier here is worth two or three of what they were before," she reminded, to grins and barks of approval.

"That's as may be," Meek agreed, "but even Courtney Bradford don't think that's enough ta force a crossin'—an' remain an effective force after we do."

Bekiaa was silent. Courtney had never been a military man, though he'd shown his mettle in combat, but the Australian engineer, self-proclaimed naturalist, and direct representative of the Union to the Republic had changed in many ways. Most recently, he'd started focusing his formidable intellect less on bugs, flying reptiles, and the plethora of other fascinating fauna on this world and more on military matters. She had to admit the strategies he'd begun to contemplate, even propose, made sense. She sighed. "I'm just frustrated. We've saat here for two weeks gettin' ready to go, and the Grik've only got more ready for us to come. I don't see an end to it. And now my friends are goin' up the Zaam-beezi, alone and unsupported. . . ." She shook her head. "Haard to sit on my aass."

Prefect Bele, Bekiaa's XO, approached at a crouch. Most could stand upright in the deep trench without danger, but Bele, his skin as black as General Queen Safir Maraan's fur, was the tallest man Bekiaa had ever known. He stopped when he found her and saluted—still crouching—a small grin on his broad face. "You are wanted at the Army HQ," he said.

"See?" Meek told her smugly. "General Kim's got somethin' up his sleeve an' wants your opinion, no doubt."

Bekiaa growled at him, but gathering her kit—which included a 1903 Springfield rifle—she stood and followed Bele back the way he had come. Zigzagging through the maze of trenches Courtney had designed, Bekiaa made a point of catching as many eyes as she could and nodding confidently at their owners. Originally resented as an upstart foreigner, she'd gained a reputation as an innovative leader and fierce fighter who'd saved the left flank of the army at Gaughala. She had few detractors now, from any legion.

"Down!" came a chorus of shouts, and she, Bele, and

all around her flopped on the timber floor of the trench as a stutter of loud reports popped in the sky nearby. *Grik case shot,* she thought. *They get more and more all the time. Enough to waste on gaal-ling fire.* Hot iron flailed the tops of the trenches, but there were no screams. After a few moments, she and Bele rose and continued on. There was no answering fire from Republic gun emplacements. They had few howitzers or mortars yet, and their 75-mm Derby guns, while capable of far greater accuracy, range, and a truly stunning rate of fire, were direct-fire weapons—just like Grik smoothbores—and wouldn't be much more effective against protected positions. They occasionally performed counterbattery fire missions, knocking out Grik guns, but that worked only against weapons they could see, and the Grik were getting better at hiding theirs. If the Grik were foolish enough to attack, they'd slaughter them in the open. But Grik artillery, primitive as it was in comparison, could do the same.

For now, Republic artillery was focused on stockpiling enough ammunition to smother the Grik forward defenses when the time finally came to strike. That, at least, was going well. The rail line had pushed almost up to the other side of the Teetgak, and hundreds of suikaa-drawn wagons made supply runs back and forth along the long forest track. The army wanted for little and had amassed a stupendous ammunition reserve. It would all likely be needed when the big push came, however, and there was no sense wasting it.

Finally, Bekiaa and Bele reached a wider part of the trench with a lot of busy coming and going. There were also thick bundles of wire running in all directions. That was another improvement after Gaughala: field telegraphy connected all parts of the army to its primary, secondary, and tertiary HQs, as well as its artillery batteries. New wireless sets, similar to those their allies used, had also been rushed to the front and *should* alleviate the confusion that had reigned at Gaughala. As some now said, "All wires lead to General Kim," and Bekiaa and Bele followed them into a heavily reinforced bunker with lots of overhead protection.

Inside, past the comm room where telegraphers clacked

away and runners sat on benches along the earthen wall, waiting to scamper to unconnected parts of the line, they found twenty officers crammed in General Kim's conference room, leaning over a map table or standing back, trying to see. Most looked up as they entered and Bekiaa noted a few resentful stares, though not as many as there'd once been. General Kim, Courtney Bradford, Inquisitor Kon-Choon, and General Taal-Gaak all smiled at their approach. General Taal, now commanding all Republic cavalry, had dispensed with his flashy armor and cape. Even Courtney now wore the standard muddy yellow-brown combat fatigues and black leather accoutrements issued to all Republic troops, though he still had his wide straw sombrero under his arm instead of the standard dark-painted helmet. Bekiaa herself probably remained the most unusually dressed, still wearing her tie-dyed camouflage combat smock, faded blue Marine kilt, and platter-shaped helmet. In battle, she'd also wear her once brilliant white rhino-pig armor. It was a mottled tan now, permanently stained with mud and blood.

"Ah, Legate Bekiaa," Kim greeted. "I'm glad you could join us."

Bekiaa shrugged. "Nothin' else going on."

Kim frowned, choosing to ignore the sarcasm. "Yes. And I'm afraid that will remain the case awhile longer. We haven't the forces to just bash across the river yet"—he shifted his gaze to Bradford and Choon, both looking as unhappy as Bekiaa, but they nodded—"and Kaiser Nig-Taak himself is reluctant to condone an unsupported frontal assault. He believes it will be too costly. We're here to discuss another way."

Bekiaa's eyes went wide with surprise before she blinked annoyance. "With respect, Gener-aal, I don't like it either, but if we wait too long, the daamn Grik'll make it impossible to get across—straight at 'em or any other way."

"Perhaps, but there are other factors to consider. First, as you know, we have confirmation that the Grik, as we speak, are finally launching the mass attack we've dreaded so long, across the strait at Madagascar. But with the impetuous move by Captain Chappelle and his *Santa Catalina* to block the Zambezi, surely soon followed by the bulk of all Allied forces along the east coast of Africa, the Grik will be hard-pressed to send more forces to oppose us here." He nodded at Choon. "The Inquisitor suspects the enemy believes we're a mere feint, a diversion, in any event."

"We *are* a diversion, of a sort," Bekiaa replied bitterly, "but it'll quit working if we stop!"

"It's already worked perhaps better than we can manage, my dear." Courtney spoke for the first time, his voice full of regret. "There are more Grik across the river than is generally known. Aerial observations put their numbers closer to *two* hundred thousand than the one fifty we previously thought."

The Republic Army had a full dozen Cantets to scout for it now, though they were careful never to show more than a few at a time. Cantets were fast two-seater biplanes, roughly resembling something called a B-1 Albatross. They had no forward firing weaponry—yet—but were equipped with a Maxim on a high mount, which allowed its observer to shoot downward, in addition to engaging enemy zeppelins. They could also carry light bombs under their wings. Many more—better—planes would soon be forthcoming as Republic industry ramped up, but even the first trickle of Cantets was a great achievement, considering the Republic had neglected aeronautics for a full decade after its first aircraft flew. They'd been considered dangerous, expensive curiosities, of little military value. They knew better now, and even these first Cantets were better than Nancys over land. The next planes might rival P-1C Mosquito Hawks, and there'd be a lot of them. The biggest choke point would be training, and Bekiaa's flying shipmates, which *Donaghey* left behind with her, had established a burgeoning flight school north of Alex-aandra.

But none of that would help them *now*.

"So, whaat do we do? Just sit here an' take potshots at each other?" Bekiaa asked sharply, tail swishing angrily.

"No," Choon said, his large pale blue eyes reflecting pleasure at being able to bring good news—before his rival (he believed) for Bekiaa's affections, General Taal, could beat him to it. "We will continue to provide a distraction the Grik can't ignore, to the extent of *crushing* the force across from us and pushing onward—as soon as we have what we need."

"And whaat's that?" Bekiaa asked dolefully.

Taal beat Choon this time. "As a comm-aander of cavalry, I have been as frustrated as you by our immobility," he said, "and have been scouting up- and downriver for possible fords." He shook his head. "There are a few possibilities, but none are ideal. The river is too deep and we will have to cross on boats and barges. Surely you can imagine how costly that would be in the face of massed artillery and musketry!"

"So we don't do it here, not initially," Choon announced triumphantly. "We continue building boats and barges in the forest behind us and bringing them up for the enemy to see, but our cavalry and engineers will also build them far to the east and west."

Bekiaa nodded, realization dawning. "We'll keep 'em maassed here while we prepare to cross on their flaanks. We'll still cross here too, but only aaf-ter those forces strike."

"Those are the bare bones of the plan," Courtney agreed. "But it will take time to prepare."

"Not thaat long," Bekiaa argued with growing enthusiasm, but Choon looked at Kim and nodded.

"I'm afraid it will still take longer than we'd prefer. Even an attack such as that, confident as I would be of success, could be far too costly and leave us crippled. We must wait for more muscle and sinew to give the bones strength."

"Wait for whaat, and how long?" Bekiaa asked darkly.

"More troops, aircraft, and particularly howitzers. And many, many more of the mortars like those the chairman of your Union was so kind to give us plans for."

Bekiaa slumped. "How daamn long will *thaat* take?" she demanded.

"They and the ammunition they require are already in production," Choon soothed. "They're amazingly simple to build, after all. More and more of your countrymen have been making the long flight to Songze, as a matter of fact, and are providing tremendous technical assistance." He shrugged modestly. "We have shared a few of our designs with them. For Derby Guns, as an example."

"Most specifically, however," General Kim continued, "we have reason to believe our *navy* might actually make an appearance, to cover our river crossing." He shook his head. "Sadly, that is least likely of all, and if the navy cannot help us at the end of . . ." He hesitated. "Sixty days' time, we will commence the operation without it."

"Sixty days?" Bekiaa practically roared. "The whole daamn war might be lost by then!"

General Kim's narrow eyelids tightened to angry slits. "Do not forget yourself, Legate Bekiaa!" He paused and his tone softened slightly. "It is my hope the delay will help minimalize casualties—and it should. The longer we wait, the more complacent the enemy will become, increasingly convinced they are a mere garrison, a check against our continued advance." He straightened and clasped his hands behind his back. "But we will closely monitor events on the Zambezi. Do *not* think we will not cross, whenever we must and regardless of loss, if it suddenly appears the war is in the balance. Even if it requires the sacrifice of this entire army." He glared around at the other officers, none of whom had spoken, but who'd all taken involuntary steps away from him. "Is that understood?"

CHAPTER
9

///// *USS* **Santa Catalina**
Zambezi River
Grik Africa

"Wilya look at that!" Major Simon "Simy" Gutfeld murmured, standing on *Santa Catalina*'s port bridgewing as the old ship led its smaller, wooden-hulled consorts upriver. Simy was short and stocky, shaped like a fireplug, but probably didn't carry an ounce of fat. His bright blue eyes always seemed to radiate an aura of excited wonder, despite the horrors they'd seen, and this was no exception. He tilted the helmet back on his dark-haired head and pointed at the sheer south bank of the river a couple of hundred yards away. It reared up almost as high as the deck he stood on. Flocks of colorful lizardbirds of all descriptions literally swarmed around them, swooping at their wake and squirting their droppings all over the decks, but that was commonplace now, and not what he was indicating.

They'd apparently left the swampy coastal plain behind and entered a river-gouged cut in an escarpment, where they began to see increasing signs of Grik habitation. There were just a few hovels at first, with fishing nets drying in the sun and crude skiffs tied to posts onshore. Most of the scruffy Grik attending them just stood and stared at the small squadron steaming past, mouths hanging open in apparent surprise. Occasionally, huge crocodiles flowed into the water from little beaches where they'd been sunning themselves, alarmed by the ships. Now and then, larger bands of Grik were seen on the ridge above. They were hunters, armed with long spears or dragging sleds heaped with meat, surrounded by clouds of flies. None of this was unexpected. They were still almost eighty miles from Sofesshk, and aerial reconnaissance had led them to believe they wouldn't see anything like a town before the bend in the river. Now, however, though there were few standing structures, Gutfeld had noticed a long series of cave dwellings dug out of the bank itself and reinforced by rough-hewn timbers. That was odd in itself, since there were few real trees around. Perhaps they used driftwood?

"Weird," Lieutenant Mikey Monk agreed, joining the Marine and raising his Imperial-made spyglass. "But they're Grik. Weird by definition. Huh. I used to think of 'em like ants, you know? Now we see 'em living in holes in the ground."

"Yeah, ants ... or crawfish. They look kinda like crawfish holes to me, the way they're built up around the entrances and all the dirt's just thrown out and, well, *shaped*." Gutfeld, off the old S-19, was born near Shreveport, Louisiana, and knew quite a lot about crawfish holes. He'd been a "motor mac" on the lost S-boat, but like Colonel Billy Flynn, killed in India, had seen prior service. In his case, he'd pulled a hitch in the USMC before joining the Navy—and the submarine service that fascinated him. It also paid more. His size made him a good pigboat sailor, but his shipmates never managed to wash the Marine out of him. Now, without a sub, he was back doing what he was arguably best at.

"Say, maybe so," Monk agreed. "Not sure which gives me the creeps more either."

Gutfeld nodded. Captain Flaar-Baa-Ris, his XO and commander of C Company, 1st Battalion, 3rd Marines, approached, stood at attention, and saluted. Flaar was a dusky yellow–furred 'Cat from Aryaal. Gutfeld returned the salute. "Whatcha got?" he asked. General quarters had finally been sounded shortly before. There were still no enemy ships in sight, but a trio of Grik zeppelins had been seen, cruising high overhead to the north, and the bend in the river where they meant to try to block the Grik breakout was just a few miles ahead. And who knew what might be in those holes? Most of the Grik on the ridge simply crouched down and tried to disappear in the scrubby brush and tall grass.

"First Baa-tallion has stood to, sur. Small aarms has all been issued, maa-chine guns is maanned, an' B Comp'nee staands ready to assist gun's crews."

"Double issue of ammo for the Allin-Silva rifles and shotguns, and the Blitzerbugs? All breastworks and boarding nets rigged?"

"Ay, sur."

Gutfeld nodded again. He didn't ask about drilling holes in the deck to bolt down the mortar baseplates. He'd overseen that himself, on both sides of the ship. They'd used mortars aboard ship before—not an ideal platform, of course—but Simon suspected they'd need to do it again, and the biggest problem they'd run into was getting the baseplates to bite. "Very well. Thanks, Flaar."

Lookouts cried out in alarm and Monk looked ahead, shading his eyes against the afternoon sun. "Oh, hell," he murmured, raising his glass again. "Smoke. Lots of it." Gutfeld shaded his eyes as well and saw what looked like dozens of columns of gray-black smoke rising in the distance, mixing high in the air to become a thick, dark haze. Unlike Kurokawa's Grik steamers, converted to burn oil, whatever approached from the west still used coal.

Gutfeld looked around. The river was very wide here, practically a lake, and recon revealed more lakes ahead, all the way past Sofesshk. But the choke-point bend was visible now, pushing into the river like a long, arched, rocky peninsula. Something like what Gutfeld imagined an extra-large mountain-fish skeleton buried in rocks might look like. Up until now, the shore had seemed most like deeply eroded soil, and little stone had been seen. That was obviously changing, and *this* Zambezi, clearly much deeper than it should be, had scoured its way down to the very bones of the earth, or the roots of the distant mountains.

'Cats on the fo'c'sle were still casting their lead lines and calling out depths. "By de maark, seven anna haaf!" came the cry, meaning there was forty-five feet of water in the deep channel they followed, conveniently marked by the enemy with painted floats. Armed and armored as she was, the 420-foot *Santa Catalina* displaced nearly 8,000 tons and drew 30 feet of water. It was believed the Grik BBs, which had to navigate the same passage, drew about the same even after whatever changes were made to them, so *Santy Cat* should be able to clear the bottom all the way to Sofesshk.

Monk nodded at the pilothouse, and Gutfeld followed him inside. Russ Chappelle watched them enter and waved them forward. "Looks like a race to see who gets to the bend first," he said. "The lookout in the crow's nest can see over that hump of rock and reports *six* Grik BBs, leading a dozen of their cruisers. Air recon says the galleys are farther back, straggling in clumps all the way past Sofesshk, and there're more BBs and cruisers gathering behind 'em. God knows where they all came from, maybe that river heading north, or farther up Lake Nalak. . . ." He shook his head. "Doesn't matter much to us. Not right now." A faint smile touched his lips. "We haven't seen it, of course, but *Arracca*'s planes've been plastering the galleys all day, which is swell, and there's damn little they can do about it." The smile vanished. "They've been steering clear of the heavies, though. They've got new defenses, like short-range rockets of their own. Or maybe they're the same old canister mortars that shoot something like case shot in the air, fused to blow about where Nancys release their bombs in a dive." He frowned. "Damn lizards must be busy as Chinamen making fireworks." He yawned, affecting unconcern. "Our guys'll figure a way around it," he assured, "but *we* have to handle the heavies for now."

The river had widened to about a mile, with the channel markers spaced roughly half a mile apart. Gauging this, Russ seemed to come to a decision. "Too much river to plug up here. We have to push it. Ahead full," he added louder, to the light-furred Lemurian at the engine order telegraph.

"Ahead full, ay!" came the reply. Amid a clash of bells, the 'Cat heaved the shiny brass handle on the EOT back and forth three times to signal a rapid speed increase. Immediately, the corresponding pointer swung to match the order with a final *clang*.

"Shit fire," Monk said wonderingly. "We're *really* gonna do this."

Russ turned to him. "Get aft to the auxiliary conn." He looked appraisingly at Gutfeld. "Your Marines are ready?"

"As ready as I can make 'em."

"Okay, Major. You might as well stay for now and see how this shapes up."

"Goddamn it!" Dean Laney snarled when the EOT gnashed to "Ahead Full." Instead of sullenly waiting awhile, however, as he usually did, he instantly responded and spun on his elaborately carved (and cushioned) stool, bellowing, "All right, step on it, you greasy little chimps! It ain't enough they wanna kill us—they can't wait to get at it!" Glancing automatically at the steam-pressure gauge, fluctuating around the 180 mark, he made a "spin it" motion at the 'Cat standing by the high-pressure steam valve. Other Lemurians, naked except for gray-blue kilts and the occasional filthy Dixie cup, blinked nervous acceptance and stiffened at their posts as more steam gushed to the huge four-cylinder triple-expansion engine crowding the compartment. A little steam fogged the space, seeping past worn seals, but very quickly the heavy heartbeat *thump-thump-kerthump!* of the engine sped up, just like a runner shifting from a jog to a sprint, and the massive, oil-streaked piston rods accelerated their eccentric pace.

Laney stood and stepped to the fireroom hatch, looking through. Four 'Cats on watch peered intently at the eight fiery ports flanking them, occasionally glancing at gauges above or tumultuous feedwater swirling in cloudy sight glasses. Compared to *Walker*'s fireroom snipes, tend-ing equally old but far more finicky "high-performance" boilers feeding her demanding turbines, these had little to do. Uncharacteristically, Laney hurled no obligatory abuse at them. He merely said, "Dog this hatch," and backed away.

For a fleeting moment, he caught himself almost missing *Walker* and all the people he'd known in her engineering spaces—even those moronic "Mice," Isak and Gilbert. He'd never really liked any of them, but he felt their absence now. Particularly since so many were dead. Covertly, he studied "his" 'Cats. He had no illusions that they liked *him*, but they respected his knowledge. They might even take a measure of perverse pride in their ability to *endure* him, and seemed to get a kick out of his weird, rebellious relationship with the skipper. That was particularly odd, since they obviously liked Captain Chappelle.

Maybe it was the stool stunt that welded them together— and to me, he reflected. When some deck apes, on a lark, swiped all the stools out of engineering—including Laney's favorite—his entire division was outraged. In complete agreement, probably for the first time, he and his snipes retaliated. Using careful planning and precise timing, they stole every single stool and chair on the entire ship—except Captain Chappelle's on the bridge—and threw them over the side. Then, despite serious pressure to blow, mainly by the XO, *nobody* in his division ratted him out. The result was new chairs and stools on the ship—including the princely one he'd just left, which just appeared one day, and a complete end to any more bullshit from the apes. *The disproportionate response,* he mused. *One thing I learned from that asshole Silva.*

In the end, despite his brief moment of nostalgia, he was relatively content with his lot, sensing a swelling . . . benevolence toward the 'Cats under his command. *They don't like me, but they maybe don't hate me either.* That was enough. Almost. He reflected back on his conversation with Kathy McCoy and the vague encouragement she'd given. *What a dish,* he thought. *After all this time, maybe she'll finally give me a chance. I've got my "baby";*

I've got a home. Maybe I'll finally even have a girl I don't have to pay to like me. . . . Then he frowned.

Not very goddamn likely, he fumed. *We're steaming as fast as we can to slam into the whole lizard navy! What're the chances me an' my baby—or Kathy—will make it through that? Shit!* "I never get a break," he mumbled, walking slowly past the throbbing engine. Shaking out a PIG-cig, he looked at it with a bitter snort, remembering it was Isak, Gilbert, and others who'd figured out how to make the waxy Aryaalan tobacco fit to smoke. *Don't miss those little turds at all.* Putting the vile thing between his lips, he lit it with a battered Zippo and sucked in the acrid pollution it discharged. He barely noticed how bad it was anymore. Even PIG-cigs couldn't compete with the reek of rancid sweat and hot, oily iron pervading the compartment—even with half the 'Cats in his division smoking now. He returned to his comfy stool. *Cap'n Chappelle's fighting for the damn cause, and down deep, just about everybody in the American Navy Clan, human* and *'Cat, is probably really fighting for Cap'n Reddy. Well, that's okay,* he grudged. *I guess I am too, in a way, even if Reddy don't like me either. But he gave me chance after chance until I wound up here. I gotta prove I deserved it. In the end, though, my main cause is this engine. . . .* He considered. *And "my" 'Cats too. And Kathy,* he added emphatically. *We're all probably gonna die, but it damn sure won't be because my baby quit on ever'body—or I did.*

"Stand by for surface action, port bow!" called Russ Chappelle. His order was quickly relayed to the lightly protected fire-control platform above the pilothouse. USS *Santa Catalina* had won the race to the bend in the river, barely, and as predicted, the Zambezi became very narrow there—so narrow that the main channel was probably little more than 250 yards wide. That was perfect for Russ's purposes, but it also meant his ship couldn't maneuver much in the action to come.

And it was coming.

They'd seen the four tall, smoke-chuffing funnels of

the leading Grik dreadnaught long before they could get a shot, and even if *Santy Cat* was barely half their size and making little smoke, Grik lookouts had doubtless noticed her as well. As she turned the corner, a monstrous dark shape loomed into view, practically nose to nose, at the ridiculous knife-fighting range of four hundred yards—and they all got an intimately close look at what they were facing for the very first time.

At a glance, the enemy ship looked like an insanely enlarged version of the old CSS *Virginia*, or "*Merrimac*," its main deck low to the water with little freeboard, dominated by a high, sloping ironclad casemate protecting two long gundecks. *Santy Cat* had fought similar ships before, admittedly much farther away, and handled them fairly successfully, but this thing and the others creeping up on its starboard flank had been altered in ways that remained imperfectly understood—until now. At least in one respect. Russ raised his binoculars while the gun crew on the fo'c'sle turned their massive training and pointing wheels to swing the 10″ rifle on target.

"Holy crap," he muttered. "Commence firing!"

"What is it, Captain?" Gutfeld asked.

"Every Grik BB we've seen had three big hundred-pounder smoothbores up front. This one only has two guns forward, in armored sponsons, barbettes—whatever—that follow the curve of the casemate, but they're *huge*! I bet they're four- or five-hundred-pounders!"

"My God."

Santa Catalina's own massive bow gun roared and recoiled back, belching a fogbank of dirty white smoke. They still used black powder in the 10″ rifle because they simply hadn't been able to test it with the newer propellants. Only the 5.5″s and other secondaries used the "new" powder. But the 10″ shell was a long conical projectile that weighed five hundred pounds itself and carried an impressive bursting charge detonated with a contact fuse. With a sound like ripping canvas, it flew downrange and exploded heavily against the starboard-side curve of the target's casemate. Iron fragments flailed the water, and what looked like a huge, long sheet of armor plate twirled away, folded and warped. But as

Russ stared through his binoculars, he drew a surprised breath.

"Holy *crap*!" he repeated hotly. "It knocked a layer off but didn't penetrate!" He turned to the talker. "Tell Lieutenant Baak he'll have to shoot straighter! Hit her square—or aim for the gun shields. And have *Amagi*'s old armor-piercing rounds rousted out of the lineup in the magazines. We might need 'em!"

Santa Catalina still carried a grand total of five of the dead battlecruiser's AP shells. The rest had been expended or turned over to the Air Corps and transformed into bombs—which had also been used up, as far as Russ knew. The Air Corps had its own lighter, somewhat-armor-piercing bombs now, but the homegrown "common" shells for *Santy Cat*'s big number one gun had been considered sufficient for any armor they'd encountered before. Now . . .

"Maybe they just added armor to the front, to get close," Gutfeld suggested.

"Maybe," Russ conceded. "But they *are* close and the front is *to* us!" He glanced at the high banks of the river on either side, even as the crew on the fo'c'sle feverishly went through the laborious process of reloading. "Signal the engine room to back us down to 'ahead slow,' and stand by to reverse the engine," he told the 'Cat at the lee helm. "We can give 'em a little rope," he added to Gutfeld.

At that moment, two enormous white clouds blossomed in front of the Grik BB, their sheer size a grim testament to how much powder its guns gulped. Freight-train roars rumbled overhead and there was a loud *crack* as the portside funnel support stays parted.

"Guess they ain't used to shootin' this close neither," the Lemurian quartermaster at the wheel quipped.

The enemy dreadnaught directly behind the first had started easing to the side, risking the shallower water on the south bank to bring its own guns to bear. One fired, quickly followed by the other, at a range of about a thousand yards. The first went wild, but the second skated off the water a hundred yards short and slammed into *Santy Cat*'s bow near her port hawse with a ringing *clang*.

The ship had almost no armor there, but the angle was such that the huge roundshot—they'd *seen* it—merely gouged a deep dent in the plates and ricocheted into the water close alongside. The tall waterspout drenching the lookouts on the port bridgewing was sufficient testimony to the energy it still carried.

"Gun number one is up!" cried one of the wet 'Cats.

Boom! Swooooosh! Blam! Another hit, almost dead center between the top and bottom barbettes, and more shredded armor flicked away amid a spray of rivets or bolt heads.

"Tough mother . . ." Russ grunted grimly. "Still, I bet that shook 'em up. It can't be easy to load those big-ass guns either." He'd been watching, and the enemy artillery had recoiled all the way inside the casemate—but how far back? Besides being bigger, the guns were longer than any the Grik had showed them before, and he was trying to imagine what kind of mounting system they used, how bulky, and how long it would take them to reload. *The gun's probably on a track, on top of a pivot. And I doubt they've got the same monsters down the sides; they'd recoil into each other.* He frowned. *Unless they have half as many, and they're staggered. Less than half,* he realized. *They couldn't put any on the old upper gundeck. Even if they weren't too heavy, there isn't room. The question is, would they do that? Sacrifice lots of bloody powerful guns for fewer superguns? Are those things really "all big gun ships," true "dreadnaughts"? They already kind of were, in a sense, but with those superguns—God, if they ever rifle them, or come up with an effective fire-control system, we might not be able to get close enough to hurt them. Even with our newest torpedoes.*

He refocused. *To load, they have to hoist a charge and shot up in front of the muzzle, place it in—we won't see that, but we* should *see . . .* Still staring through his binoculars, he observed a long wooden rod the size of a ship's topmast protruding through the armored casemate and supported by a spiderweb of lines. That's when he realized there was a narrow boom overhanging the gunports above the enemy pilothouse. Lines snaking along the sides of the rod went taut and drew it swiftly inward. Seconds later, it came back out and rose, out of the way, until it snugged itself to the overhanging boom. A second rod, servicing the lower gun, did the same. *Pretty smart,* he conceded. *No sense bringing them back inside during action. Be tough as hell to use in rough seas, though; they'd get all tangled up. And they're pretty damn vulnerable. I'm surprised we didn't cut a bunch of lines with the punches we already landed—but they're practically loaded already. I never* dreamed *they could do it so fast.*

"Back us off. Half astern," he ordered, looking impatiently down at the number one gun. A slightly rusty white-painted shell with a thin red band around the middle and a green nose lay on the loading tray. It was one of *Amagi*'s. The rammer quickly slid it into place and retracted, just as a pair of powder bags—the short section of barrel could burn only two—were laid out. The ram operated again, and a 'Cat gunner slammed the breech even as the tray folded back and the trainer started turning his wheel. *Santa Catalina* was beginning to slow, but the range between her and the first BB had dwindled to just over two hundred yards when the enemy guns roared again. Russ's old ship heaved as another shot hit her bow, smashed through, and bored deep in the ship. The other round hit as well, snapping the foremast off below the lookout's perch, spraying the bridge with chunks of hot steel and a sleet of thick paint fragments. Booms slammed to the deck, and the whole top of the mast, complete with screaming lookout, crashed down on the cargo hatch over the forward hold.

There was more screaming on the fo'c'sle, where 'Cats scrambled to clear fallen cables from the gun, even as its crew doggedly labored to bring it on target. The second Grik BB fired again and another huge shot hit, almost exactly where the first one had, but this one punched through and the portside anchor dropped with a splash, its chain shot away. Again, there was no telling where the second shot went. *Santy Cat*'s screw was beginning to bite and she was drawing away, but the enemy was barely a hundred yards distant when the number one gun, finally on target, roared its defiance. They were close enough that its own smoke obscured the hit, the report drowning the concussion of the resulting blast. Pressure shattered the windows, and orange jets of flame gushed out gunports toward the rear of the Grik's casemate. A second detonation dwarfed the first—they heard this one—as the starboard side of the target peeled upward from a roaring gust of fire and steam. All four funnels toppled to port and the burning wreck started to settle, ready charges cooking off with surges of thumping smoke.

"Reload Ayy-Pee!" came Lieutenant Baak's distinctive, yowelly voice.

"Corps-'Cats to the fo'c'sle," Russ ordered. "Wait," he told Gutfeld as the Marine started to move. "What's the range on your mortars?"

Gutfeld blinked. "All we have are the light three-inch jobs, effective to about eight hundred yards. My guys can usually drop 'em in a pickle barrel at six. On a moving ship—*against* a moving ship? Hell, I don't know."

"We're not shooting at pickle barrels today, Simy. I just want you to smother the front of those damn BBs." Realizing Gutfeld hadn't seen what he had, he quickly explained. "This whole fight's gonna be up close, brass knuckles and belly guns," he added. "You already knew that, but if you knock away all that rigging out front, they'll have a helluva time loading. Probably have to send lizards out to do it, see? Then your guys can hose 'em with mortars and machine guns while we blast 'em at our leisure. It'll be a turkey shoot!"

Nodding understanding and starting to grin, Simon Gutfeld bolted. Immediately, he ran into his XO, Captain Flaar. "Round up the mortar crews, on the double, and set up every tube that'll bear forward." He quickly repeated why. "Machine gunners will support, but fire only on command." This was punctuated by the bellow of the 10″ rifle, but Gutfeld continued without even looking. "Hopefully the mortars'll do the job, and we can help the navy stop those big bastards without taking too many licks. But like the skipper said, it'll probably come down to teeth and claws, and I don't want to waste ammo. Got it?"

What began as confused blinking turned to anticipation, and Captain Flaar's yellow-furred face spread in a grin of its own. "Ay, ay, Major!"

The Battle of the Zambezi River was never going to be a turkey shoot—Russ knew that even as he said it—but despite her early wounds, *Santa Catalina* had it mostly her way for a while. She hit the second Grik BB with a common shell as it steered away from its stricken sister, but the strike was farther back on the casemate. It punched through, seemingly confirming the speculation about armor thickness, and blew out a respectable chunk of the ship aft of the armored pilothouse. Also confirming Russ's personal opinion regarding Grik doctrines of naval warfare, the enemy then fired a badly angled broadside of twelve hundred-pounder smoothbores at a range of about six hundred yards. Two hit and knocked more holes in the old ship's bow, but now her portside 5.5˝s would bear, and the Grik never got a chance to fire again. Between Gutfeld's mortars ravaging the loading apparatus for the enemy's most lethal guns, the 10˝ rifle speaking again, and the 5.5˝s slamming through the thinner armor at will, the second Grik BB was soon another burning wreck. And as hoped, the water was shallow enough that neither sank very deep. The next BB had to come straight at *Santy Cat*, right between them, and Russ tried to get ready.

He backed his ship off a bit more, with another Japanese AP shell waiting in her main gun. *Naga* and *Felts*, unengaged so far, took station on her flanks, presenting their broadside batteries of ten fifty-pounders in support. Details busily cleared more debris from *Santy Cat*'s fo'c'sle, and Kathy and her division carried the wounded aft. Laney hadn't made a peep, and his engine had promptly answered every bell. Russ was beginning to hope they could destroy the next BB before it got off a shot with its superguns, and he'd retreated as far as he dared. At the first sign of the enemy, *Naga* and *Felts* would hammer it, while Gutfeld's Marines smothered the fo'c'sle and reloading gear with mortars. The 10˝ rifle would assassinate it.

At least that was the plan.

The wind was out of the south, and dense smoke from the ship they'd killed on that side of the channel choked the river between it and the first half-sunken BB. Another air strike from *Arracca*, the heaviest all day, roared by overhead, the small, gallant planes a thrill for the lonely *Santy Cat* to see. But from their perspective, with nothing but wreckage before them, the multitudes of the enemy beyond weren't yet real and they felt pretty good about what they'd accomplished.

"Cap-i-taan!" cried the talker. "Raa-dio report fum *Arracca*'s COFO, fly-een above!"

"Well?"

Even before the talker could respond, the bridge lookouts on both wings shouted inside. "Surface taa-gits, two six seero!"

Russ hurried to the windows and peered at the smoke ahead just as *two* Grik BBs emerged, almost side by side. "Commence firing main battery!" he shouted. "Target closest to your current point of aim. Commence firing all mortars that will bear, port to port, starboard to starboard!"

The crew of the number one gun quickly lined up on the enemy ship to the left, requiring the least adjustment. Even as they did so, Russ watched the enemy guns slowly shift and change elevation as their Grik crews did the same. Heavy *thump*s sounded aft as the first mortars lobbed into the air. *It's a gunfight,* Russ realized, his heart in his throat. But with nothing else he could do, his mind was strangely detached. *A showdown just like in the Western pictures, to see who's quicker on the draw, but here it's two ships and four gun's crews against our one.*

In the end, *Santy Cat*'s gunners won in the sense that they fired first and hit their mark. Their AP shell punched through at the very base of the casemate, and the resulting detonation savaged the two forward guns, and the armored pilothouse above it all was blown completely out. Unfortunately, *Santy Cat*'s gunners were only a fraction of a second quicker, and their heroic, professional act was the last thing they ever did. All four enemy guns fired, practically simultaneously, while *Santy Cat*'s shell was in flight, and the first of the three 400-pounder roundshot that hit *Santa Catalina* actually struck the muzzle of the 10″ rifle. The brittle iron shattered and jagged fragments shredded its entire crew. The second shot hit near the waterline, tearing a giant mouth through the forepeak and two more compartments, and ripping through the lightly armored forward magazine bulkhead. It came to rest inside after killing two 'Cats in the handling room. If it had been an exploding shell, *Santy Cat* would've ceased to exist right then. The third hit went in directly under the bridge, but hardly anyone felt it. Crashing through the officers' quarters like fragile leaves, it left a wake of personal, if inconsequential, devastation before rebounding—barely—off the heavy forward armor of the 5.5″ gun castle. From there it shot straight up, splintering through the upper deck and scattering a mortar crew behind the bridge before dropping into the water alongside *Naga*.

In that strange moment, normally reserved for the near silence of shock before the screams begin, *Naga* vomited a broadside of fifty-pound shot, and nearly every one hit the undamaged BB amid the exploding mortars Gutfeld's Marines had sent. The shot scattered against the heavy frontal armor and flailed the river. Russ shook his head to clear it and began shouting.

"Damage report! Ahead slow, come left thirty degrees to unmask the starboard battery!" He didn't know how badly his ship was hit, but it was obvious the main gun was at least temporarily out of action. "Signal *Naga* to give us some room!" He stared at the enemy through the smoke as his ship began to move, already turning slightly to port. One Grik BB was hit hard and apparently out of control, veering sharply toward its consort. With an audible crash they collided, and the wounded behemoth began pushing its sister toward the burning wreck on the north bank of the river. It wasn't dead, though. A half broadside of hundred-pounders thundered out, causing a loud crash aft and slashing the water. *Felts* fired, her accurate, powerful guns peeling armor away from the closest enemy's side.

"Number one gun's outa' aaction," the talker reported. "Muzzle's baad bent, an' a shock is knocked off. The whole crew's dead. There's floodin' for'aard, but is

mossly open seams an' sloshin' in a big-aass hole. Officers' quaar-ters is smashed. Engineerin's okay, but even
behind the armor, one o' them lass hits opened seams
an' staarted leaks. Laney says pumps can haandle it."

Russ nodded, looking through his binoculars. The
mortars or *Naga*'s roundshot had done their work on the
undamaged BB's loading rigging—and as the other
pushed it around, the forward guns wouldn't bear, anyway. *Santy Cat* had taken a beating and was probably
about to take a lot more, but they'd silenced the main
enemy guns. And the old girl still had a lot of bite down
her sides: each mounting three 5.5″ rifles, a 4.7″ DP, and
up to three of the new 4″-50 DP guns as well. They might
not be up for the heavy frontal armor they'd seen, but
all had "homegrown" AP rounds available and could fire
any direction but directly ahead. The 4.7″s could've already done that, from their new emplacements forward,
but their muzzle blasts would've hammered the main
gun crew. That wasn't a problem anymore. "Commence
firing the secondary battery!" Russ yelled, over another
of *Naga*'s broadsides. "If we can sink those two bastards
where they are, half our work is done."

What ensued was a chaotic, hellish maelstrom. The
BB still under control managed to back away from the
other before it slammed directly into the burning wreck
of the first one they'd sunk. It continued backing up until it presented nearly its own full broadside, only partly
blocked by its consort. Massive hundred-pound roundshot rumbled in from both, hammering the blocking
force. It deeply dented the armor over *Santy Cat*'s engineering spaces and punched effortlessly through everything else. Few rounds targeted *Naga* or *Felts*, but there
were enough to wreak terrible havoc, lopping off masts
and tearing great gaps in their scantlings amid blizzards
of splinters. So far, neither was badly holed, but that
couldn't last, and the death toll was horrendous. Russ
had all his Marines take what cover they could. Their
mortars were pointless now.

On the bright side, if that term could be applied to
such an appalling situation, *Santy Cat* and her mutilated
DDs were giving as good as they got. For one thing, they

remained somewhat mobile within the narrow confines of the channel, steaming back and forth and making themselves slightly more difficult targets. That required great care and amounted to little more than steaming in a fairly tight oval, but it allowed them to present fresh fire from rested crews and expose less damaged sides to the enemy. Furthermore, the modern guns mounted on the old ship were pounding deep into the enemy armor, peeling it away with every shot and exploding in the heavy wooden backing, four feet thick in places. Jagged holes began to connect the enemy gunports as more and more of their guns fell silent. Even the DDs were starting to blast through and rend Grik flesh inside the casemates. More important, by staying to fight, the increasingly shattered BBs were blocking the river themselves, and nothing as large as they were could possibly squeeze past now. Grik cruisers could still slip through, and two actually tried, quickly finding themselves caught in the middle, masking their own ships' fire as their smaller, weaker hulls earned the Allies' full focus. One was sunk and the other quickly retired, clearing the way for the BB's hundred-pounders again.

Yet even as *Santy Cat*'s damage mounted and she started looking more and more like a large battered cheese grater, Russ grew increasingly desperate to make the Grik pay for their foolishness, to sink them where they were, whatever the cost. Mikey Monk appeared on the bridge, blood streaming from cuts too numerous to count. To his eyes, nobody on the bridge looked any better. All the glass had been blown out of the windows, and though no shot had passed through the space, plenty of steel splinters or iron fragments had. Russ lowered his binoculars and stared, his expression uncomprehending. "What are you doing here?" he demanded.

"Auxiliary conn's shot away. The whole thing just fell out from under us. I was lucky." He shrugged. "Anyway, I went down to check on Laney on the way up here. I hadn't heard any bitching out of him and figured he must be dead."

"Yeah," Russ agreed loudly as the 4.7″ roared on the well deck below, just as a pair of roundshot sent geysers up alongside the battered fo'c'sle and slammed into the ship. "Is he?"

"Dead? No. Pissed as hell and standin' ankle-deep in water, but he ain't dead." Monk shook his head. "Didn't even notice me. He was too busy waddlin' around, yellin' and cussin' at 'Cats, shorin' mattresses against leakin' seams. Skipper," he added seriously, "there's water comin' in *everywhere* down there. Nothin' big, no holes exactly—the armor we added has saved us so far—but I bet half the rivets've popped. It looks like there's two hundred showerheads in the engine room, all turned on high!"

"And he hasn't made a peep," Russ said wonderingly. "I'll be damned."

"Sur!" interrupted a bridgewing lookout, her arm in a bloody sling. Russ looked at her, then past. The Grik BB that had rammed the wreck had caught fire on her fo'c'sle a while back, but with the wind blowing from the south, the blaze hadn't seemed to spread. Maybe that wasn't the case belowdecks, however, because flames were suddenly gushing from the shattered forward casemate and Grik were spilling out the rearward gunports onto the aft deck. Others climbed out the top between the funnels, braving the still-withering fire for fear of something else. Some were physically blown into the water by the pressure of the other BB's guns firing alongside, and that ship was starting to move, backing away again.

"Concentrate all fire on the far enemy ship!" Russ commanded. "Let her have it!"

The number of shrieking shells filling the air seemed to redouble, and *Felts* even managed a few shots. Her fire control had been cut when her mainmast fell. *Naga* roared, at least ten guns thundering from her less ravaged side. Two 5.5"s went off simultaneously, followed by three 4"-50s, over and over. All *Santy Cat*'s secondaries were still in action, though fallen crews had been augmented by Marines. And they were still controlled by the gunnery officer, Lieutenant Baak, on the fire-control platform. How he'd survived with so little protection remained a mystery. Even as the salvos bored in on the more distant ship, flames must've touched a magazine on the closer one at last. With a staggering roar, it simply blew up. Tons of debris erupted into the sky. Some was recognizable: two tall, crumpled funnels flipping end over end, and a massive gun was seen soaring ahead of the expanding cloud of destruction, crashing down on land.

"Take cover!" Russ bellowed.

Timbers and jagged iron hit the water, marching ever closer. Grik bodies, or parts of them, *splapp*ed the dark river almost as far as *Santy Cat*. Heavier debris rained down on the whole battered squadron. All they could see in the main channel of the Zambezi was a huge dark pall, but slowly the stiff breeze carried the worst away. What remained of the closer ship, already entangled with the first, was a jagged, flaming skeleton, already on the riverbed. Behind it, the bright paint of its new bottom and shiny bronze screws glaring at the late-afternoon sun, the fourth Grik dreadnaught was lying on its back. Hammered unmercifully, and possibly listing into a flooding side, the shock wave—or just the wave—created by the nearby blast that shattered her sister finished her, pushing her near side down until her funnels crumpled against the silty bottom.

"I'll be damned," Monk murmured. "Damn."

"Cease firing," Russ ordered, weariness seeping into his voice. The ship's guns had already fallen silent, equally exhausted.

"You think that's it, Skipper?" Monk asked, while his captain studied the river-clogging wreckage through his binoculars.

"No," Russ replied. "I don't think another battle-wagon can get through that mess, but their cruisers can. And their galleys for sure. Still, they can't know what little we've got on this side. Chances are they'll think it's more than we have, and that might make them take a breath"—he nodded at the riverbank—"until all the civvy lizards tell 'em what they saw." He sighed. "So, we may have a little time. I hope so, to make scratch repairs. Right now I don't think we'd survive an old lady in a rowboat, whacking the hull with a wooden spoon." He considered. "We should get a pretty good idea what's what from *Arracca*. Her planes were pretty busy themselves." That was certainly true. They'd even apparently made a couple of attacks on Grik heavies beyond *Santy Cat*'s view, after all. Russ had seen some diving planes and airbursts beyond the immediate congestion of battle. And it cost them. Several Nancys had retired overhead, trailing smoke, and he hoped they'd made it back to *Arracca*. At least there weren't any antiair rocket batteries nearby—yet. "I'll find out what her pilots saw," he continued. "In the meantime, get Chief Dobson to reinforce the damage-control parties with Major Gutfeld's Marines, on the double. I don't care if Dobson has to detail 'Cats to stand there with their fingers in the holes; we have to keep up power. We may have a day or so while the Grik sort things out, or we might not have any time at all. But if rising water quenches the fires in Laney's boilers, we're dead."

"Aye, aye, sir."

////// The Palace of Vanished Gods
Old Sofesshk
November 31, 1944

"Stopped? How? It cannot be!" ranted Esshk, Regent Champion and First General of all the Grik. His dark red eyes flared like bright hot lava and practically bulged beneath the parallel bony ridges tapering down his snout. His crest stood high and stiff with fury and challenge. "How could the irresistible power of the Final Swarm be halted—before it even reached the sea? And how can you *squirm* there on the floor and make such incomprehensible mewlings of defeat? To the *cookpots* with you, General Ign, if you cannot explain this to my satisfaction at once!"

"You may, of course, do with me as you will, my lord," Ign pronounced piously from his prostrate position on the moist stone pavement of the dank audience chamber in the Palace of Vanished Gods. "My life is yours, and I will happily destroy *myself* if I have disappointed you. But I beg you will hear my final counsel first."

"Hear him," urged the Chooser, fearful that in his current state Esshk would draw his own blade and slay his best general there and then before they even heard what happened. He'd never seen Esshk like this before, more like Kurokawa, who'd always been ruled by rage—

and panic—rather than the thoughtful calculation Esshk had always shown. Killing Ign would severely delay any comprehensible report, but might also be unwise for other reasons. Ign and the New Army were more devoted to Esshk than the Celestial Mother, the first time such a thing had ever occurred, but the army's affection flowed *through* Ign and there was no telling how destroying him might affect that. They could ill afford to find out now.

"Speak, then," Esshk rasped through clenched teeth, his crest quivering slightly.

"Of course, Lord," Ign said to the floor. "I was not in the van, it was not my place, yet I followed close enough in *Giorsh*, behind the cruiser swarm leading the galleys." *Giorsh*, essentially "the Place of Generals at Sea," was the traditional name for Grik flagships. The current *Giorsh* was the newest, mightiest greatship of battle built in the long, broad river leading north from Sofesshk to where the waters tumbled down from the monumental Lake of the Gods. "Even there," Ign continued, raising his head enough to roll an eye up at his lord, "I quickly sensed when things began to turn. The smaller flying machines of the prey attacked the galleys throughout the day and destroyed many of them." He flicked his own crest. "Not enough to notice, really, if there had not been so many New Army troops and their precious equipment in the van. They managed to destroy several cruisers as well, but had no success against the greatships of battle and their new defenses. All this was expected, considering that we sortied in daylight, and the losses remained a mere nuisance. They would have made no difference to our plan." He took a long breath and his voice turned incredulous, indignant.

"What we did not, *could* not have expected, was the arrival of a powerful surface ship, the prey's *Santa Catalina* itself, Lord, crouching in our *own* holy river with two or more smaller consorts. Together, they apparently mounted a most impressive defense. I could not view the battle, and the signals of those who could were quite confused, but the result was plain. Great explosions, towering columns of smoke, and the Swarm forced to a grinding halt. I have since gathered more reports, but the scope of the disarray resulting from the stoppage is difficult to—"

"But," Esshk interrupted, bulging eyes widening even farther in astonishment. It was obvious the enemy knew they were coming; they'd seen from the sky, and air attacks *had* been expected. But how could a single ship—he didn't credit its consorts—*dare* advance against them? And regardless how powerful, how could it alone throw their plans into such a shambles? "Why did the new guns on the leading greatship of battle not simply destroy *Santa Catalina* in the confines of the river? I am told it is not heavily armored and only the greater range of its weapons makes it formidable. Unable to maneuver, it should have been quickly killed!"

"The enemy chose their position well, Lord. Perfectly, in point of fact. They caught us rounding the *nakkle* leg, above the stretch of river where the digger fishers live."

Esshk's eyes narrowed. He knew the place well—and immediately understood the problem. "So, you tried to force a passage?"

"*I* did not, Lord. As I reported, I did not even know the enemy was there until the first four greatships of battle were engaged. The airships sent to scout the river ahead of us reported nothing—though the sky winds were even greater than those that swept the ground today, and they may have been pushed off course."

"*Four* greatships of battle were insufficient to sink the *Santa Catalina* or drive it away?" Esshk's tone had turned bitter again.

"Worse, Lord," Ign confessed. "It . . . destroyed them all." He hurried on before Esshk could respond. "The fault is still mine. As we have often discussed, the nature of this conflict constantly forces us to consider the changing role of generals as well as warriors, and I should have been in the van, despite tradition." He spread his arms on the damp stones. "I do not know if the outcome would have been different. Most likely, *my* first inclination would have been to attack. It is probable I would have been destroyed as well. But it is possible I may have reacted differently, viewing the situation for myself, and my failure rests on the fact that I never imagined such a scenario and never told the ships' commanders what to do if they met opposition at such a point."

"What would you have told them?" the Chooser asked, equally skeptical that Ign could—or would've—stopped the commanders of powerful ships from closing with what must've appeared to be weaker prey.

"I *hope* I would have ordered them to refuse battle and await my further contemplation, based on personal observations."

Even Esshk snorted at that. *Ign is very good, very intuitive in this new way of war,* he thought, *and has had time to consider what he should've done. But could he—could anyone—think so dispassionately in the thrall of the Hunt? Impossible. That's exactly why generals do not lead from the front.* "So the enemy is more daring and has sharper teeth than we supposed," he said, slightly less furious. "But I still fail to see how one ship could stop so much. There were more than enough ships to physically push it aside, if necessary."

"True, Lord, but at the *nakkle* leg, only one, at most two, greatships of battle could assail it at a time. The first were destroyed, preventing more from coming to grips. The wrecks have quite blocked the deep-water channel, and none of our greatships of battle can now get past them. Nor can we do anything about the blockage as long as that ship guards the bend; we cannot clear the obstruction under fire without risking adding to it."

The full realization of why Ign stopped, why he was *here*, finally dawned on Esshk. It was disaster! Catastrophe! The river was blocked and the Swarm was trapped. For an instant, he almost contemplated destroying *himself*.

"What can be done?" the Chooser asked instead, watching Esshk's crest begin to droop.

"The cruisers might still get through, though they will be confined to several constricted passages. The galleys will have more choices."

"Can you send the galleys now?" Esshk asked.

Ign chose his response with care. It had taken two hours to summon an airship to meet him onshore, then two more to fly here—under constant threat of air attack—and it was almost fully dark outside. "Our New Army can fight in the dark," he conceded. Grik had always been able to do that, but their night vision couldn't match their opponents', so they traditionally avoided it. Better training helped, and should come as a terrible surprise to the enemy. But under the circumstances . . . "Yet, as I reported, the disarray on our side of the *nakkle* leg is quite astonishing, and preparing such a thing so precipitously, and in darkness, would be extremely difficult and take many hours. Even then I expect coordination would be poor—and the burning ships would night-blind our warriors while illuminating them for the enemy. We have discussed their fast-shooting weapons before and they might shred tens, if not hundreds, of our galleys if they try to push through unsupported."

"What of the cruisers?"

"With all my worship, Lord, the cruisers would suffer the same fate in the dark, under accurate fire they can ill respond to, while attempting to avoid the wreckage around them. They would probably only further block the channel."

"Why not simply go around this *Santa Catalina*?" inquired the Chooser. Esshk looked at him blankly. "The galley warriors already carried their vessels to the water from where they hid. Have them carry them around the enemy and proceed behind him."

"A laudable suggestion, my lord," Ign temporized, "but also . . . difficult to effect. The banks are quite steep there, so the galleys would have to row a great distance back upstream. With the rainy season so recently past, the current remains swift. They *could* accomplish it," he continued, "but would then have to carry their vessels perhaps ten leagues—as much as nearly five tens of what Kurokawa called kilo'eters—before putting them back in the water. It would take days, across fairly open ground. . . ."

"Helplessly subject to merciless attack from the air," Esshk noted darkly.

"True, Lord," Ign agreed. "And not only would the survivors be utterly exhausted by the time they completed their task, but *Santa Catalina*, doubtless notified of the attempt, could simply move downriver and slaughter them at its leisure. We always knew the Final Swarm could only succeed if it scattered."

"It was just a suggestion," the Chooser said sourly. "I am not a general, after all."

A moment of contemplative silence ensued. Finally, Ign spoke. "My lords, should you choose to heed it, my counsel is this: allow me to properly plan an assault by the cruisers, to commence in a few days." He inwardly cringed.

"*Days?*" Esshk roared. "While the enemy continues to eat us from the air?" He paused, listening. The heavy mutter of many motors now rumbled in the night sky outside, echoing in through the open stone passages. It was a sure sign that the big enemy flying machines that dropped their bombs in darkness were back. They'd been absent for a couple of weeks, and Esshk had wondered about that, but now it was clear they'd been assisting in the destruction of Kurokawa. What they'd done there might succeed *here* as well. Especially if they focused on Old Sofesshk. Esshk had already clamped down on dissent after the first such desultory strike, but with the Swarm on the move, the inhabitants of the city outnumbered his guards.

"I will dispatch a ten of hundreds of my finest troops back here at once," Ign said, apparently reading Esshk's mind, "but there are purposes for the delay. First, we must assemble an unstoppable force of cruisers. Many still linger at Lake Nalak, waiting to bring up the rear of the Swarm. They must pass through the galleys, and as congested as they are, such will take care and time. Second, we must quickly alter at least a hundred of those galleys to mount the heaviest guns they will bear. They are entirely unarmed and were never meant to carry weapons of their own, but if the cruisers become blocked as well, our entire vast fleet will be of little use, and the galleys will be our only means of destroying *Santa Catalina*."

"The fast-firing weapons," the Chooser reminded.

"Many galleys will be lost," Ign agreed, "but enough should make it close enough to fire directly into the enemy's hull and sink it at last."

"Such modifications may take more than a few days," the Chooser observed.

Ign reluctantly nodded agreement, his snout brushing

the stones. "Perhaps. And I do not propose that we rely on the galleys alone. If allowed to live, I will attack first with an overwhelming number of the cruisers. *Santa Catalina* can only engage so many at once. If the cruisers quickly break her, we will not need the galleys. If not, the galleys will join the attack."

"You are wise to plan for what to do if the first—or second—plan fails," Esshk grudged. "That is rare among our race, as you know." He seemed to make a decision, his crest rising once again. "Stand, General Ign. I cannot spare you and command you *not* to destroy yourself. The blunder today was not yours alone. I myself should have accompanied you, to ensure the airships patrolled effectively, and guide you in your confusion. The airship commanders *will* go to the cookpots," he added darkly, "but you will not. That does inspire me, however." He looked at the Chooser. "How many airships remain to us, here and up the coast? They do little, now that the Sovereign Nest of Japhs is lost and the bombing of the Celestial City is suspended."

The Chooser hesitated. "There may be as many as three hundreds, Lord."

"Excellent. I want all but a handful here. They will attempt to bomb the *Santa Catalina*, of course, but more important, I want them bombing the wreckage in the channel to clear it away. Is that understood?"

Ign suppressed an urge to caution against expecting too much in that regard. Some Grik bombardiers had significantly improved, practicing on the enemy-occupied Celestial Palace. The bombs, however, while powerful enough to sink a ship and well designed for area saturation, were ill suited to the concentration required to utterly demolish a wreck. Enough of the *very* powerful sacrificial piloted bombs might have succeeded, but the Japanese teachers for their crews had long ago gone to Zanzibar. The tiny handful of trained pilots that remained could still be used, but by definition their mission had never allowed for the accumulation of the necessary experience to instruct new pilots.

"And what of the remaining 'handful' of airships?" the Chooser asked.

"One will immediately fly to inform General of the Sky Muriname that he is to bring his surviving flying machines here. I know they require different fuel, available only where they are, so that must somehow be brought as well. By airship also, perhaps. His planes have limited weapons, but we will adapt others to their use." He paused. "Issue the order yourself and ensure it cannot be interpreted as a request."

"And the others?"

"Two airships at least must fly south and scout the threat there. It is clearly greater than expected." The latest ominous reports indicated that beyond belief, the meager Republic of Real People seemed poised to attempt a crossing of the Ungee River, directly in the face of the horde already dispatched to stop it. Esshk was confident the Republic constituted a mere diversion and couldn't imagine its forces might actually succeed, but, then, he hadn't imagined that the Final Swarm might be stopped in its tracks either. It would be best to learn more about what was happening in the southern empire. "Finally," Esshk continued thoughtfully, "we must try to contact General Halik."

"If he lives," the Chooser agreed doubtfully. "We have had no word of him or his army in a great while."

"Untrue. Kurokawa claimed Halik betrayed him and escaped India to the west, perhaps into the regency of Persia. I do not believe the betrayal, particularly considering the source, but there are now . . . strange reports of war in Persia, between Regent Consort Shighat and an unknown force. It might be the enemy advancing from India, but I think it must be Halik. I can certainly imagine him strongly disagreeing with Shighat. Shighat was an associate of Ragak's, after all."

From outside came the thunder of bombs, still mostly falling on the greater mass of Grik and industry across the river in New Sofesshk, but a few might be landing in Old Sofesshk as well. It was difficult to tell. Doubtless, many were falling in the river now, hoping to hit or swamp the many galleys still passing downstream. The palace muffled the explosions, and no bomb they knew of could harm the palace itself, but they started hearing lighter, cracking detonations as rockets rose to explode in the dark, spewing fragments of iron. The rockets were a poor defense, especially at night, but were cheap in labor and materials, and easy to build. At night they relied solely on the concept that if they put enough metal in the air, some was bound to hit something. It was the best they could do for now. And it sounded like there were more planes than usual. That should make one easier to hit, shouldn't it?

"It shall be done," the Chooser assured, then hesitantly—amazed by the notion that suddenly entered his mind—he continued. "Perhaps there is yet another strategy we might pursue." Esshk and Ign both looked at him. "With the Zambezi blocked, the enemy cannot get at us either. They can bomb, and that is a nuisance, but we *do* grow better at defense. And General of the Sky Muriname has suggested better tools. Therefore, if we proceed with the full suppression of the influential Hij of Old Sofesshk, the need for precipitous action"—he bowed his head at Ign—"is less urgent. At the same time, the reports from the south concern me a great deal, and it unsettles me that we must now face two directions to fight. Perhaps . . ." If his own crest hadn't been stiffened, it would've been quivering wildly now. "Perhaps we should settle on a posture of protection here for a time, until the matter in the south is settled."

Esshk stared. "*You* say that now? You, who have clamored constantly, 'Attack! Attack!' would now turn your face from the Hunt?"

"No, Lord," the Chooser denied breathlessly. "But you yourself understand this is no conventional hunt, no commonplace war. We face no ordinary prey. If we are thwarted entire, *which has happened with this very prey before*," he reminded, "there will be no centuries of respite while we rebuild, regather, and begin to probe outward once again. This time our prey means to make *us* prey—and hunt us to extinction. We must proceed more carefully than ever before. This not only so our reforms might flourish," he lightly jabbed, appealing to their plans for absolute power, "but so our very race will survive."

Esshk spun away, his long red cape whirling behind him, exposing his widely flared tail plumage. For a long moment, he said nothing, didn't even move. Finally, he turned to face them again. "No," he said. "Your new counsel has some merit, but the time for the wide-ranging designing of battles is past. The attack in the south cannot succeed; it can only be a demonstration to draw our gaze from the greater wounded prey. And the extent of its wounds is made clear by the fact that they could only send the one iron ship against us. A daring stroke," he conceded again, "but no less an act of desperation because of that. *Now* is the time to break out. *Now* is the time to flush the Final Swarm, because now is when the enemy—our *very* worthy prey—is at his weakest and least prepared. We have reached a point where no further considerations, other than how best to effect that, will be entertained. Am I completely clear? Good."

Esshk looked at Ign. "We cannot wait days to assail the *Santa Catalina*. We must continue to press it, wound it, however we can—consistent with your excellent strategy—and with the least chance of further blocking the channel. Only that will bind it to its present position and give our airships an opportunity to destroy it. As for the rest . . ." Esshk passed his clawed hand down his jaw in thought. "With the dawn, I will join you at the bend of the river myself and we will design the next attack together."

"A great honor, Lord. The New Army—*all* your warriors—will be inspired by your presence and redouble their efforts!"

"I am sure," Esshk agreed. Then he turned to the Chooser. "You will remain at the palace. You alone have the authority, and the trust of my generals, to preside in my place. Begin the suppression you crave. It *is* time. And it may also be better, considering the sensibilities of some of the more traditional generals whom we still need, that I not be seen as part of it. Insulate our new Celestial Mother from your activities and guide her as I have done. Teach her, persuade her, ensure she understands her role. We may well need the . . . *aura* of authority she retains before all is done."

"As you command, my lord," the Chooser replied, with equal measures of anxiety and relief.

* * *

December 5, 1944

"Carefully, or I'll be gnawing your bones by the cookpot tonight!" roared First of Fifty Naxa, standing under the high, bright sun—and the heavy gun being lowered onto the reinforced fo'c'sle of the galley. His Ka'tan, Senior First of One Hundred Jash, stood with First of One Hundred Seech somewhat back, on the walkway over the rowing benches, watching with a mix of awe and uncertainty.

"We'll be gnawing *his* bones if that rickety boom snaps or the cables part," Seech hissed quietly. "And that will be our final pleasure before we are stuffed in a barge at best, or scattered among the other galleys—after this one sinks with a cannon-size hole in its bottom."

Jash made a sharp diagonal nod. He'd already lost all the extra warriors he'd rescued from the lake, to make room for the new deck and gun, and the forward three pairs of oars had been sacrificed as well. He would've lost their rowers, but they had to crew the gun. He hoped the others hadn't gone to a barge. They were all New Army warriors, after all. Somewhat annoyingly, this was all apparently considered a reward to him personally, for his instinct to save only the armed warriors spilled into the lake. The act had drawn the notice of the First of Ten Hundreds, or ker-noll, commanding the ten of galleys Jash's belonged to. And while less than a dozen of its crew had earned names—they hadn't seen combat yet— the ker-noll had specifically honored Jash by naming his galley *Slasher*. That left him torn between a sense of satisfaction and a fervent wish he hadn't saved *anyone*. Still, now that his command had a name, Jash already felt a strange attachment to it. He didn't want his crew, his own little pack, broken up, but found himself equally disturbed by the notion his *Slasher* might have a heavy cannon dropped through it and be destroyed in such an ignominious fashion before it ever met the prey.

The Swarm Fleet had no tenders, no dedicated repair ships, but with so many galleys being altered and so few repair slips in the Sofesshk vicinity left undamaged by nightly bombings, they'd found themselves alongside one of the transport barges for second-wave (second-rate) warriors. These were supposed to be towed across the strait by cruisers or tugs and land at the Celestial City after the galley warriors got their claws in it. But after a week of sitting idle while the battle at the *nakkle* leg sputtered and flared, day and night, the barge—packed with ten hundreds of warriors and all their artillery and ammunition—had exhausted the dried meat meant to get them through the crossing and first few days of battle. Those aboard had resorted to the usual expedient of eating their own, starting with the weak and sick, but a longer delay would result in a gradual diminution of combat power. It also meant that, even compared to *Slasher*, which was little cleaner than any ordinary Grik ship, the barge reeked enough for Jash to notice and be repelled. He absolutely didn't want to wind up in one like it. But the barge provided the workers, the material, and the massive (to Jash) sixteen-pounder field gun on a quickly cobbled naval truck that was inching down from the makeshift boom toward the jury-rigged firing platform Naxa stood upon.

Jash had no idea what the great gun weighed, but knew it was a lot. Most of his crew were crowded at *Slasher*'s stern to counterbalance it and give them an idea how much ballast to shift or take on to trim the vessel.

"Pull it around!" Naxa bellowed at a pair of Grik on slack taglines, staring with open jaws. Too quickly, they jumped to obey and started a slight spin. "Stop it!" Naxa snapped at another pair, and with great effort, the weapon steadied. Finally satisfied, Naxa stepped from under the gun and motioned for the laborers on the barge to ease it down. Raw wood planks and timbers groaned forlornly, and Jash felt the added weight through his feet. "Make all secure," Naxa commanded, and Grik scurried to fasten the gun to ringbolts placed around the deck. They'd rig it for firing and recoil later when a proper gun crew rowed over from one of the cruisers to show them how. A field-gun crew was already crossing over from the barge to begin training the former rowers detailed to operate it.

"Begin resuming your posts," Seech called aft. "Front-most first." As the rowers trotted forward to take their places at the benches, the galley continued to groan. By the time it leveled out at last, barely two-thirds of the positions were filled.

"This is what they told me to expect," Jash explained to his XO. "We will have to put all the ammunition in the back—the stern—to maintain proper balance. It will be awkward, carrying it to the front to use, but there is no choice. We cannot distribute the load and will already ride lower in the water than I would prefer."

"What will happen when we use up the ammunition and its weight goes away? For that matter . . ." Seech paused and lowered his voice. "I have heard the water in the strait sometimes makes waves bigger than we have seen on the lake. Those can be . . . unsettling enough. How can we survive them with that terrible, heavy thing up front?"

Jash regarded Seech curiously. "It is worse than you suppose. All gun-galley commanders were gathered to hear real sailors who have ventured into the great sea. The war has left us precious few of those, as you might imagine, and the remainder are all assigned to the great-ships and cruisers. They said, with all the weight in the front and back of our vessels, the waves in the strait will snap them in two." He shook his head with something akin to humor at the way Seech's jaw fell open. "That will not be a problem for us. Unless there is a storm, unburdened galleys can cross the strait with ease. And we *will* be unburdened by then, having dropped the great gun and all its ammunition over the side as soon as we reach the open sea."

"Well, that relieves my mind to a degree," Seech confessed.

"I am pleased to hear it—but you should also know the main reason the waves of the sea are not expected to trouble us is that few of the gun galleys are expected to survive their attack on the *Santa Catalina*. So what happens after should be of little concern to us. I am actually somewhat surprised that we were told what to do if we make it that far."

Soft, dull thumping sounds reverberated upriver, trapped by the high riverbanks and then the city, all the way from the contentious bend. They'd seen distant flashes from the airship bombs (and burning, falling airships) for three nights now, and the latest scheme, moving antiair rockets forward and using them to bombard *Santa Catalina* and her consorts, must've finally begun. Perhaps they'd be more effective in that role. It was even possible the cruisers were making their sortie, though Jash thought he would've been given warning of that. Most of the gun galleys were finished now, but few were staged, and they were supposed to closely follow the cruiser sortie when it occurred.

"Then again, perhaps we will," Jash consoled Seech. "The prey, a single ship standing against the might of the Final Swarm, cannot have things all its way forever, and it will not be expecting you or me, or our *Slasher*."

CHAPTER
11

"Wheeee!" hollered Chief Gunner's Mate Dennis Silva as he threw Petey as high and far as he could, past the wooden rail, the roiling bow wave, and out over the deadly sea of the Go Away Strait.

"Goddamn!" Petey screeched, and tumbled before flinging out all four legs and extending the membranes between them. For an instant he stalled, and it looked as if he'd drop like a stone into the churning water, but like a falling cat, he managed to orient himself with amazing speed. With a strange, undulating flap of his entire body, he bolted aft, soaring on the respectable tailwind, and crashed into the waiting clutches of laughing, chittering, hissing troops. These consisted of human Maroons from Madagascar and their Imperial cousins from the Empire of the New Britain Isles, Lemurians from all over the Alliance, and Grik-like and human Khonashi from North Borno. Still laughing, they collected Petey, pointed him back at Silva and the group gathered around him near the bow, and turned him loose. Petey took off like a rocket, squirming between the feet of three species of troops, zigging and zagging through the press, until he scrambled up Silva's leg, crawled onto his shoulder, and breathlessly cried "Eat!" in the big man's ear.

"*Good* Petey!" Silva chuckled, breaking a pumpkiny-tasting cracker in two and handing half to the colorful tree-gliding reptile.

"You're such an asshole!" Pam Cross snapped, dark hair blowing, her pretty face distorted by an incredulous frown. An unmistakable Brooklyn accent colored her words. "I thought you *liked* that little turd, an' here you are tryin' ta scare him to death!"

"He ain't scared," Silva replied in his equally thick Alabama drawl. He looked at her with his one good eye. "But what do you care? You hate his guts. I'm just trainin' him for what to do if *you* ever pitch 'eem over the side." He scratched Petey's chin while the little lizard chewed, raining crumbs. "Besides, he likes it. Only fun he can have on this overpacked scum-weenie can."

The "can" was the former Jap-Grik cruiser *Yahagi*, renamed *Itaa* by its commander, Jarrik-Fas, and it was steaming at the head of TF Gri-kakka. "Itaa" was Lemurian for "nose," and reflected the large underwater ram at her bow. Beside Pam was Lawrence, Gunnery Sergeant Arnold Horn, and Colonel Chack-Sab-At. Abel Cook, Risa-Sab-At, and Enrico Galay were aboard the other captured cruisers. They, along with *Clark*, *Saak-Fas*, and six auxiliaries trailed behind.

They'd bypassed Mahe and made an amazingly fast passage down to Grik City on the north coast of Madagascar. There they somehow packed another three hundred human Maroons and Lemurian Shee-Ree aboard the various ships, in addition to the near 2,200 troops of Chack's Brigade and the 1st North Borno. It had been impossible to take all the Maroons and Shee-Ree that wanted to go, but more might follow later as transport became available—and if there was any purpose. As it was, there was hardly space to turn around, let alone lie down, and it was utterly impossible for the troops to exercise or the cruiser's scratch crews to perform any battle drills. Fortunately, the Grik engineers knew their power plants well and were getting the most out of them.

They were also perfectly happy to continue their duties regardless of their masters—as long as they could hide below.

Physical and tactical exercises would come after TF Gri-kakka rendezvoused with USNRS *Arracca*. Three-quarters of the Raiders, including the Shee-Ree and Maroons, would board her for now, replacing the 3rd Marines and making a total "reserve" of nearly 2,500 troops, including *Arracca*'s own Marine contingent. The rest of the Raiders and Gutfeld's Marines, long separated from their comrades in *Santy Cat*, would go up the Zambezi with TF Gri-kakka. Those with artillery experience would serve as gunners for the crude but powerful batteries aboard the former enemy ships. In the meantime, all they could do was hope there'd still be somebody left to reinforce when they finally reached *Santa Catalina*.

They knew the old freighter had held the first Grik attempt to break out. Stopped it cold, in fact, and had been going through hell ever since. Due to the new obsession with comm security, however, that was about the extent of their knowledge. No doubt *someone* knew more, Tassanna-Ay-Arracca and Captain Reddy, at least. Probably Keje and generals Alden, Rolak, and Safir Maraan, and their code breakers, of course, but that might be it. If something drastically changed—like *Santy Cat*'s destruction or the Grik getting past her—their orders would change. In the meantime, the fact they were still steaming south, packed in the four stinking Jap-Grik ships and their consorts like mixed cans of human, semi-reptilian Khonashi, and Lemurian sardines, was probably a good thing.

"She's right," Lawrence chimed in grudgingly, uncharacteristically taking up for the little pest. "You can tell it scares the shit outa he." As usual, Lawrence avoided "lip words." Otherwise, he spoke almost perfect English, Lemurian, and passable Grik. And once, those who didn't know him would've sworn he *was* Grik, with the same vaguely avian-reptilian form, paring-knife teeth, and sickle claws, perfect for tearing flesh. But besides being generally smaller, his orange-and-brown, tiger-striped, feathery fur set him apart from the dingy brown and dark brown Grik; even the light and dark, rust-striped Khonashi. The Khonashi were a mixed tribe of Grik-like folk and humans, probably Malays, and were firm members of the Union. It was *very* weird having Grik-like troops fighting on their side.

"Does not," Silva denied. "He *likes* it. Why else would he keep runnin' back for more?"

"Because he's stupid," Gunnery Sergeant Horn groused. "Like me. And he doesn't like it. He likes the crackers."

"Stupid!" Petey declared, spewing crumbs.

Pam regarded Horn, hands on her shapely hips. "So what's your excuse? He give you crackers too?"

Horn frowned. "No," he said, turning to look at Silva. "Come to that, tell me again how Larry and I—both wounded heroes—'volunteered' for this suicide mission when we weren't even there."

"That's exactly it," Silva drawled. "You weren't there. I *asked* you to go to the meetin', but noo, your wimpy-assed little scratch was *hurtin'*, you said. Hell, you been a Marine long enough to know that not showin' up is the same as vounteerin' for whatever shit detail comes along!"

Gunny Horn pursed his lips in the middle of his black-bearded face. He'd actually begged off because he had a date with a pretty little Impie gal named Diania whom he was nuts about. Thank God she was safe with Sandra. True, that safety was transitory, since she'd never leave her friend, and Sandra had made it plain she was through being put off of USS *Walker*. And there was absolutely no doubt in his mind that *Walker* would eventually steam into harm's way again. . . . Absently, Horn touched the bandaged wound under his shirt. It *was* pretty small compared to the last one. He thought the dopey-looking pistol Dupont shot him with was just a .32. And as for Silva's other point . . . he reluctantly nodded agreement.

"You didn't ask *I* to go!" Lawrence accused.

"Your teensy little hole was even smaller than Horn's," Silva scoffed. "A pissant little seven-by-twenty Nambu— in the *ass*! Hell, *I* shot you with bigger bullets than that before. Lucky for you both that Japs 'n Frogs don't neither one b'lieve in manly calibers like the blessed forty-five!"

He arched his eyebrow and shook his head, as if mystified by that. "Besides, I couldn't ask; you were gone too. Prob'ly chasin' bugs to eat," he added airily, taking a huge chew of yellowish Aryaalan tobacco. "So I just naturally assumed you'd beg ta come along. What would you do with yerself if you weren't fightin' Griks with me? Prob'ly take up the ukulele, or quiltin' bees."

"No tasty 'ugs on Zanzi'ar," Lawrence moped.

"See? It's like I saved you. Again."

"You didn't 'save' him from anything, except maybe living," Pam Cross snapped, folding her arms over her breasts. "But you don't care. You don't care about anything but what you want, and you *wanted* your pals along. That's all. You didn't even care that they're hurt. Your *friends*. And you sure don't give a damn what *I* want."

"You misjudge Chief Sil-vaa this time, I think," Chack interrupted.

"How?" Pam demanded, then added "sir" a little uncertainly. In spite of being a Marine colonel, commanding what had essentially grown into a near division of very diverse troops, Chack still considered himself a mere boatswain's mate aboard *Walker*, his Home. But they weren't on *Walker*, and friends or not, Chack was the highest-ranking member of the task force until they came under Tassanna-Ay-Arracca's orders and TF Grikakka became an element of TF Bottle Cap.

"Sil-vaa knows the coming fight will be a desperate one, praac-tically a suicide mission, as Gunny Horn described it. It could also, very likely, mark the turning point in the waar against the Grik." Chack paused, blinking. "One way or another." His eyelids flickered speculatively at the troops crowding nearby, engaged in their own conversations. A small space had even been cleared for a game of marbles—a Lemurian passion. He'd lost interest in the game himself, but was curious how they managed it on a pitching deck. He shook his head.

"We've faced maany win-or-die situations before, but in faact, in most cases we could've still prevailed in the end, even if we lost." He blinked irony. "Thaat we did *not* always win, yet still find ourselves on the brink of victory—or defeat—is proof of thaat. Yet this time it's different. If we win in the Zaam-beezi River, or, more accurately, I suppose, maan-age to avoid losing, we won't win the waar, but I do think we'll fi-naally deny any real possibility of victory to the Grik." He blinked consternation. "At least thaat's my hope. We still know so little about them: their capabilities, the extent of their industry, even their borders. How much of Aaf-ri-caa must we conquer to subdue them?" He shook his head again.

"We're sure of so little, yet I'm certain of this: We're dangerously overextended, facing not only the Grik but the Dominion. Possibly the League as well. We caan't go on like this for long. If the Grik break out, we must try to stop them. They're the most immediate threat to the Western Allies and we haave no depth to our defense. Not anymore. There are settlements, industries, fortifications, but they're like skeletons; their muscle is all here. All we *haave* is here, or on the way. So, if the Grik get out, we'll haave to pull support from our allies in the east, on the other side of the world.

"They will then lose," he stated flatly. "Yet we couldn't win even then. It would all be too late, and likely end at Baalkpan, as it did before, or Maa-ni-la. Except even if we defeat them there again, we no longer have the strength to push them back. It comes down to simple math-aa-maatics. They will return, again and again, with more waarriors and better weapons each time, until we are no more. And do you think the Dominion will be saatisfied thaat we're no longer a threat to them? Thaat the League will sit idly by? No, they'll sense our doom and, like all pred-aators, strike while we're weak." He blinked with new intensity. "There caan be no victory, this time, if we lose *this* fight."

He gazed at Pam, then looked at Horn and Lawrence. "Of course Sil-vaa wanted you here because you're 'paals.' He fights better with you, and you with him." Chack managed a toothy grin. "How could you miss it?" The smile faded. "And how could you live with yourselves, any of you, if you weren't here for this, whether we lose—or maan-age not to? You've all made profound differences before. Whaat thoughts would torment you until the day you die, of whaat contributions you might've made to this operation, if the Grik are victorious at laast?" Chack looked down at his short finger claws. "I'd *much* rather die in baattle, on the Zaam-beezi River, than condemn myself to thoughts like that."

Horn grunted. "Put like that, I guess I see what you mean. Doesn't mean I'm *grateful* to the big bastard for dragging me along."

"O' course I not stay out o' this . . . fight," Lawrence said earnestly. "I just joke. Dennis jokes; I joke."

"Damn, Chackie," Silva mused. "I didn't even think of all that shit."

Pam threw her hands up. "See? What a self-centered jerk. Treats all his friends just like Petey, and doesn't give a damn what happens to 'em." She spun and stalked off, crashing through the milling troops.

"Probably should've just kept your trap shut that time," Horn murmured.

Silva stood blinking. "Well . . . damn. What'd I do? Sure, I wanted you fellas along. It'll be a hoot. You didn't really *wanna* stay out of it!" It was clear that possibility never occurred to him. He poked Horn with his finger. "Look what happened to you, last time you got benched."

"Sure, sure, and I wished I was with you a hundred times. But that gal is stupid for you, you big dope." He shooed Silva away. "Go catch her. Don't let her simmer. She'll just make the rest of us miserable—and God help us if we wind up needing her to patch us up!"

"Well, what do I say?"

"Tell her you joke," Lawrence said. "An asshole joke. She 'lieve that."

Silva seemed to think about that. Finally he handed Petey and a sack of crackers to Horn and snarled, "Here, you play with him for a while," then plowed through the troops in Pam's wake.

Chack was blinking surprise. "Sometimes I don't under-staand hu-maans at all. Is Paam really aangry?"

Horn shook his head. "No—well, yeah." He shrugged. "Kinda. Hell, I don't know." He chuckled. "If you think about it, they're the perfect pair. She loves being sore at Silva, but stays crazy for him—while he gives her plenty of reasons to bitch." He brightened. "They're like the perpetual emotion machine!"

Chack blinked perplexity, utterly lost.

Horn rolled his eyes. "And now, after all the chasing she's done to catch him, he's gone after *her*! She'll *love* that."

Chack swished his tail against the bulwark—*swat, swat, swat*—a sign of agitation, but finally understood all too well. He was mated far above his station, in his opinion, to General Queen Safir Maraan. He loved her with all his being and couldn't imagine what she saw in him. But there'd been a time when he was besotted with Keje's daughter, Selass-Fris-Ar. It was all just a great game to her, tormenting him and toying with his feelings, until it suddenly *wasn't* a game anymore. By then he'd become a destroyer-maan in the Amer-i-caan Navy Clan *and* a Maa-reen. More important, he'd met Safir Maraan. Selass was with 2nd Fleet now, fighting the Doms, and by all accounts had matured considerably—as had he. So perhaps he understood humans fine and it was only females that remained a mystery. "I don't see how that could be good for either of them," he said.

"Why not? They both live to fight, in their own way. Hell, your own sister Risa's like that too. That's the reason she and Silva—" Horn caught himself, remembering the rumors he'd heard. "Are such great pals," he finished.

Chack blinked appreciation at Horn's diplomatic diversion, but his ears flattened at the thought of Risa. *Horn is right about her, to a point. But unlike Silva, her battle joy was tempered in the action on Zaan-zi-bar. She blames herself for a costly mistake not her fault. She and Silva remain friends but she has drawn away. Perhaps she sees in him the careless self she'd always been, and is both repelled by it and mourns its loss at the same time.* Chack could sympathize. He'd hated violence in any form before the war came—and look what *he'd* become. Sometimes he yearned for that former innocent youngling-like self as well. On deeper reflection, he supposed for a moment that Silva was the only person he knew who hadn't been radically changed by the war, but realized even that was false. *Despite how he acts, Silva . . . cares more about things—and people—than when we met. That's a very good change, considering how dangerous he's become, often given such a free hand, and with an entire war to play in. We'll have to come up with something exciting for him to do if ever, with the Maker's help, we finally achieve victory and peace.*

"What's on your mind, Colonel?" Gunny Horn asked, feeding crackers to Petey. "You looked bothered all of a sudden."

Surprised that Horn, who hadn't been around Mi-Anakka as long as many, could already read him so well, Chack conjured a smile. "I'm no more bothered than usu-aal, Gunny Horn, but I appreciate your concern."

TF Gri-kakka continued south, making good time and avoiding the tempests that often stirred the strait. A few squalls tormented the troops on deck, causing frenzies of weapon cleaning and drying. In the cramped space available, this often led to altercations when someone was inadvertently poked by a cleaning rod. In truth, those instances were just excuses for frustrated troops to let off steam, but they resulted in several serious injuries. After their nearly ten-day voyage under such conditions, it came as a profound relief—despite the lurking danger—when they finally approached the coast of Africa and the sea turned cloudy with Zambezi River sediment. They'd reached the highway to the very heart of their ancient enemy, but instead of dread there was only excitement at the sight of mighty *Arracca* and her consorts silhouetted against the dark shore and setting sun.

A few weathered-looking Nancys were being recov-ered and one of the huge PB-5Ds floated alongside, minus two of its engines. 'Cats worked, apparently unconcerned, on top of its high, pitching wing. It seemed to Chack that they were patching holes in the fabric and repairing the engine mounts. As soon as the last Nancy was lifted to the hangar deck, *Itaa* was the first alongside, making fast to a broad, floating dock that led to the ship. Chack, Silva, Pam, Horn, and Lawrence led the anxious but orderly flood of troops, and when they climbed the cargo netting draped down the great Home-turned-carrier's side, arriving through a broad opening onto the hangar deck, they met Tassanna-Ay-Arracca herself, accompanied by her staff. Chack hardly recognized her. No longer a youngling, she'd reached her full height, and in contrast to the last time he saw her, she wore a high-necked white tunic with four gold stripes around the long sleeves, its tail slightly overlapping the top of a white kilt, also hemmed with four gold stripes—exactly as prescribed by Amer-i-caan Navy Clan regulations. Human trousers were not adorned and he wondered why, but shook it off. *Probably tradition,* he thought. He noted that Tassanna's uniform had been carefully tailored for comfort while accentuating her firm, youthful curves, and thought Ahd-mi-raal Keje-Fris-Ar would certainly approve of the effect. For the first time, he wished he'd worn what had come to be considered the Marine dress uniform of blue kilt and tunic, topped with white rhino-pig armor, instead of his tie-dyed caam-o-flaage combat smock. Tassanna's large bright eyes regarded them now, blinking a mixture of distinct pleasure with overtones of concern, and despite their jumbled relative seniority, impulsively lunged forward and embraced them all, even Horn, whom she'd never met.

"I am so glaad to see you," she breathed. "It's been too long! Tell me." She paused shyly. "How do the rest of our friends fare? Cap-i-taan Reddy, Lady Saan-dra, and the ahd-mi-raal?"

"Well," Chack assured her, "and doing all they can to join us here."

"Thaat is good," Tassanna said, suddenly gesturing at numerous other officers and NCOs assembling to divert the embarking troops to their assigned sections. "Let us move aside and"—she glanced up at Silva and grinned—"talk smaall until the rest of your officers arrive."

The next couple of hours were very busy as the ships of TF Gri-kakka took their turns at the floating dock, and Chack was impressed by how orderly it went. Then he remembered that despite her youth, Commodore Tassanna had been in the war from the start, her ship only their second carrier, and she'd commanded it admirably through many actions. By the time the bulk of Chack's brigade was aboard, *Itaa* had circled back around and the 2nd Battalion of Simy Gutfeld's 3rd Marines had gathered on the hangar deck, itching to take their places on the former Jap-Grik cruisers.

"Gonna be even more cramped on the ol' *Nosey*," Silva said. "She's liable to tump over." Enough Marines would join each ship to augment its gun's crews, but most would board the flagship of the task force.

"Like it won't be crowded here?" Risa snapped back, as the command group finally vacated the noisy hangar deck and made their way through bustling passageways. She and Abel Cook would remain on *Arracca* with the bulk of the troops, and she resented that immensely, still arguing that if any must stay, it should be Chack, their overall commander. Chack would've probably agreed— if he could've sent the Imperial Major Alistair Jindal or Major I'joorka, but both had been badly wounded on Zanzibar. As it was, Captain Cook, while a fine young officer, was very inexperienced, and Risa . . . He *hoped* she'd regained her balance, but her attitude remained volatile and argued against it.

"If all goes according to plaan, you will join us soon enough," he said as they mounted several wooden companionways into the base of the island on the starboard side of the flight deck. There they entered the vast waardroom, or ahd-mi-raal's quarters. Spacious as it was, it consisted of less than a quarter of what had once been *Arracca*'s Great Hall. Fine tapestries still decorated the walls, and the growth of the still-young Galla tree had been carefully diverted so it could grow up and through the space. The same effort had been accomplished aboard *Salissa* by the simpler expedient of establishing a cutting of the great tree nearly killed when *Big Sal* was almost destroyed at the Battle of Baalkpan Bay. Finding their places around a large oval table, they greeted more of Tassanna's staff as they arrived.

"You all know Co-maander Maark Leedom, I believe?" Tassanna asked, when a tall, rangy man with light brown hair joined them at the table.

"Sure," Silva said, surprised. "He was COFO at Grik City. How they hangin,' Markie Boy?"

Leedom rolled his eyes to the overhead and took a deep breath.

Tassanna coughed to kill a smile. "Yes, he was the co-maander of flight operations there, until our COFO was shot down by those most irritating Grik rockets," Tassanna informed them. "Co-maander Leedom has more experience with them thaan most and haas devised straa-ta-gems to avoid them. With the virtual abaandon-ment of Grik City for our push here, most of the planes stationed there will soon join us—where they are baadly needed, I assure you. Some will remain at Grik City under Leedom's former exec, Lieu-ten-aant Araa-Faan."

"What about Jumbo and his bombers?" Silva asked.

"Lieutenant Fisher and Pat-Squad Twenty-Two will stay in the Comoros for now," Leedom replied. "Colonel Mallory's there, or on his way, with our last two P-Forties in theater. He may shake things up, but we can't move the PB-Five-Ds any closer until we get things sorted out here. Ideally, if *Santy Cat* and you"—he added pointedly—"hold the Grik in the river, we'll build ramps at the river mouth where those two little Grik towns used to be, and move the whole squadron down."

"Thaat would be . . . swell," Chack said, thinking about how fast they could dump bombs on Sofesshk if the bombers were so close.

Tassanna's eyes narrowed. "Indeed. *If* we can hold the Grik."

"That doesn't sound so hot," Pam chimed in. "We haven't heard squat. Is *Santa Catalina* still holding?" She didn't ask, "Is anyone on her still alive?"

"Barely," Tassanna conceded. "Her people haave per-formed heroically and caused great destruction. Beyond our wildest dreams, she haas destroyed several Grik baattle-ships and nearly blocked the river with their sunken caar-casses."

"Nearly?" Chack probed.

"Grik cruisers, like yours, caan still navigate a paas-sage, and she's fought some of them as they come through one or two at a time. So far, thaat's sufficed. The problem is"—she nodded at Leedom—"the Grik are maassing a large number of cruisers and gaalleys, presumably to overwhelm her at laast. Saadly, considering the daam-age she's sustained and her dwindling aammunition, that seems likely. If they do, your cruisers and our depleted airpower might stop maany, but most of the gaalleys *must* get past. Surely enough to overwhelm the meager forces remaining at Grik City. Even all of Second Corps, if it haasn't already departed by then."

"Has it?" Risa asked.

Tassanna looked uncomfortable. "I caan't say, since I haaven't been told."

"Why not?" Chack demanded.

"For the same reason, much as I'd like to hearten him by your arrival, I caan't tell Russ Chaa-pelle in *Saanta Caat-a-lina* thaat you're here, soon to steam to his aid!" Tassanna snapped, blinking frustration. "Our communications with her have been unreliable at best. Her raadio is wrecked and her consorts baadly damaged. *Felts* still haas a raa-dio, but it's intermittent. Just as importaant, as I'm sure you understaand after the . . . traagedy north of Mahe, we haave more than one potential enemy nearby, and our communications may not be secure."

"But . . ." Pam seemed at a loss. "The League is outa here, we tossed 'em out of the whole Indian Ocean! With Kurokawa gone, who else would rat us out?"

"Kurokawa may be dead," Leedom agreed, "but some of his planes escaped—a few with radios, most likely. And we don't have a clue where they went, or if they're still in cahoots with the lizards." He looked at Tassanna. "Worse, we may not've kicked all the League ships out after all."

"What do you mean?" Abel Cook asked, speaking for the first time.

"Remember that Kraut sub we were warned to look out for?" There were nods. "Well, some of mine and Jumbo's pilots have reported sightings of something on the surface that dove before they could get close enough for a look." He shook his head. "Mountain fish don't do that; they don't care. They just wallow there and let you look 'em over. Gri-kakka, at least any we've ever seen, aren't as big as this thing's supposed to be. We have to assume that Kraut boat's still snooping around, so"—he shrugged—"comm stays tight."

Pam shivered as the conversation around the table exploded in speculation, mostly about how a League sub could possibly sustain itself out here. She had other thoughts. Grik cruisers didn't have anything like sonar to scare mountain fish away, and she'd been worried about them the whole trip down. They hadn't even seen one, to her relief, but without sonar, they couldn't have known if any ship-killing fish—or submarines—were stalking them. "Ignorance *is* bliss," she whispered to herself.

"What's that, doll?" Silva asked quietly.

"Nothin', jerk."

Silva stared at her a moment with his good eye, then returned his attention to the discussion. It wasn't going anywhere, with so little information, so he changed the subject. "You get any trouble from Grik zeps here?"

"No more bombing attempts, if that's what you mean," Leedom replied. "They try to spy on us from time to time, but we shoot them down. There haven't been any for several days. They still have a lot of the damn things, though, dispersed pretty wide after Jumbo took out a couple of their airfields, but they seem content to torment the blocking force with nightly raids. So, the good thing is, particularly if we keep comm discipline, your arrival should come as a very unpleasant surprise for the Grik."

"And thaat's your purpose here," Tassanna said, getting down to it at last.

"Yes," Chack agreed. "How soon can we go to the aid of our friends?"

Tassanna looked at him, blinking fond sadness. "The Second Baat-tallion of the Third Maa-reens haas been transferring to your ships all this time, even while *Itaa* has been fueling and provisioning. The other vessels of your taask force are doing the same from our tenders, or along the other side of this ship. We haave pilots who've taken smaall boats upriver, and they should already be aboard your ships, so . . ." She held out her hands. "You may depaart as soon as your needs haave been met. Within a few hours, I should think. And may the Maker of All Things waatch over you."

"Thank you, Commo-dore," Chack said with feeling, tail swishing behind his stool in anticipation.

CHAPTER
12

////// **Leopardo**
Lago de Vida
Nuevo Granada

*I*t had rained again for three solid days while Victor Gravois, Capitano Ciano, and the crews of *Leopardo* and the old oiler waited with growing impatience for Don Hernan to appear. The pilot had left almost as soon as they'd anchored, and there'd been no other official visits or even notice of their presence. It was as if they'd been forgotten entirely by the Dom leadership, and the only news they received came from rumors brought by an unending stream of small boats carrying strange fruits, vegetables, and some very bizarre livestock out to the ships. No one could complain about the fresh provisions, regardless of how weird, and in some ways the crews of *Leopardo* and her oiler were eating better than they had since they came to this world almost six years before. They ate so well, in fact, that there'd been little griping about being deprived of liberty ashore. That probably had more to do with the consequences of going there, however. But Gravois could—and did—complain about the way they'd been ignored via wireless to Contrammiraglio Oriani on *Ramb V*. Even if the Union frigate *Donaghey* had managed to make it to the region with a radio, it couldn't possibly triangulate their position, and the League codes were secure. Despite Oriani's admonishments to be patient, Gravois had decided they'd steam downriver the very next day, come what may, if something didn't happen. He was an admittedly arrogant man—well deserved in his opinion—and wasn't used to being kept waiting by primitive, ignorant barbarians, who hadn't *earned* the arrogance they displayed.

When the next morning dawned bright and clear except for a thin morning fog hovering low over the lake, however, the officers on the bridge were alerted by the lookouts to unusual activity ashore. Gravois set his morning tea aside and raised binoculars to look at the dock near the great stone wall. An extraordinarily ornate bireme had apparently arrived in the night and some sort of ceremony was underway, while people, brightly clad in reds and yellows, went aboard. After what looked like yet another ceremony on deck, the bireme got underway and began to approach, its scores of wet oars and red flags with twisted golden crosses flashing in the morning sun.

"It seems we've been noticed at last," Gravois commented dryly. "Please make all necessary preparations to receive dignitaries."

"Assemble a side party and rig out the accommodation ladder!" Ciano commanded. The bridge messenger raced aft to pass the word to the boatswain's mate of the watch. Pipes shrilled and running feet reverberated through the ship.

Gravois, Ciano, and most of *Leopardo*'s officers were waiting with the well-appointed side party on the ship's quarterdeck—the well deck behind the bridge—when a relatively large entourage came aboard. Most were armed guards, to Ciano's horror, wearing yellow coats with red facings and carrying brightly polished muskets. None saluted the flag, and all arranged themselves facing *Leopardo*'s side party, implying they were protecting their charge. The Italian sailors were just as surprised and affronted, grumbling and shifting with their own weapons in hand. Ciano started to protest the outrage, but Gravois touched his sleeve and shook his head. A small swarm of dignitaries, mostly priests, by their dress, but apparently a few civilians—possibly including the *alcalde* of the city?—stepped aboard and formed a tight knot. Finally, Don Hernan de Devina Dicha himself ascended the accommodation ladder, and his appearance was in stark contrast to what they'd expected.

His dress was bizarre: all dark bloodred from his neck to his shoes, with gold braid arranged like lightning flashes along the hems and seams of his cloak. A strangely shaped hat, like a broad clamshell, was a pure, glaring white, with gold trim similar to the rest of his dress. Around his neck was a heavy gold chain supporting a huge, gnarled cross sprouting what looked like hundreds of tiny spikes. A large mustache and goatee, once coal black but now iron gray with silver highlights, stood out on his upper lip and chin. Most striking of all, however, was the utter benevolence of the smile he wore on his smooth, kindly face. *"Comodos,"* he told his guards, almost admonishingly, and they instantly lowered their muskets and stood in a rigid but less threatening manner.

"Ah!" he said, the smile expanding as he advanced directly toward Gravois and Ciano. "You must be Capitaine Gravois!" He paused and afforded Ciano the slightest glance, "and Capitano Ciano! The pilot who accompanied you described you and acquainted me with your names. Welcome to the Holy City of Nuevo Granada! I am so pleased you are here, and apologize profusely that I was unable to greet you sooner! At least you have been well fed, I trust, and the provisions I caused to be sent have met with your approval?"

"Extremely well fed and much appreciated, Your Holiness," Gravois said with a bow. "May I return the favor and offer you refreshment?"

Don Hernan beamed but shook his head. "No, but I thank you. I am allowed only bloodred wine on the seventh day of our thirteen-day week. That, and the mild discomfort of hunger, are to remind me of the grace our savior received."

Ciano cleared his throat. "Yes, well. We have wine. I have been saving a fine Salice Salentino, if Your Holiness would care to sample it."

Don Hernan made a moue. "A foreign wine, crushed by heretic feet . . . Is it *very* red?"

"Quite red," Ciano assured.

"Then I accept. The color is the most important thing, after all." He looked at Gravois. "I have come in friendship to meet you all, but what I must first say is for your ears alone. I cannot allow you ashore, however. Do you have a place aboard your beautiful but apparently quite crowded ship where we might speak in private? I assure you the subject is of the utmost importance, and as much to your benefit as mine."

Gravois was startled, but quickly nodded. "Of course, Your Holiness." He looked at Ciano. "Ensure there is no one within two compartments of the wardroom, and place guards to keep it so." He gave Ciano a small regretful smile. "And don't forget the wine."

Ciano frowned but nodded. "Perhaps I might give these other gentlemen"—he gestured at the priests and civilians—"a brief tour of my ship?"

"I had so hoped you would," Don Hernan said graciously, then made a quiet comment to one of his escorts, who quickly strode to the side and called down to the bireme. Instantly, two young girls who might've been twins, both entirely naked, raced up the accommodation ladder and stood behind Don Hernan. Ciano's eyes bulged, and he knew his crew would have a similar reaction. *"Attenti!"* he barked.

"And what, may I ask, are they for?" Gravois practically sputtered, equally taken aback.

"We must be served our wine, Capitaine," Don Hernan soothed matter-of-factly.

"But . . . *they* will hear what we say. I thought you desired privacy?"

"My dear Capitaine Gravois," Don Hernan said, tremendous patience in his voice. "They may *hear*, but can reveal nothing. They cannot write, and their tongues were taken when they were infants, before they ever learned to make sounds approximating speech." He produced a solicitous tone. "And just because we have very important matters to discuss within"—he waved apologetically about at the austere warship—"such . . . martial surroundings does not mean we should deprive ourselves of beautiful things to view."

Leopardo's wardroom was rather dreary, Gravois had to confess, as he and Don Hernan sat across from each other at the long table there. The only adornments were a pair of mediocre nautical paintings and the flags of the League and the Kingdom of Italy, side by side, on the forward bulkhead. But the incongruity of the naked— and quite stunning—serving girls standing by the glasses and bottle on the pantry, utterly unself-conscious, made him ill at ease. He was used to controlling situations like this and believed it was his greatest skill, but Don Hernan had immediately created a situation that made him profoundly uncomfortable and put him on the defensive.

Don Hernan leaned back in his chair and tossed the bizarre hat on the table with a relieved sigh. "There," he said grandly, "such a disagreeable, uncomfortable object! I believe that here we may dispense with all pretense, may we not? I will first tell you much about our common enemy—more than you know already, I suspect, despite your admirable intelligence-gathering network. I have even more spies among them, spread across their entire alliance, able to deliver firsthand reports. Some do take time to reach me," he conceded, "but others of closer origin are as fresh as days, or hours."

"How is that possible?" Gravois asked, as much surprised by the information as the abrupt revelation.

Don Hernan smiled. "Suffice to say that we had suborned the Empire of the New Britain Isles long ago, and filled it with our people. With the aid of the New Britain Company, we would have controlled the Empire by now if not for the untimely arrival of those troublesome Americans, and Captain Reddy, of course. I believe you know him personally? As do I. A resourceful opponent, never to be underestimated. I have done so, to my woe, and never will again." His dark eyes very briefly turned to obsidian but quickly softened. "I understand he has been more *your* problem of late. Perhaps your schemes will even succeed in eliminating him." Don Hernan noted the growing incredulity on Gravois's face and put his hands, glittering with golden rings, on the table. "In any event, true believers remain spread throughout the Alliance, passing letters among them. Can you believe it?" he laughed. "They allow frivolous, *uncensored correspondence* between their people! That is how proceedings as far away as their war against the Grik come to me.

"As for more nearby events . . . We do not have your radio or wireless, nor have our efforts to build flying machines of our own much prospered—until recently." He smiled. "But have you seen our dragons? Imbecilic creatures, to be sure, probably like flying Grik, but they can be trained to fly to specific places and do a number of useful things—such as to retrieve packets deposited near an enemy camp and bring them directly to me. All this is how I knew what the Allies were up to, and what you were doing to thwart them. I am most appreciative of your efforts, by the way. Keeping the war so dreadfully confusing on the other side of the world has prevented our common enemy from sufficiently reinforcing his efforts here.

"Now," Don Hernan said, "I will tell you what you must know about our situation, then reveal what I know about how that affects you—and the alliance we are here to finalize."

Gravois nodded, eyebrows still raised. "Please do."

Don Hernan snapped his fingers, and one of the girls poured two glasses of wine. The other brought them both to the table. Don Hernan hazarded a taste, grimaced, then tried another. "It seems very dry," he complained mildly, then sighed. "One thing I have learned: despite my many talents, I am no general. I was disabused of that pretense most decisively and barely escaped with my life. I learned from that mistake, however, and placed one in command of my western armies, who can remedy my tactical deficiencies. Even now he draws the Allied army and its Second Fleet to their destruction at El Paso del Fuego. He has far greater resources than the enemy can possibly expect, and I am confident he will prevail." He smiled sweetly. "*You* should be grateful, since I am quite sure El Paso represents your Triumvirate's primary interest in this region."

Gravois could only bow his head. "It is pointless to deny that El Paso del Fuego is an important strategic asset," he temporized. "Denying it to the Alliance benefits us both." He leaned back as well. "I'm curious, though. I gather that your religion takes a very dim view of failure. How is it that you *survived* to take advantage of your lesson regarding the difficulties of command?" He'd meant to crack Don Hernan's composure and reassert a measure of equality, at least, as the discussion proceeded, but Don Hernan merely waved his hand.

"What I want in tactics on the battlefield might possibly be countered by my strategic awareness," he said modestly. "As far as His Supreme Holiness knows, my campaign was a great success and led to the forthcoming annihilation of the heretic horde approaching the pass—as I planned all along. None can dispute this, because not only do I bask in His Supreme Holiness's utmost favor, but only Blood Cardinals are allowed to speak with him." He shook his head sadly. "The war has cost us *so many* of those, in the strangest places. Many have evidently sought grace at their own hand at the very thought of heretic feet treading on these holy shores! Those who remain are loyal to me."

Gravois could only admire Don Hernan's audacious cold-bloodedness, and respect the way he'd turned disaster to his favor. "Most interesting. What are your plans?"

"To defeat the heretics, of course. I *can* do it alone, but your assistance would prove . . . mutually beneficial."

"You will have all the intelligence support we can provide," Gravois promised.

"And I already explained that there is little in terms of intelligence you possess with which we arc not already blessed," Don Hernan patiently declared, and Gravois blanched at the obvious double entendre. "What I desire is *material* support from this ship and your vaunted fleet of even more powerful vessels. The Allies threatening El Paso from the west are not my only concern. There are also Los Diablos del Norte—the NUS. I need their fleet controlled so I may focus on the threat from the west."

Gravois frowned. "That will be more problematic. I can promise little direct assistance. My orders from the Triumvirate are quite clear on that point."

"Your Triumvirate is as weak as your religion!" Don Hernan flared, but then visibly calmed himself. "It, like most among you, is influenced by the Catholic Church of your world, if I'm not mistaken?"

"Yes," Gravois replied stonily. He didn't believe in God, or anything resembling a "soul," but knew the vast majority of his people did. The Confédértion États Souverains, from which the League of Tripoli descended, was made up almost entirely of very Catholic countries. The Germans were a partial exception to that, retaining numerous Catholics, but also some strangely revived pagan notions. In addition, the Protestants among them were no longer persecuted, as they'd been before. But the Germans were comparatively few within the League.

"The Church here," Don Hernan continued, "the *true* Church of this world, shares much in common with yours, but there are differences that make it stronger, more decisive, less based on blind faith and more on what the faithful *see*. It is harsher in some ways," Don Hernan conceded. "But this is a harsher world by far than that from which you came. And there could not be a better tool to aid your Triumvirate in establishing its ultimate goals." He shook his head. "But if it means to limit our alliance to the weak joke it enjoyed with its client in the ocean beyond the Grik, then I'm afraid a final accommodation between us is impossible."

Gravois was stunned that Don Hernan knew about Kurokawa but realized he shouldn't have been. No doubt they'd taken at least some Allied prisoners. And then, of course, there was the spy network he'd alluded to. "It may be . . . difficult to persuade them to get directly involved. We have mighty forces"—he waved around—"this near the least of them. But there are other demands on our attention, and our resources are not unlimited."

"Ah! Resources! Another reason for your interest here," Don Hernan proclaimed.

Gravois shrugged. "Of course," he said. That was also obvious.

"But how do you mean to get them at no cost to yourselves? If you do not have the resources to join us fully and get ours as gifts from grateful friends, you can't *take* them unless you join our enemies. I doubt you could even consider that. And if you did, and they accepted you, they would expect you to commit resources to them as well!"

Don Hernan was wrong about that. Gravois had considered it but knew it was far too late. Even if it wasn't, allocation of resources, of colonies, would only deepen the division between them. And the League's strategic goal, control of the Pass of Fire, would remain unmet and it would ultimately have to face the entire Alliance alone.

Don Hernan's expression turned as sly as his face was capable of and he continued. "Only the utter defeat of our common enemy and a full partnership with the Dominion can yield what you need." He steepled his hands before him. "And perhaps you and your Triumvirate only need that little push. You have a missing ship in the Caribbean, do you not?"

Gravois was startled into nodding.

"What if I told you that the tiny wooden sailing frigate it pursued across the Atlantic ambushed and destroyed it?"

"Impossible!"

"Yet it is true," Don Hernan confirmed. "We have spies everywhere, including the Windward Islands." He smiled benevolently once more. "You might make a visit to a little bay on the island you call Martinique—but have a care for the sad wreck lying just below the surface when you do. I'm told it can best be seen at low tide."

"Incredible," Gravois murmured darkly. "So, not only did *Donaghey* make it here to consort and plan with the NUS, she destroyed *Atúnez* as well."

Don Hernan snapped his fingers for more wine. "I will give you a moment to mourn your comrades," he said.

"What did you mean earlier?" Gravois asked imme-

diately. "You said 'full partnership' instead of 'alliance.'
I doubt that was a slip. You don't seem to make many of
those," he added ruefully.

Don Hernan regarded him innocently. "What would
it mean to you? *Personally?* Power, for one thing, beyond
your wildest dreams." He glanced at the naked serving
girls. "And privileges to match." He took a sip of wine.
"To *me* it would mean an eventual amalgamation of the
League and Dominion, with the same culture, goals"—
he stared intently at Gravois—"and stronger leadership,
of course. Your Triumvirate is too timid for this world."
He blinked and leaned forward in his chair. "And, finally,
after some small modifications that would render the
True Church much reformed in the eyes of my people
and more recognizable to yours, they would share the
most unifying force of all: the same faith." He took a sip
of wine. "With one pope," he added. "Your people need
a pope," he said solicitously, "for their very souls. Just
think what a perfect union it might be! My people are
already almost fascist, as I understand the term, possibly
more than yours. And your people, already accustomed
to their leaders setting the example for how they must
think, act, even believe, will quickly accept a familiar,
stronger Church. United, such a nation, with vast resources, a huge population, incomparable military might,
and the government and church walking hand in hand,
each supporting the other . . . No power on Earth could
possibly stand against it!"

It was all so very tempting, even possible, and close
to a scenario Gravois had already considered, even
tentatively mentioned to Ciano on their trip upriver.
He loved the idea of the League and its mission to
establish a fascist world, but hated the Triumvirate and
its weak shortsightedness, the baby steps it took. Don
Hernan was absolutely right about the advantages of
his proposal. But the . . . creature sitting across from
Gravois, so confident, so serene, made him almost believe in religion after all—and feel like he was being
offered a deal by the devil himself. He broke out of the
spell Don Hernan had begun spinning with the word
"power" and barked a laugh, placing his hand on his

breast. "I presume you mean *yourself*, ruling as a partner with the, ah, secular leader of both countries?"

"*One* country by then, with myself a partner in matters of faith and culture only," Don Hernan specified piously.

"I doubt your pope would so easily relinquish his position."

"On the contrary," Don Hernan gravely denied. "His Supreme Holiness yearns to take his place in the next world, and actually feels he has lingered overlong in this one. Most tragic for one so young and wise." There seemed to be genuine admiration in his voice. "As their role is currently defined, our popes cannot live for long, constantly drawn away by their closeness to God. That is why, even at my age, I am his chosen successor. With the reforms I intend, however, I believe I can resist the call of Heaven for quite some time." He smiled again, in that amazingly disarming way he had. "More wine?" A notion seemed to strike him. "Or perhaps you would prefer one of the girls? You may have them both, if you like, but you must keep them if you do. I would have to destroy them," he continued sadly. "Only virgins may enjoy my presence." He looked directly at Gravois, who suddenly shuddered, even as he couldn't help glancing at the girls. "One of the many little changes I would like to make, if possible," Don Hernan assured.

Abruptly, he stood, emptied his glass, and retrieved his hat from the table. "There is a great deal more to discuss, but we two in particular have perhaps even more to consider before proceeding to the details."

Gravois stood as well, glancing at his own untouched glass. "Yes," he said absently. "The details." He shook his head. "For the moment, may I tempt you with a brief tour of the ship?"

"Very easily," Don Hernan enthusiastically agreed. "Please, let us first view the weapons!"

CHAPTER
13

"**G**ot another one!" Mikey Monk whooped from the starboard bridgewing as a Grik zeppelin erupted in flames and began its long, fiery fall to the ground. It sparkled against the night sky, tatters of burning fabric following, drifting downwind. Russ watched but lost sight of the sluggish meteor as it passed from view to starboard—and the muzzle flash of the 4.7″ gun below seared his night vision. No matter; he was too busy to gawk and couldn't afford distractions. He'd taken the wheel himself, something he occasionally did by accident, out of habit, but with his battered, leaky ship fighting for her life in such a confined space, he preferred to react instantly to the calls of the lookouts instead of waiting precious seconds to relay the order.

The new dual-purpose guns had never been integrated into any kind of antiair fire-control system, and that had cost the Allies dearly at the Battle of Mahe, but they'd never expected to need them against anything faster or more maneuverable than Grik zeps. Against them, however, for the very first time—even in local control—they were pure murder. The only trick was spotting them and setting the fuses right. Seeing them and

estimating altitude, speed, and direction had been aided
by a fine moon the last few nights, as well as a quick flash
in a suspected direction by one of the ship's searchlights
right before she made a turn. More than once, the river
where she would've been was churned by a pattern of
bombs, and they had a whole new respect for Grik bombardiers. A couple of bombs even hit the ship. They were
heavy, cast iron, with big black powder bursting charges
that caused serious surface damage. One hit the fo'c'sle,
irreparably wrenching the 10″ mount and blowing half
the deck timbers away, killing six Marines. Another
ricocheted off the lip of the funnel and exploded in the
water alongside, starting more leaks in the fireroom for
Laney to try to stop. Both sent chills down Russ's spine.
The first almost reached the forward magazine, and a
few inches to the left and the other would've blown *Santy
Cat's* boilers and killed her just as dead.

Other than that, though, it had been a Grik zep shoot,
and they'd knocked down at least a dozen in the nights
since the raids began. *Arracca's* planes had accounted
for twice as many, a disappointing percentage, actually,
but the Grik had gotten wise: the zeps converged from
every direction, preventing *Arracca's* P-1C Fleashooters
from catching them in big groups. The only time they
bunched up was over their target, and then, of course,
the fighters had to stay out of *Santy Cat's* protective fire.
But the zeps were fair game as they flew away, and increasingly, the fighters went after those that congregated
to bomb the wreckage in the channel. It was essential
that the channel stay blocked, and Russ was worried
about the progress the enemy might be making there.
Then there was the other new thing. . . . A bright jet of
fire arced over the point of land concealing the other
side of the bend from view and exploded well to starboard, spraying the water with hot shards of iron.

"Damn rockets!" Mikey growled, and several 'Cats
in the pilothouse nodded unconsciously, tails twitching
nervously.

"Yeah," Russ agreed. The warhead on the Grik antiair rockets was roughly equivalent to a twelve-pounder

case shot. When the bursting charge detonated, it launched a lethal pattern of iron balls and jagged shards in the same fashion. A couple of days before, they'd begun firing them at a low angle in the direction of *Santa Catalina* for the first time. They didn't do much damage even when they hit her, but they were hard on the gun's crews and anyone else not under cover. And they *could* hurt *Naga* and *Felts*, both of which were only barely controlling their own flooding. Without power for their pumps, they'd be gone already. It finally got bad enough during the day that *Santy Cat* was forced to move back, where the river widened, ceding the area closest to the blockage to probable Grik efforts to clear it.

"No big deal when they just shot 'em at our planes," Russ continued. "I mean, they knocked one down now and then, and that was too bad, but considering how many they put in the air, our guys didn't have much to worry about. But this . . . Even if they can't really hurt the ship much, they're chewing our people up. And you know they've got spotters on that ridge, adjusting their fire. It's like long-range field artillery, better than anything they've ever had." He snorted. "Better than *we* have, for that matter. And I guarantee they've figured that out and will try to use them on our ground troops."

"Still problems with that," Monk countered. "They're big, and not very mobile. Should be easy targets from the air."

Russ scratched his whiskery chin but didn't reply. He'd sent his evaluation of the threat and requested a daylight raid on the rocket batteries around the bend. They had to be fairly visible. Tassanna had been noncommittal. Apparently there were battlewagons, with their frighteningly effective antiair defenses guarding the positions, and she was getting dangerously low on Nancys. Only a few of the venerable floatplanes had been shot down, but after previous losses, *Arracca* hadn't begun this operation with anything like her full complement. And those available had been through so much that her people were starting to cannibalize them for parts. Tassanna implied she might try fighters armed with a couple of bombs, but the Fleashooters were wearing out too.

It would all come down to 1st Fleet in the end. *Big Sal* was short of planes as well, but the scuttlebutt had fast transports (razeed steam-powered Grik Indiamen prizes, for the most part) piling up crated planes for her at Mahe, awaiting her arrival. And *Madras* had a brand-new, full-strength air wing. On top of that, they *were* coming as fast as they could, Russ knew. But would they arrive in time?

"Shiit!" spat the Lemurian at the EOT, ducking as another rocket exploded right over the battered fo'c'sle. Most of the deadly fragments continued on, missing the ship, but not all. A sound like hail on a tin roof clattered back through the broken windows, just as another cluster of bombs marched across the river—and over USS *Naga*—off the port bow. A blinding orange flash lit the fo'c'sle of the already dismasted ship, and columns of dull, phosphorescent spume collapsed down on her.

"Shit!" Monk repeated, as the dual-purpose batteries hammered the sky again. A staggered pattern of bright pops lit the night. One was very lucky, or its crew was *very* good. A blue spurt of flame roiled the sky, quickly reddening and spreading across the aft section of a Grik zeppelin. It was impossible to say if it was the same one that mauled *Naga*, but it really didn't matter. Flames roared, consuming the airship faster and faster as it began to fall.

"*Naga*'s sig-naallin' wit her Morse lamp!" cried the lookout on the port bridgewing. "She's . . ." The 'Cat hesitated, watching, mentally jotting down the message. "She's sinkin'," he finally said. "That last one done her in, startin' butts in the bow. Her skipper figgers she's got maybe fifteen minutes before risin' waater drowns her fires." He hesitated again. "She's gonna try to get her in thaat gaap at the sout' side o' the river an' sink her there—if she caan do it before her bow sinks too deep. But *Naga* gots no boats! They's all tore up, like ours!" Between the heavy fighting a few days before and the bombardment of missile fragments, there wasn't a sound small boat left in the squadron.

"Maybe they can swim for it," Monk suggested lamely. "There's not as many hungry fish in the river."

Russ looked at him like he was nuts. "Not as *many*, but plenty, including freshwater sharks and more ordinary crocodiles than anyplace has a right to. Besides, how many 'Cats have you ever met who can swim?"

"Time!" came a shout, relayed from lead-slinging 'Cats on the fo'c'sle. They'd been shaken but not injured by the last rocket.

Russ turned to the talker even as he began to spin the wheel, making *Santy Cat*'s customary turn as the dark shore loomed. "*Felts* has her radio back up, right?"

"Ay, sur."

"Have her send a report to the commodore, then escort *Naga* to the gap she wants to plug." Russ knew which one her skipper meant, and it was a good idea. "She'll then stand by and take her people off—but be damn careful! *Felts* will *not* risk grounding herself. If *Naga* loses power before she's in position, *Felts*'ll take her people off immediately and burn her. Drop her anchor first, though," he added. "We don't need her drifting downstream, lighting us up." He paused. "Even if she makes it in, but it looks chancy getting to her crew, *Felts* will break off and we'll think of something else." Russ had no idea what that might be. *Santy Cat* sure couldn't help. She drew twice as much water as her consorts.

"Ay, ay, Cap-i-taan."

In the event, to everyone's relief, not only did the grounding go off as well as hoped, but the bombing soon ended. More zeppelins fell as they retreated, chased by *Arracca*'s fighters, and without *Santy Cat*'s gunflashes to help their aim, even the rockets dwindled to a stop. This seemed to confirm two things: the Grik definitely had observers, but they didn't have unlimited rockets. Finally, the only light came from the waning moon, nearing the horizon, and the fires the bombing had rekindled amid the wreckage clotting the river bend.

At some point during all this, Kathy McCoy had appeared on the bridge. When Russ noted her presence at last, he was shocked by how she looked. Her normally somewhat severe countenance was haggard and sharp with fatigue, and her dungarees looked like she'd been wallowing in blood. "Will you have *Naga*'s people brought over here?" she asked huskily.

"Uh, only the wounded," Russ replied with a guilty twinge, realizing he was about to add to her burden. "How are we doing in that regard?"

"That's what I came to report," Kathy admitted. "We've got twenty-nine dead, so far, and over a hundred wounded."

Russ blinked in alarm, but Kathy held up a tired hand. In the dim light of the pilothouse, Russ realized her hands were the only parts of her not dark with spattered blood and grime. Of course she kept *them* clean. "I'm counting what you might call minor wounds," she told him. "Stuff that would get guys sent to the rear in the old days. But our people here"—she nodded at the 'Cats around them—"can still fight through. Only about sixty are so bad they can't do *something*, and half of those'll probably die no matter what I do." She exhaled in exasperation. "I wish we could get the badly wounded fit to move, sent out to *Arracca*. . . ."

"I already thought of that," Russ told her, "and *Arracca*'s supposed to be sending boats to get them, maybe before dawn. If nothing pops—and by that I mean if the enemy sticks to the current playbook—we might even steam downriver a ways to meet them, if we can get back on station before daylight."

"That would help. Any word when we can expect . . . ?" She tapered off, but Russ knew what she was going to ask.

"Not really," he hedged. He'd received *some* word, encrypted and very convoluted, making it unclear *what kind* of boats were coming. They'd been stung so badly by their open communications, they may have gone too far in the opposite extreme. And even if he thought he'd interpreted the latest correctly, from Captain Reddy, filtered by Pete Alden and then Safir Maraan, he wasn't sure whether to be encouraged or not. *Some* help, "a spicy appetizer," was apparently on the way, but the "whole enchilada," which he expected meant all of 1st Fleet and the entire expeditionary force, was still "waiting to go in the oven." That clearly meant it was still prepping on Mahe Island.

"Cap-i-taan," said the signal-'Cat on the bridgewing, "*Felts* is headed back. *Naga* went down where it would do the most good, they say, an' they got most'a her people off." He hesitated. "Her skipper an' a couple others wound up in the water, stayin' for laast an' spikin' guns, in case the liz-aards fish 'em out. They . . . didn't make it."

"Damn!" Russ swore. He hadn't known *Naga*'s new skipper well, but she'd clearly been a fine, brave officer. He didn't voice the hope everyone shared: that she and her courageous companions had simply drowned.

The signal-'Cat's large Lemurian eyes strayed to Kathy. "There's about twenny wounded. Some baad."

"Have *Felts* come alongside to starboard," Russ told the signal-'Cat. After *Santa Catalina*'s turn, that was the most protected side, if more rockets came. "All stop, drop the anchor. Stand by to take wounded aboard. Details to prepare hoists and rig cargo nets," Russ added to the talker and a messenger.

Kathy sighed. "I better go," she said, turning, but then paused. "For what it's worth, Captain Chappelle, I think you've done okay with such a crummy hand. What's more, even the worst-hurt people I talk to think the same." She shrugged and started to leave, almost bumping into a larger form entering at the same time. "Move it, fatso," she snapped. "I got work to do."

Dean Laney stepped into the pilothouse, even filthier than Kathy. His darker dungarees didn't show grease as badly as blood, but his khaki shirt wasn't khaki anymore, and his hat was a crushed and shapeless gray mass with a bent and crooked brim. Red-rimmed eyes set in a grunge-streaked face followed the woman out. When he turned to Chappelle, his usual bitter expression had been replaced with honest exhaustion . . . and maybe a trace of hurt?

"Laney," Russ acknowledged neutrally. He hadn't seen the engineer in days, but even Monk told him he seemed like a changed man. Russ wondered which Laney this was.

"Skipper," Laney replied. Even his rough voice sounded spent.

"How's *our* baby?" Russ asked, stressing that they were all counting on *Santy Cat*'s engine.

"Toilin' away in a hot, stinkin' swamp—like the rest of us down there. Pumps're keepin' up, but can't get ahead. We plugged most of the popped rivets with bolts, where we could, or pounded Letts's gasket material in the sloshers. Wooden pegs, timbers to shore up warped plates . . ." He shrugged. "The usual. I'd'a used gum if I had any. I'm gonna rig more hoses to pumps in other parts of the ship—which we might have to run through watertight doors," he warned. "We're gettin' shorthanded, though. Guys get hurt just doin' that stuff, whether we're gettin' holes shot in us or not. Gimme some o' those Marines that're just standin' around."

Russ nodded. There were still almost six hundred Marines packed in the ship, taking a disproportionate percentage of the casualties. And except for the ones augmenting the gun's crews, they hadn't had much chance to fight back. He toyed with the notion of steaming in close enough to the blockage to let them loft mortar bombs over the rocky point. Maybe he could get planes to spot for them and they could make life hell for the Grik rocketeers for a change. But they had a finite number of mortar bombs and might need them desperately before this was done. In the meantime, the Marines he sent to Engineering would be safer from rocket fragments than in the more lightly protected parts of the ship. The question was, could they put up with Laney's shit—or would they murder him if he reverted to form? "Use as many as you need," Russ told him. "But remember, they're Marines, and we're liable to be counting on them to save our asses if things get close."

Laney waved it away. "I know that. I just need hands. It doesn't matter if they know what to do. And I'll . . . bear their limitations in mind."

Russ blinked and shook his head slightly. *A changed Laney indeed.* "Is that all?"

Laney hesitated, took a long breath, and let it out slow. "I've quit bitchin'. I promised. Doesn't mean I really understand what we're doin' here. I mean, I get what you told me—told everybody—an' it even makes sense. But, hell, we've slapped the Grik all the way back to their own yard and we're a long damn way from Baalkpan. From home. Why not back off and get stronger before the final showdown?"

Russ seemed to contemplate that. 'Cats on the bridge were pretending not to listen, but he knew they were. He thought he had a fairly good idea what their opinions were, but some might share Laney's. According to reports, a *lot* of people back home were starting to. Instead of answering the question directly, Russ walked over and sat on his chair. "What are *you* doing here?" he asked.

Laney was taken aback. "Well . . . *Santy Cat*'s here, an' I'm in her," he stated, as if that should be obvious to anyone. He realized that wasn't what Russ meant, however, and continued hesitantly. "I'm here for my baby"—he glanced in the direction Kathy went—"and maybe a few other things." He frowned, frustrated. "But it's all gonna die. *I'm* gonna die, an' I gotta wonder why. *Tell* me why. You know I'm no coward and I ain't afraid to fight, but I want a reason. 'Specially if it's gonna kill me and everything I care about." He was practically pleading now. "Give me a good reason."

"Damn, Laney. You need to lighten up," Russ quipped, earning a few accidental snorts from the Lemurian bridge watch. He sighed. "Sorry. I didn't mean that." He spread his hands. "Yeah, we could back off, lick our wounds, and build up. We might even hold the Grik back a couple years while we did it—but we'd never win in the end. We'd have to fight our way all the way back to this exact spot we've *earned* with so much blood. Not only would that cost more lives—for the same water and ground we already paid for—but the Grik would have that same time to outbreed the absolute hell out of us. They've probably got a million warriors, all told. Probably more." He pointed west. "I bet half are around the other side of that bend right now, but the rest are scattered around the Empire, or down south, facing the Republic. We'll *never* get a chance like this again. Given a couple years, we could build more ships and guns and raise a few more divisions. Hell, we might triple what we have. But we flat can't make soldiers or sailors as fast as they can, and they'll have *five* or *six* million better armed and trained troops by then. It's that simple.

"So, at this point in time, probably for the only possible time ever, we've got 'em hammered back and split up. We know they've kicked their Griklet factory in high gear, and we're facing the first full-blown crop of real soldiers they've ever made. Halik had a few—the prototypes in India—but these are the real deal, and they're just gonna keep making more. That means we gotta finish 'em before they can. And we will, if this old tub with your baby in it keeps the river blocked long enough for Captain Reddy to get here with everything we've got."

"I don't . . ." Laney closed his tired eyes. "How can you be so damn sure?"

Russ smiled. "Because we're talking about Captain Reddy—and Pete Alden, Safir Maraan, Keje, Rolak— our *friends*. Sure, they've all made mistakes before, but they've always come through in the end. Do you really doubt they'll come here as fast as they can?"

USS *Felts* was alongside now, and wounded 'Cats were rising, secured in rectangular wicker baskets. These were lowered to the deck as carefully as possible in the dark before Kathy quickly inspected them, determining the extent of their injuries, and sent them to her operating room beneath the armored casemate for the 5.5″ guns. Assistants and sick-berth attendants (SBAs) came and went.

Laney had to shake his head. "No. I *guess* not. I just hope 'as fast as they can' is fast enough—for us."

Russ took his own long breath. "Me too," he agreed. "And maybe it won't be," he admitted. "But if it comes to that, it won't be because you and me, or this old ship, didn't do our part, will it? I asked what you're doing here and you gave a straight answer. Pretty much what I expected. But *I'm* here for our friends—humans and 'Cats— to give them a chance for a life and world they can raise their kids in without the near certainty the goddamn lizards'll wind up on top, and all those kids'll just end up in a Grik cookpot someday." He shook his head. "That's *my* cause, as simple as that." He considered. "And the new Union, the United Homes, represents all our friends. It's the country I'm fighting for."

He scratched his whiskers again. "You know, it's weird. I'm not even sure what kind of country Mister Letts cooked up. I mean, I hear it's based on the same US Constitution we all swore to defend, but I haven't been home since they shook it out, so I don't really *know*. At the same time, though, Baalkpan—the Union—feels more like home than home ever did. Does that make sense? I think that's because, when you boil it down, most of us're fighting for the same things people in our situation have always fought for: each other. And if you think about it, there aren't many real civilians in this war, goofin' off and sitting it out. Most've all been on the front lines themselves, at one time or another, out here, or at Aryaal or Baalkpan—who knows where? And since we've fought with 'em, side by side with Captain Reddy and the rest, even 'Cats in the shipyards—or doing anything else you can think of back *home* in Baalkpan—still count as 'each other,' far as I'm concerned. Way more than a lot of folks I never knew and never fought beside back in the States during our 'old' war." He shook his head, frustrated, unsure he'd gotten through, but Laney seemed to be thinking about it.

"I can see that, sorta," he said. "I ain't ever really thought about it like that." His expression hardened. "Just so long as I ain't riskin' my ass for some half-baked opium dream that this beat-up tub is stickin' it out so we can 'end all wars,' or make this whole screwy world 'safe for democracy.'" He paused and squinted, rubbing his brow. "'Cause, past maybe the reasons you gave, none of that'll mean shit to anybody when we're all shot up an' sinkin' to the bottom of the river."

Russ actually laughed, but his response was interrupted. "Sur, *Felts* has transferred all her wounded an' is ready to shove off."

"Very well." Russ stood and walked back to the wheel, waiting a moment while the DD's battered shape eased away and was engulfed in gloom. The moon was almost gone, and it would get very dark when the horizon swallowed it completely. "Hoist the anchor, ahead slow. Leadsmen, report." He looked back at Laney. "I have to agree with you. And we won't be through with war even if we win. There's still the Doms and maybe the League and God knows who else. There'll *always* be war. Those idiots in the League of Nations who cooked up the notion that war is unnatural, or there's some way you can put a stop to it forever, were nuts. I'll settle for licking our current enemies and staying strong enough to fend off any more we run into, at least long enough to figure out whether we have to fight them too."

Senior First of One Hundred Jash stepped around the complicated arrangement of ropes and blocks securing the great gun on *Slasher*'s bow and stared eastward, where the tumultuous night beyond the bend was growing quiet at last. The roaring, sparkling rockets had finally stopped, their muffled, flashing *thump*s now silent. And the strange, bright battle in the sky had drifted away in various directions. All that had left him vaguely uneasy about what combat with the prey, the enemy, would be like, since—except for the rapid hammer of high-angle cannon his race had yet to master—the fighting in the air had been almost noiseless from where he was. Judging by the number of airships that fell burning to the ground, it had been extremely one-sided as well. He had no way to tell if the rockets or airship bombs had any effect other than making a satisfying racket.

He'd experienced a great deal of training—good training, he thought—but had never actually participated in battle. Nor had Seech, the rest of *Slasher*'s warriors, or any of the rest floating nearby. Having seen ordinary Uul warriors at battle play, he knew his were better, more capable, and much better armed. But the enemy was obviously better as well, or they wouldn't be *here*, and his kind wouldn't exist. More telling, all the new training was based on relatively old information, gathered and taught by the few veterans of the early India campaigns that had been sent home. The trainers, wizened warriors, elevated to Hij themselves, were confident Jash's generation could match what they'd seen of the enemy.

But surely if we have progressed, so have they, Jash reflected, again contemplating the strange feelings that stirred within him. If there was a word for those feelings in the Ghaarrichk'k tongue, which seemed to combine something akin to anticipation for a meal long deferred with what he'd imagined those in the collided galleys, tossed in the deadly water, must have felt, he'd never learned it. It bothered him.

A little more than a hundred galleys, modified in a similar fashion to his, were clustered along the south bank of the river. There were others, apparently unmodified as well, crewed by ordinary Uul warriors, and he wondered what they were for. They'd be armed in the usual way, with crossbows, spears, and swords, and couldn't be good for much, he thought. And it irked him that their more traditional commanders actually looked down on the New Army and the way they'd been taught to fight. *They've proven how useless they are often enough,* he thought with a touch of bitterness. *Maybe they're just . . . numbers, to draw fire from us. As mindless as they are, they're liable to be more of a hindrance than a help.* He put it out of his head.

None of the galleys could ground themselves here—the shore was too rocky and steep—so all their crews were condemned to spend another night afloat in the increasingly foul little vessels. Most Ka'tans didn't care if their troops relieved themselves in the bilge, or even on the benches where they sat, and the reeking miasma that resulted was overpowering. Jash had ordered his warriors to squat over the side, but that helped only a little. The sides, the oars, even the railing in many places, was streaked with dark, reeking excrement. And many of his warriors tended to keep bones and steadily riper portions of their rations for snacks, in any event. And those rations were no longer composed of foodbeasts, preserved for the stalled offensive. That was already gone. Rations now consisted of Uul inhabitants of New Sofesshk, injured or killed in the bombings, brought aboard from barges that came alongside. Some even staggered or crawled aboard under their own power, "supplying" themselves to the troops.

Jash understood this was not unusual. The Race had always fed on itself when necessary. But he was too young to remember when such was more commonplace and, despite his opinion of the quality of Uul warriors, the notion conflicted with the training he was raised with: that *all* troops had value beyond mere absorbers of projectiles and rations for the survivors. If that was true, couldn't the same value apply to Uul laborers and factory workers that kept the army equipped and supplied? That bothered him also in a vague, ill-defined way. And even more disquieting were the increasing numbers of *Hij*, already slaughtered, that were brought to the ships. Despite being skinned, they were easily discernible by the layer of sweet fat, soft flesh, and, yes, better taste. There weren't that many, but more, proportionately, than should be expected—if they were all coming from New Sofesshk. That meant some had to be coming from the older city. Probably the enemy had finally begun bombing it more diligently—something he'd expected, but couldn't possibly tell from where the galleys were gathered. But none of the Hij carcasses were torn or burned in ways they'd come to expect from those destroyed by bombs. It was strange.

"There you are," Seech said, approaching from aft. He tore a final morsel of flesh from what looked like a lower-leg bone, then tossed the bone in the water. He nodded back at *Slasher*'s complement, most already asleep on the benches. "You should rest. It will soon be dawn."

"I cannot," Jash admitted. "I feel . . . anxious."

Seech jerked his head diagonally. "Indeed. There will be a fine feed tomorrow, after we force the bend."

"Yes," Jash agreed neutrally, wondering if it would be they who were sated or the monsters in the river. The water here was choked with them now, gathering to the carrion of the sunken greatships. "All *should* be well," he said, gesturing at the ten or more cruisers gathered in the gloom. The moon had fallen from the sky, but swirling sparks rising from their funnels lit them enough to mark their places. Invisible beyond the cruisers were more galleys, countless numbers of them, poised to exploit the expected breakthrough. More distant sparks rose from the menacing form of *Giorsh*, which, along with others of her stupendous kind, were moored in the midst of the galleys to protect them from the air.

"Rest," Seech urged again. "We are supposed to begin the attack as soon as color can be seen, but I doubt it will happen that early. The plan is complicated and much must be coordinated. That is difficult enough for us, but"—he hissed at a galley full of ordinary Uul nearby—"probably impossible with the likes of them among us."

"You are right," Jash agreed, "but the attack may commence as scheduled, regardless of the confusion. Our Lord Regent Champion Esshk himself will be watching from *Giorsh*. No doubt any who hesitate will be destroyed." He considered. "The pounce may come a *bit* late, perhaps even late enough to spoil the surprise, but we will finally see what our army is made of at some point tomorrow." He glanced at Seech's barely discernible form. "We will at last discover what *we* are made of."

14

*D*awn flared in two directions that morning. Just as the sun cast its red-orange glare over the horizon to the east, promising another hot, humid day, more light of a similar color flashed and rippled on the other side of the bend. The rays of that dawn were shrouded in fog and fat columns of smoke, however, as dozens, then *hundreds*, of rockets soared over the rocky hump.

Russ Chappelle and Mikey Monk had been drinking "monkey joe" on the starboard bridgewing. Real coffee had been discovered on Madagascar—they'd even *tasted* it—but they didn't have any, and were lamenting the fact that all they had was the ersatz green-foam substitute they'd been drinking for two years. Meanwhile, they watched and waited, staring at the hazy, slowly brightening wreckage-choked pass. The significance of the date and the fact their life of total war had begun three years earlier, to the day, had been edged out by more pressing concerns. The river seemed to generate a low-lying sunrise fog for an hour or so every day, and visibility would worsen before the fog burned off. That's when the barrage suddenly began, and both were startled badly enough that, for a moment, they stood immobile.

The rockets themselves were no surprise; they'd expected them, and Russ had edged *Santy Cat* and *Felts* slightly farther back from their blocking positions than usual. The boats from *Arracca* hadn't come, and they'd steamed through the night, dead slow, screws turning just fast enough to maintain steerageway and hold their positions against the current. That used little fuel and had become routine. The extra distance was because, though the rockets could still reach them, targeting was spottier at longer ranges, particularly since their crews had to rely on instructions passed from observers. That the enemy had grasped that concept and could employ it fairly effectively was disconcerting enough, for various reasons, but what shocked them now was the sheer, utterly unexpected *volume* of fire that arced in from the invisible batteries and began exploding around where *Santa Catalina* usually lay.

More flashes lit the morning, expelling clouds of shrapnel that flailed the river over a wide area. Except for a few bangs and rattles of spent shards striking the ship, the greater percentage of the rockets were ineffective. Some continued on, however, reaching farther, and that snapped Chappelle's and Monk's reverie. Both slammed their cups on the rail and dashed into the pilothouse, Russ already shouting, "Ahead full. Left full rudder. Sound general quarters!" The EOT clattered, and the talker turned the switch on the comm circuit to Shipwide and whipped the striker in the alarm bell beside the mouthpiece, sending a frantic clanging through the ship.

Already underway, *Santy Cat* almost immediately began to turn, but it would be several minutes before her speed picked up. Meanwhile, rocket warheads started pounding her or exploding nearby and lashing her with iron. Gun's crews were cut down as they ran to their posts and grass-stuffed mattresses were blown away from stanchions. Gooseneck vents were toppled or filled with holes. A few fragments even whirred through the pilothouse, but no one was hit by anything large or fast. A few might've been struck by flying glass, shaken from the broken window frames. A quick-thinking 'Cat had slammed the battle shutters down, and that might've saved them. The shutters, intended only as splinter shields, would become large secondary projectiles if struck by a heavy gun, but were ideal for this sort of thing.

The ship's big screw bit deeper, and between that and the current, she quickly gathered speed as she headed downriver. A few more rockets hit the ship aft, one even penetrating to the dining salon, shredding the ornate tapestries and splintering the long table and many of the new chairs around it. A fire got started in the nearby officers' galley, but was quickly extinguished. Finally, the hits grew less frequent as the range increased and the volume dropped off.

"Son of a bitch!" Monk exclaimed, sucking a cut on the back of his hand. They heard the rumble of engines as some of *Arracca*'s planes passed overhead, commencing their morning recon—and attacks on targets of opportunity.

Russ wondered what their pilots thought of what they'd just seen—and what they'd report when they could see around the bend. "They're gonna pull something," he said with utter certainty. "Why hammer us like that, except to push us away—which worked," he added bitterly. "We should've just ridden it out. Bring us about," he told the 'Cat at the wheel.

"They's lotsa guys down on deck," the talker informed him. "Gun's crews on the staar-board quarter was nearly wiped out! Corps-'Cats are on the way."

"Ask Major Gutfeld to send more Marines to the guns and then report to the bridge. I think it's gonna be a busy day."

"Ay, ay," the talker agreed, then narrowed her eyes at what she heard through the earpiece held against her head beneath her helmet. "Sur!" she added urgently. "Lookout says a Grik cruiser is barrelin' through the gaap right now! An' Pee-Oh Naara-Raan says *Felts* is signaalin' that our planes see more where thaat one came from, all lined up. The planes're gonna hit 'em, but it looks like the enemy's maassin' for a major at-taack."

Russ raised his binoculars, unable to really see. There

was no wind, and the smoke from the rockets and their warheads still hung thick, joining the fog. The scout planes could see fine, however. "Very well. Have Naara signal *Felts* to send to *Arracca*: We're moving as close to the choke point as we can, to hammer the enemy as they come through. Maybe that'll make 'em lay off the rockets too, afraid they'll hit their own." He paused. "We'd appreciate as much air support as *Arracca* can give us. This might be the day for a maximum effort on her part." Russ looked at Monk. "I guess this is it. With the auxiliary conn knocked out, I want you in the steering-engine room. Make sure you detail a relay to call down course corrections in case comm goes down too."

"Aye, aye, Skipper." Monk hurried out, calling, "You be careful, sir," behind him.

Major Gutfeld arrived on the bridge just as *Santa Catalina*'s course steadied, aiming her back at the channel blockage. "I'd say 'good morning,' sir, but . . ." He shrugged.

"Yeah. What a crappy way to start the day."

Two cruisers had made it through the channel and begun to spread out. A third was already picking its way through before *Santy Cat* passed her initial blocking position. Russ could see them now: Azuma-class ironclads. The first they'd encountered in Indiaa were about 300 feet long, around 3,800 tons, and armed with twenty forty-pounder guns. Even though Allied steam frigate DDs only protected their engineering spaces with armor, they carried better, heavier fifty-pounders, not to mention more reliable engines, and the two had been considered a fairly even match. These CAs incorporated many of the improvements seen on Kurokawa's, however. Their auxiliary sail capacity was much reduced, implying better engines and possibly improved antiair capability as well. They also carried fourteen fifty-pounders, and a short hundred-pounder in the bows, on a pivoting truck. Russ expected the upgrades were based on designs Kurokawa left before his temporary break with the Grik, but it didn't much matter. They were more than a match for *Felts* now, and even *Santa Catalina* if they got close enough. The problem was, with little sea room and a fixed position to defend, this fight was starting out at fewer than two thousand yards, far closer than Russ would've preferred. *Santy Cat* had to get some hard licks in, very quickly, and her powerful 5.5″ rifles commenced firing first.

Two shells from the portside battery shrieked out and stabbed the cruiser veering right, and two more lashed out to starboard. The forward 4.7″s barked at the enemy still in the cluttered channel, and the 4″-50s just aft of the bridge boomed past the pilothouse, deafening those inside. Plates whirled away from the cruiser to the left, joined by a gush of steam, but the cruisers quickly replied with their own heavy guns, just as another salvo of rockets streaked in. Most of the big roundshot kicked up huge splashes short of the mark, but *Santa Catalina* staggered from several impacts, and her exposed gunners were flailed by rocket fragments. The 4″-50s and 4.7″s commenced rapid fire, sending salvo after salvo at their targets. The 5.5″s were "bag guns," slower to load, but they fired again within twenty seconds, punishing the maneuvering cruisers. The one on the left wasn't actually maneuvering anymore. Bleeding steam, it twisted with the current, wracked by secondary explosions. *Felts* had moved up alongside *Santa Catalina* and now turned to port, loosing a broadside of fifty-pounders into the drifting wreck, now less than 1,200 yards away. The cruiser in the channel finally slipped through the debris, however, firing one of her big forward guns. The round deeply creased *Santa Catalina*'s bow and ricocheted— almost hitting *Felts* in the stern.

"Tell *Felts* to stay back, damn it!" Russ snapped at a signal-'Cat, suddenly furious with himself that he hadn't just sent her—and the wounded she'd put aboard his ship—out to *Arracca* the night before. He'd thought he needed her for her shallow draft, but the way this fight was shaping up . . . "She's too beat up for this and has two crews on board!" he added. Another salvo hammered the cruiser to starboard, blowing away its foremast and funnel. Sparks spewed and smoke gushed low over the gundeck. Bright red flashes followed the smoke across the deck, and the ship suddenly blew up. Shattered fragments spewed across the water. *Felts* had obeyed and was turning away, but not before the cruiser to port was a helpless, settling wreck. The third cruiser fired again, however, the shot crunching deep into *Santy Cat*'s bow, and behind it, a *fourth* Grik cruiser was threading through the wreckage. "And signal *Felts* to tell Commodore Tassanna that now would be a *fine* time for some help from the air. We might even plug the last gap that big ships can pass if she can sink something in it." *Where is* Arracca's *air strike?* he asked himself. *We need it now!*

The third cruiser, already battered, turned right, exposing its fourteen fifty-pounders, just as the fourth ship fired its heavy bow gun and yet another deluge of rockets swamped the area. Most of the rockets went long this time, but a hundred-pounder and maybe half the fifty-pounders pummeled *Santy Cat* hard. Now at less than a thousand yards, many punched through. Probably only the armor bolted over her engineering spaces saved her from a fatal wound. Two hits right behind the pilothouse almost knocked the bridge watch off their feet, and there were screams aft, from the radio shack, where EMs and signal-'Cats had been working on their own radio. Yet only a moment elapsed before *Santy Cat*'s guns opened up again, punishing both cruisers.

"Left full rudder," Russ called. "Ahead slow. We're close enough, and let's give our aft guns a chance." *And get more armor between them and the engine room,* he told himself. *Many more hits from those big suckers, and they'll punch through from the front!* "Damage report!" he added, when singed and bloody 'Cats staggered out of the radio shack into the pilothouse. All of them were drenched by near misses splashing water over the bridgewing.

"No fixin' the raa-dio now," Naara said simply, supporting her left arm with her right hand. "A baall blew troo the bulkhead an' tore out the back o' the equipment. Is all gone. Lucky nobody's killed."

"In *there*," the talker agreed, "but we got caa-shul-tees all over the ship." At least they still had internal communications.

"Get on . . ." Russ looked at Naara's arm. It was bleeding and looked broken. "Get somebody on the Morse lamp and signal *Felts* to stand by close enough to see our signals after all. We still need her radio. And tell her to ask *Arracca* for some goddamn air support!"

As if Russ's frustration had finally summoned them, the drone of engines filtered through to their damaged hearing between the hammering guns. Russ raced out on the blood-soaked bridgewing, stepping over the lookout crumpled in a ragged heap. Even as one of Naara's signal-'Cats tried to get *Felts*'s attention, Russ looked at the sky. There were barely twenty planes, mostly P-1Cs, crossing in two formations, and Russ had to wonder if that was all Tassanna had left to send. The fighters were each armed with a pair of 150-pound bombs for the very first time. The older-model, underpowered Fleashooters could bear only 50-pound bombs, and then only if their guns and ammunition were removed. C models could keep their two .30-caliber machine guns and still—barely—carry the heavier load. These, like all Allied antiship bombs, were based on naval rifle projectiles already in production. The fifty-pounders were 4″-50 shells with respectable bursting charges attached to longer, finned casings filled with an incendiary mixture of gimpra sap and gasoline. The 150s were built around the new armor-piercing 5.5″ shells, just like those used by *Santy Cat*'s six casemate guns, originally salvaged from *Amagi*.

The P-1s dove into the smoke beyond Russ's view, and he assumed they were targeting more Grik cruisers preparing to force a passage. The half-dozen Nancys, each carrying two larger, heavier incendiaries, swooped down in the direction from which most of the rockets came. Huge orange-black toadstools of fire and smoke erupted beyond the rocky hump, mixed with a shattering series of explosions and uncontrolled rocket trails that tumbled and corkscrewed in all directions. Banking up and away from the inferno, it looked like all the Nancys survived the attack. Drowned by the results of that, nothing was seen or heard of the fighter strike on the cruisers until a number of Fleashooters climbed out, followed by rising columns of smoke. A pair veered back toward the cruiser Russ could see, which was making for the south side of the river. Their bombs gone, they commenced a strafing run. Waterspouts marched toward the cruiser as bullets flailed the water, then the ship. Suddenly, amid a cloud of white smoke, it almost seemed as if the cruiser exploded—but then smaller gray-white puffs blossomed in the air above it, directly in the fighters' path. One of the blue-and-white planes made it through the fog of smoke and flailing fragments apparently unscathed, but the other simply came apart and hurtled, spinning, into the river.

"Damn!" Gutfeld snarled, standing beside Russ. "Those cruisers *do* have antiair rockets or mortars, just like the battlewagons. And they're damned effective against low-flying attackers. How the hell did they teach 'em to time it just right?" He shook his head, leaving the obvious answer unspoken. The Grik had learned many things through Kurokawa's aid, of course, but also through experience and, most frightening of all, imagination. The Grik were a real, thinking enemy now, as capable of learning from and adjusting to mistakes as any other. And they'd done it at the worst possible time from the Allies' perspective, when *their* strategic flexibility was most taxed. They had to stop this breakout, and for *Santy Cat* and her people to survive, the invasion must come here as well. Nobody planned the battle that was building in the Zambezi River, and neither side had much choice about how to fight it. But the way it was turning out, it would play to the oldest and most insurmountable Grik strength of all: sheer numbers.

Russ spun and grabbed Gutfeld's arm. "We have mortars too," he insisted, "that can hammer those cruisers. I doubt theirs are designed to reach us."

At that moment, one of the starboard 5.5″s scored a critical hit against the cruiser emerging from the channel. It had just turned north, exposing its starboard broadside and clearing the way for another behind it, when flames jetted from every seam. With a thunderclap rumble, the ship burst apart, spraying itself across the water.

"Yes, sir, we do, but not a helluva lot of 'em. And our guys in the open'll get creamed by the rockets."

"We don't have a lot of anything," Russ argued. "*Arracca* is our tender, and we can't just steam out to her and resupply. Not now." He waited a moment, listening. The forward guns were still pasting the cruiser that got the plane, and the aft guns were targeting the next ship to emerge—just as two 100-pound shot slammed *Santy Cat*'s starboard side and sent everyone sprawling.

"We're holed in the engine room!" the talker squeaked. "Laney's gonna bust hisself screamin' at me!"

"There haven't been any rockets since the air strike," Russ continued, helping Gutfeld up. "Maybe they got 'em all, maybe not, but we need your mortars *now*. You've got to at least keep their heads down while they load. The cruisers' guns aren't as powerful as their BBs, but they're still tearing us apart. What good does it do to save ammo and lives for a later we'll never live to see?"

Gutfeld was nodding. "Understood, sir. We'll do our best."

"I know."

Gutfeld addressed the talker. "Call all mortar teams on deck with their tubes, on the double." The baseplates were still in place.

"Ay, Major," the talker agreed, not waiting for Russ to repeat the command.

The signal-'Cat near Russ blinked an acknowledgment to her counterpart on *Felts*. "Sur," she said, "*Arracca*'s wing lost five planes against croosers on the other side. Prob'ly sank two. But there's more, an' . . . Sur, there's hundreds o' *gaalleys* pullin' to the front, like they gonna come out too. An' they don't need that main chaannel that's left."

Russ took a long breath. *What next?* "Very well. Major, we're about to have more targets for your mortars, probably machine gunners and riflemen too."

"Aye, aye, sir."

Jash now knew what true fear was, though he still had no name to call it. The Ghaarrichk'k used other words in conversation for things that gave them unease, but if a word existed for the . . . other thing, which dwelt within all creatures, the thing that turned them prey, it was never intended for such as Jash to know. Instead, any who panicked, succumbing to the nameless impulse to survive at any cost—"turned prey"—were immediately slain out of hand. This provided an artificial antidote to fear in the form of swift and certain consequences to behavior that did, on some level, require a subjective assessment of a situation, even perhaps an individual decision. Therefore, since time began, each warrior of the Race had not only had every impulse toward individual thought suppressed unless they were granted "elevation" but had been presented with only *one* choice when the nameless dread swept upon them: obey. Death might come if they did, but there was no uncertainty about what would happen if they fled. Flight had been removed from the binary list of instinctive options, leaving only fight.

The problem was, Jash's generation of warriors had been raised to exercise their minds to an unprecedented degree. They'd been bred and indoctrinated for loyalty to their creators, of course, in the persons of Regent Champion Esshk and the Celestial Mother, but also taught to think—as one must in order to use complex weapons and employ tactics that make them most effective. They'd even been encouraged to use initiative, on occasion, when advantages presented themselves on the battlefield. None of that could be accomplished without imagining multiple options in any given situation, most especially those involving survival. For that reason, Jash, Seech, and possibly every warrior aboard *Slasher* and the other New Army galleys tasted real fear, whether there was a word for it or not, when they advanced into the maelstrom of the river bend. That they did so at all proved their loyalty was real, but also that their acuity was such that they could display yet another trait that had no name they knew: courage.

"I told you the attack would commence as scheduled," Seech shouted at Jash over the thundering drum that kept the rowers in sync. The drum was felt as much as heard, in the very fibers of the ship; otherwise, with so many other rumbling drums near and far, all the rowing would descend into chaos.

Jash allowed his eyes to rest on the burning carcass of one of the cruisers, destroyed by the enemy flying machines. Two, at least, had been gutted by bombs, and a couple others damaged. Worse, the cruisers had wounded or killed quite a few warriors with the same air-bomb fragments that tore some of the flying machines from the sky. One machine had crashed nearby, smashing two galleys. Now the whole horde of remaining gun galleys, and an equal number crewed by ordinary Uul warriors, were racing ahead of the last five cruisers commanded to force the gap.

"I told *you* that," Jash rebutted. "I also said *we* would begin late, after surprise was lost." *I did not think it would be* this *late,* he confessed to himself. *It is near to midday.* The sun was blasting down, harder than usual, as if the humid air focused its rays more intensely, and Jash felt as if he were wearing a blanket of smoldering coals. Then the sun was simply gone, choked by the smoke of the burning wrecks they passed. It only grew hotter, and it didn't seem like the airship bombing had cleared the passage in any way, serving only to reignite the jagged timbers jutting from the water—or scatter them about, creating floating hazards for *Slasher*'s lightweight hull and making rowing more difficult.

The smoke of battle and smoldering ships was heavy and oppressive, burning Jash's eyes and making breathing an effort. Smoke was always difficult for the Race, and it was doubly ironic that this new way of war produced so much. There came a crash to his right, mingled with cries of rage and alarm. He couldn't see, but suspected one of the galleys had destroyed itself on a wreck. "Watch very carefully," he told the warriors nearby, "and do not hesitate to inform the First if you see a hazard. I should resume my post," he grudged to Seech, easing back a step. He belonged at the rear of the galley, beside the warriors at the tiller, but he'd . . . needed to see, to be the first to gaze upon the enemy they must face. Seech was where he belonged, ready to call out course corrections and, ultimately, command the great gun on the bow.

"Indeed," Seech agreed, then paused, looking at him. "I will watch over our *Slasher*," he assured, "and you can rejoin me here when the prey is clear to see."

Jash nodded thanks and trotted back down the deck

above the rowers. Finally at his station again, he could barely see Seech, much less anything beyond. *Or is that . . .* Ahead, through the gloom, bright slashing tongues of flame spurted from heavy guns, pounding at something in the distance. *Surely from one of our cruisers,* he thought. There were no answering flashes, but explosions suddenly shook the cruiser and it veered sharply to the right.

"We are past the wreckage!" Seech crowed back at Jash, then his stance grew rigid and his bristly young crest rose through the gap down the center of his helmet. "The enemy!" he called back, his tone starkly less jubilant. Jash started to move forward again, but the smoke finally cleared, revealing the full panorama of the battle. He was stunned by what he saw.

Half a ten of their newest cruisers lay scattered in the broader part of the river, burning, exploding, or simply lying, half-sunk, their crews scrambling onto exposed sections or trying to escape on floating debris. Dozens of galleys had cleared the passage ahead of them, rowing swiftly, but many were already under fire. Bullets from the enemy's amazing fast-shooters stitched the water around them and spewed splinters from their fragile hulls or sprays of downy fur and blood from even more fragile bodies. Great stalks of dirty water arose among them, shrouded in smoke and foam. Jash suspected these came from the small mortars he'd been told to expect, which the Race had been unable to copy yet. One landed directly on a galley a hundred paces ahead, thoroughly shattering it and spilling its crew into the water. And the water . . . He and his were accustomed to lake and river monsters and the voracious fishes that sometimes swarmed. They even knew how to avoid them to a degree, so they could cross rivers and streams when necessary. But the Zambezi now teemed and heaved with predators of every sort, throwing up knuckles and swirls in their frenzy, and snatching struggling warriors. *There will be no avoiding the concentration gathered to the carrion here,* he realized, the unnamed tension rising in his chest.

Three cruisers, already through the gauntlet and already damaged to various degrees, were trading a furious fire with two lonely vessels lying across their path. The smaller looked something like the old-style sailing ships of the Race, of which so few remained, except it was clearly a steamer. It was just as clearly heavily damaged, though it continued to fire while its position near the larger ship afforded it some protection. The bigger one, barely as large as the casemate on the numerous great-ships it had destroyed, looked so misshapen by damage that Jash couldn't believe it was still afloat, let alone defi-ant. Some of the distortion may have been caused by the bizarre patterns of contrasting grays that covered it, but that couldn't account for all. He'd been told it was made entirely of iron instead of merely armored with it—as all Ghaarrichk'k warships now were—and perhaps that made the difference, but even from his current distance of per-haps ten hundreds of paces, he could see *through* it in several places, where heavy shot had blown holes in and out. Its smoke pipe, riddled with holes, had collapsed, as had other things, like masts, and it was generally so dented and battered that he could only guess at its original shape. Yet all that damage hadn't drawn its teeth. It still moved sluggishly, turning now to maintain its position and per-haps expose more guns and a less wounded side.

Here indeed is the greatest river monster of all, he realized. Even as he did, the closest cruiser emitted a dying screech amid a roiling plume of escaping steam that gushed out over a pair of racing galleys. The cries of their warriors echoed the sinking ship. Great bellows-driven horns aboard the command galleys roared the guttural tone for a general attack. "Full speed!" Jash snapped at the drummer near the tiller, who acknowl-edged with a hesitant nod. *At least I am not the only one with claws shredding my heart,* Jash thought. The drum-mer raised the tempo to the quickest pace the rowers could sustain for such a distance, though they'd probably be too exhausted to fight when they got there. That hardly mattered. The crew of the great gun would fight for them all—if they lived long enough. The mortars and fast-shooters had redoubled, and more and more galleys stopped, flooding, or fell off course as rowers on one side or the other were slain, their oars trailing alongside.

Though no fast-shooters had been directed at *Slasher* yet, as far as Jash could tell, a few of his warriors were crying out in pain or collapsing on their benches in welters of blood. The dead were quickly thrown over the side and replaced with reserves, but Jash wondered what was killing them. Squinting through the renewed smoke and spume, he saw many tens of the enemy lining protected rails on the target, firing garraks. The range seemed impossible; he estimated it at nearly five hundred paces now, but clearly it was not. He must do what he could to spoil their aim.

"First Seech!" he roared. "Commence firing the great gun! We are close enough to do some harm, I think." Many of the other galleys had already started firing, usually earning them the attention of fast-shooters, but it couldn't be helped. "All reserves to the front. Fire your garraks while the great gun is loaded!" He knew that was risky—the bow was crowded enough already and sparks might ignite the powder carried to the gun—but if they could suppress just a little enemy fire, it might be enough to let them achieve two or even three shots from the great gun before they were destroyed. He no longer doubted that outcome, and, oddly, the claws in his heart had relaxed their grip to some degree.

The great gun fired, slamming back against the breechings and shaking *Slasher* through and through. By some miracle of the meager breeze, the smoke cloud drifted aside and Jash saw their 16-pound roundshot fly straight into the side of the terrible ship—and bounce back into the water with a splash. But other shots were slamming through, punching holes, and he realized they must've hit an especially well-armored section. Immediately, warriors stood around the gun, firing garraks at the enemy as fast as they could. They even remembered to aim high, Jash saw, since some of their balls actually sent the enemy behind cover. A fast-shooter opened up on them, however, scattering warriors around the great gun in a flurry of splinters and blood. Out of the corner of his eye, Jash saw a pair of galleys crewed by Uul warriors race past, much faster than his heavily laden *Slasher* could manage, and almost no fire was directed at them. He wondered what they hoped to accomplish. They'd be too exhausted to use their swords and spears, even if they got alongside the enemy and climbed its high, dented sides.

"Seech is down!" came a cry, and Jash finally relented to his impulse to race forward. "Sustain this course and speed no matter what!" he called behind. A great gun on a galley beside them roared and the fast-shooter redirected its fire there, quickly felling its crew and shredding the thin timbers beneath it. The galley began to slow, and the clattering bullets sprayed the crew at the oars. Jash hardly noticed. First of One Hundred Seech, whom he'd known all his life, was lying in a twitching pile of dead and wounded warriors. *His* warriors. Seech's eyes were open, staring, but there was no inner light. That was understandable, since his entire bottom jaw was blown away and the exit hole under the back of his head was full of bloody, saltlike specks of neck bone.

The sensation Jash felt then was one fully recognized, even encouraged by the Race. It was called *hiskak*, or "battle fury," but the same training that made him susceptible to previous, unnamed feelings allowed him to control this as well. A bullet clipped a few bristles from his short crest and another grazed his arm, leaving a shallow, bloody trench. He didn't even notice. "First of Fifty Naxa still lives?" he demanded.

"Here, Senior . . . Ka'tan," came a reply beside him.

Still staring at Seech's corpse, Jash spoke. "Load the great gun. We continue the attack."

"Of course, Senior. But look there."

Jash raised his gaze. Five or six of the Uul galleys had reached the side of the enemy ship. Garraks were firing down on them, as were a few fast-shooters. Even little bombs, tossed by the enemy, exploded aboard them. Then, to Jash's astonishment, two of the galleys suddenly detonated with a force sufficient to obliterate themselves and several galleys nearby, heeling the great ship over. Before it could recover, another blast-shattered galley exploded against the rusty red, barnacle-encrusted bottom that was exposed. A great pall of smoke spread from the scene, and for a moment there was no firing at all.

In that instant, Jash had a profound revelation. He'd

believed the Uul galleys were sent to divert attention from his more valuable warriors, but it had been the other way around. In a way, he had to admire Regent Champion First General Esshk's ruthless strategy, but resented not only the willful waste of New Army warriors, but the fact that Esshk hadn't told them the ultimate plan. It would've worked, anyway, and many more gun galleys—and their crews—might've survived, pressing their attacks less fiercely, firing from farther away. Beyond this resentment—another new sensation—Jash also felt something akin to humiliation and betrayal, realizing that despite his devotion to Esshk and the Celestial Mother, Esshk, at least, valued him—and Seech—no more than the lowliest, most mindless Uul.

"Damage report!" Russ demanded, rising shakily from the deck. He noted there was blood on his hands and wondered where it had come from. *Oh.* The Lemurian quartermaster's mate at the EOT was down, his helmet gone, along with a big chunk of his head. About the same time the galleys blew up, a shot had struck the pilothouse, spinning a battle shutter inside like a warped saw blade. Another 'Cat shoved the dead one out of the way while Russ grabbed the wheel again.

"Lec—" The talker coughed on smoke filling the bridge. "Lectric comm is out. Laney's on the voice tube, says there's baad floodin' in the fireroom an' engine room both. Them goddaamn gaalleys blow a *big* hole under the armor. Engine room's floodin' faster, an' ain't nothin' he can do. Pumps can't keep up, an' we'll lose those when the waater gets the boilers."

Russ nodded. He'd expected as much, and known immediately his poor *Santa Catalina* was doomed at last. Still, her job wasn't finished. "Detail everybody who can stand, not fighting, to bring up all the ammo they can get their hands on before the magazines flood. Stow it in the air castle, the casemate." He hesitated. "Even the sickbay." Those were still the most heavily armored parts of the ship, and all six 5.5"s were still in action. The same couldn't be said for the deck guns, but Russ didn't know if that was due to damage or dead crews.

Major Gutfeld swayed through the hatch from the starboard bridgewing, face blackened, eyes red; brows, lashes, and beard mostly singed away. "That was bad," he murmured simply. "I lost a lot of people."

"Yeah," Russ agreed, steering directly for the open gap in the channel ahead. No less than four Grik cruisers were through now, and though most were damaged to some degree and had stopped firing for the moment, probably as surprised by the galley "bombs" as anyone, that wouldn't last when they saw where he was heading. "And it gets worse," he continued. "We're sinking. Nothing for it. Our only chance is to try to block that last little gap and turn this tub into a fixed battery."

Gutfeld was staring at him, wide eyed. "Yeah," he said. "I guess so. What can I do?"

"Keep those damn galleys off us. I don't know if we'll make it as it is, but any more holes'll put us down right where we are, savvy?"

"Aye, sir," Gutfeld agreed, and bolted out the hatch to rejoin his Marines.

"Cap-i-taan," cried the talker. "Laney wants to send his people up!"

Russ handed off the wheel to a 'Cat with blood matting the fur on his face and lurched to the voice tube. The noise coming out of it sounded like a freight train going over a waterfall. "Laney? Can you hear me?"

"Yeah. I gotta get my people outa here! We're done!"

"Send as many as you can, but keep us going ten more minutes."

"Shit! I can't promise *two* minutes!"

"You *will*, if it's the last thing you ever do!" Russ yelled. "You want to prove you're an officer, a *man* worth respect? Now's your chance. Give me full ahead, right now, and keep the throttle open until I say so—or you damn well drown, you got that?"

The EOT clanged behind Russ. "I got it—an' so do you. All I have left," Laney shouted back, his voice tinny and strained. "But it'll only last as long as it lasts. Don't you get it? We're fillin' up and I can't even slow it down. My baby's *done*, an' there ain't a goddamn thing *anybody* can do about it, see? I want my people the hell out, right now." There was a short hesitation. "I'll stay myself, an' make sure you get the last turn she'll give."

Russ felt a stab of guilt but didn't let it touch his voice. "Fair enough. Everybody out . . . and you too, when the water reaches the fires. With or without your baby, I still need you."

"Sure, sure. No sweat. I love this damn engine your cockeyed scheme stole from me, but it ain't worth dyin' for. Not when there ain't no help for it."

Russ stepped back to the wheel, taking it in both hands. There was a slight surge in speed, but not much. The ship was getting too heavy with water coming in. The surviving cruisers had opened fire again, as had a couple more of *Santy Cat*'s guns. A steady chatter came from machine guns and riflemen as the tortured old ship bulled through the floating debris and clustered galleys. Another one blew itself up about forty yards away, killing galleys all around but doing no further damage to the ship. Other galleys were probably destroyed by shot from the Grik cruisers. Russ felt a new, faint shudder through his shoes as the hull, lower in the water by the moment, dragged across the riverbed.

"Just a little longer, baby," he muttered.

A fifty-pound shot struck the port bridgewing and caromed away, right before a shaken signal-'Cat stepped through the hatch, blinking at the huge dent. She shook her head. "We got four more Grik croosers comin' up-river *behind* us," she stated, voice flat. Russ was stunned. There might still be that many already engaged, it was hard to tell, but *four* more? *We're totally screwed.* "Where the hell did they come from? Why didn't *Arracca* stop 'em, or at least warn us?"

"Sur." The 'Cat hesitated, sparing a blink of compassion for her exhausted, desperate skipper. "*Felts* is a floatin' wreck, all her maasts gone. Her raa-dio's been out for a while. I tole you. . . ."

Russ nodded. He remembered now.

"But however they get paast her, *Arracca* ain't abaandon us. Her laast planes're comin' up the river too, right behind the croosers. *Arracca*'ll come too, I bet, it comes to thaat. We gonna *block* this daamn river!" Russ didn't know whether to laugh or cry. If *Arracca* came herself, their mission might still succeed, but at what cost? Grik airships couldn't miss something the size of the huge carrier, and their bombs would eventually burn her to the waterline. It was a disaster.

At that moment, there was a bursting, gushing sound, like a great bubble of gas moving through the intestines of the ship, amplified a thousandfold, and a plume of sooty steam engulfed the upper deck around the fallen funnel. Russ tried the wheel but could hardly move it. The steering engine was dead. "Give me a hand!" he shouted. With two 'Cats helping, he managed to heave the helm hard over, a spoke at a time, until the water-logged, coasting hulk finally turned slightly to port just a few hundred yards shy of the mouth of the passage and all the wreckage she'd made. Then, with a rending screech of steel against underwater rocks and a final, bouncing lurch, her fo'c'sle barely ten feet above the surface of the river, her boilers drowned, and Dean Laney's "baby" dead, USS *Santa Catalina* came to rest at last.

Heartsick and emotionally spent, amid a furiously renewed fusillade of hammering shot that pounded the wreck with a deafening roar, Russ impulsively reached over and shoved the EOT handle to Finished with Engine. He was surprised when the pointer from below slowly, deliberately, clanged five times to match the command. *Laney really stayed to the end,* he realized, suddenly hoping the ship's asshole engineering officer wasn't already dead on his feet, mortally scalded or about to drown.

Like the water rising in his ship, an unexpected, hopeless gloom surged in Russ and he was jarred by the faint cheering that began to rise over the sound of battle, growing louder by the moment. The signal-'Cat stared aft.

"What the hell's that about?" Russ demanded.

"Them Grik croosers," the 'Cat jabbered excitedly. "They ain't Griks! They're *ours*! All is flyin' the Staars an' Stripes o' the Naa-vee Claan!"

Hope roared against the despair that had threatened to engulf Russ Chappelle, and he realized his *Santy Cat* would only truly die when all her people were gone. He started shouting orders. "Get more hands shifting ammunition, supplies, anything they can think of. And secure every mattress and piece of plate they can find to the rails! This old ship's last fight has just begun," he added grimly.

Jash and Naxa had been jockeying their bullet- and shrapnel-wracked galley through the jumbled flotsam of their assault. Quite a few undamaged galleys had become entangled in the confusion and little fire was directed at them. Others were swamped, shot to pieces, or overwhelmed by the effects of the blasts. Naxa managed to fire the great gun at the crippled enemy a couple more times, as did other galleys, but the effect was difficult to discern in the chaos, each shot inevitably summoning a blistering hail of retribution from fast-shooters, garraks, even the high-angle bombs. Nearly a third of *Slasher*'s warriors had been heaved over the side or lay bleeding in the sloshing bilge. Twice more, Jash ordered his warriors to pause their rowing and fire garraks at the enemy, concentrating their aim at the fast-shooters, but he couldn't tell if they had any effect. All the while, return fire slaughtered his warriors in the most hideously efficient manner imaginable, leaving Jash furious and frustrated by his inability to respond in kind. Worse, his fragile vessel was filling with water and becoming logier. Soon he and all his warriors would die—for nothing.

"The great gun will be our end," Jash said at last. "It must go over the side. And all its ammunition as well."

"If we return without it . . . ." Naxa began.

"With it, we will not return at all," Jash interrupted emphatically, and immediately set his warriors to the task of slashing the tackle holding the gun in place and throwing the heavy shot into the river. When the splashes subsided, the battered galley rode a little higher and the inrush of water could be contained with buckets.

"The enemy has stopped on the north side of the channel near the middle of the river," Naxa observed. "Perhaps it has sunk?"

Jash spared a glance from a plume of smoke he'd been watching approach from downriver, just in time to see *Santa Catalina* deal a punishing salvo at the closest cruiser, already fighting a fire and trying to get around behind it. "If so, it does not seem to have affected how deadly it is. Still, we may have unexpected assistance." Ships were approaching, more cruisers of the Race. Excitement rose among the galleys at the sight of the un-looked-for aid. There were three, no *four* of them, steaming rapidly in from the east. Then a moan of dread drifted across the water and Jash's relief turned to horror as the new arrivals immediately fell upon the battered nestmates, firing directly into them at point-blank range. The first they encountered was blown apart by concentrated, stabbing muzzle flashes and crashing iron. It quickly began to drift and fill. The other friendly cruisers, an equal number now, with the latest running the gauntlet of the motionless, misshapen wreck, began to fire back, focusing on the traitorous ships, rapidly closing to what Jash was sure must be a mutually destructive range. That's when his disbelieving eyes finally recognized a profound difference.

Throughout his short life, he'd watched the banners of the Ghaarrichk'k change, evolving away from the many flags of various regencies, ships, even armies. The bloodred of the Celestial Line was a constant, but the water and airship fleets had adopted a red circle, representing the Giver of Life, cradled within the traditional *Kakrik* swords of the Race. Behind them, more red lines radiated outward in all directions on a white field, symbolizing expansion and conquest. This had become the banner of the New Army as well, and only some of the regencies still differed. The flag the intruders flew, streaming from every mast as if nailed in place, was the same striped banner as the still-fighting wreck they'd been sent to assault.

"How . . ." Naxa began, noticing as well, as the battle they'd thought was won quickly intensified to newer heights of close-range ferocity. Virtually ignored now, the iron ship that, nearly all alone, had defied the might of the Final Swarm was free to snipe at targets of opportunity— and focus its fast-shooters on the galleys once more. In addition, another stream of enemy flying machines flew over to make attacks beyond the bend. A few dove on the galleys, ripping them with bombs and fast-shooters of their own.

"I do not know," Jash ground out, "but we are being slaughtered to no purpose. We can do no more against the iron ship. It has already sunk, I think, and we have not the power—or anything resembling a plan—to over-run it."

"You say we should . . . stop the attack?"

Jash barked at Naxa. "We no longer attack *now*! The battle has moved beyond us and we merely mill about and die. We are but a tithe of the Swarm, even of the New Army, but it, even we, have greater value than *this*," he said bitterly. "We must save as much as we can. Sound the gathering-away horns!" he said louder.

"On whose authority?" Naxa asked incredulously.

"Mine."

"But . . . you are not a general, even a ker-noll! You are merely a Senior First!"

"There are no ker-nolls left!" Jash snapped. "If any lived, they would command us to attack or withdraw—something! Someone must take it upon himself to decide. I shall, if no one else."

"They will *destroy* you!" Naxa warned.

"We will all be destroyed if we do nothing," Jash replied, waving up at the small flying machines, turning for another pass. "At this moment, I do not much care if they destroy me—or promote me."

A First of Ten had already run aft to adjust the wooden valves on the large boxlike compression horn. Pressing down on the bellows with a clawed foot, he produced a loud, low-frequency rumbling sound that carried far over the water. The cruisers were too distant or firing too furiously to hear, but the galleys—those that could—began to turn from the slaughter and make their way back toward the tangle of wreckage blocking the river. They'd slip through how and where they could.

////// *USS* Santa Catalina
Zambezi River
Grik Africa

*T*he cruiser fight that ended the Second Battle
of the Zambezi River had been a brutal affair.
Santy Cat had pounded the enemy cruisers as
they passed her, so the prize ships of TF Gri-kakka arrived in better shape than their opponents. But their
crews were a scratch bunch, less familiar with their ships
and weapons than the Grik, for a change. Deprived of
the primitive fire control that made even *Felts* and her
kind equal to Grik cruisers at long range, they'd had no
choice but to get close, do things the old-fashioned way,
and make it a barroom brawl. By dusk, all the Grik cruisers had finally been pounded down, their smoldering,
shattered hulks protruding from various parts of the
broader river beyond *Santa Catalina*, the water around
them frothing with predators feeding on their crews. But
they'd kicked the guts out of two of TF Gri-kakka's cruisers in return, and both were in a sinking condition.

To Dennis Silva's intense frustration, Chack had directed USS *Itaa* to keep her distance from the worst of
the fighting, unwilling to risk the helpless Marines
packed aboard and unable to fight effectively with them

underfoot. That left the other three cruisers at a further disadvantage, but they still prevailed—at great cost. Now their boats were busy removing survivors, after they'd added themselves to the river blockage. Amazingly, *Felts* still lived, and even towed one of the sinking cruisers to a conspicuous gap herself.

"Goddamn," muttered Dennis Silva, staring at the shattered wreck of *Santa Catalina* in the smoky gloom of the dying day as USS *Itaa* tentatively crept alongside, almost like a young girl visiting a disease-wracked old woman on her deathbed.

"Goddamn," Petey said, but it wasn't his usual grating shriek. It was as if he was mimicking the big man's tone as much as his words. Maybe he was even conscious of the mood behind the words for once.

"She's been through it," Gunny Horn agreed, stunned that anything could've endured so much damage and floated as long as it had. "Looks like somebody shot a case of shotgun shells into an oil drum." He thought about his analogy. "Which is probably why it took so much to kill her. The waterline and engineering spaces were armored, and everything else is so thin, solid shot just punched through; didn't make holes that spread . . ." He shook his head. There was still little accounting for it, and what he was really doing was trying to keep his mind off how many humans and 'Cats had been equally unprotected by the old ship's thin plates. The cheering that began again as line handlers secured *Nosey* to the wreckage proved that, somehow, there was still life in the motionless sieve.

A voice came from the battered bridgewing, carried over the cheering by a speaking trumpet. "I need your pumps! We're trying to save as much ammunition as we can, but the magazines are flooding!"

Silva cupped his hands. "Is that you, Russ?"

Chappelle didn't hear him, but he did hear Chack when the Lemurian replied in that curious, carrying way his people had. "Of course. Whaat-ever we caan do. We haave the rest of Major Gutfeld's Maa-reens aboard as well, and will begin sending them across if we caan make faast." He waved out at the river behind him. "All our boats are otherwise occupied. Caan you lower something to cushion our contaact?"

"Yeah. We'll tie lines to mattresses and drop them over the side." That's when Silva realized some of *Santy Cat*'s misshapen aspect was due to the lumpy bedding lining her rails. Once *Itaa* was secured to the wreck, Lemurian Marines started across. The bulwark along the forward well deck was low enough that they actually had to climb down to it. Sailors carried hoses across and *Itaa*'s pumps soon had water jetting back into the river. They'd never keep up, but they might slow the flow.

Chack, Silva, Lawrence, and Horn met Simy Gutfeld, Mikey Monk, and a somewhat dazed-looking Russ Chappelle beside the collapsed funnel on *Santy Cat*'s upper deck. All were clearly exhausted and as battered-looking as the ship, and Russ looked a little punch-drunk, like the shock was finally starting to set in. When *Itaa*'s searchlights lit the darkness, he visibly flinched.

"I don't think that's a good idea. The Grik have spotters for their rockets."

"They shouldn't bother us tonight," Chack assured him. "*Arracca*'s planes demolished their baat-teries pretty thoroughly. No doubt they'll bring up more and site them with greater care, but we should be safe for now."

"But the zeps . . ."

Chack blinked agreement. "They may come, but we'll finish as soon as possible. After thaat, with all the smoke and no moon, they'll be lucky to hit us."

"Relax, Russ. You did swell," Silva said. "We got it from here."

Chappelle glared at him sharply. "What the hell's that supposed to mean?"

Chack blinked soothingly. "As soon as we traansfer the Maa-reens and all the supplies we brought, the cruisers and *Felts* will carry your wounded and ours out to *Arracca*." He hesitated. "They'll also take you and your entire crew—all but a few experienced gunners."

"Now, wait just a damn minute," Russ flared. "This is still my ship! No *way* I'm leaving her!"

Chack's tone hardened. "I sympaa-thize with your

feelings, but you *will* leave," he said. "Those are my orders as your relief, Commo-dore Tassanna-Ay-Arracca's orders as your direct superior, and Cap-i-taan Reddy's orders as Supreme Comm-aander of all Allied Forces and the high chief of your claan." Chack's tail whipped behind him, casting a shadow on a splinter-torn deckhouse like a writhing snake. "In case you are wondering, considering the . . . defi-aant way in which you initiated this aaction, these orders in no way reflect their disapproval of whaat you did," he continued more softly, blinking complete sincerity. "Quite the opposite. I understaand you're to be promoted, in faact." He smiled, revealing sharp canines reflecting red from the distant flames. "You may haave heard we recently aaq-uired a slightly laarger, more powerful ship, thaat desperately needs an experienced crew."

"*Savoie*?" Russ breathed. "Shit! I can't handle a damn *battleship*!"

Chack gestured around. "I dis-aagree, and so does Cap-i-taan Reddy." He gave a very human shrug. "If you caan't, there's certainly no one else who caan, and you—and your surviving crew—have the most experience in the closest thing we've had."

Russ gazed around, speechless. "But . . . to leave her," he murmured at last.

"She ain't a ship anymore, buddy," Silva said, gently for him, "she's a fort—a knife right in the lizards' guts, thanks to you. Now they're gonna give you a big-ass *sword* to swing around, so quit whinin'."

"What about me?" came a gruff voice. They turned and saw Lieutenant (jg) Dean Laney following a pair of stretcher bearers helping gather the wounded on deck. Pam and her division had immediately gone to *Santy Cat*'s sickbay and begun organizing with Kathy. Laney's face was red and glistening under a shiny layer of the curative polta paste. His arms and hands beyond where his rolled-up sleeves had been were wrapped in loose bandages.

Silva's face twisted into a beatific grin. "Why, if it ain't the spook o' Dean Laney, the biggest, fattest asshole in the Asiatic Fleet! You here to haunt me?"

"There ain't no Asiatic Fleet no more—an' I ain't no goddamn ghost."

"Good," Silva said, his tone darkening. "Then you get to stay here with me, rifle in hand, fightin' the numberless hordes o' evil." He paused and his good eye narrowed. "Just like old times, right?"

Laney looked away, but Russ spoke up. "If I go, I want him. *Savoie*'s going to need an engineering officer too."

Laney stared at Chappelle as if in shock. He was even more stunned to see Monk reluctantly nod agreement.

"Hey," Monk murmured aside at Horn. "What was that between Silva and Laney?"

"Long story," Horn whispered back between his teeth. "From before the old war, back in China." Absently, he reached for the tooth under his shirt, dangling from a leather thong around his neck. "You know they used to be pals, right? Well . . . not anymore. Just as well Laney's getting off this busted tub. I doubt the Grik would have a chance to get him."

Monk frowned. "I used to feel the same way. Now? I dunno."

"There you are, you dumb ox," Pam snapped at Laney when she appeared behind another stretcher case. "Kathy was askin' about you. Said you had a talk comin'." She grinned expectantly. "Wouldn't want to be in your shoes if she's pissed!"

For reasons no one could understand, Dean Laney suddenly smiled. "No," he said, "I wouldn't either."

Chappelle stiffened, eyes catching the arrival of small boats in the water bearing survivors from the sunken prize cruisers. "Those . . . there are *Grik* in those boats!" He turned to a Marine manning a machine gun at the rail nearby, but Lawrence stopped him. "Don't shoot!" he said. "Yes, there are Grik. They are engineers in the cruisers, *our* cruisers . . ."

Russ looked at him incredulously.

"Long story," Silva said, unconsciously echoing Horn.

The transfer went as quickly as possible, but the sound of Grik airships forced them to shut off the searchlight. Apparently, Chack had been right, and the smoke and darkness hid them sufficiently that only a few bombs were even dropped, lashing the south side of the river and the shore beyond. Visibility must've been fine up high, because several airships fell to fighters off *Arracca*. The *Nosey* moved away, full of wounded and *Santy Cat*'s crew. If all went as planned, she'd transfer her cargo to *Arracca* and be back by dawn, or a little later, along with her lightly damaged consort, USS *Ris*, meaning "Chin." *Ris* took *Itaa*'s place and pumping operation and began removing the rest of the wounded before off-loading more supplies, all while the little group continued to discuss the battle—and what came next. One by one, strangely reluctant it seemed, Monk, Laney (with assistance), and finally Russ left to gather their meager possessions, and then returned.

Generators and drums of gasoline were shifted, along with new, smaller, tripod-mounted searchlights to replace those lost. Water butts, cases of rations, medical supplies, and more ammunition—all things that would hopefully sustain them for a while—came across. "Great! More mortar bombs," Gutfeld exclaimed, watching crates come aboard. Others had already arrived, but some had been lost on the sunken cruisers, and he never felt like he could have enough. This particularly since they knew the Grik would be back, probably in great swarms of galleys. And given the losses they'd suffered, there was every expectation they'd break with tradition and try a night assault at some point.

"Some of those are new," Chack told him with a predatory smile. "I think you'll like them." Gutfeld nodded, now watching the last of *Santa Catalina*'s crew go over to *Ris*. He and his Marines would stay, even those who'd been through so much already, and he had to be somewhat envious of those leaving. "Sure," he said. "Can't wait to try 'em. What do they do?"

"I guess it's down to us," Monk said, glancing around while Chack talked to Gutfeld. *Santa Catalina*'s future, such as it was, was no longer their responsibility and he was focused on her past, what she'd achieved, and what she meant to him. Kathy McCoy was personally helping Laney across to the *Ris*, and Monk was sure tears had joined the shiny paste on the man's blistered face.

"Yeah," Russ agreed, also looking around, seeing the same things as his XO, but different things as well. *Santy Cat* had been his, practically since they found her and refloated her. She'd made him what he'd become, just as surely as she'd turned Dean Laney into a man. But he and Monk and Laney had saved her first, and made her what she'd become as well. Then they'd used her up. Somehow, though, he didn't think she minded. They'd never refloat her after *this*; she was too far gone. But she still had a critical, different part to play, just as they did, and he decided that was probably how it ought to be. Finally, with a deep sigh, he turned and clumsily handed Silva a rectangular wooden case. "That's Captain Reddy's pistol," he said huskily. "You remember—the one we found on this old girl so long ago. It's an old Colt revolver that Baalkpan Arsenal thought about copying before we settled on 1911s. They polished off the rust, dolled it up, and nickel plated it as a gift to the skipper, but he said it should stay with the ship." He gestured around. "Like you said, she isn't really a ship anymore, but one thing Captain Reddy promised me was that if things ever got bad enough that I was down to counting on that old pistol, he'd do his damnedest to get here before it ran out of ammo." He paused. "There's fifty rounds in the box."

Silva hefted the case. He'd admired the Colt back when they were trying to copy it, and it had been his input that made them decide on the easier-to-manufacture 1911s. Even so, the allure of the six-shooter and powerful .44-40 cartridges it fired had been attractive. That he had it back here made him feel . . . odd. "Sure," he said, and grinned. "Thanks. I'll take care of it, though I doubt the skipper'll feel bound to that same promise when it comes to me!"

Russ and Monk shook hands all around and finally went aboard *Ris*. When the battered cruiser backed away and vanished in the smoky darkness, Chack stood slightly apart, tail lashing. He was now in complete command to a degree even Silva couldn't argue with. "Very well," he said loudly. "Let's finish stowing all these supplies and rigging the protective plates." They'd brought more armor plates from Kurokawa's stockpile on Zanzibar. They were all fairly small, just a few hundred pounds each, and might've been meant for the raised scantlings on his cruisers. They were perfect for lining these rails, even rigging overhead cover from shell fragments. "Make sure the raa-dio sets are as well protected as possible, and as far from one another as praac-tical. I don't intend to lose communications. Otherwise"—he paused—"those of you who saw aac-tion today, get some rest. I doubt the Grik will come again tonight. Even they can't absorb repeated thraashings like you gave them. Nor do I think they'll come with the dawn, but their rockets might—and we must be ready. Aaf-ter that? We must be ready for anything."

Just as Naxa had warned, Jash was summoned aboard the monstrous greatship *Giorsh* as the bloody dawn caught him leading his leaking, decimated little flotilla weakly past it, heading upriver in search of a place to beach the shattered galleys before they sank. Naxa, to his obvious resentment, was also required aboard *Giorsh* as Jash's senior subordinate First. "They will destroy us *both* for what you did," he seethed, sure he was already doomed, and disdainful of Jash's wrath. Jash said nothing, actually agreeing, and wasn't even angry at Naxa's outburst. One after the other, they climbed the rope ladder to an open port near the center of the thickly armored casemate of the flagship and stepped inside.

"Continue upriver," a First of One Hundred called down to *Slasher*, confirming their fate in Jash's mind. He'd never see his warriors or his brave little galley again.

"Destroyed!" Naxa hissed low. The officer turned to them and said, "Follow me."

The First led them forward along the heavy-beamed lower gundeck, past massive cannon dwarfing the one *Slasher* had borne. Uul sailors and gunners stared as they passed, observing their appearance with indifferent eyes. Jash wished he could've freshened himself, even for this. His tunic and armor were stained black-red with blood and burned gunpowder, and the bloody gash on his arm had begun to throb. A stairway appeared before them in the gloom—there were few lamps—and the officer led them up it, and then another stair ascending from the next gundeck above. Finally, they found themselves in a compartment with inward sloping sides, probably near the top of the armored casemate. It was full of busy Hij, drawing pictures on thin, rigidly stretched and trimmed skins. At a glance, Jash recognized the pictures as maps, like he'd seen during training, only these depicted the wreckage-strewn, watery battlefield beyond the bend. None of the Hij met his gaze.

Stopping in front of a heavy wooden door with guards on either side, the officer scratched loudly on it. "They are here, Lord General," he said through a small grating.

"Send them," came the reply.

Looking significantly at his charges, the officer opened the door and gestured inside. Instead of following, however, he merely closed the door behind them. Jash and Naxa caught the slightest glimpse of the general, seeing only his short red cape and brilliantly polished armor, before flinging themselves to the deck.

"You cannot know me, but I am Second General Ign, Supreme Commander—after Regent Champion First General Esshk, of course—of all the Ghaarrichk'k armies," came a gruff voice. "Rise," it continued, and to Jash's amazement, it might've even held a touch of amusement. "I have been where you are and have not the time or desire to prolong your uncertainty."

Glancing at each other with wide eyes, Jash and Naxa stood and discovered for the first time that they were alone with the general. Ign turned and regarded them with an intense, orange-eyed stare. "Without reflection, without thought, answer me at once: Why did you withdraw from the battle, causing others to do the same?"

"Because Senior Jash ordered it," Naxa blurted.

Jash blinked, the answer so obvious to him, but realized he had better speak. "Lord General, the battle was over."

"It was not! It continued for several hand-spans," Ign countered emphatically. "Not only why, but *how* could you, a mere Senior First, *choose* to go against your orders?"

"With my utmost worship, Lord, *our part* in the battle was over long before we retired." Jash paused. "It might even be said that it was over before it began." He straightened as far as his forward-leaning posture allowed. "I did not go against my orders. I obeyed them fully—until it was no longer possible to continue. In the meantime, highly trained members of the New Army were being destroyed to no purpose and I . . . I *did* take it upon myself to preserve as many warriors as I could. Not only so they would not turn prey, but so they would be available to fight again. Perhaps"—he hesitated again—"in a fashion more consistent with their training."

"It was not for you to decide how any warriors, new or otherwise, should be used," Ign snapped, teeth clacking.

"No, Lord," Jash agreed, lowering his eyes to the deck. "But new commands were needed and none were forthcoming. We were taught that in battle, particularly against *this* prey, commanders can sometimes be slain. In such cases, a new thing must happen; junior officers must be prepared to take up their leader's sword, become leaders themselves, and continue the fight."

Ign seemed to consider that. "True, in principle, but not only has that never yet occurred—until today—but you did *not* continue the fight!"

"Not today, Lord General. As I said, our part in the battle was done. We could no longer kill the enemy. We could only continue to die. I did what I thought I must to ensure that as many warriors as I could influence would survive to fight *tomorrow*."

It was Ign's turn to stare, eyes wide. "Indeed?" he said, then shook his head. "Quite remarkable." He snorted something like a derisive laugh. "It is clear to me that you recognize the battle today was a fiasco—which it was, in many ways—and may even wonder why *I* have not been destroyed." Ign was right. That question *had* occurred to Jash. "The answer is simple, really. Though the initial plan was mine, First General Esshk was not only in personal, direct command, but he altered the plan in certain unfortunate ways. These included pushing it forward in the face of confusion and poor coordination. The arrival of additional enemy elements was unforeseen, but would have made no difference if the *Santa Catalina* had been more quickly destroyed."

Ign's eyes narrowed. "Do not interpret this . . . explanation as criticism of the First General. He is the greatest living general of the Race and the finest Regent Champion we could ever hope for." He swiped at the air with his claws as if fighting an unseen enemy. "But all this is so new, everything we do or face these days. Newer even than Esshk can absorb at times." He paused. "And it *takes* time to adjust, I know full well. As do you, it seems." Ign's nostrils flared above his sharp front teeth, and he took a long breath. "Thankfully, we have the numbers for time. More numbers still, thanks to your quick thinking, Senior. And the making of good officers such as you *proves* that time remains our asset, not the enemy's."

Jash was dumbfounded. He'd come aboard expecting to be destroyed, not praised. He was almost unable to follow the Second General's next words. "And the attack was not a complete fiasco. The primary target, the *Santa Catalina*, was immobilized, if not destroyed. That alone might have ensured victory if not for the arrival of other enemy ships. We could have simply sent the Final Swarm past it in the dark. Still costly, perhaps, but acceptably so. Unfortunately, we can apparently get no other large warships through the entanglement of wrecks, to protect the Swarm from water or sky while it remains in the confines of the river. The enemy cruisers alone might run the galleys down and smash them in their hundreds! First General Esshk believes too much of the Swarm would be slaughtered before it disperses at sea." Refocusing on Ign's words and tone, Jash got the distinct impression the Second General had advocated that course regardless, and Esshk had overruled him. Ign practically confirmed it when he continued. "The First General is emphatic that *Santa Catalina* be overwhelmed. He believes concerted efforts toward that end will draw the enemy cruisers to its aid and concentrate them, where our rockets, gun galleys, even assault galleys, may destroy them as well. The enemy cruisers are just like ours and are vulnerable to rockets, the smaller cannon, even firebomb throwers."

Jash was watching Ign carefully now and was astonished to hear uncertainty, possibly even disagreement, in his tone. "It will be some time before another attack can be prepared," Ign went on. "As you observed, there was great loss and disarray. Your *Slasher* and the rest of the galleys you preserved will be repaired, but you will not join the next attacks in the river. Those will be"— Ign's jaws clacked the equivalent of a frown—"more old-fashioned affairs, performed by warriors better suited to such tactics. Instead, Senior Jash, you are henceforth elevated to the rank of First of Ten Hundreds, 'Ker-noll,' as it has come to be known. I will need such as you when we finally break out and smite the enemy at the Celestial City itself. The galleys and warriors you saved are yours, plus however many more it takes to complete your complement. Train your warriors well, however you see fit." He stared hard at Jash again, the seriousness of his expression plain. "Do not think, because of this, that you are free to become *too* creative, but I expect great things of you, Ker-noll Jash. Do not disappoint me."

"Am I to be Senior First now?" Naxa prodded as they rumbled down the stairs to the lower gundeck. Naxa's sudden cheerfulness was in stark contrast to his earlier mood.

"Perhaps," Jash temporized, thinking. He was relieved, of course, but also troubled, both by his new responsibility and the fact that he and his force would be out of the fighting for a time. And even as he thought he'd had enough combat to last him awhile, he was somehow senselessly disappointed that he couldn't return to it at once. The battle—the sheer waste of it all—had simultaneously repulsed and thrilled him. *Is that normal?* he wondered. *Yes. Certainly for Uul. But they would have been slain out of hand for doing as I did. I was promoted. Clearly, to Second General Ign at least, the New Army* does *have more value than Uul. But what of First General Esshk? Ign said he'd changed the plan, probably including the part most costly to us.* Then he had a more troubling thought. *Why did Ign even tell me that, despite his protestations on Esshk's behalf? It makes no sense. And does General Esshk know of my elevation? What will he do if he did not, and later discovers it?* Jash flicked the thought away. *NOT for me to concern myself with. I am a ker-noll now, a First of Ten Hundreds! I will soon have more than enough to worry about.*

"Prepare a boat," Jash instructed the First of One Hundred who'd greeted them so perfunctorily, only barely suppressing the urge to flare his short crest in dominance and rub the First's snout in it. "I must return to my command."

CHAPTER 16

////// 2nd Fleet Allied Expeditionary Force (AEF)
Army of the Sisters
Sister's Own Division
December 12, 1944

The architecture of the Dominion city of Dulce was different from any of the other places the Allies had been, down the entire Pacific coast of South America. Other cities used as much adobe as stone, and few buildings were made with any apparent desire to impress. The *alcalde*'s palace at Guayak had boasted a few arches and some stacked, square columns, but even the Temple of God had been plain on the outside, usurped from local, less-demanding faiths. But seaport or not, Guayak was on the frontier of the Dominion, as were cities to the south, and hard-line Dominion control and intolerance of earlier cultures had been asserted only within the last generation there. Strict Dominion control of Dulce and points northwest (probably all the way to the desert hell just south of the NUS), and eastward down the northeast coast of the continent, at least as far south as the mouth of the Amazon River, had been in effect for 150 years. All was ruled from the Templo de los Papas in the Holy City of New Granada, twelve hundred miles away.

Dulce, like all cities "beloved by God and His Supreme Holiness," it was said, was made of intricately fitted, carved, and painted stone. Most of the long, narrow buildings were geometrically arranged around a great central square and had two stories. In the middle of the square was a stepped pyramid temple, at the top of which people were routinely "brought to grace" by the Blood Cardinal, with the help of his priests. In other words, it was the place where slaves, prisoners, and pretty much anyone out of favor with the church was tortured to death for the edification and entertainment of the faithful masses.

Dulce would've been a tough nut to crack from the sea. Two large fortresses protected the fine, deep harbor the city encompassed, but it obviously never occurred to anyone that an enemy might attack by land. Only a hastily erected wooden palisade protected against such an approach, and at the moment, Major Blas, Sister Audry, Arano Garcia, and Captain Ixtli were standing on the top of a low hill three miles away, watching the palisade—and a gratifying quantity of other inflammables—burn.

Six hundred yards to their left, from the top of another hill, four batteries of twelve-pounder "Naa-po-leons"—twenty-four guns in all—spat sparkling tongues of fire into the moonless night. Fused case shot traced sputtering arcs across the sky and flashed brightly over the city, followed by a continuous low rumble of thunder. This was maintained by the three other grand batteries similarly situated at other commanding points, not to mention the hundred mortar tubes adding their weight to the barrage.

"They're over here, Gener-aal," they heard, and First Sergeant Spook and a Vengadore private led a mounted General Shinya and several Impie officers to their vantage point. They saluted as the visitors dismounted, and Shinya left the Impies holding the horses. "As you were, my friends," he said.

"Good evening, General Shinya," Sister Audry said.

"Colonel," he replied. "Colonel Garcia. Captain Ixtli." He allowed a wry smile to touch his lips. "Major Blas."

"We goin' in there tomorrow?" Blas demanded without preamble.

"Colonel Dao Iverson will attack with the Sixth Imperial Marines, the Eighth Maa-ni-la, and the Third Frontier Regiment." Frontier troops were somewhat irregular volunteers from the Imperial colony of Saint Francis. Most were armed with standard Allin-Silva breechloaders now, but some still carried massive weapons designed to take down the huge, dangerous continental fauna that haunted the vicinity of their colony. Their discipline left a lot to be desired, but their tenacity in battle didn't.

"Sure thaat'll be enough?" Blas asked skeptically.

Shinya nodded. "More than sufficient by then. Reconnaissance has revealed fewer than two thousand Dom troops in the city. They were probably a local garrison, primarily artillerymen, trained to man the heavy guns in the forts—few of which can be moved or brought to bear on our assault." He stroked the sparse mustache he'd begun cultivating on his upper lip. "I'm actually surprised the city wasn't abandoned. Indications from General Ansik-Talaa, approaching Puerto Limon, are that it's being evacuated by sea."

"They cannot do that here, with your fleet offshore," Captain Ixtli observed.

"No," Shinya agreed. "But I'd expected them to retreat north, toward Corazon, or at least Puntarenas or Nicoya. Those are the last two strongholds between here and the Pass of Fire. Our scouts"—he nodded at Ixtli—"are convinced that Corazon and also Aguas Rapidas are already packed to overflowing with refugees." He paused. "And perhaps as many as one hundred thousand troops."

"Swoo!" said First Sergeant Spook, a word many Lemurians had adopted to simulate an impressed whistle. X and XI Corps together numbered only sixty thousand, now including more than seven thousand local volunteers. 2nd Fleet had another thirty thousand Imperial Marines embarked or on the way—the last of their reserves—which would become XV Corps when it landed.

"The Maker only knows how many civilians will be there," Blas said thoughtfully.

"And most will be willing combatants as well," Ixtli stated grimly.

Engines rumbled in the darkness and firebombs erupted in the city below, largely concentrated in apparent assembly areas behind the palisade. Shinya saw Sister Audry cover her mouth with her hands as more and more of the antipersonnel bombs exploded and Nancys off *Maaka-Kakja*, *Raan-Goon*, and *New Dublin* bathed the city with fire.

"I do not like the merciless aspect of war against the Dominion any more than the rest of you," Shinya said through his perpetual frown. "We may as well be fighting Grik instead of people. But as Captain Ixtli reminds us, there are few noncombatants among the enemy. They certainly don't differentiate between ours." He pointed at the city, now bright with lurid red flames. "They should've evacuated. They couldn't have hoped to stop us here. Instead, they chose to slow and bleed us—and they will—but not enough to matter. There aren't any lizardbirds, and our planes can attack unimpeded. Finally, with a sufficient supply of ammunition from the fleet, our artillery can bombard the city without pause. No solid shot will be used, except against walls and palisades. That should provide a minimum of rubble cover for the enemy to resist our final assault. It's scheduled to begin in two days."

"Why go in at all?" Blas asked. "Why waste lives? With unlimited aammo, we could just flaatten the joint."

"Or go around?" Sister Audry suggested, horrified by the suffering below. She imagined she could almost hear the screams of burning children.

"That would leave a concentrated, hostile force in our rear," Shinya said. "And relying entirely on bombardment will take too long. Even while Colonel Iverson conducts the bombardment and assault, the rest of the army will press on. Iverson will rejoin as soon as Dulce is secure." He clasped his hands behind him. "I suggest you all try to get some sleep. I hope to increase our pace as much as the more difficult terrain ahead will allow." He started to turn away.

"I'm surprised you aren't using the Sister's Own Division for the aass-ault," Blas said acidly. "We've got every other shitty job you've come up with." The others were surprised by her bald statement, but it was significant that no one chastised her for it, even Sister Audry.

Shinya looked at Blas, his narrow eyes unblinking in the glow of the distant destruction. "Believe it or not, I understand your sentiment. But every competent workman—or general—uses his very best tools for the task at hand." His gaze passed to Garcia, Ixtli, Sister Audry, and then back to Blas. "And I'm saving you for Corazon." He took a deep breath while that sank in. "Hopefully, by then, conditions will have changed. Our attack there will be a joint operation involving Second Fleet and everything that remains at our disposal. It's even *hoped* the New US will finally do their part and launch a simultaneous attack on Boca Caribe on the east side of the Pass of Fire, preventing the enemy from reinforcing their fleet on this side of the pass." He shook his head. "I won't count on that, however. I'm sure Lieutenants Reynolds and Faask are doing their best to hurry our new allies along, but my expectations are low. Perhaps now that Captain Garrett and USS *Donaghey* have joined them, the NUS can be better persuaded of the urgency for haste and how fleeting this opportunity might be." Nodding, he turned back to where his horse was waiting. "We resume the march at oh four thirty," he called over his shoulder.

"Another long daamn day," First Sergeant Spook grumped.

Blas nodded down at burning Dulce. "Longer for them."

USS Matarife
South of Puerto Limon
December 12, 1944

The former Dom frigate USS *Matarife* crept carefully inshore southwest of the enemy port city of Puerto Limon. The sky was dark and overcast, so even if there'd been a moon it wouldn't have betrayed them. Approaching such a rocky shore with only captured charts of unknown accuracy was another matter, however, and Greg wasn't sure the low visibility was a good trade. Then again, since they couldn't broadcast their friendly intentions, they might be in more danger from their own people than the enemy. They'd seen tall columns of smoke all the previous day, marking XI Corps' line of advance as they paralleled the mountainous coast. Once they were even fired on by a battery of what looked like Impie field artillery clattering down to the beach and unlimbering on the gravelly sand. *It was a dumb move,* Greg Garrett thought. *If we'd been Doms, we could've wiped that battery out with* Matarife's *bigger, more numerous guns.* They'd drawn away instead. No doubt the artillerymen proudly reported repulsing a heavy Dom frigate, and Greg just hoped General Ansik didn't have any aircraft on call. If they appeared, their only defense would be to run up the Stars and Stripes and hope their flag would save them— but that could also undermine their reconnaissance mission if any Doms happened to notice. They were probably safe from that here. Doms ashore would have trouble spreading the word, and few enemy ships had been sighted, mostly far out to sea.

Either way, the battery proved that XI Corps was on the prowl within twenty miles of the big Dom port, and the Nancy would at least have some friendly troops below if it ran into trouble. Greg wondered if General Ansik would keep pushing all the way to Puerto Limon, and whether he'd been given the word to attack the place or not.

"Six faaddoms!" came the muted cry from forward, where 'Cats were heaving the lead.

"Very well," Greg said, trying to judge the distance to shore. It looked to be about a quarter of a mile, but it was hard to tell. "We'll anchor here," he told Mak.

"Ay, ay, sur," replied his XO, immediately calling for the sails to be taken in and the anchor released. "Aanchor prob'ly won't hold on this bottom," he advised.

"It won't have to for long. I only plan to be here long enough to see our flyers on their way. Put the Nancy in the water as soon as you're ready, if you please."

The anchor splashed and the ship slowly swung around downwind, away from shore. Sure enough, the anchor started to drag, but it would arrest their progress sufficiently. A boom rigged specifically for the purpose dipped toward the Nancy, which had only been brought on deck, assembled, and fueled after dark. Greg watched the shadowy shapes of men working under the supervision of his own petty officers. Most of *Matarife*'s crew were members of the NUS Navy at present. It wouldn't do to have 'Cats running all over the ship when they poked their noses in the Pass of Fire. But though the Nussies were all experienced sailors, they'd never launched an airplane before, and Greg hoped they wouldn't damage the fragile craft.

"Easy there, you tailless freaks!" shouted Chief Bosun's Mate Jenaar-Laan, his rough voice carrying throughout the ship. Greg winced, sure he'd be heard onshore. "I'll poke a hole in every one o' you fishy-skinned, furless baas-tards for every hole you poke in that plane! Belay there! It's staart-in' to spin!"

"Boatswains are the same in every navy, and regardless of their species, it would seem," Captain Anson remarked with amusement, appearing beside Greg with Fred and Kari.

"I guess," Greg agreed distractedly as the Nancy swayed out over the water. Finally, the boom lowered and its hull kissed the relatively calm wave tops, and he started to relax.

"Okay," Fred huffed. Understandably, he'd been at least as concerned as Greg. "I guess we're up," he said. The few belongings they'd take were already in the plane. These amounted to Blitzerbug SMGs and several magazines for each, a single change of clothes, and food and water. With a third passenger and extra fuel, they'd even removed the .30-caliber machine gun from the nose. Fred hadn't been too sorry to see it go, since he'd never flown with one, anyway, and his plane would be nose-heavy enough as it was.

"Be careful," Smitty Smith told them. "Dulce's closest, and with part of Second Fleet parked in the harbor, landing there should be safe enough. Last chatter we picked up, before splitting off from *Donaghey*, was all about a fight brewing in the city, though." He shrugged in the darkness. "Up to you. But you should have enough fuel to make Manizales. It's a good ways back from the front, and that's where the bulk of the fleet still is."

"That's our primary destination," Fred confirmed. "We'll only divert to Dulce if we have to."

Kari raised a board with a chart pasted to it. It was the most up-to-date they had, combining certainty with Anson's best guesses. They knew Second Fleet had compiled much better charts now, and bringing back copies would be a priority. "We'll get there," Kari said. "If we ever get going," she added.

"Yes, the time has come," Anson agreed. He looked at Greg. "Honestly, though, what do you think your chances are of managing the second part of your mission?"

Greg scratched the stubble on his chin. He'd have to shave twice a day to fully tame it. "Pretty good, or I wouldn't risk my people." He glanced at the rigging surrounding them. "We had to rig *Matarife* back like she was so the Doms wouldn't catch on too quick. That's a shame, because the changes made her faster. Other than that, her quarterdeck and poop are too high, her bow's too bluff, and her foremast is raked too far forward. Compared to *Donaghey*, she's a slug—but she's still faster than anything we're likely to meet. If the wind is kind, that includes Dom steamers. Still, our best bet is to keep the enemy thinking we're all on the same side. The ex-Dom sailors who came over to us should help with that—if they're on the level," he added worriedly. He'd never trust a Dom officer—of any age—again, but the Nussies swore the common sailors they captured were another matter. Almost invariably, as soon as they realized their enemies weren't the monsters they'd been conditioned to believe they were and their own officers were the true monsters in comparison, they were happy to become devoted residents of the NUS. A surprising number even joined the NUS Navy. Considering what would happen to them if they were recaptured, that took more guts than could easily be imagined.

With a final farewell, Kari and Captain Anson dropped down in the forward cockpit of the Nancy, squirming to adjust their parachutes and get as comfortable as possible on the modified wicker seat. Anson displayed uncharacteristic concern when Kari helped him with the parachute straps. He was thrilled by the idea of flying for the first time, but it hadn't occurred to him that he might have to jump from the plane for some reason. "Don't worry, Cap-i-taan," Kari told him. "Naancys are very reli-aable. An' if it does craap out, we prob'ly won't jump, anyway." She pointed at the wing struts, engine, and propeller behind them. "Ridin' it down is safer sometimes."

Fred slid down the lifting line onto the wing and unfastened the hooks. Then he dropped into the aft cockpit, turned on the fuel and the ignition, and primed the carb. "Contact!" he called, rising to grasp the pusher prop in front of him. He propped the engine awkwardly, unaccustomed to what was usually Kari's job. He finally managed it without mulching himself and then strapped himself in. With a last wave at those watching on *Mata-rife*, he gunned the engine, and the plane wallowed away from the ship, blowing spray off the wavetops. Soon, the Nancy was lost in the darkness, and the only thing Greg could see was the blue exhaust flare and the phosphorescent wake churning around the hull. Finally, the engine roared and the wake began to race away to the northeast, disappearing entirely when the Nancy bounced into the sky. Greg raised his telescope and followed the glowing exhaust as it circled around and headed west-southwest over the beach, the jungle, and the mountains beyond.

"God help them," he said as the engine noise receded. Fred and Kari would suffer at least as much as any Dom defectors if they were forced down and found themselves in the hands of the enemy again, and it was clear the Doms knew about Anson. God knew what imaginative misery he'd endure if caught. "All hands, stand by to get underway. Let's have the staysails on her, Chief Laan. We'll weigh anchor as soon as she has some headway on her."

"Cap-i-taan!" called Mak-Araa. "Look at the shore!" Greg raised his glass again and caught a series of lights flashing at them from the beach. "It's a Morse lamp!" he exclaimed, surprised.

"Yah. Did you caatch what it said?"

"No, but I think it's repeating." A signal-'Cat joined them and they watched as the flashing continued, the 'Cat pronouncing the words as they came. "I'll be damned," Greg said. "They want us to send a boat ashore!"

"They sent the proper code prefix," Mak observed skeptically.

"Yeah. I guess the enemy might've gotten it somehow, but that's no Dom on the lamp. The signal's too sure." He paused. "And there's no warning prefix. But it does carry the 'urgent message' suffix." He came to a decision. "Send the appropriate countersign and have them stand by," he told the signal-'Cat. "Call away the whaleboat," he added. "You take it in, Mr. Mak, with half a dozen armed sailors. And don't bring more than two visitors back."

"Ay, ay, Skipper."

It took almost an hour for the whaleboat to be prepared and manned, motor through the brisk surf close to the rocky beach, and then return. It was so dark, Greg suspected Mak was being extra careful, but it was past 0300 now, and he wanted to be far from shore when the sun came up. Lieutenant Mak was obviously of the same mind, because he practically bounded aboard, followed by two men in the mottled camouflage garb of General Ansik's XI Corps. They saluted Greg.

"Captain Andreis," said the taller of the two, with a thick brown beard and the usual long Imperial mustaches. "C Battery, Eighth New Britain Artillery, at your service," he said. "An' me companion is Lieutenant Robbins, First Battalion, Twenty-First Imperial Marine Regiment. We, ah, was the ones that fired on ye earlier today, thinkin' ye was a bloody Dom. When we saw how slow ye was creepin' along the coast, we hoped ye'd anchor nearby. We scampered ahead tae catch ye, plannin' tae have another crack at ye with the dawn."

"Then we're both fortunate you thought better of it," Greg said wryly. "But what made you realize we weren't Doms?" he asked.

"General Ansik told all forces advancin' along the coast tae watch fer an Allied ship. USS *Donaghey*, in point o' fact." He waved around. "But this's a Dom frigate if ever there was one. We never thought she might be otherwise until ye dropped a Nancy in the water an' it took off. The Doms got no Nancys."

"Very well. I can accept that. But what 'urgent message' do you have for us?"

"Two things, sir, an' a request. First, we have wireless communications, an' whatever yer mission, we can pass word tae General Shinya. The Doms already know where we are." Andreis shrugged. "Aye, an' *ye* can send from here for that matter, an' none'll be the wiser, if ye have wireless gear aboard. I assume this ship's a prize?"

"She is, and we don't. I may take you up on your offer. We've been avoiding transmissions in case the League is listening."

"We suspected as much, an' a clever precaution it is. We saw a big steamer on the horizon just three days ago, headin' south-southeast. A lethal-lookin' bugger she was too, bigger than the dear *Walker*, which I seen when she first came tae New Scotland. She had to be a Leaguer, consortin' with the Doms, an' ye'll need tae keep a watch fer her."

Greg looked meaningfully at Mak. "They're getting bolder in this hemisphere," he said. He looked back at Andreis. "Is that all?"

"Aye, other than the request. Shinya's given General Ansik permission tae assault Puerto Limon. The defense is scant, much like Tenth Corps found at Dulce, an' control of a port on this coast'll allow the NUS tae land supplies an' troops. I can't think of a better ploy tae help us take the port than if ye brought yer fine Dom frigate in the harbor an' raised the devil with the enemy while we attack from shore. Can ye help?"

Greg rubbed his face. It was tempting, and more in line with how he'd originally hoped to employ *Matarife*. Finally, he shook his head. "I'd love nothing better, Captain, but we have our own mission—that could get chancier than it already is if we're seen helping you and word gets ahead of us."

Andreis couldn't hide his disappointment, but nodded. "Aye. I presume ye'll be tryin' tae have a look at defenses on this side o' the Pass o' Fire? I understand. The advantage this ship'll give ye could quickly expire." He straightened. "In that case, we'll take our leave an' let ye get underway."

"Thanks, Captain, and good luck." Greg extended his hand. A short time later, Mak was taking their new friends back to the beach, along with a message about the Nancy to be sent to Shinya. It didn't take Mak nearly as long the second time, and soon he was back aboard. "Whaat'll we do now?" he asked.

"Accomplish our mission," Greg replied, "which I'm confident we can do—if that damn Leaguer didn't already reverse course and head back where we're going. Let's get underway."

////// *USS* Matarife
Caribbean
December 13, 1944

USS *Matarife* hated the wind anywhere much forward of directly abeam, particularly when the sea was rising and starting to pound her bluff bow. Her high fo'c'sle stayed drier than *Donaghey*'s would have, but taking a direct course, the frankly astonishing leeway she made would've had her aground in a few hours. Greg Garrett had no choice but to tack the ship back and forth in a generally northeasterly direction throughout the night and most of the following day. Lookouts reported an increasing number of ships, but *Matarife* didn't draw any undue attention. With the faded red sails of a warship and her Dom flag, a surprising number of merchantmen actually drew away from her path. The former Doms among the Nussie crewmen said that was because their navy often took prime sailors from their own civilian ships—unless their owners were very rich and powerful.

The wind and seas finally eased toward dark, and *Matarife* shortened sail but continued east for a while before coming about and making for the southern approach to the southeastern side of the Pass of Fire. Hopefully, she'd arrive around dawn.

"Shipping on this wallowing turd makes me appreciate the old *Donaghey* even more," Smitty Smith grumbled, walking the dark quarterdeck with Greg and biting off half of a cigar. Crunching the mouthful into a wad, he put the other half back in his pocket. Greg reflected that there were probably guys in the west, still stuck with Aryaalan tobacco, who might kill Smitty for the rest of that cigar. He'd once been a smoker himself, but couldn't stand Pepper, Isak, and Gilbert's PIG-cigs. That helped him avoid getting readdicted here, where real tobacco was plentiful, so he guessed he owed the squirrelly Mice and their 'Cat partner one. He looked at the sky and saw that the overcast was beginning to clear and occasional stars could be seen.

"She doesn't handle very well, by our standards," Greg agreed, "but she's got teeth." *Matarife* actually threw considerably more iron than *Donaghey* in terms of weight of shot. There were thirty-two 24-pounders on the main gun deck and sixteen 9-pounders on the quarterdeck and fo'c'sle, including a pair of chasers on each. None had been as effective as *Donaghey*'s eighteen- and twelve-pounders, because she hadn't possessed even the rudimentary fire-control system *Donaghey* enjoyed. That was no longer the case. The bronze guns themselves were good quality, meticulously maintained, with smooth, consistent bores. The iron shot was a little less consistent in diameter, but the wads would keep it fairly well-centered in the bores. More important, the same elevation marks had been made on the gun trucks, and windage marks were on the decks behind them. There was a plumb bob in a glass-sided box in the maintop, and an electrical circuit carried current for the primers, which would be inserted in the vents during action.

That had all been the easy part, and would allow *Matarife* to fire relatively well-aimed salvos at a distance instead of indiscriminate broadsides at close range. The hard part was providing sufficient electricity, since *Donaghey*'s little wind-powered auxiliary generators were only intended to charge batteries to run her comm gear. They couldn't make enough juice for the long runs to the guns, and no one wanted to strip *Donaghey*'s main generator, even temporarily. She *had* spares, but there was only one complete engine to power them. The problem was solved by installing one of the spares spun by the engine from Fred and Kari's battered Nancy.

That had caused something of a scene. The plane was in rough shape but could've been fixed, and nobody was happy about gutting it, least of all Fred and Kari. Greg put a stop to the argument, which grew loud enough to cause alarm a surprising distance from the Santiago docks, by roaring, "Have you both forgotten there's a *war on*?" In a lower tone, he'd then promised them *Donaghey*'s plane—to keep.

"It's getting a little lighter," Smitty now said, squinting south, raising an Impie-made telescope. The Nussies had binoculars, but the magnification was poor and their glass wasn't as good. "I bet that's that Boky Kreeb joint on the chart," he said, then consulted the pocket compass now barely visible. "Probably about two, two, zero." He looked at Greg. "Pretty impressive navigation, Skipper, considering all the mushy zigzagging we did, and we never got a good sun sight yesterday."

"Boca Caribe," Greg corrected absently, "and Lieutenant Mak deserves the credit." He still missed Lieutenant Saama-Kera, killed in action, but Mak-Araa was shaping up pretty well. Dawn was coming fast, and Greg looked for himself, quickly finding the focal length of his telescope after long practice.

The Dom city was six or seven miles away and he couldn't see it, especially the shoreline, very well, but all this area was very mountainous and the city crowded high into the foothills. A disconcerting number of local mountains were active volcanoes, especially to the west, probably surpassing Jaava and Sumaatra with their density. Greg didn't know if the haze he was trying to penetrate came from them or the sea. A few lights still flickered in the vanishing darkness and helped outline the masts of ships along the docks or anchored offshore. As the light continued to improve, he saw dark smoke rising from distant funnels. That probably marked them as warships, or at least military transports. Oddly, the first Dom steamers they'd ever seen had been the latter.

Nobody appeared to notice *Matarife* as she passed. If they did, they apparently gave her little thought. It was too far to see signal flags, anyway. *Matarife* sailed on.

The forenoon watch trudged tiredly on deck, and Mak relieved Smitty a few minutes before 0800. "Shoreline'll start crowding us soon as it angles northwest," Smitty warned the XO. "Recommend you come to three, three, zero within the next hour or so." He glanced at the sails. "If the wind'll let you. I don't know what it's going to do. Don't think *it* knows yet. It's getting brisk again, but gusty." He straightened. "I stand relieved," he proclaimed, then slumped again and made his way below. Greg longed for his own bunk after the exhausting tack on tack the day before, but figured things would start to hop as they penetrated deeper into an area the Doms had never allowed anyone to enter. Their captured charts gave them a good idea what to expect in terms of navigation, but nobody had any idea what they'd run into otherwise.

"I missed Bocaa Caa-ribe," Mak said, glancing astern. There were occasional settlements, little more than fishing villages along the coast, but there'd be nothing bigger, as far as they knew, until they saw Rio Grabacion seventy-five miles to the north. The Doms liked big forts, but apparently relied more on their navy to protect this side of the pass.

"Didn't miss much, as far as I could see. We didn't get close. Maybe a squadron of warships. Probably a fort. Strategic position or not, they seem to have some kind of fort at every town big enough to support one."

Mak nodded and swished his tail. "Prob-aably more worried about raids, in the paast, thaan anybody aac-tually trying to take the paass itself."

"Probably. The NUS didn't want it. Hell, *we* wouldn't want it if we didn't need it to link up with the Nussies and whip the Doms. I can imagine advantages to *having* it, if we ever do, the biggest being keeping it away from the damned League."

Greg Garrett probably hated the League even more

than he hated the Grik. After more personal experience with the Dominion, he hated its leaders and depraved culture just as much, but considered the League the biggest long-term threat to all they'd accomplished. Granted, he'd been off the Grik front for a while and knew things were desperate there, but Captain Reddy was there to handle it. Like many in the Alliance, he had much more faith in his former skipper and current clan chief than Matt would've considered appropriate. "We have to keep the League's claws off the pass," he continued. "None of the Allies can stand against them alone. The NUS damn sure can't, and the League'll pick the Nussies off at their leisure if they can keep us out."

Lieutenant Jeremy Ortiz, the officer who came aboard with the NUS sailors and was acting as *Matarife*'s first officer, had joined them. Like most Nussies, he wore thick muttonchops on his cheeks—despite the fact that he looked much too young to support them. *Probably has the same problem I do,* Greg thought, scratching the dark bristle already spreading on his face. Ortiz nodded very seriously. "I agree with your assessment entirely, and admit I believe that our alliance with you now was the result of divine providence."

"I don't know about that," Greg demurred, "but it's a good thing for both of us."

Mak had been quiet, apparently deep in thought. Finally, he spoke, changing the subject. "Cap-i-taan Gaarrett, I under-staand there's some kind of ca-naal near here, made by people, on the world you came from, but nothing like the Paass of Fire. How do you think it got here?"

Greg shrugged. "Who knows? I've heard lots of theories. Courtney Bradford leans toward the notion of a big meteor—a giant rock falling from the sky—way bigger than the ones we see at night. . . ." He hesitated. Many Lemurians believed falling stars were souls sent from the Heavens to inhabit younglings at birth. "Anyway," he continued, "a great big rock, maybe a mile wide, might've hit, fast as a bullet, and blown a hole in the ground. Over thousands, maybe millions of years, the hole washed out and turned into the pass. Mr. Bradford—and others—also think all the volcanoes in the region might've blown their tops all at once and done the same thing."

"That is the consensus of many natural philosophers within the NUS," Ortiz agreed.

Greg rubbed his chin. "Or maybe a smaller meteor lit the fuse on the volcanoes, and that's why there's so many still around?" He shook his head. "I don't know. Not my problem."

"Unless they all blow their top while we're close by," Mak suggested with an edge. "It'd be our problem then."

Greg laughed. "They might, I guess, but I doubt it. Some of the volcanoes on the west coast spew all the time, I'm told. That's why they call it the Pass of Fire. But relax. I figure they're like a pop-off valve on a steam line, making sure the pressure bleeds off before it splits wide open."

Mak chuckled nervously.

As it turned out, *Matarife* had to tack back out into the Caribbean as the wind came around more out of the west. More Dom ships were seen, a few steamers able to sail directly into the wind, making for the pass itself. Greg suspected they were carrying troops and supplies to El Corazon to face General Shinya and Second Fleet when they arrived. He also knew there were only certain times of day they could squirt through with the tidal race, and that was supposed to be an interesting ride. *Maybe some of 'em crack up,* he hoped. The afternoon watch had just come on when the lookout at the masthead warned of dark smoke on the horizon, which quickly resolved into a column of approaching ships. All had red sails furled on their yards.

"Four steamers, staar-board bow, eight t'ou-saand five hunnerd tails—yaads!" came the confirmation. "Dom ships o' the line!"

"Anything smaller? Faster?" Greg called upward.

"There's a sail to the sout'—could be a fri-gaate like us—screenin'. But is too faar. Nuttin' else right now."

Greg was pleased by the report. The 'Cat at the masthead knew exactly what was important to him; whatever the other sail might be, was it in a position to interfere? He paced for a moment in front of another pair of 'Cats at the wheel. Lieutenant Ortiz technically had the conn, but understood that was a courtesy. Still, when Greg suddenly straightened and said, "Steady as you go," Ortiz couldn't hide his surprise.

"But . . . Captain Garrett, we are sailing almost directly at them."

"Yeah, and they're coming right at us. Closing speed's what—maybe twelve knots?"

"About thaat," Mak agreed, blinking curiously at Greg.

"Do you mean to *fight* them?" Ortiz asked incredulously.

A ghost of a smile touched Greg's lips. "I sure hope not. I have every confidence in my crew and the Nussies you brought aboard to fill it out, but we're not here to fight—and four liners against this one dumpy frigate make for slightly longer odds than I prefer. Trouble is, with this west wind, we can go north, south, or anything eastward in between. I want to go north, but if we sheer off now, for no apparent reason, they might get suspicious. We'll *ease* north a bit," he decided, and spoke to the 'Cats at the wheel. "Come left to zero six zero, if you please." He turned back to Ortiz. "I'm betting those liners have someplace to be. Based on their heading, they're probably beefing up the defenses at the pass—on one side or the other. Let's try not to distract them." He scratched his chin. "All the same, let's clear for action, but don't run out the guns." He looked at Mak. "And let's get all the 'Cats out of sight."

Matarife made her slight course correction and her sails were subtly adjusted. Soon it was clear she'd pass to the north of the enemy column, probably just a little beyond the effective range of the Doms' guns—unless they altered course as well. They didn't. When they were just inside two thousand yards, west-northwest of the enemy, the new Nussie lookout cried, "On deck! Signal flags on the lead steamer!"

"We'll reply and see what happens," Greg said. One

of Ortiz's sailors had joined the NUS Navy off this very ship after *Donaghey* captured her. He was still uncomfortable around Lemurians, but grateful for his freedom and a new, less oppressive life. He was also almost pathetically grateful to Greg Garrett personally, despite the action that killed so many of his former comrades. His loyalty and gratitude were particularly appreciated now because he'd been one of very few ordinary seamen aboard *Matarife* who could read and write a little. He'd been learning letters and numbers, essentially striking to become a signalman, and that's why he knew the ship's number and countersign—the appropriate response to the enemy's hoist.

Greg crossed his fingers as the unusual pennants soared up the halyard. *Matarife*'s countersign would probably be out of date, but if the Doms knew her, they'd also know she'd been gone awhile. Instead of cannon fire, different flags replaced the first ones high on the enemy's mizzenmast. Another former Dom, with years of service in the NUS Fleet, quickly conferred with the signalman. "They ask where we are bound."

Greg had expected that, considering the ship probably should've put in at Puerto del Cielo on her return, far to the southeast.

"Tell 'em we were sent straight to Puerto Dominio with dispatches for the *alcalde* there."

Two more flags replaced the first hoist, and Ortiz told Greg the first simply meant "urgent dispatches" and the second was their destination. That was fine with him—if it worked. The two former Doms and Lieutenant Ortiz breathed a collective sigh when a final hoist was seen.

"Essentially, it means 'carry on,'" Ortiz said.

"You know their signals?" Greg asked, surprised.

"Yes. The basic ones we just exchanged haven't changed, in my memory. Somewhat arrogant, don't you think?"

"Kinda stupid, you aask me," Mak interjected, still crouching behind the bulwark, out of sight. Of course, the Grand Alliance had been just as complacent for a while, Greg reflected.

"Fortunate for us, however," Ortiz continued a little harshly. "Had they not accepted the countersign, the only response would have been pursuit, ending with an overwhelming quantity of roundshot."

"Chance we had to take," Greg said, glancing at his watch while the big enemy warships passed to the west, the smell of coal smoke now on the wind. "Don't shorten sail, but let's spill a little wind so it doesn't look like we're slowing down. We can't go much farther east before we turn north or we'll never see . . ." He paused, trying to remember the unfamiliar name.

"Rio Graab-aass," Mak said with a grin, tentatively standing and staring aft.

"Rio Grabacion," Greg corrected, his memory jogged.

By early afternoon, as soon as the enemy squadron was hidden by its own haze on the horizon, *Matarife* turned sharply to three two zero north, with just as much westing as her sails would bear. Ironically, Greg now had to be thankful they'd undone the rig improvements *Donaghey*'s crew had made during the ship's refit, because otherwise they probably would've already been caught. As the afternoon wore on, and the closer they got to Rio Grabacion, the more ships they saw. Most were merchantmen, but there was the occasional sailing warship. They sighted a couple of light craft, rigged like brigs, but also another frigate. All they did in each case was exchange numbers and continue on. Apparently, only higher-ranking Dom officers commanding more powerful ships really cared what they might be up to. Ortiz explained that *Matarife*'s captain might be—probably was—senior to the commanders of anything equal or smaller in size. For them to demand an explanation could be considered a mortal insult. Most likely, their skippers probably thought it odd that *Matarife* didn't demand to know what *they* were doing.

The distant coast had never been entirely lost from view, except occasionally from deck, but it slowly grew into another sharp, hilly shoreline almost identical to Boca Caribe across the bay, channel mouth, gulf—whatever best described it. Soon, even Rio Grabacion could be seen, also situated just like Boca Caribe and extending a considerable distance inland, climbing the terraced flanks of low mountains. The only differences were that there were two forts, one on each side of a narrow river mouth, and there were even more Dom warships at anchor.

"I don't like this," Greg muttered. Smitty, Mak, and Lieutenant Ortiz all stood together, gazing over the fo'c'sle rail. "Counting the probably six or seven liners at Caribe, the four we saw crossing, and the . . . dozen or so here?"

"Looks like fifteen heavies," Smitty supplied. He was on the leeward corner of the fo'c'sle, and he spat over the rail.

"Okay," Greg continued, "but that's still a lot. Twenty-four ships of the line, on this side of the pass."

"Twenty-four at *least*," Mak corrected, "and an unknown number of frigates, steam, and sail. Where are *they*?"

"Right. And who knows what's at Dominio, or dispersed to other ports we hadn't even planned to scout." (Greg had dropped the confusing *rios*, *bocas*, and *puertos*.) "Not to mention what we haven't seen still at sea." He shook his head. "No matter how you cut it, there weren't *supposed* to be as many as we've already spotted. And if there're more here than we figured, what's waiting for Second Fleet on the other side of the pass?"

"Your concern mirrors mine, Captain Garrett," Ortiz pronounced. "The Doms must know the NUS Fleet is massing against them, and that would explain their numbers . . . but only on its face. I should think they'd still be more concerned by the proximity of your Second Fleet in the west, it having already done them such grievous harm and its apparent intentions more obvious. Given the admittedly ponderous nature of past NUS Fleet movements, they can't know how soon we mean to strike—or that we'll coordinate our attack with yours, can they?"

Greg shrugged. "I don't know. Maybe somebody goofed up our recon west of the pass, or whoever's supposed to catch their spies over here isn't getting it done. One way or another, either their fleet's bigger than we ever thought, or they build new ships even faster than the Grik. Or," he continued, scratching his chin, "they don't *need* as many ships in the west, for some reason. Maybe something nasty—"

"On deck!" came a cry from above. "All them liners

up ahead got steam up. Four haas pulled their hooks aan is headin' out torrd us!"

Greg raised his glass again, then gritted his teeth. "Sure enough. They're not buying it and they're coming for us on sight." He glanced at Ortiz. "Nobody to the south or already at sea was suspicious, which can only mean spies from Cuba—at least—got here before us." He snorted. "Should've waited for us to get closer. They could've just blasted us from anchor."

"Prob'ly didn't want us baashin' up the town with stray shot."

Greg nodded. "Maybe. Especially since, with the wind still out of the west, they might be faster than us if we just run with it."

"Which we must, if we still want to see what awaits at Puerto Dominio," Ortiz pointed out.

Greg didn't reply. Ortiz was right, and that final visit remained part of their mission, but Greg was increasingly skeptical of success. Not only would they still come away with only a rough estimate, but if spies had spread the word as far as Rio Grabacion, they'd doubtless already warned Puerto Dominio as well. Greg swore under his breath. One of the things that frustrated him most was that they'd practically wasted *Matarife*—at least in regard to what Greg would've preferred to do with her. But if these Doms already knew they had her, the rest would soon enough, and his original, more adventurous scheme would've been suicide, anyway. It was probably just as well they'd discovered her cover was blown, and at least they'd picked up a little information to ponder.

"We'll try to get a look at Dominio," Greg finally announced, looking at the Nussie runner hanging back behind Ortiz. "Pass the word aft; come right to zero eight zero. And crack on," he added. "Every stitch she'll wear goes aloft. Rig the stuns'l booms."

Provisions for "stuns'ls," or studding sails, were not as conspicuous as the improvements they'd made to the rigging, so they'd kept them in place. *Matarife* had never worn them for her former masters, but they could easily be hoisted and secured to the ends of her yards. Once aloft and properly adjusted, they drew a lot more wind and might be enough to keep them ahead of their pursuers. If not, they'd have to turn southeast and put the wind on *Matarife*'s quarter. That was the only—almost—sure way to outrun the enemy steamers. Then again, maybe not. Who knew what the Doms had been up to? They might've improved their engines. Greg was increasingly positive they'd improved the damaged ships that made it back after the Battle of Malpelo. Probably with armor. Was that why they were so confident in the west? Finding answers to those questions might be the most important thing they could still do.

"Aye, aye, sir!" the messenger said, and hurried aft. Almost immediately, the ship began to turn away from the still distant but now clearly approaching Doms.

The stuns'ls helped, speeding them along at almost seven knots in the moderate airs, but with wind *and* steam, the four Dom liners slowly gained during the long afternoon. Greg pressed on, however, confident the Doms were topped out at their apparent eight knots—and that *Matarife* could make ten with the wind on her quarter if she was forced to veer away from her objective. About 1700 hours, with barely an hour of visibility left, the big bow chasers on the leading Dom ship started trying the range. The first shot fell far short, but her gunners knew their stuff and the line was pretty good. Each successive shot came closer.

"How much farther?" Greg asked Mak. They were back on the quarterdeck, standing near the wheel.

"Eight or ten miles," Mak replied, shaking his head, blinking frustration. "Even if we get there, it'll be daark an' we won't see anything."

"Yeah," Greg reluctantly agreed.

"More smoke fine on the port bow!" cried the lookout. "Bear-een seero four seero! Range ten t'ousaands! Smoke an' two sails. The sails is slaan-teen sout'!"

"They're trying to box us," Smitty said.

Greg pursed his lips and nodded. "I guess that's that. Damned if I know how they cut it so fine. This bunch up ahead must've been sent looking for us from Dominio." A roundshot, probably a twenty-four-pounder from their pursuers, splashed close alongside, wetting them with spray. Greg sighed. "Sound general quarters," he said. The ship had been cleared for action all day. The insistent gonging of the pipe bell commenced, taken up by others amidships and forward, and Marines rattled their drums at the companionways. 'Cats and men raced from below and started preparing their guns. 'Cat Marines, armed with breech-loading Allin-Silvas, climbed the ratlines, and NUS Marines lined the rails with rifle-muskets between the lighter upper deck guns. The four-cylinder engine out of Fred and Kari's Nancy fired up below, spinning up the generator, and Greg motioned Smitty aloft to his station with his eyes.

"We gonna fight 'em now?" Smitty asked over his shoulder, rushing to the shrouds.

"Yeah. A little, at least."

Lieutenant Ortiz had learned a lot about *Donaghey*'s, and now *Matarife*'s, fire-control system, but hadn't seen it in action. That meant he couldn't appreciate what a force multiplier it could be. "We are vastly outnumbered," was all he said.

"Yeah. So? You want to surrender?"

Ortiz's face reddened. "Of course not. But any resistance at this point invites crippling damage. We should steer south and retire now while we can—and before the Dom frigates gain enough to cut us off."

"Relax," Greg told him. "We'll be fine." He shrugged. "Or maybe we won't. But with our primary mission so hashed up, there's one more thing I want to know. Stand by to come right, to one six zero," he called to the 'Cats at the helm. Then he waited while all stations reported manned and ready. Another pair of shot whooshed by, one flapping the main and fore courses as it punched ragged round holes in them. "Get rid of that damn Dom rag and run up our battle flag," he ordered. The Stars and Stripes of the American Navy Clan quickly replaced the red and gold of the Dominion. It was a big flag, easy to see, but unlike *Donaghey*'s, there were no battle names embroidered on its stripes. Besides helping to sink *Atúnez*, this would be *Matarife*'s first action for the Grand

Alliance. "Stand by for surface action starboard," Greg called, and his order was repeated. Finally, he turned to the 'Cats at the wheel and said, "Execute."

The 'Cats quickly spun the wheel, and blocks squealed as sheets were hauled. "Commence firing," Greg called above. Smitty called down elevations through a speaking trumpet. There were no voice tubes on *Matarife*. The elevations were based on his range estimates and were matched to the marks on the carriages. "Fifteen degrees right!" he added, and 'Cats and men shifted their guns with handspikes, matching the marks on the backs of their carriages with those painted on the deck. Ortiz, as acting first lieutenant, had memorized the commands expected of him during drills and now yelled, "Prime!" Gun's crews pricked the charges in the guns through the vents and inserted electric primers.

"Clear!" the gun's crews shouted, stepping away from their weapons.

"All clear!" Ortiz reported. "Battery is ready."

"Firing!" shouted Smitty, waiting for the plumb bob in the glass box to cross the mark that signified the ship was level. Several seconds passed before he was satisfied enough to close the firing circuit. *Matarife* heaved as all her starboard twenty-four-pounders fired in a single instant, spewing jagged tongues of bright yellow fire and a fog bank of white smoke that quickly gushed back over the ship and downwind to port. Greg had plenty of time to focus his glass before a tight pattern of shot shattered the sea a hundred yards short and slightly left of the Dom. *Pretty good,* he thought, *considering the range.* The guns were already being reloaded as youngling Lemurians and Nussie boys brought charges up from below. Smitty was calling corrections. Greg chuckled when he saw the wide-eyed expression on Ortiz's face. *Wish we had some exploding case shot to fit these twenty-fours,* Greg thought. *The range is still a little long for those, but it would really get Ortiz's attention if we blew that Dom out of the water with a single salvo!*

Another pair of Dom chasers crashed in the sea nearby, aft, but *Matarife*'s sudden course change—and the accuracy of her first broadside—had probably rattled the enemy.

"Clear!" came the chorus of shouts from below, shaking Ortiz out of his astonishment. "All clear, battery is ready!" he managed.

"Firing!"

Another broadside salvo vomited from *Matarife*, and Greg watched very closely. Smitty was right on target this time, just a few shot missing the mark completely. The enemy sails shivered violently, and the foremast started to lean. With a gathering rush, it rumbled down, taking the main topmast with it, and the entire, entangled mass plunged into the sea. Immediately, the lead Dom liner veered to port as the wreckage pulled it around.

"Reload?" Ortiz asked. The other three liners had been strung out behind the first but were bunching up now, in disarray. They'd been completely unprepared for how quickly their leader was disabled, not to mention the range at which it was accomplished. A belated, stuttering broadside spat from the crippled Dom as her portside guns were revealed, but their gunners had probably fired without great care on the orders of some outraged officer. None of the shot came close. Greg considered.

"Cease firing," he ordered at last. The one Dom, maybe all four of them, were at their mercy, but knowing the common sailors aboard them were as much victims of the Doms as they were made him shy from wanton slaughter. Besides, he thought he'd seen what he was looking for. "But we'll reload, if you please. There's still a chance we'll have to fight past the frigates running south. I kind of doubt it. The moon won't be up until well after midnight and it'll be dark as hell."

Ortiz stepped briskly back to him. "But, sir . . . that was amazing. We can win a great victory here."

Greg waved to the east. "Those other ships'll be up before long," he cautioned. "We *can't* take 'em all. And we need to get word back about everything we've learned. Part of that, it looked to me, is that Dom liner we hammered had armor plate bolted on."

"Are you certain?" Mak asked.

"No. It could've been the range or the angle, but I saw some of our shot skate off her bow and hit the water. May be nothing, but if they have even thin armor at their bows, think what they might wear over their engineering spaces. On top of everything else, Admiral Sessions—not to mention Admirals Jenks and Lelaa—needs to kick that around."

CHAPTER 18

////// USNRS **Arracca** *(CV-3)*
TF Bottle Cap
Off the Mouth of the Zambezi
December 15, 1944

"   I hope you have a pleas-aant flight," Commodore
       Tassanna-Ay-Arracca told Russ Chappelle, Mikey
       Monk, and Dean Laney as they prepared to step
into the launch floating inside the great carrier's boat bay.
The launch would take them out to the big PB-5D Clipper
floating alongside *Arracca*, and the plane would fly them
directly to Mahe, where *Savoie* now awaited their arrival.
The rest of *Santa Catalina*'s exhausted crew had departed
almost immediately, aboard USS *Ramic-Sa-Ar* and the
battered *Felts*, as soon as she received emergency repairs.
Felts was in no shape to fight or even sail; all her masts
had been shot away. But her hull was essentially sound
and she could steam. *Ramic*'s place in the screen would
be taken by the very last Scott-class steam frigate, USS
Revenge (DD-22). She'd actually been completed after
James Ellis and was the third Allied ship to bear that
proud name.

   "I guess this is it, then," Russ said, extending his hand.
He was anxious to go, yet still somewhat reluctant, and
he looked past Tassanna at his surroundings as if to find
a reason to stay. There was nothing where he was. The

large bay was a holdover from *Arracca*'s life as a sailing Home that hunted gri-kakka for their meat and oil, and the long, narrow boats that chased them had been kept here, ready to race directly out of the ship in pursuit of their prey. It had been an ingenious expedient that allowed quick egress and kept the people from having to stow the boats above, where they'd be in the way, susceptible to deterioration, and would have to be lowered the precarious distance to the water below. Unfortunately, not only did the heavy doors enclosing the space present formidable engineering and time-consuming construction challenges, but they represented a natural vulnerability in the otherwise incredibly stout hull. No large ships were built with them now, and even the very first purpose-built carrier, *Maaka-Kakja*, which otherwise followed traditional hull designs, had dispensed with the boat bay. And there were no gri-kakka boats left in *Arracca*. Instead, a shoal of motor launches floated there, ready for rapid dispatch to floatplanes in distress or the occasional Mosquito Hawk that had to ditch. Quickly getting to those was essential for their pilot's survival in this malicious sea.

Tassanna took Russ's hand and blinked encouragement, correctly gauging his emotions. "Cap-i-taan Reddy needs you, *Saavoie* needs you, and we will all need her when you get her ready to fight."

Russ stared down. "I just . . . It's really hard to leave my ship while she's still fighting."

In addition to the incessant night bombing, which inflicted terrible casualties on the fixed battery that *Santa Catalina* had become, the Grik had finally made another move against her and her cruiser consorts the day before. They'd expected it, and even had photographs of the preparations to look at, taken from a high-flying Nancy and its observer/copilot equipped with a Brownie camera. Brownies had been the most common cameras brought to this world by the crews of *Walker*, *Mahan*, and S-19, and a couple of functioning examples had even been discovered aboard *Santa Catalina*. Steve Riggs, the Minister of Communications and Electrical Contrivances, often in consultation with Enrico Galay, had been in charge of making the 120 film they required. They'd practiced developing techniques on old film in the cameras, and when they were finally successful, the 'Cats had been amazed by images from another world. Steve, Alan Letts, and a few others who'd seen the pictures had experienced almost surrealistic emotions. The worst were when the pictures depicted friends they'd lost, happily posing in front of still-familiar sights in a very different Philippines and China.

In any event, the blurry photos from the "new" equipment allowed Tassanna to warn Chack, and he'd been as ready as he could be when the usual preparatory rocket barrage ended and hundreds of galleys, full of thousands of warriors, swept in to strike with the sunrise. It had been a near-run thing; the cruisers couldn't get between *Santy Cat* and the wreckage-choked river bend to break up the assault with their rams, and modern weapons or not, Chack had his hands full. Particularly when the cannon-armed galleys got close. The absolute worst, however, were the ones equipped with firebomb throwers, which inflicted terrible casualties and left *Santy Cat*'s splintered wooden decks burning far into the night, making her a fine target for Grik zeppelins, which punished her even more. Still, not a single Grik warrior made it aboard, but that was solely due to a profligate expenditure of ammunition on the part of the defenders. Tassanna had dispatched all she could spare upriver—she couldn't leave her fighters helpless against Grik zeps—and was worried there wasn't enough .30-caliber ammunition in the entire theater to feed *Santa Catalina*'s hungry machine guns. Especially if such attacks continued. They had to expect they would.

"There *is* some good news," Tassanna stated. "We now know where some of the enemy airship bases are. I've had Naancys with extra fuel tanks following the departing attackers at a discreet distaance, and they've discovered two of them."

"Great," Monk said. "Now you can hammer 'em."

Tassanna blinked regret. "Soon," she assured. "The problem is, COFO Leedom suspects there are at least *four* primary air-fields. If we attaack the two before we find the others, the enemy may determine how we found them and become even more evasive. That could make it more difficult to discover the rest." Her tail swished and her tone hardened. "I would like to find at least *one* more before I ask Col-Noll Maall-ory to direct Jumbo to attaack them with his heavy bombers. Aafter yesterday, however . . ." She paused. "Haaf is better than none. We must take some of the pressure off Chack. I've given COFO Leedom just another week to pinpoint the finaal air-fields. Then, whether he does or not, we will attaack what we caan in daylight, when all the zeps are on the ground."

"Might be costly in daylight," Laney groused. "If they got them goddamn rockets guardin' 'em."

Tassanna blinked. "We will not know until we try. The Naancy scouts couldn't tell in the darkness. There could be no rockets, or there could be maany." She blinked determination. "I will also ask for an immediate strike if we see another mass gaalley attaack building—though even massed, it is difficult to destroy enough of them to seriously haamper their operations." She brightened. "We haave some replacement air-craft, as you saw, aarriving on fast traansports, direct from Baalkpan. Others—more dilapidated, I fear—came from Grik City. Most that were stationed there haave been sent south to operate from air-fields improvised by Ian Miles and his irregulars haraassing the dwindling Grik in the jungles of Mada-gaasgar." Her eyes narrowed. "Still," she said, "even the new aarrivals barely returned us to one part in three of our complement, and in the end, holding the river must primarily remain Chack's responsibility." She looked steadily at Russ with her large, shining eyes. "Ensuring thaat his sacrifice and the one you already made has meaning will rest in no small paart with you."

It was cloudy and actually fairly cool for a change when the big Clipper thundered in and landed on the water in the harbor on the northeast end of Mahe Island the next morning. They'd stopped at the Pat-Wing 22 base on the Comoros Island of Mayotte for fuel, but the flight crew discovered a bad oil leak from the starboard outboard engine. That meant they had to change planes, which was a tedious and painful process for some of *Arracca*'s wounded flyers they'd brought with them. After a couple of hours, during which Russ, Monk, and Laney all sacked out in Jumbo Fisher's tarred canvas–covered bamboo HQ, *Santa Catalina*'s groggy senior officers boarded the "new" plane. It was a longer-serving veteran and *looked* worse than the other, with its patched holes; its faded, salt-washed paint; and plenty of oil-stain streaks of its own, but the engines sounded healthy, and Jumbo had pronounced it his personal favorite. It had survived the sinking of USS *Andamaan*, as well as numerous raids over Sofesshk. Thus, somewhat dubiously reassured, they continued on their way and reached Mahe at about 0700.

The relatively small harbor, nestled against some modest mountains, was incredibly (too vulnerably, in Russ's view) packed, just as it had been before TF Bottle Cap sailed for the mouth of the Zambezi. A lot had happened since, and though some of the residents were the same—USS *James Ellis* and USNRS *Salissa* were back after supporting the operation against Zanzibar, and the fleet carrier USS *Madraas* and USS *Sular*, the great Grik BB–turned–armored transport, apparently hadn't moved—there were a number of new additions. Some of the new cargo ships based on enlarged versions of Scott-class steam frigates had arrived from Austraal with more troops to cram on the little island, their tents now crawling up the denuded flanks of the mountains. Another dozen MTBs were there, half tied to their own wharf on one of the little islets in the harbor, the other half patrolling the narrow channel. A couple of the remaining steam-sail frigate DDs patrolled offshore, but the rest were undergoing dockside repairs.

With the defeat of Kurokawa, the air threat had been diminished, but Ben Mallory, back from Mayotte himself, had a constant combat air patrol over the island. Jumbo had told Russ that Ben's two remaining P-40Es had been brought from Zanzibar on *Salissa*'s hangar deck, where they'd been joined by the banged-up specimen that made it ashore after the Battle of Mahe. That damaged plane represented almost the very last of their reserve of parts. A final two P-40s were still in Baalkpan and might be ferried out, but Russ didn't know if that had been decided.

Swirling clouds of lizardbirds dwarfed even the human and Lemurian bustle. The occupation of their island had resulted in a boom for the avian predators. The invader's refuse was much appreciated, as was the smorgasbord of dead and injured fish churned up by the activity on the water. But what drew Russ's attention most, staring through the waist gunner's opening in the wallowing fuselage of the Clipper, was the massive angular form of *Savoie*. USS *Savoie*, *now,* he corrected in his mind. The great French battleship, a true superdreadnaught from the Great War, was certainly imposing, even under her various scars. Guns seemed to bristle in all directions, and she exuded an aura of indestructibility.

That was a false impression, of course, countered by the many rusty scorch marks and the dried, diagonal slime lines testifying that nearly her entire stern had been submerged. She might've even sunk if she hadn't been beached. But she floated level now, and smoke hazed the top of her forward funnel while the one aft of a battered seaplane catapult was being re-erected. Interestingly, even while repairs proceeded, painters were already at work, starting from the bow, applying the ragged "dazzle" scheme. Soon, hopefully, she'd be ready for action—and she was *his*.

Russ still couldn't believe Captain Reddy had taken his old destroyer up against her, virtually alone. Of course, the battleship's attention had been intensely—and painfully—focused elsewhere at the time. *Even so, for Matt to attack her in his aged, battered* Walker, *and then* capture *her* . . . Russ shook his head. He and his people had been through a lot, but seeing *Savoie* reminded him they hadn't been the only ones. *That's something easy to forget when you're in the thick of it,* he realized.

On two engines, the Clipper rumbled up to a pier where another PB-5D floated, surrounded by a cluster of Nancys, tiny in comparison. The engines clattered to a tired stop, and line handlers secured the plane. Russ, Laney, and Monk were the first ashore, anxious to get out of the way so the wounded could be moved, and Russ was stunned to see Admiral Keje-Fris-Ar, generals Pete Alden and Muln Rolak, Colonel Ben Mallory, and even Commander Steve Riggs—who'd been in Baalkpan, the last he knew—standing in front of a company of 'Cat troops, rigid at attention.

"Pree-sent . . . aarms!" Rolak shouted. He and the other officers snapped crisp hand salutes while the troops raised their Allin-Silva rifles vertically in front of them.

"*Santa Catalina* arriving," Pete Alden roared.

A massive lump formed in Russ's throat and he blinked rapidly. Somehow, he managed to return the salute as sharply as he ever had. Monk and Laney did the same. They held it there for a long, long moment before Rolak finally belted, "Order aarms!" Then, "Rest!" When he did that, the troops went to the position of parade rest, but Keje, Alden, Rolak, Riggs, and Mallory advanced and shook their hands. Keje actually embraced them, disconcerting to them all, particularly Laney.

"You did *very* well," Rolak said, eyes blinking earnestly in his gray-furred face.

Russ straightened. "I lost my ship," he said simply.

"And you ever expected *not* to?" Keje asked gently, red-brown eyes blinking in the white fur surrounding them. The rest of his pelt was the color of rust, but the war had aged him. Rolak was much older, but his hide was gray all over and already so lined by scars, he never seemed to change. "Please spare us—and yourself—any pretext that your aac-tion could haave possibly ended any way but worse," Keje continued. "You saw the necessity and did the best you could with what you haad. We haave all been forced to do the same too often. Accept our praise—and the mercy of the Maker of All Things—with a glaad heart. You deserve them."

"You went up the Zambezi knowing you'd lose your ship—at least—and did it anyway," Pete agreed. "As it turned out, it was the right thing to do. And she's not lost yet," he consoled. "In the meantime, in the finest tradition of the American Navy Clan, no good deed goes unpunished, and we have another project to dump on you."

"I heard," Russ replied somewhat wryly, glancing at *Savoie*.

"She's not as bad off as you'd think," Steve Riggs said, a grin on his boyish face. He paused. "I flew out from Baalkpan as soon as I could with a new level-crosslevel we copied from *Amagi*'s. It's the same one we put in the new cruiser, USS *Fitzhugh Gray*," he said by way of explaining his presence. "That was one of the things *Savoie* was missing. We figure Gravois swiped it or threw it over the side before leaving her to Kurokawa. I'm not sure we could've licked her otherwise."

"*One* of the things?" Russ asked.

"I'll get to that. First, as I said, she was in pretty good shape electrically and otherwise. The Frogs must've taken care of her. There was quite a bit of recent neglect, but nothing we can't sort out now that she's patched, pumped out, and floating. Hell, she could fight *now* if she had to. We just don't have enough people with the slightest clue how to operate her, much less fight her. Another one of the problems Kurokawa had."

"As to that," Pete began, somewhat hesitantly, "almost sixty Japs volunteered to help." He frowned. "I honestly don't know what to tell you about that. They all came from *Amagi* originally—obviously—but swear they hated Kurokawa and the Grik. Say their world, their emperor, *our war*, is gone. Given a choice, they'd rather join former 'honorable enemies' in the American Navy Clan than anything else that's available."

"Japs! No way!" Laney blurted.

"Shut up, Laney." Russ rubbed his short blond beard, thinking. "But Japs . . . Jeez, how can we trust 'em?"

"As to that, believe it or not, we put one in command of the new cruiser. Toru Miyata."

Russ looked startled. "Yeah? Well . . . he's different. He's like Shinya and already fought with us, going in the Cowflop after that fat Grik broad they worshipped."

"And besides you—and maybe some of those sixty Japs—he's the only person we had available who's conned a big warship," Riggs said. He nodded at Keje. "Not counting our carrier skippers who sometimes *think* their ships are battlewagons with flight decks. But we damn sure can't spare any of them."

Russ shook his head. "I don't know. I'll have to think about it. Maybe talk to some of them." He shrugged. "I'll have all my *Santy Cat*s, right?"

"Of course," Keje promised.

"And Ka . . . Surgeon Commander McCoy?" Laney asked. If his face wasn't already red and peeling, he might've blushed.

Keje looked at him and blinked amusement. "If thaat is whaat she waants."

Russ looked out at *Savoie* again. "Okay, so we're probably good for engineering, but we'll have to work up everything else. Maybe the Japs can help, maybe not. Did we get any of her former crew?"

Pete grunted. "Just a handful. The XO for one, but I wouldn't trust him as far as I could throw the ship. Scuttlebutt is, Captain Reddy had him and the rest of the Leaguers, including twenty-odd ground crew for the Macchi-Messerschmitts Colonel Mallory whacked, flown back to Baalkpan for Henry Stokes to squeeze."

Ben curled his lip. "Most either really don't know much or keep squawking about being neutral! Shit. I think I'd rather trust the Japs."

"No foolin'?"

Keje blinked distaste. "It is true. I caannot believe all subjects of the League could be of such . . . poor quality, unfortun-aately for us, but these remind me most of the 'Honorable' New Britain Comp-aany creatures we dealt with in the Empire of the New Britain Isles."

Russ frowned, then turned to Riggs. "Okay, what're some of the 'other things' *Savoie*'s missing that helped Captain Reddy beat her?"

Riggs assumed an expression that implied he'd hoped Russ had forgotten that train of thought for now. "Well, in addition to the level-crosslevel, Gravois apparently took or tossed the fire-control computer for the main battery."

"Oh, wow," Monk groaned.

Riggs held up a hand. "We're working on that," he

assured hastily. "We already started building them based on *Amagi*'s computers for her 5.5″ secondaries. USS *Gray* has two, and they're . . . a few of the things on her that actually work."

"What's that supposed to mean?" Russ asked, and Riggs looked pained.

"One thing at a time, huh? Anyway, we never thought we'd need anything that big, so we parted out what was left of *Amagi*'s 10″ gun directors. They wouldn't've worked for *Savoie*'s thirteen-and-a-halfs anyway. But when we did the new ones for Gray, we made 'em expandable, with provisions for add-ons, see?"

"Add-ons?" Monk asked skeptically.

"Yeah, like geared modules that'll accept input for different-size projectiles. They'll allow for weight, velocity, diameter—the works. We damn sure never expected thirteen-fives, but we're working on it, and even sent a couple projectiles home so they can start making them." He frowned. "That might take a while."

"So, basically, even when we get a crew worked up, *Savoie*'s stuck in local control," Russ stated.

"Just her main battery. There are directors for her secondaries. And we *will* get the other computer sorted out."

"How fast?"

Riggs gulped. "A month. Maybe two. Three to get it here and installed, tops."

Russ ran his fingers through his hair. "Okay. I'll believe that when it happens. That just leaves two questions. At least until I can get aboard *Savoie* and see things for myself. First, why isn't *Fitzhugh Gray* here already, and when can we expect her?"

Riggs looked embarrassed. "I, uh . . ."

"She's a piece of junk," Pete snapped.

"I wouldn't say *thaat*," Rolak soothed, but glanced at Keje to continue.

Keje blinked annoyance. "They haad to tow her back to Baalkpan during her sea triaals. There is word of some steering daamage." He glanced at Riggs. "The ex-plaan-ations are vague, but clearly she did not deserve such a distinguished name!"

"Crapped out on her trials, huh?" Monk murmured. "So I guess we don't count on *her*."

"Not right away," Keje agreed sourly. "What was your laast question"—he smiled—"for now?"

Russ looked at him steadily. "Just this: When are we going back upriver to relieve the Third Marines on *Santy Cat* and *Arracca*?" He waved around. "When is this army going to move and kick hell out of the Grik?"

"The troops are ready now," Rolak said firmly. "We await only a few thousand more, already on their way from Baalkpan and Madraas." He glanced at Pete. "And sufficient traans-sport, of course."

"You mean *Tarakaan Island*, stuck up at Zanzibar, with *Walker* in her repair bay?"

Keje looked uncomfortable. "She is not essen-tiaal, but would make things faar easier. And we hope the Republic armies threatening the Grik from the south will further divert their attention." He blinked a mild rebuke and his tail swished rapidly behind him. "But *Waa-kur* could possibly be the greatest source of delay, not only because we might need her to fight, but because we"—he waved around the anchorage—"maany, maany, people need her to just be there."

Russ scratched his beard again. "You know, that's a little irrational—and maybe a little unfair too. My God, Keje—Admiral—hasn't she been there enough? She can't perform miracles and she can't last forever. One of these days she'll be gone. I get that she's a morale builder, but what kind of hit would morale take if she got blown to smithereens right in front of everybody?" Russ was heating up and knew it, but he couldn't stop. "What if it was her instead of *Geran-Eras* that took that fish in the battle north of here? Would the whole damn war be lost?"

Rolak, urbane as usual, shocked Russ with a single word: "Possibly."

"You're kidding, right?"

"No. I honestly *doubt* thaat would be the case, but one never knows. Thaat old, worn-out . . . *glorious* ship has been a large part of every major success we haave achieved. It's impossible to caal-cu-late how her loss might affect the resolve of our forces. And if Cap-i-taan Reddy

himself was lost, the impaact would be even more severe."
He looked at Keje. "But I differ with my brother Keje in
one profound respect: if I had *my* way, Cap-i-taan Reddy
would steam his ship baack to Baalkpan as soon as she is
seaworthy and stay there until the waar is won."

"*Paart* of my heart says the same," Keje agreed, "but
it would never happen. Not even if Chairman Letts com-
maanded it." He coughed. "So we use him—and *Waa-
kur*—how we caan. I haave no illusion that *Waa-kur* is
the equal of our greater ships. Certainly not your *Saavoie*,
Cap-i-taan Chaa-pelle. But nothing else inspires our
people as she does. Her worth in that regaard faar out-
weighs her meager tonnage or actual com-baat power."
He blinked meaningfully at *Savoie*. "And sometimes she
does perform miracles, with the Maker's help." He
straightened. "Fi-naally, though this may sound selfish,
the *rest* of my heart waants Cap-i-taan Reddy here. He
is our Commaander in Chief, after all. He haas already
implied thaat he will not wait for *Waa-kur* to be made
whole again and might even abaan-don her."

Keje shook his head. "I doubt thaat would be a well-
liked choice among our troops, but if it comes to it,
Cap-i-taan Reddy will leave his ship because, most of
all, we need *him*." He bowed to Pete. "Not because he
will be in the forefront of the fight this time, I hope.
Thaat will be for you, Gener-aal Alden, and you, Gener-
aal Rolak. And Gener-aal Queen Safir Maraan. *You* will
meet the Ancient Enemy on his home ground at long
laast. But we need Cap-i-taan Reddy for his wisdom, and
that most indefin-aable of things we Mi-Anakka rarely
heeded before this waar began: his luck." Keje smiled,
blinking sadness. "My brother Adar saw it long ago. How
else could Cap-i-taan Reddy haave survived so long,
through so much, preserving our cause as he did so, if
not for the will of the Maker of All Things? Is it even
possible to imaa-gine otherwise? I caan't." He returned
Russ Chappelle's steady gaze. "Nor caan maany thousands of troops who must endure the fight to come. *They*
need him there."

///// **USS Walker**
Allied-Occupied Zanzibar
December 17, 1944

"hen I said 'Never again are you throwing
me off this ship,' this isn't exactly what
I had in mind," Sandra said wryly, slipping through the open hatch and looking around Matt's
new stateroom. Matt was seated at a little desk/table,
large enough for two or three to gather around, and he
smiled up at her, setting a pile of paperwork aside. He
did so with relief and often longed for the time when
there *wasn't* any paper, besides what *Walker* brought to
this world, but there was no getting around it now. With
help from the Empire of the New Britain Isles, the paper
(and all the forms printed on it) coming out of Baalkpan
and Maa-ni-la was thinner and finer all the time. The
Impies had been making paper for almost two hundred
years, and Doocy Meek often said the Republic of Real
People was built on a foundation of the stuff. But paperwork was absolutely essential to the management of a
global war, and Matt was glad he had Keje and his staff
to handle most of it. His portion was focused primarily
on strategy in the west, and accumulating the resources
to carry that strategy out. He got constant updates on
other theaters, including analysis from Henry Stokes,

but that was as much a matter of form as a means of explaining why certain resources were or weren't available.

He knew he had it amazingly easy compared to Chairman Alan Letts, who not only *had* to focus much more broadly but also had to coordinate supply for the various "pointy ends" in the face of a contentious, diverse, and increasingly selfish Union Assembly. As official CINCAF, Matt could've still interfered in operations anywhere he wanted, but he'd made it plain that he trusted those on the scene, and felt too removed to jostle their elbows. With his more comprehensive view, Alan Letts was increasingly the real Commander in Chief of All Allied Forces, and that's exactly how Matt thought it should be, if the Union was to thrive.

Still, comparatively light as his paperwork undoubtedly was, Matt was glad to see his wife, and happy for the diversion. "Me either," he said, leaning back on his stool and gesturing around with mock modesty. "It *is* a little extravagant for my taste," he added with heavy irony, "but it'll have to do. Have a seat." He waved grandly at a stool. Sandra rolled her eyes and carefully did so. The growing weight of her swelling belly was making her back hurt.

Originally reserved as a commodore's stateroom, spanning the width of the deck, like the wardroom below on most four-stacker destroyers, Matt's new quarters were located in the forward part of the bridge structure, directly under the pilothouse. Never used for its original purpose on *Walker*, the stateroom had been segmented by bulkheads to provide additional space for the bulkier comm gear, filled with lockers for spare parts for the same, and generally shrunk to less than half its original size. The remaining space had been used for general storage ever since. But Matt's emergency cabin above, forming the rear bulkhead of the pilothouse, had also served as a charthouse and sound room. With bulkier equipment now there as well, even the tiny space reserved for his little bunk had vanished.

As a compromise to his duty—and his wife—Matt had moved into the roughly 10-foot-by-12-foot remnant of the stateroom. The problem was, it had only a fraction

of the floor space that implied, since it was cut in half by
the triangular shape of the forward bridge structure behind the number one gun. He instructed the shipfitters
to install the desk, a small sink, a mirror, and a few lockers for his clothes and effects. Finally, he had them bolt
rings to the bulkheads to sway a hammock in the tiny
space that remained.

Matt was still smiling at Sandra, glad she'd recovered
enough to engage in a little humorous vexation. She certainly *looked* better, beginning to regain some weight
and heal her complexion from the ravages of exposure.
She might not yet have the radiant glow that women in
her condition often exhibited, but she had assured him
that both she and the baby were fine. "What?" he asked.
"My old stateroom's not good enough for you?"

Sandra frowned. "It's not that, and you know it." Then
she managed a small smile of her own. "I'd *hoped* when
you conceded to my demand that we stay together, we'd . . .
you know, actually get to *stay* together. I wasn't expecting
this end run. You're a lot sneakier than you look."

Matt shrugged. "This is the best I can do," he said
seriously. "From a practical standpoint, my old quarters
keep you close to the wardroom" (that was Sandra's
battle station, doubling as a surgery. The large, green-
topped table under a hanging light was her operating
table). "And this keeps me one ladder away from the
bridge."

"But they both keep us apart," Sandra grumped.

Matt had begun twiddling his Baalkpan-made lead
pencil. Now he set it down. "I agreed to rescind the prohibition against 'mates' serving on the same ship. With
the realities we face, that was probably stupid from the
start. But we don't have room for separate staterooms
for every married couple in the fleet, so the prohibition
against, ah, 'conjugal relations' aboard ship has to stand.
Again, like before, if everybody can't do it, neither can
we. We have to set the example." He raised an eyebrow.
"Besides, Chairman Letts pushed legislation through
the Union assembly that all pregnant females be taken
off combat status and, preferably, sent home. I used my
pull as CINCAF and High Chief of the American Navy

Clan to keep you here as essential to the war effort—but I felt like a heel, and it's the best I can do."

Sandra sighed. "I know, and you're right. I just wish, for a little while, we could have a real married life. Especially after . . ." She shook her head. Matt scooted his stool closer and held her gently. "Sure," he said. "And we will someday. We knew this was going to be tough from the start," he added, remembering how they'd hidden their feelings so long during the "dame famine," refusing to give in when, for all they knew, there were a grand total of two, then only half a dozen, human females on this entire world. That was long over now, but they still couldn't just do what they wanted. Not only was it their duty to set an example, but hopefully, the American Navy Clan would last a long time after they were gone. Both were conscious of the precedents they set and the traditions that would be established, based on them.

Sandra leaned back and looked around. "Okay," she said, "but you really need to liven this dump up." She grinned. "Get some pictures. Maybe some drapes over those two portholes."

Matt laughed. "All I want is a picture of you—and our kid, when it comes. Alan says we'll be able to do that soon, but right now all the cameras and the film they can make are being used for recon."

Sandra smiled wistfully. "'He,' not 'it.'" She patted her stomach. "Adar said this is your son."

Matt was taken aback. "When? How could he have known?"

"He said he could . . . hear his voice, there at the end." She shook her head as her eyes began to fill. Matt held her again until they were interrupted by a Lemurian messenger rapping lightly on the bulkhead.

"Yes?" Matt said.

"Co-maan-der Spaanky aasks you come."

"I'll be right there." He looked at his wife.

"I'm fine," she assured.

"Okay. We'll talk about this more. You want to come?"

"No." She smiled. "I've got to liven up *my* new quarters." She shook her head. "Actually, I want to go to *Tara*'s sickbay and do my rounds."

"Take Diania."

Sandra snorted. "Like I could go anywhere without her! She's worried about Gunny Horn, and that just makes her more protective of me than she was before. She's so sweet, but I'm starting to feel smothered."

"That's fine by me. Even with her hand messed up, she's as dangerous as one of Chack's Raiders. I like having her to watch over you." Matt stood and walked to the hatch. "Same problem?" he asked the messenger.

"Ay, sur."

"Okay." He looked back at Sandra. "See you later," he said, and stepped out onto the deck between the bridge structure and the amidships deckhouse. Following the 'Cat, he rumbled down the companionways to the forward berthing space under the wardroom and moved forward between the folded racks. All the damage had been repaired in here, but in the passageway beyond, flanked by shredded compartments for galley stores, sparks arced and lit the gloom. It was here that a single 13.5″ shell had blown through both sides of the ship—sideways—and pretty much wrecked frames 23, 24, and 25. The problem was, not only had those frames and the surrounding plates been repaired before, but the weight of the number one 4″-50 was almost directly above, and Spanky was deeply concerned about the structural integrity of the ship.

"Hey, Spanky," Matt said, coming up behind the shorter, reddish-haired man, standing in his signature pose with his hands on his hips. "What've you got?"

"Afternoon, Skipper." Spanky pointed. "This isn't going to be as easy as I figgered—not that I ever really figgered that in the first place," he said. The compartments on each side of the passageway had been torched out, exposing the twisted frames. Those that protruded from the starboard side of the ship had already been cut away before a simple patch was applied. Now that the ship was in *Tarakaan Island*'s repair bay, the patches had been removed from both sides. Workers could be seen, standing on scaffolds, outside the ship.

"You need more time," Matt guessed.

"Hell yes, I need more time!" Spanky almost

exploded. Chief Jeek looked back from where he was supervising a cut, suspecting the outburst was aimed at him and his repair crew. Seeing the captain, he returned to his work.

"You know people are dying right now—*friends* of ours," Matt began.

Spanky turned to him, face redder than the hair and whiskers around it. "Don't you think I know that . . . sir?" He waved his hands in frustration. "We've done the impossible often enough to make it seem routine, but goddamn miracles—if you'll pardon the expression—take a little goddamn longer!" He nodded back at the twisted frames to port. "We can't just keep slappin' tape on her and expect her to fight. We have to do this right—and there just ain't *no way* to do it right anymore! These frames are *gone*, completely shot out. And we can't just straighten what's left and rivet in replacements this time." His voice cooled. He'd been venting, and even if Captain Reddy was willing to take it, he didn't deserve it. "I'm sorry, Skipper, but we gotta go deeper." He stamped the warped deck plates under his feet. "Pull this up and tie in lower. Higher too, up in the chief's quarters."

"Welding won't cut it?" That had been their first hope.

"No, sir. The 'Cats back in Baalkpan've worked their own miracles, coming up with good electrodes and learning to make good enough welds to build a whole damn ship, I bet. But *Walker*'s got too many different kinds of steel in her. Always did, for that matter, and it's even worse now. The same method won't work on her. The welds'll be too brittle, or won't stick." He passed his hand over his face. "I'm not a great welder and don't like welded ships—you know that. Too many stories about problems before the war. That doesn't mean I wouldn't weld this mess up if I could. I just don't think it'll hold." He paused and nodded at Jeek. "The 'Cats have the only solution I see."

"And that is?"

"You went aboard *Ellie* and saw how she was framed . . ."

"Sure, the same as us, but like all 'Cat designs, they diagonally reinforced her between the frames with riv-

eted angle stringers." Matt looked at Jeek. "You want to
do that here?"

"Ay, sur," Jeek replied, tilting his chief's hat back on
his head. "It'll work," he urged, "but we gotta peel some
decks an' plates off her. Them stringers'll give us more
thaan twice the st'ucture to rivet to. Make her *daamn*
strong again!"

"How long?"

"Maybe . . . a month," Spanky answered tentatively
for Jeek.

"That's too long," Matt stated definitively. "We can't
stay here that long." He paused. "*Tara* can't, and neither
can I." He looked at the deck. "I know we've got fine
people on the scene, perfectly capable of doing everything that can be done without me holding their hand,
but . . . I *need* to be there, where our people are fighting."
He shrugged helplessly and looked up. "I don't suppose
Tara could carry *Walker* down to Mahe?"

Spanky looked horrified. "I can't imagine any way to
secure her well enough to ride down to Mahe in *Tara*'s
repair bay. If we hit anything but perfect weather, she'll
fall off her blocks like the poor old *Stewart* did in Surabaya. That'd wreck her." He shook his head. "And if we
hit really rough weather, with *Walker* floppin' around,
she'd probably wreck *Tara* too. Besides, we'd have the
same problem after we got her there. The whole reason
to take *Tara* is to load her up with troops and equipment.
Can't do that with *Walker* in her. Here or there."

"What's the answer, then?" Matt asked, a hint of near
desperation in his voice. He could hardly bear to just
abandon his ship. He would if he absolutely must; he
wouldn't let the invasion languish, or what was left of TF
Bottle Cap die, solely for the sake of preserving one old
ship, no matter what she meant to the Alliance—and
him—but there had to be a better way.

Judging by Spanky's concerned, thoughtful expression, he felt the same. "Give me just *one* more week," he
said at last. "We'll drill out the rivets, get *Tara* to lift the
plates off the deck and sides, and set 'em ashore. We'll
go low first, set the stringers below the waterline, and

replate up to that. Then *Tara* can wash us out of her belly and scram. Have *Ellie* come back and escort her down. You can go with her. We'll finish up the rest of the work on *Walker* here, alongside the dock."

"How are you going to do that with *Tara* gone?"

Spanky shrugged. "Our people can do it themselves if we get one of Kurokawa's cranes up and running." They'd already pulled a lot of machinery, parts, and tools off of Zanzibar and sent them to Mahe, but the cranes had been left behind. Their boilers, at least those they could easily salvage, were gone.

Matt zeroed in on that. "What about power?" he asked.

"We'll take one of the replacement boilers out of *Tara* or fix one of the busted ones here. Hell, between me and Tabby and that squirrel Isak, we can, by God, *make* a boiler if we have to. Our engineering plant's in good shape and none of the snipes've had anything to do for a while. Most are on liberty."

Despite how much work remained, it was all in a relatively confined area and too many people would just get in the way. About half the crew was on extended shore leave. *They've earned it,* Matt thought, *but God knows what they find to do. If Silva was here, he'd be off hunting Japs or Grik, even after I told everyone to leave them alone. Especially since they seem too busy hunting each other—and staying away from us—to make a nuisance of themselves.* Then again, he'd heard that the Japanese had built a kind of officers' club, and it, as well as Kurokawa's HQ, had survived pretty much intact. *And Kurokawa had some kind of wine-making going on. They've probably built a still by now, making seep from polta fruit—or alcohol from who knows what else they've found.* He couldn't pretend to be upset about that. They *had* earned a break, and there'd been few opportunities for any real liberty on this world. *Hmm,* he considered. *Then again, there's probably quite a bit of conjugal visitation going on as well. And there are a lot of female 'Cats and Impie women on* Tara. *They go ashore too. . . .*

Spanky seemed to be following his line of thought. "The shore patrol pretty much leaves 'em alone. Just protects 'em from incursions by the former inhabitants, keeps 'em from hurtin' themselves, and makes sure they're back aboard when they're supposed to be."

"That's fine," Matt said, "but you'll need all hands to make your scheme work." He realized belatedly that he'd just effectively endorsed Spanky's plan. He hoped he wasn't grasping at straws. *Walker* was more than just a ship to many, but she also represented a disproportionate concentration of the most highly trained veteran sailors in the American Navy Clan. *Savoie* needed experienced hands of all sorts, as did the new construction back home. It made no sense to let them languish here if *Walker* couldn't be quickly repaired.

"That's okay." Spanky grinned. "They're probably bored to tears by now, anyway. Only so much drunken debauchery any sailor can take." Matt coughed sarcastically, but Spanky's expression turned serious. "And there's not a man or 'Cat who wouldn't trade their liberty for a *year* if it meant getting this old girl back in the fight."

Matt hadn't thought of that, but he suspected it was true. He knew what the thought of leaving her was doing to him, but to her crew, her people, she was home. The majority of the few original destroyermen aboard had probably hated her once. He had himself, to a degree, wishing for a more modern, capable command. That had changed profoundly. And her predominantly Lemurian crew had always loved her in their peculiar way, which was closer to affection for a community, an extended family, or a beloved hometown. They came and went over time, of course, often promoted and transferred to other ships, other Homes, and some had been given commands of their own. But *Walker* would always be special to them, even more than to the Alliance in general. And as flagship of the American Navy Clan, she was practically the capital of their state in the Union, as such things were reckoned. *No,* Matt realized. *No one will lightly abandon her, and they might not be good for much elsewhere if they did. And they certainly won't complain about the work, compared to the alternative.*

The deck in the forward berthing space thudded behind them and Sonny Campeti, *Walker*'s gunnery officer, hurried in. He had a perplexed, almost . . . stunned look on his bearded face. "Captain, XO, there's something you need to see."

"What is it?" Matt demanded.

"It's . . . Please, sir, just come look for yourself, sir. You won't believe it if I tell you. I *saw* it and still don't believe it myself!"

Matt and Spanky looked at each other, blinking. "Okay, Mr. Campeti. After you."

From *Walker*'s deck, nestled low in *Tarakaan Island*'s repair bay, they couldn't see what had Sonny so ruffled, so they mounted the brow and strode up to *Tara* herself. The excited jabbering of workers paused as they passed, and Matt looked at them curiously. They wore expressions or blinked emotions similar to Campeti's. Finally, standing near one of the DP 4″-50 tubs flanking *Tara*'s forward starboard crane, they looked at the northwest entrance to what Silva had dubbed Lizard Ass Bay. There, beneath swirling lizardbirds and the gray smoke rising from her aft funnel, was a sight none of them had ever expected to see: USS *Mahan*, DD-102, had arrived.

"Well, I *will* be damned!" Spanky blurted, just as Tabby raced up the brow to join them. She never went ashore to "play," still nursing what even she must finally realize was a hopeless love for Spanky. No one doubted that Spanky loved her too, but not like *that*, and their relationship remained complicated. In any event, the lightning speed of the scuttlebutt must've reached her in the aft engine room just as quickly as Matt and Spanky were informed.

"Is thaat . . . ?" she began, gasping.

"Apparently so," Matt confirmed. There was no mistaking *Mahan*'s distinctive outline, which had been truncated not once but *twice* in combat on this world. Her forward third had literally ceased to exist when Jim Ellis rammed her into *Amagi* and detonated a load of depth charges rolled into her bow at the height of the Battle of Baalkpan. She sank but was later raised, and had a new bow built and a new bridge structure attached to the front of her amidships deckhouse. That shortened her by the length of her forward fireroom, and she had only two tacks and boilers now, but she'd retained the same combat power as her sister—if not her speed. Then, during the night action ending Second Madraas, somebody's torpedo—they'd assumed it was a wild one from *Walker*, but Matt now suspected it came from a League submarine—blew her new bow off. That time, *Walker* towed her in, but she'd been all but abandoned, considered too far gone to justify the effort to fix her again.

Apparently, someone on the scene disagreed. She obviously had a third bow now, and was seaworthy enough for the long voyage here. Matt shook his head, still unbelieving. The last they'd officially heard, she remained in Madraas with little more than a caretaker crew aboard. She *had* finally been moved into one of the unpowered floating dry docks, but she was there only because, with the logistical demands of First Fleet, no ships large enough to tow it to Mahe or back to Andamaan could be spared. Matt remembered there'd been rumors that *Mahan*'s caretakers were doing a bit more than just keeping her pumps going and killing vermin as they crept aboard, but this . . . "Did you know?" Matt asked Spanky, incredulous.

"Hell no!"

Ed Palmer joined them, along with Chief Jeek, Pack Rat, Paddy Rosen, even Min-Sakir "Minnie." And now Sandra approached, followed by Diania and a herd of *Tara*'s human and Lemurian medical personnel and crew. Matt spun to Ed. "Did *you* pick up anything about this by wireless? Radio?" he demanded.

"No, sir, I swear!" Ed squinted at the approaching ship as she made her turn, less than a mile away. One of the Lemurian 4˝-50 gunners handed him an Imperial telescope. "She's hoisted a signal," Ed informed them.

"What's it say?" Sandra asked.

Ed snorted. "It says, 'Don't shoot. It's really me.'" The crowd exploded into amazed laughter.

When *Mahan* was secured alongside USS *Tarakaan Island*, two Lemurians and a dark-skinned woman clambered aboard, all in whites. They saluted *Tara*'s flag and then the SPD's 'Cat OOD, who'd rushed to meet them, his tail whipping with excitement. Matt was even more amazed to see that the most senior of the three, a yellow-and-tan-striped female Lemurian, was a lieutenant (jg). The other two were ensigns. The ranking 'Cat cleared her throat. "Lieu-ten-aant jaay gee Tiaa-Baari an' ensigns Toos-Ay-Chil an' Sonyaa request permission to come aboard." The OOD blinked helplessly at Matt, who shrugged and nodded. "Permission graanted," the Lemurian managed. Toos was a gruff-looking older 'Cat with dark brown fur. His name indicated he was originally from Chill-Chaap. If so, he was one of a few former residents alive and must've been traveling when the Grik hit there. The Impie gal, for that's clearly what Sonya was, was no taller than the Lemurians and looked a lot like Diania. Not as pretty, but they could've been sisters. The three turned to Matt, braced to attention, and saluted once more.

Matt returned the gesture almost absently, staring at them. Then he looked down at *Mahan*. Up close, she looked pretty rough, only half-painted and streaked with rust. And the new bow looked a little crude—but in a sturdy sort of way. Otherwise, however, she appeared ready to fight. There was a brand-new DP 4″-50 on the fo'c'sle, and *Mahan*'s other original guns were trained fore and aft behind the bridge and on the aft deckhouse. Undamaged 25-mm tubs flanked the catapult aft, though there was no plane. And the portside torpedo tubes—at least—were loaded.

Matt frowned, noting again that only one boiler was lit. He turned his gaze back to Tiaa-Baari. "What the hell are you doing here, and how did you do it?"

"Sur," Tiaa said, rigid as a statue, tail hanging motionless, almost straight down. "We had the bow built, onshore, for a while. Before we ever got in dry dock. There really waasn't much else wrong with her, 'cept maybe the number one boiler . . . an' thaat could'a been fixed if we haad the people an' parts. Coulda been here way sooner with just a little support from Gener-aal Linnaa-Fas-Ra."

Linnaa commanded VI Corps in Indiaa, which was supposed to be preparing to move south and join the rest of the expeditionary force at Mahe. There were security issues in Indiaa; Halik wasn't too long gone, and there were lots of dangerous predators there. But Linnaa and his troops weren't doing any fighting. The only ones actively employed were Colonel Enaak's 5th Maa-ni-la Cavalry and Dalibor Svec's Czech Legion—and *they* weren't even in Indiaa anymore. They were still shadowing Halik's army as it rampaged through Persia, killing other Grik. Still, Linnaa constantly made excuses for his delays, and Matt recalled that his most valid one had involved a severe shortage of escorts for his transports— a role *Mahan* might've filled if she'd been repaired more quickly. Matt's expression darkened. And it was Linnaa himself who'd assured them for so long that *Mahan couldn't* be repaired. . . .

Tiaa misunderstood his expression. "I'm sorry if we did wrong, but we joined the Navy Claan to fight. *Mahaan* was *made* to fight. We were doing nothing at Madraas."

Matt smiled and nodded at the ship. "Not nothing, obviously. But if Linnaa wasn't helping, was actually trying to prevent your coming, how'd you manage it? And"—he looked quizzically at Ed Palmer—"why didn't somebody let us know you were coming?"

Tiaa blinked rapidly. "We haave no raa-dio, no wireless. An' as for the other." She hesitated. "Gener-aal Linnaa may still not know we're gone."

"Really? My God!" Sandra exclaimed. "Is he that far out of touch?"

"The scuttlebutt is, he never goes outa thaat paalace Kurokaa-wa occupied when he was there, so yeah. His staaff says all he does is gripe about the new Union, and figger out ways to draag his tail."

"Daamn Sulaarans!" Pack Rat snarled. "Always yaankin' *ever'body's* tails!"

"That's enough," Sandra scolded. "There are plenty of honorable Sularans. Many are fighting alongside us. Some are aboard *Walker.*"

"Them ain't the ones I'm daamnin'," Pack Rat said, sulking. "It's the high-ups like Linnaa, always thowin' wrenches in the works!"

"So," Matt said, looking appraisingly at Tiaa and her comrades. "You just . . . snuck out, and people back in Madras are covering for you."

"Ay, sur." Tiaa blinked pleadingly. "I know—maybe—it waasn't right, but . . . did we do right?"

Matt barked a laugh. "You certainly did." He turned to Palmer. "Chairman Adar was always soft on Linnaa, for political reasons, but this is beyond the pale. I doubt Chairman Letts will be as forgiving. Draft a dispatch for immediate transmission to Madras; copy Chairman Letts." He paused, considering. "And the Madras Navy Yard, attention the commander of the Marine contingent there."

"Sure, Skipper. What'll I say?"

"General Linnaa is to be relieved and arrested at once and charged with conduct detrimental to the war effort. We'll add specifics later. In the meantime, his XO will assume command. He'll get Sixth Corps moving as fast as he can, or *he'll* be replaced. Make sure the Marine commander understands that."

"But, sur," Tiaa said. "The CO of the Maa-reen contingent is a lieu-ten-aant!"

Matt grinned. "Then he might wind up a corps commander if he can't find somebody who'll get Sixth Corps off its ass. Now"—he nodded at *Mahan*—"I want to see what you did. Especially how you fixed the bow. We have a few structural issues to deal with ourselves," he added ironically. "And maybe you have some engineering problems?"

"Ay, sur."

Matt turned to Tabby. "Find Isak and join us on *Mahan*. Maybe between everybody, we can sort this all out."

Two hours later, Matt, Sandra, Tabby, Isak, Tiaa, and Sonya were in *Mahan*'s wardroom, drinking iced tea. Spanky was drinking the vile Lemurian coffee—none of the real stuff had made it out of theater yet—and spitting Aryaalan tobacco juice in a cuspidor made from a 4″-50 shell on the deck beside his stool. All the 'Cats were smoking PIG-cigs, to Isak's satisfaction, and Matt was thankful when Diania, present as Sandra's assistant, opened all the portholes, letting the acrid fumes escape. To no one's surprise, Ensign Sonya had been presented as *Mahan*'s acting engineering officer, and she was seated between Isak and Tabby. Ensign Toos had gone over to *Walker* to inspect her damage and make any suggestion he could. He'd once been a shipwright, building the enormous seagoing Homes in Baalkpan, giving him a talent for robust structural engineering. He'd even participated in *Walker*'s first rebuild. Unlike most Lemurians, he'd quickly embraced the advantages of steel construction and been instrumental in designing *Mahan*'s repairs.

"So," Matt began, "*Mahan*'s hull is obviously sound." ("Sound" was an understatement. There was still no armor—that would've made her too heavy forward—but after examining how the new bow was framed and attached, no one doubted she was stronger than she'd ever been.) "But what's the story in Engineering?"

Tabby blew smoke out of her very feline nose, something that always jarred Matt's sensibilities. "Her boilers are shot, both of 'em. They need an overhaul, baad," she said.

"Shot?" Sandra pressed.

"It's the goddamn tubes, mostly. They're crap, just like ours were," Isak snapped in his reedy voice. He lowered his gaze. "S'cuse me talkin' like a damn deck ape, Lady Sandra."

Sandra rolled her eyes. Governor Empress Rebecca Anne McDonald had bestowed the title upon her, along with a knighthood for her husband, but since few really understood the significance and so many already called Matt "sir," it was her title that had slowly grown in use throughout the Alliance. Discouraging everyone who used it had grown more tedious than accepting it. Especially now that even *Walker*'s oldest hands were using it too.

"Lucky *Tara* still gots plenty o' new tubes that stupid Lapsajik"—that's how Isak pronounced Laap-Zol-Jeks's name—"brought out from Baalkpan Boiler an' Steam Engine Works. Even still have a couple of his monkeys to help put 'em in."

"The brickwork inside is pretty shot too," Tabby added, blinking at Sonya. "She says it's the same she had at Second Madraas, which got shook up when she was hit. They've done the best they could, but praactic'ly had to swipe everything they got from the yaard, includin' the new number one gun! That daamn Linnaa!"

"I wonder if we could get away with hangin' him?" Spanky mused.

Matt grimaced. "Probably not." He looked at Tabby, the gray fur on her face wrinkled around a thoughtful frown. "But *Tara* has plenty of firebrick too."

"Yah," Tabby agreed. "We overhaul both boilers— might as well do it right—an' it'll take about a week."

Matt nodded, then looked at Spanky, his decision made. "That's the same week you'll have to get *Walker* fit to float, but then you're on your own." Everyone was surprised by that, and the 'Cats blinked furiously. Matt regarded Tiaa. "You've done a remarkable job, getting *Mahan* here. Ensign Toos is your XO?"

"Ay, sur."

"Hmm. I want him to stay here and help with *Walker*. I'm sure he'll make a good first officer, with his experience with damage control! But both of you are lieutenant commanders now."

Tiaa's amber eyes, already large, grew wider. "Thaank you, Cap-i-taan Reddy!"

Matt frowned. "The part that's going to be hard to take, and just as hard for me to dish out, is that I'm going to have to relieve you of your command."

Tiaa blinked acceptance, mixed with disappointment. "Of course. I never expected to keep *Ma-haan*. I've never been in aaction, and in honesty, we were lucky to even make Zaan-zi-bar. Besides the engineerin' issues, just findin' here was haard! We don't have a proper naavigator aboard."

Matt's eyes widened and he cleared his throat. "Very well." He looked around the table. "I'll assume command of *Mahan* and Tiaa will be *my* XO—for now."

"Me?" Tiaa murmured, astonished. "*Cap-i-taan Reddy's* XO?"

Matt smiled at her. "If you don't mind. I know it might be awkward, and you can request another assignment, but I'd really like to have you stay."

"Mind? *Aawk-ward?* In honesty, I . . . do not feel quaal-i-fied for such an honor!"

"The honor's mine, Commander Tiaa," Matt replied earnestly. "This ship is more yours, as are the people you've commanded, than anyone else's now. I have no doubt you'll overcome any . . . inexperience you may have very quickly. I did," he added cryptically, then looked back at the others. "In one week, *Mahan* will escort *Tara* to Mahe, where she'll begin embarking troops and equipment for the full-scale invasion of Grik Africa." He considered. "Tabby? You'll come too, to assist Lieutenant Sonya in Engineering." He glanced at Spanky. "Don't worry, I'll make sure you don't have to build a boiler to power a crane." There were chuckles. "We'll also take Paddy Rosen, who can help *Mahan*'s quartermasters get up to speed. Paddy and Tabby can share the duties of first officer. Is there a gunnery officer? Torpedo officer?"

"Aah, no, Cap-i-taan," Tiaa said.

"Take Campeti and Bernie Sandison," Spanky suggested glumly. He didn't want Matt to leave but understood why he had to. If he did, Spanky wanted him to have the best.

"No, you'll need them. And when *Walker* does come down, I want her power hitters on deck. I'll take Pack Rat for gunnery, and Torpedoman First Fino-Saal. Who else do we need?"

"Does *Mahan* have a surgeon?" Sandra demanded.

"Yes, Lady Saandra," Tiaa said. "We, ah, stole a good corps-'Caat from the Maa-reen contingent at Madraas. He was contemplating slow, painful poisons to try on Gener-aal Linnaa, an' I thought it best to take him away. But he can't compare with your skill!"

"Few can," Matt agreed fondly, but looked squarely at Sandra. "I won't try to make you stay behind this time, but you'll have to go aboard *Tarakaan Island*. *Mahan* has even less space to spare than *Walker*." Sandra started to object, and Matt raised his hand. "Or you can stay with *Walker*. I only ever promised not to throw you off *her* again. But those are your only choices."

Sandra bit her lip but finally nodded. There was no

arguing with Matt's logic. *Mahan* was very cramped. And at least she'd be near him. Matt finally looked at Spanky and took a deep breath. "As for you, get our girl fixed. When she's ready for sea, I don't know if you'll be able to bring her straight down or have to take her to Madras and escort Sixth Corps." He leaned back and snorted in frustration. He'd finally told Spanky more about what the League had in terms of ships and forces, sufficient to disturb anyone's sleep. So far, only he, Ben Mallory, Keje, Safir Maraan, and Alan Letts and his staff of snoops, of course, were fully aware of the near-impossible odds they faced beyond the Grik and Doms. Henry Stokes was trying to pry more intelligence from the Leaguers they'd sent to Baalkpan, but Matt only really trusted the information he'd received from another source. . . . "I don't like anything that's going on," he continued, "and there's still at least one League pigboat out there. If it comes nosing around, I want it hammered." Belatedly, he turned back to Tiaa. "How's *Mahan*'s sound gear, by the way?"

Tiaa shifted uncomfortably. "It's the older style, best suited for frightening mountain fish. We were lucky *Ma-haan* didn't lose her sound head with her bow. I doubt we could've scaa-venged another." She brightened. "But we have a *good* sound-maan, with the very finest ear!"

CHAPTER
20

////// USS Santa Catalina
Zambezi River
Grik Africa
December 20, 1944

"Well, they're at it again," Silva fumed, feeling as much as hearing the airship bombs exploding in the river. The dull *thump-thump! thump!* was like an erratic external heartbeat pounding against *Santa Catalina*'s fractured ribs, and transmitting through her entire prostrate form. And since the ship's own heart had been stilled entirely, Silva felt a brief stab of irrational, superstitious dread. *Like a tomb robber hearin' sounds or movement where there shouldn't be none,* he thought. He shook it off. He was less superstitious than most sailors, particularly the Asiatic Fleet variety, who'd been in constant contact with various extremely superstitious cultures, but that didn't mean he was entirely immune to the creeps. He glanced at the Lemurians assigned to help him in the wrecked ship's machine shop. *I wonder how the 'Cat's're takin' it,* he thought. Some, especially those from land Homes, oddly enough, were extra sensitive to the willies. *Prob'ly 'cause they live in cities, surrounded by dark, scary jungles.*

"O' course they're at it again," Lawrence agreed, snapping his jaws to catch a weary yawn. "It is night."

Petey said nothing, merely scrunching tighter to Silva's neck and blinking his luminous eyes nervously at the overhead, as if expecting it to fall on them at any moment. Silva also sometimes wondered, very fleetingly, what Petey thought about all this—if he thought about anything at all besides food. His former life flitting from tree to tree on Yap Island couldn't have prepared him for the confusing—and very loud—life he'd endured since leaving. Then again, Yap was a wildly dangerous place, and he might've already lived longer than he would have there.

The electric lights flickered when more bombs exploded closer, probably jostling the two semiportable generators tied into the ship's circuits in the upper level of the engine room. They were powered by the same water-cooled four-cylinder engines developed for Nancy floatplanes. That made them pretty heavy and was the reason they were only semiportable. Only one was running now, making sufficient electricity for the machine shop. Hopefully, they'd isolated all the submerged circuits. They probably had, but you never knew, and even if the reeking water of the river was just a few feet beneath the deck Silva stood on, it was unlikely to rise and threaten them with electrocution. It was already as high inside the ship's torn hull as it was outside. That might change if they were still here—if they survived—for the rainy season, but for now the river was actually slowly dropping.

None of their light was visible to the enemy. Hatches were kept carefully shut and holes were stuffed or covered, rendering the dank, murky, rust-growing space even more stifling and disagreeable than it would otherwise have been. Unfortunately, the suffering Silva and his assistants endured might be for nothing. There was a bright new quarter moon, and with Chack unwilling to blatantly advertise the wreck's position with muzzle flashes from her remaining dual-purpose guns, the Grik were flying lower and might see the ship, anyway. A few more planes from *Arracca* helped, and they could go after Grik zeppelins directly overhead without fear of friendly fire, but the enemy seemed to have an inexhaustible supply of airships, and pulverizing what was left of the old ship had apparently been their sole focus for almost two exhausting, hellish weeks. It was starting to feel like *Santa Catalina* had the attention of all the Grik in the world.

Silva flipped the power lever up on the engine lathe, and as it whirred to life, he murmured reflectively, "This poor sunk bucket is the most pulverized damn thing I ever saw." No one heard him over the moan of the electric motor and roaring gears in the headstock, so he looked at Lawrence and raised his voice. "Chickenshit dark-sneakin' zeps! Me an' you flew right over ol' Kurokawwy in one. In *daylight*!"

"They thought us on *their* side," countered the Sa'aaran. Only he seemed comfortable in the humid heat of the workshop.

"Trivvy-allitees!" Silva proclaimed grandly, focusing his good eye back on his work and advancing the tool post toward a cylinder of spinning brass. Just before he touched the metal with the cutter, another pair of bombs exploded in the water close enough to shiver the ship and rake it with iron splinters.

"Daamn, *them* was close," said one of the two 'Cat Marines detailed to help, who'd leaned over to watch. Silva didn't mind the audience but could've used some *real* help, and wished they'd kept at least a couple of *Santy Cat*'s crew—a machinist's mate, for instance. He could do the work himself easily enough but had other things to do. And he didn't like being below while they were under attack.

"Yeah," Silva grunted. "Been too many o' those. Too many hits too," he added darkly. That was certainly true. The ship had been directly struck several times, increasingly over the last few nights. In contrast, daylight had been a time of relative peace, with only a few rockets coming in. *Maybe the flyboys in the clippers finally found where they make the damn things an' flattened the joint,* he thought. "Those last ones probably opened up some seams." He snorted. Then he grinned. "Might've even sunk us. Good thing we're already sunk, huh?"

"Not . . . hunny," Lawrence griped, and Silva's grin faded.

"No, it ain't funny, really. This old ship never was much, but she was somethin'. An' she had heart, y'know? So did all the 'Cats we've lost, before an' since we got here," he added. The attack that came five days before had cost them more than two hundred killed, with nearly three hundred wounded—mostly from burns. Many who weren't too bad off had stayed aboard to fight, but for all intents and purposes, that single battle cut the 3rd Marine Regiment in half. They couldn't sustain losses like that, and Chack wasn't ready to call on his brigade for reinforcements that would be just as vulnerable. Silva agreed, and was trying to even the odds a bit. His first notion—actually Horn's—was to pump fuel oil over the side and light it when the Grik got close. Satisfying as that might've been, they were in a river, and the enemy always came at them from upstream. Such an attempt would probably be futile, and more dangerous to them than the enemy. Silva seized on the notion, however, and was trying something else.

"Where's Horn and that little monkey with the sprayers?" he demanded loudly, just as a naked man and Lemurian Marine, sopping wet, appeared in the hatchway. They'd been in the fireroom, diving in the mucky, dark, filthy water, feeling for the burner nozzles to retrieve. Diving was a profoundly unnatural act for any 'Cat, and Horn didn't like it either, but he was too big to squirm in tight places. His main job was to be there to assist (and encourage) the 'Cat, and fish him out if he got in a jam. "*There* you are!" Silva said. "About damn time." He glanced aside at Lawrence. "Guess we did cut out all the sunk circuits, since they didn't get boiled alive!"

"Not funny," Horn snapped, unknowingly echoing the Sa'aaran. "We got five. That enough?" he added, snatching at an old, worn mattress cover "fart bag" Lawrence tossed him for a towel.

"Nobody laughs at my jokes no more," Silva lamented, shaking his head. The 'Cat handed the nozzles to Lawrence and accepted another towel. Lawrence held them up to the light, examining mostly black cylinders about the size of D-cell batteries with tiny holes in one end, then dropped them in a can of gasoline mixed with oil. "How do they look, Larry?" Silva asked.

"They're rusty, and seen hard use."

"They don't have to be new er perfect for this, just not a ball o' rust."

"Then they'll do," Lawrence stated.

"That's enough," Silva informed Horn.

"Do for what?" Horn demanded, pulling on his skivvies, dungarees, and shoes. He'd wait before he put on the tie-dyed smock. It was too hot. More explosions shook them, and they glanced at the flickering lights again.

"I'm tryin' to make caps that'll screw down an' hold 'em in place in a bigger fittin' that'll screw on the end of a pipe. Like a long, wizardy wand! Clamp a hose to the pipe an'—hopefully—we got somethin' even better than Grik firebomb throwers at close range."

With pumps no longer required to keep the water out, he intended to repurpose them to pump fuel oil through the wand at high pressure, either simulating a flamethrower or creating a mist of fuel over the enemy before lighting it. He wasn't sure it would work like that and might have to enlarge the holes, but it was worth a try. The wand was for control, and also—if it failed—to make the things a little safer to operate. He'd already threaded the pipes and made the outside of the bases and all but one of the caps, but he'd needed the nozzles themselves for final measurements before boring the inside of the fittings.

"Hopefully?" Horn practically moaned. "Why don't any of your ideas ever have 'I'm damn sure this will work' in there somewhere?"

"I'm damn sure this'll . . . do *somethin'*," Silva replied. "That make you feel better?"

Just then, a series of heavy detonations hammered the ship forward, and without the cushioning effect of water beneath her keel, the old *Santa Catalina* transmitted the jarring blows through her bones, knocking everyone in the shop off their feet.

"Hit the breaker!" Silva shouted, rising and flipping the lathe power handle down. He snatched his helmet and weapons belt and headed for the hatch. Lawrence lit a small fish-oil battle lantern just as the lights went out, and they all exited the compartment and clattered up the companionway. Before they emerged on the main deck, Lawrence raised the glass globe on the lantern so one of the 'Cats could blow it out. He needn't have bothered. The moon was directly overhead, but that was the least of their worries. Met by shouts, running figures, and cries of pain, they looked forward and saw that the entire ship beyond the bridge structure was engulfed in flames. Hoses, also powered by gas-engine pumps, were already beginning to play on the roaring, thundering inferno, but it was so *big*. Worse, it was spreading on the water downstream.

"Goddamn!" Silva blurted. "They busted one of the fuel bunkers wide open!" All the bunkers were flooded to some degree, but fuel oil and water don't mix, and oil floated on top. Now the very thing Dennis hoped to use against the Grik was threatening to consume them. A harried-looking Major Gutfeld and a squad of Marines appeared, rushing forward. "Whatcha need, Simy?" Silva asked.

"Come with me, or stay the hell out of the way."

"Fair enough," Silva said. "C'mon, fellas. We'll know pretty quick if we can put the fire out—or need to start gettin' people off."

"What if we have to abandon?' Horn asked.

"Then the whole plan's in the crapper an' we'll be lucky to survive. Like usual."

There's a science to fighting an oil fire on a ship with plenty of other flammables of its own. Unfortunately, the Marines occupying *Santa Catalina* knew nothing about that. Chack and Silva did, and they did their best to direct the hoses at the ship instead of the flames, actually trying to herd the fire back without spattering and spreading the burning oil. The idea was to isolate the fire and maybe even wash the burning oil out of the bunkers and cut off the surface flames from returning with the hoses. It was a different kind of battle from what the Marines were used to, but a battle nonetheless. And all the while, at least at first, more bombs continued to flail the ship and firefighters, with hot fragments of iron that mowed them down in rows. Then, after the last zep either expended its bombs or fled from the fighters, ready ammunition for the forward 4.7″ guns began to cook off, forcing them to retreat, and the fire gained again.

"Hey, Chackie," Silva called when he got a glimpse of his friend through the roiling smoke to port. "Ain't exactly how I'd planned to spend my evenin'. What're the chances of a nice, long liberty when this is done?"

"You may get one sooner thaan you'd like," Chack yelled back over the crackling roar. "Though the distraactions ashore *here* may not be as aa-musing as you'd prefer. Then again, in *your* case . . ." Chack returned his attention to the work at hand, pointing out some wounded Marines to the stretcher bearers. "Carry them aaft," he ordered, "and have Surgeon Lieu-ten-aant Cross begin sending all the wounded up and aassembling them on the faantail. Tell her I'm not sure we can keep the fire in check, and her patients must be prepared to abaan-don."

"Abaan-don?" Gutfeld's XO, Flaar-Baa-Ris, almost squeaked at Chack. Her C Company was most involved where Chack was, and the flames seemed to turn her yellow fur to gold.

Chack looked at her. "We must be ready."

"But . . . with respect, Col-nol, if we bail off this hulk, how're we gonna stop the goddaamn Grik?"

"I don't know, Cap-i-taan," Chack replied. A heavy detonation jarred the deck beneath their feet, and flames gushed up from the ragged hole that had been the forward cargo hatch. Chack's eyes flared. "Baack! Everyone baack! Drop your hoses, graab the wounded, and run for the stern!" He looked at Silva, who was already repeating his commands more physically, literally hurling people back.

"What is it?" Flaar asked. Chack didn't take time to remind her that they hadn't considered it necessary to secure any of the ammunition for the wrecked 10″ rifle in the forward magazine. The shells wouldn't fit anything else and most of the big bags of powder in the largely flooded compartment were soaked. The terrifying operative word just then was "most." They should've done something with the bags on the top racks somehow, even if they only swam in and tipped them into the water, but they'd been a little busy and actually hoped to figure out a way to retrieve the powder, without getting it wet, and use it. Now it was too late.

"Run," Chack simply said. Most of the firefighters and those trying to help them made it past the forward part of the armored casemate before the dry powder bags—and many of the damp ones—went up. The forward part of the ship bulged outward, the fo'c'sle deck peeling up like the lid on a sardine can, scattering flaming deck planks into the sky. Then, even as the Marines picked themselves up and continued scrambling aft, one of the 10˝ common shells, its fuse cap blown off and ignited, detonated deep inside the ship. When it did, it set off as many as twenty more.

"Holy shit!" COFO Mark Leedom exclaimed through the voice tube by his head at the Lemurian observer in the aft cockpit. He was flying a Nancy and had personally accompanied this protective sortie himself, not to shoot down zeps but to follow the survivors. And his plane wasn't carrying guns or bombs, only extra fuel tanks to take it as far as it could go. "Jasper, get TF Bottle Cap on the horn right away and tell Commodore Tassanna that *Santy Cat* just . . . blew the hell up!"

"Jeez, wilco," came Ensign Jaas-Rin-Paar's shaky reply. "Whaat we gonna do?"

"Well, that blast did one good thing. It lit up some zeps hanging over the bend in the river, turning northwest. Now I know where they are, I can kind of see 'em with the moonlight and their exhaust flares."

"We never seen Grik zeps wit'draaw nort'-wes' before," Jasper acknowledged. We gonna follow 'em?"

"That's why we're here. Pass our course along to the commodore too."

"Ay, ay."

Leedom glanced one last time at the roaring inferno below and shook his head. "Jesus. Poor bastards."

*   *   *

Commodore Tassanna-Ay-Arracca was standing on the bridge of her great Home-turned-carrier, staring west, when a signal-'Cat brought her the reports from her COFO. She thought she'd seen a sudden pulse of light on the horizon, but believed it was her imagination. *Arracca* was too far away to watch the bombing, but now she knew she'd probably glimpsed the end of *Santa Catalina*—and an awful lot of friends. At least maybe Leedom was on the trail to another airstrip. If they could find that . . . She stiffened and turned to her talker. "Have COFO Leedom's executive officer report to me on the double." She considered. "And majors Risa-Sab-At and Abel Cook as well." She turned to stare out the windows again. Abel was the first to arrive, boyish face concerned, just as the signal-'Cat informed Tassanna that they'd heard from one of the prize cruisers. There *were* survivors on *Santa Catalina*, and the cruisers were closing to render assistance. Still . . .

Risa stepped into the pilothouse, along with Leedom's deputy, Commander Riaar-An-Fas. Riaar had been COFO before Leedom arrived but was never comfortable with the role. She'd been glad to be superseded. Now Tassanna was about to dump a COFO's load back on her. "The ground around the former Grik villages at the mouth of the Zaam-beezi is suitable for air-craaft?" Tassanna asked, already knowing the answer. Leedom himself had gone ashore with an armed party to reconnoiter.

"With care, a graass strip could be prepared," Riaar answered, blinking caution.

"Very well. We're about to close the shore and staart ferrying everything related to air operations on this ship over there; people, paarts, tools, fuel, ord-naance . . . everything." She blinked consolation at Risa. "I have no news of your brother, Chack, but his brigade—*your* brigade—is going ashore as well. Not to fight but to provide security and help build the air-strips. I was told this would be as simple as filling holes and collecting rocks. Not very de-maanding on its face, but it must be done as faast as possible because"—Tassanna turned back to

Riaar—"we will fly the entire Third Air Wing ashore with the dawn."

"But, Commo-dore . . . What of the ship?" Riaar stopped and shook her head. "It caan't be done in any event! We caan't possibly . . ."

"There will be no aar-gument, and it *will* be done," Tassanna stated, blinking harsh disapproval. "I haave ordered it and you have the entire crew and Chack's Raider Brigade—praac-tically a division—to accomplish it. As for this ship, it carries fifty 50-pounder guns in addition to its more modern armaa-ment. It was rebuilt to protect itself against sur-faace taa-gets before the enemy threat from the air became so extreme. It has fought sur-faace aactions before and will steam upriver and do it again." She nodded at Risa and Abel. "You will be baack aboard by then, minus a security force suitable to protect the aar-strip from local predaa-tors. No Grik haave been seen in the vicinity." She paused. "Thaat is all. You're dismissed to begin prepaar-ations. We all have a great deal to do." She turned to the signal-'Cat. "Inform CINCWEST and CINCAF of our intentions."

"But . . . dawn?" Riaar practically wailed.

Tassanna's severe blinking softened. "The wing will fly its usual sortie but laand onshore. I understaand it may take time to transfer everything required to sustain it, but time is a luxury we haave lost. So hurry."

Dennis Silva had been blown flat onto the splintered deck, his nose slamming the brim of his helmet, the helmet coming off and sliding away. He was aware of the noise and heat of the blast behind him, but his impact with the deck had severely narrowed the degree of consciousness he could devote to anything. A single imperative glared brightly above all else, however, and he staggered to his feet, spitting blood draining down from his sinuses, and hurried unsteadily away.

Gunny Horn was already sitting up, tilting his helmet to protect his face from the heat of the blaze, but saw his friend get up and stumble aft, like he was in a trance. He didn't see Petey, but that didn't mean the little tree-glider was hurt, just that he was gone. He usually made himself scarce when things turned sour. Lawrence moaned beside him, snatching Horn's attention, and the Marine quickly flailed at the Sa'aaran, knocking smoldering embers off his smock. Horn still wasn't wearing his and supposed he'd have flash burns, at least. He wasn't hurting at the moment, though, and quickly helped Lawrence to his feet. "You okay?" he demanded.

Lawrence nodded but didn't look sure. Horn physically pointed him at the half-dozen 'Cats around them. Some were still, others starting to roll around and scream. "Get those guys aft. I'll send help." That wasn't necessary. Other 'Cat Marines were already racing up to pull their hurt comrades away from the roaring flames.

"H'vere are you going?" Lawrence demanded.

"To check on Dennis. I'll see you in a minute." Without another word, Horn bolted in the direction Silva went, barely catching a glimpse of him bowling some milling 'Cats aside and almost falling down a companionway toward the rear of the armored casemate. Horn followed, suspecting he knew where Silva was going—even if his friend didn't. Wounded suddenly packed the companionway, clawing their way up from the sickbay. Some walked, others crawled, and a few were being carried. Smoke was pouring up behind them and Horn fought his way down, trying not to hurt anyone but forcing his way through. Down another set of crowded metal stairs, he started hearing shrieks of outrage. The voice was strident and very familiar.

"What the *hell* do you think you're doing? What . . . No! Don't touch . . . *Put me down!* We have to get these people . . ." There was a series of hacking coughs before the word "out," considerably weaker, came to him. He ducked into the sickbay and saw in the dim, smoke-hazed light of the oil lanterns and the one bright light hanging over a bloody table (they still had electricity, anyway) that Silva had thrown Pam Cross over his shoulder like a sack of grain and was carrying her back toward him and the companionway behind. Pam was kicking and writhing and raining blows on him. Horn snatched a bloody rag from a pile, dunked it in a basin, and wrapped it around his head. Silva looked steadier now, but his battered face was set in an expression of grim determination and his one eye gleamed with a singular purpose.

"Quit hitting him!" Horn coughed urgently. "At least on the head. He might have a concussion!"

"But I have to get . . ." The rest of Pam's words disintegrated in a coughing fit. Her eyes were red and streaming, and snot poured from her nose.

"You have to let him get *you* out," Horn shouted through the damp rag after her, as Silva deftly ducked through the hatch. "And see to *him*! He's *not* okay. I'll finish up here. There's not many left." When Silva and Pam were gone, Horn quickly surveyed the space. *Not* any *left that'll live,* he thought, but grabbed a pair of unconscious 'Cats by their arms and started dragging them through the hatch to the companionway. Almost there, a corps-'Cat and an SBA, also with cloth around their faces, relieved him of his burden. Another pair dove into the even smokier sickbay, checking for life and snatching crates of medical supplies. "Give me those," Horn shouted. "Get more!"

Hours later, it seemed, Gunny Horn weaved his way drunkenly through the press of Marines on the fantail and finally found Lawrence squatting by Silva. The big man was lying on the deck with his head propped on his helmet. Lawrence must have brought it. Petey was cringing under the pile of Silva's weapons nearby. Over the rail, one of the cruisers was standing by, and wounded were sliding over by breeches buoy. The other cruiser had added its hoses to the effort forward, and when Horn looked that way it seemed like the fire was smaller now. He was too tired to care.

"There you are, Arnie," Silva said, his voice distorted by his swollen nose and a broken lip. "I figgered you burned up."

"Back to your usual asshole self, I see," Horn croaked. "No, I didn't burn. Nearly choked, though. How are you feeling?"

"I'm swell," Dennis replied. Then he conceded. "My head's a little sore. Last thing I remember was hittin' the deck with my face. Then I woke up here." His gaze caught

Pam's approach and he added, "What the hell happened, and why's she so pissed at me?"

Pam knelt in front of him, roughly feeling his forehead. "You got some swelling. Prob'ly have a concussion too, and you'll have a pretty bruise. Your stupid head's too hard to break, though." She straightened. "I'm pissed because you took me from my duty!" she snarled, her Brooklyn accent sharp with fury. "You prob'ly *killed* people I could'a saved!" She turned to Horn and raised a wooden vial of polta paste. "You have burns. Lemme at 'em."

"Sure," Horn said, moving slightly away. Pam followed, and Horn lowered his voice. "Lay off the big goon, wilya? He wasn't in his head." Pam's face clouded with fury again, but Horn plowed on. "He really wasn't. And by the time we got down in the sickbay, you were about the only one left to save—I checked. We got as much else out as we could, and might even get back in. It didn't burn, last I saw. But you need to cut Dennis some slack."

"Why?" Pam demanded.

Horn hesitated. "He gets . . . focused on what he's doing—we all know that—and sometimes he comes up with some pretty over-the-top stunts." That was putting it mildly. "But I may be the only one who's ever seen him like . . . he was before. Back in China," he added. Everyone knew Horn and Silva had a history there, that something none of them talked about had taken place that bound the two men—and even Laney—in a way no one understood. Horn waved it away. "That's for another time. Maybe he'll tell you someday, maybe not. But the point is, he was knocked stupid then too, and the one, the *only*, thing on his mind was trying to save this little Chinese girl." Horn shrugged. "All she ever did was shine his shoes and fix his blues after he blew them out in bar fights, but . . . I don't know, she just *mattered* to him somehow, when hardly anybody else in the world really did." Horn shook his head. "She was just part of the story, and it's a doozy, but the fix she was in got me, him, Laney—and a few others in a, uh . . . 'situation' that ramped up into us almost starting a full-blown war between us, the Japs, the Chinese, maybe even some other countries, way before the real war ever kicked off."

Pam was looking at him wide-eyed. "Is that how you got his tooth?"

"Huh? Well, yeah. When he was . . . like that. Knocked some sense into him." He chuckled. "Didn't *stop* him, but made him start thinking—which probably saved all our lives." He looked at her. "Anyway, my point is, when he got that way this time, the only thing on his mind was to protect *you*. Would it have made any difference if there was still something you could do in the sickbay? No, he would've done it anyway, because just then *you* were the only thing in this whole screwed-up world that *mattered*, *see*? So if you love him like I think you do, just . . . lighten up a little. God knows we're liable to need him, and even if he doesn't show it, it distracts him when you're sore at him. Especially when he doesn't know why."

"And he *really* won't know why right now?" Pam pressed.

Horn shook his head. "Not a clue." He suddenly grinned. "I take a little of that back. I think he gets a kick out of it when he knows why you're sore, but right now he's just hurt. Take care of him."

Pam bristled. "I have a *buncha* guys to 'take care of,' thank you," she replied with terse sarcasm, but then her firelit face softened somewhat. "Including you. Lean down so I can smear some o' this goop on your back." As she did so, she quietly said, "Thanks, Arnie."

Colonel Chack-Sab-At was suddenly beside them. He looked terrible: his smock was torn and charred, his brindled fur was singed, and his amber eyes were puffy and wet. Horn hadn't seen him since the blast and was afraid he'd been killed. That would've left Simy Gutfeld in charge. Gutfeld was a good Marine, but they needed Chack—just as they needed Silva.

"Yes," Chack said, his voice rough, "help Chief Silva as best you can." He stared forward, apparently distracted. "I believe we'll soon have the fire under control. The explosion in the maag-a-zine blew the whole bow away, which let most of the remaining oil out of the daam-aged bunker." He blinked, but the gesture—usually so full of meaning among Lemurians—conveyed nothing but exhaustion. "The forwaard four-point-seven guns are gone, and perhaaps half the four-inch-fifties are out of aac-tion. We've suffered many caas-ualties, and those still fit to fight are worn completely out."

He looked at Pam. "The only consolation is, if the Grik haad been ready to come at us now, they already would haave." He gestured around. "And they could've swept us off this wreck with a feather duster." He scratched at the singed fur around his nose and it crumbled away. "But they *will* come," he declared with certainty, "and even if we're able to remain aboard, it'll be haarder than ever to repel them." He sighed. "So please do ensure that Chief Silva is ready to supervise repairs to some of our guns and finish his flame weapon—we still have fuel in the aft bunkers—and that he caan fight, of course. We may need that most of all."

Dawn, behind and to the right, was creeping up on Mark Leedom and his backseater, slowly brightening the alien landscape of Grik Africa below. It was cold at nine thousand feet, and they were higher than Lemurians found comfortable. Part of this had to do with the temperature—only 'Cats from the Republic of Real People seemed truly used to the cold—but it was mainly because they seemed to require more oxygen than humans. They were prone to hypoxia at anything much over seven or eight thousand feet. Fortunately, the Grik had the same problem, maybe worse, and only flew their airships at high altitude to make attacks. Ordinarily—like now—they flew much lower, and the zeppelins Leedom had pursued all night, slowly increasing in numbers from the initial three to the current eleven, had been cruising below three thousand feet.

As far as they knew, Grik zeps still had no stations on top of their envelopes for observers, but the enemy flight was a formation in name only. A scattered gaggle was a better description, and Leedom had climbed so high only shortly before to avoid being seen by any stragglers as the light improved. That same light began to glare sharply on the enemy aircraft and further reveal the weird land below.

Leedom had never been to Africa—*any* Africa—except to bomb Sofesshk. He hadn't even seen real photographs of the old one before he came to this world. All he knew came from Tarzan pictures, and he'd imagined the whole thing choked with jungle, just like Borno. The scrubby floodplain with islandlike clumps of trees along the Zambezi had seemed an aberration. Apparently it was, but it was even stranger here. High, jagged, snow-capped peaks jutted to the west, and an enormous lake, like an inland sea, was appearing just ahead. Down below looked like a patchwork of . . . different-colored jungles, mostly greenish, but some tinged with blue, even red. All were separated by grassy prairies teeming with groups of massive beasts or huge herds of smaller ones. Mark couldn't even try to describe them at this altitude but got the impression he'd never seen anything like them before.

And the birds! The sky close to the ground practically convulsed with flying creatures of all shapes, colors, and sizes. Most were probably the size of ducks or geese, but some looked as big or bigger than Grikbirds, or even the plane-size flying reptiles Greg Garrett had described on Mauritius. Leedom had never seen so much *life* congested in one place, with the possible exception of flasher fish when they swarmed. It was awe-inspiring—and frightening. Particularly when he realized there were a lot of fairly typical mud-hut, warrenlike Grik settlements scattered below as well. Most were situated near streams or clustered along the massive river now curving back toward the south end of the lake from the west, but to see so many of their enemies after flying so far from Sofesshk made him contemplate—maybe for the first time—just how wildly outnumbered the Allies were. If there was a bright side, it was that they finally knew not all Grik were warriors, or even capable of fighting effectively, no matter how individually frightening they might be. One on one, hand to hand, the lowliest Uul could tear anybody apart. But the simplest weapons negated their physical advantage. And the Allies still had better weapons. Mark hoped that would be enough.

"How're you doing, Jasper?" he called back to his backseater.

"Got a headache, an' a little numb in the fingers. I okaay, though. Draawin' pit-chers."

"Good."

"On'y one thing," Jasper continued, and Mark knew what he was going to say.

"Yeah, we're bingo fuel. We gotta turn back pretty soon. We should have a tailwind, though, and that'll help. I'm gonna push a little farther."

"I'm game . . . but I'd *really* raather not haafta' waalk baack."

"You an' me both."

They flew on, the roar of the in-line engine above and between them lulling their tired minds. Mark Leedom was yawning with fatigue and saw Jasper in his little mirror doing it almost constantly, the thin air probably to blame. Finally, perhaps half an hour after they should've turned back, and with Mark feeling increasingly irresponsible for not doing so, he moved his goggles to wipe away the dry gunk around his eyes. Then he blinked. "Hey," he said, "does it look like those zeps are descending?"

"De-scending!" Jasper replied, but his tone sounded giddy.

I need to get him down, Mark thought. "Try to focus," he shouted.

"Yeah. Sure," Jasper said, more like himself. "Yeah," he continued after a moment. "They're lower now, an' more bunched up. I think they're headed for thaat clearin' on the east side o' the lake. Hey! There's zeps on the ground there! Maybe a dozen. More!"

"You're sure?" Mark demanded. Ordinarily, he'd never ask such a thing. Lemurian eyesight left his in the dust, but Jasper wasn't quite himself.

"Sure, I'm sure," he responded tersely. "An' please quit yellin'. I tole you my head hurts!"

"Okay," Mark said, banking right and turning into the morning sun, hoping there'd be less chance of them being seen. "Then let's get out of here before they spot us." He hesitated. "Have you been keeping up with our position?"

"Gettin' it current now," Jasper replied apologetically.

"Good. As soon as you do, send it. Now we know

where three Grik airfields are. Maybe that's all there is. Either way, it's time for Jumbo and Colonel Mallory to hit 'em with the big boys. We're getting out"—he heard Jasper's yawn through the speaking tube, even over the roar of the engine, and grinned—"and down. Stay awake, and you'll feel better soon."

"Yah. Just in time for the long-aass flight back! But we gonna make them slinkin' lizaard baas-tards *pay* for what they done to *Saanty Caat*!"

"You bet."

////// Kakag
Grik Africa
December 22, 1944

General of the Sky Hideki Muriname sponged sweat off his balding head with a grimy rag and readjusted his precious wire-rim glasses. Then he tried to squirm back into the narrow gap between the engine and the mount fairing on the starboard wing of the DP1M1 torpedo bomber. The planes, with their twin nine-cylinder radials, were armed with a copy of the Type 89 machine gun and could achieve 180 miles per hour while carrying a short-range torpedo or a thousand pounds of bombs. Muriname considered them his finest achievement, even greater than the AJ1M1c fighters he'd designed. The Allies had bested his fighters—rather depressingly easily—but still had nothing that could match his bombers, as far as he knew. The closest things he'd seen, their small Nancy flying boats, had been terribly effective at first and retained the advantages of range and of being deployable anywhere there was water to land on, but they were comparatively slow and couldn't carry the load his bombers could. The problem was, the Allies had a lot of them and just kept making more.

The handful of fighters and bombers he had left, including the old Type 95 floatplane—a final relic of *Amagi* tied to the shore of a nearby river—totaled less than thirty planes. They'd been all he could salvage during the disaster at Zanzibar, and all the tediously constructed industry and painstakingly trained workers required to build them had been destroyed or captured. Even if he was inclined to start again, virtually from scratch, it might take years just to replicate what he'd already achieved. The Allies would have far better planes by then, and frankly, he didn't think he had years. One way or another, he believed the war would likely be decided within a year at most.

Either the Allied gamble to go all in would finally crush the Grik—which he now knew to be in considerable domestic disarray despite, or because of, Esshk's attempts to consolidate power—or the gamble would fail and the Allies' fragile lines of support would collapse as the rampant Grik rolled up their tenuous trail of outposts all the way back to their source. In the first case, the best he and his people could hope for was incarceration. On the other hand, if Esshk won and the Allied threat was neutralized at last, Muriname suspected his services would no longer be required. Ultimately, however, and just as important, he *wasn't* inclined to start again, not for Esshk and the Grik, so there'd be no more planes for him—from them.

It was miserably hot and humid at the little grass strip he'd had the foresight to have cleared in the jungle near the Grik city of Kakag, barely two hundred miles southwest of Zanzibar. The Grik ground crews he'd positioned there, with fuel and as much ordnance as he could divert without catching Kurokawa's attention, had built little huts to protect his people and supplies, but overhead protection for the planes (and those working on them) was sadly lacking. Kurokawa had known about the airfield but would've been furious to discover Muriname's diversion of resources to support it. *Kurokawa did the same thing to the Grik, to build his base on Zanzibar,* Muriname mused as he groped upward for the fuel-line attachment. The glare of the sun above made it nearly impossible to see anything in the shadow of the motor. *So why does it give me such satisfaction that I used that madman's same methods?* he wondered. Then he knew. *Because I did it to* him, *and I'm alive because of it. And he is probably dead.*

"Pliers," he said to the Grik ground crew, watching in amazement as their leader, practically their regent, performed physical labor in front of them. Muriname usually discouraged his pilots, even the Grik pilots, from doing that, but the fitting he was trying to connect was in a very cramped place and such chores were difficult for Grik. They had longer fingers, yet even those that kept their claws filed short had trouble manipulating small screws and tools in confined spaces. And Muriname didn't have any human ground crew at all. Since his very life might depend on how well the clamp was seated on the fuel line, he preferred doing it himself.

"Your tool, Lord," a small Grik said, passing the pliers. It spoke with an exaggerated deference that would've made Muriname laugh if the creature, with its jagged mouthful of teeth and scimitarlike claws—on its feet, at least—didn't still look so terrifying. Muriname grunted instead. With one hand holding the clamp on the line, he reached up with the pliers and compressed it until it slid over the bulge. When he released the springlike clamp, it tightened down, holding the line in place. He backed out and mopped his head again while the Grik stared at him as if he were magical. He sighed. Terrifying or not, he could sometimes almost think of them as people. He'd grown somewhat attached to the first draft he'd taught to fly the dirigibles he'd designed, but he'd hardened himself against such sentiments after they were so badly wasted. Still, a degree of . . . acceptance had crept back upon him regarding *these* Grik, and particularly the pilots he'd trained. They tried very hard and did remarkably well, even better in some ways than his remaining Japanese, since the way they had to orient themselves in their aircraft allowed them to perform maneuvers that were difficult for humans. *Face it,* he told himself. *You are proud of them.*

Grunting again, he tossed the rag on the ground and paced away, leaving the Grik to wrap things up. His HQ was a mere shack at the edge of the cleared strip, but at least there was shade. Heading for it, he was intercepted by Lieutenant Ando—his XO, now that Iguri was dead or captured. Ando was very young for the job, but he was a good pilot, passionate about flying. He was pointing to the southwest.

"Another messenger approaches, General of the Sky!" he said loudly. Muriname shaded his eyes and saw the Grik airship approaching low over the trees bordering the strip. "They'll probably insist more vigorously that we move our planes south, to support their attacks against the enemy on the Zambezi," Ando speculated with a side glance at his superior.

Muriname slapped his thigh with a fist. "No doubt." He sighed. "Assemble a detail to assist them, then bring them to my headquarters. I'll refresh myself and await them there."

"Of course, General of the Sky."

Muriname paced on, brooding. Entering his hut, he stripped off his shirt and quickly washed his face and torso in a basin. Then he pulled on a new tunic. *At least we have plenty of clothes,* he mused. The Grik had been making such things for them for a long time, and stores had been quickly diverted here. Glancing briefly at the roughly sewn seams, he didn't wonder how they did that, but he was always curious how they weaved the material itself so fine. He shook his head and stepped into his open-sided "office" and sat on a wooden chair by a table. His Grik servants had already placed four bowls of water on the table, and that meant they'd seen how many Grik dignitaries were approaching. *There'll be two of them, and one bowl each for Ando and myself,* he suspected. He was right. Ando followed the Grik inside and motioned them to a pair of rough wood, saddlelike stools the servants had also brought. Muriname stood, immediately recognizing one Grik as Hij Sich'k, the same interpreter that came here before, and several times to Zanzibar. He was dressed in common Hij fashion, in a red breechcloth arranged like a diaper and a short red cape with slashing Grik characters painted in black around the hem. He wore no armor and carried no weapons and was remarkably thin, with an extraordinarily narrow snout.

"May I present Seventh General Gookir," Sich'k carefully enunciated in Grik—which Muriname understood well enough when spoken slowly.

"We're honored by his visit," Muriname replied just as carefully, gesturing at the bowls of water. "Would you care to refresh yourselves after your flight?" Both he and the interpreter could speak some of the other's language by now; Muriname had to speak a little Grik to communicate with his pilots, but each continued to pretend they couldn't. Since Sich'k wouldn't stoop to "foul" his mouth with Japanese in front of General Gookir, Muriname wouldn't say a word of Grik. Sich'k performed a sharp, diagonal nod and spoke to Gookir. Gookir was as large and powerful as Sich'k appeared frail and wore the polished breastplate, helmet, and short cape of his office. The only thing different that Muriname hadn't seen before was that the leather armor on his arms and shins up past the knees was dyed or painted as red as his cape. Gookir snapped a string of guttural, hissing syllables, emphatically gesturing southward, essentially demanding why the General of the Sky and all his flying machines remained here so long after they'd been summoned.

"Tell him we continue repairs, and all the fuel and ordnance we sent south in carts were drawn by mere Uul laborers, plodding at the pace of a slug. It will do First General Esshk no good if my planes are there, exposed to enemy attack, without even the fuel or weapons to fight."

Sich'k conveyed this to General Gookir, who obviously didn't understand any Japanese.

"The airfield they demanded has been finished," Muriname understood Gookir to say, "and the Uul laborers have been joined by others; those that die are replaced. They make good time now and will have their things in place in a matter of days."

"Very good," Muriname said, nodding. "Tell the general to summon us again when all is ready, and we will come."

Sich'k spoke, but Gookir's eyes flared and his crest stood up. "No!" he snapped in Grik. "They will come *now*. They will come with the fuel and weapons they carry and attack that troublesome wreck that blocks the river. *Then* they may await their things at the airstrip!"

"That's not only unwise but also impossible at present. Less than half my planes have had the proper maintenance for such a long flight. I'd lose a third—a ten—of them before we ever got there. And they're quite irreplaceable," he reminded.

Gookir began to pace. "Then send those able to make the trip now. Follow with the rest when the maintenance is complete," he snapped.

"It's never wise to split one's forces," Muriname began to lecture, Sich'k translating word for word, and Gookir whirled to face Muriname and Ando. "You talk to me of what is wise? Then I remind you that it is *most* unwise to antagonize First General Esshk! We need your flying machines now, and you will deliver at least some of them at once." He paused. "Let me also remind you that the sword that is never drawn has no use. It is never cleaned, its edge never sharpened . . . and, occasionally, it is discarded. Only the useful sword is looked upon with favor, fed with blood, and kept always at one's side. Come at once; come today. Be of use or be discarded."

Muriname clouded. "How dare you speak to me that way? A *seventh* general! I'm *first* General of the Sky, second only to General Esshk himself in the chain of command!"

"I speak as First General Esshk has commanded me," Gookir rumbled. "I speak his words, directly from him to you."

Muriname stared. Finally, he nodded. "Very well. Return to First General Esshk and tell him, directly from me, that *some* of us will come today. The rest will come when our maintenance is complete."

"I will tell him what I see, not what you say. We remain here until the first flying machines depart."

"You will not!" Muriname practically roared. "I won't be watched over like an Uul laborer! Leave now. You'll just be in the way otherwise, and I have much to do."

Gookir began a strong retort when Sich'k told him what Muriname had said, but Sich'k continued, speaking softly, placating. Finally, he turned to Muriname.

"I have learned you Japhs quite well, I think, and assured him you would come to battle because you have said so. Your word, your *honor*, drives you beyond what threats can accomplish. I also told him that his remaining here would insult you to such a degree that you might change your mind. In that case, it would be his fault, not yours, if you stayed away." He took a long breath and exhaled loudly through his long, narrow snout. "Therefore," he continued, "we will leave." His eyes narrowed. "But you *must* come. As he said, the weapon not at hand when needed is of no use. And in warning, First General Esshk has grown more difficult to please, even as his power to see his will done has increased more than you can imagine." He snapped his jaws shut, then ventured, "That is all I may say on that matter. But I strongly urge you to show yourself of use. . . . Or the next time I come, the visit will be most unpleasant for us both."

"Such vile, loathsome creatures!" Ando burned breathlessly as they strode back across the airstrip, the Grik zeppelin fading in the distance over the trees. "For them to imply you might avoid any task you've committed to . . . It's beyond bearing!"

Muriname watched him as they walked, surprised by Ando's genuine outrage. They'd all avoided certain death in Kurokawa's service, after all, when they flew here as the defense of Zanzibar collapsed. But they'd been unable to find the enemy carrier, all their own airfields had been overrun or were under attack, and they had only so much fuel. They would all have died to no purpose if they'd remained. Besides, even Ando recognized that Kurokawa had been mad. Perhaps that's how he reconciled their actions? "I'll take the fighters down," Ando continued, "if that meets with your approval, of course. If so, how soon can you bring the bombers?"

Muriname stopped walking, forcing Ando to pause and look at him. "None of this meets with my approval, Lieutenant," he said. "None at all. It never has."

Ando's eyes widened. "What do you mean, sir?"

"Simply this: I will no longer serve the Grik. They *are* vile and loathsome and don't even remotely understand honor." He gestured. "That Hij Sich'k believes he does, to the extent he thinks he can use our concept of it, backed by threats, to control us. But there has been no real honor in anything we've done since we came to this world—and I'm sick of it!"

"But . . ."

Muriname sighed. "Tell me, Lieutenant Ando, what was Kurokawa to you?"

Ando looked confused. "He was my lord, sir, and the representative of the emperor on this world."

Muriname pursed his lips. "He was your *captain* where we came from, where you were merely a seaman second class," he said, almost brutally. "It was *I* who advanced you, not he. True, he still represented the emperor—at first—until he tried to supplant him over time as his madness deepened, to *become* him in our minds, binding our honor to him alone. All while aiding the Grik in their abominable cause and sacrificing those most loyal to him for *his* purposes. Not the emperor's!"

"Then . . . are you my lord?"

Muriname became frustrated. "No. I'm your commander. What I'm trying to say is that we have no lord here, besides our honor and our conscience, and neither of those things will allow me to aid the Grik anymore."

Ando ran a hand across his face, trying to concentrate. "But you have, sir! Just days ago you forwarded them our plans for the copies of the Type Eighty-nine machine guns we developed on Zanzibar!"

"Only to buy time, Lieutenant. They desperately desire weapons to counter the Allies, particularly what they call 'fast-shooters.'" He shrugged. "So I gave them plans for those and other things. I doubt they'll understand them, and they certainly can't make them without our help. *We* can't make any more without the sophisticated machinery and specialized steelmaking facilities we lost on Zanzibar!" He nodded at the planes gathered around the airstrip. "Our only value to them is what we can do to advance their hunt and exterminate all who oppose them. Kurokawa joined their hunt, as he said others have done before. But *what* others? Have you seen them? What became of them after they were no longer of use? That League serpent, Gravois, said their spies reported that the Allies had determined they were often extermi-nated, or their survivors planted on Madagascar for the hunting pleasure of highly placed Hij. Some have even joined the Allies now—but none still fight with the Grik. What does that tell you?"

"That they're even worse than I thought," Ando al-lowed, "but what of *our* honor, having pledged ourselves to them? Can we concern ourselves with anything be-yond that?" He looked at the planes himself. "I did not hate Americans in the world we came from, but in ser-vice to the emperor, we were at war with them when we came here. Lord . . . Captain Kurokawa did what was necessary to continue that war. I agree he was mad and had other motives, but what else could he do?"

Muriname shook his head. "We were at war with *America*! Not a handful of Americans on a couple of small ships. We were certainly not at war with a world full of beings we never knew existed. And the America we fought is not here, any more than our Nippon or our emperor! Kurokawa fought for vengeance and ambition, not because he thought it was what the emperor would have us do! Honestly, Ando, what do you think the em-peror would desire of us if he knew everything about our situation?"

Ando had no reply. "What will *you* do?" he asked instead.

It was Muriname's turn to rub his face. "I don't know—other than that I cannot help the Grik again." He consid-ered. "Nor can I join the League. If anything, they've shown themselves to be more treacherous than the Grik. I suspect our planes would be most welcome to the Do-minion, but I know little of them. What I do know sup-ports my suspicion that they're the most repugnant of the three." He paused. "Have you considered that the Amer-icans, their Imperial allies, and their ape-man friends are the *only* ones who have behaved with any honor at all?" He sighed. "It must be them. I *must* go over to them." He balled his fists at his side. "But how? I'm not . . . insensitive to the fact that they were our enemies on another world. But others of us have joined them, you know. One even commands their armies against the Dominion." He said that with a tone of wonder.

"I . . ." Ando began hesitantly, then stopped.

"Yes?" Muriname prompted.

"You're *not* my lord?"

"No. You're bound to obey me as long as you remain with me, but I won't demand your oath."

"So I'm also free to choose as my honor and conscience dictate?"

"You are."

Ando looked tortured. "Then I must, most respectfully, honor our commitment to General Esshk. I understand why you can't, and even sympathize. Your arguments are most compelling."

"What can you offer Esshk?" Muriname waved around. "These planes are mine."

"Are they?" Ando challenged. "If you're not our lord, how can everything be yours? In any event, you placed me in command of the fighters. They, at least, are mine."

Muriname had to nod at the justice of that. Not all would defect with him. Perhaps most wouldn't, and he'd have to let them all decide. Even the Grik. But they weren't "normal" Grik, and knew that others like them had fought with the Allies at Zanzibar. So joining the enemy's hunt might seem less unnatural than might otherwise be the case. Besides, many would surely follow him, considering him their "lord" no matter what he said. Muriname determined then and there that he must have all the bombers. Any he couldn't crew would have to be destroyed. They were the only bargaining chip he had that might protect him from Captain Reddy—and his wife.

"Very well," he said sadly. "As many fighters as you can find pilots for are yours. We'll gather my—our—entire command and put the choice before them. Then you can fly south and die for General Esshk," he added bitterly.

"I can't lie to Esshk on your behalf," Ando warned. "That will only get me killed. But I won't volunteer the information that you're not coming either." He managed a small smile. "You've already told that lie and it should give you several days to arrange whatever meeting you can with the enemy." The smile vanished. "When they do ask where you are, however, I'll tell them—and the next time we meet, we must be enemies."

CHAPTER
22

////// **Giorsh**
December 24, 1944

It was almost dark when the pitiful few hundred galleys, of *ten* hundreds—almost one part in three that remained of those they'd built to carry the Final Swarm to the Celestial City—gaggled back past the mighty *Giorsh* from the clotted *nakkle* leg, where they'd fought all day. Regent Champion and First General Esshk was beside himself with fury, pacing and ranting for all to see on the open fo'c'sle of his great flagship.

"Repulsed again!" he practically shrieked, his crest so rigidly erect it almost vibrated. "It is *impossible*! There can be no more than six or seven hundreds defending that pathetic wreck that blocks the river, yet they threw back a hundred times their number. *Again!* It cannot be borne!" He rounded on General Ign, who'd been pacing with his lord since he joined him, to describe the action he'd seen. No one else would draw near, and the rest of Esshk's advisors huddled at the base of the sloping casemate beneath the monstrous forward guns protruding from it. "Who is to blame?" Esshk roared. "Find someone to *blame*!"

"Of course, Lord First General," Ign almost simpered. Inside, he smoldered. *There is only* one *to blame, and I needn't search far.*

"Address me as Regent Champion at present," Esshk snapped petulantly, gesturing wildly at the tower of smoke around the bend, glaring bright under the setting sun. "I will have no association with what happened today!"

"Of course, Lord Regent Champion." Ign hesitated. "I will scourge whoever is responsible," he swore, "and destroy him with the traitor's death. But our true advantage did not quite amount to a hundred to one."

"Yes, yes, I know. They still have their flying machines and cruisers—*our cruisers*, before they were stolen—and their detestable fast-shooters that allow few to fight as many, but even then only incompetence and terror could have thwarted us. The traitor's death is too lenient for the culprit!"

Ign's mind soared to agree but quavered at the concept. *No,* he thought. *Esshk is my lord, the greatest general of the age, and he is, for all purposes, the Celestial* Father *of all the Ghaarrichk'k now. I cannot blame him!* Ign was one of only a very few who understood Esshk and the Chooser's ultimate aims, and he supported them wholly. Not only was it essential and far past time that warriors lead their race, but they also must be worldly and wise. No Celestial Mother had ever been a warrior— *More than that one time in her life,* he amended—and their cloistered lives made them anything but worldly. Real wisdom could never naturally occur in them. *It is time for a warrior. It is time for Esshk. It is time for me,* he told himself again, *to stand at Esshk's side as First General and Vice Regent!* Esshk would never be called Celestial Father, of course, but he would be such in all but name. *And all these things will come as we reconquer every speck of ground we've lost, rolling the enemy back and back until we eat the marrow from their bones, in their most distant places. But first we must get past the wreck of the* Santa Catalina.

"It was more than just the flying machines and cruisers, Lord," Ign informed him, "though with no cruisers of our own to counter theirs, they crushed countless galleys beneath their rams. Still, the wreck was almost surrounded, the cruisers nearly overwhelmed. The day was almost ours at last—until their *Arracca*, the monstrous carrier of flying machines, stood in to the rescue. Not only is it large enough to turn warriors prey at the sight of it, but at such close proximity, it is heavily armed with cannon of the old style and new. It went directly alongside the wreck and lashed on, allowing hundreds of troops to reinforce those so close to death. No one could have foreseen such a thing—not even the . . . designer of the battle."

Esshk closed his eyes, and his narrow, muscular shoulders slumped. "Perhaps," he allowed, grasping at the excuse. "But what do we do now? The Swarm remains strong, but we meant to transport much of it on barges once the enemy scattered, hunting the galleys. Of the galleys themselves . . . their numbers dwindle."

"Can we not bomb *Santa Catalina* again? And the carrier as well?" Ign asked, but Esshk slowly shook his head.

"I did not wish to distract you with this news while you organized the assault over the past few days, but the Lord Chooser learned from reports that still pass first through the Palace of Vanished Gods that, just a day after our airships struck such a heavy blow and paved the way for *today's* disaster"—Esshk would've snorted fire if he could—"three of our remaining primary airfields were attacked and destroyed. Destroyed! Somehow the enemy prey discovered where they were at last. Only the one near Lake Galk survives, and there are few airships there. It is the farthest from the fighting," he added bitterly. "Perhaps even worse, now," he continued, "few, if any, of the galleys we lose can be replaced for some time. Nor will there be any more cruiser hulls. The enemy was not content to destroy only our airfield and airship manufacturing yards at Lake Ukri; they attacked there again and again. Surely you noticed that the larger bombers have not come here for some days? In any event, they burned the yards and much of the stockpiled timber on the east shore of Lake Ukri, where we focused the construction of lesser vessels. The yards for greatships of battle on the northwest coast of Lake Nalak are intact, but those ships are of little use to us now." He paused. "Finally, the rocket works across the river have suffered sorely. It is fortunate we have others, and none of the major gunpowder-mealing centers have been found, but we must be more sparing with our rockets until production can match the demand."

He hissed furious frustration and spun away, fluttering his long red cape in an arc behind him. He stood silent for a long moment, staring at the darkening smoke in the distance, past the bend. The sun had gone down and the sky in the east was a brooding purple-brown. "In any event," he ground out, "we have less than five tens of airships left and must use them wisely. We need them for communications now more than anything. Particularly with our forces in the south," he added cryptically, but didn't elaborate. "And to continue the search for General Halik in Persia." He blinked dismay. "He *must* be there, but none of our airships sent to find him have returned. The enemy must be intercepting them, possibly from Indiaa or Zanzibar."

Ign considered that. He didn't know Halik, or really understand how Esshk could be so sure he even still lived, but for whatever reason there was no doubt his lord was unusually fond of the missing general. "Then what shall we do here?" he asked.

"I summoned General of the Sky Muriname most insistently," Esshk replied. "You know he actually has Ghaarrichk'k pilots for some of his machines? We must make more of them as soon as we can, and train more of our race to fly them. Then we will have no further use for the tiresome Japhs." He growled frustration. "But that, like everything, will take time!"

"The General of the Sky will come?" Ign asked skeptically.

Esshk sneered. "He and his larger machines remain delayed, a matter of 'repairs,' I am told, but he sent his smaller machines to counter those of the enemy. They are at the small airship field north of Old Sofesshk. We have not used it since it was first attacked and the enemy will not expect us to now. Besides, the flying machines have been carefully hidden in the forest surrounding it." He stopped, suddenly thinking furiously. "I meant to use them immediately, but then I could do so only once, since

their specialized fuel and weapons have not yet arrived."
He looked at Ign, his eyes narrowing with resolve. "We
will wait until we are ready for the next assault, and then
use them with surprise. Even with the arrival of the enemy flying-machine carrier, the defense of the *nakkle* leg
must be desperately weakened. They do not risk those
ships lightly, and it cannot operate its flying machines
and fight at the same time. Perhaps they ran low enough
on them that they could be of little further assistance?"
He clacked his teeth. "Speculation. There were quite a
few flying machines in the air today, not so?"

"Yes, Lord."

"Still, we must have hurt them, as they have hurt us,
and they must be growing weak in numbers and ammunition for their weapons. If nothing else, we forced them
to use a great deal of *that* today! But we retain the advantage if we can just bring our full weight to bear." His
jaws suddenly opened in a savage grin and his eyes were
alight. "So we will do what we have not before. We will
mount an all-out attack, with as much of the Swarm as
we possibly can, advancing onshore with heavy batteries
as well as on the water."

"But, Lord! They will see! They will prepare and
slaughter our forces before they are even in position."

"Not if we do what they least expect!"

Ign just looked at him, waiting.

"We begin the attack at night, of course! Not just in
the darkness before the dawn but in the deepest black
of night."

Ign was shocked but intrigued. They'd almost done
that once before, and at the time it would've been hopeless. Now, however, with the proper preparation, fast and
deadly flying machines of their own, and particularly
with their primary target immobilized . . . "The confusion will be so great, we may lose nearly as many as we
did today, just in collisions on the water," he warned.

"That is why you will plan it carefully, plan it yourself.
Lead the attack *yourself*!"

Ign gulped. He wasn't afraid to fight or die, but he
never wanted to be the cause of one of Esshk's furious
fits, like the one he'd seen that evening. The traitor's

death could be a mercy compared to what might happen. *Then again, with enough time—and without excessive meddling—it can be done.* He straightened and a surge of . . . not confidence, exactly, but something more akin to the eager acceptance of a difficult challenge gripped him as notions became possibilities, and possibilities began to form into plans. *So be it. I will gladly stake my life on the battle taking shape in my mind,* he swore. "In that case, I will relate an observation of note," he said carefully. "One of the returning galley crews discovered a gap in the wreckage that cruisers, at least, might take advantage of. We must confirm that, but if it exists, I will plan a night attack in which the leading galleys mark the gap for as many cruisers as we can push through. We could be upon the enemy before they know it, with vast numbers and heavy fire from the water and the land— all before they can engage us at long range. As day comes, the Japh flying machines can support us."

"Excellent!" Esshk enthused, warming to the plan that belonged to them both. Never had Grik generals truly collaborated to such a degree, and it was a satisfying, almost giddy experience. General Ign felt it too, and was amazed by the change in his lord. It was almost as if this terrible day had never happened.

"There are only two great things left to consider," Ign ventured.

"They are?"

Ign took a long breath. "First, such an attack will take time to plan, since there will be *tens of hundreds* of small things to prepare. More specifically, we must *practice* for it. Just as a warrior learns the sword, or one of the New Army teaches his muscles to load his garrak without thought, they must all be able to mount this attack as if with their eyes closed! There is no other way it can succeed."

"Time is of the essence, Second General Ign," Esshk said severely, but his crest lowered slightly in acceptance. The Chooser's counsel had taken root—perhaps too late—and his obsessive rebellion against the constant delays was what had caused the day's disaster.

"Indeed, but nevertheless."

Esshk paced back and forth several times, but at least he had himself under control. Ign was relieved. Seeing their lord in such a state couldn't have been good for any warriors watching nearby. "What is the second thing?" he asked at last.

"You realize, Lord, at this point, even a victory at the *nakkle* leg now could wound us too deeply to launch the Final Swarm at the Celestial City at once." Ign was making a statement, not asking a question.

It was Esshk's turn to take a long breath. "Such has occurred to me," he conceded. "But we cannot let that deter us. Doing nothing, or continuing as we have, will *never* loose the Final Swarm. It remains trapped here until the river is clear. See to it, Second General Ign." He paused, his gaze intent. "The plan now forged must be honed to the keenest edge. That shall be your task. Take us down the river—and across the strait!"

Ign left *Giorsh* in his personal galley, larger than the standard and equipped with a narrow but comfortably appointed pavilion amidships, sufficient to accommodate his senior staff. Few of those were present, having already been dispatched to begin specific preparations. First they must determine what was left from today. Those warriors—those *troops*—had been savaged, yet apparently none had turned prey. They had simply, finally, withdrawn. *They must be reorganized, as I did with Ker-noll Jash's force, and prepared for use again. Guns and galleys must be gathered, as well as sufficient cruisers.* They were running short of those. He paced his pavilion as the rowers propelled him to his destination. All *our warriors must be reorganized, and training for their specific assignments begun,* he thought, *yet all has to be hidden from the sky!* He groaned to himself. How to do that? *How can we make something seem it is not there when it is? Particularly when we are conserving rockets. Most we shoot at the sky are wasted, but they do keep the enemy cautious. Should we save them all for bombardment? They are effective against surface targets—especially if the great enemy carrier remains where it is. But then their flying machines will feel even freer to observe what we do from the air!* Suddenly, he remembered the odd coloration of the enemy ships, with their strange patterns. *Their warriors dress in such a way as to make them more difficult to see as well. Perhaps we can do the same? Somehow hide ourselves in plain sight?* He'd have to consider that.

Everything he wanted to do would take time, probably longer than Esshk would permit, but Ign had girded himself to insist—to the extent of offering to destroy himself and forcing First General Esshk to take sole command. *He might do it,* Ign knew. *So certain of success after the enemy ship/fort was so badly damaged by our bombing, he'd delegated me to merely organizing the assault today, to his limited specifications, as best I could. Esshk owned the failure, and his greatest fury had no doubt been directed at himself, his command to "find someone to blame" a desperate, hopeful deflection. But if he fails alone on the scale we now contemplate, there can be no one to blame but himself. Even the Chooser might turn against him. If we both fail, the blame might be sufficiently diluted for us both to survive.* Ign growled at himself. *But we will not fail this time.* Still, in case they did, he had other preparations to make.

It was long past dark when his command galley edged up to a pier supported by the ravaged hulls of galleys that still floated but were too badly damaged to repair sufficiently for battle. Others, in better shape, were tied to them. In the gloom, they looked just as dead, since there were no torches to mark them and their crews mostly slept. None of these warriors had been involved in the debacle that day; they'd already faced another, and Ign was conserving them. He hoped to good effect. To his satisfaction, he and his aides were challenged immediately, as soon as they set foot on the pier.

"I am Second General Ign," he proclaimed to the two guards armed with muskets, bayonets fixed. "We know," they gushed simultaneously, and threw themselves to the dock at his feet, taking care to protect their weapons, he noted. "I am here to see Ker-noll Jash. Fetch him at once!"

One of the guards leaped up and hurried away, his short tail plumage fanned as wide as it was able. Ign turned to the other. "Rise. Make a light before I trip and fall in the river. If the enemy attacks from the air tonight, we will hear him in time to douse the flame. Besides, I doubt they will waste their bombs on a single torch."

"Of course, Second General!" the guard practically yipped, fumbling for flint, steel, and tinder in a pouch on his belt. Very quickly he'd struck a light, and a single tall torch blazed on the pier. Jash and his second in command, Senior First Naxa, trotted down the booming, bouncing planks, closely followed by the messenger, until they arrived in front of Ign. He could tell they were wondering if they should go down on their bellies as well, but Ign spoke before they could decide. "I am relieving you of your duties here," he said brusquely. Jash looked stunned, then glanced helplessly around, unable to speak. Ign continued relentlessly. "You will abandon your galleys at dawn, as others arrive to occupy them. When they do, you will take all the warriors under your command to a place a half day's march upriver, where others like you will begin to form."

"Like *us*, Lord General?" Jash ventured.

"Yes. Warriors who have not only proven themselves in battle, but have proven they can think. More important, that they can cope with . . . setbacks. Not many such survive," Ign added with a snort, "though perhaps a few have joined those ranks today."

"The attack," Jash asked carefully, "it was a setback?"

Ign jerked a diagonal nod. "First General Esshk used the term 'disaster,' and that might be a better description. In any event, now we will prepare to strike with the entire Swarm. As much as we can put afloat."

"Then . . . why take us *out* of our ships, Lord General? Why take us off the water?"

"Because even the lowliest Uul can pull an oar and die, Ker-noll Jash," Ign snapped brutally. "I have other plans for those like you." His voice softened slightly. "My sire was a seafaring Hij, and I began my training for war at sea, so I can understand the attachment you have formed to your galleys. But I want you to refresh the meager training you received in the new discipline of defense."

Naxa's stubbly young crest bristled, and Ign held up

a clawed hand. "I know. It is still considered unworthy by many, but *you* were bred for it, if insufficiently prepared. I want you to learn it well, but I also want you to think about it, make suggestions to your instructors. They know of you and *will* listen."

"But . . ." Naxa seemed devastated. "While we train, we will miss the battle? Perhaps the greatest battle that ever was?"

"That is possible," Ign acknowledged. "Or I may send for you and keep you with me, adding to my Personal Guard. . . ." He hesitated. "Regi-'ent," he said at last, tasting the word. "I will lead the attack from shore, flanking the enemy with as many cannon as we can move. First General Esshk will command on the water." Ign hadn't suggested this to Esshk just yet, but was sure his lord would agree. He remained of the old school, after all, in which generals never actually drew their swords in battle. Protected by *Giorsh*'s mighty armor was the best place for him. "Be warned, however," Ign added, "that I do not mean for you to face battle in the attack." His crest fluttered and he glanced at the dark galleys, most of their crews still sleeping. "Oh, some of you will die; I have no doubt the enemy will bomb and shoot at us." His eyes narrowed and his crest flared high. "But just as I no longer ever expect our plans to go entirely as designed, this enemy has taught me that he will *never* do as we expect. If you do find yourselves facing the enemy weapon to weapon onshore, we will all have great need of your defensive skills." He sighed. "And your understanding of when the time has come to withdraw." He cocked his head to the side. "If any of us manage to live through that, then rest assured that the 'greatest battle that ever was' will come sometime later, and you will play a most prominent part."

USS Santa Catalina

"Thumped 'em again," Silva said, gazing over the bullet-dented plates and stuffing-leaking mattresses secured to the stanchions. His tone wasn't triumphant, however; it was just tired. He was leaning against a mangled, red-soaked mattress on the ravaged hulk's starboard-side upper deck, his blood-crusted cutlass still in his hand. He needed to clean it before shoving it back in the scabbard at his side. Countless Grik bodies and the remains of bullet-splintered, smoldering galleys bumped and pirouetted against the ship's perforated sides as the current swept them along. It was a macabre, surrealistic sight, its ghastliness and scope only hinted at by the lurid light of other galleys burning more fiercely. Silva was surprised how many bodies there were, only a few occasionally twitching or heaving slightly in a desultory fashion as things below merely picked at their food. "Water boogers've got finicky," he observed, guessing even the voracious crocodiles and other predators must've been satiated at last, but not before paving the whole bottom of the river with bones.

"Appaar-ently," Chack agreed, equally exhausted, leaning on the rail beside him. He didn't even have the energy to pick the dry, crusty blood out of his fur. He couldn't possibly have gotten it all. Though somehow uninjured, they were both splashed with gore. The Grik had actually gained *Santy Cat*'s decks before *Arracca* finally steamed alongside, and all the survivors had resorted to the bayonet and the cutlass. Chack's Brigade, led by Risa, Cook, and Galay, had streamed across to bolster their ranks and finally turned the tide, but not before Simy Gutfeld's Marines were savagely mauled. Gunny Horn and Lawrence joined them, moving slow. Petey was probably still hiding.

"Pam's going across to *Arracca* with the wounded," Horn said, for Silva's benefit. "There're a lot. More than even *Arracca*'s medical division can handle." He waved to port. "So Pam'll be staying aboard her, and they have to get underway in case Grik zeps come—or they start shooting rockets."

Dennis grunted and shrugged.

"I thought us got all their zephs," Lawrence said, his voice distorted like a man with a broken nose by a long slash across his snout. Miraculously, he was the only one of the four who'd been wounded.

"Maybe, maybe not," Horn speculated. "Can't take the chance."

"How the hell are they gonna turn her fat ass around?" Silva asked. "River's wide here, but the deep channel's too narrow, ain't it?"

"We will back *Arracca*'s 'faat aass' to where the chaannel widens again," came an amused, almost little-girl voice behind them. They turned, and there was Tassanna-Ay-Arracca; Chack's sister, Risa-Sab-At; and Major Enrico Galay.

"There's my girls!" Silva said as he moved to embrace the Lemurian females, grinning for the first time since the battle ended. (He always wore an unnerving grin of some sort during combat, but no one was quite sure what it meant, or even if he knew.)

"Chief Sil-vaa," Chack growled, "Ahd-mi-raal Tassanna and Major Risa are both your superior officers. You caan't simply claasp them to you when you meet!"

"Of course he caan," Tassanna said, returning the hug. Then she moved to embrace Chack, Horn, even Lawrence. Risa took her turn with Silva, and the hug lasted long enough for Chack to cough irritably.

"Enough of your grumping!" Risa scolded her brother. "*You* reminded me how import-aant Dennis is to me at Zaan-zi-bar. How import-aant all my friends are! Especially at times like this." She backed away. "Go see Paam," she urged Silva.

Gutfeld limped up, his trouser leg cut away and a bloody bandage wrapped around his upper thigh. "You should go across to *Arracca*," Chack told him.

"Oh, I'd love to," Gutfeld said. "But with such a little scratch, compared to the real wounds over there, I'd be embarrassed." Others began to join them, shuffling tiredly toward the gathering. Tassanna glanced around, seeing only "original" defenders—what was left of the 3rd Marines. Major Cook was using several hundred of Chack's Brigade to rig repairs to the defenses; carry provisions, water, and crates of ammunition across; and take the wounded and dead aboard *Arracca*. They were doing everything they could to get the collapsing colander that had been a ship ready for yet another attack like they'd endured that day. Looking at the faces around her, 'Cat and human, Tassanna wasn't sure that was possible, no matter what they did.

"Listen to me," she said. "I think, perhaaps, this haas gone on long enough. You've shaattered every aassault the enemy haas made, destroyed untold numbers of their waarriors, and devastated their gaalley fleet. I . . . believe we might be able to stop them from the comparative safety of the open water now, in the strait. I *must* retire with *Arracca*. I caan't leave her in range of their rockets, or motionless beneath attaacks from the air." Her tail flipped back and forth, and she blinked pleadingly at Chack. "Come with me. We've established an air-field at the mouth of the river, improved the Grik forts there, and landed heavy guns. We have a foothold on the enemy's ground, awaiting only the rest of First Fleet and the expeditionary force's arrival. You haave done your duty and more."

Chack blinked regret. "We caan't," he said. "All you say is true, but you only tell haaf the tale. With raad-io, we have the straight dope."

He looked around and continued, raising his voice. "The sea-lanes are cut until the entire fleet can come with *Ellie*"—he grinned in wonder—"and *Ma-haan*, I was aa-stonished to hear. And hopefully *Waa-kur* as well. But they're needed to protect against a sub-maa-rine lurking in the strait. There haave been more reports, and the sub-maa-rine is confirmed, though the Maker knows how it can remain so long. One of Jumbo's Clippers even dropped bombs on it before it could submerge, but there was no sign it was daam-aged. The upshot is, there'll be no more supplies thaat caan't be flown in for us"—he nodded at Tassanna—"or for TF Bottle Caap and the new forts on the coast. More planes will trickle in, but most must be held baack for First Fleet." He blinked mild reproach at Tassanna for her well-intentioned deception. "So, the strait is now too dangerous even for *Arracca*, as you know. She must stay in the shaallows at the river mouth. And that mouth is too wide, with too many fingers, to contain the many hundreds, if not thousands, of gaalleys still remaining to the enemy. Paarticularly if they make their paassage in the dark." He shook his head. "We must keep holding them here, where they *caan't* sneak paast and where our dwindling aam-u-nition will have the greatest effect at the shortest distaance." He looked at Silva. "We must keep punching them in the gut."

Silva arched the brow over his good eye, then shrugged, and Chack looked back at Tassanna. "It's decided. We stay." He considered. "Most of the First Raider Brigade will reinforce us here—there's no space for all—but the rest will embaark on the cruisers *Ris* and *Itaa*. They'll take all the mortars we caan't employ here and form a ready reserve, but also be prepared to pursue other opportunities."

"If thaat's whaat you think is best," Tassanna said, frowning.

"It is. First Fleet and Ahd-mi-raal Keje, gener-aals Alden, Rolak, and my mate, Safir Maraan, *will* come soon. *Cap-i-taan Reddy* will come soon. When they do, we'll haand them more thaan a beachhead. We'll give them a baattle already haaf won!"

There were tired cheers. They weren't the cheers of enthusiasm, but they carried acceptance and resolve. That was all that mattered.

After Risa, Tassanna, and Galay left, the four of them leaned on the rail again, and Gutfeld grimaced and sat on a winch.

"Opportunities?" Silva asked.

Chack had been sure he'd pick up on that. "Yes, but not the sort you so enjoy. The Grik have slaammed us, head-on, over and over again." He quirked a wry smile. "They must be getting tired of it. After they recover from today, they'll almost certainly try something different— and we must be ready to counter any 'opportunities' *they* may try to seize."

Brevet Major Abel Cook approached and saluted, his boyish face grim in the flickering light. Petey was standing on his shoulders behind his neck, tense and alert.

"There you are, you chickenshit little skink!" Silva proclaimed. "Oh! Not you, Mr. Cook. Glad to see *you*. I mean that leech stuck to your neck."

"Shit!" Petey cawed, and launched himself at the big man, resuming his usual perch and sniffing for food. He'd taken to digging his claws into Silva's shoulders, like a cat making bread, when he was most insistently hungry, and Silva hated it. "Quit that, you little turd!"

"Turd!" Petey screeched adamantly. "Eat! Goddamn!"

"No!" Silva snapped harshly. "Eat later. No food now."

Petey bonelessly collapsed around Silva's neck and uttered a low, desolate moan.

"Oh, my God!" Abel chuckled, and somehow, everyone found it within them to laugh.

"Go ahead," Silva simmered. "Yuk it up. Don't know how I ever wound up with the little flyin' snake gut in the first place. Why don't you take him, Mr. Cook?"

"Thank you, no. I already feel rather unprepared for my current duties, standing in for Major I'joorka. The responsibilities inherent in nurturing such a sensitive and delicate creature as Petey are quite beyond me." Cook turned to Chack. "We're almost finished transferring wounded and supplies, and *Arracca* will be shoving off soon. What do you want the Raiders remaining aboard, and myself, to do next?"

"Get some rest, Major Cook," Chack ordered. "You'll need it." He looked at Silva. "And *you* go see Paam. I know you think it's un-maanly to betray true feelings toward your mate—"

"She ain't my mate," Silva interrupted.

"I consider her so, and so does she."

"Whoop-tee-do. If anybody's my *legal* mate, it's Risa! Why, we—"

"Chief Sil-vaa! Go! I rarely give you direct orders, but I am now—and I also order you not to tell Paam you went to see her because I ordered you to!"

"Aye, aye, Chackie." Silva grinned. "You take all the fun outa ever'thing, but you're the boss. Just remember, if any 'opportunities' of my sort do rear up, I want in. I wanna play somethin' new."

////// *Grik City*
December 28, 1944

A hazy yellow morning glared across Grik City Bay, washing the largest concentration of Allied shipping ever gathered on the Grik front of the war in tarnished, fluid bronze. Fluid, because there was already a great deal of activity on the water, and boiler smoke, highlighted as well, seemed to pour into the sky. Hundreds of small boats and barges scurried between the ships, distributing everything from ammunition to water barrels, and larger vessels took turns alongside the big new oilers, or visited clusters of smaller oilers of the older sort. Frequent bombings had prevented the construction of large, fixed, tank batteries at Grik City, so for the most part, they'd always floated in the bay.

"Alan Letts worked wonders getting so many support ships sent down," Matt observed. He was standing with all the First Fleet brass—plus a few others—on the observation deck behind *Big Sal*'s pilothouse. They'd gathered for the meeting he'd called as soon as *Mahan* escorted *Tarakaan Island* in just before dawn. *Tara* had moved to the docks to begin embarking II Corps, and *Mahan* was anchored close alongside *Big Sal*, taking on fuel. Her paint job had been completed during her short boiler refit, and now she sported the same "dazzle" scheme as most of the other ships.

"Indeed," Keje rumbled beside him. "But this is nearly all we haave left. More ships are building as we speak, but I understaand he stripped aaux-iliaries from all our possessions as far east as Baalkpan itself."

"There's not even enough transport left at Madras to bring Sixth Corps down," General Pete Alden agreed. "We'll have to turn this around as soon as we free it up." He shook his head. "Jeez. This is a pretty big anchorage, way bigger than Mahe's, but it looks just as packed." Pete and General Muln Rolak, along with their I and III Corps, had never been here. Matt remembered there'd probably been nearly as many Grik ships in port when they attacked and took the place, but their Indiamen had been clustered tightly together on the southwest end of the bay and the huge Grik dreadnaughts were mostly near the docks. The middle of the bay had been relatively clear. The majority of the Allied ships were anchored in the middle now, and the sheer size of some of them was enough to alter even Matt's perspective. Big as they were, even the Grik BBs were kind of small compared to *Big Sal*, USS *Madraas*, and USS *Tarakaan Island*. USS *Sular* had been converted to a troopship from a Grik BB, but looked bigger with all the landing dories bulking up her sloping sides.

And then there was USS *Savoie*, of course. Not as long as a Grik BB, but more massive above the waterline. She wouldn't participate in the coming operation—her crew and repairs weren't ready—but with the end to Grik air raids here, she'd steamed down from Mahe on two engines. Matt figured she'd be just as safe, and fully combat ready or not, Russ Chappelle assured him she *could* fight. *Savoie* would continue to work up her crew while adding a powerful deterrent to anyone trying to enter the bay while the rest of them were gone.

Besides, unless they sent *Savoie* all the way back to Madraas, here was the only place she could complete her renovations. Mahe had turned into a ghost town almost overnight. A Nancy patrol squadron, an oiler, and six motor torpedo boats were all they'd left behind. Even

the Austraalan engineers who had been building air-
strips were brought down. Nat Hardee would miss his
MTBs, but he'd received ten more from the Filpin Lands,
enough to bring his squadron up to strength. Only his
and one other boat had veteran crews, however. The rest
had been wiped out on Lizard Ass Bay.

The new MTBs, countless tons of supplies, munitions,
fuel, and a half-dozen more tanks Alan Letts squeezed
from the production budget arrived aboard twelve heavy
haulers. Like the new oilers, these were wooden steamers built on the up-scaled lines of Scott-class steam frigates. Fatter, longer, virtually unarmed, and with only two
masts for auxiliary sails, they had impressive cargo ca-
pacities and required a minimal crew. More were being
built in Austraal as fast as engines and boilers could be
sent, and they'd bring continuous reinforcements straight
from there as the campaign progressed. No longer would
Austraalan troops have to be taken to Baalkpan for
training before heading to the front. That was the hope,
anyway.

Otherwise, the harbor was crowded still more with
older, more conventional transports, oilers, and all the
other auxiliaries the fleet required. Most had been gathering at Mahe and came down with the fleet, but many
came straight from Baalkpan, La-laanti, Aryaal, Andamaan, even Madraas, braving the terrible sea and its
monstrous denizens without escorts. More than one was
overdue. The sailing steam frigates and AVDs still in
service, despite their distinguished records, weren't up
to the kind of fighting TF Bottle Cap had reported, and
most would be sent back to Madraas to escort VI Corps
down. They still had their AMF-DIC equipment, designed to acoustically discourage mountain fish. It might
do the same to any submarines the League left creeping
around. Careful Lemurian ears might even be able to tell
the difference—and the ships did carry depth charges. A
few steam frigates (DDs) would remain, redesignated as
APDs—fast destroyer transports. They could be used to
get Marines ashore quickly, if necessary, probably under
fire.

Finally, there was USS *James Ellis* and USS *Mahan*.

Ellie hadn't been here before either, and caused a stir when she arrived because she looked just like *Walker*. Some were disappointed she wasn't *Walker*, but all were excited by what her presence implied: that the Allies could make more. *Mahan* caused excitement as well, more among those who knew her than those who didn't. Most of the former exhibited the same incredulity Matt still shared to some degree as he stared down at her, riding peacefully at anchor. He shook his head. *She's mine now—for now. Tiaa's shaping up fine, and I'll turn* Mahan *back over to her as soon as* Walker *arrives.* It didn't look like that would happen in time, however, and he realized he'd likely be going into battle aboard a ship other than *Walker* for the very first time. The thought made him uneasy. He glanced at the horizon to the north, the morning clouds still purple and orange, wishing for *Walker*'s distinctive shape and that of their new cruiser. Both would've come in very handy.

"What do you think, my brother?" Keje rumbled beside him, and Matt jerked, surprised he'd allowed himself to drift. He applied a false smile.

"I'm sorry, Keje. What was that?"

Keje nodded at General Queen Safir Maraan. "She said Col-nol Will is concerned about Hij Geerki's Grik workers and what they will do after we're gone." Colonel Will, commanding the Maroons and Shee-Ree, was present with some of his staff but seemed content to let Safir speak for him, so Matt looked at Safir. She was standing with Pete Alden and Muln Rolak, and it was the first time they'd been together in a very long time. Also gathered were the commanding officers of many of the ships around them, the COFOs of *Big Sal*, *Madraas*, and the Grik City air defense. Even Ben Mallory had flown in to join them from the Comoros, leaving Jumbo behind. They'd tapered off their bombing attacks on Sofesshk over the past few days, gathering strength and forces for a major effort. Only ground-attack aircraft from *Arracca* and the airstrip she'd established could really help their friends on *Santa Catalina* at the moment.

"Do you think they'll be a problem?" Matt asked Safir. She blinked denial and shook her head. "No. We work them, saal-vaaging Grik wrecks and improving defenses, but they've never been so free." She blinked again. "Or well fed. Any desire they may haave had for things to 'go baack to normaal' is gone."

"Geerki thinks so as well?" Rolak questioned. The remarkably ancient Geerki had been his "pet" for a time, but had proven himself loyal more than once.

"He does," Safir assured.

"But what of the Gareiks Colonel Miles is chasin'?" Will spoke up. "If he dan't kill 'em all, thar'll be naught but us tae stop 'em when ye laeve!"

Matt nodded. They'd been through all this before, but he understood how Will felt. The man was no coward— he wanted to go with them—but he wasn't keen on being left with such a small force to defend against such a potentially large one. "If Miles can't finish them off and there's too many to stop at the walls"—he shrugged—"let 'em have the crummy joint. Pull back to the waterfront and evacuate aboard *Savoie* and her tenders. They'll get you out. Or you can cross the Wall of Trees and take to the jungle. Link up with Miles. It really won't matter. The few Grik that get in here will already be weak and starving."

"They'll eat Geerki's civvy Grik," Pete warned, and Matt pursed his lips. "Yeah, I hadn't thought of that. Not much we can do about it either."

"We could pull them out with the Shee-Ree and Maroons," Sandra said quietly, speaking for the first time since greeting her friends.

Pete looked at her, amazed. "We can't have a buncha damn *Grik* running loose on Russ's battlewagon!"

Russ Chappelle chuckled. He and Mikey Monk were standing with some of the other ship commanders. "Believe it or not, Pete, we've already *got* Grik on *Savoie*."

Pete looked even more surprised. "I never saw 'em at Mahe."

"They don't get out much," Russ quipped. "They do behave themselves, though." He looked at Matt. "I can take some of Geerki's friends, but not all. A lot might still feed the Grik."

"Not for long," Rolak said philosophically. "And not

enough to strengthen them after their ordeal in the swaamps"—he nodded at Will—"or the effort of overwhelming the defenses here. Once we win our battle with First Gener-aal Esshk, any Grik here should be simple enough to remove."

Will, looking from one to another, finally voiced the question nagging them all. "But . . . What if ye—*we*—cannae boot the Gareiks back out because . . ." His expression twisted into a grimace. "Because we cannae!" he simply said.

"You mean, what if we lose?" Sandra replied. She looked around and continued simply, without raising her voice. "We won't. We can't." She waved around the harbor. "This is it, all there is. All that's left of the grand vision we dreamed when we first met. Sure, we'll get more ships, more troops, more supplies, but if we wait any longer, *Santa Catalina*—and everyone in her we love—will be gone. Wasted."

Russ Chappelle nodded grim agreement, and Sandra's voice finally started to rise. "*Now* is the time to take advantage of their sacrifice, while they're still alive, still blocking the river!" she said. "Now is the time to add our attack to theirs and take the fight to the Grik!" Her gaze fell on Safir. "If we wait, they'll all have died for nothing and we'll be right back on the defensive again. And we'll stay on the defensive this time," she warned, "all the way back where we started." She shook her head, eyes flashing with steely determination. "No," she snapped. "We didn't come all this way just to wait for the perfect situation. That'll *never* come. And we haven't endured all we have, lost all we have, just to say, 'Time out! We're not ready!'" She pointed vaguely southeast. "That's where the fight is, and it's happening right now. We're not too early for it—we're almost too damn late!" Her hand strayed to the bulge in her belly. "It's time to do what we came here for. For those we've lost"—she gently patted the bulge—"and those to come. But also for each other and *ourselves*." She lowered her voice again and even managed a smile, but her eyes had begun to fill. "We'll do it so we can live our lives and raise our young, at least for a time, without the *torture* of this war hanging over us."

"She's right," Matt agreed, putting his arm around her. "We won't lose, *because* we can't. And we can't abandon those who've given us this precious time." He looked at everyone, just as his wife had. "We go, and we go today." He looked at Safir. "What's your status?"

"As you know, Second Corps began embarking as soon as *Taara-kaan Island* touched the docks." There was no hesitation in Safir, not with Chack fighting for his life on the Zambezi. She'd had her troops ready for quite a while. "The only delay will come from re-aaranging some of what *Taara* carries in her repair bay, to combaat load her, as you say. The taanks"—she stumbled slightly over the unfamiliar word—"all eight of them, including the two that survived the attaack on Zaan-zi-bar, are already loaded in the special landing barges they require, but we must move them if they need to laand before all our aartillery and other supplies. Gener-aal Rolak says they should be in the middle. The first out should be laanding craaft with troops, maa-chine guns, mortars, and light aartillery. Taanks next, then heavy aartillery, more troops, and supplies."

"That's how Chack figured it at Zanzibar and it seemed to work pretty well," Matt agreed.

"Yes, but it haas slowed us down."

"How long will it take?"

"Perhaaps the rest of the day," Safir admitted miserably.

Matt looked at Pete and Rolak. "But First and Third Corps is still embarked. You're just loading the new divisions that got sent here?"

"Aye, sir," Pete agreed. "A few hours, tops."

Matt looked back at Safir, a tight knot forming in his chest. Long ago—and occasionally still, from time to time—he'd wished he could just lay the awesome responsibility that'd been dumped on him at the feet of another. How many thousands had died under his orders? How many times had he gambled with their lives—with the very survival of all their people on this world? And now he was about to do it again. He took a deep breath. "Let me know as soon as Second Corps is fully embarked," he told Safir. "Go over yourself and set fire to their tails."

He raised his voice so all could hear. "Generals Alden and Rolak, Colonel Mallory." He nodded at Keje's commander of flight operations with a slight smile. "COFO Tikker," he added, then glanced at his *Mahan* XO, "and Commander Tiaa-Baari will remain here with Admiral Keje and me for further discussions."

Tiaa's eyes widened in horrified surprise. She was profoundly uncomfortable around so many giants of the Alliance and had no idea why she was there in the first place.

Matt continued. "Everybody else, return to your ships. Complete fueling, ammunitioning, and victualing as soon as possible." He glanced at Russ. "You stay too. Since you're stuck here, you might as well help work out a schedule to speed things up." He turned to the rest once more. "This entire task force *will* be underway by nightfall."

December 30, 1944

Two nights and three excruciating days out of Grik City Bay, most elements of First Fleet designated to participate in the operation to rescue TF Bottle Cap—and take the war to the Grik—finally appeared off the mouth of the Zambezi River. Some of the new heavy haulers had broken down and been towed back, but that was probably inevitable given the speed with which they'd been designed, thrown together, filled with cargo, and sent to the front. Other ships, civilian freight haulers for the most part, had straggled badly. But every member of the Amer-i-caan Navy Clan, or anything that might've been considered a warship, for that matter, had made it. Terrified as many must surely be, nobody was willing to miss this.

From the captain's chair in *Mahan*'s pilothouse, Matt studied the hazy, darkening smear ahead that was the continent of Africa. He couldn't imagine how they'd cram the whole task force up the Zambezi, especially since the only place they could possibly turn anything big around, short of Sofesshk itself, was lousy with wrecks. And *Ar-*

racca was already upriver, halfway to where *Santa Cata-lina*'s people might need immediate assistance. Matt was most concerned about Tassanna hanging so close to her shattered consort because most of her planes were ashore and she thought *Arracca*'s guns could make a difference.

"Surfaace con-taact! Bear-een one five seero! Range tree t'ousand yaads!" the bridge talker behind him suddenly shouted. Matt spun to face the relatively tall, skinny 'Cat and felt a little disoriented yet again. "Bridge talker" wasn't a permanent rating or classification in the navy—except aboard USS *Walker*, where the diminutive Minnie and her equally tiny mates monopolized the duty through their professionalism and, frankly, the simple fact that they could always make themselves heard and understood. In such a mixed-language navy, understanding could never be taken for granted. Fortunately, Matt understood *Ma-han*'s current talker perfectly well. "Crow's-nest lookout reports some-teen' like a big gri-kakka with a weird back fin floatin' on the surface. He don't know whaat it is."

Matt raised his binoculars and stared twenty degrees to starboard of *Mahan*'s—and the task force's—line of advance. The coast was sharper, darker now, and the contact might've remained invisible without the glare of the setting sun washing across its distinctive shape, brightening the splotchy, rusty gray of its conn tower and long, lean hull. In spite of the warm, humid air gushing through the pilothouse, Matt felt ice water pour down his spine.

"All ahead full. Come right to two four zero," he ordered as calmly as he could. "Sound general quarters. Surface *target*"—he stressed the word—"looks like a Kraut *submarine*. Big sucker. Maybe a type nine?" He shook his head. It was too far, and what type it was meant nothing to anyone on *Mahan* but him. "Inform *Ellie*—and Admiral Keje—that we're attacking." He thought about ordering *Ellie* to come up to give him a hand—but what if there was more than one enemy sub? They were best off sticking with the procedure they'd come up with for this situation: mountain fish generally fled from the acoustic hammering they took from the DD's sonar and the AMF-DIC of the sound-equipped auxiliaries. If a sub was picked up, probably initially distinguishing itself

by not fleeing and then by the different returns the
soundmen and 'Cats now knew to look for, the auxiliaries and deep-draft freighters would form a protective
screen around *Big Sal*, *Madraas*, *Sular*, and *Tarakaan
Island*. The closest modern DD would attack while the
other stood by to assist or respond to other threats. "Ask
Keje to vector his combat air patrol to the target, but tell
Ellie to hang back until we call her."

"Ay, ay, sur!"

Pack Rat had apparently dropped on his belly and
slid forward to hang down from the fire-control platform
above the bridge—holding on to the stanchions with his
toes or tail, for all Matt knew—and was staring at him
upside down. "We gonna *shoot*, Skipper?" he asked as
Mahan rapidly accelerated, white water surging up
around her propeller guards.

"You bet your ass. Quit hanging there like a possum
and get the main battery ready to fire!"

"Ay, ay, Skipper! Main baattery's maanned an'
ready!" Pack Rat glanced aft and blinked annoyance.
"Torpedoes an' secondaries is laaggin'." Then his face
vanished. Matt should've chastised him more sharply for
the unorthodox stunt, but just couldn't make himself.
Pack Rat knew what to do, but he was no officer, and this
was his first chance to act like one. Matt would have
Tiaa-Baari talk with him later. He raised his binoculars
again. "What's the target doing?" he asked.

"He just . . . sittin' there," the talker replied, blinking
uncertainty. He obviously didn't know what else to say.
That's when Matt realized he'd made a big mistake. He
was used to the instant (if sometimes exasperatingly laid-
back) professionalism aboard *Walker*, her veterans—'Cat
and human—able to perform their duties with hardly
any thought. And every one of them knew exactly what
he wanted when he asked a question. He'd grown spoiled
and forgotten how to act around an entirely green crew.
He'd completely forgotten how green *he'd* been just a
few short years ago! Despite SOP at GQ, Commander
Tiaa-Baari, XO or not, had no business at the auxiliary
conn in combat, not yet, but that's where she'd bolted as
soon as the alarm sounded. *She's got the brains, initia-*

tive, and guts to go far, but she's got a lot to learn. I should've told her to stay on the bridge! She's proven she knows how to handle the ship, but now she needs to learn how to fight it. Have to fix that . . .

"Commander Tiaa to the bridge on the double," he shouted. "Talker, ask the lookout what that pigboat's doing *besides* just sitting there! Is it blowing air, trying to submerge? Is it manning guns? What's its heading? Speed?" Matt quickly paced to the starboard bridgewing and stared forward. "Range!" he barked directly up at Pack Rat, bypassing the confused talker, who was trying to get the information Matt asked for while still reciting readiness reports. They'd done a lot better in drills, but this was taking way too long.

Tiaa pounded up the ladder onto what used to be the amidships deckhouse and raced to his side. "Reporting as ordered, Cap-i-taan!" she cried.

"Nineteen hundreds," Pack Rat quickly shouted back, but then he also hesitated. "Taagit course an' speed is . . . nothin'. He's just sittin' there, Skipper!"

Matt shook his head, staring at what was definitely a Type XI boat. *What the hell?* he roared inside his head. He turned to Tiaa. "That's gotta be the same boat that's been snooping around down here for weeks. Hasn't even made a secret of it. And surfacing right in front of a task force on its way to, hopefully, even the odds against the Grik isn't—*can't be*—a benign act. Particularly based on past experience. I think this is another League attempt to lean on the scales, to keep us from relieving *Santy Cat* and let the Grik break out."

Tiaa was nodding quickly, but her eyes blinked doubt. Matt didn't catch it, or thought she was just as shocked as he was that they'd be this bold. His eyes narrowed. "*Or*," he continued, "maybe they bobbed up for a better look to see if we brought *Savoie*. I doubt word got out to the League by radio from Zanzibar that we took her, but that sneaking sub might've *seen* us do it and reported. Rizzo's Italian ground crews spilled that they'd been expecting ammunition resupply by sub. . . ." He suddenly nodded to himself. "*That's* why the damn U-boat's still hanging around out here: to find *Savoie* and put a spread of fish in her! Sure, we might kill the sub, but balanced against us having *Savoie*, the League probably considers it expendable."

"But . . ." Tiaa finally broke in, still blinking uncertainty. "*Saa-voie* was expend-aable too, was she not?" The U-boat was plainly visible to her by now from the pilothouse. And it *was* just sitting there. "Maybe the sub-maa-rine crew don't feel expend-aable. Maybe they just wanna talk?" Tiaa could hardly believe she'd dared to disagree with Captain Reddy, but to her amazement, he gave her an encouraging nod. Then he took a deep, bitter breath. "Maybe," he agreed. "More likely, though, even if they do, it's just to delay us more." His voice hardened. "And we can't wait to find out. *Big Sal* will be in range of her fish shortly, unless she changes course. More damn delays, whether that's their aim or not, and the League's caused us enough of those." He snorted. "Besides, I *told* Gravois what we'd do if we caught their damn sub poking around after he left." He looked up at Pack Rat's expectant face, peering down at him again. "Commence firing!"

The talker finally announced, "All stations maanned an' ready," just as the salvo buzzer rang. Unlike *Walker*'s, *Mahan*'s buzzer was still the original, and even after being sunk, it sounded mostly like it should. *Raaaa—Blam!* The number one gun fired at one thousand yards, missing long. A big splash rose up far beyond the target and *blam!* the second round was already on the way, missing even farther. Pack Rat had ordered an up ladder but blew his initial range. "Check fire!" Matt heard his shout. "Down five hundreds! Commence firin'!" But at twenty-five knots, *Mahan* had already closed the distance and the next shot fell long as well.

"Damn!" Matt muttered, staring through his binoculars. The sub was going down fast, the setting sun lighting the spray as air jetted from ballast tanks. A shell finally came close, arcing right over the sub's deck gun as it vanished underwater, but Matt shook his head in frustration as the last shot hit empty water in about the same place.

"Cease firing!" he ordered. "Stand by, depth charges. Reduce speed to fifteen knots."

"Sound will find him," Tiaa assured, but her eyes were blinking shame. Worse, the number two and three guns' crews behind the bridge, which hadn't been able to fire because of the angle, were shouting heated insults at the number one gun crew—which was yelling angrily back. A few jeers were normal, even acceptable, but this wasn't, and Tiaa clearly didn't know what to do about it. It dawned on Matt that getting *Mahan* ready to fight had tightly welded her people together in one way, but their goal complete, they'd never really become a *crew.* They had a chief bosun's mate—in name—but Matt suspected the burly, no-nonsense Ensign Toos he'd sent to *Walker* had been the ship's disciplinarian. He snatched up a speaking trumpet and leaned out over the bridgewing. "Silence fore and aft!" he roared. "This is not a baseball game! It's a ship of war, under my command, in *my* American Navy Clan! His eyes focused on Torpedoman First Class Fino-Saal, whom he'd appointed acting torpedo officer. Well, he was good at other things too. "You're *Chief* Saal now, chief bosun's mate. Sort out the deck division POs as you see fit and get this crew squared away." He turned to face forward. "After we kill this damn sub," he grated. All that remained on the surface was a smear of gold-tinged white foam.

"I got him!" came a cry from inside the charthouse, and Matt strode in to look at a brown 'Cat listening intently to a set of earphones. There was no scope for his equipment, only a large vacuum tube, like a tuning eye, which glared brighter with each sound pulse as they neared the target. It couldn't tell them anything about what the sub was doing, however, and the 'Cat's eyes were clenched shut, in any event. "He's turnin' away, goin' deep," he said.

"Can you do that out here, over the chart table?" Matt demanded. The 'Cat looked up at him and blinked. "Sure! I mean, ay, sur!"

"Then come on!" *This is turning into a sick joke,* Matt realized, *and it's all my fault. I drilled them as best I could with the time I had, but I didn't bring enough core people to do what I didn't think of and check the little things. Little things that grow huge,* he added with frustration at himself. The 'Cat followed, trailing the long wires to his earphones, and stared down at the chart while Tiaa made a mark along a straight edge and looked at him expectantly.

"Ten de-grees leff," the 'Cat said, and Matt nodded at Paddy Rosen, who'd also been growing increasingly incredulous. They'd had that sub served up on a platter, and now it was getting away.

"Lost con-taact due to short range!" the 'Cat suddenly announced.

"Very well. Set the charges for medium depth. We'll drop on time," Matt said, looking at his watch, then glancing meaningfully at the talker, who gulped and switched the comm circuit knobs to the depth-charge racks and torpedo mounts, whose crews would fire the Y guns. Matt looked back at his watch and counted the seconds down. "Fire the Y guns," he ordered. Seconds later, two wrinkled bronze drums blasted into the air on either side of the ship, splashing into the sea about eighty yards away. "Roll two," Matt commanded, and another charge dropped in their wake from each of the two cramped racks astern.

They'd finally done away with wooden barrel charges, and the new ones were copies of the MK-6 depth charges *Walker* and *Mahan* brought to this world, with the exception of the bronze casings. They relied on a simple, adjustable, pressure-sensitive detonator and were extremely reliable weapons. Unfortunately, they were also sadly ineffective against submarines. They worked very well frightening mountain fish away (though once in a while, an apparent "old bull" became more annoyed than afraid), but dropping them close enough to damage a maneuvering sub was problematic. Chief Gray once said it was like shooting at bats with a pistol in the dark. With this green crew? It was probably more like throwing rocks.

The sea spalled and purple spume rose high in the air behind them. "Right standard rudder. Bring us around," Matt ordered. As soon as they were back on course, he looked at the sound-'Cat. At first he shook his head, then tensed.

"Con-taact! Same con-taact! Is still movin' away . . ." He shrugged. "Maybe five hundred yaads, five or six knots. I think is still turnin' away from the traack of the taask force."

Matt considered. "Have Keje continue on into the shallows at the mouth of the river. *Ellie* will join us to kill this Leaguer before he gets away."

Ellie and *Mahan* hunted the sub for two hours while the task force steamed past, long after dark and into the night. Contacts became fewer and further between— whoever this U-boat skipper was, he was good—but whenever the hunters scented their quarry, they pounded the sea unmercifully. Usually, when the turbulence cleared and *Ellie* tried to pinpoint the enemy again, it took a while, because she always started looking in the direction of the task force. Each time, however, as she widened her search, the enemy was always found moving *away*. That made no sense. They'd expected he'd continue trying to close and do some damage. Curiously, he never did. That was smart, if he was trying to save his skin, but he'd eventually been driven far enough away that he'd never have a chance to pick off any Allied ships.

Finally, getting low on depth charges and with all contact lost, Matt had to accept that the U-boat had escaped. With their searchlights on, *Ellie* and *Mahan* hurried to catch up with the task force back across the area they'd hunted. Perry Brister reported what might've been a small oil slick, but no debris was seen. Disappointed they'd missed a good chance to kill one of their tormentors, but glad they'd at least driven it away and prevented damage to any of the ships in their care, *Mahan* and *Ellie* rejoined the task force already riding at anchor above the silted river fan, where the depth averaged only six or seven fathoms. If the sub came after them now, it might get some licks in against some of the ships blocking the big boys with their own hulls, but it would be easy to kill. Matt instructed Commander Brister and *Ellie* to refuel and load more depth charges alongside one of the tenders, then keep up a sonar picket for the rest of the night. He then threaded *Mahan* in among the gaggle of ships and went alongside *Salissa* for the same purpose— and for one final conference. A long accommodation ladder had already been rigged, and they'd raised it high enough that Matt, with Tabby in tow this time, only had to step across from the fo'c'sle. It was still a long way up, but Matt reflected that it was a far more dignified way to ascend the dizzying heights to *Big Sal*'s hangar deck than the first time he'd climbed even higher on a bouncing, swaying rope ladder.

Gaining the hangar deck amidships, he saluted aft out of habit, even though *Salissa*'s flag of the United Homes flew above the superstructure "island" almost directly above. Then he saluted the OOD before asking permission to come aboard. The side party gathered to welcome him was fairly large and loaded with brass, consisting of Keje and generals Pete Alden, Muln Rolak, Safir Maraan, and Fan-Ma-Mar from III Corps. Tikker and *Madraas*'s COFO were there, but Ben Mallory was already ashore at the airstrip Tassanna had built.

Several division commanders were also there to greet him, such as generals Taa-Leen of the 1st (Galla), Rin-Taaka-Ar of the 2nd, and Mersaak of the 3rd. Even General Grisa, finally recovered from wounds he'd received at Grik City, was back in command of Safir Maraan's 6th Division. Matt was glad to see Lieutenant Colonel Saachic of the 1st Cavalry Brigade. They'd probably need his cav, and Matt only hoped his Me-naaks hadn't gone nuts on their transport. The longer they were at sea, the harder they were to manage on land.

All these people were old friends and he was glad to see them, glad they were here, but he was most surprised to see Sandra standing between Keje and Rolak. She'd made the trip on *Tarakaan Island* and must've come over as soon as she anchored. With her being a little over seven months along, he didn't like her doing *anything* quickly. Seeing his expression, she rolled her eyes. "*Tara*'s going upriver with the assault and I knew you'd throw a fit if I stayed in her," she defended. "*Big Sal* is *not* going upriver"—she patted Keje's arm—"and this is like my second home. *Tara* let in enough water to flush

a pair of Nat Hardee's PT boats," she explained, realizing the real reason for his concern, that she'd come
over in some small, open boat. "Nat brought me over
himself, on the Seven boat." She grinned. "Number aside,
not many things left in our navy have been luckier than
it has!" She watched his relief turn to frustration. "I take
it your fishing trip didn't go so well?"

Matt shook his head. "I think we put a few hooks in
him, but he shook 'em out." He sighed. "Probably my
fault. *Mahan*'s crew is green as grass. I wish she had more
experienced hands." His expression firmed when he
glanced at Tabby. "Her power plant's in good shape, and
I think everybody else'll be okay, now they're over their
first-shot jitters. As for the pigboat, Perry Brister found
a little oil slick, but I'd bet it's still out there." He brightened. "But if it *is* losing fuel, it can't hang around. Its
skipper'll have to go wherever his fuel is." He shook his
head. "I wish I knew where that tenacious bas—fella calls
home."

"We will find it—or him," Keje consoled. "And if he
is leaking, our scout planes may find him more easily
now."

"I hope so."

"Now that the pleas-aantries are behind us," Rolak
interjected wryly, "how soon will we move upriver? The
plaan is as set as it can be, as long as the situation remains
the same with *Saanty Caat*. Our recon photos, maaps,
assignments—all are in readiness. Again, as long as there
are no changes."

Matt looked oddly at Rolak. "You think there will
be? Is something unusual cooking upriver?"

"Not thaat we know of," Rolak replied, looking at his
Imperial watch. He'd picked up the importance of precise timekeeping for military purposes quicker than most
'Cats. Of course, he and Safir were from Aryaal and
B'mbaado, two of only a few Lemurian Homes that had
routinely engaged in warfare—usually against each
other—before the Grik came. "As of eighteen hundred
hours, when we received our laast update, all was quiet."
He grinned. "But of *course* there will be changes! There
always are. And of course the Grik will cook something

unusual for us to adaapt to." He rubbed his furry chin. "Thaat's one reason, as carefully as we haave plaaned this operation, I'm glaad we also allowed for some flex-ibility. Baarring the unexpected, however, I ask again: When do we move?"

Keje waved around. "We caan't attempt it in dark-ness. It will be difficult even in daylight. Few of our comm-aanders haave ever maaneuvered within the con-fines of a river before." He shrugged. "I haave not. USS *Revenge* has well aac-quainted herself with the chaannel and caan lead us in with the dawn." He grimaced. "She puts out new chaannel markers every day, but increas-ingly, Grik raiding paarties move them. We must not allow any of our laarger ships to run aground or strike a snaag. If thaat happens, we will be in the same fix as the Grik." He scratched the beardlike mane around his own chin and blinked thoughtfully. "Yet another reason to make haste: if we linger, the Grik might try to slow or stop us with snaags, or even attempt mines of some sort."

"Agreed," Matt said. "And it'll take a while before the Grik even know we're here. Best not to give them time to react at all." He yawned and reached over to take his wife's hand. "Let's get on with the meeting, shall we? I hope there's not too much left to kick around—and there's some chow. I'm starved." He grinned. "And beat. Keje, if you don't mind—*Big Sal* being a naval reserve ship, after all—I'd like to stay aboard with my wife to-night." He frowned. "This could be a long operation, and there's no telling when I'll see her again."

"Of course," Keje agreed. "Lady Saandra's stateroom is always ready." He blinked understanding that turned to unease. "We should all try to make it an early night. Tomorrow will be a great and terrible day."

Whatever happened, there was no denying that.

Pete Alden looked at the others. "There isn't much left, unless anyone has some last-minute confusion about what's expected of 'em, or suggestions that occurred to 'em as they digested the plan. I still wish we could adjust the order of the landings more easily, based on what's going on when we get there, but there may be no room to shift things around. *Sular* and most of First Corps have to go first, followed by *Tara* and most of Second Corps. Follow-up elements and Third Corps will be in smaller ships, and we can be more flexible about where we send them in. Let's look at the latest recon photos and try to narrow that down some more." He looked at Tikker. "And I'd like to go over the air-cover assignments one more time." Tikker, *Madraas*'s COFO, and Keje nodded.

Finally, Pete stared pointedly at some of the other officers, his gaze lingering on Safir Maraan before it passed. "Mainly, I want to make damn sure everybody's still on the same page regarding our objectives. We're here to relieve TF Bottle Cap, establish a firm beachhead with defensive depth, and choke off the Grik Swarm in the Zambezi for good. If anybody gets any bright ideas, they better keep 'em on the tactical level or run 'em by me first. Is that understood? This'll be the biggest contested landing we've ever made, way bigger than Grik City. We have three corps on paper, but the numbers are more like four. That *should* be enough to accomplish our mission."

He glanced at Matt, acknowledging the curt nod to continue, and his expression turned hard. "I can finally tell you all that the Republic Army in the south is about to get off its ass and try to force a crossing of the Ungee River. Granted, they've kinda been waiting on *us* to get off *our* ass, but things are startin' to jump. More troops and weapons are on the way, and we *will* continue the assault toward Sofesshk when we have sufficient forces, but let me be clear: We're not gonna win the war tomorrow. We can *lose* it tomorrow if somebody screws up by the numbers, or gets wild-ass notions an' starts makin' shit up as they go . . . again. We're about to park our big, fat, bristly ass right on the Grik's front porch, and they *ain't* gonna like it." He shrugged. "My guess is, they'll pull out all the stops to boot us out, and there's a helluva lot more of them than us, so we gotta do this smart, see? That's the only way. And we can't risk massive casualties. We're gonna lose a lot of people," he conceded grimly, "no getting around it. But once we get in, get *dug* in tighter than a tick, we'll start pilin' *their* dead asses up in heaps just like we all did together at Flynn's Lake." He nodded at Matt. "Except this time, with secure supply lines, we won't have to count every shot we take."

Safir Maraan knew exactly who Pete was most concerned about when it came to slipping her leash. He hadn't been at Grik City when she'd almost single-handedly turned what was supposed to be a destructive raid in force into a full-scale invasion, but he knew what happened. Her ambitious redefinition of their objectives worked, but it had been very costly. Worse, it left their entire long-term strategy against the Grik in almost unsupportable disarray. She'd learned her lesson the hard way and was through trying to win the war by herself, on the fly. "Fear not, Gener-aal Aalden," she said. "I will behave."

Pete suddenly grinned. "Not sure I'd ever expect you to go *that* far. As General Rolak inferred, and Silva always says, plans are for shit. But even when they go in the crapper, we gotta keep the *reason* for 'em in mind, and keep fighting as a team."

Safir grinned back and there were a few nervous chuckles, but Matt, at least, was sure Safir Maraan would never just run wild again. "Okay," he said lightly, breaking the tension. "Great. Let's get this over with." He yawned again. "But chow first." He looked at Keje and raised a brow. "You wouldn't happen to have any of Courtney's *real* coffee aboard, would you?"

CHAPTER
24

////// Battle of the Ungee River
South Soala Riverfront
December 30, 1944

Regardless how long Legate Bekiaa-Sab-At had yearned for this attack to begin, she was nervous. She feared they'd waited too long, and so much depended on success! If they were badly defeated, the Grik army at Soala could immediately march north and add its weight to the Swarm battling TF Bottle Cap on the Zambezi. If Bottle Cap was overwhelmed, Madagascar was next. And the situation on the Zambezi had reached such a critical point that no matter how gallantly her friends—and family!—had held, failure would mean not only the loss of Madagascar, and probably the war, but also a virtual avalanche of Grik descending back on Soala. The Army of the Republic would be destroyed no matter how the battle went today. She shook her head. *One thing at a time. I can't think about that. I have to focus on the fight here, now.*

She glanced right and left. There was no moon, and the stars were hidden by a high, thin overcast. The riverfront where they'd quickly (with considerable chaos) launched hundreds of boats and barges to carry ten legions of men and 'Cats across a quarter mile of open water was utterly steeped in darkness. Even better, though no lights were ever allowed on the south side of the river, the Grik side practically glowed in the night vision–destroying glare of hundreds of cookfires. And General Kim had wisely forbidden his troops to fire on the Grik at night, precisely so they'd continue this moronic practice. They might even think it made them more secure, and nothing like what was about to occur could ever happen in the dark. Surprise was everything, not least of which was the prevention of many casualties during the long, slow river crossing.

"Look who I caught hiding with the troops!" Optio Jack Meek exclaimed quietly, pushing a tall, slightly thick-bodied man close enough for Bekiaa to make out his distinctive features. It probably wasn't really necessary to whisper—yet—but the need for silence had been impressed on everyone, and NCOs had carefully checked to make sure nobody even loaded their rifles until they were told. A single shot might cost hundreds of lives.

"Good work, Optio," Bekiaa said, putting her hands on her hips and looking up at the man before her. "I suspected you'd try a stunt like this," she told Courtney Bradford harshly.

"It's no bloody stunt," he replied stiffly, "and I resent you characterizing it so. I'm here on principle, and this is as much my battle as yours. I'm not entirely useless in a fight, you know." He gestured back in the direction of Kim's HQ. "He doesn't need me now, and you may need every soldier"—he shifted the long-barreled Krag slung on his shoulder—"and rifle you can get."

Bekiaa's anger gushed away and she felt nothing but admiration and fondness for Courtney Bradford. He'd already done so much for all of them, and he wasn't exactly young anymore.

"I aapol-o-gize for calling it a stunt," she said, "and I know you caan fight. Maybe you even *deserve* to fight. But whether Gener-aal Kim needs you now or not, he will later. And the Aall-i-aance needs you even more!" she stressed. "There may be other Aallied representatives at Songze, even Alex-aandra now, but you're still their superior—and Cap-i-taan Reddy's direct representative to General Kim." She shook her head. "I'm no diplo-maat,

I'm a Maa-rine. Even if I live, I could never do whaat you do so easily." She blinked amusement, unseen. "People *like* you, and thaat's more impor-taant to our cause than one more rifle." She nodded back toward shore. "Please return to the comm-aand post," she pleaded. "I'll have troops escort you if I must, and thaat *will* deprive me of soldiers I might need. Besides," she mused more quietly so only Courtney could hear, "don't aass-ume thaat Gener-aal Kim won't desper-aately need your aad-vice before this baattle's done. He's come a long way, but this is only his second great aaction. The first since Gaugh-aala. You've seen *many* aactions." She grinned. "He might still need some pointers."

Courtney finally slumped. "Oh, bugger all," he mur-mured. "Very well. And no one needs to escort me. I know the way." Suddenly, he embraced Bekiaa tightly. "Do be careful, my dear," he insisted. "I've lost so *many* people I love. I don't think I can bear to lose another. God keep you." He turned and pushed aft through the gathered troops toward the back of the barge in the dark-ness. "God keep you all," he said louder.

"A good man," Prefect Bele said. He must've joined her while she was focused on Courtney.

"Yes."

"But this is not the place for him."

"No," Bekiaa agreed. She pulled her new watch from a pocket sewn under her dingy rhino-pig armor and looked at it, angling the face to catch the glow from across the river. The watch, a gift from Inquisitor Choon, was Republic-made and she marveled again at its size, con-sidering the complexity inside. It was half the size of Im-perial watches and almost as small as some she still occasionally saw on the wrists of the original destroyer-men. She could also wind it without inserting a key—another advantage over Imperial designs, and a common-place example of the technically advanced nature of Republic industry and expertise. At the moment, how-ever, the watch told her nothing. It was just too dark. *No matter,* she thought. *We'll know when it's time.* Right then, some distance away, upriver and down, twenty more legions were already crossing. It was unrealistic to expect they'd manage it without any notice at all, but the vast bulk of the Grik army was in front of Bekiaa and was about to have a strakka of confusion and destruction blow across it before it had much chance to shift troops to its flanks.

Bekiaa and the ten legions around her waited in relative quiet for another hour while the tension ratcheted up. Rapid flashes started lighting the darkness to the east, downriver, accompanied by the long-delayed thump of heavy guns. There was no way to tell whose they were, but the wireless operators with the force would get the news to Kim, and he'd start the big show when he thought the moment was right. Bekiaa made her way to the very back of the barge, joining a group of Gentaa standing near a contraption they'd brought aboard.

Gentaa are . . . odd, she thought. They looked like a cross between humans and 'Cats, but Courtney was sure they either were a separate species indigenous to this world or came from another so long ago they might as well have been. Their culture was just as strange. Loyal to the Republic, they excelled at support roles within its armed forces even if they didn't—usually—directly join them. Bekiaa understood there were exceptions, primarily in the navy, but those were frowned on by the Gentaa themselves. They'd apparently—very lucratively— cornered the heavy-labor industry throughout the Republic, almost to the exclusion of everyone else. They worked on the docks, in the factories, on the rail lines, and in the mines as a highly cliquish, cooperative labor class. Courtney likened their system to something he called a racial labor union, which benefited the nation and itself. The hale enjoyed a good living, and the injured or aged were taken care of.

In any event, though the Gentaa didn't fight, there were lots of them with the army. They were the teamsters and logistical laborers every army needed, and they worked for the engineering officers. They'd built all the boats and barges the army was using now. And just because they weren't soldiers didn't mean they ran no risks. The ones around the small engine with its long propeller shaft, as well as others at the front of the barge with broad steering oars to help fight the current, would cross with the troops, sharing their danger. Bekiaa knew they trained with weapons to defend themselves, but she'd never seen them use them. Even at Gaughala. She wondered if they would today. "All ready?" she asked them.

One of the Gentaa straightened and looked at her. The only thing she could tell in the dark was that he was taller than she was and had a shorter tail. Generally, however, Gentaa appeared slightly more human than Lemurian, with features less feline, and their fur tended to lighter shades. It was also shorter than that of Republic 'Cats, which, longer and thicker than Bekiaa's in the cooler climes they called home, made Gentaa fur about as long as that of more equatorial 'Cats, like Bekiaa herself.

"All is ready," the Gentaa simply said.

Bekiaa blinked skeptically at the little engine. "And you can steer with thaat?" she asked. She'd been briefed on what to expect, but had her doubts.

"Yes, some. Once the propeller is lowered, we can shift the thrust from side to side a short distance"—he glared around them—"if your soldiers will stay clear."

"They will," she assured, but remained unconvinced the little motor could move the big barge. Fixed engines and protruding propellers would've made the barges too heavy and vulnerable to quickly move, however. This had to work.

"Then move them," the Gentaa said. "We will soon be underway." His tone wasn't particularly impolite, but there was no deference to her rank. She was used to that from Gentaa. Before she could turn and give the command, the entire Republic side of the river suddenly lit up with a vision-searing flash, accompanied by the ear-splitting, staccato concussion of more than two hundred 75-mm guns, the nearly seventy 105-mm howitzers they'd gathered, and untold numbers of light Allied pattern mortars.

"Take in the lines!" she shouted as the hawsers holding the stern of the barge to the dock were already coming aboard. "Shove off, and clear a space around the shaaft," she added. "Get us underway as soon as you have space to drop the prop," she told the Gentaa, then turned to stare forward. The higher-velocity 75 mms were already impacting the distant shore or snapping brightly in the air above. Mortar and howitzer shells exploded behind the enemy breastworks, and even as she watched, the rumble behind and ahead became continuous. The noise was so great, she never even heard the little engine start. All around them, hundreds of narrow boats with many oars—much like she'd seen in the harbor at Alex-aandra—dashed ahead, filled with lightly armed troops. They'd be the first ashore to secure a landing area for the more heavily armed troops on the barges before the enemy could get their "shit in the sock." Judging by the hellishly destructive firestorm falling on their positions, the Grik should have a hard time with that.

Imperceptibly at first, the barge Bekiaa shared with two hundred troops of her 23rd Legion began to move. The rest of her legion was crammed in other barges nearby. Bekiaa unslung her '03 Springfield and pushed her way to the bow, where Prefect Bele waited.

"Jesus," Bele murmured, staring at the maelstrom of fireballs, flashing detonations, jetting earth, and swirling smoke. Amid it all would be searing shards of iron and tumbling body parts. Bekiaa looked at her tall companion, remembering he was a Chiss-chin of some kind. She'd never asked for details of his faith and didn't care. Her own belief in the Maker of All Things had wavered from time to time, in the face of all she'd seen, but that internal struggle was hers alone. Bele was a great soldier, becoming a great friend, and how he chose to worship the Maker couldn't have mattered less.

The barges, their linear formation starting to bulge as they battled the growing strength of the current, crept slowly closer to the inferno ahead. Bekiaa raised her telescope and saw that the fast boats were more jumbled, but already surprisingly close to shore. A cannon blast blossomed in the opposing breastworks, quickly followed by another. *Can't get 'em all,* Bekiaa told herself. The artillerymen behind her must've thought otherwise, and showered the positions with shells—even as more Grik cannon opened up. Some were starting to find their mark. One longboat suddenly stalled under a tall column of spray, its oars in disarray as it began to fill. Another shattered more catastrophically, spilling its occupants in the water. Bekiaa shuddered. There weren't as many water monsters in the rivers as in the coastal seas, but there were still a lot. And since there was little reason for anyone on this world to learn to swim, the chances any would find their way to shore were remote.

The first Grik guns to fire had probably been loaded with case or roundshot—possibly for some time—but, increasingly, heavy charges of grapeshot churned the water and shredded boats. One looked to Bekiaa as if it had been slapped, and when the splashes around it finally dissipated, none of the platoon-size crew remained sitting on its benches. The boat twirled away downstream. Collisions were increasing as well, as boats attempted to avoid the thickening hail of projectiles, and all the while, Allied shells kept falling.

Bekiaa redirected her glass as the first boats drove up on the red sandy beach. Grik muskets were firing now, kicking up clouds of dust around running forms. Some fell, but others raced to the base of the breastworks and started throwing grenades over the top.

"They're gettin' slaughtered," Optio Meek murmured beside them.

"They are doing their job," Bele retorted. "And they are not being slaughtered," he added thoughtfully. "Many more are making it ashore than I feared would be the case." The barges were a little over halfway across and starting to take fire as well. Huge splashes sprouted all around them, but Bekiaa didn't see any hits—yet. No doubt there would've been more fire if the defenders hadn't been distracted by the first wave of boats. To Bekiaa's dismay, however, it looked like the covering artillery fire had already started reaching longer, falling farther behind the closer defenses. She knew they had to do that to avoid hitting their own people, but it seemed too soon. Then, almost deafening her, two thunderous reports rolled across the water, originating from her right. She turned just as two more shots slammed out, sending shells shrieking across to detonate against the breastworks to the right of where their first troops were attacking. The breastworks literally shattered, blowing themselves, cannon, and parts of Grik in the air. The Grik defenses had been beefed up to protect against direct fire from the 75 mms across the river, but couldn't begin to stand against the 150-pound, high-explosive, 8″ (210 mm) shells that now began systematically obliterating them. Bekiaa had been expecting it—hoping for it—but the sudden appearance of the spark-spewing, twin-turret, Republic gunboat *here*, on waters it never could've reached on its own, still came as a shock.

"The navy has arrived," Bele said dryly.

"I see it, but I still can't believe it!" Optio Meek shouted gleefully.

Princeps-class "monitors" were about two hundred feet long and fifty feet wide, and displaced close to 1,200 tons. They'd been designed for harbor defense, however, not blue water, and with a very low freeboard they couldn't survive a voyage through the perpetually storm-lashed seas around the horn. Considered obsolete, if still potent, with their respectable armor and heavy breech-loading guns, two had been disassembled months before and carried by rail to the new Republic shipyards at Songze. Practically helpless against *Savoie* when she arrived at Alex-aandra and sat on the war effort there so long, they could still, it was believed, make a good account of themselves against anything the Grik had to offer.

Reassembling them and getting them back in the water had been a nightmare, however, particularly since the yards at Songze were already stretched to capacity by other projects. It had remained uncertain if they'd arrive in time. They had—or at least *one* had. Perhaps the other was still supporting the downriver crossing? Roundshot immediately started whacking the monitor, most careening off in the dark. A couple hit the pilothouse, and even it seemed proof against Grik field guns, but Bekiaa doubted the people inside would shake the impacts off as easily. Jagged holes appeared in the two smoke-streaming funnels, stanchions were knocked away, and boats were turned to kindling, but the ship kept firing as if it barely noticed these little insults.

Recovering from her happy surprise, Bekiaa refocused on matters at hand. "Commence firing!" she ordered. Stationed in the bow of about half the barges were pairs of Maxim guns and their crews. At less than a hundred yards, they sent tracers over their own people on the beach and brought them down to smother the tops of the obstacles they faced. They went through belts very quickly, and all the troops detailed to stay with them, provide security, and replace gunners if they were killed had more belts draped across them.

"Here we go," Bele said, gritting his teeth as the beach approached. "Get down!" There wasn't room for everyone to hit the deck, but most crouched or took a knee. Bekiaa wished they could've built up the sides of the barges to provide protection from small arms, at least. This quickly became a more pressing concern when, with the nearest defensive structures demolished, the monitor raised its guns and started dropping hell beyond them. Unfortunately, no bombardment could wipe out every obstacle, and Grik cannon and musket fire resumed against the barges as they started grinding ashore. Men and 'Cats fell around Bekiaa amid the crack and thump of heavy lead balls hitting wood and flesh. Splinters flew and troops screamed. Others just dropped. Both Gentaa at the forward steering oars cried out and tumbled into the water. Peering over the low rail, Bekiaa shouted, "Haang on!" and with a crunching, scraping sound, the barge ran aground.

"Go, go, go!" Bele roared, standing aside while troops streamed past. "Machine-gun squad, stand by!" They would set the weapons onshore and help push them forward on their low wheeled carriages. More of the 23rd's barges landed beside them, smashing over abandoned longboats, and clouds of grapeshot and musket balls tore into them as well. Machine guns continued to reply, however, giving cover as troops raced to join their comrades at the base of the breastworks that were still intact. Bekiaa eyed the gaping holes the monitor made off to her right as she ran, breath coming in great gasps, but she pushed on. The gaps weren't for her.

Most of the light infantry she finally joined huddling

at the base of the breastworks were also from the 23rd, but quite a few men and 'Cats from other legions were mixed in now. It didn't matter. They'd used all their grenades and were probably getting short on rifle ammo. Her wave had plenty of both, and more grenades showered over the top while relieved troopers pillaged ammo crates.

"Fill your cartridge boxes! Quickly, quickly!" Bele roared. "Get those machine guns up here!" he added, watching the weapons' clumsy advance over bodies and broken ground. "*Carry* them!" he shouted, frustrated. Then he pointed ahead. "Straight to the top!"

"Let's go!" Bekiaa yelled, her voice carrying farther than Bele's, despite their difference in size. A thunderous roar accompanied the 23rd to the top of the breastworks, and it spread along the length of the assault as more legions joined the charge. Machine guns, dozens of them, slammed down on the peak of the barricade and immediately put fire on the second barrier their aerial recon had warned them to expect.

Bekiaa took an instant to survey the hellish scene. Grik corpses and parts of them were scattered all over the reverse slope. Some still moved, dragging their torn bodies along the ground. Cannon had been upended, partially buried, even bent and broken by direct hits, and a reeking miasma of blood, ripped bowels, and feces lingered with the low-lying smoke. Republic artillery still pounded more distant positions, and the flashing explosions and geysering earth and timbers almost as far as she could see riveted her attention for an instant. But there were also a lot of Grik musket flashes directed back at them, and the *vroop!* of balls passing close shook her out of her reverie. That's when she saw hundreds, maybe thousands, of Grik hurrying in between the barriers to fill the gap the monitor made. "Prefect Bele!" She pointed.

"Pass the word," Bele shouted. "Even-number guns will keep firing across. Keep their heads down. Odd-number guns and riflemen, engage the enemy reinforcements! Grenades!"

The 23rd wasn't the only legion to use those tactics, and the Grik, rushing in from the flanks at the bottom of what amounted to a ravine, began dying under a merciless fusillade. Even these different, more disciplined Grik couldn't take that kind of punishment forever, and some started running up the fallback berm to join their comrades holding there. Others swarmed up to attack their tormentors, bayonets fixed.

Sword to sword, spear to spear, one on one, only the most skilled man or 'Cat could cope with almost any Grik. They were bigger than 'Cats and just as fast, and brought other weapons, like vicious teeth and claws, to the fight. Only a disciplined shield wall and superior weapons opposing rampaging hordes had allowed the Allies to prevail in battles of that kind in the past. Abandoning swords, spears, and crossbows for muskets as their primary weapon gave the Grik greater standoff firepower and lethality, but made them possibly less effective at close-quarters combat—particularly when facing breech-loading rifles, also equipped with bayonets and wielded by soldiers taught to use them well. The screaming, shooting, clashing collision at the top of the breastworks was louder than the artillery fire—and Bekiaa was right in the middle of it.

"Protect the machine gunners!" she yelled. They didn't carry rifles and couldn't shoot in the middle of the press. She fired her Springfield, shot after shot, as fast as she could work the bolt, and Grik tumbled back. She didn't have time to reload when the rifle ran dry, and slammed its bayonet in the side of a Grik trying to skewer Optio Meek. It shrieked and rolled away.

"Thankee, Legate!" Meek cried, quickly emptying his revolver at another pair of Grik. Besides the copies of MG08 Maxim machine guns, 11-mm revolvers carried by officers and NCOs were the only multishot firearms in the Republic Army. Current-issue rifles had strong bolt actions but no magazine. Bekiaa suspected that would change.

Bekiaa parried a bayonet aimed at her middle and drove her own into her attacker's throat. "Don't thaank me," she gasped. "Get a daamn rifle! How maany times I gotta tell you?" She hissed when a sharp, triangular point barely pierced her rhino-pig armor and pricked the back of her right shoulder. She spun, but Prefect Bele had already smashed the Grik's skull with the butt of his rifle. He reversed the weapon and stabbed another. Bekiaa took the few seconds she had to strip another clip into her rifle before starting to shoot again.

A machine gun clattered nearby and she realized its front must've been cleared of friendlies. In seconds, another joined it—and another. Only then did she feel the pressure on her legion beginning to fade. "They're pulling baack!" she shouted. "Pour it in 'em!" Troops started shooting again as they finally found time to reload. Bright flashes and white smoke chased the remaining Grik, starting to stream directly away toward the fallback berm. A roar erupted to Bekiaa's right and she realized the Grik weren't just running from them; they were fleeing the arrival of troops from the second wave of barges who'd charged straight through the gap the monitor made and continued running right up to the top of the second barricade. Once there, they started shooting, throwing grenades, and finally hosing Grik with enfilading machine-gun fire, tracers sparkling right and left.

Bekiaa looked around as the incoming musketry quickly tapered off. "How baad?" she asked Bele, wondering what his estimate of their casualties might be. He was covered with blood but didn't seem hurt. On the other hand, the back of her shoulder was starting to burn, and she winced, blinking at the sky. That's when she realized she could begin to see a brightening beyond the smoke blanketing the battlefield. The long dark night was almost past. This assumption was confirmed when ten Cantets roared low overhead, three small antipersonnel bombs slung under each wing. The army now had thirty of the swift little planes, though they'd never revealed more than four to the enemy.

Bele glanced around as well and blinked. "I don't know. I really don't think we lost too many, considering. We're still effective if that's what you're asking. My God, the Twenty-Third can fight!" he added proudly.

"Yes, it caan," Bekiaa agreed. "An' we already knew thaat." She blinked ruefully. "Gener-aal Kim's straa-ti-gee seems to have worked after all; these Grik *haad* grown complacent. They haad no clue about the chik-aash we were gonna dump on 'em." Her tail flicked, betraying an anxious unease. "Gaugh-aala was haard. This was easy. But I bet it'll never be this easy again."

"The Grik learn, but so do we," Bele comforted her. "And we learn faster, I think."

"I hope so." Bekiaa pointed across where the Grik had gone. "This fight's not over yet. Let's move while our new best friends . . ." She squinted and blinked surprise. "That's Kim's own First Legion." Day was spreading fast and she could see the pennant of the 1st waving atop the next obstacle. She raised her voice and pointed across the abattoir below at the next enemy position. "Follow me! Let's get over there while the First keeps their daamn heads down!"

The gruesome view from the top of the second Grik position was much like the first, and Bekiaa supposed she had the new howitzers and mortars to thank for that, as well as the fact the Grik were still wedded to breast-works instead of trenches. She hoped they hadn't learned their lesson. The artillery fire now fell on North Soala itself, blasting much of the city to rubble beneath a monstrous plume of reddish dust. They'd lose the heavy mortars as they edged past their extreme range, but the howitzers were doing fine work. Even the 75 mms were more help now that they were firing at longer range, at a higher trajectory. Bekiaa was slightly lower here than she'd been on the first breastworks but had a better view of the vast panorama of battle beyond.

Ten legions were fighting hard on the distant left and things looked pretty rough for them. The city was almost intact there, and the enemy had plenty of obstacles to defend. There was fierce fighting in the rubble, for that matter, and Bekiaa wasn't sure which would be harder to overcome. The Grik left (on her right) was starting to come unwrapped. About five miles away, where the river shifted slightly north, she could barely see the twin smears of rising coal smoke from the other monitor and wondered if its presence made the crossing easier there as well. In the middle . . .

"They're running," Prefect Bele said, amazed.

"Cap-i-taan—I mean, Centurion!" Bekiaa called past him to one of her Lemurian officers. She still thought of centuries as companies. "How's the aammo?"

"More comes!"

"Very well."

"There aren't many civvy Grik takin' off," Optio Meek observed, staring though Repub binoculars.

"Prob'ly not maany left," Bekiaa stated flatly. "Maybe the biggest difference between us an' the Grik. We're tryin' to defend our people. Grik move in to defend a place—an' eat everybody there." She pointed at another dust cloud rising to the north. "Gener-aal Taal's caav-alry came across with the downriver force. Looks like he's finally gettin' to play. He'll hit those runnin' Grik like a scythe," she added with satisfaction. The Cantets weren't waiting, and seemed to focus all their attention on the fleeing enemy mob as they dove and swooped above it. Little bombs fell and flames roiled up.

"What'll *we* do?" Meek asked.

Bekiaa nodded to the left. "Still haard fighting there. Send a runner to First Legion. They prob'ly got one of the wireless sets. Make sure they've told Gener-aal Kim the same things we've seen, an' inform him we're headin' thaat way, to hit those holdout Grik in the aass! Make sure our aar-tillery knows too," she quickly reminded.

"What should the runner pass to the First Legion commander?" Bele asked with a growing, expectant grin. With the appointed rank of legate, Bekiaa could technically order other legions to support what she wanted to do in battle, as long as it didn't conflict with specific orders from a general—particularly General Kim.

Bekiaa considered. "He's secured his objective, just like us. Easier thaan expected too." She paused and blinked regret. "For some of us." She nodded to the left again. "Not easy over there, though." She shrugged. "Tell him he can come too, if he waants."

CHAPTER 25

///// *USS* **Santa Catalina**
Zambezi River
Grik Africa
December 31, 1944
0120

"*D*amn, it's smoky. I can't hardly catch a breath," Silva grumbled, glaring at the glowing cherry on the end of the PIG-cig dangling from Gunny Horn's lips. Silva, Horn, Lawrence, Risa, and Simy Gutfeld were trying to relax behind battered armor plates wired to the remaining stanchions as far forward on *Santa Catalina*'s portside upper deck as they could get. Beyond that point was nothing but twisted wreckage. The bright side was, the total destruction of the sunken bow had reduced the low-deck acreage they had to defend from Grik boarding attempts, and the wreckage presented a barrier to the upper decks as well. Fifteen or twenty of Gutfeld's Marines and Chack's Raiders were close by, lounging against the armor or sleeping on deck. A .30-caliber machine gun stood sentinel over them, wrapped in an oilcloth against the falling damp.

Horn sucked a final lungful from the vile paper tube, then tossed it with a grimace. "Me either, but that wasn't to blame." He nodded at the south shore, lost in haze and the darkness of night. "Air strikes on Grik rocket batteries must've started some pretty big grass fires this time, on both sides of the river."

"It's not that 'ad," Lawrence said, even though he and their Khonashi troops seemed more susceptible to the ill effects of smoke inhalation than humans and 'Cats. "You are all just lose your . . . air in lungs, standing around. No exercise," he added with a self-satisfied snort. He'd been working out with Chack's Raiders on the aft well deck and fantail every day. Petey stirred from Silva's shoulders and looked at Lawrence with big, glowing eyes. With a dismissive "*Kack*," he settled back, and Lawrence quickly looked away, probably to hide his desire to snatch the useless pest and twist his head off.

"Well, I for one am haappy our lonely staand may be near its end." Risa sighed. Word had quickly spread that First Fleet had finally arrived off the river mouth and would begin moving to their relief at dawn. That meant they *should* start getting appreciable assistance by the end of the following day. The news had inspired a celebratory air among the defenders of the shattered, sunken fort, and Risa seemed infected by the mood herself. That worried Silva. Risa had always been one of the finest, most enthusiastic Grik killers he'd ever fought with, and their personalities meshed so well that they'd become — some said — more than just best friends, with the same almost-perverse talent for remaining oddly cheerful under the worst circumstances. But Dennis had noticed a striking change in Risa. It began after her brilliant but bitter stand at the Wall of Trees during Second Grik City, and became especially evident after their assault on Zanzibar. She'd lost some of her habitual liveliness and no longer reveled in the fight. He wasn't sure how she'd take it if they discovered their "lonely stand" wasn't quite over after all. Something about all the smoke was nagging at him, and he thought it was too early to relax. Particularly since the Grik hadn't much pestered them for an entire week. They damn sure hadn't forgotten they were there, and that could only mean they were cooking up something ugly — and probably big.

"I don't know," Simy said thoughtfully, scratching his temple up under his helmet. It had been so long since any of them bathed, he was sure he had lice—or the local equivalent. "There couldn't be much grass or brush left around here to burn." Apparently, he was also still thinking about the smoke. "Maybe they're burning their latrines." He wrinkled his nose. "Stinks bad enough."

"Since when've the Grik ever gave a crap—where they crapped?" Silva asked. "I never seen 'em use no latrines." He moistened a finger and raised it. "Wind seems mostly outa the south right now," he declared. "Fires from bombing around the bend shouldn't spread that far upwind."

"Maybe a zep or plane crashed. Or maybe they're trying to choke us out," Horn speculated.

Silva grimaced. "Could be. Or . . . maybe they're hidin' something." He raised his voice to the other 'Cats nearby. "Any o' you monkeys hear anything?" A couple of Raiders looked at him, blinking curiosity, but shook their heads. A Shee-Ree blinked thoughtfully but didn't reply. "Weird," Silva muttered. "'Cause I think I do." He glanced around at his friends. "I can't hear high-pitched stuff worth a shit anymore." He tossed in a grin. "'Specially women's voices. All I get's this squealy whine, see? Like a dry bearing. But maybe I've got to where I can hear low-pitched stuff better. Does that make sense?"

"Maybe," Horn agreed. "But what do you hear? What do you *think* you hear?"

Silva shrugged noncommittally. "You know, stuff. Kind of a thumpin', groanin' sound. Might just be this old ship settlin'."

"No," Risa agreed unhappily, "I hear something too, now thaat you mention it."

Horn's eyes widened. "Grik?"

"Could be," Silva said. "Hey, maybe they're tryin' to put the sneak on us?"

"Then it's a *good* sneak," Lawrence retorted. "I don't hear anything."

"Me either," Horn objected, "and it's the middle of the goddamn night. Grik don't attack at night!"

Silva rolled his good eye. "You know better than that. And what if the reason you don't hear nothin' is because your ears ain't as screwed-up as mine? Think how stupid that'd make you feel." He looked at Major Gutfeld.

"Whaddaya say, Simy? You got those fun new mortar rounds we ain't got to use yet. Let's have a show."

"Whaat's going on?" came Chack's voice from the darkness aft, and their commander, accompanied by Major Cook, moved to join them.

Horn nodded at Silva. "This knucklehead thinks there's Grik out on the water, sneaking up on us in the smoke."

Chack looked at Risa, then at Gutfeld. "Whaat do you think?"

"He could be right," Risa said. "I hear something too."

Gutfeld shrugged. "I don't know. I guess it can't hurt to check."

Chack seemed to consider, his tail slashing back and forth. Finally, he nodded. "Very well. Loft some staar shells. At worst, as I heard Chief Sil-vaa say, it'll give us a show."

"Aye, sir," Gutfeld agreed, and limped slightly aft, then up on the remains of the deckhouse where the funnel once stood, calling for his forward mortar section to ready its weapons. "Stand by to fire four illumination rounds," he ordered.

"Commence firing when ready," Chack called. After several moments there came two deep, metallic *toonk*s. Seconds later, two more. Four bright flashes blossomed high over the wreckage-strewn river, yellow-orange bursting charges replaced by rapidly brightening red-orange flares that drifted lazily north under little parachutes and foggy sparks. They were dazzling enough to hurt the eyes, even through the low-hanging smoke, but interesting as the new star shells were, all eyes were quickly drawn to the water around them.

"Holy shit!" yelped Gunny Horn, instinctively snatching the heavy Browning automatic rifle from where it stood against the bulkhead. He'd been lugging the precious BAR as his personal weapon since he came aboard and never went far without it. Any sense of security it gave him now was probably transitory, because it looked like the entire river between them and the wreck-choked bend was alive with giant, crawling bugs, glowing a bloody, neon red. But they weren't bugs; they were galleys—hundreds of them—all filled with Grik. Countless more were behind them, picking their way through the sunken ships, and there was something else. . . .

"Cruisers!" Risa shouted. "There's at least one tryin' to squeeze through! Probably more!"

"Staand to!" Chack roared. "All haands, maan your baattle stations! Commence firing to repel boarders!" He spun to Abel Cook and saw the terror reflected on his young, smooth face. "Prepare the close-in defense weapon Chief Sil-vaa devised, on the double—but haave a care!" he cautioned.

Cook shook his head and determination scoured the fear away. "Aye, aye, Colonel!" He rushed purposefully aft.

Just then, through the smoke lying heavy on the water between them and the half-mile distant southern shore, dozens—scores—of yellow-red flashes rippled in the gloom, blossoming in the night, spewing their own dense clouds of smoke.

"Guns!" Silva stated simply, almost admiringly. "They laid down a smoke screen to sneak a buncha damn *cannons* on our flanks!" Even as he finished speaking, heavy shot started slamming the ship. Many of Gutfeld's Marines and Chack's Raiders had been resting near their positions, but there was a great deal of tumult as other 'Cats, men, and Khonashi, both human and Grik-like, poured up from the illusory security they'd chosen below, adjusting accoutrements and donning helmets as they ran. A case shot exploded overhead, scything down a group thundering up a companionway, sending screeching bodies tumbling down on others crowding the stairs. More shells exploded, most long or short, but sharp, hot iron sleeted the savaged ship.

"Goddamn lizards!" Silva bellowed, dropping behind the dented armor plate near the closest machine gun, while its two-'Cat crew ripped the cover off and inserted a belt. "Who said they could have explodin' shells? That ain't fair!"

Chack, Horn, Lawrence, and Risa had quickly joined Silva under cover. Now Chack spoke to his sister. "Take charge here," he told her. "I'll send as much firepower for-waard as I can. We *must* keep them from gaining a foothold! Make it hot enough that they'll prefer to circle around and approach from aaft." His eyes flicked to Silva. "Then Major Cook can try your latest contrivaance—and may the Maker protect us!"

The first mass of galleys was almost on them—it had been that close, the surprise nearly total—yet *Santy Cat*'s defenders were starting to respond, flailing them with fire from Allin-Silva breechloaders and stuttering Blitzerbug SMGs. Another star shell thumped in the air, joined by mortar bombs from all the sections as they came up. Steamy explosions convulsed the river, tossing galleys on their sides or shattering them in the middle. Grik spilled out, swirling away and sinking, their shrieks tearing the night. The nearby machine gun yammered, throwing geysers of water—then splinters and flesh—into the air. Others joined in, and then they were all almost deafened by the blast of a 5.5″ gun just below, ranging for the first distant cruiser. Lawrence was carefully, methodically, firing shot after shot from his Allin-Silva, probably accounting for two or more Grik with each 450-grain, .50-caliber bullet he sent. That was something he'd learned from Silva, whose "big sumbitches line up; little sumbitches bunch up" mantra always implied it was a waste to kill just one Grik when your bullet could punch through two. Risa hadn't fired yet but had her Blitzer up, peering around, trying to judge the flow of the assault and see where it might land the heaviest. All the while, musket balls smacked and spattered against the iron armor.

"Get yer idiot head down, wilya?" Silva scolded her.

Risa ignored him, but finally fired a long burst and then dropped down, her face bleeding from cuts caused by flying bullet fragments. "It's haard to tell—there's so maany of 'em!—but the attaack seems to be maassing here, right in front of us."

Chack nodded and turned. Keeping low, he started to trot away. "Where're you going?" Gunny Horn called after him.

"To send more troops, as I said," he replied. "And to the comm shaack while the aaeri-al still stands, so we can get word of this attaack to Cap-i-taan Reddy." He blinked something Horn didn't catch. "I caan imagine little he can do to hurry his advaance, but he needs to know whaat's haappening—and we'll need all the air he can give us, if we live till dawn."

"Makes sense," Silva said philosophically, sliding his massive "Doom Stomper" over the plating and taking aim at the Grik on the steering oars of a distant galley. He fired, and the heavy recoil rolled him back. Flipping the breech open, he inserted another monstrous, one-inch round and took aim again. "Ha!" he exclaimed. His first shot had killed both oarsmen, and the galley, still churning forward at full speed, slammed into another, slicing it in half. He chose another target and fired again, the thunderous report almost rivaling the 5.5″ from where they were. Horn slid his BAR over the armor, blinked, then blasted a much closer target, spraying twenty rounds of .30-06 into the boarders huddled at its bow. They jerked and danced, falling in the water or sprawling on the splintered deck. Dropping his magazine, he slammed in another.

Silva fired again, causing Horn to jerk. "Quit playing with that damn toy!" he shouted. "There's Grik right over the damn side, *straight down*!"

"Grenades!" Risa yelled as more troops rushed to join them, some falling and skidding on the deck as shrapnel or Grik musket balls slashed at them.

"Always tryin' to smush my fun," Silva moped, but relented, gently setting his beloved weapon aside and unslinging the Thompson SMG from its usual place across his back. Popping up, he sprayed another galley, his arc of brass glittering in the dying flare. "More star shells!" he shouted.

The cannon on the bank rippled another salvo and the wreck reeled, people screamed, and Silva started tossing grenades over the side from a satchel someone handed him. Bloody columns of spume rose to drench them. "What a shit storm," he grumped, risking his good eye for a peek over the plating. Two of the 5.5″s were firing now, and they'd hit the cruiser picking its way through the wrecks fairly hard. It was afire forward, but still moving. Soon it would be clear—and more would likely come. "Lizards really caught us with our pants down this time. Wonder what they'll do next?"

"Who cares 'hat they do," Lawrence said. "Us gotta kill they, herd they apht."

"Sure thing, little buddy," Silva agreed. "Don't wanna miss *that* fun." Suddenly, he groped for the familiar shape of Petey around his neck, but the reptile was gone—as usual. He caught himself hoping the little twerp found a safe place to hide.

The pressure was building and galleys bumped against the hull. Grapnels would come next, and the fighting would get very close indeed. At least the cannon onshore had stopped for the moment, but surely only to prevent hitting their own warriors, possibly disrupting the assault. And, apparently, there was plenty of pressure to go around. Dennis couldn't tell if they'd actually herded any Grik, but a bright orange glare lit the night from aft with a hungry, rushing *whoosh!* Silva looked and watched as burning fuel oil spurted from a pair of the wands he'd made, arcing out and playing across dozens of galleys stacked against *Santy Cat*'s flank. Grik writhed and screeched in the roiling flames, withering like moths over a campfire. The galleys took fire, and the grapnels they'd flung were quickly cut away. Burning ships drifted downstream, entangling others and setting them alight as well. "Looky there!" Silva hooted gleefully. "It worked!" He'd been pretty sure it would, but was a little worried his cobbled-together flamethrowers would work *too* well, or they'd have trouble getting the pump engines running in time. Apparently not. A rapid clanging, hammering sound diverted his attention and interrupted his celebration as more grapnels fell on their position.

"We need one o' those hoses up here," Risa shouted at him. Dennis only shook his head. Near the bow, the current might keep burning galleys pressed against them, and that might be bad. Then again, things were getting bad, anyway. . . .

Marines and Raiders hacked the ropes, but there were too many to get them all before the first Grik started topping the armor on the stanchions, toothy mouths gaping wide in the middle of cries lost in the roaring tumult.

One of the machine gunners was physically jerked over the side, and another Grik hopped aboard in his place. Silva took a step back and stitched the beast with a three-round burst that shattered its neck and head. There was more rapid weapons fire as Blitzers joined in, their stutter punctuated by the boom of buckshot from Allin-Silva shotguns. But Grik were piling aboard quickly now, some with muskets with fixed bayonets, others with old-style sickle-shaped swords and wickedly barbed spears, all of which were more than sufficiently lethal for the kind of fight shaping up.

Calmly, Silva slung his Thompson and drew his 1911 Colt and 1917 Navy cutlass. He knew without looking that Risa, Horn, and Lawrence would all be there beside him. He did note that most of the other defenders had likewise taken up close-quarters weapons or fixed bayonets. "All right, you fuzzy, lizardy bastards!" he roared. "Let's cut a rug!"

USNRS Salissa *0300*

Matthew Reddy was buried in a desperate dream featuring the river he'd finally reached. The problem was, it wasn't really a river but a great, monstrous funnel deeper than the Wall of Trees was high. Far deeper than that. It was deeper than the terrible sea, and it was made entirely of bones. Worse, everything he cared about—*Walker*, all her people, even Sandra—was perched precariously on the rim of the funnel, teetering, tipping, almost falling in. And the only thing keeping the ship that way seemed to be the bones themselves, moving, shifting, jutting upward and snapping against the tired iron hull, pressing just long enough to keep it steady. Yet every now and then the funnel demanded a sacrifice and he was forced to choose who'd next venture in. He didn't *know* they were adding their bones to its structure—he didn't want to know—but, then again, somehow he did. And he was pretty sure whose bones were shattering themselves to keep his ship, his people, his *wife*, safe. But it wasn't for him. It couldn't possibly be for him. . . . Could it? He shuddered and railed against that thought in his sleep. If he really believed he, his hubris, his *arrogance*, was what was feeding the funnel, he'd gladly make the sacrifice it really wanted and jump in the bottomless hole himself. *How* gladly he'd do that probably horrified him most of all. . . .

The popping, banging of the bones against the hull became a banging on the door of the stateroom he was sharing with his wife, and he opened his eyes in the dark. He couldn't have been asleep for long, just long enough for the dream to start, and he groggily rolled off the sleeping cushions onto the floor and stood. He was slightly disoriented, wondering where his new hammock was and how he'd fallen out without hurting himself. But the deck wasn't steel and the hammock wasn't there. "Just a minute," he murmured, finally remembering where he was, then added, "Who's there?"

"Diania," came the urgent reply. "I hate tae wake ye, but ye're needed at once!"

"Come in, Diania," Sandra said, rising as well. Her voice husky, resigned.

"Now, wait a minute . . ." Matt objected. All he had on were his shorts.

"Diania will have a light," Sandra said, ever practical. "You'll need it to dress." *Big Sal* had electric lights in many critical areas, but they'd never been installed in her living quarters.

Quickly throwing on his clothes in the light of the lamp while Diania carefully avoided his eye and helped Sandra dress, Matt dashed to Keje's conference room, or Great Hall, just down the passageway.

Keje was already seated at his large, ornate dining table, but he wasn't there to eat. There was a great bustle of coming and going, and two successive waves of messengers left thick pages of Lemurian paper piled in front of him. Keje grunted at the last, then looked up at Matt's approach. "Hot tea," he called to his steward. In the absence of Courtney's coffee, hot tea had a growing following. Matt even preferred it to the prospect of returning to monkey joe.

Tikker crashed through the door, followed immedi-

ately by Captain Atlaan-Fas and Commander Sandy
Newman. Atlaan was basically Keje's flag captain, and
Sandy was his XO. Sandra and Diania followed at a more
dignified pace, and Keje stood, blinking apologetically
at Sandra, then turned to Matt.

"The Grik have launched a major aassault on *Saanta
Caatalina*," he informed them, blinking brief but deep
anxiety. It was enough for them to see how worried he
was, however, quickly substantiated by his bleak, almost
formal statement. "Col-nol Chack has sent thaat the
Third Maa-rines, and his Raiders, are fully engaged by
shore baatteries, gaalley-borne waarri-ors, and an unknown number of Grik cruisers."

"Cruisers?" Matt snapped, briskly massaging the bridge
of his nose.

"Thaat is the report," Keje confirmed. "The aar-tillery
numbers perhaaps a hundred pieces, initially revealed on
the south baank of the river, supporting the first assault.
More are on the *north* baank now. All must've been
moved up under cover of darkness, perhaaps over sever-
aal nights, and the smoke Chack reported earlier was
probably made to screen the enemy's final prepaar-
ations."

Matt nodded bitterly, wondering if all their own careful preparations had already gone up in smoke. "How
bad?" he asked.

Keje took a long breath, held it, then blew it out. "The
Grik have gained *Saanta Caatalina*'s decks in sever-aal
places and the fighting has turned quite desperate. Col-
nol Chack believes the attaack might prove to be . . .
overwhelming."

"What are we doing about it?" Sandra asked.

Keje suddenly blinked furiously and his tail transformed into a whipping cobra flailing the air behind his
stool. Somehow, he kept his voice under control when
he replied. "Tassanna—*Arracca*—has launched the few
planes she retained aboard, configured for ground attaack." He straightened. "For reasons I will touch on in
a moment, those planes were told not to return to *Arracca*, but to fly to the new air-field to re-aarm and refuel.
Ben Maallory is already pre-paaring a strike with other

planes already at the air-field." He nodded at Tikker. "I summoned my own COFO for advice on what else might be done." He looked directly at Matt, his large rust-colored eyes rock steady. "But regarding *Arracca*, I specifically refused Commodore Tassanna's request to move her ship upriver to support *Saanta Caatalina*—again. Shortly after, all communications with *Arracca* were lost." He glanced down at his hands and realized they were clasping each other in front of him. He abruptly put them behind his back. "I strongly suspect Commodore Tassanna has . . . disre-gaarded my orders."

Matt nodded. "She's been upriver before, while we were lollygagging around between Zanzibar and Grik City. She thinks she has a better handle on what's going on than we do. Maybe she does."

"She doesn't," Keje insisted. "The Grik will be expecting her this time. Waiting for her."

"Possibly."

"Well . . . what did *you* expect *her* to do?" Sandra demanded, glaring at Keje first, then Matt. "*You're* the ones, both of you, who showed her what to do in situations like this!"

"Whaat are you taalking about? We never showed her to disobey orders!" Keje denied.

"Maybe not, but you've given her the example, good or bad—over and over—how to throw caution to the wind when people you care about are hanging by their fingernails." Matt frowned, and Keje's blinking redoubled as they both went back to a terrible night when poor little *Walker* tried to *tow* Tassanna's former massive Home, the great *Nerracca*, out from under *Amagi*'s guns. It hadn't worked. Ultimately, *Nerracca* and thousands of her people, including Tassanna's own father, had been blotted out. But they'd tried, perhaps against all reason, and Tassanna must always try as well. Matt still visited that night in his dreams, and his failure burned just as sharply now as it had then, but he recoiled from the . . . special nightmare Tassanna had been forced to endure. Keje's only "failure," which he labored under for increasingly personal reasons, was that he'd been too far away to help. It was just as real to him, however, and Matt and

Keje both refused to meet Sandra's eye for a long moment, before her voice suddenly cracked like a shot.

"Stop! Both of you. Quit feeling sorry for yourselves. I was there too, remember?" she asked Matt. "You did all you could," she reassured him, then glared at Keje. "And if you'd been closer, *Amagi* would've gotten *Big Sal* too. The question is, What're we going to do about this? How do we save our people and salvage the plan *this* time?" she challenged.

The messengers stopped in their tracks and the murmured conversations of Keje's staff went silent. Then Keje's steward arrived with the tea, and even though everyone was still standing, he walked slowly around the table as if oblivious to the tension, filling mugs and setting them down.

"Thanks," Matt said, raising his mug and smelling the steaming brew. Tilting it to his lips, he quickly gulped it down, savoring the molasseslike sweetener he'd come to love as much as the 'Cats did. "What *I'm* going to do is take *Mahan* and *Ellie* upriver now," he said flatly. "Tonight. As soon as I can get aboard *Mahan* and *Ellie* can join her. The rest of First Fleet will proceed with the operation as planned." He glanced at Sandra. "At the very least, I have to stop any cruisers that leak past *Arracca* and *Santy Cat*. We can't let 'em get among our transports." He snorted. "And we've actually got to try to be careful where we engage them too. There are several places in the river where, if we sink 'em there, they can choke us off all by themselves!"

"I expected this decision," Keje admitted, "and already directed *Ellie* to move alongside. Even now she threads her way through the anchorage." He blinked, troubled. "But what if you miss the channel and run aground yourself?"

"*Revenge* is already positioned in the mouth of the river, waiting to lead us all in," Matt mused. "We'll take a couple of her people as pilots."

Keje seemed satisfied by that, but Sandra wasn't. She suddenly felt like she'd practically goaded them into action, and the thought generated a wave of nausea. Matt appeared to notice the discomfort sweeping across her frustrated expression, and Sandra realized she hadn't goaded anyone but herself into recognizing what had to be done. Matt and Keje had obviously known all along. Feeling foolish and even slightly ashamed, she shook her head and managed to fix a sad smile on her lips. Reaching up, she put her hands around Matt's neck and pulled his face down to hers. "Save our people," she murmured, kissing him, then grinned more naturally. "But be careful, sailor."

Matt responded with a confident nod, but his guts twisted as he realized he was about to jump down the "funnel" himself, after all.

Ker-noll Jash, Senior First Naxa, and the newly formed Slasher Regiment (Jash was still almost bursting with pride that his new force had a name, and a highly appropriate one, in his view) had joined Second General Ign's Personal Guard, just as Ign had said. Moving and positioning six tens of great guns to the south bank of the river nearest the enemy had been a grueling experience, however, especially since it had to be done quickly, in the dead of night, while gasping from the exertion and choking on the smoke blowing across them from the long line of brush fires built farther to the south. Jash knew other warriors had moved a "mere" four tens of guns to the north side of the river but hadn't envied them. The terrain was much rougher there.

All seemed worth it when together they watched—and felt—every gun in the grand battery roar simultaneously at the distant target in the smoky, murky night. None of them had ever seen so many field cannon fire at once, and it was a stirring, blood-quickening, amazingly deafening experience. More stunning yet to Jash was how many projectiles hit on or near a target he couldn't even see before the enemy deployed their curious flying flares. And he noted that few of the pointers of guns had made significant corrections before they fired. He wondered how that could be. He was enthralled by the drumming of shot hitting the distant wreck and the thunderous snap of the magical new exploding shells bursting in the air and slashing the enemy from above, and knew he had to learn more about field artillery.

"How do they do that?" he'd ventured to Second General Ign. "How can the . . . gunners"—he'd stumbled on the unfamiliar word—"so well prepare to strike an invisible target?"

Ign huffed. "This war teaches us lessons all the time, new things to make and new ways to use those things. As for the latter, do you imagine that you and your regiment are the only ones to receive special training? You have been learning defense," he'd said, gesturing down the slope in front of the pounding guns where Jash's regiment was directing an equal number of Uul warriors as they dug shallow trenches in the hard red soil. Ign's personal troops stayed back, behind the guns, and Jash suspected many of his Slashers would never hear properly again, but they toiled on, oblivious to the thunder. "Defense is something I doubt we will test today," Ign had continued, "but this is a good exercise, and one must never think himself too sure about anything regarding this enemy."

He'd nodded at the gun line. "Our gunners receive special training as well, first upon the many greatships of battle we cannot bring to this fight. But their advanced teachers are some who have learned new things in battle and survived. We had few of those to begin with," he'd conceded, "but there were enough *to* begin. Now there are more. And as you were seen to be special by those who knew what to look for, so were our gunners. Few rank above First of Ten, but all are Hij. They *must* be Hij to learn the things you question." Ign blinked and shook his head, the flashing guns lighting his orange eyes. "Even I do not fully understand *how* they do what they do. I only know that accomplished gunners, given a precise bearing and range—things our seafaring Hij have been . . . induced to reveal how to determine"—he'd paused to cough in the smoke, but continued—"as well as the *much* better equipment we have provided them, of course, can accomplish what you see, time after time. That is all I must know—for now." He coughed amusement. "Like you, I would learn more when there is time."

Ign had looked thoughtful. "We have tried to train parts of our New Army and fleet to be very good at specific things, and I think we have succeeded. The enemy, in contrast, seems very good at many things at once. I cannot yet say which I think is best, but consider it possible that our weakness, *my* weakness, may be that we have focused overmuch on specifics, unable to accept that many of our race can learn a broad range of skills. You, for example, were first primarily raised to use the newest weapons in attack. That should have been simple enough and fully sufficient for our purposes in the past. Yet then it was decided to teach you to attack from galleys, which you also had to master. Immediately, you were then expected to learn to operate a great gun." Ign's crest had fluttered. "That you might also do *that* well, with so little practice, was perhaps too much to expect at the time, but you survived." Ign snorted. "You not only survived, you *taught yourself* to lead, so I sent you and your troops to learn defense." He'd nodded past the booming guns again. "At this also you seem to have excelled. Now you show interest in the great guns of the land—field artillery. Perhaps I will send you for gunner training next. It might be interesting to discover how much you can absorb, because training all our warriors to fight in different ways could be the only way to defeat an enemy who apparently already can."

The great guns had gone silent as the distant swarm of galleys enveloped the shattered, smoking wreck, and the growing staccato of small arms merged into a constant, clattering roar. The work in front of the cannon had also stopped, as hundreds of snouts turned toward the climax of the battle on the river.

"Back to work!" Jash had shouted, and Ign gurgled a chuckle.

"In spite of what I just said about focus, I am glad to see you still so attentive to your assigned task. Still, I doubt we will actually need the defenses you prepare. As soon as their *Santa Catalina* has finally fallen, we will disperse and conceal these guns and troops. The enemy's flying machines will seek their revenge and we have little protection against them here. Nor can you provide it with your works in the time we have. Let your warriors take a moment to enjoy the end of that troublesome obstacle once and for all, and revel in the loosing of the Final Swarm. We will join it soon enough ourselves and return the world to its proper balance as we drive the enemy—our *prey*—before us once again, as First General Esshk, the Celestial Mother, and the Vanished Gods themselves have all decreed we must."

But *Santa Catalina* wouldn't fall.

The fighting went on and on beneath the sputtering flares, the booming mortars savaging the tightly packed galleys, which often swamped one another in their zeal to close with the prey. The great guns of the enemy, protected within the shattered hulk, continued to blast at the cruisers as well, as they picked their way through the wreckage at the bend of the river. The first of these was burning forward, bright flames washing aft as it picked up speed to clear the way. More fire spewed near the wreck and Jash thought it was doomed at last, but quickly realized the enemy was somehow *directing* the flames at the galleys around it—which were immediately engulfed. A new sound joined the battle: the agonized squeal of burning Grik. Everywhere the gushing fire sprayed, more galleys and more warriors were consumed.

"Terrible, terrible," Second General Ign murmured. "But perhaps fitting after all."

Jash looked at him in surprise. The general's crest had risen to stand almost straight up on his head as he spoke, but there'd been an unmistakable hint of admiration in his tone. He saw Jash watching him. "Prey they are and will always be, but there can be no doubt they are *worthy* prey. Of course they are, to have resisted us at all. That they drove us to this is remarkable." Seeing Jash's expression, he knew he had to explain, somehow. "Don't you see? With every setback they inflict on us, they make our ultimate victory greater. They are the worthiest prey we have ever faced, and we who bring them down will never be forgotten."

Jash had trouble imagining that a warrior, *any* warrior,

even a second or first general, might be known beyond his time. Such a thing had never happened, but the idea . . . intrigued him.

"Many names will be forgotten *tomorrow*, including yours, Second General Ign, if this assault also fails!" came a loud voice behind them. Ign and Jash turned to see a Ghaarrichk'k even bigger than Ign step down from the open door of a carriage drawn by thirty warriors in polished armor. Jash had never seen First General Esshk, but immediately knew him. He wore bronze armor, redly reflecting the gouts of flame, and the long red cloak of the Regent Champion flowed down around his feet. There was also only one being on earth who'd ever speak to Second General Ign so. Jash and Ign dropped to their bellies in the same instant. Senior First Naxa had slunk a few steps away before he too dropped.

"Stand!" Esshk said, striding quickly forward. "Before your entire force lies useless on the ground!" Jash and Ign had barely regained their feet before Esshk resumed. "Why have you stopped firing? The fate of the battle, the Final Swarm, hangs in the balance, yet you do nothing!"

"I thought you were aboard *Giorsh*, awaiting the signal to advance with the Swarm," Ign temporized, pointing. Another cruiser had slipped through the tangle. "If the cruisers can do it, the greatships might, with daylight."

"I came to witness the end of that nuisance," Esshk snarled, pointing at *Santa Catalina*, "and our final, triumphant breakout. The *world* awaits beyond that heap of wreckage!" he roared. "Yet what do I find? *Defeat*," he hissed, "pulling more heavily on the scale than ever before. How could you design such a disaster? It is good I came to relieve you of the burden of this battle you have made! Open fire!" he shouted at the gunners, staring back with jaws agape. "Pound that thing out there until there is no life on it!"

"Many of our own warriors are on it now," Ign reminded mildly. "And despite the apparent chaos, which all battles display to best effect, *Santa Catalina must* soon fall."

"Quicker with the weight of these guns," Esshk stated.

"So . . . I am truly relieved. You directly command here now?" Ign asked carefully.

"I do. Remove yourself at once . . . but do not destroy yourself. I would speak with you again when this is done." He glared down his snout at Jash. "Is this the prodigy you so praised?" He waved at the digging Slashers. "Is this meager jumble the result of my benevolence on his behalf?"

Jash started to speak, but Ign slammed his elbow against the leather armor over Jash's torso.

"It is, Lord," Ign said.

"If this is all he has learned from you, you may take him away as well."

Ign bowed. "Then in light of my past service, I request that we be allowed to stay and observe how you salvage the battle I so poorly devised." He glanced at Jash. "Help *him* unlearn my poor example."

Esshk hesitated. He needed to appear reasonable in front of all these troops. *Ign's* troops. "Oh, very well," he said, as if it meant nothing. Then he spoke lower, more hesitantly. "In light of your service, as you said, I would . . . spare you the shame of that." He raised his voice again. "But wallow in it if you must. Just stay out of the way." He glared back at the artillery line. *"Open fire!"* he repeated.

The great guns thundered again, the pressure pounding Jash's chest, but they couldn't add much to the roiling turmoil inside. He worshipped First General Esshk above even the Celestial Mother, but this . . . He'd never imagined such capriciousness. The battle in the river was a mess, to be sure, but it was also all but won. Naxa glared at him as if Jash were somehow responsible for nearly getting *him* killed again, and quickly turned away.

"Do not judge First General Esshk too harshly," Ign whispered near Jash's earhole. "Remember what I said about not being forgotten? He needs to be remembered for this more than we. More important, our race must remember it was he who won this battle and began our rise to victory."

Jash didn't understand. "Will we be required to destroy ourselves?" he asked.

"You? I doubt it. Myself? Very possibly." Ign hesitated. "Unless, of course, First General Esshk manages to lose the battle he appropriated. I truly hope that doesn't happen." He gestured out at the fighting. "But those are not all mere Uul warriors over there. I would expect some Uul to turn prey under fire from our own guns, but most would continue fighting. It is the Way." He looked directly at Jash. "If *you* were over there, however, already winning the fight, and realized your own race was deliberately firing on you for no reason you could see, what would you do?"

Jash took a deep breath and considered a moment, but had no ready reply. "I would think the bombardment was a mistake and pause, protecting my troops as best I could until it was corrected," he finally confessed.

"Exactly," Second General Ign said. "You would *think*. You probably wouldn't flee, but you might stop pressing your attack." He looked at Esshk, striding back and forth behind the bellowing guns, bodyguards clustered around him. "He made you. He made *me*; better tools to fight this new kind of war. But I suspect even now he does not fully understand us and expects us only to fight with greater skill in the same old way. With overwhelming numbers that might still succeed, he has toiled very hard to improve the *quality* of his quantity. But the enemy has proven time and again that the quality of quantity alone is rarely sufficient anymore."

Jash agreed—he thought—but remained confused. He was still very young, after all. He was perhaps most confused that Ign remained so loyal to Esshk despite what Jash saw as a terrible betrayal. His own worship had almost immediately collapsed into resentment in the face of the fundamental unfairness he'd witnessed, and he found himself cast upon a tumultuous sea of uncertainty.

Together, for a long moment, they watched the effect of the bombardment. Solid shot still pounded the distant wreck, and exploding shells sparkled away into the night to pop brightly over the target, their glare pulsing in the smoke. It was hard to tell through the rumbling reports, but it seemed as if the withering fusillade of small arms diminished somewhat. The enemy would be taking cover and he wondered if his counterparts, fighting over there, were directing their warriors to do the same.

"We will still win," Ign said abruptly. "The return fire from the enemy is concentrated more toward the back of the ship. Our warriors have certainly gained the forward part—but their attack *has* slowed. Perhaps they have even taken the armored section where the enemy's greatest guns have been protected against us? Look: another of our cruisers has negotiated the tangle at the *nakkle* leg and is not under fire!" Suddenly he tensed and stared hard in the fiery, smoky gloom. "There!" he said sharply, pointing at a massive, deeper darkness moving up from behind the *Santa Catalina*.

"I think I see," Jash said, squinting. The smoke had finally overwhelmed him. He was having trouble breathing and his vision was blurry with the water that filled his eyes. "What is that?"

"Our salvation, I suspect," Ign replied. Considering what he'd said, his tone was surprisingly bleak. "First General Esshk is no fool. He will never destroy us as long as we are of use. I am distressed to say he may soon need us once more." He took a step forward.

"Where are you going, Lord General? We were commanded to stay out of the way."

"I must convince First General Esshk to restore my command," he stated simply, "so I can put fire on *that*." He pointed again at the massive dark shape even Jash now recognized.

"Will he?"

"I think so, when he recognizes the threat. Just as I said he must be seen to win this fight, it is even more important that he not be seen to lose it."

Just then, the side of the great . . . blackness on the water suddenly belched long, wicked, sparkly tongues of flame at them. Before they heard the report of the salvo, more than twenty shells, larger and more powerful than anything the Grik were firing, exploded above or among the firing line. Gun's crews went sprawling or were tossed in the air, and several of the great guns themselves were shattered or thrown on their backs, crushing their crews. A couple of shells detonated among Jash's Slashers, and he was already running toward them even as Second General Ign strode faster toward where Esshk and his entourage had halted their pacing.

"You are not supposed to be here!" Naxa snapped as Jash went past him.

"What will they do? Destroy me?" Jash snarled back. "Get back to work!" he bellowed at his warriors. "Dig!" More huge flashes lit the night, and the air crackled with the approach of more big shells.

CHAPTER
26

////// *USS* **Santa Catalina**
Zambezi River
Grik Africa
0230

*D*ennis Silva and Gunny Horn dragged Major Gutfeld aft through the growing melee sprawling across *Santa Catalina*'s ravaged upper decks. Gutfeld had been hit in the leg again, with a musket ball this time. Raiders and Marines, impossibly intermixed, were falling back all around them, pausing to shoot at smoke-blurred targets or jabbing bayonets at anything that got too close. Silva didn't know where Risa and Lawrence were; they'd been separated in the crush. He hoped they'd made it through—or around—the rampaging Grik controlling the forward part of the ship. The latter wasn't impossible; the Grik seemed hesitant to venture below and fight through dark passageways the defenders knew so well. And the boom of a 5.5″ proved they hadn't gotten into the air castle/casemate yet.

A Grik musket ball snatched the PIG-cig right out of Horn's mouth, flecking him with smoldering bits of cherry. "Shit!" he yelped, trying to brush sparks away with the back of his right hand, still wrapped around the BAR. Someone running past smacked the long barrel, and his fist, backed by the heavy gun, punched him in the mouth, splitting his lip. *"Shit!"* he shouted again.

"I think even the lizards want you to quit them nasty things," Silva grunted, heaving Gutfeld up on his shoulder.

"Put me down, you big ape!" Gutfeld snapped. "I can walk!"

"Not fast enough, Simy," Silva replied. "An' we gotta scoot!" He started running while Horn fell in behind, BAR leveled.

"Thank 'em for their concern for me, wilya?" Horn quipped back.

"Sure thing," Silva replied, spraying a group of Grik that had gotten around in front of them with his Thompson. They fell kicking on the deck. He'd been forced to leave his Doom Stomper behind—it had been the big rifle or Simy—but it wouldn't have been very effective at the moment, anyway. He slowed to step over the Grik he'd just killed. "These boogers said, with their dyin' gasps, they don't give a shit about you; it's just even with all this other smoke, your PIG-cigs is makin' 'em gag."

Horn backed over the corpses. "Good. I'll fire up another, quick as I can."

A flurry of shots *vroop*ed past, clattering against a bulkhead and warbling away. "Agghh!" Gutfeld groaned. "Dammit! One caught me!"

Silva gritted his teeth but couldn't stop to check him now. The musketry was increasing and the hair on the back of his neck seemed to tell him that Grik bayonets were right *there*. Finally, the portside stair down to the aft well deck was just ahead, and a heavy line of Raiders and Marines had formed a barricade, bristling with shiny, "friendly" rifle muzzles and bayonets. All were shooting as Silva and Horn hurried directly at them, both large men trying to will themselves smaller. Seconds later, they reached the barricade, and Silva tossed Gutfeld on the reverse slope of mattresses and wooden crates before he and Horn scrambled after him. More stragglers joined them, stiffening the line, but there weren't many. They must've been among the last to fall back.

"Thanks for not shootin' us," Silva told a 'Cat Marine, coughing between deep breaths.

"I never *seen* you," the 'Cat confessed matter-of-factly, firing again. "Caan't see *nothin'*."

Silva blinked his good eye. "Then what the hell're you shootin' at?"

"Thaat way. Griks're thaat way."

"'That way' ain't a target, shithead." Silva raised his voice and yelled at a corps-'Cat. "Get the major aft—he's hit twice. Once in the leg. I don't know where else." Settling beside the 'Cat who, probably like the rest, missed him only out of dumb luck, Silva inserted another twenty-round magazine in his Thompson and rested it on the breastworks. "Hold your fire!" he shouted, their front clear for the moment. "Wait'll you got somethin' to shoot at!" There must've still been plenty of targets above on the deckhouse and over on the starboard side of the ship, because the shooting there continued unabated. Only a couple of mortars were still running, dropping bombs among the galleys, and there were no more star shells. Silva wondered if the mortars had pulled back or been overrun.

"You takin' charge here?" a Raider asked him.

"Not if I can help it. Why? Who's supposed to be in charge?"

"Major Risa," one 'Cat cried, reminding Silva that his friend might still be forward somewhere. Others shouted "Galay" or "Gutfeld." Silva didn't know where Enrico Galay was either, but Gutfeld was out of it. "'Ajor Cook to First," a Khonashi called. Even as he did, another hot blast of liquid fire *whoosh*ed out on more galleys trying to come alongside aft, prompting more crackling shrieks.

"Major Cook's busy," Silva said. "Where's your lieutenants? And where's Chackie—Colonel Chack?"

"No'ody knows," replied the Khonashi. "No'ody else alive, directly o'er us, an' us're all 'ixed."

Silva sighed, but Gunny Horn barked a response. "Mixed or not, you're all Raiders or Marines. Don't tell me you gotta have an officer to tell you how to fight!"

"Not how, just where," retorted an ancient 'Cat in Marine rhino-pig armor.

"Why, looky here! It's Moe! How are ya, you ol' scudder? I ain't seen you in a coon's age!"

"I seen you, thaat's why you not see me," Moe replied. "I aall-ways say, bein' roun' you will get me killed." He grinned, displaying his few remaining teeth. "I too young to die." Silva saw the first-sergeant stripes on the sleeve of Moe's combat tunic, so he seemed to be the highest-ranking NCO present.

"Okaaay," Silva said equably. "I reckon right here's good for now." His eye caught a renewed mass of movement in the smoke. "Here they come!"

Muskets crackled and the Grik charged, straight into the massed, rapid fire of breech-loading Allin-Silvas, Horn's BAR, several Blitzerbug SMGs, and Silva's Thompson. Blood sprayed and downy fur exploded into clouds, thickening the smoke. Bodies piled up on deck, twitching, squirming, mewling in pain—but more Grik ran over the top of the heap, jaws agape, teeth bared, pressing on. "Up!" Silva roared. "Meet 'em with your steel!" Blitzers kept hammering, but Silva dropped his empty Thompson and grabbed his Colt and cutlass again. The cutlass swung and clanged off a musket barrel after chopping through the stock and the Grik's fingers. The creature shrieked and died when somebody else shot it. Silva reeled when another musket slammed down on top of his helmet, but he put two bullets in the Grik that swung it.

Suddenly, another Grik a few yards in front of him just . . . exploded. Pieces of it sprayed more Grik to its left, impaling them with shattered bone. A big hole appeared in the side of the deckhouse. Another shot had a similar effect farther forward, splattering several more Grik. Then there was a series of pops overhead and jagged shards of hot iron slashed down, killing Grik and defenders alike.

"Down!" Horn shouted. "Back behind the barricade! Open fire, pour it in!" Silva dropped down, firing his pistol with a muffled *Pop! Pop-pop!* "Stupid damn Grik've started shelling us again," Horn yelled. Silva had figured that much, but didn't know why. The fire would be hard on the defenders, but most probably had a little cover at least. As he'd just seen, it would be worse for the Grik trying to root them out. Pieces of the exploding shells that flew upward were starting to fall, and a chunk glanced off his helmet as he raised his head to see.

The Grik charge had stumbled but was still boring in. Some of its weight was gone, however, and rifle and SMG fire kept it beaten back—especially when *another* salvo of Grik shot pounded and exploded over the ship.

Silva raised his voice in glee. "Hot damn, they're doin' our work for us!"

"Look! Look!" cried Moe, pointing behind to the left. Silva had to wipe the gunk out of his good eye before he saw a massive dark shape loom up out of the gloom. Cook's flamethrower lit the night, and Silva realized *Arracca* was back. Effortlessly, the great Home-turned-carrier demolished her way through the crop of galleys, grinding them under and smashing them aside. Her two DP 4.7″ guns opened up on the cruisers sneaking through the gap, as the portside half of her fifty big fifty-pounder smoothbores roared a broadside at something Silva couldn't see. Tassanna had flatly refused to relinquish any of her ship's heavy armament, specifically in case of situations like this. Doubtless she'd secured the ship from air operations in favor of surface action, something all carriers once practiced, but *Arracca* was the only carrier in the west still armed with enough guns to wade into a brawl.

Santa Catalina's riddled wreck groaned as *Arracca* came alongside, pulping more galleys and countless Grik between their hulls. Abruptly, to Silva's surprise, Chack was standing beside him, oblivious to the shot still raining down or zipping past. Besides the calm on his unblinking face, he looked like hell; scorched fur and uniform utterly covered in blood. "You've done well," he said, "but now we must prepare to abaandon this ship. Hold here as long as you caan while the rest fall baack to the well deck and go aboard *Arracca*. Help is on the way," he assured, "but our position is hopeless."

Silva gestured forward. "Why fold now? We're holdin' okay, an' *Arracca*'ll block most of the shore batteries from hittin' us. They can't do much to *her*."

Chack looked at him. "But their rockets might, and they'll almost surely use them now. Besides, you may hold here, but our defense on the staar-board side is falling apaart. *Arracca* caan't shield both, and there are caannon on the north baank as well." Silva hadn't known that, but he'd been pretty preoccupied. The fighting here had been loud enough to mask anything going on to starboard. He finished stuffing a massive wad of Aryaa-lan tobacco leaves in his cheek and nodded.

"Jeez. Okay, we'll hold. Just tell us when it's time to skeedaddle." He paused then, his eye looking away. There was something he hadn't allowed himself to think about, but if they were leaving, he had to now. And Chack had a right to know. "I, uh . . . sorta lost Risa. Forward," he said at last. "She was just there, fightin' like a wildcat—then she wasn't. Larry too."

Chack blinked rapidly then, suddenly realizing how much inner pain Silva must be feeling. "Risa is safe," he assured. "Laaw-rence as well. Risa *is* . . . wounded," he conceded cryptically, "but Laaw-rence helped her out through the inside of the ship. Quite a few escaped thaat way, but the Grik are in the ship now. You must waatch behind and beside you."

Silva only nodded, but Chack could tell a heavy burden had been lifted from him. "How's Simy?" Silva asked. "We fetched him out."

"I don't know."

A droning roar came from forward, produced by the portable bellows-driven horns the Grik favored for issuing simple commands on the battlefield, and everyone was depressingly familiar with this particular nerve-wracking note; it was the call for a general charge. Another roar rose from hundreds of Grik throats already aboard—and maybe thousands still waiting to join them. The smoke swirled around a tightly packed, rampant mob.

"*They're* protected from the shore batteries too," Horn said nervously, slamming another magazine in his BAR. "They'll push like hell now."

"They ain't protected from *those* batteries," Silva replied with a huge grin, nodding up at *Arracca*'s towering sides. Below the carrier's hangar deck, but still higher than they were, the gaping muzzles of twenty-five 50-pounders protruded from open gunports, quickly shifting, depressing. Silva emptied his pistol into the charging Grik, then ducked behind the barricade. "Better hunker down, fellas!" he called. "My guess is, all them guns is packed to the gills with canis—"

Arracca's gunners took their time, carefully aiming each huge piece. Even so, they fired close enough together that the individual reports were swallowed by what seemed a single, stupendous, point-blank crash. A fog bank of smoke thicker than anything they'd experienced gushed down on the ship—as did a rumbling, clattering, ricocheting storm of *thousands* of three-quarter-inch balls. The Grik charge was blasted away, literally smashed, and all that remained was a long, gruesome heap of shredded tunics, armor, weapons, shattered bone, and unidentifiable gobbets of flesh.

Silva jumped up like a jack-in-the-box. "That's the style!" he howled.

"Get down, you idiot!" Horn snapped. "There's *more* of 'em, you know? And some of our guys caught some bouncers."

"You should maan-age here well enough, after all," Chack agreed, moving back in a crouch. "Send your wounded to the well deck to be taken aboard *Arracca*. I must direct the withdraw-aal from the staar-board side. You may pull baack as you see fit, but don't get cut off!"

"Sure thing, Chackie! Have fun!"

Chack blinked consternation. He was just as exhausted as anyone after their long ordeal, but it looked like the end was near, one way or another. He actually embraced that, since First Fleet and its expeditionary force was so near at last, and he hoped—if he lived—he'd soon be reunited with Safir Maraan. Together, they'd see the beginning of a new phase in the war against the Grik. He couldn't describe anything about their current situation as "fun," however. Still blinking, he disappeared in the swirling smoke. Silva laughed.

The battle was intensifying everywhere, though Silva's view was largely limited to the narrow corridor in front of him, imposed by *Arracca*'s looming bulk and the riddled superstructure opposite the splintered deck. The Grik massed and charged several more times as their numbers were replenished. Each time they were annihilated by the defensive fire of Silva and Horn's scratch platoon and *Arracca*'s devastating gusts of canister. Otherwise, Silva got only occasional glimpses to confirm what he *thought* was going on, based on where the fighting sounded fiercest. And Chack—or somebody—sent word from time to time, trying to keep him apprised so he'd know when it was time to pull back.

Arracca's portside guns fired continuously, hammering Grik cruisers and the massed battery on the south bank. USS *Ris* and USS *Itaa* had obviously come up with *Arracca* and were probably doing the same. A few planes from Tassanna's airfield did what they could, but it was difficult to support the fight on the river in the dark. Silva suspected they were concentrating on the shore batteries. None of their solid shot was reaching Silva's position anymore, but occasional case shot still exploded overhead. Worse, a few Grik rockets started lofting in from the other side of the bend, probably fired without orders, but more were likely on the way. Silva glanced aft, surprised how quickly the wounded had been transferred to *Arracca* and now *Ris* or *Itaa*—he couldn't tell the former Grik cruisers apart—which had snugged up against *Santa Catalina*'s fantail. It was blasting grapeshot down the wrecked ship's starboard side, and Abel Cook was spraying burning fuel over there as well. Flames lapped up over *Santy Cat*'s side but didn't find much left to burn.

Or has it been quick? Silva wondered. He had no idea how long they'd fought, and even if dawn was approaching, he wouldn't be able to tell through all the smoke. He narrowed his eye. Raiders and Marines were spilling down the ladder to the well deck from the starboard side, firing back the way they came. Some were falling as musket balls tore into them. Troops guarding the removal of the wounded slammed a volley at the pursuing Grik, but they barely slowed, flowing after the other blocking force in a slashing tide of death. "Time to beat feet," Silva said, tilting his helmet at the growing rout.

"Through *that*?" Horn demanded incredulously.

"Hell no." Silva pointed up. 'Cats aboard *Arracca* were casting lines and lowering another cargo net down the ship's towering side. Horn looked at it and cringed. Floating debris from all the galleys crushed between the ships had kept them from actually touching, and there remained a daunting gap. Realizing the cause for his friend's concern, Silva grinned. "Just play like you're a grasshopper!" Silva gazed at their motley force. "Lightly wounded, if you think you can make it, go now. The rest o' you dopes get some lines secured around the worst cases. We'll all shove off together once they're clear."

The evacuation of Silva's little force went better than he'd expected for a few minutes, while a chaotic, pitched battle raged astern. There was nothing he could do to help back there, so keeping a watchful eye aft, he continued getting what he and Horn increasingly considered their guys off. By the time the unwounded were climbing the cargo net, however, they'd been seen by the Grik swarming aft—where *Arracca*'s guns wouldn't bear, even if there weren't still friendlies back there.

"Get a move on," Horn urged the 'Cat above him on the netting as he climbed. He'd discovered the gap wasn't all that great, with the proper motivation. *"Hurry up!"* he shouted as musket balls started slapping the thick wooden hull around him. "Shit!" he added as the 'Cat cried out and fell. Another stiffened and went limp, dangling from the net. They were climbing through a storm of musket balls and splinters now. Their troops already at the top, as well as some *Arracca* 'Cats, were shooting back, but they had to be careful as well.

Silva had almost reached the vast opening to the hangar deck when the entire ship seemed to heave, bashing his knuckles and bouncing him on the net, which whipped like a shaken blanket and slammed back against the hull. One of the Grik-like Khonashi lost his grip and dropped screeching toward the roiling water below. He didn't make it. Whatever caused *Arracca*'s heavy lurch had finally driven her hard against *Santa Catalina*'s butchered side, and the Khonashi's scream chopped off as he was mashed between the ships.

"Aww, *hell*!" Silva muttered, a sudden chill coursing down his spine. The firing fell off as *Santa Catalina* was jolted as well, and Silva, Horn, and the rest of their survivors clambered past the stanchions onto the massive, practically empty hangar deck. "Empty" was a relative thing, however. There were few planes, mostly heavily cannibalized wrecks, but lots of people. Most were gathered in an impromptu hospital area aft, being triaged by harried-looking corps'-Cats, but many were running back and forth, trying to move the injured. Haggard troops were being organized to defend the bay openings, provide cover for those remaining on *Santy Cat*'s fantail, or pull more wounded aboard.

To Silva's secret delight, he almost immediately saw Lawrence, standing as if waiting for him—with the Doom Stomper in his arms. A *very* nervous-looking Petey cringed behind what Silva—with a startled blink—recognized as his own sea bag. Petey immediately bolted forward and up to his customary place behind Silva's neck. For once, for now, he didn't squawk about food or anything. He didn't make a peep at all.

"*There* you are!" Silva declared at Lawrence as if he'd caught the Sa'aaran deliberately malingering. "Where the hell've you been? An' I hope you didn't scratch my darlin' rifle—or bang my poke around too bad. You know Captain Reddy's pistol's in there!"

"Hvat you care?" Lawrence snapped back. "You just 'eave it 'ying there! Your stu'id 'ag too. Lucky you, I, and so' others go 'ast our quarters." His outrage dimmed. "I got Risa apht, and Colonel Chack send I to get her here. She's hurt in the leg."

Silva's facade faded as well. "She's okay?"

Lawrence hesitated and didn't answer directly. "Lieutenant Cross is 'ith her." He jerked his snout toward the greater mass of wounded.

"What the hell hit the ship?" Gunny Horn demanded. "It almost shook me off." He shuddered, probably remembering the Khonashi who fell.

"We get *raammed*! Raammed baad!" cried a 'Cat running past. Silva, Horn, and Lawrence all shared horrified looks and rushed to port, where many others were moving. They were closely followed by the mixed group of defenders that had latched onto them.

Nearing the portside hangar bay, they were lit by a blazing inferno below. A Grik cruiser, maybe the first to break out, and which they'd seen set afire by *Santa Catalina*'s guns, was fully engulfed in flames. Somehow, probably steering belowdecks, its crew had aimed it at *Arracca*, and all her guns couldn't sink it before it hit her hard. Peering over the side, heat blasting his face, Silva saw that the damn thing had bashed a big, deep hole in *Arracca*'s side with its underwater ram. Hoses were already starting to play on the blazing wreck and steam billowed, forcing Silva back.

"We haave to get underway at once," said a familiar little-girl voice nearby, and Silva wrenched his head around to see Commodore Tassanna-Ay-Arracca standing with several officers. She'd obviously hurried down to see the damage herself.

"But, Commodore!" one of the officers protested. "We caan't push the wreck from the wound it made, and it will *tear* away if we move, making the wound even larger!"

Tassanna glared at him. "It will tear away as it sinks as well, *after* it sets us afire!" She looked at Silva, her huge eyes filled with a sadness not unlike another he'd seen there before. "Chief Sil-vaa," she said formally. "This ship has haad many upgrades, including some ingenious modifications to her waater-tight integrity, but they were added, not built in. I don't imaa-gine they caan preserve it for long. On my way here I already received word of flooding beyond the bulkheads. The pumps could still control it, but we must tear away from that"—she pointed at the inferno alongside—"before it burns us all. In doing so, I expect further daam-age that will overburden the pumps." She took a deep breath, blinking too rapidly for Silva to decipher the meaning. "This ship—my Home—must sink."

Silva nodded slowly, eyes never leaving hers. "That's more than likely so, Tassy—I mean, Commodore. What're we gonna do?"

"We will get underway, lightening the ship as much

as we can, and fight our way through the Grik cruisers until I caan beach us there." She pointed at the sloping bank on the south side of the river, where the Grik batteries were emplaced, still firing. Seeing Silva's expression, she explained, "It's the only place in reach thaat an assault force—including the surviving Raiders, Maa-rines, and every soul aboard this ship not serving her guns, might successfully get ashore."

"In the face of sixty damn guns," Silva brooded.

"I doubt there's more than thirty left in action," Horn piped up sarcastically. "Probably just a measly half-million Griks defending them too."

"Nevertheless," Tassanna said, "I see no other option." She turned to a messenger. "Cap-i-taan Saaeen will get underway, making a wide turn to port that will ground us as close as possible opposite the south-shore battery. Once we're grounded, the starboard guns will fire on the baattery while the portside guns continue to engage the enemy fleet. I'll be up shortly." She hesitated. "Hopefully in time to beach the ship myself." The messenger saluted and fled.

"What about Chackie an' the rest still on *Santy Cat*?" Silva demanded, a kind of desperation growing in his gut. He wasn't afraid of the hellish fight to come, but they couldn't just leave their people behind!

"Sever all connections to *Saanta Caatalina*," Tassanna told another messenger. "Make sure Col-nol Chack understaands the situation. *Itaa* and *Ris* will continue his evaac-uation. Hopefully, we'll draw most of the enemy's attention when we move." She turned back to Silva. "It's all we can do for them. In the meantime, I'll open the aarmories to every member of this crew. The weapons are the old-style rifle-muskets, for the most part, but nearly everyone has received basic training in their use, and they're still better than what the Grik possess, it seems." She looked directly in Silva's eye and blinked challengingly. "*You* will haave nearly three thousaand combat-aants, added to the remainder of the Raiders and Maa-rines we took aboard. I suggest you use your experienced troops as NCOs to form detaachments as every cook, mechanic, clerk, even pilot on this ship aarives to be aarmed. You have very little time."

Shit, Silva thought, stunned. *I know I told Chackie I wanted to play somethin' new, but* this *ain't what I had in mind. I can't LEAD such a thing!* He did a quick mental inventory. *Risa's hurt. So's Gutfeld. Don't know where his XO, that yella'-furred 'Cat named Flaar, is, or Major Galay neither. They're prob'ly still with Chackie, if they're still livin'. An' sure as shit, Chackie'll be the last one off* Santy Cat, *no matter what.* No doubt other junior officers had made it aboard, but it suddenly dawned on Silva that he and Horn probably *were* the only ones with a reputation . . . crazy enough for everyone—Marines, Raiders, and sailors alike—to follow on a suicidal stunt like this. He sighed. "How're we gonna do it? No matter how close you get, we can't just wade ashore."

"*Arracca* still has bays for gri-kakka boats in her sides. Inside are twenty-four motor launches for recovering daamaged floatplanes and retrieving aircrews from the waater. One or two may be down for repairs, but at least twenty should be operational. They're very faast and should each carry twenty-five troops. That gives you at least five hundred for your initial laanding, which, aac-companied by our bom-baardment and any aar support I caan summon, should come as a complete surprise to the enemy. The boats will continue to carry people as long as they're able—and there are any left."

A great rending crash thundered through the ship, rattling the heavy timbers beneath their feet as *Arracca* began to move. Silva looked out at the Grik cruiser, a little lower in the water but still burning fiercely, and saw it start to jackknife. Its bow, deep in *Arracca*'s guts, gouged and twisted with a terrible, booming, splintering rumble. Tassanna blinked rapidly, as if feeling the pain in her own side. "I must leave you now," she said. "More Grik cruisers are already on the loose, and I must continue to fight my ship. You have even more to do."

For the first time in a while, Silva realized the guns were still firing and heavy shot was still pounding the ship. Unlike the later purpose-built fleet carriers, *Arracca*'s sides were thick enough that only the heaviest roundshot could really hurt her. But Silva had a sudden fear that other Grik cruisers might try to ram, seeing what the first had accomplished. "Aye, aye, Commodore," he said, then looked at Horn, Lawrence, and the rest who'd followed them and still stood by. To his disappointment, Moe wasn't there, and he didn't even know if the old 'Cat had even made it aboard. Finally he blinked, almost apologetically. "Looks like we got our work cut out for us," he said grimly. "I hope Chackie gets ashore double quick to take over, but as of now, we're all a buncha goddamn officers."

CHAPTER
27

////// Ign's Grand Battery
South Bank of the Zambezi

S econd General Ign pulled First General Esshk
out from under the smoking earth and shattered
bodies of his entourage. An enemy shell had
detonated almost as it touched a caisson full of ammunition, and its resulting explosion—and that of two other
caissons positioned rather carelessly nearby—managed
to accomplish slight craters in the hard ground beneath
them and probably accounted for seventy or eighty Grik.
The splinters, shell fragments, and pieces of closer Grik
had flattened Esshk and his escort.

"I yet live," Esshk managed, somewhat surprised,
staring intently up at Ign.

"Yes, Lord," Ign replied, abruptly and very thoroughly
examining Esshk for wounds. He was covered with the
blood of his companions but seemed unhurt. Only three
of those companions managed to rise, however, and resume their far-less-protective encirclement. A few others
still moved, but they'd never be whole. Ign shouted for
warriors to end their misery. Seeing Esshk trying to rise
as well, Ign helped him to his feet. "You must leave this
place at once!" he shouted over another salvo of shells
exploding among the guns, shocked by his own boldness.
Shortly before, Esshk had essentially condemned him to

death, yet now Ign's words and tone—directed at his lord—sounded dangerously like a command. Esshk either was still too stunned to notice or fully agreed. "Direct the battle from elsewhere," Ign pleaded. "We cannot lose you here!"

Esshk hacked dusty phlegm. "You are right, of course." He paused. "And I was . . . mistaken to reproach you as I did." He paused. "I have experienced the fury of the enemy's weapons before, when they wrested the Celestial City from my grasp. I haven't had occasion to endure their direct, deliberate attention since," he continued ruefully, "and sometimes forget how quickly they can force us to alter our plans, regardless how meticulously prepared. We rush to embrace their weapons, but never seem to achieve parity. Even as we match what we have seen, they field better"—he waved his hand to indicate the flashing guns on the water, heralding another incoming salvo—"or make what we copied infinitely more effective!"

Most of the shells exploded among the furiously digging warriors this time, and Ign flinched, hoping Kernoll Jash wasn't hit. "I beg you, Lord General," Ign implored, "leave this to me. You must direct the rest of the battle and ensure the greater plan proceeds."

"Indeed," Esshk agreed, straightening, smoothing his bloody cloak. Blood made the red garment, lit by gunflashes, seem spotted black. "All I said earlier is forgotten. I do tend to less patience than I once had," he added—as close to an apology as he could come. "I go now to send the signal to loose the Final Swarm at last." The pounding from great guns on the river had slackened, and they realized one of the burning cruisers had apparently rammed the great flying machine carrier that came to *Santa Catalina*'s aid. "If we are fortunate," Esshk continued with growing excitement, "the enemy on the river has been dealt with. Perhaps it will burn, even explode! If not, the several of our cruisers now approaching or already engaged should keep it busy. It *can't* stop the Swarm now, particularly if our warriors simply ignore it and rush past. Continue your bombardment, Second General Ign! I hope to maneuver *Giorsh* through the blockage in the river after the rest of the Swarm is loose. You will join me in her then."

"It will be my greatest honor," Ign proclaimed, but his tone was still urgent as he watched *Arracca*'s smoke- and fire-glare-blurred shape. She *had* been rammed and was fighting the flames of the burning cruiser, attacking the boarders on *Santa Catalina*, and directing occasional shots at the other closing cruisers—even as they pummeled her in return. Amazingly, however, though it was hard to be certain with such dismal visibility, Ign thought she'd actually started moving. He could only think of two reasons for that. "But do hurry from here, Lord," he begged, then paused. "I would be grateful for one final indulgence."

Esshk looked at him questioningly, and Ign nodded toward *Arracca*. She *was* moving, sluggishly but certain. "That ship came to aid the other. It has been seriously . . . inconvenienced, at least, but must have removed many of the warriors fighting on its consort. We already know, against all reason at times, our enemy rarely abandons its warriors to certain death. I don't think *Arracca* would leave *Santa Catalina* without the bulk of its survivors aboard. Perhaps it is in peril of sinking or being stranded as its consort was, but I doubt it is fit to escape—even if it was disposed to do so."

"Then . . . ?" Esshk trailed off.

"I expect it will either smash its way into the gap we exploited," Ign predicted, then hesitated. "Or perhaps . . . I do not think it impossible that it may try to put those warriors ashore here."

Esshk's eyes widened, incredulous. "Why? What could they possibly gain? They must be sadly depleted, a very few hundreds left at most. And you just said they do not abandon their people to certain death!"

"They have, rarely," Ign stressed, "when they had no other choice, or the prize was worth the sacrifice."

Esshk was still confused. "What makes your position such a prize?"

"The same things that induced me to place our batteries here: the shallow-water approach that would prevent their captured cruisers from getting too close, sloping terrain that allows us to fire over the heads of our infantry, and the level ground beyond that made it simpler to move our guns in the first place. All make this an excellent spot for the enemy to attempt a landing. And"—he waved at the devastation around them—"as you can see, we have been seriously depleted as well."

Esshk seemed unconvinced. "It would still be a pointless gesture. Mere revenge against the annoyance you caused them—extreme annoyance, no doubt," he hastened to add. He was still somewhat chagrined by the way he'd treated his most loyal supporter. "Yet even if the enemy gained this position, the initial wave of the Final Swarm consists of only one part in four of the forces arrayed to exploit its success. Their few hundreds would be swept aside by the hundreds of thousands close at hand, which can quickly be called upon."

"Nevertheless," Ign persisted, knowing that calling upon such numbers, many still afloat in barges, and their timely arrival were two different things. "Whether for mere vengeance, or as part of an unfolding plan we cannot know, it is a possibility. I would request that you order several regiments of our new troops to reinforce this position, as well as the one across the river."

A few shells started bursting overhead again, possibly from one of the cruisers moving out from behind the shattered wreck in the river. *Arracca* seemed to be heading directly for the gap and the cruisers emerging from it, still . . .

Esshk turned and began striding quickly toward his carriage. Somehow it and most of the detachment detailed to draw it had been spared the earlier wrath of *Arracca*'s guns. "Very well," he said, stepping aboard the carriage. "I will make a preparatory command that two regiments—a division, you call it?—stand ready to join you, if the need arises and you send a messenger. Otherwise, dawn is not far away and you must disperse your guns and troops, as planned, before the enemy wreaks his vengeance from the sky!"

Jash arrived beside Ign, breathing hard, as First General Esshk's carriage pulled away. "Your orders, Second General?" he panted.

Ign looked at him. "Why are you winded? Certainly you are not still concerned about our fate?" he added wryly.

"No, Second General, but some of my subordinates are. I have been forced to run back and forth along our line and personally order our infantry back to their labor."

Ign's jagged teeth bared. "We are back in favor. Kill who you must to establish that fact." Out on the water, *Arracca*'s guns were firing on the cruisers—and back at them again, the shell bursts short at first, but quickly getting the range. More important, it seemed as if she'd begun a turn to port, something she wouldn't do unless her steering was damaged—or she was heading here, toward them. "And tell them they are soon likely to practice their defensive training very intimately." He turned. "Runner! I doubt First General Esshk will expect you so quickly, but catch his carriage even if you must run yourself to death. I believe we will need the reinforcements he promised." He looked back at Jash. "You have your orders as well!"

Jash bolted back down the slope, waiting until the guns loosed another ear-numbing blast toward the enormous ship now clearly bearing down on them. Racing forward, he was enveloped in their smoke. "Senior First Naxa!" he called, coughing, almost falling in the invisible trench his warriors were scooping from the hard red earth.

"What?" Naxa replied sullenly.

"You can't see it, but the enemy greatship approaches, and Second General Ign is convinced it will disgorge a landing force. Prepare the troops!"

"What do I care what anyone destined for the cookpots says?" Naxa replied insolently. Jash's young crest flared through the top of his helmet. "Second General Ign is back in command—as I told you he would be—and ordered me to kill anyone who defies his orders. Now, do you still doubt or did you merely misunderstand?

Must I repeat myself?" Jash bared his teeth in a feral snarl Naxa had never seen from him.

Naxa's own crest lay flat. "No, Ker-noll." He spun toward the staring troops. "Dig!" he howled. "For your lives!"

Commodore Tassanna-Ay-Arracca grimaced, sharp teeth bared, ears laid back, as she conned her ship—her Home—in the tightest arc it was capable of to bring its flooding, battered, smoldering hulk back opposite the battery on the south bank of the river. And USNRS *Arracca* gave its all for this last dash, somehow achieving eight knots while exchanging a furious fire with three Grik cruisers whose initial expectation must've been that Tassanna meant to plug their last gap with her ship. In truth, she'd been tempted to do just that, but such an act, so far from a feasible landing, would not only doom her immobile ship to rockets, bombing, fire ships—who knew what?—but would doom all her people as well. And for what? If First Fleet, in all its might, couldn't stop the leakers, even the full Swarm now, they were all doomed, anyway. Instead, Tassanna completed her turn, with *Arracca* thundering and booming, spitting, and taking heavy shot, while she calculated known water depths and angles of approach, and tried to imagine the depth and density of the silt. Her heart wilted when she first felt the bottom through the deck beneath her feet, and it almost stopped when *Arracca*'s nearly 14,700 tons, loaded with all the inertia she'd achieved, drove deep into the soft, mucky silt. But it wasn't all silt. Beneath it protruded the same stone skeleton that dominated the bend in the river, and the jagged, rocky bones tore at *Arracca*'s hull as it pounded across them to within two hundred yards of shore. That's when her single huge screw tried to beat itself apart and the massive ship finally shuddered to a stop.

Tassanna took a long breath in the sudden silence of the pilothouse. Homes were designed for gentle groundings, even flooding down for various purposes, but few had any illusions *Arracca* would ever move from *here* again. And she wasn't as perfectly parallel to the shore as Tassanna had hoped to take her, lying about thirty degrees off, but all her starboard guns would bear on the enemy position, and her portside guns could still engage the cruisers on the river. She'd have to be satisfied with that. She shook herself and broke the funereal silence with a harsh command loaded with all her grief and a terrible rage at this Ancient Enemy that had cost her so much. "All personnel who haaven't already done so—including this bridge crew—will report to the aarmories and take whaatever small aarms are left. Staand ready to join the laanding force." She looked at the people around her, all Lemurians, all family—some literally so—and her voice softened slightly. "I will remain here, comm-aanding the gun's crews and aammunition haandlers," she said, and no one even contemplated arguing. She turned to her talker. "Paass the word to Mr. Sil-vaa: aaway all boats!"

Twenty motor launches, each packed far beyond capacity with thirty-five, even forty troops, began surging out of *Arracca*'s portside gri-kakka boat bay as fast as they could—and the plan went straight in the crapper. They were supposed to circle until all were out, then speed around the hulk toward shore together. The trouble was, three Grik cruisers were closing fast, firing faster, and whether they saw the small boats or not, their shot was falling all around them.

"Shit!" Silva roared. "Okay, let's go straight around. Send to all boats," he shouted at the comm-'Cat and his battery bearers, crowded among the heavily armed and loaded troops. "Everybody goes straight in, no stoppin'. The smoke's thick as hell, with *Arracca* blastin' the shore—an' the shore shootin' back. *Use* the smoke. Even thick as it is, nobody can get lost if they steer for the shell blasts an' gun flashes." He hesitated. "Once they get *around* the goddamn ship!" he added as a precaution. He was used to the small groups he surrounded himself with in situations like this knowing what he meant, regardless of what he sometimes actually *said*, but this was a whole new world for him. *Better to overexplain than just assume nobody's stupid enough to go chargin' ass straight out at a Grik cruiser instead o' the beach!* he thought. The Lemurian coxswain beside him spun the wheel and the launch sped east amid the shot splashes along *Arracca*'s looming side. Silva turned to see several boats already following and hoped everyone got the word. Suddenly, *Arracca* wasn't beside them anymore and the coxswain immediately turned south.

Gun flashes and shell blasts weren't all that lit the riverbank. Silva could barely hear their motors over the cannonade, but *Arracca*'s remaining planes—and who knew who else's—were swooping low through the smoky darkness, their target obvious, dumping a gratifying number of firebombs on the enemy gun line. Long, roiling mushrooms of flame seared the night and there were numerous secondary detonations as ammunition limbers and caissons went up. "Get those flyboys on the horn!" Silva shouted at the comm-'Cat.

"Ay, ay." A moment later the 'Cat said, "I got COFO Leedom!"

"Good. First thing, ask him what it looks like from above. What can he see?"

"He see okaay. Thick smoke, lots, but is low lyin' an' the brush fires is dyin' down. They see fightin' pretty good. Fightin's makin' most'a the smoke now."

"Swell." Silva wiped sweaty goo from his eye. "Ask him what it looks like around *Santy Cat*."

A moment later, the Lemurian shook his head. "Looks all done. *Saanty Caat*'s burnin'. Lots of gaalleys is burnin' too, but more is just millin' aroun'. All the croosers is move awaay from her."

Silva frowned, not sure what to make of that, but out of time for questions. "Okay. Tell Leedom to burn as many lizards onshore as he can, fast as he can, but *we'll* be on that beach in about three minutes. He burns any o' us, I'll shoot his sorry ass down myself. We probably can't mark targets with smoke until daylight, but we'll try to describe what we want him to hit. See if he gets that."

"He gets it," the comm-'Cat said a moment later.

Silva nodded and fished out his tobacco pouch, cramming a huge wad of yellowish leaves in his left cheek. He'd brought his Doom Stomper, slung on his back—one never knew when the huge weapon might come in handy—but he couldn't shoot it with a chaw on the right without risking a hell of a bruise. Petey was too scared to complain about the sling or the heavy barrel that mashed him when Silva moved. He was too scared to do anything at all but hang on the back of Silva's neck and make himself as small as he could. Silva wondered why he didn't just stay on *Arracca*—and that started bothering him in a vaguely superstitious way. *Little shit always seems to just* know *the safest direction to scram. But this ain't a safe direction a'tall. He's probably too addled to know anything right now.*

As an arguably superstitious gesture of his own, Silva had taken the wooden case with Captain Reddy's Colt out of his duffel, dumped the box, and stuffed the long-barreled pistol in his belt. Forty-four of the fifty cartridges bulged his pockets, and six were in the cylinder. The Colt replaced the even longer-barreled flintlock pistol he'd carried for a very long time, for no good reason he could think of just then. He'd started to simply pitch it over the side, but, to his surprise, Lawrence grabbed it from him. *Fine,* he'd thought. *Who cares?* Now he wondered if Lawrence was wearing the fancy but battered old flinter like he always had, and that led to another uncomfortable thought: except for Petey, who couldn't possibly count, he was all alone.

He wasn't literally alone, of course; almost forty 'Cats, Khonashis, Imperials, and probably even a few Maroons and Shee-Ree were crammed onto the boat. But for the first time he could remember—almost since he'd faced his abusive uncle with a grubbing hoe—Dennis Silva had embarked on a major undertaking without anyone he knew to . . . well, *talk* to. Anyone to show, by his manner and banter, that he wasn't afraid. He didn't know why that was important, because he *wasn't* afraid of the fight to come, or even to die, but suddenly, amazingly, he felt a growing, undefinable dread. Only one thing ever really scared him before, and that was the . . . weakness Pam put in him. So maybe he was just a show-off like she always said. Or maybe what scared him about Pam was the *responsibility* he felt toward her? To protect her and keep her safe, even from himself.

That could mean only that the unfamiliar culprit now

was responsibility itself, and, boy, did he have it in spades this time! That had to be it. All his pals were in other boats, commanding what amounted to regiments, and he was in charge of them all. To top that off, Pam and Risa and Tassanna, not to mention all their wounded, were trapped on *Arracca*—which Petey had fled for *this* stunt *he* was leading. At that moment, Dennis Silva was suddenly so terrified of screwing up that he was absolutely sure he would. He had no idea how to cope with that. He'd seen plenty of terror—it was all around him now—but he'd never, *ever* felt it! What the hell was he going to do?

A huge splash erupted in the water alongside, and the nasty, putrid, Grik-filth water of the Zambezi gushed across him. Another roundshot from the shore battery nearly hit another boat close by. A young (human) Khonashi sitting by his feet jerked and looked around, wide-eyed, his helmet loose enough that it moved independently. Who knew what he'd been through already? Everyone on this boat was a veteran of hard fighting, but the youth looked just as scared as Silva felt—and confidence welled within Silva that he'd found his "cure." He brusquely patted the boy on the shoulder. "Hey, kid. What's your name?"

The young Khonashi looked up, startled, eyes even wider, if possible. "You . . . you talk I?" he asked, voice cracking, incredulous. Human and Grik-like Khonashi spoke the same language, of course, so none used words with Ms, Ps, or anything requiring lips. The human members of the tribe could do it; they just didn't.

"Yeah, I'm talkin' to you."

The kid blinked as if to ask why, but finally answered, "Uda."

"Uda, huh? You got the jitters?" Uda had no idea what jitters were but seemed to understand. "Me too," Silva confessed. "But only 'cause I thought I was doin' somethin' new. Fact is, ain't none o' this really new. We're goin' over there to kill a buncha Griks—same as we been doin' for weeks, months—hell, years for some of us. They're gonna try to kill us," he confessed. "But we're better'n them, see?" Silva noticed more and more were listening now, even as the incoming fire intensified. He raised his voice. "Sure, they're ugly an' scary," he continued. "No offense," he added to a pair of watching Grik-like Khonashi, "but they ain't *hard*. They ain't been through what we have. All this time on *Santy Cat*, the fight on Zanzibar . . . Hell, me an' Gunny Horn had a en-tire *ship* drop on us in North Borno!" He nodded at Uda. "I bet you was there." He searched the faces staring back. "An' don't none o' you think all that—all we been through—was for nothin'. It was for *this*! It was to make this *easy*, stacked against the rest, an' them nasty Grik boogers ain't ready for *us* a'tall." He shook his head and grinned in that . . . disconcerting way he had, watching the cannon flash. "I still can't see shore through the gun-smoke, so they damn sure can't see us. They're just blas-tin' away at *Arracca*, shootin' bad enough to come close to us from time to time. So when we hit that beach right in their laps, they're gonna squirt." His eye narrowed. "An' then we're gonna kill the absolute hell outa them lizardy sons of goats!"

He was right, to a degree. The battle-weary Marines and Raiders in his first wave were much harder than even Ign and Jash's New Army warriors. But nothing about the coming day was going to be easy for anyone.

CHAPTER 28

////// *South Bank of the Zambezi*

Amazingly, nineteen of *Arracca*'s twenty launches roared up on the beach, and more than six hundred wildly mixed Marines and Raiders poured into the knee-high water around the boats and surged ashore. Immediately, the launches, refloated with their burdens gone, reversed their engines and backed away. Only one boat had been destroyed by the hasty, startled artillery directed at them as they emerged from the smoke, hit right on the cutwater by a sixteen-pounder solid shot that scattered it and its occupants like toothpicks less than thirty yards out. Almost half its complement actually managed to flail their way in through the neck-deep water they'd found themselves in. River monsters might've gotten some, but most of those had probably fled the pounding pressure of the artillery duel between ship and shore. With a growing roar and the seemingly magical appearance of the various units' battle flags whipping among them, Silva's assault force swept forward like an incoming tide.

All at once, Dennis Silva discovered several things: First, *Arracca*'s counterbattery fire and the air attacks had hammered the gun line harder than he'd really expected. Less than twenty guns were still in action, and all they seemed to have was solid shot and exploding case. Both were hell on massed infantry in the open—which was what he had at the moment. Solid shot simply blew through as many troops as were gathered in front of it in a straight line, and killed or maimed others to the side with secondary projectiles, pieces of equipment, even bone. Case shot, with fuses cut to zero, exploded at the muzzle and fanned its fragments out in a killing swath. It was less effective than canister or grape, but still deadly. But these guns, apparently supplied for a long-range bombardment, didn't seem to have any canister or grape, and that was one blessing, at least.

What Dennis also hadn't expected, so focused on the enemy guns, was the two or three thousand Grik *infantry* shallowly entrenched in front of them. They'd clearly been just as surprised as the artillery, and their first pattering fire was rushed and relatively ineffective. Some of it stayed that way as the assault thundered up the beach, closing the short distance, spraying bullets from Blitzerbugs and Allin-Silvas. The regiment directly in front of them, in the center of the line, started bleeding warriors as they closed, many tossing away their weapons and bolting for the rear. *Grik Rout!* Dennis exulted. But the two flanking regiments—and the one on the right, in particular—managed stunning, point-blank volleys that staggered Silva's own force, chopping down men, 'Cats, and Grik-like Khonashi in murderous waves. It was too little, too late. Grenades booming, bayonets flashing, and Blitzers yammering, the heart of the charge slammed into and through the trench, pounding up the gentle grade toward the waiting guns. More Raiders and Marines poured through the gap, pushing up the trenches on either side and slaughtering the steadier Grik from the flank.

The most important thing Silva learned was that at the moment, he wasn't really in charge of anything. These Marines and Raiders, mixed as they were, had all received the same training and knew exactly what to do. He had only to set the example and maybe shout the occasional reminder to refocus their attention. "Keep rollin' 'em up!" he roared, his order echoed by the 'Cats and quickly spreading to the entire force. *"An' get those damn guns!"* That said, even burdened with his various weapons (and an utterly terrified Petey, who accomplished only occasional squeaks but grimly hung on), Silva emerged from the final lingering effects of his funk and became the killing machine he truly was. He slung his empty Thompson and pulled his cutlass and 1911, hacking and shooting anything that came in reach.

"Pull them back!" Ign roared. "Pull the guns back before we lose them all!" He spun to Jash, jaws clenching, teeth grinding. "I must pull back as well, and you must give me time."

Jash was overcome with shame. "My defense . . . I never imagined it would collapse so quickly!"

"It wasn't *your* defense that failed, Ker-noll. I never gave you the chance to develop it! Then *I* arbitrarily simply threw my Personal Guard forward, to the right of the Uul *you* suggested I withdraw to the guns! The same Uul that immediately broke!"

"They were surprised," Jash halfheartedly defended.

"So were the rest, but I'm sure your Slashers and my Guards could have held them better and longer alone. Recall what remains. Form them to stop the pursuit of the guns, if you can. I should have allowed you to dig the fallback trench you yapped about when you arrived after all," Ign added ruefully.

"You can still do it," Jash shouted over the rising roar of battle. "Look." He pointed. "Even our Uul-turned-prey are not as craven as they once were. Many have rallied around the guns. Set *them* to digging trenches when you have retired a safe distance! If I can rally what is left of my Slashers and your Guard, we may slow the enemy's advance long enough for you to place the guns there as well, and it will serve as a position to gather the reinforcements First General Esshk must send!"

Ign shook his head in wonder. "You have already become a better general than I," he admitted. "It will be as you say, if either of us can manage our parts. Whatever you save of my Guards are now yours. If you live . . ." He shook his head and said no more except: "There is no time. We must hurry."

As it turned out, there was little hurry after all. Six hundred disorganized troops had blown three thousand out of their defensive position, but *couldn't* effectively pursue. And the enemy commander clearly had other priorities in any event, as Jash watched the fast little boats shuttle back and forth between the beached behemoth and shore in the growing light of the new dawn. Hundreds were landing, *thousands* quickly digging trenches and throwing up breastworks of their own. None of the Grik guns still in action—mainly because they'd still had crews—were taken. Probably half of those captured could quickly be put back in service, but their ammunition had to be mostly spent or destroyed. Exhausted runners succeeded in communicating Jash's orders to both "his" now widely separated regiments, which had simply pulled away from contact along the riverbank. They were both marching toward Ign's growing defense, giving the long-range enemy weapons a wide berth. Several warriors broke away from the Slashers and trotted toward where Jash, with a couple of Firsts from the Guards, stood in the tall prairie grass roughly four hundred paces from the strengthening enemy position and two hundred from Ign's.

Jash knew he was still in range of enemy rifles, but their warriors seemed too busy digging to bother with him. He raised his gaze to the river and his young crest rose. Far from being over, the great battle on the river still raged. *Santa Catalina* was utterly doomed at last, its wreck blazing from end to end. Four cruisers of the Race harried two others like them, flying the huge, tattered, striped banners of the enemy, as they tried to fight their way toward *Arracca* and shore. Both were battered and slow, gushing steam. *Arracca* still fired in their defense, her heavy shot peeling armor off their attackers and slowly wrecking them as well, but she didn't fire with the same sustained fury as before. *Even such a monstrous thing as that must eventually exhaust its ammunition,* Jash supposed.

Somewhat inspiring, however—if less than he'd anticipated—was that the Final Swarm had indeed been loosed. Three more cruisers had already rushed past the battle, avoiding it as best they could, steaming directly downriver. In their wakes swam hundreds of galleys, oars flashing in the probing rays of the rising sun as they also avoided the obstinate combatants. A few were wrecked by shot and some were rammed under, but most merely cruised past the fighting. Jash glanced at the sky, surprised the enemy flying machines hadn't returned. Tightly packed as they were, the galleys would make a tempting target, but he was more concerned about the force Second General Ign was massing behind him.

"Ker-noll Jash!" Naxa exclaimed excitedly as he and the other Slashers approached. "I am so pleased you are not dead." He jerked his snout down at their former position. "What a mess."

"Indeed," Jash agreed, actually relieved to find Naxa alive as well, despite how fickle he'd proved. *Then again,* he realized, *capriciousness appears ingrained in our race. Second General Ign seems immune—as had First of One Hundred Seech.* It dawned on Jash with a mixture of surprise and pleasure that he, at least, had remembered *one* warrior past his time. "Come," he said. "I have seen enough. We must join Second General Ign at once. The longer his force grows in the open, the more vulnerable it is to air attack." He gestured downhill with his own snout. "And the longer they have to prepare, the harder it will be to destroy them."

"*General* Silva!" Major Simon Gutfeld called sarcastically as he dropped over the side of a motor launch and limped heavily toward him. Gutfeld had two wounds in the same leg and a bandage wrapped around his torso, blood seeping through under his arm, and Silva was frankly amazed he could stand, much less move.

Lawrence snickered in his annoyingly hissy way, and Silva rolled his eye. "Good God a'mighty, don't call me that! You here to take over?"

"Hell no," Gutfeld denied. "I'm wounded, and you're doing fine. Where's a chair?" He grinned. "Surgeon Lieutenant Pam Cross told me I could only come out to play if I took it easy."

"Lucky she let you come at all," Dennis moped. "Damn

woman'll lord it over you unmerciful, you ever show her a scratch. How's Risa?"

"Worse than me," Gutfeld hedged, quickly adding, "but she'll be okay. Last I saw, she *had* a chair, sitting there, yelling at the walking wounded to help Pam get all the wounded ashore."

Silva frowned. "What about *Arracca*?"

Simy shook his head. "She's finished, Dennis. You can't see it, but a good bunch of galleys are after her now, on the other side. She's low on ammo and there's no infantry left aboard." He shrugged. "Tassanna can't keep the lizards off for long and means to burn her once enough of 'em scramble aboard."

Dennis was stunned. "I'll swan." Tassanna burning *Arracca* would be like Alan Letts burning Baalkpan.

"Yeah."

Gunny Horn joined them. Of the three leaders of the assault against the guns onshore, he'd been the only one wounded—by a musket ball that grazed his cheek and left a red furrow in the black beard on his face. Now he was gesturing angrily at the sky. "Our planes could keep 'em off her! Where the hell are they? It's full daylight now and they ought to be buzzing the whole joint!"

Gutfeld was nodding. "I got the full dope. Air is waiting for the Grik army to bunch up more in front of you— hitting them now'll just keep them spread out—and they're waiting for those Grik cruisers that got past to run into Captain Reddy, coming up the river. He'll stop 'em," he said matter-of-factly—and nobody doubted that—"and then the air'll hit the galleys as they stack up behind. That's the plan, anyway."

"Goddamn plans," Silva snorted, lips twisting as if the very word smelled bad. "Damn galleys're thick as can be out there *now*," he disagreed, pointing at the river.

"And the air *is* coming for them," Gutfeld objected. "I think I hear 'em now, as a matter of fact."

Silva glanced at him and back at the water and slowly nodded. He heard planes too. Then his eye went wide and a great flash reflected off it. "Holy—" One of their lamed cruisers, full of *Santy Cat* survivors and still trading fire with two others, had suddenly exploded. The concussion and expanding cloud of debris swept away a dozen Grik galleys and rolled the closest, equally battered enemy cruiser on its beam ends—where it stayed and filled.

"What the hell?" Horn demanded.

"Signal 'lags on *Arracca*!" Lawrence said urgently. Horn had an Imperial telescope and quickly raised it, reading the flags a 'Cat was whipping around in one of the hangar bays. Before he could report, a comm-'Cat raced up, started to salute, but then just blurted, "Grik *baattle-ships* is comin' through the gaap!" she practically wailed. "T'ree of 'em is seen, so faar. An' our air is report enemy *planes*!"

"Bullshit!" Gutfeld roared. "Calm the hell down! Grik BBs can't get through that tangle upstream—and they damn sure don't have any *planes*! Ours are coming in, though. Look!"

Simy Gutfeld was right—and wrong. Three Grik BBs actually had forced their way through the gap at last. It was one of their monstrous forward guns that had smashed the crippled cruiser. But Allied planes had also arrived. At that moment, all of *Arracca*'s fourteen remaining P1-Cs and Nancys swooped out of the sun, aiming at the galleys assaulting the port side of their Home. Machine guns yammered, shredding the flimsy craft, and light bombs tumbled down on top of them. Then, in the blink of an eye, two Nancys were blotted from the sky as they pulled up from their attack. A third staggered, suddenly trailing smoke. This because, unfortunately, Simy was wrong about something else: the Grik did have planes.

"Jumpin' Jesus! It's the *Japs*!" Silva shouted in amazement.

Colonel Chack-Sab-At stepped slowly aft, limping slightly, holding a bandage pressed firmly against his side where a Grik bayonet had bidden him—the very last person off the wreck of *Santa Catalina*—farewell. Now he unconsciously avoided *Itaa*'s great guns as they recoiled inward, trying to keep his eyes on the sooty, debris-choked spot where USS *Ris* had ceased to exist. *So many good people,* he lamented, *put through so much, only to end like that.* He didn't have words for how he felt as his tear-sheened eyes searched for struggling figures in the water. He didn't expect to see any, and he wasn't surprised. He did see the three huge Grik dreadnaughts creeping around the bend, however, and his amber eyes burned with hate. He wanted to go after them, kill them, but that was impossible. There were still two cruisers dogging *Itaa*, bashing her apart even as she returned the favor, and they'd be lucky to make it to shore as it was. He glanced at the sky. *Where are our planes?*

Hardly noticed, Major Enrico Galay paced beside Chack, hovering. They were all exhausted, but Chack had also lost a lot of blood. He'd seen young Major Abel Cook wounded and carried aboard, watched Gutfeld's gallant and equally young Lemurian XO, Captain Flaar, repeatedly bayoneted and torn apart. He'd basically witnessed the death of half his Raiders and Gutfeld's Marines, and now he'd seen *Ris*'s death, along with so many others he knew. Still, Galay wasn't concerned whether Chack would continue on regardless, until he was dead or his job was done. He worried only that the young Lemurian they all admired and relied on so much might simply collapse.

"There are our planes!" Galay said excitedly, pointing barely a hundred yards ahead at the space between them and *Arracca*—a space so choked with Grik galleys that the enemy cruisers had finally been forced to bear away.

"Taarget the gaalleys now, Cap-i-taan Jarrik!" Chack shouted toward where Keje's cousin Jarrik-Fas stood beside the wheel. "And see whaat more speed you can coax from this ship. We must run her as far aground as we can." He turned to Galay, as if emerging from a daze. "Do we have comm?"

"Just now repaired. The aerial was shot away," Galay replied, glad to see the renewed energy in his commander. Nancys and Fleashooters roared past just ahead, flailing at the galleys.

"Jaap planes!" shrieked a lookout, and Chack blinked to hear something so unexpected. Then he saw them.

They *were* Jap-Grik planes, just like they'd seen at Mahe and Zanzibar! But what were they doing here? An instant later, when two Nancys were destroyed and another wrecked, he knew. "Report this to Cap-i-taan Reddy at once!" he shouted. "How maany are there?"

"Cap-i-taan Reddy knows!" came a response from the talker by a bank of voice tubes behind the tiller. "Our planes seen 'em! We got more pursuiters on the waay—" The talker's voice rose. "But they was all loaded for ground attaack! Is gonna be a while. For now, we got only *Arracca*'s six pursuiters in the air!"

"Signaal their flight leader to lay off the gaalleys and attaack the Jaaps!"

"Ay, ay, Col-nol!"

"Brace yourselves!" Jarrik-Fas roared through a speaking tube. Chack turned to stare at the shore, coming up fast, and Major Galay actually grabbed him and pulled him to the deck, onto his lap.

Silva's eye was fastened on the surreal dogfight that erupted over them as six Fleashooters tangled with eight or ten Jap-Grik fighters, the like of which he'd never, ever, expected to see again. And it was the *same* Jap/Griks! The same green-and-sky-blue planes wearing the very same glaring red meatball! Shouts tore his gaze away and he watched as the battered cruiser—the last to leave *Santy Cat*, so *hopefully* Chack was in her—bash its way ashore. It was going slower when it hit and wasn't nearly as big, but it didn't draw as much water as *Arracca*, so it made it to within fifty yards of shore before it ground to a halt. But the way it lurched and juddered, it probably encountered just as many rocks with its frailer hull.

"Take over here," he said, handing his Doom Stomper to Lawrence. "Keep movin' every able body with a weapon to the line." With that, he was off and running toward an empty launch that was shoving off. Gutfeld and Horn both looked at Lawrence, holding the big rifle as if that meant he was now in charge. Quickly, the Sa'aaran leaned the weapon against a crate, part of the massive pile of supplies they'd been taking off *Arracca*, in a gesture that implied "Not me!" All three started shouting orders for more boats, more hands.

With Silva directing the 'Cat coxswain—the only other person in the boat—to head for *Itaa* instead of returning to *Arracca* for another load, the launch rumbled out to the newest wreck this tragic stretch of river had claimed. A lot of the galleys that'd been strafed were just milling around, too damaged to continue or unsure what to do. Silva sprayed a clip from his Thompson at one, earning a few returning shots. "Hey!" objected the coxswain.

"Shut up!" Silva growled, inserting another magazine. For good measure, he emptied that one at a Jap-Grik plane zooming overhead, firing at *Arracca*.

"You gonna get 'em *aall* shootin' at us!" the Coxswain complained.

"Nothin' new about that." Another strafing Jap-Grik plane swooped on *Arracca* but suddenly developed a dark smoke trail. Silva realized it had a P1 on its tail. Starting to spin, the Jap-Grik arced down and slammed into the top of *Arracca*'s flight deck, exploding and spewing burning fuel. Furious, Silva saw the P1-C Fleashooter impact *Arracca*'s side, most of the aircraft's tumbling, burning carcass scattering itself inside, on the hangar deck. Another Jap-Grik fighter pulled up and barreled away. "Goddamn Japs!" Silva seethed, but in reality he had no idea whether the enemy shot the Fleashooter down or the *Arracca* pilot, untrained in dogfighting, had been too focused on his target. It didn't matter. *Arracca* was burning now, and with almost everyone but Tassanna, her gun's crews, and some of the worst wounded ashore, there was no one left to fight the fires.

"No puttin' that out," Silva growled as they neared *Itaa*'s savaged side. "At least Tassanna'll be spared burnin' her own Home." Looking closely at *Itaa* for the first time, he was amazed it made it to shore. Its armor had been beefed up by Kurokawa and it was probably tougher than the new Grik cruisers, but it had taken a hell of a pounding. Only a stump remained of the mainmast, and the foremast was completely gone. The funnel, amazingly still streaming gray oil smoke (as opposed to the black coming from the coal-fired Grik), was a sieve. Half the ship's big guns were dismounted and her bulwarks had almost been battered away, exposing the shambles around the few guns still in operation. Aside from all that, the rocks she'd run up on had torn her bottom out, and her stern, still afloat, was quickly settling.

"Chackie!" Silva called. "Chackie! Where's Colonel Chack, goddammit!"

"Here!" shouted down a form, but the face was unrecognizable through the blood-clotted, smudged, and fire-curled fur.

"Get your blotchy tail down here so I can get you ashore!"

Chack glared past the growing defensive position at the just as quickly growing Grik horde beyond. "Is the enemy about to attaack?"

"Whadda you think?" Silva demanded incredulously. "O' course they are. It's what they do! We may have a minute er two, but that's all the more reason to get you ashore to take *goddamn charge*!"

"Tassanna raad-ioed that you've done well enough on your own," Chack countered. "I haave to get these people off, and there are three Grik BBs bearing down." A huge splash right alongside almost tossed Silva from the boat, underscoring Chack's point.

"Which you can't do a damn thing about!" Silva stressed.

"He is right," agreed Jarrik-Fas, whom Silva did recognize. He and Enrico Galay had joined Chack by the splintered rail. "Take your troops ashore; prepare for your battle on land." Jarrik blinked. *"Arracca* is abandoning even now—she must." It was true. The fire on the flight deck had almost burned itself out, but the hangar deck, its timbers long soaked with spilled oil and fuel, was already becoming an inferno. Steam gushed from the bays as fixed water sprinklers fought the blaze, but with the great ship's boiler rooms flooding and no one left in them, the pumps were already dying. If more evidence was required, *Arracca*'s guns had finally gone silent, and great splashes erupted on her unengaged shoreward side as the huge, rectangular wooden rafts she'd used at anchor for seaplane docks slapped down. Silva had no doubt Tassanna meant to use them to quickly off-load the last of her people.

"This ship," Jarrik continued gruffly, "afloat or not, is still on the water. It remains her and her crew's duty to engage enemies of the Union on the surfaace of any waater, no maatter how putrid!" He actually grinned. "And need I remind you, Col-nol, that I still out-raank you at sea—where I believe your permanent raank of boatswain's mate second has somewhat . . . staag-nated?"

Chack gazed at the older Lemurian he'd looked up to all his life, then tightly embraced him. A heavy shot struck *Itaa* aft, and a plane roared by overhead. "Go," Jarrik said. "You waste time."

"Yeah, get a move on, Chackie," Silva agreed anxiously, looking west. Six more launches had joined his, and all the precious little vessels were in danger. The closest Grik BB was little more than a mile away now, and someone cried, "Get down!" as a Jap-Grik plane strafed them, launching splinters and little geysers of spray.

"All Raiders, Third Maa-rines"—Chack glanced at Jarrik and saw his nod—"and any other personnel not essential to fighting this ship will enter the boats alongside as quickly and orderly as you caan." He hesitated and blinked something close to sick desperation. "This includes waalking wounded, but those too baadly hurt to move must stay aboard for now." His voice turned harsher. "Do not forget your weapons, and any aammunition you caan find! I haave no use for un-aarmed troops!"

One boat was smashed by a huge ball from the looming Grik dreadnaught, but the rest managed to pack in almost two hundred bloody, dazed, utterly exhausted Raiders, Marines, and sailors. And despite Chack's orders, more than a few were carried—including an unconscious Abel Cook, strapped to a stretcher. All the while, *Itaa*'s remaining fifty-pounders hammered at the approaching juggernauts, most of her shot bouncing off their armor. They had actually slowed in the meantime, clearly for the very purpose of minimizing the damage

Itaa could do, and yet stayed in their line of battle like they had all the time in the world. That left only the first to continue *Itaa*'s systematic demolition. The ones behind started hammering *Arracca* (pointlessly, considering the volcano of flames she'd become), and occasionally ranged past her, their heavy roundshot striking within the perimeter Silva and his friends had established. Most of this fire was ineffective, but occasional screams were heard.

Five launches reached the shore, spilling their precious cargo. The others had towed *Arracca*'s huge rafts away from the blistering heat of the burning Home, and finally every element of the first opposed "invasion" of Grik Africa that was likely to make it ashore had done so. Yet behind it was a scatter of burning and smoldering wrecks that, even in death, were still molested by mighty, unassailable leviathans. Around those great ships, swarms of galleys churned downriver, apparently unconcerned by their feeble presence. Why a tithe of them didn't simply land and overwhelm them from the river, no one knew. Perhaps the burning *Arracca* kept them away or they were so single-mindedly focused on their long-delayed attack across the strait that they didn't care about the spent survivors. Perhaps they'd even been ordered to ignore them. The beachhead was no real threat, after all. It couldn't expand and it couldn't retreat. Sooner or later, sufficient forces would gather to rub it out. That couldn't take much longer. Beyond the breastworks on the gently rolling, grassy plain to the southwest, a rapidly growing army of Grik warriors massed.

A handful of *Salissa*-marked Fleashooters suddenly arrived to challenge the Jap-Grik planes—*Arracca*'s last ones had been destroyed or driven away—but they were inexplicably few. *Salissa*'s pilots were better-trained and more experienced dogfighters, however, and showed up just as the Jap-Grik fighters had started focusing on the landing force. Their strafing runs were disrupted, and another wild aerial melee flared above them. But where were the rest of *Salissa*'s and *Madraas*'s Air Wings? Where were their Nancys, loaded with firebombs?

With experienced junior officers and NCOs now helping sort things out and others racing up to deliver a blizzard of reports regarding who'd been sent where and what they'd salvaged, Chack, Silva, Horn, Galay, and Lawrence first followed Gutfeld to where the wounded were being gathered, close enough to feel the heat of the burning carrier but protected by it from fire of the Grik BBs. It was a heartbreaking scene of misery, with torn bodies laid out under the sun on the hard red soil. Corps-'Cats and SBAs were doing their best, but they were overwhelmed. Silva was relieved to see Pam's exhausted, harried form moving quickly, triaging patients and instructing that some be taken to where canvas awnings were going up under Commodore Tassanna's direction. That was a relief as well, both that Tassanna had survived and that she was keeping herself from focusing on her loss.

"Hey, sailor," came a slurred, cheerful voice, and Silva and Chack knelt beside Risa. "Hiya, doll," Silva said when he saw her, but a huge lump in his throat threatened to choke him. Chack's sister, and one of Silva's *very* best friends, didn't look as bad as many others, and the analgesic seep was doing its work, but Lawrence's description of her wound hadn't come close to preparing Dennis for what he saw. A Grik musket ball had hit her square on the shin, under her knee, and shredded flesh was the only thing holding her leg. Somehow, Silva couldn't imagine the vivacious, fun-filled Risa he'd always known stumping around on one leg, and it scared him to think what she might do when the seep wore off. Clearly, Chack felt the same as he caressed her furry face with his hand, tears dropping unashamed.

"I'll be baack up on the line with you guys, soon as I'm paatched up here," Risa promised, eyes blurry.

"Of course you will," Chack agreed.

"Sure," Silva said, his own eye starting to fill. Impulsively, he leaned down and kissed the blood-matted fur on her forehead.

"Cut thaat out, dummy," Risa chastised him. "Paam's around here somewhere. She sees that, she'll beat you up an' cut off my booze."

"Yeah. Too bad," Silva agreed as he and Chack stood.

"Me an' Chackie'll check back in a spell." Leaving Gutfeld with an SBA to change his dressing, the rest of them trudged silently up past the corpse-choked Grik trench toward where the gun line had been. It was still there, only all thirteen serviceable guns had been turned to face outward and the new trench and breastworks—incorporating the wrecked guns as well—were built around them.

"There isn't much ammo for the captured pieces," Horn reported. "Enough for maybe six shots apiece, split between case and solid shot. We got a handful of old six-pounders out of *Arracca* before the fire spread too far; some of her people went back aboard, heaved them over to the cargo-bay doors, and dropped them in the water with lines secured to their lunettes. They brought the lines and a couple of limber chests ashore, and we dragged the guns in like big fish. One broke a couple of spokes, but it should be okay. Even better, we got off a whole six-gun battery of the new mountain howitzers, and about three hundred rounds of canister for them." The howitzers were very small guns, too light to fire solid twelve-pounder solid shot, but they excelled at close range with canister and shell. They'd originally been loaded aboard *Arracca* for the Raiders and 3rd Marines to use if the opportunity presented itself, and each had been disassembled and packed in three easily managed crates. "There were more in the ship, but all in flooded compartments," Horn apologized.

"You did well to get whaat you could," Chack told him. Just then, a large Grik case shot burst overhead, raining fragments past their defenses. "We should spread out," Chack told them grimly. "Gunny Horn, please see how things progress on the left side of our line. Major Gaa-lay? Inspect the right. Laaw-rence, Chief Sil-vaa, with me." More shells exploded, sending troops scurrying for the new trench. The Grik dreadnaughts had apparently worked their way down to antipersonnel munitions at last, or just got tired of wasting solid iron. Even so, the bombardment only came from the second and third BBs. The first was still pulverizing *Itaa* with its monstrous forward 400-pounders. A pair of Jap-Grik planes broke loose from their attackers and swooped over, churning the hard red dirt with their two wing-mounted machine guns.

"Goddammit!" Silva shouted, shaking his fist at them. "Where's the rest of *our* planes?"

"That's what I intend to find out," Chack replied, arrowing toward a hastily dug-out CP. It was basically a hole with crate timbers and soil piled on top, but he recognized the antenna aerial. Ducking inside the cramped space, Chack, Dennis, and Lawrence coughed dust filtering down from yet another nearby blast, and Silva recognized the same comm-'Cat who'd been in his launch. It wasn't easy, since his gray-and-brown-striped fur had already turned red with the dust.

"Comm is all jaammed up!" the 'Cat cried, knowing exactly what Chack was about to ask. "Baad snaafu! Almost all our planes was loaded for ground an' ship strikes comin' in, an' Jaap-Grik planes jumped on 'em. Tore the Naancys up baad. Most pursuiters had no aammo for their guns, overloaded with bombs, but tried to keep Jaaps off Naancys. Big mess. Naancys got told to drop their bombs on the galleys already downriver an' get the hell baack to the caar-iers. Fleashooters got called baack to re-arm with gun aammo to escort the Naancys baack here. They hurryin'!"

Chack took a long, calming breath, and Silva rolled his eye. "Goddamn Kuro-kawwy! Still a pain in the ass even after he's dead!" He pointed outside. "Those are *his* planes, *his* pilots, y'know," he told Chack.

"Of course," Chack agreed, tail swishing. "Clearly, some survived to flee Zaan-zi-bar. The question is, Did some of his torpedo bombers also escape?"

"That's bound to be somethin' else Keje an' Captain Reddy is worried about," Silva said. "They'll have to keep some pursuit ships back to protect the carriers, dammit!"

"Hvat a 'ess," Lawrence agreed gloomily.

"There's nothing for it," Chack said, tone brisk. "First Fleet *is* coming and *will* aassist us as quickly as it caan. Of that I haave no doubt."

"Me either," Silva agreed. "I just hope they don't get here in the nick of time to bury our dead asses."

"Thaat will *not* haappen," Chack snapped, wincing at the pain in his side. He pressed harder against the bandage and looked at the comm-'Cat. "Aall the same, please specific-aally, *offish-aally* inform Cap-i-taan Reddy and Ahd-mi-raal Keje-Fris-Ar from me that *Saanta Caatalina*, *Arracca*, and *Ris* are all destroyed. *Itaa*'s . . . beached wreck now defends us against a growing number of Grik *baattle-ships*. Maany of the enemy's undaamaged cruisers now head downstream with their gaalleys. Either we are out of range of their rockets or they haave not been released to engage us, but we're under air attack and bom-baardment, and eight to ten thousand Grik haave thus far gaathered beyond our works. More aarrive continuously.

"Opposing that, we have perhaaps five thousand survivors from all our ships and combaat units combined, only two-thirds of which are aarmed and caan be considered effective. Less than *haaf* my Raiders and Maa-rines still live, and I doubt haaf the survivors are fit to fight. So," he continued, his voice growing harsher—even Chack had his limits, it seemed—"in the face of these vaarious difficulties, this beachhead is currently held by perhaaps eight hundred combaat troops and—hopefully—as maany as twenty-five hundred sailors. We haave maany wounded, little food, almost no drinking water, no mortars, and few caannon. Worse, we only sal-vaaged enough small aarms aammunition for about an hour of sustained firing. Not thaat we'll *laast* an hour against the force opposing us without aar-tillery or air support, if it chooses to make a determined aassault." He paused, thinking, then shook his head. "Send thaat."

"*G*oddamn it!" Matt Reddy bellowed, surprising everyone in *Mahan*'s pilothouse. Captain Reddy almost never swore, and the Lemurian bridge crew recognized the phrase as a second-tier curse, reserved (for those who didn't sling it about habitually and meaninglessly) for extremely intense frustration. That didn't mean they thought his outburst was unjustified. Their mission had started well, with *Mahan* and *Ellie* making good time, but then, about an hour and a half before dawn, their very long and difficult morning had begun.

First, they'd run into the advance trickle of Grik galleys making their way downriver to the sea. *Mahan* was in the lead and *literally* ran into one, shearing off all its portside oars and swamping it immediately. But unlike *Arracca* or the captured Grik cruisers, *Mahan* and *Ellie* couldn't just bash their way through countless galleys, regardless of how fragile the smaller vessels were, without accumulating damage to their thin-skinned bows and vulnerable propellers. Reluctantly, considering that First Fleet's arrival was probably still unsuspected by the Grik—no enemy airships had ventured near, and spies would take time to carry word to their leaders—Matt was forced to order *Mahan* and *Ellie* to "light 'em up" with their searchlights. This might shorten the distance scouts had to carry reports, but hopefully the Grik would think the leading edge of their swarm had only run into a supply run for *Santa Catalina* by the captured Grik cruisers. They had searchlights of their own, provided by Kurokawa. The light helped them avoid collisions and kill Grik with their machine guns, but Matt was surprised and concerned by how quickly the galleys thickened on the river—and shot back at them with muskets.

The powerful smoothbore muskets, probably about .60 caliber, like the ones the Alliance first had, fired a soft lead ball that tended to spatter even against the relatively thin steel of the DDs. They left dents, to be sure, but couldn't do any real damage to the ships. The same couldn't be said for the wooden boats on the davits, bridge windows, or searchlights. Matt was even beginning to worry about the torpedoes in their lightweight tubes. Worse, exposed personnel manning the machine guns (and starting to use a *lot* of ammo they might badly need later) had only the mattresses hooked to stanchions for protection, and *Mahan*'s and *Ellie*'s dead and wounded were starting to pile up. Matt finally ordered his two ships to simply avoid as many galleys as they could. What chance did they stand against the tightly packed mass of First Fleet behind them?

Then, just as the first hint of gray began to color the eastern sky and a luminous, flashing orange glow could be perceived to the west, everything else went to hell at once. They'd long been aware of *Santa Catalina*'s urgent situation and suspected Tassanna's disobedience to Keje's order that she not, under any circumstances, put *Arracca* in similar danger. They'd known nothing of her participation in the battle until after she'd been rammed and Tassanna radioed her desperate plan to beach the ship and assault the south bank so she'd have someplace to land TF Bottle Cap's survivors. Matt had still been confident the situation could be salvaged by the massive air strike already sortied from *Big Sal* and *Madraas*, but then the flight—entirely configured for ground attack—got bounced by perhaps a dozen Jap-Grik fighters. Before they knew what hit them, twenty-two Nancys (nearly a third of the complement of both carriers) and four Fleashooters were swatted from the sky. The marauders fled, probably to refuel and rearm.

Keje had to recall the strike. The pursuit ships had to rearm with ammunition for their guns, and the unprotected Nancys couldn't just swan around until they returned. Nor could they land on the water with bombs under their wings. And not *all* the Fleashooters could rejoin the strike when it was ready again. If the Grik had fighters, they might have some of Kurokawa's torpedo bombers too. Some of the pursuit ships would have to protect the fleet. Keje did order all the planes to drop their bombs on a concentrating gaggle of galleys and several cruisers Matt couldn't yet see, but that was small consolation set against the mounting desperation of Chack's and Tassanna's radio pleas.

Finally, and what had just inspired Matt's intemperate outburst, not only did a cluster of Grik cruisers finally appear, blasting away, in one of the narrowest charted stretches of the river, but *Mahan*'s second salvo from her numbers one and two 4″-50s apparently got hits that were just a bit too lucky—and fully consistent with all the *bad* luck they'd endured so far. The target belched steam from a hit amidships, but the worst damage must've been to its helm or steering. Abruptly, it veered away to starboard, slamming into the rocky, steep-sided shore. There was just enough light for Matt to see Grik fall *onto* the cruiser through his binoculars, plummeting down from the crushed warren of cave dwellings Russ Chappelle first reported. It would've been bad enough if the enemy ship settled there, but its crew immediately reversed its engines, grinding off the rocks even as it started to fill. Maybe it was instinct or maybe it was deliberate—no one would ever know—but all Matt could do, even as galleys surged past his ship and the next cruiser opened up with its heavy bow gun, was watch the first one sink, rumbling and booming and spewing steam from splitting boilers. It finally came to rest, beam on, bulwarks barely visible, effectively blocking the river. Debris, coal dust, and bodies from the wreck were already swirling past them as huge crocodiles—and other things—nibbled at the latter.

"Goddamn it," Matt said again, lower, clenching his fist. There was no glass left in the pilothouse windows, but musket balls whanged off the battle shutters. A pair of machine guns on the port side opened up on the galleys, and a big splash sprouted mere yards off the port bow as the next cruiser fired again. Less than half a mile away, those guns could gut *Mahan*.

"All stop," Matt ordered. "All astern, one third. Back us away. Signal *Ellie*. Have Pack Rat resume firing the main battery at the following cruisers."

"Aye, aye, Captain," Paddy Rosen said. With enough light to see, they didn't need the pilot anymore, and Paddy was probably the best helmsman in the fleet. Certainly the most experienced with *Walker*—or *Mahan*. He'd been conning the ship with the wheel in his hands, but Tiaa-Baari had the deck. Neither complained when Matt essentially ignored that. Tiaa blinked misery, as if this whole situation were somehow her fault. Matt sensed her mood and offered a small, fleeting smile. "It's just war, Commander. Crazy stuff happens. Sometimes there's nothing you can do about it."

"We caan still get paast," Tiaa urged hopefully, gauging the gap between the wreck and the high cliff on the north side of the river. Paddy looked dubious, and Matt wasn't so sure either. And there were still those other cruisers. This was the absolute worst place this could've happened, and he realized, belatedly, he should've expected it for that reason alone.

"Aacting torpedo officer Fino-Saal asks why don't we blast the wreck with torpedoes?" the talker passed on.

Matt considered that but shook his head, doubting torpedoes alone would do the trick. *Maybe we could use depth charges too?* he thought. *Won't work,* he decided. *Even if the torpedoes shatter the wreck, we'll have to creep across it to drop the charges—all the while a sitting duck for following cruisers.* "No," he murmured regretfully. "Not a bad idea, but we'll have no way of knowing if it worked until we get past—or get snagged. We need something quick, but it has to work. Maybe more than once," he added gloomily.

"*Arracca* is aground," the talker reported. "The laandeen party haas taken the baattery, but they're gettin' haammered by Jaap-Grik planes. There's a big enemy force aassembling to attaack. . . ." The 'Cat talker blinked rapidly in horror. "An' three Grik *BB*s is shellin' 'em now!"

"That's just dandy," Matt growled. *Mahan* had backed sufficiently far that the cruisers were only barely visible beyond a gentle bend. The river was widening again astern, and Matt wondered if the Grik might try to force the passage themselves. At least here he could sink them more safely—but he'd have to *wait* to do that, and who knew how many more were on their way? He stood and paced to the chart laid out on the table, covered with broken glass. "The river starts widening back out a few miles past the wreck. We *can't* just sit here. Get Commander Brister on the horn and see if he has any ideas."

Perry Brister brought *Ellie* alongside *Mahan*, and he and Matt conferred for some time via their speaking trumpets. Perry's first instinct was the same as Fino-Saal's, but he agreed it would be risky, and whoever chanced it—he volunteered *Ellie*—might add their own wreck to the Grik cruiser. They could ask for air strikes, but both suspected the only short-term result would be further delay to the air support Chack and Tassanna so desperately needed. Paddy advocated dumping depth charges from their motor launches, but exploring that suggestion revealed several weaknesses. First, how would they get the boats (full of explosives) in the water and past the teeming galleys full of musket-armed troops—and through the fire of the waiting Grik cruisers? Second, with the charges set so shallow, how would the boats get clear without destroying themselves? Finally, after everything else, how could they possibly know if they'd successfully removed the obstacle? This line of speculation was rendered moot when inspections revealed the launches in question were too shot-up to float for long, in any event.

Late morning turned to early afternoon, and galleys still swept past the stationary DDs, giving them as wide a berth as they could. The Grik had seen that *Mahan* and *Ellie*, conserving ammo, fired only on those that came too close. Another sortie had finally flown upriver, pounding the Grik opposite Chack's position and ineffectually attacking the BBs giving their friends so much grief. But aside from killing a few hundred Grik and possibly stalling their assault, all the air attacks seemed to accomplish

was to disperse their infantry a little more than usual—
they'd already dug *more* trenches—and temporarily
raise the bombardment by forcing the BBs to maneuver.
But *thousands* more infantry were seen hurrying to reinforce the enemy onshore, and the BBs seemed in no hurry
to follow their galley swarm. They'd long since silenced
Itaa's last guns, and it appeared as if slaughtering Chack's
command was their only purpose for now. At least the
Jap-Grik fighters had quit the scene. The P1s had accounted for six or seven of them, and the rest only occasionally returned in pairs when there were gaps in the air
cover. That meant their airfield had to be very close, but
there was no time to look for it now.

By late afternoon, with the sun dropping into their
eyes, Matt and Perry had settled on a desperate plan.
They'd secure *Ellie*'s anchor chain to *Mahan*'s stern, and
the two ships would rush forward together, laying as much
fire on the enemy cruisers as they could. *Mahan* would
drop both her anchors near the stern of the wreck, attempting to hook it, and together the two DDs would try
to pull it around. It was a reckless scheme, and Matt embraced all the disastrous scenarios mounting in his mind
so he might prepare for them. In too many cases, however,
there was absolutely nothing they could do if things went
wrong. With both ships' engines at full astern, the chain
linking *Ellie* to *Mahan* might part. If that happened, *Mahan*'s younger sister would surge backward unexpectedly,
probably slamming her rudder hard over and smashing
stern-first into the cliff. Or *Mahan*'s anchors could tear
loose, or her own chains break, sending *both* DDs into a
full-speed, colliding catastrophe. Worse, it might not
work at all, and both ships would be stuck pulling their
guts out, relatively motionless, while the cruisers smashed
them apart. Matt was reluctant to ask *Mahan*'s heart-
breakingly willing crew to run such a risk, but he simply
couldn't think of anything else. They were running out
of time, and the longer they waited, the more would be
stacking up beyond the wreck, waiting for them. It was
now or never.

"The detail is ready aaft to take in *Ellie*'s chain," Tiaa
told him.

"What about the torch detail?" Matt asked. Tabby had eight 'Cats belowdecks forward, standing by to race up on the fo'c'sle with a torch and long hoses from the oxygen and acetylene bottles positioned below. Their job, probably under heavy fire (thus the large party all armed with Blitzers), was to cut the chains if they had to. Matt tried to forbid Tabby from leading the party herself, but she reminded him she was, hands down, the best torch in the ship.

"I feel more and more helpless," he murmured, low enough even Tiaa probably didn't hear over the blowers. "Nobody minds me anymore. First Tassanna, now Tabby. The Grik damn sure don't do what they're supposed to! What's next?"

His question had been rhetorical black humor, but he got his answer almost immediately.

"Comm-aander Tiaa! Cap-i-taan Reddy!" cried the talker, his voice incredulous, eyelids a blinking blur. "Crow's-nest lookout reports . . ." He paused to get himself under control. "*Salissa* an' . . . it looks like *Tara-kaan Islaand* an' *Sular* beyond, is all steamin' upriver behind us!"

"What?" Matt demanded, racing out on the bridgewing to see for himself. There he stood, oblivious to the resurging musket fire and resultant clatter of .30 cals above and behind, just staring at the massive shapes churning upriver. They were quite close. Understandably, the crow's-nest lookout—stuck up there in the heat all day, unable to expose himself to descend—had grown less attentive to events behind them. And there'd been no word by radio.

"Sur! Sur!" Tiaa urgently cried, unwilling to actually grab him. "Please come inside! You gonna get shot!"

Matt spun and strode directly to the talker by the TBS transceiver on the aft bulkhead of the pilothouse. Her eyes went wide at the sight of his furious expression. "Get Admiral Keje on the horn right now. Admiral Keje *himself*."

"Ay, ay, Cap-i-taan!"

"Whaat you think they're doin' here?" Tiaa asked.

"That's what I mean to find out. Keje probably got

bored," Matt added bitterly. "Or General Alden whipped him into it, hoping to find another place to land and march to Chack's relief. Who knows?"

Much quicker than Matt expected, implying Keje was waiting for the call, the talker handed him the headset. "The ahd-mi-raal," she said.

Matt crammed the earpiece up under his helmet and spoke into the microphone. "I sure hope you have a good reason for this," he almost snarled. "You were supposed to keep *Big Sal* safe! Those were your orders, and moving her here against them is gross insubordination." He didn't add that Keje was supposed to keep his wife safe too, and try as he might, he couldn't banish that thought.

"I do keep her safe!" Keje quickly countered, voice almost pleading. "Not only do the naarrow confines of the river at this point better protect *Salissa* from possible enemy torpedo bombers, I did not tell you I was coming specificaally so those planes, which we know have raadio, would not discover it—and report it to the Grik." Matt seriously doubted that was the main reason Keje told him nothing, but it actually was a good one. "Most of my planes are now conducting an attaack upriver. With the loss of so maany of *Arracca*'s planes, Tassanna's aarstrip is more than sufficient to accommodate them. Paarticularly after we landed the maa-jority of our ground crews and augmented the fuel and ord-naance stores there." He took a breath. "We really should name that aar-strip, something heroic, profound . . ."

"You're starting to ramble, Keje," Matt warned.

"Yes," Keje replied, somewhat stiffly, "and I haave no reason to." He sighed. "You are my brother, my commaander in chief, and I did not disobey you lightly. But your advaance has been staalled all day while our people, our *friends*, continue to suffer, and their peril only mounts. With the full agreement of Gener-aal Aalden and long before you detailed the—forgive me—wildly irresponsible solution you are about to attempt, I realized thaat blind obedience under these circum-staances was contraary to my greater duty, for the reasons I already stated, and more." The deep breath he took became a sigh. "This ship—my *Home and state*—may now be an aar-craft caarr-ier, but above that, as you so often remind me, it is first and foremost a waar-ship of the United Homes and Graand Alliaance. Perhaaps *Salissa* is not fit for the baattle-line, as you also repeatedly insist, but she remains better than your tiny DDs at other things besides simply carrying aar-craft. Do not let your concern for her blind you to thaat and force you to make a risky, possibly futile, costly, and utterly unnecessary attempt—when I bring you a better way."

Matt blinked, taken aback, but when he spoke again, his voicc had lost its edge.

"Okay. I admit I'm stumped. What've you got?"

"Simply this: I ask that you move *Mahaan* and *Ellie* aside and let *Salissa* paass."

"What the hell?"

"Hear me," Keje insisted. "Though you caannot, *Salissa* can *raam* paast the wreckage of the cruiser as if it were not there."

"Whoa!" Matt objected. "Talk about risky. Those cruisers are pretty stout; *Arracca* was built a lot like *Salissa*, and one of 'em basically sank her by ramming. You stick that fat tub and we're done."

"Never fear," Keje replied, maybe a little huffy over Matt's description of his ship. "You forget—after the Baattle of Baalkpan, *Salissa* was baadly daamaged and raather more comprehensively reconstructed than *Arracca* was later modified. There is a difference. As haave we all, I've closely studied Grik cruisers. They are stout, as you say, but *Salissa* can certainly crush one from the side. The engines may scraatch her bottom as she crumples them," he conceded, "but she *caan* get past!"

Matt looked around, realizing everyone in *Mahan*'s pilothouse was watching him. The machine guns outside had started firing again, and more musket balls whanged off the ship. The Grik were getting stirred up at the sight of such massive reinforcements, and the thunder of *Salissa*'s big muzzle-loading cannon, blasting great swaths of canister, had probably been shredding galleys all the way upriver. None could hear Keje's end of the conversation, particularly over the increasing roar of battle, but they must've caught the gist from what Matt said. They'd been ready to try his stunt, no matter what, but were clearly hopeful there was another way.

"Okay," Matt finally agreed. "We'll give it a try. But even if you grind the wreck to paste, there's at least two more cruisers past her, probably more by now. You'll have to stand against 'em alone until most of the wreckage you churn up washes downstream." Matt wasn't too worried about that. *Salissa*'s flight deck might get damaged, but even without armor she was still tougher than the cruisers. And though her armament had been reduced to make more room for planes (and keep Keje out of the battle line, Matt mused ironically), she still mounted twenty 50-pounder smoothbores and retained two of *Amagi*'s 5.5″ secondaries. Six of the new DP 4″-50s had been installed as well, replacing a pair of 4.7″s, and she still had four twin-mount 25 mms and *lots* of .30-caliber machine guns.

"Have you thought," Matt asked soberly, "that even if this works, you might have to do it again—and again? At least until the river widens out. Even then it might be a slow grind, fighting our way *all* the way." He took a long breath and closed his eyes, then added brutally, "It might be morning before we get there, and nobody left to save."

"I haave thought of thaat, my brother," Keje answered, equally grim, "and aac-tually expect it to be the case. But you expected to fight all the way from the staart. Only this blockage delayed you." His tinny sigh came to Matt through the earpiece over the louder rumble of guns. "And if our friends are indeed lost to us when we arrive, their souls waatching from above will know we tried— and they will still see the vengeance we wreak on their behaaf."

"Very well," Matt agreed. "Let's get on with it and pray to God—the Maker—that it works. We've wasted enough time."

CHAPTER 30

"Why have you not attacked?" First General Esshk demanded of Second General Ign, even as he slid down into a covered section of the new, deeper trench Ign's troops had been frantically digging all day. Ign glanced up, not recognizing Esshk at first, silhouetted against the setting sun. And even his voice reinforced the initial confusion. Gone was the deep, commanding self-assurance that always permeated it. In its place was a somewhat higher-pitched tone, bordering on apprehensive desperation.

"First General Esshk!" Ign finally replied. "I thought you were in *Giorsh*!" Ign had, in fact, believed *Giorsh* was one of the three greatships of battle bombarding the enemy position. The flagship of the fleet was no longer painted white to distinguish it from the rest. While useful for signaling purposes, so other shipmasters always knew where to look for guidance, it also tended to single out the flagship for disproportionate attention from the enemy.

"*Giorsh* remains beyond the *nakkle* leg," Esshk replied. "I never even made it aboard. First came your unexpectedly precipitous request for reinforcements here"—Esshk gestured around—"which I immediately acted upon." That was certainly true. Despite the damaging air attacks that began late in the morning, Ign had amassed more than twenty thousand well-armed New Army troops and almost as many cannon as his grand battery had possessed. The difficulty in bringing up the latter had been profound, however. Arduous as it was to move the big guns in the first place, the enemy flying machines had focused heavily on them, disabling many and slaughtering their carefully trained crews. "And yet to be honest, Second General Ign, your situation here very quickly lost its place at the fore-front of my concern."

Ign's orange, slit-pupiled eyes widened and his crest fluttered. "Indeed? May I ask what else has transpired?" *And what brought you back here,* he didn't say aloud.

"You may, since you will have to deal with most of it directly. There have been . . . developments," Esshk conceded. "First to reach me, after yours, were rather tortu-ously delivered reports of events in the south, on the Ungee River. Airships were only able to bring them partway, not only because of the threat in our skies"— Esshk's own eyes grew wider—"but because the Other Hunters staging their impudent 'distraction' at Soala have revealed dangerous flying machines of their own! Messengers were forced to carry their reports some dis-tance before being flown as close to here as they dared. Only then could they proceed on foot once more. *Crack the bones* of that ridiculous Kurokawa for never sharing his rapid means of communications with us!" he spat in frustration, teeth gnashing emphasis. Regaining control, he continued. "In any event, this very morning the Other Hunters launched a massive, well-coordinated assault across the Ungee. Early indications are that their attack could succeed."

Ign was thunderstruck. He'd never been as complacent as Esshk regarding the Other Hunters, but he'd never imagined they could cross the Ungee in the face of the force arrayed there either. *Then again,* he considered, *look what has happened here.* This entire day had been overwhelmed by the impossible.

"In addition," Esshk continued relentlessly, "reports from Kurokawa's Japhs who joined our hunt in the air have confirmed that all the enemy's First Fleet, which we believed incapable of consolidating itself so quickly, has indeed arrived off our shore and is currently forcing its way upriver *here.* A . . . large percentage of the Final Swarm making its way to the sea in galleys has already been destroyed. We have fed them directly into the enemy's jaws, morsel by morsel," he added bitterly. "For what good it will do, I already sent orders to stop the galleys out there"—he gestured at the river, where, sure enough, most of the hundreds of galleys in view were now just milling about—"and dispatched messengers east, running along the riverbanks, to signal all galleys past our view to return at once, or ground their ships and make their way back on foot. The cruisers must stand and oppose the enemy."

If Ign was thunderstruck before, now he felt as if the lightning had burned him to the bone—as did Jash, apparently. He'd scrambled up, probably to make a report, and heard everything. He'd never even known the Other Hunters existed, and his gaping jaws betrayed surprise about a great many things.

"Finally," Esshk said with a measure of affected disdain, "I also received word directly from the Palace of Vanished Gods that the Celestial Mother herself has expressed 'concern' over these various reports. Reports to *her*," he emphasized. "Which means either she has developed a network of informants on her own—quite astonishing—or the Chooser, left perhaps overlong as her sole guardian, has been indiscreet. Possibly for purposes of *his* own," Esshk added darkly. "I must return to the palace to discover the extent of our troubles there." He glared at Ign. "You, however, must force yourself to imagine not only that the enemy on the river might manage to fight his way here, but that the Other Hunters have succeeded in crossing the Ungee and destroyed the force at Soala. Based on that assumption, we must reconsider all our plans accordingly. So I ask again: Why have you not attacked?"

Ign was baffled by Esshk's apparently random train of thought. "I have been waiting. . . ." He paused. "The enemy flying machines have retired for the moment, doubtless to refuel and rearm. But their attacks are more frequent, with greater power." He nodded understanding. "More evidence that the rest of their fleet does indeed approach. At the same time, the trenches constructed by Ker-noll Jash and other troops you sent have protected those inside them amazingly well. We are safe here and so are the additional forces you send me, once they arrive. Some are somewhat shaken by their experience in the open and need time to recover," he confessed. "But, ultimately, we serve our purpose. The enemy cannot attack *us*; they are trapped."

"But they *will*," Esshk insisted, "when—if—their reinforcements come. And the enemy before you has provided a perfect place for them to land. You *must* attack at once before their flying machines return. If you get close enough, quickly enough, the flying machines cannot strike you without killing their own, and you have more than enough troops to swarm them under, depriving them of the claw hold they have gained." He paused. "If you cannot . . ."

"Yes, Lord," Ign actually interrupted, his tone weary. "I will, of course, destroy myself at once."

"No!" Esshk snapped. "As I was saying, in the unfortunate event that you cannot overwhelm the enemy and they land more troops, you must save as much of your force as you can. Most specifically yourself"—he glanced at Jash—"and as many of your apprentices as possible. The enemy fleet cannot pass the blockage at the *nakkle* leg any easier than we . . . and we will make it even more difficult if it comes to that."

Utterly shocking Ign and Jash, and it was probably fortunate no one else could hear, Esshk's tone turned almost pleading. "You will begin to design defensive battles on ground of your choosing, as well as in the south. We cannot *ever* allow this enemy and the Other Hunters to combine."

Esshk sighed deeply, and they finally saw a glimpse of his mental and physical exhaustion. "All my grand schemes have been overturned. I have already sent runners summoning every warrior in the Empire. We have even contacted General Halik at last. When all are gathered, no force on earth—combined or not—can overwhelm us. But I grow uneasy that the whole war will become one of defense. I suppose there are advantages to that in terms of numbers and supply—such is actually what that creature Kurokawa advocated from the start—

but it was never possible. *The Ghaarrichk'k do not fight defensive wars!"*

"Until now," Ign said softly, and Esshk reacted as if he'd been struck.

"Perhaps," he whispered, "and I . . . do not know how . . ." His voice firmed. "You and the army you made must form the spine of that war."

Ign nodded but couldn't escape the irony that Esshk had probably wanted him dead just a few hours before, and now implied that he had the very survival of their race in his claws. He looked at Jash. "Sound the preparatory horns. We attack in one hundred breaths." He looked at Esshk. "Go, Lord. Be safe. The Celestial Mother cannot lead, and all relies on you. But you must prepare yourself. If I can destroy the pitiful survivors before us, the enemy will find it more difficult to land." He hesitated. "But they *will* most likely land. They will continue to bomb us from the sky, and their fleet will be as safe from ours as ours from theirs. So, for a time at least, the Ghaarrichk'k *must* fight a defensive war. But as this enemy taught us and you yourself have seen, the greatest might can shatter against a strong defense. And as the enemy has finally come to us in attack, so will we one day return to them."

Tassanna's Perimeter

The brush-fire smoke had long died away, but great new gouts of pink smoke, colored by the red setting sun, suddenly billowed from the enemy trenches, and shrieks tore the sky as shells came in. Some burst long raining shrapnel between the Allied trench and the hospital tents, but enough of them sleeted sizzling shards directly down on the defenders. Screams erupted in the trench, and even Silva tried to crawl under his helmet. He cursed Petey for taking up so much room, then hissed at Chack as the shells kept coming. "Lawsy! Them damn lizards're gettin' too good at this artillery shit— *Gad!*" he exclaimed when a sputtering shell actually landed in the trench just yards away before it blew, blowing their hearing and showering them with dirt clods, blood, and pieces of people. They were only eighteen-pounders, compared to the hundred-pounders from the Grik BBs, but their gunners seemed better at setting fuses.

The hellish bombardment continued for what seemed an hour but couldn't have been more than a few minutes. It was incredibly frustrating not to fire back, but the range was long for mountain howitzers and they simply didn't have enough ammo for the long guns. Still, the shelling was so intense that Silva was sure they must've lost a few of their own guns and crews, anyway. Then, suddenly, distant horns bellowed and the barrage lifted all at once. Silva, Chack, and many others slowly raised their heads to peer over the top of the trench and scanty breastworks. Petey looked too, only to utter a squeaky "Skirp!" and finally bolt away, back down toward the beach.

Silva didn't even notice. Thousands of Grik had risen from their own trenches like a surging tide. Even more alarming, they didn't just immediately wad up into a charging mob, but paused to adjust their alignment and raise their bayonet-tipped muskets to something like the position of port arms in front of them. Dozens of battle streamers unfurled in the breeze, and to the raucous blare of other horns, they stepped off into a loping advance.

"Holy shit," Silva blurted. "These're trained soldiers, just like Kurokawwy's an' them lizards down on the West Mangoro!"

"Trained to fight shoulder to shoulder, just like *we* were at Saay-lon," Chack countered. "We'll slaughter them," he growled. Silva had no doubt of that, but also doubted they'd ever get them all. His concern was shared by most. "Here they come!" rose a chorus of shouts from many throats—human, 'Cat, Khonashi—but all one people at that moment, ready to fight to the death and bound more tightly by the certainty they were about to.

Chack stood. "All baatteries! Commence firing!"

Five howitzers, loaded with case at first; nine Grik eighteen-pounders; and three Allied six-pounders had survived the shelling. They all opened up at once, the staggered reports pounding their ears, muzzle flashes and vent jets stabbing the gathering twilight. Shells and roundshot ripped downrange and burst in front of the charging ranks or plowed great furrows of blood and gore. Grik artillery—and their gunners—might've improved dramatically, but the veterans in the Allied trench, even using captured guns, were professionals. Grik fell in oval swaths of riddled bodies, as if gigantic shotguns blasted them from the sky.

"Oh yeah," Silva urged. "Hammer 'em! Chew 'em up!" He was distracted when Commodore Tassanna-Ay-Arracca and several of her officers plunged into the trench beside him, all armed with a variety of Allin-Silvas, rifle-muskets, and Blitzerbugs. To his consternation, Pam slid into the trench behind them, Simy Gutfeld and an armed corps-'Cat helping her with a dazed but determined-looking Risa. His first attempt to berate them all died in his throat when he saw Risa's manic blinking and realized she now had no leg at all beyond the bloody bandage wrapped around her knee and thigh. He gulped. "What the hell're you doin' here!" he finally managed.

"Same as you," Pam flashed back. "About to get killed. An' you'll let us do it how we want, or so help me, I'll kick you in the balls so hard, they'll pop out your ears!"

"I will fight to the laast," Risa proclaimed, softer, wan, almost fey, but just as unwavering. Her slack face suddenly became animated and she blinked delight. "Here we are all together again! My brother." Chack spared her an understanding blink. "My 'mate.'" She grinned at Silva, then clasped Pam's hand tightly in hers. "And my best friend in all the world! I am surrounded by faamily. How could I aask for better compaany at a time like this?"

Tassanna looked at her, blinking affection. Beyond her, Arracca still blazed. It would take a long time for something that size to burn to the waterline, even with occasional internal ordnance explosions and ruptured fuel lines feeding the fire. Itaa, what was left of her, burned too. She'd been entirely demolished. "My Home is gone," Tassanna said. "The only one that remains to me is whaatever place my people, my faam-ily, make their staand." She raised a Blitzerbug. "This raagged hole in the earth is my Home now, and I will defend it."

Silva grunted, laying his Doom Stomper across the breastworks and taking aim. "Crazy damn wimmen," he groused. In his heart he had to agree with them, but he'd never admit it. And unlike that morning, he had no fear. "I don't know what kinda 'time like this' you dopey broads're goin' on about. All I see is a chance to kill a whole shitload o' Griks. Okay," he muttered lower, "big lizards line up, little lizards bunch up. . . ." He fired.

"Howitzers, load caanister!" Chack roared, gauging the distance. "Rifles, present. At three hundred yaards . . . *fire!*"

The Grik charge withered under the awesome volley of two thousand canister balls and nearly three thousand rifle bullets. And with the enemy running practically shoulder to shoulder, it was almost impossible for any of the projectiles to miss. But there were just so *many* targets. The gaps in the line were quickly filled by more panting Grik—just as other gaps appeared when Allin-Silvas kept firing independently and the two .30-caliber machine guns they'd salvaged off *Arracca* opened up, toppling shrieking Grik in windrows. Rifle-muskets fired slower, ramrods flashing in the last light of day. Many sailors were either too panicked or unfamiliar with the weapons to load them properly, or even forgot to cap them. Unaware they hadn't fired because of the deafening din, they repeatedly loaded charges and bullets on top of one another. If they suddenly remembered to cap them now, their barrels would burst. But the vast majority knew what they were doing and added a respectable volume to the cloud of lead the Grik charged against. Silva's Doom Stomper got off six punishing rounds that rolled him back each time, but he probably killed a dozen or more Grik as the huge bullets torc through the ranks. Finally, reluctantly, he laid the big rifle aside and slipped the Thompson off his shoulder. The Grik wave was getting close now, visibly depleted but still outnumbering the defenders four or more to one. At a hundred yards, however, the Raiders', Marines', and sailors' fire was even more effective. And on top of the blistering canister coughing from the stubby howitzers, Chack had one more surprise.

The captured guns were loaded with gravel, shards of iron from the case shot that galled them all day, broken pieces of Grik weapons—anything that came to hand. Added to this were the howitzers, of course, but also about two hundred Allin-Silva shotguns ready to blast out twenty .30-caliber pellets per shot, and as many as six hundred fully automatic .45ACP Blitzerbugs—not to mention Horn's BAR and Silva's Thompson. When all the cannon fired their final defensive gust of canister and improvised shot at around forty yards, that was the signal for every SMG, shotgun, and pistol to open up.

The effect was devastating. The whole front rank of the charge collapsed as if swept by an invisible scythe, and the follow-on ranks tottered and staggered as well. But then, the roughly ten thousand Grik who were still able finally fired back. They were winded and rushed and their aim was poor, but probably a third of the defenders instinctively dropped behind the protection of their breastworks or were blown back by the impact of big lead balls. Tassanna and Pam both cried out and fell, just as Chack roared, "Baayo-nets up! Out of the trench! Meet them in the open!"

Silva had his '03 Springfield bayonet but nothing to affix it to, and he didn't want to leave the girls. But he couldn't just wait with them until the Grik poured into the trench. With a fleeting glance at Pam and Tassanna, unable to tell how bad they were hit but seeing them still moving, he jumped up and mowed down a semicircle in front of him with the Thompson. Only then did he realize he hadn't seen Risa with the others. *No time for that!* He dropped his empty magazine, inserted a fresh one, and started firing controlled bursts. Chack was beside him, the bayonet on his trusty Krag jabbing and stabbing, the rifle firing occasionally. Simy Gutfeld was there too, fighting with an Allin-Silva, his limp hardly apparent.

And then, to his horror, Silva saw Risa. She'd hobbled into the open, using a Grik musket for a crutch, and was shooting a Blitzer one-handed, like a pistol. Blitzers were too heavy for that, and she'd swing it up, fire a short burst, and let it drop for a moment before repeating the process. Most frightening to Silva, and probably unknown even to Risa, she was blinking . . . *contentment.* Silva's Thompson was empty and he dropped it on the ground, pulling his cutlass and 1911 again. Hacking frantically at one Grik and stabbing another—shooting it with his pistol for good measure—he roared over the battle, "Goddammit, Chackie! Your nutty sister . . ." A tangle of Grik swarmed around him and he slashed one across the throat. A shower of blood blinded him and he fired his pistol twice in the direction he'd seen a bayonet thrusting at him. A different bayonet skated off his ribs, and he shot in that direction too, trying to wipe blood out of his eye with his sword arm.

"I got Risa!" Simy yelled, pounding and stabbing his way toward her. Silva saw her blinking, disappointed, at her empty weapon, but then got very busy again. Somewhere above the racket he heard the drone of airplane engines. *About damn time,* he thought. *Hope they're ours. . . .* The slide on his 1911 locked back and he had no more magazines. Nearly decapitating a Grik with a backhand stroke with his cutlass, he found the opening to his holster with the pistol muzzle and dropped it in. Then, without even thinking, he pulled Captain Reddy's gleaming Colt from his belt. The full-house black powder .44-40 loads made it buck and roar and kill in a most satisfying manner.

Jash had made the charge right among his Slashers and now fought directly beside those that remained, loading and firing their garraks slightly back from the "clash of claws," the ancient term for the point of contact with the enemy where the most vicious, visceral fighting occurred. Second General Ign had directly commanded him to keep his distance, to "preserve his Slashers' temper" after their earlier reverse, but Jash suspected the order had been mostly intended to preserve *him.* Even then, the charge had been terrible, unlike anything he'd ever imagined, and his survival owed little to his position in the attack. The galley battle, under such murderous fire from enemy fast-shooters, had been bad enough—as bad as he thought it could get—but *this* . . . Half his Slashers, now counting Ign's Guards, died in that meager five-hundred-pace assault. He'd watched them shredded by canister, riddled by bullets, even pulped by random solid shot. Clearly, the artillery barrage hadn't been as effective as he'd hoped. And now to see the desperate abandon and single-mindedness with which the enemy fought, face-to-face, bayonet to bayonet, close enough to see their snarling faces twisted with rage, hear their shrill, furious, or agonized cries . . . He'd always been told the enemy *couldn't* fight like this; they were too weak, too sensitive to loss. He doubted that now, in general, but also clearly saw how brutally a proper defense could bleed any attack, even one as overwhelming as he and Ign believed this was. More important, he saw how *he* could've stopped the amphibious attack that morning, or at least made it just as costly. For all he and his Slashers had learned during their training for defense, *this* was the true lesson he must remember. If he lived.

The firing had all but stopped in the midst of the wild melee before him, replaced by the thunder and clash of garraks grinding together like spears. Squeals of pain and howls of fury intermingled in an all-encompassing roar that muted the few shots still coming. A short, muffled stutter drew his eyes to one of the tree prey, a "Lemurian," nearby, fighting in the open with only one leg. He lowered his garrak, amazed. No member of the Race would ever do such a thing! A missing limb was a mortal wound, and warriors who lost them either died on the battlefield or went to the cookpots. None would keep fighting; there was no reason. It was best to cut your own throat or make yourself as comfortable as possible for the time you had left. He was even more amazed to see a human actually fighting to reach the Lemurian, to render *aid*—and was almost disappointed to see them both fall under a fusillade from his Slashers when they saw a gap to shoot through. Oh, but then! A one-eyed giant he thought he might've glimpsed in the predawn fight, already killing with thoughtless fury and matching skill, suddenly became a machine of death! Armed only with a sword and one of the strange hand garraks, he slew his way toward his fallen comrades as effortlessly as one of the great herbivores of the plains ate grass. *No,* Jash thought, *there is no comparing* that *to an herbivore. It is more like one of the great predators that take a hundred Ghaarrichk'k armed with spears to slay!*

"You must kill *that* one," he directed the troops around him as they loaded their garraks, not even sure why. The enemy was finally crumbling here in the middle. Soon, the attack would push through and roll them up to the side, just as the enemy had done to them that morning. Even as that thought came to him, however, he felt a pressure on his own right as warriors surged against him. He also realized he'd been hearing the roar of flying machine engines for several moments but had been too absorbed by what he'd seen to take proper heed. Now he did.

A formation of the small blue-and-white planes, so similar to the "fighters" of the Japhs, was swooping down on the rear of the assault, toward *him.* Fast-shooters in their wings flashed in the gathering gloom. Then he heard the clatter of the fast-shooters as warriors started falling, flailing on the ground. Worse, something was definitely happening on the right—and the enemy in front had taken advantage of the attack's hesitation to reload their small fast-shooters and mow his warriors down again.

"Ker-noll!" Naxa shouted. "The enemy is out of their trench, *attacking* on the right! They are led by a giant with black fur on his face, firing one of the big fast-shooters in his *hands*!" Jash was confused. The enemy was out of its trench here as well. . . . And Naxa's report had doubtless been exaggerated even before he heard it, but there was another giant before him, with lighter-colored fur. How many giants did the enemy have? Jash and Naxa both crouched as more planes roared by, spitting bullets, scattering troops, kicking up great clouds of dust. Jash hurried to the rear, where he could see, and was horrified to watch the right side of the attack peeling back, away from the enemy, and firebombs *did* fall then, scorching the retreating troops with mushrooms of flame.

"We still have them *here*," Jash snapped. "I smell their

blood! Their throats are bared to our teeth!" Naxa just looked at him, and in that moment Jash knew *this* First of One Hundred would finally do whatever he asked without complaint or resentment. Yet, unbidden, he suddenly remembered First General Esshk's words and Second General Ign's last command: "Don't spend all your troops on this." That's when he knew he was in great danger of doing just that, even if the attack succeeded. To emphasize that, he heard the distant, growing thrum of the recall horns.

"We must pull back," he told Naxa reluctantly. "Send runners to the other ker-nolls and ensure they hear the horns." *There must be a* single *ker-noll to command the entire attack next time,* he smoldered. *Or Second General Ign should have come himself. There is no need for independent coordination of a mob, but an* army *needs a commander on the scene. That is something else I learned today.* "Tell the ker-nolls to order their troops to spread out, to run for our trenches. There is no danger of pursuit, but the flying machines will burn us all if we stay together!"

Naxa looked doubtful. "If we just flee, won't our own warriors still behind us think we turned prey and kill us?"

"No," Jash assured, hoping he was right. "Not if we re-form as we near our lines, before we reenter our trench. It will be difficult and we will be vulnerable then as well, but we must attempt it." He paused. "And not only so we won't be killed." He'd taken command of a larger force in disarray once before and realized it was time to do so again. "Pass that *order* as well."

Jash's Slashers were already pulling back, his overheard command circulating among them. He was sickened by what they'd endured, only to fail, but was more than satisfied with his troops. He'd discovered another new feeling that day, something else that required a word. Satisfaction was part of it, but there was more of something else as well. With a final glance at the one-eyed giant kneeling by the fallen human and Lemurian and shooting his hand garrak amid a field of dead,

covered with too many of his Slashers, Jash suspected
he knew a word for how he felt—and was fairly certain
he'd meet the giant again.

The whole grassy plain between the two trenches was
burning when Silva and Chack carried Risa back down
in the trench and up the other side. Gunny Horn and
Lawrence followed, carrying Major Simon Gutfeld. Both
were dead, riddled and bloody. Enrico Galay and several
others were behind them, loaded down with their weapons. Horn, Galay, and Lawrence had already been fighting their way toward the center when the whole Grik
attack fell apart, the end beginning when Horn, desperate to take some heat off his troops so they could at least
reload, wrapped leather cartridge box slings around the
barrel of a .30-caliber machine gun, picked it up, and
advanced behind it. Lawrence joined him with Horn's
BAR. The leather cooked and so did Horn's left hand,
but it started the bubble that eventually popped. Not that
any of them much cared about that just then.

Pam's face was covered with blood, streaming from
under her hair, where a Grik musket ball had blown a
hole in her helmet and cut her scalp. She didn't seem to
notice, except to occasionally dab at the blood in her eyes
with her sleeve as she worked on Tassanna. The commodore had a more serious wound in her upper right
shoulder. Both stared in horror, and tears gushed through
the drying blood on Pam's face, when Risa and Gutfeld
were gently laid down to join the long row of corpses
growing behind the trench. Horn looked grim as he took
his BAR back from Galay and sat heavily, exhausted,
breathing hard. The fur on Chack's face was wet with
blood and tears, and his eyes were bright in the light of
the burning prairie.

Silva's face was like stone, and he'd pointedly avoided
looking at Risa's. He hadn't looked directly at anyone at
all, in fact, since they'd found him beside his friend on
the battlefield. At first he hadn't even responded; he just
knelt there, slowly ejecting spent, blackened brass cartridges from the Colt and inserting six more from his
pockets. Now he gazed at Gutfeld. "I'll swan," he said

roughly. "Now ol' Simy's gone too." He sighed. "He was a right guy, an' went out good, but this ain't no right kinda war no more." His voice turned bitter. "Good folks dyin', fightin' goddamn *vermin*!" Finally, reluctantly, his eye turned to Risa's face at last, and a huge fat tear raced down his grimy cheek. Hesitantly, he caressed her furry chin and gently closed her mouth.

"Go to him," Tassanna whispered urgently to Pam.

"He don't need me," Pam hissed back. "He don't need anybody."

Tassanna blinked reproach. "You are *not* that stupid."

Pam motioned helplessly at the bloody compress between the 'Cat's chest and shoulder.

"I am well enough. Go. He needs you more thaan I right now."

Silva jumped slightly when Pam wrapped her arms around him. "Jeez," he started to snap, then he slumped. "Hiya, doll," he finally managed, looking at her. "You look awful."

Pam snorted wetly. "You don't look so hot yourself."

Silva shrugged loosely and looked at Horn. "We'd all be goners if Arnie an' Larry hadn't waded in when they did, hittin' 'em on the flank. Lizards still get too focused on what's right in front of 'em. Good thing, I guess." His eye strayed back to Risa. "She an' Simy gave 'em a show too. Somethin' about her made the Grik up close not wanna tangle with her."

"Baddest-ass 'Cat Marine they ever saw," Horn whispered. "Nobody in their right mind would've gotten close, one leg or two. And Simy . . . Shit!" he exclaimed abruptly and stood.

"Where are you going?" Chack asked.

"I'm . . . I have to check on my people on the left."

"Rest first," Chack ordered, offering his canteen. "Drink. I haave a little left. Let Laaw-rence drink as well, then give the rest to Paam for the wounded." He looked toward the enemy position, but it was obscured by smoke and flames. And Nancys were stooping on it now, washing the trench with fire. "The Grik will not attaack again tonight, I think, but will probably soon resume their bombardment. If not from laand, then the river."

"All the more reason to get them squared away," Horn insisted.

Chack snorted. "You fought your first aaction as a senior officer today, yet you are an NCO to your core. Don't you think the Raider and Maa-rine NCOs under your comm-aand can maan-age without you a while longer?"

Horn nodded reluctantly and sat heavily again, taking a sip from Chack's canteen.

"We haave been through much today," Chack said gently, finally kneeling beside Risa himself, opposite Silva and Pam. He glanced at Tassanna watching them. "Together we haave lost much as well." His gaze swept around, encompassing Lawrence and Galay, all the survivors and the slain, then went down to the beach where *Arracca*'s flames illuminated the wounded gathered there. More were headed down, many more, most on stretchers or carried in blankets. He wished he could protect them better, but there were more wounded than fighters now. Particularly with no water, the fighters needed to conserve what energy they had left for improving their position and fighting, or the wounded stood no chance at all.

Finally Chack's gaze settled on Silva. "I know you loved Risa in your way—prob-aably the same way I did." He shook his head. "I will never aask again, because it doesn't matter. Whaat you need to know is thaat Risa loved you too." He looked at Pam. "And you. Just as importaant, you must know she died on *Saanta Caatalina*, not here, as soon as she lost her leg."

"Bullshit," Silva snapped. "An' you're an asshole. She was never the sort to just give up! An' they got wooden legs an' such now that would'a had her back in the fight. Maybe not in the middle of it," he conceded, "but in it."

"Perhaaps," Chack said, then sighed. "But you knew Risa. Do you doubt the waar was already killing her, little by little, even before her wound? The waar had become her life, as it haas for too many of us—her brothers and sisters—and one way or another it had reached a turning point. She thought it had turned *against* us here and we'd all be together in the heavens this night. She sought an end consistent with her nature.

An escape from her wound, in a way, but also from the waar. She may still be right about our fate," he added grimly, "but she was also wrong, because whether we survive or not, Cap-i-taan Reddy, First Fleet, and Gener-aal Aalden's expeditionary force will be here tonight or tomorrow and the waar *will* turn." He gestured at the smoldering battlefield. "The enemy remains more numerous than we and is haarder now thaan ever. We've forced him to learn new things, and he's done it too well. We must also learn, since I expect this will be the laast time we fight as *we* almost always haave: behind breast-works as they come to us to die.

"No," he continued, "the war will turn to something we caan't imaa-gine in our darkest dreams as we take it to the Grik in *their* streets, among *their* homes, in places they must defend. Thaat, my brothers and sisters, will be a haard slog, as you would say, and perhaps Risa is well out of it." He sighed again. "And it caan't last much longer; we're too tired and so are the Grik." He blinked thoughtful determination. "We'll destroy them within a year—or they'll destroy us just as quickly in this terrible, wrongful place." He also caressed Risa's face. "It was she who made me a waarrior, a soldier," he confessed. "But her spirit was already ebbing, and I would've spared her what I fear is yet to come if I could." Abruptly, he stood. "So I rejoice thaat she is now at rest," he said, though his tone belied his words, "and her soul will rise to the Heavens. She waatches us even now, and would scold us for our grief."

"Are you done?" Pam asked sharply. "Okay, my turn." She shrugged. "Sure, I was jealous o' Risa"—she squeezed Silva hard—"even though I had no call. I guess it was because she got to fight, more than anything, an' all I ever get to do is patch everybody up when they're done." She stood. "But I'm gonna do my job, just like she did, to the bitter end. If she's really watchin', that's what she'll expect of all of us." She paused. "What's that?" she demanded, poking Silva's bayonet wound, clearly visible through his ripped T-shirt. He winced. "Gonna need stitches. Again. Are you shot in the ass again too?" she demanded of Lawrence.

He shied away. "I not shot at all—just Grik 'lood."

"Good. Make way for Gunny Horn. Lemme see your hand."

The BBs on the water—there seemed to be four of them now—all opened up, lashing the position with exploding shells, and they tumbled back down into the trench.

"Gonna be a long night," Silva grumped.

"They're pulling back their galleys," Chack observed, seeing the smaller oared ships churning upstream in the light of the flashing guns.

"Yep," Silva agreed. "They must'a finally got the word that Captain Reddy's comin'. They're gonna need all them warriors pretty soon."

A big shell burst forty yards away, fragments whistling around them.

"And we're going to need all of ours," Chack agreed.

CHAPTER
31

////// January 1, 1945

*T*he dusk barrage was fairly brisk and caused more suffering among the beleaguered defenders, but it lasted only about half an hour before the four Grik BBs and (they estimated) six cruisers sullenly ceased firing. That seemed to coincide with a belated effort to reach them with a few rockets from beyond the bend, but of the twelve that came, only one landed in the perimeter, and it did no damage. Chack estimated the range at about three miles, so now they knew the distance at which the repurposed air-defense weapons were ineffective against surface targets. After that, except for an occasional shot from the entrenched batteries across the charred plain, it remained mostly quiet for the rest of the night, and the BBs and cruisers just sat out there, waiting. There were about a hundred Grik galleys too, seen by a scouting motor launch, lingering out of sight beyond *Arracca*'s smoldering corpse. There was little doubt what *they* meant to do at dawn. The rest of the galleys had been glimpsed rowing back upriver, their dreams of crossing the strait and reconquering Madagascar at least temporarily crushed.

Chack was up all night reorganizing the defenders and distributing what little ammunition they had left. There was no water left at all, besides what could be taken from the river and boiled. Nobody was ready to drink the filthy brown ooze straight. Not yet. Silva, Horn, and Lawrence helped Chack until he sent about a third of their force and both machine guns down to the beach under Major Galay. That effectively eliminated Horn's and Lawrence's independent "commands" and left less than two thousand still in the trench. Chack told his groggy friends to get some rest near the center of the line, where they could quickly move wherever they were needed, and they gratefully trudged away. Chack came by as the sky began to brighten and found them all clustered together among the sleeping troops. Lawrence was curled in a ball at the bottom of the trench, and Horn was snoring loudly. Pam, just relieved and probably more exhausted than any of them, was curled up against Silva's side, oblivious to the fact that Petey had returned from . . . wherever he went and draped himself halfway across her shoulder as well. Chack started to pass on and let his friends rest a little longer, but he caught a flicker reflected in Silva's open eye. He stopped and crouched.

"Them Griks on the river are waitin' for Captain Reddy," Silva whispered. "They're gonna make a stand."

Chack nodded. "I expect them to attaack us here as well, from the water and the laand."

Horn had stopped snoring. "So, what's the dope? You get any on the radio?" he asked thickly. "Is First Fleet going to get here in time?" he asked more specifically.

"First Fleet has been fighting all night," Chack said, "not only against enemy ships but to baash its way across their wrecks. *Salissa* has liter-aally been doing that, crushing sunken cruisers beneath her or aside." He shuddered. "While considered an excellent expedient at first, I don't think Ahd-mi-raal Keje expected to have to do it so often, and even *Big Saal* caan only take so much. The river finally broadens, however, and they will get here," he emphasized, "but I caan't say when, or whether it'll be in time for us. The gaalleys are obviously prepaaring to attaack from the river with a force at least equal to what I sent to face them, but I suspect that is only to weaken this position—which it haas done," he confessed. "There is movement in the enemy trench, and

I expect his greatest effort here." He stood. "I will be baaack. I may as well begin prepaaring our troops to face the day. You might waant to do the same." With that, he strode away.

Pam sat up and stretched, dropping Petey behind her back. "Agh!" she hissed, jumping up. "You little *shit*! I thought you were somethin' . . ." She shook her head. "Weird dreams." She took an unsteady step. "I better get back to work down at the tents." She paused and looked back at Silva. "Be careful, Dennis."

"You too, doll. See you after a while."

"Little shit eat?" Petey inquired, eyes still closed as he crawled back up on Silva.

"Not yet," Silva said, also standing.

"You think they'll come?" Horn asked.

"Yeah. No. Who knows?"

"How much ammo you got?"

"None for my Tommy gun or forty-five, sixteen rounds for the Doom Stomper, an'"—he displayed the nickel-plated Colt—"thirty-two rounds for this thing, not countin' what's in it." He smirked. "Thirty-eight total. That's how long the skipper has to save our asses." He climbed out of the trench and unbuttoned his trousers in the direction of the enemy. He could see them now, the day brightening quickly. "Sonova goat," he murmured. "Just look at them lizards! Practically paradin' into their formations! Never thought I'd see such a thing."

Snickering, several Shee-Ree joined him in urinating toward the Grik. In their culture, they were claiming a possession. Silva chuckled as he buttoned back up. "I'm so dry, I'm surprised I had the water for that—but at least I got to take a piss on Grik Land itself!" He slid back into the trench.

"So, this is it, huh?" Horn asked.

Silva ignored him. "Hey, you remember a fella named Mack Marvaney? Gunner's mate third, I think, or maybe he was still just a striker then. Stood us all around at that dive in Shanghai—can't remember its name—after that fight with those Brit gunboat swabs?"

Horn tried to concentrate. "Yeah, maybe."

"Poor bastard didn't last hardly twenty-four hours on

this shithole world. Goofy lizards on Bali got him, first time we ever really went ashore. Different kind o' lizards from Grik, but still smart, see?"

"You thinking maybe he was the lucky one?" Horn asked.

Silva looked at him, surprised. "Hell no! Just think of all the fun he's missed!"

Horn was mystified. "I swear. You shift gears faster than anybody I ever knew. Most people might at least have to double clutch it after losing a pal like Risa. Aren't you still chopped up about her at all?

Silva considered. "Yeah, I'll miss her," he admitted, "an' I expect I will as long as I live. But you know, either ol' Chackie's right an' she's still with us, havin' a peek from time to time . . . or she ain't. No use worryin' about it—except when I'm in the crapper. He's right about one thing, though: this war changed her from all fun to all gun—an' if there's one thing I've learned, you can't take nothin' for granted. That's why I rared up an' asked Pam if she wanted to get hitched."

Horn was even more amazed. "What did she say?"

"'No way in hell,'" Silva replied, as if it hadn't fazed him at all. Maybe it hadn't. "Who knows what that really means, comin' from her? But I asked, an' she had her chance, so I ain't got that hangin' over my head no more. That's what matters, right? I figger Risa went out as good as anybody'd want to, an' did her heap o' livin' with no regrets. Me too—or me either." He waved his hand. "Whichever."

That's when they heard the planes. It started as a dull drone but quickly grew to a thunderous roar. High above was a formation of twenty big Clipper flying boats, heading right for the enemy across the plain. Dark objects began tumbling down in long streams, exploding into roiling toadstools of fire right across where the Grik were preparing their assault. The pattern wasn't very tight and a few firebombs actually fell uncomfortably close to the Allied trench, but there were *hundreds* of them, and they completely wrecked the tight attack formations. Oddly, the Grik scattered so quickly and efficiently it looked like they'd been trained for it—or told to expect the command—but an awful lot were caught and Silva was dancing up and down in the trench, joined by Lawrence and hundreds of others. "That's the style!" Silva whooped. "Burn 'em up, burn 'em down, cook their goddamn *bones*!"

One of the Clippers coughed black smoke and started to spiral down. That's when they realized that Jap-Grik fighters were after them. But the bombers had an escort, and P1-Cs pounced on the attackers and quickly shot two out of the sky.

"Yeah!" Horn shouted hoarsely, joining the celebration. Silva looked back at him, grinning, only to see the swarm of galleys crowding in toward the beach—but Nancys were bombing them as well, and galleys burned and flaming Grik threw themselves into the water. The two machine guns opened up and the closest galleys spun away, out of control, fouling the ones behind. And there, sprinting into view from the east, huge bones in their teeth, were USS *James Ellis* and *Mahan*.

"Jumpin' Jesus, look at that!" Silva bellowed. "That's *Mahan*, by God!" He looked upriver where the BBs and cruisers waited, already firing their big forward guns, splashes rising high around the racing DDs. "You'll never hit nothin' as fast as them, you fat bastards!" he taunted at the top of his lungs. "Get ready to eat some slimy, shiny *fish*!" He gleefully held out his arms as if embracing the scene, but suddenly sobered. "Damn," he said. "*More* Jap planes!"

USS Mahan

"Sur-faace taa-gits dead ahead!" *Mahan*'s talker echoed the unnecessary report from the fire-control platform above. The river was very wide here, as they'd known, but all ten enemy warships were in full view as soon as they rounded the final bend: four BBs on the left, six cruisers on the right. All were stationary, probably at anchor. *They're expecting us,* Matt knew, *and hope lying at anchor will improve their gunnery. It will,* he conceded, *but it'll also make them sitting ducks!*

"Come right to three zero zero. Signal *Ellie* to do the same and take the lead." *James Ellis* was faster and could easily pull ahead. "Tell her to keep a sharp eye out for wrecks too," he reminded. "There's a lot of 'em scattered around out there." *And some are ours,* he reminded himself grimly, catching his first distant glimpse of *Santa Catalina*'s shattered, smoking hulk and *Arracca*'s still-burning wreck in the shallows. "Main battery will commence firing at the far left BB," he ordered calmly. Turning to Chief Fino-Saal on the port bridgewing, he said, "Target the next BB in line with the number two torpedo mount, two fish."

"Ay, ay, sur!" Fino had already started tracking, and he looked through the sights on the director again. "Range, twenty-six hundreds, bear-een, two four five. Speed," he added gleefully, "nuttin'! Two mount, match pointers. Staand by tubes two an' four!"

The salvo buzzer rang, and guns one, two, and four barked simultaneously, sending bright tracers converging toward the first target. All three hit—there would've been hell to pay with Pack Rat if they hadn't, at this range—and brittle armor was blasted away from the frontal slope of the huge ship's casemate. A huge splash erupted in front of them, sheeting water through the shattered windows. There was no point closing the battle shutters for this fight; they wouldn't stop anything and would only make it hard to see. "Russ Chappelle was right," Paddy Rosen declared. "Those're damn big guns! Good thing it takes 'em so long to load!"

And a good thing they're relying on their bow guns instead of turning to give us broadsides, Matt thought. *They'd eat us up, then. So it's also a good thing our air recon told us how they were situated so we* could *just come in blasting away like this!*

"Fire two! Fire four!" Fino called, and two Baalkpan Naval Arsenal MK-6 torpedoes arced out amid swirls of white smoke and plopped hard in the water. As soon as the concave splashes dissipated, foamy trails arrowed straight at their target.

"Jaap planes!" came Tiaa-Baari's voice, loud enough to be heard through the fur around the talker's ear. Matt

had decided, for this action, he needed Tiaa at the auxiliary conn after all, in case one of those monstrous Grik
roundshot hit the bridge. The talker repeated what they'd
all heard and continued. "Ten Jaap *bombers*, she stressed,
comin' up behind us!"

"Air action aft!" Matt shouted, pacing out on the starboard bridgewing and looking astern. They were a perfect target for a run like this! "All machine guns, open
fire when the enemy is in range! Helm, stand by for evasive maneuvers."

But the bombers seemed to ignore them. Astonished,
Matt watched them fly far overhead as if the DDs weren't
there. They were clearly some of Kurokawa's torpedo
bombers, complete with twin engines and big red meat-
balls, but they made no attack. The number one gun, *Mahan*'s only dual-purpose 4˝-50, might've had a chance if
they had, but the rest of her guns were all originals and
couldn't elevate high enough to engage aircraft. *Ellie*'s
could, and Matt saw her tracking the targets, pointers and
trainers spinning their wheels like mad. He was distracted
when two massive waterspouts rocketed into the air alongside Fino's target. Seconds later, two more torpedo blasts
rocked another Grik BB, *Ellie*'s target, no doubt. Then
two hits staggered *Mahan* at once, and the whole ship was
smothered by splashes. They'd finally strayed far enough
abeam of the undamaged BBs for their broadside guns to
bear, and their gunnery had *much* improved since the last
time Matt—or *Mahan*—faced them. Another hit struck
Mahan amidships on the starboard side, just under the
bridge. Matt lurched back into the pilothouse.

"Grik cruisers haas got underway an' is comin' right
at us!" the talker told him, his voice pitched high. *Ellie*'s
hit too!" Nancys and Fleashooters were swarming the
enemy now, hammering the cruisers in particular, which
were starting to weave and fire their antiair mortars,
putting up a curtain of iron fragments and balls for the
planes to fly through. But the pilots knew about them
now and kept their distance. That made their bombing
less effective, but they lost fewer planes.

"Damage report," Matt demanded. "Let's get our
other portside fish on the way," he told Fino.

"Caa-sul-tee on the two mount!" the talker said. "It won't train!"

"Swell," Matt growled. "Signal *Ellie* to stand by to come about to one three zero. We'll hit 'em with our starboard fish. Main battery, except for the number one gun, concentrate on the cruisers. Number one will engage the BBs in local control." The salvo buzzer rang, and three more shells converged on the BBs before Pack Rat switched targets. "Execute the turn," Matt ordered. Even as *Mahan* heeled, another heavy blow shook her fo'c'sle, but most of the shot churned the water in front of her, where she would've been. *Grik're getting* way *too good at this,* he thought, troubled by the implications. *If we'd been on the open sea, in a battle line instead of a knife fight, it could've been even worse.*

He saw one of the Jap-Grik bombers burst into flames and fall, but also noticed something very strange. There was a gaggle of pursuit planes after them as they turned back toward the fight, but the one that fell—then another one!—actually had several Jap-Grik *fighters* between them and the chasing P1-Cs! The Fleashooters got one of those, but a *third* bomber staggered out of the formation . . . which *looked* like it was making a torpedo run on the remaining Grik BBs! That didn't make any sense at all.

"Cap-i-taan!" cried the talker. "We're gettin' . . . screwy traans-missions, sayin' they're Jaaps—on our side!" Matt blinked, then strode to the talker as the salvo buzzer rang again and the guns roared. "Give me your headset! Who's this?" he demanded in the microphone, trailing the cord behind him as he stepped back out on the wing to watch the attack.

"This is General of the Sky Hideki Muriname," came a static-scratched, accented voice, "formerly of the Japanese Imperial Navy. Do I have the honor of addressing Captain Reddy?"

"Yeah."

"Then allow me to quickly state my purpose." At that moment, torpedoes dropped from the seven remaining twin-engine planes, and they pulled up and scattered, several fighters and maybe a dozen P1s after them. "I would never have served the Grik if given a choice, and will no longer, regardless of your decision." All seven torpedoes exploded against the side of the last two Grik BBs. Two hit one and five hit the other. That one exploded under a tall column of rising smoke and debris. All four were now either sunk or sinking, and that left only five cruisers to deal with. One of those was already a drifting wreck. "But I hope," the voice continued with an added tone of satisfaction, "that now, at last, I can return to the path of honor and serve *you*—along with whatever remains of my bombers after this day."

"I'll have to think about that," Matt said rather lamely. This was the last thing he'd ever expected to happen. *I'll also have to have a long talk with Sandra about this Muriname,* he decided.

"I understand your hesitation," the voice agreed, "but would appreciate it if, for the moment, you will instruct your fighters to focus on the planes trying to destroy my bombers. Not all my pilots—and some are Grik—made the same decision as I."

"What? That you were on the losing side?"

"Not at all, and there isn't time to explain. Let it suffice for now that for the very first time since I came to this world I actually *had* a choice and picked your cause. Others did not, and I can't speak for them. But"—Muriname's voice was increasingly anxious—"the number of light bombers and trained pilots I can give you is dwindling as we speak."

That was certainly true. "All right, I'll call off my 'Cats, but you'll fly due east—under escort—until you come to an airstrip on the south bank of the river mouth. Land there and sit in your planes until you're told what to do."

"Of course, Captain Reddy, and thank you. I will be glad to refuel and rearm—with something—and return to the fight."

"No. Just do as you're told, and we'll talk later." Matt paused. "And if any of your planes try to go anywhere *but* the airstrip, we'll shoot you all down."

"I understand," Muriname said.

Matt handed the headset back to the talker. "Get COFO Tikker on the horn and tell him to lay off the Jap bombers. Kill the fighters but protect the bombers, then escort 'em to Tassanna's airstrip."

"What the hell's goin on?" Rosen asked, chain of command momentarily blown away by his astonishment.

"The damnedest thing," Matt replied, shaking his head. "What shape's *Ellie* in?"

"The same as us," replied a signal-'Cat on the port bridgewing. "Light caa-sul-tees an' some big holes shot in her, but no serious dam-aage."

"Good." Matt's eyes strayed to the unrecognizable heap of twisted, fire-blackened junk that had been *Santa Catalina*, then swept to the wreckage closest to the south bank of the river. Four Grik BBs were stacked up there, one burning furiously, one gone, and two settling on their sides amid great clouds of steam. Beyond was *Arracca* and *Itaa*—and what was left of the forlorn hope that came upriver in the first place to salvage the entire war and maybe save them all. God only knew how much it cost. "We'll both come about and finish the cruisers so *Tara* and *Sular* can start getting people ashore to expand our beachhead—and finally bring some relief to the ones who gave it to us."

It didn't take long. *Mahan*'s and *Ellie*'s greater speed and maneuverability, as well as the Grik cruisers' dogged determination to maintain a tight line of battle, allowed Matt and Perry Brister to dodge broadsides and keep their distance while they systematically pulverized the Grik ships with rapid salvos from their much more accurate guns and improved armor-piercing shells. When the Grik squadron was reduced to creeping, smoke-streaming hulks, Matt ordered them finished with torpedoes—certainly overkill at that point—but Matt was in a hurry. Even as the last cruiser's expanding cloud of debris was still splashing in the water, he turned to Tiaa-Baari, who'd joined him on the bridge. "Do we still have any boats that'll float?"

Tiaa blinked reflectively, tail swishing slightly. "The ship's caar-penters haave been working on them all morning—or were until the aaction begaan. The port side motor launch haad been plugged, but was demolished by the shot thaat disabled the number two torpedo mount. The whaleboat was never badly daam-aged, how-ever, an' was repaired first. I looked at it on the way for-waard an' it seems fine."

"Very well. Call away the whaleboat. I'm going ashore." He smiled at Tiaa. "*Mahan* is yours, Commander." He shrugged. "She always was, by rights, and I appreciate the loan. Take care of her."

CHAPTER
32

Second General Ign and Ker-noll Jash gazed out at the wreckage of their division. Both knew it wasn't as bad as it seemed, since the troops had scattered, as ordered, when the enemy flying machines came. Since then, the planes had been drawn to the battle on the water, and they'd been largely ignored. Still, the devastation around them was bad enough, and a great many New Army warriors lay dead, crisped by flames, and the smell of roasted meat lay heavy in their snouts.

"We can still attack," Jash said almost dismally, yet pleased (he still lacked a more fitting word) that so many troops had regathered after their dispersal.

"First General Esshk only required that we launch another attack this morning, in coordination with the expected assault from the water, if it appeared likely to succeed," Ign grated. "It did, so we prepared." He took a long breath. "With our warships and the galley force destroyed, our own force in disarray, and all the enemy's flying machines free to focus entirely on us, should we attempt to proceed, further sacrifice is meaningless." Naxa and several other lower ranks had gathered round, but Ign looked only at Jash. "As I stressed yesterday, as even First General Esshk began to see, we must preserve as much of this force as we can. There are many New Army warriors, but few have faced the enemy as closely as you and survived. We will need the wisdom you earned." He gestured at the breastworks across the blackened, corpse-strewn field and saw the flags above them, the striped one with the starry blue field, and the green one with what looked like a broken ship painted on it in black.

Downriver, another monstrous flying-machine carrier, much like *Arracca*, and two other huge ships, one clearly rebuilt from one of their own greatships of battle, were approaching. All around them, smaller ships of indeterminate purpose streamed by. The two fast, sleek ships of steel had taken positions guarding against another Ghaarrichk'k sortie around the *nakkle* leg, but Ign knew, despite the still-vast fleet beyond, no such sortie would come. One ship at a time, squeezing past the wreckage there, could only add to it now. *Perhaps that's what we should do,* he reflected. *Block the passage completely—for now our positions are reversed.* He shook his head.

"Do you know why the enemy came as he did?" he asked.

"Of course," Jash replied. "He was desperate to stop the Final Swarm."

"Which he did," Ign stated brutally. "But still he comes. There will be more warriors aboard those large ships, and probably the small as well, *experienced* warriors—troops— that have fought our race before. They will be armed with many weapons such as the worst we have faced, and perhaps new things as well. And they come now not just to stop us but to destroy us all. They will *end* the Race and all that we are if they can, just as we tried to do to them."

"All the more reason to attack!" Naxa blurted, but then flattened his short crest in abject apology for his impertinence.

"No," Ign denied, "we must gird ourselves for their inevitable attack." He waved at the hasty trenches. They hadn't saved everyone, of course, even those who hadn't ventured into the open, but they'd helped. "And we must dig," Ign said. "We must prepare better trenches—deeper, longer, better defended from the air—and we must dig them in their hundreds, all the way from here to Sofesshk itself." He briefly closed his eyes. "Perhaps even beyond." He looked back at Jash, and when he spoke again, his voice held a trace of irony. "So, you did not 'miss the battle' after all. Tell me: Did you learn as much as I hope?"

"Yes, Lord General. I believe so."

"Good. Because the time for thoughtless attack, for the sake of attack, is over if our race is to survive. And it seems the greatest battle that ever was is about to begin."

"I'm sorry about Risa, Gutfeld, all the rest. So many!" Matt said dismally. "We came as fast as we could."

Chack merely nodded, but his tail was like a whip, snapping back and forth. "But you did come, as you said you would," he replied, "and maany still live because of it." The tiny foothold Tassanna's desperate decision established had rapidly expanded during the day as, completely ignoring the "plan," the expeditionary force immediately started landing in the order it arrived. *Tarakaan Island* spawned Nat Hardee's MTB squadron again to beef up their security and patrol capacity, and start marking the numerous less visible wrecks as best it could. *Tara* then nudged as close into the shallows as she dared. Safir Maraan and most of her II Corps crowded ashore at once. Safir's reunion with Chack had been joyous but bittersweet, surrounded by the tumult and chaos of disembarking troops and equipment, but absent so many—especially Risa. Only after *Tara* backed away and turned directly downstream—Matt wanted her back under the umbrella of Leedom's and Tikker's pursuit planes at Arracca Field (that name now official) and away from any possible rocket attacks—were I Corps and General Pete Alden able to land in *Sular*'s motor dories. Some of the dories and *Arracca*'s seven surviving launches then carried Tassanna and the wounded out to *Salissa*, which would leave the following day and revert from battering ram to aircraft carrier once again. Besides, she'd need *Tara*'s attention to whatever damage she'd taken that they could get to. III Corps would be brought in by those same dories from the smaller ships, but only after enough space could be made and the perimeter sufficiently expanded and improved. The primarily Austraalan construction battalions would be very busy for a time.

Pete and Safir, of course, wanted to immediately drive

the Grik that recon flights reported retreating from the nearest trench, but Matt vetoed that, seconded—to his surprise—by Rolak. Rolak calmly reasoned that any force chasing the Grik now would be disorganized, unprepared, and next to impossible to support until they got the mess here sorted out. And given the evidence of trenches and Chack's confirmation that these Grik were *soldiers*, not a fleeing mob, such a pursuit would be dangerously exposed. Instead, beneath a sun that was setting on the first official day of the Allied invasion of the Grik homeland, within a bubble that formed in the middle of all the tremendous activity required to land thousands of troops and thousands of tons of equipment, munitions, and supplies, there was relative peace for the larger reunion of many old friends.

Pam, even wearier than when Silva saw her that morning, was preparing to go out to *Salissa* as well. For now, she gravitated to Silva's side, despite the eyes on them, and he had to practically hold her up. Sandra, with considerable awkwardness, considering her advanced condition, had come out from *Big Sal* with Keje. He, along with Diania, practically fluttered around her in concern before Matt could embrace her and take her hand in his. Somewhat shyly, Diania then moved to stand near Gunny Horn, who, just as touchingly shy, couldn't take his eyes off her.

Perry Brister came ashore from *James Ellis*, leaving Ronson Rodriguez in command while *Ellie* and *Mahan* shelled the Grik battery on the north bank and the MTBs scouted the blockage at the river bend. Even Abel Cook managed to attend, accompanied by Enrico Galay. Cook's wounds were mainly painful burns on his torso and a few rocket-shrapnel fragments from the same blast that had severed his hose. Lawrence, of course, stood at Silva's side, opposite Pam. Many others, including 1st Division's General Taa-Leen, 6th Division's General Grisa, and Colonel Saachic of the 1st Cavalry Brigade, had come and gone, to pay their respects or just say hello, but there was a great deal to do and they'd all have to get at it.

The first discussions of dispositions and requirements

past, the group settled into an awkward but necessary near silence while they simply absorbed one another's welcome presence—and the enormity of what had passed and what they were about to embark upon. Inevitably, perhaps, Petey shattered the moment. "Eat *now*! Goddamn!"

Silva thumped him on the head. "Silence in the ranks, you little turd. I got nothin' for ya yet."

"Eaaat!" Petey pleaded.

"Really, Chief Silva," Sandra scolded fondly, "you shouldn't neglect your faithful pets so." She offered Petey a piece of the crunchy, sweet biscuit the army practically subsisted on in the field, which tasted like hardtack flavored with pumpkin and molasses. It exploded in a cloud of crumbs when Petey took it.

"Ol' Larry don't bellyache about it," Silva countered.

Lawrence hissed. "I *not* your . . . goddan' haithhul het!"

Silva looked at Matt. "I gotta say, that last part o' the fight was pretty weird . . . Japs killin' Griks, an' Japs killin' Japs. Chackie caught some of it on the radio. What're you gonna do with Murry-nammy?"

Matt glanced at Sandra, at the indecision on her face. He'd left that up to her, since she knew Muriname better than anyone, even Gunny Horn, and had a better feel for his character. "We'll have to see," he temporized. "He did bring us those six torpedo bombers—plus two more and two fighters that weren't in the attack." He smiled slightly. "We may also wind up with *Amagi*'s old Type Ninety-five floatplane. Muriname had it flown to Zanzibar, but there's nobody there. Spanky and *Walker* already left a couple of days ago. Jumbo's going to send a Clipper up with some fuel." He brightened. "Colonel Mallory, Tikker, and Leedom are excited about the bombers. We've been working on our own, of course, but these might give us a leg up—and they're already here, where we can use them."

"It'll take longer to decide if we can use Muriname and his people," Sandra said. Then she winced, and Matt looked at her with concern, pulling her closer. She'd seemed uncomfortable ever since she came ashore. *It won't be long before our baby comes,* he realized. *Please, God, don't let it be here. And let it inherit peace!*

"Hang Muriname," Pete Alden growled, staring out at the jumble of wrecks, near and far. "Pretty damn convenient how he showed up after we didn't need him."

Matt wasn't so sure about that. There'd still been two BBs and six cruisers, a heavy load for *Mahan* and *Ellie* alone. And just one lucky hit apiece from those big Grik guns could've tipped the scale. "It was a mess," he decided aloud, "but it worked. Somehow it worked. We're established here now, and just as important, the Army of the Republic made it across the Ungee River." He smiled at the surprised expressions. Few knew that yet. "They'll be coming up from the south"—he nodded at Pete, Safir, and Rolak—"and we'll start figuring out how to push the Grik from here." He hesitated, smile fading. "Don't get too excited. We've all been through a lot, but I think our hardest fighting is still to come. Everybody agrees the Grik are finally getting wise, and their rockets were an unpleasant surprise. Who knows what else they'll come up with? We know from experience that desperation can breed brilliance. So stay on your toes."

An excited comm-'Cat approached, accompanied by a familiar, ancient Lemurian Marine.

"Why, there you are, Moe, you old scamp!" Silva exclaimed. "I thought you was a goner. How come you didn't come play with me, Larry, an' Arnie? I thought we was pals."

"I didn't waant to get dead," Moe replied. "'Sides, Major Cook needed me more thaan you. I'm *his* first sergeant."

"Surs," the comm-'Cat interjected urgently, trying to hand Matt a message form. "Col-nol Maallory reports from Arracca Field!"

Matt waved the form away even though, based on the 'Cat's happy blinking, it might not contain bad news for once. "Just tell us."

"Sur! The Col-nol begs to report thaat the cruiser USS *Fitzhugh Graay* haas aarived."

Covered by the pleased exclamations, Silva leaned toward Lawrence and whispered, "Right on time, huh?"

The comm-'Cat was waving the form. "But thaat's not all! She's not aa-lone!"

"*Walker*?" Matt guessed hopefully. He'd been following Spanky's progress but hadn't expected his ship for another day or two. *She must be in top shape for Spanky to push her,* he thought.

The comm-'Cat looked a little crestfallen, but perked up. "Yeah! *Waa-kur*'s here—an' some-teeng else!"

"I'll be damned," Silva whispered at Horn this time. "First fight *Walker*'s ever missed. Just as well, an' I'll be glad to see her. B'leve I'm ready to get back in the Navy War." Pam poked him in the ribs—his wounded ribs—with her elbow, but the blow didn't have its usual enthusiasm behind it either.

Matt was impatient now. "*What* else?"

"A sub-maa-reen! A *Ger-maan* sub-maa-reen!" the 'Cat proclaimed triumphantly. "It surrendered to *Waa-kur*! Just popped up on the waater right in front of her with a white flaag already tied to the . . ." He looked at the message.

"Periscope shears?" Matt prompted, amazed.

"Yeah! I mean, yes, sur."

"What did her cap-i-taan say?" Rolak asked.

"Her cap-i-taan, not much, but another maan's in chaarge an' says he's known to Cap-i-taan Reddy." The 'Cat looked at the form again. "Waal-burt Feedler? Says he's been trying to surrender for a while, but keeps gettin' shot at!"

Everyone went silent as they all exchanged glances. Cook, Galay, and Moe might not know what had passed between the Alliance and Oberleuitnant Walbert Fiedler of the League of Tripoli, but everyone else did now.

"I'll be damned," Matt said, eyes wide. He didn't know what Fiedler was up to or how he, a pilot, had gotten on the sub, but he immediately worried what news he might have. *It would have to be something big for him to bolt the League entirely—and bring a whole sub's crew with him,* he thought. "I'm kind of anxious to hear what Fiedler has to say for himself," he understated dryly.

"I'll be damned too," Silva said. "In one day we got Japs surrenderin' to us, now Krauts. The war's as good as won!" He sobered when he saw the excitement wane and knew his stupid crack was what killed it. Chack's arm tightened around Safir Maraan and his gaze shifted glumly to the first funeral pyres already burning. Risa wasn't on one yet but would be soon—and there'd be many, many more. "Hey, Arnie," he asked Horn. "What day's today, anyway?"

"January first or second—I think. Hard to keep track. But no earlier."

"The first," Sandra confirmed, "and Chief Silva's right. It's hard to imagine now, but things are looking up." Her hand rested on her swollen belly and she looked up at Matt with a tender smile. "It's a whole new year, full of new beginnings, and if the war isn't 'as good as won,' it's farther from being lost than it's ever been. I thank God for that, and I'm grateful to all those we've lost who brought us to this point." She turned to face the others, and her voice turned hard. "Now, as I promised Adar as he was dying in my arms, let's finish the job!"

*////// The Palace of Vanished Gods
Old Sofesshk*

"*D*o not concern yourself: the prey will *never* tread the soil of the sacred city," First General Esshk told the newly elevated Celestial Mother. He'd risked a flight in the black airship shortly after dark and arrived at the palace to find his nominal ruler in a state of great apprehension, actually *pacing* outside with a harried-looking Chooser and her sister guards.

"But the Final Swarm was thwarted!" the Celestial Mother challenged. "Even now it straggles back in darkness, the warriors abandoning their galleys and fleeing ashore!"

"It was not *thwarted*, Giver of Life," Esshk defended, "merely repurposed, and the warriors do as I commanded. They do *not* flee! I beg you to consider: the Swarm was dispatched to cross the Go Away Strait and destroy the prey at the Celestial City." He paused and dramatically glanced about as if bewildered. "Yet even as it proceeded to do so, the prey came *here*! Never could I have imagined such a fortunate turn of events!"

"*Fortunate?*" the Celestial Mother demanded, amazed.

"Of course. They have served themselves up to us in our own lair! What prey ever did such a foolish thing?

As surprised as I by such abnormality, the Swarm was cast into some disarray," he conceded. "But now we can gather it upon the land, where proper battles are designed, and crush the prey at our leisure."

The Celestial Mother, her grand, young, coppery frill tentatively lying flat, finally stopped pacing and faced him. "Truly?" she asked. "My tutors who tell me of the past say nothing like this has ever happened."

"Of course it hasn't!" Esshk responded, deciding her tutors would probably have to be replaced. They'd been specifically warned against informing the new Celestial Mother that anything that happened—or anything Esshk did or told her—was in any way unusual. "Does the prey embrace the predator? Does it step blithely into its open mouth?"

The Celestial Mother looked away. "No," she said at last. "But there is much that makes no sense. . . . I wish I were older and knew more." She faced Esshk again. "And with you away so much and only the Chooser to counsel me, I sometimes cannot decide what to think."

What has that ridiculous Chooser said? Esshk wondered, glancing at the shorter creature at the Celestial Mother's side—now apparently trying to make himself even smaller and inconspicuous. "It is not for you to waste a single thought on," he assured. "Go inside. Rest. Eat. I must begin reorganizing the Swarm. The sooner that is done, the sooner we will devour the prey." He regarded the Chooser. "Come, Lord Chooser, I would consult with you—and there is one I would have you hear." He looked back at the Celestial Mother. "By your leave, Giver of Life?"

He hurried away with the Chooser in his wake, and as soon as the Celestial Mother and her entourage were out of earshot, Esshk hissed, "What nonsense have you been filling her head with?"

The Chooser's crest would've flattened in panic if he hadn't kept it rigid by artificial means. "Nothing! Her tutors . . ." He paused. "And distant as it has been, the flashing and smoke of battle has been visible at times. She questions." He took a few more breathless steps to keep up with Esshk's longer strides. "Who would you

have me hear?" he ventured. Esshk stopped abruptly
when they met a gathering of warriors and several . . .
other beings in the gloom. *Humans!* the Chooser
realized. *Japhs!*

"This is . . ." Esshk paused. "Tell me again what you
are called."

One of the men bowed. "I am Lieutenant Mitsuo
Ando. I was General of the Sky Muriname's executive
officer."

"Where is your lord?" Esshk demanded.

Ando hesitated. "I have no lord now but you."

Esshk grunted. "Muriname turned against us," he
explained to the Chooser, "but Ando remained loyal,
destroying or driving away others who went with Muriname. He has only a few flying machines left, but proposed a scheme that may have merit. You know more of
our ability to make weapons. Hear him."

"Very well," the Chooser said, looking at Ando. "What
will you say?"

"First, I must ask: Can you still build airships? I
understand the enemy destroyed some of your facilities
for doing so."

"We can and will," the Chooser declared, "though it
will take time to restore our capacity. And aircrews must
be trained."

Ando gestured to his companions. "We can help with
that. Another question: How many of the piloted bombs
remain?"

The Chooser glanced at Esshk. "Many, though few
have been retained ready for use. Your former lord considered them extremely wasteful in time to build them
and train their operators, particularly since our airships
can only carry one, and the enemy's ability to intercept
them improved. Ordinary bombs, in larger numbers,
were deemed more effective."

"Very true," Ando nodded. "But what if you could
put dozens, *hundreds* of piloted bombs in the air at once
without even risking your airships?"

"But . . ." The Chooser glanced at Esshk again. "How?"

Ando smiled. Unlike Muriname, he had no regard for
the lives of the Grik pilots he'd trained. The fact that none

he'd had in his fighters survived only proved they could never be as good as humans. Trusting them with *planes* had been a terrible waste of good machines. But Grik pilots were good enough for what he had in mind now. "You have flying bombs, plenty of potential pilots . . . and rockets to get them in the air. We will have to build bigger rockets and probably ramps or cradles to launch them from, but they should fly. Long enough, at least."

The Chooser gaped. "That can work!" he agreed enthusiastically, but his excitement quickly faded. "But perhaps only once. And the smaller, faster enemy ships that plague us so will be very hard to hit. With much of the war to come likely confined to land, they might just leave."

"The enemy will still have to supply his army," Ando disagreed. "And supply ships are *not* hard to hit. Besides, you still have a powerful fleet on the lakes. For the enemy to advance, he must counter your ability to bombard his troops onshore. He will still need his navy, and with piloted rocket bombs and more airships, you can still destroy it."

The Chooser looked thoughtful. "What will we call this new weapon and those that use it? Something so ingenious should have a name."

"May I have the honor of considering that?" Ando asked.

Esshk looked at him. "*If* it works, you will be the new General of the Sky. Naming the weapon you devised will be up to you."

At the Mouth of the Zambezi

The German (League) submarine *U-112* rode at anchor just offshore from Arracca Field in the broad fan of the Zambezi River. It was a very large Type XIB boat, inspired by the same design philosophy as the French submarine the Allies sank after it attacked their raiding force headed for Madagascar more than half a year before. With a length of 115 meters and breadth of 9.5, it was longer than USS *Walker*, anchored to port, and probably as heavy as the new Allied cruiser lying to starboard. Amazingly, *U-112* was almost as heavily armed as the cruiser as well, fitted with four 127-mm (5″) guns mounted in two twin turrets positioned forward and aft of the conn tower. The tower itself sported two 37-mm and two 20-mm antiaircraft guns. Of course, its most lethal weapons could be fired from four torpedo tubes in the bow and two more in the stern. Capable of more than twenty-five knots on the surface and with its tough pressure hull protecting essential running gear, it was more like a submersible light cruiser than a typical U-boat. To support that role, it was equipped with a cramped, watertight compartment intended to accommodate a folding Arado AR 231 floatplane for scouting purposes, but the 231 turned out to be a piece of junk, and nothing else was ever built to fit. Ultimately, the space was used to augment the boat's already respectable fuel capacity and further expand its impressive range.

For all that, *U-112* hadn't been a very successful design. It was slow and difficult to trim underwater (also similar to its French counterpart in that respect), and several damaging bumps from large, inquisitive predators hadn't helped. Just as significant, few of its class were ever made, and even fewer spare parts for its unusual features were aboard the tenders meant to support the multinational fascist fleet that somehow wound up on this . . . different Earth to become the League of Tripoli nearly six years before. And those years of diminishing maintenance and long clandestine deployments hadn't been kind. Probably one of the reasons the League had essentially written it off—along with its crew of a hundred German sailors.

Oberleuitnant Kurt Hoffman leaned on the conn-tower rail, staring at the new cruiser in the gathering dusk. None of its main guns were pointed at them, but Hoffman had no doubt they were being watched very closely. For that reason, and the fact that he and Oberleuitnant Walbert Fiedler were expected aboard that ship very shortly, he'd donned his least battered khaki jacket and least crushed black-brimmed, white-topped hat. Fiedler, placed aboard by the passing *Leopardo* and its oiler—the last time *U-112* had been able to fuel—was dressed much the same, in the best they could come up with. Like everyone aboard, both had beards, though Hoffman's was red and Fiedler's was a dark blond.

"Most impressive that they could build something like that in so short a time," Hoffman said, nodding at the cruiser.

"Very," Fiedler agreed neutrally, "though by itself, it's sadly inadequate for what lies before it."

"Still," Hoffman said, almost bitterly, "we have added nothing half as significant to our forces in the even longer time we have been on this world."

"*We* are not the League anymore, Kurt," Fiedler reminded forcefully, then sighed. "And the League did not have to. Merely maintaining what it already has requires almost as much industry as it took to build that." Of course the League *couldn't* maintain everything and had no intention to. Particularly less valuable (and reliable) assets like *U-112*. Oh, Hoffman had been assured that help would come, but everyone knew how empty that promise was. And in the meantime, *U-112*'s bunkers were almost dry in the middle of an ocean that was hostile both above and below, and they were virtually out of food. Combined with its crew's dissatisfaction with the League in general and Walbert Fiedler's persuasive arguments, surrender and asylum became the only option.

"And the most significant thing the Allies have accomplished is their Alliance itself," Fiedler continued. "We will not be trusted at first," he cautioned. "We can hardly blame them for that. But we will eventually be accepted."

"Among so many different peoples . . . so many races," Hoffman murmured dubiously.

Fiedler laughed. "There are just as many peoples and odd races in the League," he reminded. "The only difference here is the status of those races." He turned serious. "Do *not* make the mistake that these nonhumans are *Untermensch* of any sort. Many of their leaders are not human."

Hoffman frowned, and Fiedler knew he and many of

the crew might find that hard to accept. "Subhuman" races and species in the League weren't persecuted as they'd begun to be in Germany before it entered the Confédértion États Souverains, but they weren't equals, and certainly had no power. Hoffman was probably wondering again whether they'd done the right thing.

"What were we supposed to do, Kurt?" Fiedler demanded. "We were *abandoned*—just as the League will disdain the entire German contingent as soon as it is no longer needed. You forget: I was alone with Gravois for a long time. His attitude was clear and reflects that of the Triumvirate's leadership. At the same time they fear us and seek to control us, they scorn us because we are relatively few. The French will marginalize the Spanish next, though I can't see them succeeding with the Italians, but we Germans are already becoming *Untermensch* in the League ourselves, in terms of authority."

Hoffman grunted. "You know this Kapitan Reddy so well? He will not make us fight our own people?"

Fiedler shook his head. "I cannot say that with certainty now, with the news we bring. It is actually probably a good thing we were sufficiently forgotten that we could still eavesdrop on secure League communications," he mused. "But this alliance between the League and Dominion—you cannot *imagine* the depravity of the Dominion—is more shameful than the assistance we gave Kurokawa. I shall oppose *anyone*, even Germans, who would fight to support such a union. But unlike the members of the Triumvirate, even our German leaders yapping for scraps around the bigger table, Kapitan Reddy is a man of honor."

Now Hoffman sighed. A motor launch was approaching from USS *Fitzhugh Gray*'s side. "So, how much will you tell them?"

Fiedler looked at him. "This time? *We* will tell them everything, and promise our full support. We have no choice, and *our* honor demands that we choose a side at last. To our credit, I think, we have done so—regardless of the privation that forced our hand. Yet we cannot now pick and choose to what *degree* we will do the honorable thing. Kapitan Reddy will smell the League on us like excrement if we try, and he will never trust us. What good can we possibly be to our people then?"

Hoffman nodded at the cruiser again. "So, even so weak, you think they—*we*—might prevail?"

Fiedler frowned and turned to look at *Walker*. Even repaired from her most recent damage, she still looked battered and worn. But he knew what she'd been through and what she'd accomplished. Still . . . "In all honesty, I can't see how. Then again, what our new friends lack in combat power, they more than make up for in courage, determination, ingenuity." His frown faded and became a grin. "And luck! You are a U-boat commander in the deadliest sea mankind has ever known. Surely you must believe in luck above all things!"

Army of the Republic
North Soala
Ungee River

General Marcus Kim, Inquisitor Choon, and Courtney Bradford, accompanied by a mounted security detail, found the 23rd Legion's tired pickets guarding a fairly clear street in a largely intact portion of northwest Soala. A few thatch-roof buildings still smoldered where Cantets had dropped firebombs to support the twelve legions (including the 23rd and 1st, which reinforced), but beyond the safe range of the Republic's indirect fire capacity, the battle had degenerated into a hovel to hovel—often hand-to-hand—infantry fight through the mazelike warren of two-and three-story adobe buildings. One of the sentries scampered to collect Bekiaa-Sab-At. He returned with her quicker than expected, along with Meek and Bele.

"Legate Bekiaa, Prefect Bele, Optio Meek," General Kim said, nodding a greeting. "I'm glad to see you all well."

Courtney Bradford peered at them more closely in the dim light of the picket's lantern. They were alive, but he wasn't sure they were well. All were covered in dust, caked on the blood and sweat beneath. Bekiaa looked worst of all, her fur thickly matted and her rhino-pig armor, which hadn't collected as much dust, splashed with dark, dry blood. She moved slowly, stiffly, and her eyes were bleary. She looked like she'd been sleeping nearby and the sentry woke her.

"You look terrible, my dear," Courtney said, concerned.

"Thaanks," Bekiaa replied wryly. "I must've conked out," she added, confirming their suspicions. "See, there was this nice, soft pile of rubble, an' I couldn't help myself."

Kim chuckled, something he hadn't been able to do after the army's last battle. "We won't keep you from your rest very long. You've certainly earned it. I'm told that your attack in the enemy's rear, in company with the First Legion, provided a much-needed distraction from the flanking force. You have been commended by General Modius—again. I think he is much taken with you."

"He's a good maan," Bekiaa said.

"An' savin' his arse is becomin' a habit," Meek added sourly.

"Optio!" Choon snapped, but Kim raised his hand and gently waved the admonition away. Everyone knew Meek was no mere optio. He'd originally been assigned to Bekiaa by Choon himself—not to spy, exactly, but certainly to keep an eye on her. She'd since earned his wholehearted support.

"I believe Optio Meek was enjoying a well-deserved nap as well, Inquisitor," Kim said. "We will all need rest before we pursue the enemy."

"Which we need to get at as quick as we can," Courtney agreed grimly before continuing in a more customary, animated tone. "We just heard via wireless that First Fleet and its expeditionary force have not only stopped the Grik attack down the Zambezi, but two corps have already landed east of Sofesshk." He frowned. "*Un*fortunately, the blocking force was badly mauled. Worse, though we expected it, the Grik can now focus all their vast forces on General Alden on their own land, close to their base of supply—unless we keep some of those forces occupied." He removed his sombrero and mopped sweat off his forehead with a rag. "Quickly, aggressively pursuing the army we defeated here should have that effect."

Bekiaa was nodding. "Yeah. Preferably before they haave a chaance to shake off their scare an' get their aact together," she mused, her tail swishing now as she became more alert and animated as well.

"It will take a few days to reorganize the army," Choon said, thinking aloud. "It was not too badly damaged this time, but there is great confusion. Now that we control the Ungee River, we can establish this city as *our* new base of supply. We expended a great deal of ordnance, and some, at least, must be replaced. Perhaps General Taal's cavalry can continue to harass the enemy, keep them moving past defensible positions..."

"Gener-aal Taal caan't do it alone," Bekiaa countered. "He'll need weight behind him." She gestured around. "The Grik paanicked at first, but controlled it—I saw." She looked at Courtney. "There was no widespread Grik rout. They didn't just run away; they regrouped, orgaanized a rear guard here, an' retreated in a relaa-tively orderly fashion, considering the pasting Taal an' the Caan-tets gave 'em." She looked thoughtful. "Pretty daamn impressive, aactually."

"Indeed," Courtney said, nodding. "Our friends in the north evaluated the enemy performance much the same." He looked at Kim. "The Army of the Republic is across the Ungee River, but there are more rivers ahead, in rough country. Beyond, and before we can hope to link up with General Alden, there's a dreadfully flat and open plain. That may be to our advantage," he conceded, "or very possibly not. I sincerely doubt the Grik—*these* Grik—will so woefully underestimate this army again."

Puerto del Cielo

Capitaine de Fregate Victor Gravois stared moodily out at the great stone fort at the mouth of the River of Heaven. *Leopardo* had been obliged to remain at anchor there for an entire week, awaiting final sailing orders from Contrammiraglio Oriani. This after her excruciatingly long (if well-fed) stay on Lago de Vida at New Granada, while Gravois and Don Hernan finalized the treaty of alliance—and came to their own understanding. *At least I* think *we have an understanding,* Gravois admitted gloomily. He didn't trust Don Hernan, and the irony that he'd finally met someone even more devious, cunning, and ambitious never struck him. But he was . . . uncomfortable with the arrangement they'd made, since so much of their hidden agenda relied on Gravois's machinations within the League—maneuvers he'd never survive if they were discovered—and Don Hernan faced virtually no risk at all. Still, he was confident he could deal with the OVRA, and there were many he could recruit to his cause. Finally, of course, he was going home at last, preparing to reenter his own environment, where the players and rampant intrigues were as familiar as his own hand. *Now,* he snapped to himself, clasping his hands behind him, *if only Oriani will stop dawdling and release me from this mosquito-infested wilderness, I can return to the comforts of my villa by the sea from which I can lay the groundwork for my bigger plans.*

"Capitaine Gravois," Capitano Ciano said, moving to join him by the rail. His voice was neutral, but when Gravois looked, he could see Ciano's lips were twisted in an expression of disgust. Less than a kilometer away, several small bundles still smoldered beneath the charred crosses on the beach. In the seven days *Leopardo* had been at anchor, they'd been "treated" to the spectacle of group crucifixions and burnings at the base of the great stone fort five separate times. Even to members of the League of Tripoli, hardened to the necessity of barbarity by their conquest of the Mediterranean, the depravity of the Dominion was hard to bear. The crew was most affected, but Ciano was obviously starting to feel the strain. "I cannot imagine why we are so desperate for allies that we must soil ourselves so," Ciano murmured.

"Things will change," Gravois replied cryptically, then caught himself. He liked Ciano and considered him a candidate for inclusion in his plot, but the time wasn't right. "The Dominion, by association with the League, will learn more civilized behavior," he explained more safely.

"I wonder if that's possible," Ciano responded darkly, "or if the opposite is more likely true." He turned to Gravois and faced him. "We have our orders at last," he said.

"Good. How soon can we sail?"

Ciano hesitated, and if anything, his expression turned more bitter. "As soon as we fuel. We will then leave the oiler and carry the treaty to Ascension Island. Oriani will forward it to Tripoli along with our recommendation—as his own, no doubt—that substantial naval forces be prepared for deployment here to safeguard our ally's control of the strategic passage to the Pacific. *Leopardo*, along with you and I, will then return to Puerto del Cielo"—he sent a shuddering glance back at the beach—"where we will stand by for further instructions or further opportunities to consult with Don Hernan, at his convenience."

A white-hot fury rose in Gravois's breast and he struggled mightily to contain it. "How long?" he managed to ask.

"I have no idea," Ciano practically snarled, yanking his hat from his head and running fingers through his sweaty hair. He was angrier than Gravois had ever seen him. As angry as Gravois himself. "You know the state our capital ships are in; maintenance is so often neglected, and they've rarely ventured past the strait of Gibraltar. Months, at least, I suspect," he spat, clenching his fists and glaring at the charred crosses. "More months here, watching *that*. I always knew Oriani was a *pezzo di merda*, but never expected him to stoop this low. Damn him! Damn the OVRA. And damn the League that allows creatures like him to thrive!"

It took Gravois several moments to contain his own rage; this would certainly complicate things. . . . Or would it? He practically felt his mind shift gears and start racing with new plans, new schemes. *With a significant percentage of the fleet here, away from the League and largely commanded by men I know, men as dissatisfied with the Triumvirate as I and possibly open to . . . alternatives . . . my ultimate plan might actually be* easier *to effect.* He looked at Ciano, still simmering beside him. *I can even test that theory,* he realized, *and now might be the perfect time, after all.*

"Yes," he murmured. "Damn the League."

South of El Paso del Fuego

"Colonel Sister Audry! Major Blas!" came the rather annoying voice of Governor-Empress Rebecca Anne McDonald's aide, Lieutenant Ezekial Krish. Blas groaned, wondering if Rebecca sent Krish to pester her or to inflict her on Krish. She was pretty sure Rebecca was her friend, but either could be the case.

"Over here," Sister Audry called, beckoning. Krish and several other members of Rebecca's personal guard trotted their horses, each leading another, back down the column of weary Marines, Vengadores, and Jaguar Warriors struggling up yet another steep grade. The whole country was nothing but hills and mountains, Blas reflected, an uncomfortable number of which were active volcanoes. "Colonel Garcia and Captain's Ixtli and Bustos are with us as well," Audry reminded reproachfully. Krish tended to disregard them, and she wouldn't have it.

Krish's face reddened as he saluted. "Of course. I brought enough horses for you all. General Shinya desires that you join him at an overlook near the front of the column."

"Where?" Audry asked, and Krish pointed near the top of the peak they were winding up the side of. Audry glanced worriedly at Blas. Lemurians didn't do well where the air was thin. "Isn't that a bit high?" she asked.

Krish smiled condescendingly. "Not nearly as high as we have been. It just looks so because the lowlands here are almost at sea level."

"How *smaart* you are, Mr. Krish," Blas mocked, raising her gaze to the promontory he'd indicated. "C'mon," she said, "at least thaat one's not smokin' an' throwin' fire around." She looked back at Sergeant Koratin. "Why don't you come? One horse'll carry us both." She really wanted Koratin's input on the campaign, especially in front of Shinya, but Koratin just shook his head. Blas shrugged. "Okaay. Keep 'em movin'. If you let 'em stop, they'll stiffen up an' you'll never get 'em goin' again.'"

X Corps' advance had slowed to a crawl, taking far longer to negotiate these mountains than the higher, harder ones they'd traversed before. But X Corps was worn down and everyone knew they were marching toward, potentially, the bloodiest confrontation they'd ever had with the Doms. Blas figured they'd lost a couple hundred troops to straggling every day. Many caught up but some didn't, and the army was bleeding out even before the fight.

They mounted and followed Krish up the winding columns of tired men and 'Cats. Sooner than expected, just around a jagged spur, was a relatively flat mountain meadow where the leading regiments were already spreading out, making camp. Krish led them up a narrow path to a craggy outcrop a hundred feet above the meadow, where they found Shinya, Rebecca, Saan-Kakja, and General Blair. Much to their surprise, none of the other regimental or even division commanders were there.

"Good afternoon," General Tomatsu Shinya greeted them crisply, while Rebecca and Saan-Kakja embraced Audry and Blas. They warmly welcomed Garcia, Ixtli, and Bustos as well. Blas gazed at the stunning view to the northwest. Several smoking mountains stood on both sides of what looked like a wide bay, the late-day sun shimmering on the water. It wasn't a bay, however, and they were among the first Allied personnel to view the almost mystical Pass of Fire from the ground. Even at this distance, perhaps fifteen miles, her sharp eyes saw sprawling villages all around the water, more ships than could be counted—their masts intermingled—and a very densely populated area largely surrounded by tall, zigzagging walls glowing bright white in the sun's final rays. *That must be El Coraa-zon an' the fort the flyboys described,* she thought, *where Gener-aal May-taa an' his aarmy is waitin'.*

"Where's everybody else?" she asked, looking at General Blair.

Shinya didn't allow him to respond. "You've all seen

the maps we've compiled, based on those we captured," he said. "They're constantly updated by scouts"—he nodded at Ixtli and Bustos—"and aerial reconnaissance." He frowned. "Those updates are essential, and you'll start seeing them daily now because this General Mayta is an industrious man. He continually strengthens the defenses around El Corazon and changes the dispositions of his troops." He shook his head. "But maps never give the full effect, and this place allows us a panorama of the ground itself that we won't likely see again. Look upon it and commit it to memory as best you can." He handed Blas an Imperial telescope, but she glared at him and passed it to Audry. Her naked eyes were almost as good, and Audry was their colonel, after all. Audry took a brief look and then handed the telescope to Garcia.

"As you know and now see, our objective could be difficult," Shinya continued. "Mayta's force is believed to be larger than Tenth and Eleventh Corps combined. The fleet remaining at his disposal is also larger than originally thought, and we must assume it's been improved in some way. Observation planes have reported little interference by Grikbirds of late, but that doesn't mean there aren't many here. It could only mean Mayta doesn't care what we see—or *wants* us to see certain things." He blinked dissatisfaction in the Lemurian way. "Honestly, I'm inclined to take our time and develop a careful strategy. Too much remains unknown and the stakes are enormously high. Add the fact that El Corazon is not lightly named. It's the heart of the western Dominion, possibly second only to New Granada itself, and is also the heart of the enemy's control of this side of the Pass of Fire. I suspect they'll defend it . . . fanatically."

He took a deep breath and glanced at Governor-Empress Rebecca. "Unfortunately, we don't have as much time as I would wish. A representative of the NUS now with Second Fleet has confirmed collusion between the Dominion and the League of Tripoli, obviously—to me—because of the strategic importance of the pass. Bad enough that the Doms should have it, but backed by the League, they could hold it against us forever. That would prevent any possible cooperation between us and our

NUS allies." He smiled wryly. "They're understandably anxious about that, since they'd then be alone, at the mercy of the Doms and the League. They're adamant that we strike at once and are preparing to attack the east side of the pass with their fleet, while landing a ground force of their own at the mouth of the river leading to the very heart of the Dominion." He blinked dubiously. "This in spite of some inconclusive but troubling observations made during Captain Garrett's bold scout in his prize, *Matarife*."

"I don't like it either," Rebecca said, "but we are running out of time, and the NUS is determined to eliminate the Dom threat before the League can become a significant factor." Her small voice hardened. "So am I. Simultaneously with the NUS attack from the east, High Admiral Jenks and Second Fleet will also strike there"— she pointed at distant El Corazon—"landing another entire corps. They will land every Marine from every ship if they must," she added grimly. "We, on the other hand, as has long been planned, will support the landing with an attack on El Corazon from the landward side." She managed a small smile. "None of this is news to any of you, and I'm sure it's well known to the enemy as well by now. That's why you, the leaders of the Sister's Own, are here."

"Over time, each regiment and each division in the army has asked for the honor of leading the attack on the Pass of Fire when it comes," Shinya said, looking into every face. "But I brought you here alone to tell you first that the Sister's Own Division will not only lead the attack, as I promised, but you'll all be involved in planning it. Your division has the most combat experience in the army, and you all bring valuable and unique insights about the enemy to the planning table. We must combine them." His gaze finally fell on Blas. "And, unlike your experience at Fort Defiance, you must all be aware of every aspect of the plan we make if it's going to succeed."

For a moment, no one said anything; then Blas blinked amazement. "I'll be daamned!" she blurted. "Did you just *aa-pologize*?"

Shinya's frown deepened. "Take it as you will, but let

there be no mistake: we may well be facing the greatest battle ever fought in this hemisphere. We're unprepared, underequipped, and, even with reinforcements, we might be outnumbered." He glanced at Rebecca. "We also have very little time to remedy any of those things, so let's make the most of it."

CAST OF CHARACTERS

(L)—*Lemurian, or Mi-Anakka*
(G)—*Grik, or Ghaarrichk'k*
Lt. Cmdr. Matthew Patrick Reddy, USNR—CINCAF (Commander in Chief of All Allied Forces).

First Fleet Elements

USS *Walker* (DD-163)

Cmdr. Brad "Spanky" McFarlane—Minister of Naval Engineering.

Cmdr. Bernard Sandison—Torpedo Officer, Acting XO, Minister of Experimental Ordnance.

Cmdr. Toos-Ay-Chil (L)—First Officer.

Surgeon Commander Sandra Tucker Reddy—Minister of Medicine and wife of Captain Reddy.

Lt. Sonny Campeti—Gunnery Officer.

Lt. Ed Palmer—Signals.

Surgeon Lieutenant Pam Cross

Chief Boatswain's Mate Jeek (L)—Former crew chief, Special Air Division.

Chief Engineer Isak Reuben—One of the original Mice.

Chief Gunner's Mate Dennis Silva

Earl Lanier—Cook.

Wallace Fairchild—Sonarman, Anti–Mountain Fish Countermeasures (AMF-DIC).

Min-Sakir "Minnie" (L)—Bridge talker.

Corporal Neely—Imperial Marine and bugler assigned to *Walker*.

Lawrence "Larry the Lizard"—Orange-and-brown tiger-striped Grik-like Sa'aaran.

Pokey—"Pet" Grik brass-picker.

Diania—Steward's Assistant and Sandra's friend and bodyguard.

Gunnery Sergeant Arnold Horn USMC—Formerly of the 4th (US) Marines.

USS *Mahan* (DD-102)

Lt. Cmdr. Matthew Patrick Reddy, USNR

Cmdr. Tiaa-Baari (L)—XO.

Chief Quartermaster Patrick "Paddy" Rosen—First Officer.

Lt. Tab-At "Tabby" (L)—Engineering Consultant and First Officer.

Lt. Sonya—Engineering Officer.

Chief Gunner's Mate Pak-Ras-Ar—"Pack Rat" **(L)**—Gunnery Officer.

Torpedoman 1st Class Fino-Saal (L)—Acting Torpedo Officer.

Juan Marcos—Officer's Steward.

USS *James Ellis* (DD-21)

Cmdr. Perry Brister

Lt. Rolando "Ronson" Rodriguez—XO.

Lt. (jg) Suaa "Suey" Jin (L)—Sound Man, Anti-Mountain Fish Countermeasures (AMF-DIC).

Lt. (jg) Paul Stites—Gunnery Officer.

Lt. (jg) Johnny Parks—Engineering Officer.

**Chief Bosun's Mate Carl Bashear
Taarba-Kaar "Tabasco" (L)**—Cook.

Salissa Battlegroup
Admiral Keje-Fris-Ar (L)

USNRS *Salissa* "Big Sal" (CV-1)
Captain Atlaan-Fas (L)
Cmdr. Sandy Newman—XO.

1st Naval Air Wing
Captain Jis-Tikkar "Tikker" (L)—Commander of Flight Operations (COFO), 1st, 2nd, 3rd Bomb Squadrons; 1st, 2nd Pursuit Squadrons.

USS *Tarakaan Island* (SPD-3)
In self-propelled dry dock.

USS *Sular* (Protected Troopship)
Converted from Grik BB.

Frigates (DDs) Attached

Des-Ron 6
Awaiting new ships or appointments:
Captain Jarrik-Fas (L)
Lt. Stanly Raj—Impie XO.
Cmdr. Muraak-Saanga (L)—Former *Donaghey* XO and sailing master.
Lt. Naala-Araan (L)

Des-Ron 10
USS *Bowles***
USS *Saak-Fas***
USS *Clark***

MTB-Ron-1 (Motor Torpedo Boat Squadron Number 1)

> 11 x MTBs (Numbers 4, 7, 13, 15, 16, 18–23)
>
> **Lieutenant Nat Hardee**

Assault Force

1st Allied Raider Brigade—"Chack's Raiders" or "Chack's Brigade"

> **Lt. Col. Chack-Sab-At (L)**
>
> **Major Risa Sab-At (L)**—XO, Chack's sister.

21st (Combined) Allied Regiment

> **Major Alistair Jindal (Imperial Marine)**—1st, 2nd Battalions of the 9th Maa-ni-la, 2nd Battalion of the 1st Respite.

7th (Combined) Allied Regiment

> **Major Enrico Galay**—Former corporal in the Philippine Scouts; 19th Baalkpan, 1st Battalion of the 11th Imperial Marines.

1st North Borno Regiment

> **Brevet Major Abel Cook**—Temporarily in place of Major I'joorka.
>
> **1st Sergeant "Moe" the Hunter**

Land-Based Air

Mahe Field—Army/Navy Air Base Seychelles

> **Colonel Ben Mallory**
>
> 3rd (Army) Pursuit Squadron (3 x P-40Es, 2 serviceable)—Remnants of 4th, 7th, 8th Bomb Squadrons; 5th, 6th, 14th Pursuit Squadrons

3rd Pursuiters

> **2nd Lt. Niaa-Saa "Shirley" (L)**
>
> **S. Sergeant Cecil Dixon**

At Grik City, Mahe, and Comoros Islands

USS *Madraas* (CV-8)—8th Naval Air Wing.

USS *Sular*—Protected troopship converted from a Grik BB.

AEF-1 (First Fleet Allied Expeditionary Force)

General of the Army and Marines Pete Alden— Former sergeant in USS *Houston* Marine contingent.

I Corps

General Lord Muln-Rolak (L)

1st (Galla) Division

General Taa-leen (L)

1st Marines; 5th, 6th, 7th, 10th Baalkpan

2nd Division

General Rin-Taaka-Ar (L)

1st, 2nd Maa-ni-la; 4th, 6th, 7th Aryaal

II Corps

General Queen Safir Maraan (L)

3rd Division

General Mersaak (L)

"The 600" (B'mbaado Regiment composed of "Silver" and "Black" Battalions); 3rd Baalkpan; 3rd, 10th B'mbaado; 5th Sular; 1st Battalion, 2nd Marines; 1st Sular

6th Division

General Grisa (L)

5th, 6th B'mbaado; 1st, 2nd, 9th Aryaal; 3rd Sular

1st Cavalry Brigade

Lt. Colonel Saachic (L)

3rd and 6th Maa-ni-la Cavalry

"Maroons"
>   **Colonel Will**
>
>   Consolidated Division of "Maroons," Shee-Ree, and Allied Advisors

III Corps
>   **General Faan-Ma-Mar (L)**

9th & 11th Divisions
>   2nd, 3rd Maa-ni-la; 8th Baalkpan; 7th, 8th Maa-ni-la; 10th Aryaal
>
>   **Hij Geerki (G)**—Rolak's "pet," captured at Rangoon, now "mayor" of Grik POWs at Grik City.

Preparing for Deployment
>   **XII Corps**—Half-trained Austraal volunteers with rifle-muskets.
>
>   **XIV Corps**—Militia out of Baalkpan, Sular, and B'taava.

Land-Based Air
>   **Lt. Araa-Faan (L)**—Commander of Flight Operations (COFO) at Grik City.
>
>   **Lt. Walt "Jumbo" Fisher**—Pat-Squad 22, Comoros Islands.

TF Bottle Cap

Arracca **Battlegroup**

USNRS *Arracca* (CV-3)
>   **Commodore Tassanna-Ay-Arracca (L)**—High Chief, 5th Naval Air Wing.
>
>   **Lt. Cmdr. Mark Leedom**—Commander of Flight Operations (COFO).

USS *Santa Catalina* (CA-P-1)
>   **Cmdr. Russ Chappelle**

Lt. Michael "Mikey" Monk—XO.

Lt. (jg) Dean Laney—Engineering Officer.

Surgeon Cmdr. Kathy McCoy

Stanley "Dobbin" Dobson—Chief Bosun's Mate.

Major Simon "Simy" Gutfeld—3rd Marines.

Frigates (DDs) Attached

Des-Ron 9

USS _Kas-Ra-Ar_**

    Captain Mescus-Ricum (L)

USS _Ramic-Sa-Ar_*

USS _Felts_**

USS _Naga_***

The Republic of Real People

Caesar (Kaiser) Nig-Taak (L)

General Marcus Kim—Military High Command.

Inquisitor Kon-Choon (L)—Director of Spies.

General Taal-Gaak (L)—Republic Cavalry Commander.

Courtney Bradford—Australian naturalist and engineer, Minister of Science and Plenipotentiary at Large for the Grand Alliance.

Captain (Brevet Major) Bekiaa-Sab-At (L)—Military liaison from the Grand Alliance and Legate under General Kim; now directly commanding the 23rd Legion.

Optio Jack Meek—Bekiaa's aide, Inquisitor Choon's liaison, and Doocy Meek's son.

Prefect Bele—Bekiaa's XO.

TFG-2 (Task Force Garrett-2)
    **(Long-Range Reconnaissance and Explora-
    tion)**

USS *Donaghey* **(DD-2)**
    Cmdr. Greg Garrett
    Lt. Mak-Araa (L)—XO.
    Lt. (jg) Wendel "Smitty" Smith—Gunnery
        Officer.
    Chief Bosun's Mate Jenaar-Laan (L)
    Surgeon Lt. (jg) Sori-Maai (L)
    Marine Lieutenant Haana-Lin-Naar (L)
    Major "Tribune" Pol-Heena (L)
    Leutnant Koor-Susk (L)
    Alferez (Ensign) Tomas Perez Mole—League
        prisoner (Spanish).

USS *Matarife* **(Prize Ship)**

In Indiaa and Persia

Allied Expeditionary Force (North)

VI Corps
    General Linnaa-Fas-Ra (L)

5th Maa-ni-la Cavalry
    Detached Duty, shadowing General Halik
    Colonel Enaak (L)

Czech Legion
    The Czech Legion, or "Brotherhood of Volun-
        teers," is a near-division-level cavalry force
        of aging Czechs, Slovaks, and their conti-
        nental Lemurian allies, militarily—if not
        politically—bound to the Grand Alliance.
    Colonel Dalibor Svec

At Baalkpan

> **Cmdr. Alan Letts**—Chairman of the United Homes and the Grand Alliance.

> **Leading Seaman Henry Stokes**—Director of Office of Strategic Intelligence (OSI; formerly of HMAS *Perth*).

> **Cmdr. Steve "Sparks" Riggs**—Minister of Communications and Electrical Contrivances.

> **Lord Bolton Forester**—Imperial Ambassador.

> **Lt. Bachman**—Forester's aide.

> **Leftenant (Ambassador) Doocy Meek**—British sailor and former POW (WWI), representing the Republic of Real People.

> **Surgeon Cmdr. Karen Theimer Letts**—Assistant Minister of Medicine.

> **"King" Tony Scott**—High Chief and Assemblyperson for the Khonashi of North Borno.

USS *Fitzhugh Gray* (CL-1)

> **Cmdr. Toryu Miyata**

> **Lt. Cmdr. Ado-Sin (L)**—XO.

> **Lt. Robert Wallace**—Gunnery Officer.

> **Lt. Sainaa-Asa (L)**—Engineering Officer.

> **Lt. (jg) Eno-Sab-Raan (L)**—Torpedo Officer.

> **Ensign Gaat-Rin (L)**

> **CPO Pepper (L)**—Chief Bosun's Mate.

Eastern Sea Campaign

> **High Admiral Harvey Jenks**—CINCEAST.

Second Fleet

> **Fleet Admiral Lelaa-Tal-Cleraan (L)**

USS *Maaka-Kakja* (CV-4)

> **"Flag" Captain Tex Sheider**

492   C A S T   O F   C H A R A C T E R S

Gilbert Yeager—Chief Engineer; one of the original Mice.

3rd Naval Air Wing

2nd Lt. Orrin Reddy—Commander of Flight Operations (COFO), 9th, 11th, 12th Bomb Squadrons; 7th, 10th Pursuit Squadrons; Orrin Reddy, though as reluctant as his cousin to assume higher official rank and still stubbornly considering himself a 2nd Lt. in the US Army Air Corps, has been named "Flag" COFO of Second Fleet.

Sgt. Kuaar-Ran-Taak "Seepy" (L)—Reddy's "backseater."

USS *New Dublin* (CV-6)—6th Naval Air Wing.

USS *Raan-Goon* (CV-7)—7th Naval Air Wing.

Line of Battle

Admiral E. B. Hibbs

9 Ships of the Line, including HIMSs *Mars*, *Centurion*, *Mithra*, *Hermes*, plus:

USS *Sword*—Former Dom *Espada De Dios*.

USS *Destroyer*—Former Dom *Deoses Destructor*.

Cmdr. Ruik-Sor-Raa (L)—One-armed former commander of USS *Simms*.

Lt. Parr—XO; former commander of HIMS *Icarus*.

Attached DDs

HIMSs *Ulysses, Euripides, Tacitus*

HIMS *Achilles*

Lt. Grimsley

2nd Fleet Allied Expeditionary Force

Army of the Sisters

General Tomatsu Shinya

Saan-Kakja (L)—High Chief of Maa-ni-la and all the Filpin Lands.

Governor-Empress Rebecca Anne McDonald

Lt. Ezekial Krish—Aide-de-camp.

Surgeon Cmdr. Selass-Fris-Ar (L)—Daughter of Keje-Fris-Ar.

X Corps

3 divisions Lemurian Army and Marines, 6 divisions Imperial Marines, 4 regiments "Frontier Troops"; total 10 divisions with heavy artillery and support train

General James Blair

Colonel Dao Iverson—6th Imperial Marines.

Captain Faal-Pel "Stumpy" (L)—1st Battalion, 8th Maa-ni-la.

Sister's Own Division

"Colonel" Sister Audry—Benedictine nun; nominal command.

"Lord" Sergeant Koratin (L)—Marine protector and advisor to Sister Audry.

Major Blas-Ma-Ar "Blossom" (L)—2nd Battalion, 2nd Marines, and the Ocelomeh (Jaguar Warriors).

"Captain" Ixtli—Blas's acting XO.

Lt. Anaar-Taar (L)—C Company, 2nd Battalion, 2nd Marines.

Spon-Ar-Aak "Spook" (L)—Gunner's Mate, and 1st Sgt. of C Company, 2nd Battalion, 2nd Marines.

Colonel Arano Garcia—"El Vengadores de Dios," a regiment raised from penitent Dominion POWs on New Ireland, augmented by disaffected Dom Christians represented by **"Captain" Bustos,** who replaced Ximen, KIA.

Teniente Jasso—Garcia's XO (Pacal's replacement).

XI Corps and Filpin Scouts
General Ansik-Talaa (L)

In Contact with New United States Forces
Lt. (jg) Fred Reynolds—Formerly Special Air Division, USS *Walker.*

Ensign Kari-Faask (L)—Reynolds's friend and "backseater."

Enemies

Japanese
General of the Sky Hideki Muriname

Lieutenant of the Sky Mitsuo Ando—Muriname's XO.

Grik (Ghaarrichk'k)
Celestial Mother (G)—Traditional absolute, god like ruler of all the Grik, regardless of the relationships between the various Regencies.

General Esshk (G)—First General of all the Grik, and Regent Champion Consort to the new Celestial Mother.

The Chooser (G)—Highest member of his order at the Court of the Celestial Mother; prior to current policy, Choosers selected those destined for life—or the cookpots—as well as those eligible for elevation to Hij status.

General Ign (G)—Commander of Esshk's New Warriors.

First of Ten Hundreds (Ker-noll) Jash

In Persia
General Halik (G)

General Shlook (G)

General Ugla (G)
General Orochi Niwa (Japanese)

Holy Dominion
His Supreme Holiness, Messiah of Mexico, and by the Grace of God, Emperor of the World
Don Hernan de Divina Dicha—"Dom Pope" and absolute ruler, Blood Cardinal.
General Mayta—Commander of the Army of God.

League of Tripoli
Capitaine de Fregate Victor Gravois (French)
Oberleuitnant Walbert Fiedler (German)
Capitano di Fregata Ciano (Italian)
Contrammiraglio Oriani (Italian)—Organizations for Vigilance and Repression of Antifascism.

In Allied Custody
Capitaine Dupont (French)

SPECIFICATIONS

American-Lemurian Ships and Equipment

USS *Walker* (DD-163)—Wickes- (Little-) class four-stacker destroyer. Twin-screw steam turbines; 1,200 tons; 314' x 30'. Top speed (as designed): 35 knots. 112 officers and enlisted (current) including Lemurians (L). Armament: Main, 3 x 4"-50 + 1 x DP 4"-50. Secondary, 4 x 25 mm Type-96 AA, 4 x .50 cal MG, 6 x .30 cal MG. 40-60 MK-6 (or equivalent) depth charges for 2 stern racks and 2 Y guns (with adapters). 2 x 21" quadruple-tube torpedo mounts. Impulse-activated catapult for PB-1B Nancy seaplane.

USS *Mahan* (DD-102)—Wickes-class four-stacker destroyer. Twin-screw steam turbines; 960 tons; 264' x 30' (as rebuilt). Top speed: 25 knots. Rebuild has resulted in shortening and removal of 2 funnels and boilers. Forward 4"-50 is on a dual-purpose mount. Otherwise, her armament and upgrades are the same as those of USS *Walker*.

USS *James Ellis*—Walker-class four-stacker destroyer. Twin-screw steam turbines; 1,300 tons; 314' x 30'. Top speed: 37 knots. 115 officers and enlisted. Armament: Main, 4 x DP 4"-50. 4 x .50 cal MG, 6 x .30 cal MG. 40-60 MK-6 (or equivalent) depth charges for 2 stern racks and 2 Y guns (with adapters). 2 x 21" quadruple-tube torpedo mounts. Impulse-activated catapult for PB-1B Nancy seaplane.

USS *Sular*—Protected troopship converted from Grik BB. 800' x 100', 18,000 tons. Twin-screw, triple-expansion

Baalkpan Navy Yard steam engine. Top speed: 16 knots. Crew: 400. 100 stacked motor dories mounted on sliding davits. Armament: 4 x DP 4"-50, 4 x .30 cal MGs.

USS *Tarakaan Island*—Self-propelled dry dock (SPD). Twin-screw, triple-expansion steam engine; 15,990 tons; 800' x 100'. Armament: 3 x DP 4"-50, 6 x .30 cal MGs.

USS *Santa Catalina* (CA-P-1)—Protected cruiser; formerly general cargo. 8,000 tons, 420' x 53', triple-expansion steam, oil fired. Top speed (as reconstructed): 10 knots. Retains significant cargo/troop capacity, and has a seaplane catapult with recovery booms aft. 240 officers and enlisted. Armament: 6 x 5.5" mounted in armored casemate. 2 x 4.7" DP and 5 x 4"-50 DP in armored tubs. 20 x .30 cal MGs. 1 x 10" breech-loading rifle (20' length) mounted on spring-assisted pneumatic recoil pivot.

USS *Savoie*—26,000 tons; 548' x 88'; 4 screws. Top speed: 20 knots. 1,050 officers and enlisted. Initial armament: 8 x 340 mm (13.5"), 8 x 138.6 mm (5.5"), 8 x DP 75 mm (3"), 5 x quad-mount 13.2 mm, 24 x 8 mm.

USS *Fitzhugh Gray* (CL-1)—Four-stacker light cruiser. Triple-screw, steam turbines; 3,800 tons; 440' x 45'. Top speed: 30–35 knots. 211 officers and enlisted. Armament: Main, 3 x 2 DP 5.5". Secondary, 5 x DP 4"-50, 2 x 21" quadruple-tube torpedo mounts, 6 x twin .50 cal. MG, 6 x Y guns (with adapters), 80 MK-6 (or equivalent) depth charges for 2 stern racks. 2 x impulse-activated catapults for PB-1B Nancy seaplanes.

Carriers

USNRS (US Navy Reserve Ship) *Salissa* (*Big Sal*, CV-1)—Aircraft carrier/tender, converted from seagoing Lemurian Home. Single-screw, triple-expansion steam engine; 13,000 tons; 1,009' x 200'. Armament: 2 x 5.5", 2 x 4.7" DP, 6 x 4"-50 DP, 4 x twin-mount 25 mm AA, 20 x 50 pdrs (as reduced), 50 aircraft assembled, 80–100 in crates.

USNRS *Arracca* (CV-3)—Aircraft carrier/tender converted from seagoing Lemurian Home. Single-screw, triple-expansion steam engine; 14,670 tons; 1009′ x 210′. Armament: 2 x 4.7″ DP, 50 x 50 pdrs. Up to 80 aircraft.

USS *Maaka-Kakja* (CV-4)—Purpose-built aircraft carrier/tender. Specifications are similar to *Arracca*, but it is capable of carrying upward of 80 aircraft, with some in crates.

USS *Madras* (CV-8)—Purpose-built aircraft carrier/tender. Second of 4 smaller fleet carriers (9,000 tons, 850′ x 150′). Faster (up to 15 knots) and lightly armed (4 x Baalkpan Arsenal 4″-50 DP guns—2 amidships, 1 each forward and aft). Can carry as many aircraft as *Maaka-Kakja*.

USS *New Dublin* (CV-6)—Same as above.

USS *Raan-Goon* (CV-7)—Same as above.

Frigates (DDs)

USS *Donaghey* (DD-2)—Square-rig sail, 1,200 tons, 168′ x 33′; 200 officers and enlisted. Sole survivor of first new construction. Armament: 24 x 18 pdrs, Y gun and depth charges.

Dowden class—Square-rig steamer, 12–15 knots, 1,500 tons, 185′ x 34′; 218 officers and enlisted. Armament: 20 x 32 pdrs, Y gun and depth charges. Nearly all survivors of this class have been converted to AVDs (destroyer/ seaplane tenders) or APDs (fast transports).

****Haakar-Faask class***—Square-rig steamer, 15 knots, 1,600 tons, 200′ x 36′. 226 officers and enlisted. Armament: 20 x 32 pdrs, Y gun and depth charges. Nearly all survivors of this class have been converted to AVDs (destroyer/seaplane tenders) or APDs (fast transports).

*****Scott class***—Square-rig steamer, 17 knots, 1,800 tons, 210′ x 40′. 260 officers and enlisted. Armament: 20 x 50 pdrs, Y gun and depth charges. Nearly all survivors of this class have been converted to AVDs (destroyer/seaplane tenders) or APDs (fast transports).

Auxiliaries—Most heavy hauler, transport, and oiler hulls are now based on enlarged lines of Scott-class DDs. Virtually unarmed, they require small crews due to a vastly reduced sail plan and more reliable engines. Some fast, clipper-shaped vessels are still employed as long-range oilers. Fore and aft rigged feluccas remain in service as fast transports and scouts.

***Respite Island*–class SPDs**—Self-propelled dry dock. Designed along similar lines to the new purpose-built carriers, and inspired by the massive seagoing Lemurian Homes. They are intended as rapid-deployment, heavy-lift dry docks, and for bulky transport.

USNRS *Salaama-Na* Home—Unaltered, other than by emplacement of 50 x 50 pdrs. 8,600 tons, 1014′ x 150′. 3 tripod masts support semirigid "junklike" sails or "wings." Top speed: about 6 knots, but capable of short sprints up to 10 knots using 100 long sweeps. In addition to living space in the hull, there are three tall pagodalike structures within the tripods that cumulatively accommodate up to 6,000 people.

***Woor-Na* Home**—Lightly armed (ten 32 pdrs) heavy transport; specifications as for *Salaama-Na*.

Aircraft

P-40E Warhawk—Allison V1710, V12, 1,150 hp. Top speed: 360 mph. Ceiling, 29,000 ft. Crew: 1. Armament: 6 x .50 cal Browning MGs, and up to 1,000-lb bomb.

PB-1B "Nancy"—W/G type, in-line 4 cyl 150 hp. Top speed: 110 mph. Max weight: 1,900 lbs. Crew: 2. Armament: 400-lb bombs.

PB-5D "Clipper"—4 x 10 cyl, 325 hp radials. Top speed: 145 mph. Max weight: 7,400 lbs. Crew: 5–6, and up to 8 passengers. Armament: 5 x .30 cal, 2,500-lb bombs/torpedoes.

P-1C Mosquito Hawk or "Fleashooter"—10 cyl, 325 hp radial. Top speed: 255 mph. Max weight: 1,640 lb. Crew: 1. Armament: 2 x .30 cal Browning MGs in wings.

Field artillery—6 pdr on stock-trail carriage—effective to about 1,500 yds, or 300 yds with canister. 12 pdr on stock-trail carriage—effective to about 1,800 yds, or 300 yds with canister. 3″ mortar—effective to about 800 yds. 4″ mortar—effective to about 1,500 yds.

Primary small arms—Allin-Silva breech-loading rifle (.50–80 cal), Allin-Silva breech-loading smoothbore (20 gauge), 1911 Colt and copies (.45 ACP), Blitzerbug SMG (.45 ACP). M-1917 Navy cutlass, grenades, bayonet.

Secondary small arms—Rifled musket (.50 cal), 1903 Springfield (.30–06), 1898 Krag-Jorgensen (.30 US), 1918 BAR (.30–06), Thompson SMG (.45 ACP). A small number of other firearms are available.

MGs—1919 water-cooled Browning and copies (.30–06). 400–600 rpm, 1,500 yds.

Imperial Ships and Equipment

Until recently, few shared enough specifics to be described as classes, but they can bc grouped by basic size and capability. Most do share the fundamental similarity of being powered by steam-driven paddle wheels and a complete suit of sails, though all new construction is being equipped with double-expansion engines and screw propellers, and iron hulls are under construction.

Ships of the line—About 180′–200′ x 52′–58′, 1,900–2,200 tons. 50–80 x 30 pdrs, 20 pdrs, 10 pdrs, 8 pdrs. (8 pdrs are more commonly used as field guns by the Empire.) Speed: about 8–10 knots. 400–475 officers and enlisted.

Frigates—About 160′–180′ x 38′–44′, 1,200–1,400 tons. 24–40 x 20–30 pdrs. Speed: about 13–15 knots. 275–350 officers and enlisted. Example: HIMS *Achilles*, 160′ x

38', 1,300 tons. 26 x 20 pdrs. New construction follows the design of the Scott-class DD.

Field artillery—The Empire of the New Britain Isles has adopted the Allied 12 pdr, but still retains numerous 8 pdrs on split-trail carriages—effective to about 1,500 yds, or 600 yds with grapeshot.

Primary small arms—Allin-Silva breech-loading rifle (.50–80 cal), rifle-musket (.50 cal), bayonet. Swords and smoothbore flintlock muskets (.75 cal) are now considered secondary and are issued to native allies in the Dominion.

Republic Ships and Equipment

The Republic has finally begun construction of blue-water warships, though details are scant.

Coastal and harbor defense vessels

Princeps-class monitors—210' x 50', 1,200 tons. Twin screw, 11 knots, 190 officers and enlisted. Armament: 4 guns in two turrets, 4 x MG08 8 x 57mm (Maxim) MGs on flying bridge.

Field artillery—75 mm quick-firing breechloader loosely based on the French 75, but without the geared traverse. Range: 3,000 yds, with black powder propellant and contact fuse exploding shell.

Primary small arms—Breech-loading bolt-action, single-shot rifle, 11.15 x 60R (.43 Mauser) cal. **Secondary small arms**—M-1898 Mauser (8 x 57 mm), Mauser and Luger pistols, mostly in 7.65 cal.

Republic military rank structure—As reorganized, it is still a combination of the ancient and the new, with a few unique aspects. The Army of the Republic is commanded by General Kim. Each division, also commanded by a general, is still ordinarily composed of 6 legions. Legions have 6 cohorts, led by a colonel. The senior cohort commander (and XO) is the prefect, and roughly equivalent to a major. The remaining cohorts are led by senior centurions (captains), who still command one of the 6 centuries in the cohort through their senior optio (2nd lieutenant), who has a junior optio (like an ensign) as his assistant. Other centurions are roughly equivalent to 1st lieutenants. The Republic also has provisions for temporary, special-purpose rank appointments. A military tribune may be given specific tasks requiring them to outrank all prefects and below, as well as single-ship captains. A legate may supersede the colonel of any legion for a specific purpose, unless countermanded by the general of the army the legion is attached to. Likewise, legates act as commodores at sea.

Enemy Warships and Equipment

Grik

New, unnamed class of Grik BBs (ironclad battleships)—800′ x 100′, 27,000 tons. Twin-screw, double-expansion steam engine. Top speed: 10 knots. Crew: 1,300. Armament: 3 x 15″ 400 pdrs (2 forward, 1 aft), 24 x 100 pdrs, 24 x 4″ AA mortars.

***Azuma*-class CAs (ironclad cruisers)**—300′ x 37′, about 3,800 tons. Twin-screw, double-expansion steam engine, sail auxiliary. Top speed: 12 knots. Crew: 320. Armament: 20 x 40 or 14 x 50 pdrs, and 1 or 2 x 100 pdrs. 4 x firebomb catapults or 6 x 4″ AA mortars.

Tatsuta—Kurokawa's double-ended paddle/steam yacht. It was also the pattern for all Grik tugs and light transports.

Aircraft—Hydrogen-filled rigid dirigibles or zeppelins. 300′ x 48′. 5 x 2 cyl 80-hp engines. Top speed: 60 mph. Useful lift: 3,600 lbs. Crew: 16. Armament: 6 x 2 pdr swivel guns, bombs.

AJ1M1c ("M" for "Muriname") Fighter—9 cyl, 380 hp radial. Top speed: 260 mph. Max weight: 1,980 lbs. Crew: 1. Armament: 2 x Type 89 MG (copies) 7.7 x 58 mm SR cal.

DP1M1 Torpedo Bomber—2 x 9 cyl, 380 hp radials. Top speed: 180 mph. Max weight: 3,600 lbs. Crew: 3. Armament: 1 x Type 89 MG (copy) 7.7 x 58 mm SR cal. 1 torpedo or 1,000 lb bombs.

Field artillery—The standard Grik field piece is a 9 pdr, but 4s and 16s are also used, with effective ranges of 1,200, 800, and 1,600 yds, respectively. Powder is satisfactory, but windage is often excessive, resulting in poor accuracy. Grik field firebomb throwers fling 10- and 25-lb bombs, depending on the size, for a range of 200 and 325 yds, respectively.

Primary small arms—Copies of Allied .60 cal smoothbore percussion muskets are now widespread, but swords and spears are still in use—as are teeth and claws.

League of Tripoli

Leopardo—Leone-(Exploratori-) class destroyer. 372' x 34', 2,600 tons. Twin screw. Top speed: 30 knots. Armament: 8 x 120 mm, 2 x 40 mm, 4 x 20 mm, 4 x 21" torpedo tubes. 210 officers and enlisted.

Holy Dominion

Like Imperial vessels, Dominion warships fall into a number of categories difficult to describe as classes, but again, they can be grouped by size and capability. Despite their generally more primitive design, Dom warships run larger and are more heavily armed than their Imperial counterparts.

Ships of the line—About 200' x 60', 3,400–3,800 tons. 64–98 x 24 pdrs, 16 pdrs, 9 pdrs. Speed: about 7–10 knots. 470–525 officers and enlisted.

Heavy frigates (cruisers)—About 170' x 50', 1,400–1,600 tons. 34–50 x 24 pdrs, 9 pdrs. Speed: about 14 knots. 290–370 officers and enlisted.

Aircraft—The Doms have no aircraft yet, but employ "dragons," or Grikbirds, for aerial attack.

Field artillery—9 pdrs on split-trail carriages—effective to about 1,500 yds, or 600 yds with grapeshot.

Primary small arms—Sword, pike, plug bayonet, flint-lock (patilla style) musket (.69 cal). Only officers and cavalry use pistols, which are often quite ornate and of various calibers.

After being transported to a strange alternate Earth, Matt Reddy and the crew of the USS Walker *have learned desperate times call for desperate measures, in the return to the* New York Times *bestselling Destroyermen series.*

Time is running out for the Grand Human and Lemurian Alliance. The longer they take to prepare for their confrontations with the reptilian Grik, the Holy Dominion, and the League of Tripoli, the stronger their enemies become. Ready or not, they have to move—or the price in blood will break them.

Matt Reddy and his battered old destroyer USS *Walker* lead the greatest army the humans and their Lemurian allies have ever assembled up the Zambezi toward the ancient Grik capital city. Standing against them is the largest, most dangerous force of Grik yet gathered.

On the far side of the world, General Shinya and his Army of the Sisters are finally prepared for their long-expected assault on the mysterious El Paso del Fuego. Not only is the dreaded Dominion ready and waiting for them, they've formed closer, more sinister ties with the fascist League of Tripoli.

Everything is on the line in both complex, grueling campaigns, and the Grand Alliance is stretched to its breaking point. Victory is the only option, whatever the cost, because there can be no second chances.

Ready to find
your next great read?

Let us help.

Visit prh.com/nextread

Penguin
Random
House